She knew she should be blissfully happy, but here in the noisy, crowded room she felt alone and frightened . . . tonight she had a strange feeling that something horrible was about to happen, as if they were sitting on the edge of an earthquake, as if a gaping chasm had opened at their feet . . . But that was stupid. Soon it would be the start of a new year. Ted was home, and the family were safe and well – what was there to be afraid of?

Peter Ling wrote his first published novel when he was eighteen. After a career in journalism he became a television scriptwriter, and with Hazel Adair he created the much-loved series *Crossroads* which ran for over twenty-three years. He has scripted episodes of *Dr Who* and *Dixon of Dock Green* and has written plays and serials for radio. Married with four children, Peter Ling now lives in East Sussex.

By the same author

Happy Tomorrow
Crown House
Crown Papers
High Water
Flood Water
Storm Water

Halfway to Heaven

PETER LING

ORION

An Orion paperback
First published in Great Britain by Orion in 1994
This paperback edition published in 1996 by Orion Books Ltd,
Orion House, 5 Upper St Martin's Lane, London WC2H 9EA

Copyright © 1994 Tropstar Ltd

The right of Peter Ling to be identified as the author of
this work has been asserted by him in accordance with the
Copyright, Designs and Patents Act 1988.

A CIP catalogue record for this book is available from the
British Library.

ISBN: 0 75280 276 3

Printed and bound in Great Britain by
Clays Ltd, St. Ives plc

Family Trees

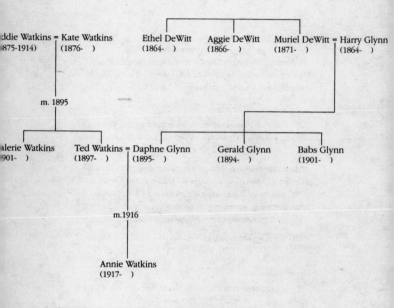

ddie Watkins = Kate Watkins   Ethel DeWitt   Aggie DeWitt   Muriel DeWitt = Harry Glynn
(875-1914)   (1876-)   (1864-)   (1866-)   (1871-)   (1864-)

m. 1895

alerie Watkins   Ted Watkins = Daphne Glynn   Gerald Glynn   Babs Glynn
(901-)   (1897-)   (1895-)   (1894-)   (1901-)

m.1916

Annie Watkins
(1917-)

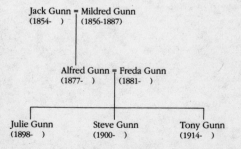

Jack Gunn = Mildred Gunn
(1854-)   (1856-1887)

Alfred Gunn = Freda Gunn
(1877-)   (1881-)

Julie Gunn   Steve Gunn   Tony Gunn
(1898-)   (1900-)   (1914-)

*Many years too late,
this book is dedicated
to my father and mother,
with love and gratitude.*

AUTHOR'S NOTE

I must express my gratitude to all those people who have so kindly helped me: to Richard White and Leslie Adams, who both checked pre-war legal details; to Gerry Savage at Upper Norwood Library, who allowed me to consult their local history collection; to the BBC, who gave me permission to include an extract from their Outside Broadcast commentary at the scene of the Crystal Palace fire on the night of 30 November, 1936; and above all, to Melvyn Harrison and his colleagues at the Crystal Palace Foundation and Museum. I have drawn upon several of their publications – not least, their brilliant compilation *The Crystal Palace Is On Fire!* Without them, this book could never have been written.

Although I have tried to ensure that as far as possible all the known facts are accurate, this is first and foremost a novel. For dramatic purposes I have had to telescope time occasionally, and invent a few non-existent streets, shops and houses; all the characters are completely imaginary, with the exception of Sir Henry Buckland – who passed away in 1957, at the age of 87 – and his daughters, Irene and Chrystal, who I am happy to say still provide a living link with the glorious history of the Crystal Palace.

BOOK ONE

1919–1923

Chapter One

HE WAS RUNNING – running as if his life depended on it – and perhaps it did.

Up the steep gradient of Anerley Hill, Ray never slackened his pace. By now his lungs were bursting and he was taking great gulps of air, straining his ears for the sound of footsteps coming after him. At this time of the evening the shops were all in darkness, but he saw the lighted windows of the pub on the corner. Only another few yards to go . . . If they caught him now, he'd be done for.

A quarter of a mile away, halfway up the hill, Valerie Watkins crumpled up a letter and threw it into the waste-basket beside her dressing table.

A moment later, she picked it out and smoothed it flat. She was tempted to read it once more, but what was the point? She already knew it by heart; it wasn't very long – just a single page in Eric's sprawling handwriting. And she had known what he was going to say, even before she opened the envelope. She had always known, really.

She tore the paper in half, then tore it across again and again. When it was a handful of scraps, she dropped them into the basket. She didn't want anyone else to read it – her mother, her sister-in-law, the dustmen – she wanted to destroy the letter once and for all, and forget it.

She looked into the swing-mirror on the dressing table, and her face gazed back at her – pale and uncertain. Automatically, she straightened her petticoat; she had been about to get dressed for the evening when Mum came upstairs, apologising.

'Oh Val, this letter came for you while you were at work. Sorry, I should have remembered it before.'

And she had waited until her mother left the room before she opened the envelope. Well, it was all over now. But what was she going to do? How could she celebrate New Year's Eve, and her brother's homecoming, when her heart was breaking?

'Don't be so stupid,' she told herself sternly. 'Hearts don't break; they only hurt for a while. You'll get over it.'

She was determined not to cry. She wouldn't let the others know what she was going through. Whatever happened, she wasn't going to spoil the evening for them. What did it matter if Eric had decided to marry that other girl? It wasn't the end of the world, was it?

Suddenly she turned her head, listening. Somewhere far away, she could hear the sound of running footsteps, coming nearer. For one ridiculous moment she felt a thrill of hope. It must be Eric – he'd changed his mind – he was hurrying to tell her so—

But her reflection looked back at her with scorn, telling her that this was nonsense. It couldn't possibly be Eric; he'd gone for good.

All the same – somebody was running . . .

When he got to the Sackville Arms, Ray heard the sound of singing and laughter coming from the public bar – they were doing a roaring trade tonight, everybody was out celebrating – but although he had a painful stitch in his side, he did not dare to stop, and raced on around the corner.

The side street was long and narrow, lit by a single gas-lamp at the far end. He was almost sobbing with relief as the darkness closed around him. Then he felt a sickening lurch of fear – he could still hear footsteps behind him, and they seemed to be getting closer. When he reached Number 37, he raced up the front steps, fumbling in his pocket for his doorkey, but it slipped through his shaking fingers, tinkling on to the step.

Desperately, he turned at bay to face his pursuers, his back pressed against the door . . . but there was nobody in sight, and no sound except the heaving of his lungs and the beating of his heart. He had been running away from the echo of his own footsteps.

Sweating with relief, he scrabbled for the key and let himself into the house; the door crashed shut behind him.

Downstairs in the basement kitchen, the sound disturbed a sleeping child; she uttered a single, anxious cry. Two women looked at one another, and stood up.

'There now, he's woken her.' The older of the two, Kate Watkins, clicked her tongue in disapproval. 'That'll be our Mr Duke. These young men, they don't stop to *think* . . .'

Her daughter-in-law was already stooping over the two-year-old, stroking her hair and saying quietly, 'It's all right. She's gone off again already – she only stirred in her sleep.'

They heard the young lodger's feet rattle on the lino as he ran upstairs. Vexed, Kate settled herself again in the armchair by the kitchen range, saying, 'It's all very well, Daphne, but I'll have to have a word with him. He's got no consideration, rushing in and banging about like that.'

As he crossed the second-floor landing, Ray Duke heard someone call his name from one of the rooms. It was Valerie, the landlady's daughter. He saw the door-handle turn, and hurried on; he didn't want to speak to anyone now. He scrambled up the last flight, into his attic bedroom, and slammed the door.

Panting, he put a match to the candle on the bedside table, then flopped down on top of the counterpane, trying to get his breath back, waiting for the pain in his side to go away.

There was a knock at the door; he tensed immediately. 'Who is it?' he asked.

'Me – Valerie. Are you all right?'

What the hell did she want? He answered gruffly, 'Yeah, I'm OK.'

'I was a bit worried . . .' The door opened a couple of inches. 'May I come in?'

'I s'pose so.' He sat up, still wearing his cloth cap and his raincoat, which he pulled defensively around him. 'What d'you want?'

'I couldn't help wondering—' Valerie stepped into the room, caught in the glow of candlelight.

It was the first time anyone had been into his room since he had moved into Sackville Road a couple of weeks ago. He stared at her. She was in her dressing gown – loosely belted, so he could see her petticoat beneath, bare legs and bare feet.

Seeing his expression, she knotted the belt more firmly and explained: 'I was getting changed when I heard you running up the street. You seemed to be in such a hurry, as if you were running away from something.'

He wanted to tell her to mind her own damn business, but as she moved a step nearer the bed, he changed his mind. She was only about nineteen – not a bad looker, either. 'Yeah, I was running away.'

Still breathless, he told her the story in fits and starts – how he had been on his way home when he saw two hulking great brutes set on a little old lady and snatch her handbag. He'd tried to help her, but then both men turned on him.

'Two of 'em there were,' he went on, 'bigger than me – I wouldn't have stood a chance. So I made a run for it. They both came after me, but I was too quick for 'em – I got back indoors before they could catch me.'

'You were lucky, but why didn't you go to the police station?' asked Valerie.

'I didn't stop to think. Besides, I wasn't feeling very proud of meself, running away like that. Didn't help the old lady much, did I?'

'At least you tried – that was very brave. But you should report it to the police. They might want you as a witness.'

'I dunno about that. It was dark – I never got a proper look at 'em.'

'Well, I'm glad you're all right.' Self-consciously, she indicated her dressing gown. 'I must finish getting dressed. We're waiting for my brother to come home – he's been away in the Army, you know.'

With that, she left the room. Ray crossed to the door and made sure it was properly shut, then, with a sigh of relief, he took off his raincoat. Diving into one of the pockets, he pulled out a small beaded handbag and emptied it on to the counterpane. Three gold sovereigns, five half-crowns – and some small silver and coppers. Nearly four quid altogether. Because he had come up behind her, the old woman never saw his face. By the time she had screamed for help and people started chasing after him, he was halfway home.

Taken all round, it had turned out pretty well, really.

In the kitchen, Mrs Watkins glanced across at her granddaughter, asleep on the old sofa.

'You want to watch out, Daphne. If she tumbles off onto that tiled floor, she could have a nasty fall.'

'She won't. I piled up the ironing in front of her, to stop her rolling off the edge.'

Kate Watkins laced her fingers together, then started again on another tack. 'Look how she's crumpled up Ted's clean shirts; you'll have to iron them all over again before he can wear them.'

Daphne Watkins smiled. 'She's made herself a little nest . . . I can easily run the iron over them. I just wanted to have all his clothes clean and aired before he comes.'

'And when's that going to be, I'd like to know?' Not for the first time, Kate looked at the clock on the dresser. 'It's getting so late – Annie should have been in her cot long ago.'

'She might as well sleep down here as up in the bedroom. It won't do her any harm; Ted's bound to want to see her as soon as he comes in.'

'Yes, I suppose so. I'm sorry, Daff.' Kate gave her daughter-in-law an apologetic smile. 'I'm fussing again, aren't I? Only I thought he'd be home before now.'

'So did I.' Daphne smiled back. 'He'll be here soon.'

A silence fell, marked by the tick of the clock and the flicker of flames in the grate.

Ted Watkins had been away for a long time. He had served in the Forces for three and a half years, and today he was returning to civilian life. When he joined the Army in 1916, there had been just enough time for a whirlwind courtship and a hasty wedding before he was packed off to the trenches in France. Nine months later, little Annie was born, and since then Ted's leaves had been brief and infrequent. He was allowed the luxury of two weeks at home after the Armistice was signed in 1918, but he hardly knew his baby daughter.

Once the fighting was over, they had all imagined that the troops would be discharged and sent home, but it wasn't as easy as that; the British had to keep a strong force in the occupied territories, so Ted had spent most of 1919 on duty in the Rhineland.

But today it was all over. This was the last day of the old year, and Ted was coming home for good – home to the little terraced house in Sackville Road, halfway up the hill to the Crystal Palace – home to his family.

'Funny to think we'll soon be in nineteen-twenty.' Kate repeated the date, trying out the sound of it. 'Nineteen-twenty . . . It'll take some getting used to. The nineteen-tens seem to have gone on for such a long while.'

It had been an eventful decade for everybody, and tragic for many. Kate Watkins' husband Eddie earned his living as a commercial traveller, and never had any ambition to get into uniform, but when the war broke out he responded to the recruiting campaign. Under the influence of Kitchener's hypnotic glare and accusing forefinger, he had decided that his country needed him, and although he had been almost past the age limit, he had volunteered to join up and do his bit. Within a few weeks, he was killed in action at Mons.

Two years later, Kate had scarcely come to terms with the loss of her husband when her son – christened Edward after his father, but always known as Ted – had joined up in his turn. She tried to be brave, and forced a smile when he marched away, wondering if she would ever see him again.

Luckier than his father, Ted went through his Army service without a scratch and tonight, as the last hours of the old year ticked away, he was on his way home, to be reunited with his mother, his wife, his baby daughter – and his sister.

Kate and Daphne looked up as the kitchen door swung open and Valerie joined them.

'Well?' She looked round the room. 'Ted not here yet?'

'Not yet, Val,' said Daphne. 'Very soon now.'

It was easy to see Val was Kate Watkins' daughter. When they went out together, even total strangers remarked on the resemblance. By now Kate was generously plump, and at fifty-three her chestnut hair was turning grey, coiled into a bun on top of her head, kept in place with tortoiseshell combs; while Val, at nineteen, was pleasantly curved, and her gleaming curls hung loose over her shoulders.

'You've taken your time,' said Kate.

Valerie tried to smile. 'I've been slaving away at the dressing table, dolling myself up for His Lordship's benefit. How do I look?' She did a twirl, showing off her new dress. Romantically long and loose, in pale violet crepe de Chine, it had a dropped waist and came down to a few inches above her ankles.

'You look lovely,' Daphne told her. 'I hope Eric appreciates it.'

'Oh, I didn't mean him – I was talking about Ted!' Valerie had not realised how hard it would be just to say Eric's name, but she forced herself to go on. 'Eric's not coming after all. He wrote and said he couldn't get away this evening. He's been so busy since he moved to Raynes Park – he's got heaps of other people to see.'

Kate and Daphne looked at her, not knowing what to say.

'But I thought—' Kate began. 'You and Eric—'

'It really doesn't matter!' Valerie even managed a little laugh. 'We were only friends because of working in the same office, and now he's moved away I don't suppose we shall be seeing each other very often, so . . .' Then she stopped – there was nothing else to say.

Daphne broke the silence. 'Well, we're all going to have a wonderful time this evening – Eric doesn't know what he's missing! And you'll be the belle of the ball.'

'It's not exactly a ball,' said Kate. 'They get a very rough crowd at the Sackville Arms, by all accounts. If you spill anything on that dress, it'll never come out. Crepe's a devil for stains.'

'I'll take care, Mum,' said Val. 'Oh, talking of rough crowds, do you know what happened to our new lodger?'

Glad to change the subject, she told them young Mr Duke's story, and they all agreed that it was terrible the way innocent people got assaulted and robbed nowadays. Kate said she didn't know what the world was coming to.

'And he's not much more than a boy himself,' she added. 'Only seventeen, he told me.'

'Well, it was good of him to try and help the old lady.' Val looked at the clock. 'It's almost ten – what time did Ted say in his letter?'

'He didn't say a time, just "See you Wednesday night" . . . If he's not here soon, we can forget about going out.' Daphne stretched, and smothered a yawn. 'I'm quite tired already.'

'What?' Val swung round, dismayed. 'But we've got to go – it's all arranged!'

'No, Daff's quite right,' Kate chimed in. 'The Sackville will be shutting any minute – they close at ten o'clock.'

'Not tonight, Mum, they've got a special licence for New Year's Eve. Besides, it's meant to be a welcome home for Ted!' Then she broke off at the sound of the knocker on the front door.

Daphne's heart beat a little faster. 'There he is now.'

'It might not be.' Val was on her way up the basement stairs already. 'I'll go and see.'

The house was on four floors. The big old-fashioned kitchen was in the semi-basement, with the area steps outside – and on the floor above, the hall opened on to a front sitting room with folding doors leading into what had once been a dining room. Now the back room had been converted into a bedroom for Daphne and little Annie and – when he was at home – Ted. On the second floor were two more bedrooms, for Kate and Valerie, and on the top floor, the attic bed sitting room, let out to single lodgers.

Listening intently, Kate and Daphne heard the front door slam.

'He'll wake that poor little mite again—' began Kate, but Daphne said, 'That's not Ted. It sounds like a girl—' and a moment later Val returned, followed by Daphne's sister, Babs Glynn.

'This is a surprise!' exclaimed Daphne, as Babs pecked her on the cheek. 'What are you doing here?'

Babs' china-blue eyes opened a little wider as she replied coolly:

'As a matter of fact, I was invited.' She advanced on Kate with her hand out. 'How do you do, Mrs Watkins? So nice to see you.'

Val's words tumbled over each other. 'In all the excitement it went clean out of my head. I ran into Babs at dinner-time, and I told her about Ted coming home tonight and us going out to the Sackville to celebrate and see the New Year in and all that . . . So I asked her if she'd like to come along and join the fun. Well, we're all family, aren't we?'

'You see?' Babs turned to her sister reproachfully. 'I hope you don't think I'm the kind of person who turns up without an invitation.'

'I hadn't really given it much thought, either way,' said Daphne pleasantly. 'But it looks as if you've had a wasted journey, because Ted hasn't arrived. I don't think we'll be going out after all.'

Babs had begun to unfasten her coat; her fingers froze on the last button. 'What do you mean?' She turned to Valerie. 'I thought you said Eric What's-his-name was going to be here? Hasn't he turned up either?'

Once again, Val had to launch into an explanation – Eric had been unavoidably detained, wasn't it a nuisance? – while Daphne watched and listened sympathetically.

Daphne was twenty-five, and Babs was nineteen, but they were separated by more than a difference in age. At first glance no one would have taken them for sisters. Daphne was gently attractive, slender and fine-boned, her straight fair hair cut in a becoming fringe; beside her, Babs, all blonde curls and pink-and-gold prettiness, looked dazzling.

Daphne turned to her sister. 'If Ted doesn't turn up soon, we'll just have to stay here and drink a toast to the New Year in cups of cocoa.'

'Don't be ridiculous!' Babs undid the last button and let her coat slip from her shoulders. She was wearing a dance dress in shot silk which changed colour as it caught the light, rippling from peacock-blue to sea-green with every movement she made. Raising her voice, she said sharply: 'I didn't come all this way for a cup of cocoa. Of course we're going out!'

On the sofa, little Annie stirred again, and began to whimper. Daphne picked her up at once, cradling her daughter and saying softly, 'It's all right, lovey, it's only Auntie Babs. Yes, I know, it's long past your bedtime, isn't it? Let's take you upstairs.'

The child relaxed contentedly against her mother's breast, and was asleep before they left the room.

'Well, this is a washout, I must say,' said Babs. 'I'd been looking forward to this evening.'

'We were looking forward to seeing Ted, as well,' remarked Kate. 'It's a real shame he couldn't get here.'

'He might still be on his way,' said Val. 'Why don't we go to the pub anyhow? If he turns up later, you can tell him where to find us, can't you, Mum?'

Kate looked horrified. 'You can't go into a public house by yourselves – three young women on your own? I never heard of such a thing!'

'No, we certainly can't.' Babs too rejected the idea. 'Whatever would people say?'

'All right, then.' Val had another brainwave. 'We'll get Mr Duke to take us.'

'Mr Duke?' Babs frowned. 'Who's he?'

'Our new lodger – Raymond Duke. He's got the top floor,' Val explained.

'Oh, really? What's he like?'

'I don't think that's a very good idea,' Kate broke in. 'He's only been here a couple of weeks. Besides, he's under eighteen – they wouldn't let him in.'

'They won't bother about that tonight!' said Val, her eyes dancing. 'Let me go up and ask him. He might like to go out – I expect he could do with something to buck him up.'

'We don't really know anything about him—' Kate was still arguing, but Val was already running upstairs.

When she knocked on Ray's door for the second time, he sounded rather flustered.

'What do you want?' he asked. 'I mean – who is it?'

'It's me again. Can I come in?'

'No, you can't. It's not convenient.'

'But I want to ask you something.'

'Oh. Well, you'll have to wait.'

Raymond was standing in front of the washstand in his vest and socks; he had been sponging himself in cold water from the ewer in the basin, because he was hot and sticky after running so fast. He finished towelling himself and began to scramble into his clothes, calling out: 'I'm just getting dressed – I won't be long.'

Pulling on his shirt, he buttoned his stiff collar and tied his tie quickly, then plunged into his trousers, his waistcoat and his jacket. Why did everything take twice as long when he was in a hurry? But he wouldn't let her in until he was fully dressed, neat and tidy; he even made her wait while he laced his shoes and ran a comb through his hair.

At last he opened the door. 'Well, what do you want?' he asked.

'Goodness, you look smart,' she said. 'Were you thinking of going out?'

'I might. I hadn't really decided.'

'Oh good, because that's what I came up to ask you. I wondered if you'd like to come round to the pub, to see the New Year in?'

'What, take you out, d'you mean?' He eyed her speculatively. 'You're a proper bobbydazzler in that get-up . . . Yeah – I'll come with you, if that's what you want. Where do you fancy going?' He couldn't believe his luck; no girl had ever offered herself to him like this, and he moved towards her eagerly.

Quickly, Val sidestepped. 'I didn't mean just you and me.' She explained about Ted having been delayed, and how they couldn't go into a pub without a male escort.

'Three of you?' Ray Duke's face fell. 'I couldn't run to that – I'm a bit short of the readies tonight.'

'Oh, that's all right. I wasn't expecting you to treat us – we'll pay for ourselves,' she assured him.

'Honest?' He cheered up again. 'Oh well, that's different. But it doesn't have to be a pub, does it? How about somewhere a bit smartish, with a band – somewhere we could dance? How'd you fancy me as a partner, eh?' He put his arm round her waist and pulled her closer, turning her to face the mirror above the washstand. Looking at their reflection, she saw the colour rising in his cheeks, and the glitter in his eyes.

'We'd make a handsome couple, wouldn't you say?' he asked, and his voice sounded husky and excited, close to her ear. 'D'you know what? I've been thinking about you ever since the day I moved in. I've had my eye on you all along, Valerie. You don't mind if I call you Valerie, do you?'

'No, but—' She pulled away from him. 'We'd better go down; the others will be waiting.'

'Let 'em wait. We've got things to talk about, Valerie – personal things.'

All at once she began to laugh – and she couldn't stop laughing. He grabbed her arms, saying, 'No, listen. I'm serious—'

'I'm sorry, but I can't help it. The thing is – before we go out, don't you think you ought to tuck your shirt in?'

He had changed in such a hurry, his shirt-tail was hanging out; furiously, he stuffed it into his trousers.

'It's not funny!' he snapped.

'I know it's not. I'll go down and tell them you're getting ready.'

She hurried away, and he heard her still laughing on the stairs. Silly cow – for two pins he wouldn't go out with her at all. But then he heard her saying to her friends, 'Mr Duke's going to take us – isn't that nice of him?'

Sulkily, he put on his street coat and his cap and followed her. When he entered the kitchen and was introduced to Babs, his mood changed once more. To hell with that stupid, sniggering girl – Barbara Glynn was a regular knockout . . . She flashed a brilliant smile as they shook hands, then asked him: 'Excuse me, I'm told you're only seventeen. You don't think they might turn us out, do you? It would be so embarrassing.'

He squeezed her hand. 'No, I'm eighteen,' he told her. 'You got nothing to worry about.'

Kate looked up. 'You told me you were seventeen when you moved in.'

'I've just had my eighteenth birthday,' he improvised rapidly. 'Right, are we all ready? Where's Mrs Watkins?'

When Daphne came downstairs, having settled Annie for the night, Val explained the change of plan, but Daphne said she'd stay and wait for her husband – so in the end Ray set out with two young ladies, one on each arm.

It seemed very quiet in the kitchen when they had gone. Kate stretched out and patted Daphne's hand, saying, 'What a shame. Not a very good start to the New Year, is it?'

'What do you mean?'

'Poor old Val. I don't care what she says, she'd set her heart on that Eric taking her out. And it's disappointing for you as well; I don't expect we'll see Ted tonight now. The buses will have stopped running.'

'Oh well, I'll wait up till Val comes home, anyway.' Daphne lifted her head, catching a distant sound.

'What is it? Annie's not woken up again?'

'No, listen – there's a car coming. It's drawing up.'

Out in the street, a taxi stopped at the kerb with the engine running. A young man in a shabby overcoat got out and unloaded a canvas kitbag and a battered suitcase on to the pavement, then paid the driver.

'Keep the change, mate. And a Happy New Year!'

As the cab pulled away, the front door opened and the hall lamp shone out into the night, catching Ted Watkins like a spotlight. He dropped the bags, smiling broadly and holding out both hands, as Daphne flew down the steps into his arms.

'I knew you'd get here,' she said, as they kissed one another.

'I told you I would, didn't I?' he laughed, then lifted her off her feet, swinging her round in his embrace. 'When did I ever let you down?'

From the doorway, Kate called out: 'Come in, for goodness sake! Carrying on like that in the street!'

Ted carried his luggage into the hall and kissed his mother. 'Home at last,' he said. 'How've you been keeping, Mum?'

'I'm not so bad. How about you, then – throwing your money away on taxis? Couldn't you have walked from the station?'

Ted grinned. 'I got the cab at Waterloo, didn't I?'

His mother gaped at him. 'All this way? You must be barmy – how much did that cost you?'

'Never you mind! It was worth it – every penny.'

'Want your brains tested, you do. I don't suppose you bothered to have any supper, either. Come downstairs. We can do you egg and bacon—'

'It's all right, Mum. I had a ham sandwich at Waterloo.'

'That's not all you had, I bet,' Daphne scolded him fondly; she had tasted the whisky on his lips.

'Well, it was a special occasion, saying goodbye to all my pals – so to save time we held our first Regimental Reunion there and then, in the station buffet.'

Daphne laughed. Ted could always make her laugh – nothing would change that, but he seemed different somehow – mysteriously older. His face was still boyish and his smile full of mischief, but his forehead had some wrinkles she didn't remember and there were shadows in his eyes that she had never seen before.

When they went down to the kitchen, Ted took off his coat, looking around and asking: 'Where's the rest of the family, then? Where's young Annie? Where's our Val?'

'Annie's asleep,' she told him. 'Val's gone round to the Sackville.'

'Pub-crawling at her age? All on her own?'

'Course not. She's got Babs with her and our new lodger, Mr Duke. They wanted us to go and join them, but it's a bit late for that now.'

He checked the clock. 'Still half an hour till midnight – plenty of time.' He began to put his coat on again, despite Daphne's protests.

'But you've only just got here! You're not going out again already? I thought we could have a bit of time together, on our own—'

He kissed her again. 'Sweetheart, we've got the rest of our lives together. Mum won't mind keeping an eye on Annie while we nip out for half an hour, will you Mum? I mean, if they're expecting us at the Sackville, we can't very well disappoint them, can we?'

She looked into his soft brown eyes, and her heart melted. When had she ever said no to him?

'All right,' she said. 'Let's go.'

By now the saloon was crowded, but Babs had managed to bag a table in the corner. She and Val put their coats on Ray's chair while he fought his way to the bar.

'Now then!' Babs settled herself comfortably. 'I want to hear the whole story – what's happened to your friend Eric? After everything you said, I was looking forward to meeting him.'

'I probably said a lot of stupid things. It turns out he wasn't quite as keen as— well, I don't think I'll be seeing him again.'

'You poor thing.' Babs gave a nod in Ray's direction. 'Still, you certainly don't waste any time, do you, finding yourself someone else already?'

'Mr Duke? Don't be silly, it's not like that. I told you, he's our lodger. I've hardly spoken to him till tonight.'

Babs shrugged. 'Well, he's not bad-looking, but I must say he's a bit common, isn't he? Not really our sort.'

Val smiled. 'I don't know what "our sort" is! We weren't exactly born with silver spoons in our mouths, were we?'

'You know very well what I mean. What does he do for a living?'

'He works at Fabers Furnishings, up the road.'

'Well, there you are – a shop assistant!' said Babs, as if that settled the argument. 'Look out, he's coming back.'

Shining and triumphant, Ray managed to carry three glasses to the corner table without spilling them. 'Here we are. One squash for Valerie, one port and lemon for Barbara, and half a pint for yours truly. Bottoms up!'

'Chin-chin,' said Babs, and sipped her drink.

'How much do I owe you?' Val fumbled in her purse.

'No, no – this is on me,' Ray told her.

'But I asked you to get them,' said Val. 'You must let me pay—'

'Wouldn't dream of it – my pleasure,' he said. 'It's not every day I get to take out two lovely ladies. Cheers, dears.'

Babs smiled thinly. 'Very kind of you to say so.'

Beaming, he looked from one to the other. 'D'you mind if I ask – are you two cousins, or what?'

'No, just friends,' Babs told him. 'Daphne's my sister, and she's married to Val's brother Ted. He should have been here tonight, only he seems to have got lost.'

'So that's how you got to know each other?'

'We've known each other ever since secretarial college,' Val chimed in. 'It was at a tennis party. I took Ted, and Babs took Daff—'

'And they just clicked, eh?'

'Clicked?' Babs raised her eyebrows. 'They got engaged.'

Nudging Ray, Val murmured, 'Babs' family are a cut above our lot. They've got one of those big houses in Crystal Palace Park Road.'

'Is that a fact?' Ray was impressed. 'Nice class of property round there, I'm sure.'

'We like it,' said Babs modestly. 'And whereabouts do you come from, Mr Duke? Do your family live in London?'

'No, they're in America,' answered Ray, as casually as if he had said: 'They're in South Norwood.'

'Your parents live in *America*?'

'Yeah – California. They went out there on business years ago. I went with them, when I was a kid.'

'Well, I never!' Babs gazed at him with new interest. 'You actually lived in California?'

'That's right – near Hollywood. Dad's got money in the moving picture business. Later on they sent me back here, to boarding school; they didn't want me to grow up talking like a Yankee.'

'But now you've left school, couldn't you go back and join them?'

'Oh, I will – in a year or two. I'll come into a legacy when I'm twenty-one, and then I'll have nothing to worry about. But Dad believes in young chaps starting at the bottom and making their own way in the world.'

'And that's why you work at Fabers Furnishings?' said Val.

'At the moment – but I won't stay there long. Faber's not a bad old stick, only it gets a bit humdrum, the same old job, day after day.'

'I know what you mean. I felt like that when I was at Catchpolls – you know, the drapers in Sydenham?' said Babs, then hastened to add: 'I wasn't serving the customers myself. I had a secretarial post in the office – book-keeping and correspondence and so on – but the work was very monotonous, and they were so strict about timekeeping . . . If I was just a few minutes late in the morning, they were quite offensive. In the end I had to give in my notice; I'm not used to that kind of behaviour.'

'Do you mean you're out of work now?' asked Ray.

'Well, I'm between posts, so to speak,' Babs replied delicately. 'I don't have to work, of course, but I like to keep myself occupied.'

'Now there's a funny thing!' exclaimed Ray. 'Phyllis Carter – she works in the office at Fabers – she'll be leaving soon to get married, so the boss is looking for someone to take her place . . . I could put in a word for you if you like.'

'Well, that's very kind of you, Mr Duke—'

Babs was interrupted by Val, who suddenly jumped up and began waving. 'Look, it's Daff and Ted! Coo-ee! Over here!'

There was another family reunion. Ted embraced his sister and greeted Babs, who presented her cheek to be kissed, then Val introduced him to Ray. They managed to grab two more chairs, then Ted insisted on buying another round of drinks, and pushed through the crowd to the bar.

'Isn't this wonderful?' said Val. 'All of us together again.'

'Yes, wonderful,' said Daphne.

She knew she should be blissfully happy, but here in this noisy, crowded room she felt alone and frightened. She never liked pubs much at the best of times – that was one of the differences between her and Ted – but tonight she had a strange feeling that something horrible was about to happen, as if they were sitting on the edge of an earthquake, as if a gaping chasm had opened at their feet . . . But that was stupid. Soon it would be the start of a new year. Ted was home, and the family were safe and well – what was there to be afraid of?

She made herself smile. 'Everything's wonderful,' she repeated.

When Ted came back with the drinks, he apologised. 'Sorry I kept you waiting, but the landlord's organising a whip-round. It seems some old dear in the public bar had her handbag snatched earlier on tonight – left her practically stony-broke, poor old soul, so we were all chucking a few bob into the kitty.'

As the conversation became general, Val turned to Ray. 'She must be the one you saw. Perhaps you ought to go and speak to her.'

'What for?' he asked. 'There's nothing I can do.'

'You could ask her if she needs a witness.' Val began to stand up. 'I'll come with you, if you like—'

'*No!*' He pulled her down, muttering, 'I told you, I never got a proper look. I didn't really see anything . . . I'd only make a fool of myself.' Uncomfortably, he glanced round the table but the others weren't listening.

Ted had already changed the subject, and was saying to his wife and sister-in-law, 'Guess who else I saw just now, propping up the bar? Your old man!'

'Father?' exclaimed Daphne. 'He's here?'

Ted grinned. 'Large as life, and twice as sinful.'

'It's not funny, Ted.' Babs tossed her head. 'You didn't speak to him, did you?'

'Course I did! He seemed very pleased to see me. I invited him to come and have a drink with us, for auld lang syne.'

'I hope you're joking!' Babs warned him. 'Because if that man has the nerve to come and talk to us, I shall walk out of here and go straight home!'

'Oh, he's not that bad. You should make allowances—'

'After what he did to poor Mother?' said Babs indignantly.

'Well . . . Anyhow, he might not come over. I'm not sure he heard me properly, as he was talking to three people at once – chatting to the landlord, offering to paint a new signboard for the pub, trying to buy half a bottle of sherry from the off-licence on tick, and wheedling the barmaid into going round to his studio to model for him!'

'Typical,' sniffed Babs. 'I think it's disgusting – he ought to be locked up.'

Mystified, Ray asked Val: 'Is she talking about her father?'

'I heard that,' Babs cut in. 'As far as I'm concerned, he isn't my father any more. He walked out on his wife and family years ago – and I don't want anything to do with him.'

Daphne tried to intervene. 'Mother and Father never really got on—'

'So your Dad doesn't live with you any more?' Ray pursued. 'In the big house?'

'I should think not!' Babs told him. 'He lives in some awful lodgings in Penge – practically a slum, by all accounts – and serve him right.'

Then she averted her face, as a disreputable elderly man joined them, an unlit pipe clenched between his teeth and a shapeless tweed hat on the back of his head.

'So there you are!' he barked, squinting round the table. 'Good to see you, Daphne. Babs, how's the world treating you?'

She did not reply, but kept her gaze fixed on the engraved mirror on the opposite wall. Ted stood up, offering the old man his chair, and said: 'You remember my sister Valerie, don't you?'

'Do I? Yes, of course I do. Pretty face – splendid figure – Peter Paul Rubens would have made you into a masterpiece, my girl. Come and see me if you feel like having your portrait painted – drop in any time.'

'Sit down, Father,' Daphne told him. 'You're looking well.'

'Mustn't grumble.' He placed a half-bottle of sherry on the table and added, 'Though I don't know why people say that – I always enjoy a good grumble myself.'

Ted completed the introductions. 'And this is our new lodger, Mr Duke – Raymond Duke.'

Ray reached across the table to shake hands. 'Pleased to meet you.'

'You may be – she isn't!' Harry Glynn pointed his pipe-stem at Babs. 'Ashamed of her dear old Dad, my little girl is. Don't worry, Babs, I'm not stopping – got to make my way home before my landlady locks me out. I've bought her a little present. She's rather partial to a drop of sherry in the evening – I'm hoping it might mellow her a little.'

Daphne sighed. 'I suppose you're behind with the rent again?'

'Since you mention it, I must admit—'

He had been speaking loudly, but now his voice was drowned in a sudden surge of noise. The landlord clanged the brass bell above the bar and bellowed: 'Stroke of midnight, ladies and gents! Ring out the old year and ring in the new – a happy nineteen-twenty to one and all!'

Then they all stood up, hugging one another, linking arms and singing discordantly: '*Should auld acquaintance be forgot, and never brought to mind . . .*'

'Happy New Year, my darling,' Ted whispered in Daphne's ear, and kissed her. 'This is going to be the happiest year of our lives – I promise!'

She could only just make out the words; by now the place was like bedlam, and they were being jostled and buffeted by people trying to dance.

'Let's go home, Ted,' she said urgently. 'Just the two of us.'

He smiled. 'Whatever you say, sweetheart.'

It took them some time to make their way through the crowd, and when they reached the doorway they met Daphne's father again.

'Time I was heading for home,' he said. 'Good night, you two – and a Happy New Year.'

In the saloon, Ray was shouting hopefully at Babs through the din: 'How'd you fancy a dance?'

She shrugged. 'Might as well. Val, look after my coat and bag, will you?'

'Just a minute.' Val pointed to the table. 'Your Dad's gone without his bottle of sherry – you ought to go after him.'

'Why should I?' asked Babs. 'What did he ever do for me?'

'Don't be like that. Ray – how about you?'

'Why me? I don't even know him.'

'We can't leave it there, can we?'

In the end they all went outside, expecting to find Harry in the street, but he had already disappeared.

'He can't have gone far,' Val persisted. 'Anyway, it's nice to get a breath of air. It was like an oven in there.'

So they set off down Anerley Hill, and soon saw the old man ahead of them; a hobbling silhouette under the street-lamps.

'You can run after him if you want to,' said Babs, standing still. 'I'm not speaking to him.'

Val called and waved, but it was no good. 'He can't hear us. Ray, do take it, please!'

Reluctantly, he began to jog-trot down the hill. The two girls watched as he reached Harry Glynn and handed over the bottle. Faintly, they heard Harry expressing his thanks before continuing on his way.

'Miserable old brute,' muttered Babs. 'I hope he drops it.'

When Ray rejoined them, he said: 'Well, that's that. Let's go back in the warm and have that dance you promised me.'

But Babs had changed her mind. 'Sorry, I must go too. It was getting very rowdy in there – besides, it's awfully late.'

'Right, then. I'll walk you home,' he offered immediately.

The girls exchanged glances, and Babs said, 'I don't think so, thanks all the same.'

'You don't want to go all that way on your own,' began Ray. 'I'll keep you company.'

'We'll all go,' said Val. 'The walk will do us good.'

Ray tried to argue, but the girls were in agreement, so they set off together along Thicket Road, past the boundary fence that enclosed the Crystal Palace grounds. Though it was dark, they caught glimpses of the lake shining between the trees, and the awesome replicas of prehistoric monsters, keeping watch over the island.

Babs chattered as they strolled along, but Valerie couldn't help wondering what might happen on the way back, when she would be alone with Ray. If he tried anything on, she'd box his ears and make a run for it.

As it turned out, she need not have worried. Frustrated in his plan for a tête-à-tête with Babs, Ray returned to Sackville Road in stony silence, hardly bothering to speak to Val at all.

When Harry Glynn let himself into the boarding house, he saw a light in the front window, which meant that his landlady was still up. He pushed open the parlour door and looked in; she was sitting at the round table, with playing cards spread out over the red chenille cloth.

'You shouldn't have waited up for me, Miss Preece,' he told her.

An oil-lamp above the table threw a glow upon the middle-aged woman in a Spanish shawl; it picked out her thin features dramatically, making her eyes into black holes, like the sockets of a skull.

'Fancy yourself, don't you?' she retorted. 'What makes you think I was waiting for you?'

'What are you up to, then?' He glanced at the cards, laid out in neat rows. 'Looking into the future, to see what nineteen-twenty has in store for you?'

'I never read my own fortune,' she told him. 'I've been amusing myself with a few hands of Patience, that's all.'

'Did you win?'

'Not once. The cards weren't on my side tonight; the luck ran against me . . . So what have you been doing? Drinking and carrying on as usual?'

She lifted her head to look up into his face, her eyes rimmed with kohl, and her hair red with henna. Putting his hand on her shoulder, he could feel her bones beneath the silk shawl.

'Gad, you're a fine woman,' he said. 'Here, this is a little gift – to bring you luck in the New Year.'

He presented her with the half-bottle. The moment she touched it, her expression changed; she seemed to shrink into herself, and the colour drained from her face.

'What's wrong?' he asked. 'Aren't you well?'

'Where did you get this?' she gasped.

'I bought it for you at the pub. I thought you'd be pleased.'

'It's so cold – cold as the grave,' she said, and fear crackled in her voice. 'Who else has handled it?'

Before he could answer, the bottle slipped between her fingers. It fell into the fireplace, smashing to pieces in the grate.

'What the devil are you playing at?' exclaimed the old man indignantly. 'Throwing it away – what d'you mean by it, eh?'

They looked down at the broken glass, and the dark liquid seeped across the fireplace tiles, like a gush of blood.

'It was touched with evil . . .' she whispered. 'It was like shaking hands with death.'

Chapter Two

IT WAS ALMOST like spring; everyone said so.

Val had bagged her favourite seat on the open-topped bus – upstairs, right at the front; from this vantage point, she could see everything. Although it was the end of February, she could feel a touch of warmth from the setting sun. She threw back her head, enjoying the mild weather. Soon the buds on the trees would begin to show green; her spirits lifted at the thought.

It had been a long, dreary day at the office, but that was nothing out of the ordinary – most days were like that. Val had a job as a typist and filing-clerk with an insurance company in Brixton High Road, and found it very dull. The rest of the staff were middle-aged or elderly. She shared a poky little room with two other female clerks – gloomy spinsters of uncertain age and uncertain temper – and since Eric had left the firm she looked forward to the end of each day like a release from prison. But she wouldn't let herself think about Eric. Soon, she hoped she would forget him altogether.

Suddenly a dusty sparrow, swooping down from a rooftop, almost flew into her face, swerving away at the last moment with such a look of astonishment at meeting a human being in mid-air, Val laughed out loud. The conductor, collecting fares on the top deck, glanced at her suspiciously.

'Did you say something, miss?'

'No – I was just laughing, that's all. Take no notice – I'm getting off at the next stop.'

She stood up and swayed along the bus, then ran down the curving outside stairway. Jumping off at the stop in Upper Norwood, she walked through to Church Road. By now the sunset had turned the western sky into a brilliant spread of gold, orange and crimson, as loud and joyful as a brass band . . . For a moment she thought her imagination was playing tricks – it even *sounded* like a brass band – then she realised that she was listening to the notes of a cornet cascading from an upper window, above Gunns the the greengrocers.

Stepping into the shop, she found Alfred Gunn weighing out Brussels sprouts for an elderly customer, while at the other end of the shop his son – a young man with tousled, unruly curls – was absently polishing apples on his apron as he read the top sheet of a pile of old newspapers, used for wrapping vegetables.

Val went over to him, while the melody of *Lily of Laguna* floated down from above. 'Somebody's fond of music,' she remarked.

'That's Grandad,' said the young man, without looking up. 'Potty about music, he is. What can I do for you, miss?'

'I want three apples, please.'

'Right you are.' Still absorbed in the news item, he began to pile apples on to the scales; he went on until there were nine or ten apples in the big brass scoop.

Val was about to say something when Mr Gunn called down the length of the shop: 'Steve! What are you playing at? Reading the paper when you're supposed to be working! Motor-racing again, I'll be bound!'

The young man mumbled, 'Well, I couldn't help noticing—'

'I don't pay you to daydream! It was three apples you asked for, wasn't it, miss?'

Red-faced, the young man looked at her for the first time. 'Oh, sorry. Didn't you say three pounds?'

He had large dark eyes, and there was something very appealing in his expression. Val heard herself saying: 'Yes – three pounds. Thank you.'

Mr Gunn was taken aback. 'Beg pardon, my mistake. All right, Steve, don't stand there gawping. Wrap 'em up and look sharp about it.' He turned to greet another customer. 'Good afternoon, madam. What can I do for you?'

The young man caught Val's eye, and a slow smile spread over his face, as he said softly, 'You didn't really want three pounds, did you? I can put some back.'

'No, that'll be fine,' she told him. 'An apple a day keeps the doctor away. I'll be very healthy.' Then, as he wrapped them in the newspaper, she added: 'You're keen on motor-racing, are you?'

'That's right.' He glanced at her and asked, 'I don't suppose you're interested in cars?'

'Not really. I'm like your Grandad – potty about music.'

'You ought to meet him some time.' He grinned at her as she paid for the apples, and she smiled back.

When she left, the cornet was playing a cakewalk, and she swung along the pavement in time to the rhythm. She felt ridiculously happy, and she didn't know why. Then she realised: for the first time in months, she had talked to a young man easily and naturally. And she was looking forward to seeing him again, next time she went to the greengrocers. Then she scolded herself for being so absurd. Hadn't she learned her lesson yet? It was no good; sooner or later, you always got hurt. She wasn't going to make that mistake again.

A voice from nowhere startled her. 'Hello, Valerie. You look very pleased with life.' Raymond Duke had come out of the shop next door – Fabers Furnishings.

'Hullo, Ray. Just finished work?'

'Yeah – old Faber's locking up, and I'm on my way home.'

'Then we can keep each other company down the hill,' said Val. She didn't particularly like Ray Duke, but she was prepared to be pleasant. As he fell into step beside her, she added: 'The music's cheerful, isn't it?'

'Blooming row, if you ask me. Old Mr Gunn's at it all day long, blowing that rotten trumpet. If you heard it as often as I do, you'd soon get sick of it.'

'Think so?' Val changed the subject. 'Isn't it a lovely evening? Such a beautiful sunset.'

'Can't say I noticed.' He glanced at the sky, which was turning to amethyst and mauve, then dismissed it, continuing: 'I'm glad I ran into you – I got something to tell you.'

'Oh?' She looked at him in surprise. 'What's that?'

'It's about Phyllis Carter, her that works at our shop – the one I told you about. She finished last week – wedding next Saturday, then she's off to Brighton for the honeymoon.' He sniggered. 'I bet that'll teach her a thing or two, eh?'

Valerie shook her head. 'Sorry, I don't know what you're talking about.'

'I told you – the boss is advertising for another secretary. He's put a card in the window.'

'And you thought I might be interested? Well, that's very nice of you, but – I don't know . . . I suppose it would save on bus-fares, if I could walk to work—'

He cut in impatiently. 'No, not you. I was thinking of that friend of yours – Babs.'

'Oh, I see.' Val decided she didn't really like Ray Duke at all. 'I thought you meant me.'

'Course not. You're fixed up already, aren't you? The thing is – do you think she'd mind if I called round now and told her there's a vacancy?'

When they reached Sackville Road, Valerie took him down to the kitchen. They walked in upon a domestic scene: Daphne was bathing little Annie in a tin tub on the hearthrug, while Kate warmed a towel by the fire. They all looked up when Ray walked in, and Annie held out her arms, saying, 'Dadda' – then stopped, pulling down the corners of her mouth as she realised her mistake.

'She thought you were her father,' said Kate, as Daphne lifted the baby out of the water. 'Mind her back, dear. Shall I have her now?' She took her granddaughter on her lap, enfolding her in the bath-towel, while Daphne emptied the tub into the sink and dried her hands on her apron.

'Ted usually gets home about this time. What was it you wanted, Ray?'

He began to tell her about the vacancy at the shop, concluding: 'So I thought, if your sister's still looking for a job, p'raps I ought to go round and tip her the wink? Only I don't like to barge in without being asked.'

'I said he'd better have a word with you first,' Val put in. 'I mean, he doesn't want to rush in where angels fear to tread!'

'Angels?' Ray frowned, rather confused. 'What's angels got to do with it?'

Daphne smiled. 'I think Val means that my family are a bit set in their ways. Some of their ideas are rather old-fashioned.'

'Specially your Mum,' Val pointed out. 'It's only fair to warn him.'

'Well, yes, she can be a little – I don't know how to put it—'

'Try "la-di-da",' suggested Ted, from the doorway.

Deep in conversation, they had not heard him coming down the stairs. Annie began to wriggle off Kate's lap, calling out: 'Dadda! Want my Dadda!'

He kissed Daphne, slapped Val's bottom in passing, and scooped up his baby daughter, while she squealed with delight.

'I was just telling Ray about Mother,' Daphne explained. 'He's offered to walk round to Belmont, because there's a job going at Fabers and he wondered if Babs would be interested.'

'That's very good of you, old man,' said Ted, 'but you'll have to mind your Ps and Qs with my respected Ma-in-law. It's a bit like dropping into Buckingham Palace for a chat with the Queen. Don't forget to kneel down and kiss her hand when you arrive. You needn't be so formal when you go out – just bow three times and walk backwards.'

Seeing the look on Ray's face, Daphne said, 'He's pulling your leg – she's not that bad. A bit snobbish, perhaps.'

'A bit?' Ted chuckled. 'She'll tell you all about her late-lamented father, the great financier Montague DeWitt. A big man in the City, according to her – practically a millionaire.'

'A millionaire, eh?' Ray's expression changed. 'Is that a fact?'

'It's just Ted's nonsense!' Daphne interrupted. 'He wasn't a financier, he was a stockbroker.'

'Same difference. Honest, the first time Daff introduced me to the old girl and said we were going to be married – me, a commercial traveller for a pickle factory – she practically had convulsions. She impressed on me what a mighty step I'd taken, when I picked a DeWitt to woo. I thought she was doing bird impersonations.'

'That's enough!' Kate scolded her son. 'Whatever will Mr Duke think of you, talking about Mrs Glynn like that? She's always been very pleasant to me whenever I've met her.'

'Which is once in a blue moon!' Ted was unrepentant. 'At the church, on our wedding day, I had my work cut out to stop Mum curtseying in the vestry!'

Daphne broke in again. 'Ted, do shut up for goodness sake. If Ray wants to go round to Belmont and see Babs, out of the goodness of his heart, I'm sure they'll all be very grateful.'

'Where's Belmont?' Ray was looking confused again.

'That's the name of the house,' Val enlightened him. 'Where we went, the night we walked home with Babs. You know the way, don't you?'

'Yeah. Well, if you really think it'll be all right, I'll call round this evening.'

By now Ray felt more determined than ever. He had to get inside Belmont, to meet Babs again – and her family.

It was quite late when he reached Crystal Palace Park Road. He had gone to some trouble over his appearance, putting on his best blue suit and a clean shirt and slicking down his hair. He took a deep breath as he opened the front gate. The gravel drive was overgrown with weeds, though he scarcely noticed that – he had eyes for nothing but the tall building looming over him. It seemed even bigger than he'd remembered; four storeys high, it had a square Italianate tower, and the windows were framed in Virginia creeper. A light shone behind lace curtains at one of the first-floor rooms.

Plucking up his courage, he tugged at the iron bell pull, which set up a jangling somewhere in the depths of the house. He waited for what seemed an eternity, but nothing happened.

'They got to be at home, if the light's on,' he thought. 'P'raps they're all deaf.'

He tried once more, letting the bell peal for several seconds; again there was no response. His courage was ebbing fast, and he was about to turn tail and retreat when he heard footsteps on the gravel behind him. Turning guiltily, he found two people advancing on him – a tall young man in his middle twenties, with a toothbrush moustache, together with an older woman. Over fifty, she had a face like a parrot – a beaky nose and a parrot's unwinking, suspicious stare.

'What are you doing here?' she squawked.

'I – er – I wanted to see Babs,' he blurted out, and knew at once that he had said the wrong thing. 'Miss Glynn, I mean.'

The young man drawled, 'But does Miss Glynn want to see you, I wonder?'

'Do we know you?' The parrot lady thrust her face closer, peering at him. 'Who are you?'

'Ray Duke. I live with the Watkinses at Sackville Road.'

'I might have guessed,' said the lady sourly. 'What shall we do about him, Gerald?'

'Better go inside – no point arguing the toss out here,' said the young man, putting his key into the door. 'After you, Auntie.'

They entered the house, where a gas-globe shone dimly from a wall-bracket. Gerald pulled at one of the little hanging chains beneath it, saying, 'Now then – let's see if we can throw some light on this.' With a hollow roar, the gas-mantle flared into a dazzling white, and he scrutinised Ray carefully. 'You live at my sister Daphne's house, do you? Did she send you round here?'

'No, sir.' Ray despised himself for speaking so humbly. 'I mean to say, she didn't send me, but she said it'd be OK if I come here.' He corrected himself quickly. 'If I *came* here . . . I've got some news for Miss Babs, you see, about a job.'

'Really?' Gerald led him to an upright chair beneath a stag's head on the wall. 'You'd better wait – I'll see if she's available.'

The parrot lady added sternly, 'Stay there, and don't touch anything.'

He sat down, and they went away. A draught blew across the black-and-white tiled floor, nipping at his ankles. He was impressed by the house, and by their effortless superiority, and his feet were cold.

When Babs appeared, he was on the point of disobeying orders and slipping off home, but she stopped him imperiously. 'Mr Duke! Where are you going?'

He hesitated. 'I – I dunno really. P'raps I didn't ought to have come. P'raps I should have sent a note.'

'What for? What do you want?'

So he told her about the job at Fabers, and she began to ask questions about the duties and the hours and the wages.

'How many other people are working there?' she wanted to know.

'Just the three of us at the moment. Mr Faber and me – and Tubby.'

'Tubby?'

'Tubby Dingwall – he does the heavy work, carrying furniture around and all that. When we have deliveries, he drives the van.'

'I see. And they're both respectable men, are they?'

'Course they are. I wouldn't be working there if they wasn't, would I?'

'I hope not . . . And there's no female staff then, apart from me?'

'No, you're the only lady.'

When she smiled, it was like the sun coming through clouds. 'I think you're rather a dear,' she said. 'Come and be introduced to Mummy. She wants to meet you.' She took his hand and squeezed it. 'I'll show you the way. She's upstairs, in her sitting room.'

He let himself be led up the wide staircase; the Turkey carpet was worn and faded, but he didn't notice that – he was feeling more confident now.

The sitting room was large, but so cluttered with furniture it seemed quite crowded. There were several armchairs, two sofas, and various tables, bookcases and china cabinets; so many pictures hung on the walls – landscapes, portraits and still lifes in heavy gilded frames – that the green damask wallpaper was almost completely covered. A fire burned brightly in the grate beneath a marble overmantel crammed with vases, ornaments, two displays of stuffed hummingbirds under glass domes, and a clock that had given up telling the time at ten past eleven. It was the most ornate, expensive-looking room Ray had ever seen.

Beside the fireplace, propped up on cushions in the biggest armchair, sat a large lady with silver-grey hair brushed up on top of her head, and a tightly curled fringe along her forehead in the style of the dowager Queen Alexandra. Like Alexandra, she had been a beauty in her day. Even now, carefully powdered and rouged, she gave an impression of faded glory.

Extending a heavily ringed hand, she said in a deep, aristocratic tone: 'How do you do? Babs, dear, won't you introduce your new friend?'

'This is Mr Raymond Duke, Mummy. Mr Duke – my mother, Mrs Glynn.'

'I am delighted to meet you. Sit by me, where I can see you.'

With an effort, she lifted her feet from a tapestry stool. A vague gesture indicated that he should sit down; hypnotised, he did so. The warmth of the fire and a cloud of perfume enveloped him. She fixed him with lustrous violet eyes and said, 'I see so few people these days. This is a rare pleasure.'

Babs explained that Raymond worked at Fabers Furnishings, and had offered to introduce her to Mr Faber in connection with the office vacancy.

'A furniture shop?' Mrs Glynn sighed. 'I'm afraid none of our family has ever been involved in trade, Mr Duke.'

'But I thought Babs – Miss Glynn—' Ray turned to her and stammered, 'didn't you say you worked at Catchpolls, the drapers?'

'*Not* in the retail department,' Mrs Glynn enlightened him. 'She was on the management side. I hope Mr Faber realises how fortunate he is, to be offered a young lady with Babs' ability and experience.' All the time she was speaking, she fidgeted with a collection of small objects on a round table beside her chair: a silver-covered prayer book, a tiny brass bell in the form of a crinolined lady, a heartshaped pearl brooch, a cut-glass scent bottle and a lace handkerchief.

Ray watched her closely, following every movement of those ringed hands, observing everything they touched.

'Don't worry, Mrs Glynn. I'll put in a good word for her,' he said.

'How very kind.' Muriel Glynn turned her head as the door opened and another woman came in. 'Ah – I don't think you know my sister Agnes? Aggie dear, this is Mr Duke. He's a friend of Babs, and is going to help her find some employment.'

Skinny and sallow, with haunted eyes and hairpins slipping from wispy white hair, Agnes bore little resemblance to her sister. Her hand in Ray's was frail and brittle, like the skeleton of a bird.

'So nice to meet you, Mr Duke,' she twittered. 'My dear, isn't it time for your medicine?'

'Later, Aggie. Not when we're entertaining guests.' Her words were not unkind, but Aggie flinched as if her sister had slapped her.

'Yes, of course. Excuse me,' she whispered, backing away. 'I should have realised. So sorry to have interrupted you . . .'

Muriel touched the little brass bell. 'I shall ring when I want you, Aggie.' Her hand hovered over the collection of treasures, and she said to Ray, 'You've been so obliging, Mr Duke. Let me give you something, as a little memento.'

He switched on a bright, expectant smile as she selected the silver prayer book – he might be able to get a few quid for it, with a bit of luck – but she turned the pages until she found what she was looking for; a pressed flower – dark blue, paper-thin and dusty.

'It's a gentian – not rare, but very precious. My dear father brought it back from a walking-tour in Switzerland. I would like you to have it.' She laid it reverently on his palm; he tried to look suitably grateful, wondering what the hell he was going to do with it. 'Papa was a DeWitt, you know – a very great gentleman.'

'Yeah, I bet he was. Thanks a lot.'

Ray folded the dry flower up in his handkerchief, thanking his lucky stars he had a clean one with him, and put it carefully into his breast pocket. As he did so, the door opened once more and Ethel Glynn entered the room. Gerald followed, brushing crumbs from his moustache.

'Very decent sandwiches, Auntie Ag – not half bad,' he said, as he strolled across to his mother.

'Gerald dear, did you have a good day at the office? Let me introduce you – my son Gerald, Mr Duke – and my eldest sister Ethel. They are both involved in the property business, at Hawkins and Company Estate Agency. Ethel, this is—'

'Thanks, Mu – we've already met,' Ethel cut in sharply. 'We found him on the doorstep.'

'Don't say that, Auntie!' guffawed Gerald. Taking his place in front of the fire, he lifted his coat-tails to enjoy the warmth. 'You make the poor chap sound like a parcel!'

'That's not a very nice thing to say, dear.' Muriel turned to Ray. 'Well, Mr Duke, now you've met the entire family, I believe?'

'Yes, I have.' To keep the conversational ball rolling, Ray added:

'Matter of fact, I had the pleasure of meeting your husband as well, a few weeks ago.'

At once the temperature dropped. There was a long and terrible pause, broken by Agnes, who remarked bravely, 'Dear me, there must be an angel passing overhead – isn't that what they say?'

Ignoring her, Muriel addressed Ray in measured tones. 'You are mistaken, Mr Duke. I no longer have a husband.' Moistening her lace handkerchief with a few drops of cologne, she pressed it to her temples. 'I imagine you were referring to my estranged husband? I would be grateful if you would not do so again; we never mention him in this house.'

With a shaking hand, she returned the scent bottle to its place, but her sleeve caught the edge of the table and knocked it over, sending precious knick-knacks flying in all directions. Everyone rushed to pick things up, while Muriel closed her eyes, saying faintly, 'Perhaps you should bring my medicine now, Agnes. I'm feeling rather exhausted.'

At the end of the evening, Ted stood up, saying to Daphne: 'I've got to make an early start. I'm on the long run – South Croydon and Purley. I think I'll have a bath before bed.'

Daphne stood up too. 'I'll fetch you a towel from the airing-cupboard,' she said.

Unfastening his collar, he took off his tie. 'I wouldn't say no to a nice glass of beer, while you're at it. Would you bring me one on your way up? I'll leave the bathroom door ajar.'

She said doubtfully, 'Don't you think you should lock it? Suppose Val wants to go to the bathroom – or your Mum?'

'Oh, they were both tucked up in bed long ago. Be a pal, Daff – a hot bath and a cold beer, and I'll be halfway to heaven.'

The bathroom was at the back of the house, on the half-landing. Ted turned on the taps, then struggled with the old-fashioned geyser, lighting a taper and poking it in. At the third attempt, the gas lit with a startling explosion; he hoped it hadn't woken Annie, who was asleep in the bedroom only a few steps away. Hearing no sound from her, he began to undress.

When Daphne pushed the door open, he was sitting in the bath soaping himself. She was in her nightdress now, and handed him the glass of beer. 'There you are,' she announced. 'I'll be off to bed, if there's nothing else.'

'There is.' He took a swig of beer, then winked. 'Do us a favour and scrub my back, eh?'

'Now then – none of your nonsense!'

'I thought that was one of the things you had to promise in church – to love, honour, obey, and wash your husband's back?'

'You're a terrible man, Ted Watkins. Oh well – just this once.'

He handed her the soap, then presented her with his broad shoulders, shining and sun-tanned. Working up a lather, she said thoughtfully: 'Matter of fact, there's something I've been meaning to say. I was thinking – Annie's getting to be quite a big girl now. She doesn't really need me all the time, like she used to. So I was wondering – wouldn't it be a good idea if I was to go back to school?'

'School? I thought you'd got your diplomas and certificates already?'

'No, I meant go back to Carmichael Road – teaching.'

When Ted and Daphne met, she was the youngest member of the English Department, teaching Grammar, Composition and English Literature at Carmichael Girls' School. She had continued to teach there after they were married, until she had to give up work before Annie arrived.

'What d'you want to do that for?' he asked. Leaning forward with his head down, his voice sounded hollow and muffled. 'I'm making enough money to support you and the offspring, aren't I?'

'Of course – but a little extra always comes in handy. And I'm sure your Mum wouldn't mind looking after Annie. I'd only go back part-time to begin with.'

'To begin with? How long's this going on?'

'Well, when Annie starts kindergarten, I could go full-time. If we get her into Carmichael Mixed Infants, I can take her with me in the mornings and bring her home after school.'

She had stopped soaping him, and he straightened up. Looking at her over his shoulder, he was no longer smiling. 'You've got it all worked out, haven't you?'

'I thought we agreed: when Annie was old enough, I'd start teaching again – that's what we said.'

'That's what *you* said, but there was a war on then. Nobody knew what was going to happen. You might have had to support the whole family . . . Things are different now. I've got a weekly wage-packet – there's no need for you to go out to work.'

'But I want to! Don't you understand? I enjoy my work.'

'Maybe later on, when the babe's older. Like you said, when she

41

starts school herself, that might be different – but not yet. I'm the breadwinner in this family, not you.'

'I didn't know you felt like that about it.' Disappointed, she went on lathering his back, and felt him begin to relax under her hands.

'I expect you're a bit bored, stuck at home all day,' he went on gently. 'I can understand that. I get pretty bored myself, a lot of the time, trudging round with the sample-case and the order-book, trying to talk South London into buying pickles!'

When Ted left school at fifteen, his father had just resigned from his job as a traveller for Mulligan's Pickles in order to join the Army. The firm took on the young school-leaver in his place, at first as an errand-boy, but very soon, since there was a shortage of manpower, Ted was given his father's old job and took over his customers.

The war dragged on. As soon as he was old enough to go into uniform, Ted left the firm, like his father; unlike his father, he came home safely. When he returned to Mulligan's factory, he was given a hero's welcome and resumed his old duties, with a small rise in salary. And now, just over a month later, he wondered if the last two years of the war had been nothing but an impossible nightmare; it sometimes felt as if he had never been away at all.

'It's not much of a job, really,' he went on. 'But I don't have the qualifications to do anything else, so I may as well make the best of it. I get on all right with the customers, that's the main thing. I suppose I could have done worse.'

'And it must be better than the Army,' she tried to console him.

'Better? Yes, in a lot of ways – but we had some fun as well, you know. It wasn't all killing, and being killed.' She felt his muscles beginning to tense, and continued to massage his smooth, slippery skin. 'Mmm – that feels good.' He grunted with pleasure, then looked over his shoulder again with a wicked gleam in his eye. 'But I tell you what'd be even better . . . Why don't you take off that nightie? You don't want to get it wet, do you?'

'Ted!' Though she pretended to be shocked, a little thrill of excitement ran through her. 'I think perhaps I'd better lock that door after all.'

Then she slipped off her nightdress, seeing her own reflection – a pale pink ghost in the steamy mirror – and Ted opened his arms invitingly. 'Come on in – the water's lovely and warm.'

'There isn't room for two in there,' she protested, but he reached out for her.

'We'll make room somehow,' he said. 'If we both squeeze up tight.'

As she stepped in, he took her in his arms, and the soapy water slopped over the edge.

'What will your Mum say, if the floor gets flooded?' she began, and then could say no more, for he stopped her mouth with kisses. She surrendered herself to his warm, wet embrace, and more and more water splashed on to the bathroom lino.

The following morning, when Babs arrived at the furniture shop in Church Road, Ray greeted her impatiently.

'I thought you said you'd be here at ten?' he demanded. 'You're late!'

'Oh, am I? Does it matter?'

She had been in two minds about what to wear; at first she had put on her pretty white shantung with the broderie anglaise round the neck, but then her mother had said she should wear something plainer, in case it put ideas into anybody's head, so she'd changed into her maroon wool instead.

'It's nearly quarter past,' said Ray. 'Old Faber was going out to an appointment, but he waited specially – he won't be best pleased.'

He led her down a strip of carpet, through a forest of wardrobes, to a partitioned area with frosted-glass windows and a sign that said Private. Straightening his tie, he knocked on the door.

'Come in.'

There were two desks in the office, a small one with a typewriter, a filing-tray and a vacant upright chair – and a large one, covered with circulars and catalogues, and a candlestick telephone. Behind this desk Mr Faber sat in a swivel chair. Seeing Babs, he half-rose to his feet.

'This is Miss Glynn, sir,' muttered Ray.

'How do you do?'

They shook hands, and she found herself looking up at him. He was a tall man in his early forties, with fair, greying hair already receding from his temples, and his eyes had dark rings under them.

'Thank you, Duke – that will be all,' he said. 'Try not to slam the door, please.'

Slightly resentful, Ray went out. If the door did not exactly slam, it closed with unnecessary force. Mr Faber winced and looked at his watch. 'I can't give you very long, Miss Glynn. I have to go out shortly.'

'I'm sorry I'm late,' she said. 'It was my mother.'

'Your mother?'

'She's an invalid – almost bedridden. I have to do everything for her.'

'I'm very sorry to hear that.' He frowned. 'But surely, if she's so dependent on you, how would you be able to take this job?'

'Well, I've got an auntie – Mummy's sister, who lives with us. She's elderly herself, but she can manage little jobs around the house.'

'I see. May I ask how old you are?'

'I'm nineteen.'

'Nineteen . . .' He examined his fingernails. 'It must be a worry for you. Do you feel you could leave home each day, with an easy mind?'

'I shall have to. After all – Mother's in God's hands,' she said, with a tremulous smile. 'And I promise I'd never let you down, Mr Faber.'

Looking at Babs, he realised he was smiling too. 'I'm sure you wouldn't,' he said. 'Very well – let me tell you what the job entails.'

He outlined her duties, showing her where the account books and the correspondence files were kept, teaching her how to make out bills of sale, and lay out letters on the company's headed stationery. Then he asked her some questions about her last job at Catchpolls, and she showed him the grudging reference they had given her when she left. The manager had not been able to resist a barbed reference to 'occasional differences of opinion over time-keeping'.

Mr Faber read this, then glanced at her sympathetically. 'Your poor mother was the reason for that, I expect?'

'Well, yes. She can't help it. Sometimes she'd keep me talking at her bedside – almost as if she couldn't bear to let me go.'

'I can understand that. I appreciate your difficulties, Miss Glynn; my own wife is an invalid. Sick people can be very demanding, can't they?'

'Oh, they can, Mr Faber.' She bit her lip. 'It's wonderful to find someone who really understands.'

He cleared his throat and told her he would be pleased to offer her the post of secretary, and asked how soon she could start work.

They agreed she would begin on Monday next, and shook hands once again; then he went off to his overdue appointment, telling Ray he could take the Situation Vacant card out of the window.

Ray watched him go, then turned to Babs. 'You've got the job, then?'

'I have,' she told him happily. 'I start next Monday.'

He grabbed her and gave her a smacking kiss, as a heavily built man with a drooping moustache emerged from the stockroom at the rear of the shop.

'Hello, hello – what's all this?' asked Tubby Dingwall. 'Who's your ladyfriend, Raymond?'

Rather flustered, Babs allowed herself to be introduced, and Ray explained that she would be joining the staff after the weekend. Tubby tapped the side of his nose and said: 'All right for some, eh? I can see I'll have to keep an eye on you two lovebirds, or you'll be canoodling in the corner every time Mr Faber's back is turned.'

'It's nothing like that, I assure you,' said Babs, with icy politeness. 'Mr Duke was just congratulating me on my new appointment. We're only acquaintances, really.'

Tubby gave her a knowing look. 'Take my advice, you want to keep it that way, girl. If he tries taking you through the beds and mattresses to test the springs, don't you let him!'

Holding her head high, Babs left the shop. Ray caught her up beneath the striped awning.

'Take no notice of old Tubby,' he said. 'He don't mean nothing.'

'I sincerely hope not,' she retorted. 'If he speaks to me like that again, I shall report him to Mr Faber. At least *he's* a gentleman, thank goodness. Anyway, I must be going—'

Ray stopped her. 'Aren't you going to say thank you?'

'What for?'

'Well, you know – getting you the interview. It was me persuaded the old man he ought to see you.'

'I'm very grateful. Goodbye.'

But he wouldn't let her go. Gripping her arm, he went on: 'How about you and me going out for a bit of a celebration tonight? We could go to the flicks if you like. there's a good picture on this week – Charlie Chaplin in *Shoulder Arms*.'

'I don't like Charlie Chaplin much; I think he's rather common.'

'But it's supposed to be his best ever. Come on, how about it? Meet me outside the Electra at seven o'clock.'

She looked into his eyes, and saw the glimmer of something she could not understand – something secret and mysterious. It scared her a little, but it excited her too.

'All right,' she said. 'If you like – seven o'clock, then.'

This time she did not keep him waiting, but arrived on the dot. He bought the tickets, and they went inside. Down at the front, a plump lady with bangles was playing an upright piano, but Ray suggested they should sit as far back as possible.

'If I'm too close, that piano-playing gives me a headache,' he said firmly, leading the way along the back row.

Then the lights dimmed and the film began. As Ray had promised, it was Chaplin on top of his form, yet the audience did not laugh much. The scenario had Charlie packed off to war as a foot-slogging private in the trenches, dodging enemy shells and camouflaged within a canvas-and-plaster tree. It must have seemed very funny when it was filmed, half a world away in Hollywood; here in South London, where there was scarcely one household that had not suffered the loss of a husband or sweetheart, an uncle, brother or cousin, the humour fell a little flat.

Ray, who was not bothered by such considerations, would normally have enjoyed the comedy – but tonight he had other things on his mind.

Throughout the film, he made a series of stealthy advances upon Babs, letting his foot touch hers, his knee nudging her leg, sliding his arm along the back of the seat until his hand rested on her shoulder. She did not appear to notice, neither withdrawing nor responding, but gazed fixedly at the flickering black-and-white images on the screen.

Greatly daring, he leaned closer still and whispered in her ear: 'You're driving me barmy. You're lovely, you are . . .'

She did not seem to hear, and he brushed his lips across her cheek, but when he began to work his way towards her mouth she pushed him away.

'Stop it,' she whispered fiercely. 'Don't do that!'

Deflated, he huddled back into his seat and tried to concentrate on the film instead.

By the time they left the cinema, he had recovered his confidence, and as they passed a poster in the foyer advertising 'a laugh a minute – starring the one and only Fatty Arbuckle – coming next week!' he said casually: 'My mother and father know Mr Arbuckle very well. He's a wonderful bloke, one of their best friends. Last time Dad wrote, he told me all about a party they went to at Mr Arbuckle's house. One of those big Hollywood do's – swimming pool, champagne, balloons – the lot.'

'Very nice,' said Babs coolly.

'And this is Mr Arbuckle's latest picture – Dad says I shouldn't miss it. What d'you say we come again next week, eh?'

Outside on the pavement, Babs turned to face him. 'Thank you all the same,' she said, 'but I'd rather not.'

'What's the matter?'

'You know very well. If I'd realised you were that sort of person I'd never have come here tonight.'

'It was only a bit of fun—' he began sulkily.

'Then I'm sorry to disappoint you; I'm not that kind of girl. And don't bother to see me home – I'll go on the bus. Good night!'

He watched her walk off briskly into the darkness; anger and frustration knotted together in his guts.

'Just you wait, you stuck-up bitch,' he thought. 'I'll get you, one of these days. You'll see . . . Then you'll be sorry.'

When Babs got home, she found the family in a state of uproar. They were all gathered in her mother's sitting room, and everyone was talking at once.

'What's going on?' she asked.

Gerry rolled his eyes to heaven. 'Mother's lost one of her little treasures. I've had to move all the furniture and roll up the rugs, but it's nowhere to be found.'

'What are you talking about?'

Aunt Ethel, on her hands and knees at the fireplace, was digging into the ashes beneath the grate with the poker. Raising her voice, she called shrilly to Babs: 'You haven't seen it, have you? Your mother's little pearl brooch?'

'The one shaped like a heart; it was one of the last things dear Papa gave me,' said her mother tragically. 'If we don't find it, I shall never forgive myself.'

'It can't have vanished into thin air,' said Babs. 'When did you have it last?'

'I'm not sure. It was on the little table this morning – at least, it was there last night. Such a fine piece of jewellery. I've always loved that brooch.'

'Try to remember where you saw it,' Babs urged her. 'It can't have gone far.'

'Have you looked in the coal scuttle?' suggested Aunt Aggie.

'Don't be silly, Aggie, how could it possibly get into the scuttle?' Muriel reproved her sister. 'It hasn't got wings, dear. Somebody must have moved it.'

Smoothing his moustache with his forefinger, Gerald said, 'Look here, we don't want to waste any more time arguing, do we? You can rule out Auntie Eth and me, because we've been at the office all day.'

'Well, I certainly haven't touched it,' said Babs. 'And obviously Mummy hasn't got it, so . . .'

They were all looking at Aggie.

'Come on, Auntie,' Gerry said wearily. 'What have you done with it this time, old dear?'

'Agnes, how could you?' screeched Ethel. 'You promised faithfully you wouldn't be naughty again.'

'Just put it back, Agnes, and we'll say no more about it,' added Muriel. 'Tell us the truth, dear. What have you done with it?'

Confronted by their accusations, Aggie burst into tears. 'I'd tell you if I could,' she sobbed, 'truly I would . . . But if I did take it, I must have forgotten, because I've been thinking and thinking, and I've looked everywhere – only I can't *remember* . . .'

Weeping like a child, she let Ethel lead her away to her room, and was put to bed.

Chapter Three

'*HOW MUCH?*' ASKED Ray, incredulously.

'Two pounds ten,' repeated the jeweller, removing the magnifying lens from his eye. 'Maybe I could stretch a point and call it two pounds, twelve-and-six, but that's the top whack.'

Between them on the counter, the pearl brooch looked suddenly small and tawdry.

'But it's got to be worth more than that. They're real pearls—'

'Sorry, sonny-boy.' The jeweller shook his head. 'They're artificial, and the setting's not silver – it's pinchbeck. Wherever you got this, you want to ask for your money back; you've been sold a pup.'

Although they had done business together several times, Ray had not been very forthcoming about the little trinkets he had 'come across', and the jeweller had never asked any questions.

'Two pounds, twelve shillings and sixpence – take it or leave it.'

Ray muttered uncomfortably, 'I can't take it back – I bought it off of a bloke in a pub. Call it two pounds fifteen – OK?'

'Well, seeing it's you . . .' The jeweller pulled open a drawer beneath the counter and started to rummage in a cashbox.

About to hand over the brooch, Ray suddenly had an idea. 'Hang on – I've changed my mind. I know somebody else who might be pleased to have it.'

'You won't get a better price anywhere, I can promise you that.'

'Never mind.' For the first time, Ray smiled. 'Money isn't everything.'

'Alleluia! Alleluia!' sang Valerie, at the top of her voice. 'Praise the everlasting King.'

The choirmaster nodded and said, 'That's better, it's coming along. Now let's try the second verse.'

He raised his baton slowly, then brought it down swiftly, and the choir launched into: 'Praise Him for His grace and favour, To our fathers in distress—'

But he was already tapping the baton crossly on the music-stand and calling out: 'No, no, that won't do at all!' He glared at them. 'Those dreadful cockney vowels are creeping in again. Do you realise that in a few weeks' time you are going to be welcoming our King and Queen? What do you suppose they'll think, if they hear you singing like that?' He exaggerated the lazy South London accent: '*Prize 'im for 'is grice and fiver* . . .'

Some of the girls began to giggle, and he reprimanded them sternly. 'Quiet, please! It's *not* funny. Let's try again, and this time I want you to imagine Their Majesties are standing here beside me. One, two—'

'*Praise* Him for His *grace* and *favour!*' they chanted dutifully, and got to the end of the verse without further mishaps.

Val was usually one of the first to get the giggles, but tonight she didn't see the funny side of it; this was a very important occasion – the first time she had set foot inside the Crystal Palace for six long years. All through the war, it had been closed to the public, since it was converted to a Naval Training Centre, officially named HMS *Victory VI* – affectionately known as HMS *Crystal Palace* – housing around thirteen thousand sailors. This year, on 1 January, the Navy had evacuated the premises and the slow, laborious process of repair and redecoration had begun. Now, a few months later, preparations were under way for the grand re-opening on 9 June. The official ceremony was to be carried out by His Majesty, King George V, with a full accompaniment of military bands, orchestra and massed choirs, augmented by local musicians. Among them was the Penge and District Choral Society, which is why Miss Valerie Watkins, one of their youngest members, was now throwing back her head and singing with might and main: 'Alleluia! Alleluia! Glorious in His faithfulness.'

This evening, they were only accompanied by a single upright piano, but outside the rehearsal room there was a continual thudding of hammers and the regular to-and-fro of saws ripping through planks. The builders were hard at it, working overtime to get the job finished.

At that point they were interrupted again. When the door opened, the background noise became louder than ever. Goaded, the choirmaster began irritably, 'I thought I said we were not to be disturbed!' Then, in a change of tone, 'Oh, I beg your pardon.'

The newcomer inclined his head gravely. 'Forgive me. I wasn't sure if you were aware of the time. It's nearly half-past eight.'

His appearance was striking. Fifty years old, with a light summer coat thrown over his shoulders, he had the bearing of a much younger man. He wore a suit of grey plus-fours and a grey homburg hat on his head, set at a jaunty angle. From his trim military moustache to the gold watch-chain across his waistcoat and the silver-topped cane in his hand, he made a deep impression on some of the lady choristers.

'Ah, thank you for reminding me, sir,' murmured the choirmaster. 'We've been working so hard, I hadn't realised . . .'

'I hesitated to interrupt, but my workmen are about to pack up for the night, so I shall be locking the doors shortly.'

'Of course, of course.' The choirmaster addressed the musicians. 'As ever, ladies and gentlemen, time is the enemy, and we have to leave. We shall continue at the same time next week. I look forward to seeing you then.'

A buzz of chatter arose as the singers began to gather up hats, coats and music-cases; the man in the homburg remained for a few moments, in conversation with the choirmaster, then joined the flowing tide of men and women leaving the rehearsal room.

Valerie wasted several minutes looking for her scarf – could she have dropped it somewhere? She searched under the rows of folding chairs without success then, as she went to put on her street coat, she found the scarf tucked into one of the sleeves. About to leave, she noticed the silver-topped cane propped up in the corner by the door, and interrupted the choirmaster, who was deep in discussion with the pianist about an awkward rallentando.

'Excuse me, but I think the gentleman left his stick behind.'

'Who? Oh, the General Manager. How tiresome – I suppose I should go and look for him.'

'Don't bother – I'll find him.' She took the stick and set off quickly.

In the dusk, the central nave of the Palace was a vast, shadowy space; half-built partitions were dwarfed by huge columns that disappeared up into darkness. High overhead, Val could see the first stars, twinkling through the great vault. The aisles were still thronged with singers and workmen, making their way to the exits, homeward bound.

She craned her neck, looking for the General Manager. When she saw him, she broke into a run and caught him up below the Crystal Palace clock. He glanced at her quizzically and pointed upwards.

'Eight-thirty exactly. Time you weren't here, young lady!'

'Yes, sir – only you forgot this.' And she handed him his walking stick.

He raised an eyebrow. 'Bless my soul, so I did. How very good of you.'

'Not at all. Good night, Mr Buckland.'

She turned to go, but he stopped her. 'You know who I am?'

'Yes, sir – you're the Manager. I read about you in the newspaper.'

'Did you indeed? And you must be a member of our choir. Are you a professional singer?'

'No, sir. I'm a clerk in an insurance office.'

'Really? And is this your first visit to the Crystal Palace?'

'Oh no. Mum and Dad used to bring me here before the war, when I was little. I thought it was the most wonderful place in the world.'

'And what do you think of it now, eh?'

'I still think so, and when they've finished getting it ready, it's going to be better than ever.'

'Quite right – it will be.' He checked his watch against the huge dial, high above them. 'Time for me to lock up; let me see you off the premises.'

The last stragglers were leaving as they reached the main exit, and he added, 'Perhaps you wonder what I'm doing here, so late in the day? I like to keep an eye on things, as far as I can. Fortunately I only live just round the corner, so I spend a good deal of time here. I dare say that seems strange to you.'

'No, sir.' Valerie smiled. 'If I was in charge of the Palace, I'd be the first here in the morning and the last to leave at night.'

'Would you?' He looked at her more closely. 'Yes, I believe you would . . . May I ask your name, young lady?'

'Watkins – Valerie Watkins.'

'If you don't think I'm being inquisitive, Miss Watkins – do you live hereabouts?'

'Ten minutes away, halfway up Anerley Hill – five minutes if I run!'

'And I've kept you talking – you'd better start running, or your mother will worry!' He gave a short bark of laughter, then added more seriously: 'But let me say one thing before you go. I'm going to need some more office staff here, because we have a great deal of

52

work ahead of us. If you should ever think of changing your job, would you let me know?'

Valerie's face lit up. 'When can I come and see you, sir?' she asked.

'How soon can you start?' he said.

It was a dull day, and Babs had been given a job that was even duller. Mr Faber had gone to an auction sale. As a rule, Fabers Furnishing did not deal in second-hand goods, but he had heard there were some interesting pieces and he might pick up a bargain. Before he left, he had given her a stack of bills to type and send off. It was dreary, repetitive work, and after half an hour she was very bored indeed. Abandoning the typewriter, she took this week's copy of *The Young Ladies' Companion* out of her desk drawer, and turned to the latest instalment of the serial. When the door opened, she tried to slip the magazine under the accounts file, then relaxed as Ray walked in.

'Oh, it's you,' she said. 'You might knock, another time.'

He smirked. 'Having a nice read, were you? All right, I won't split on you to His Nibs.'

'It's none of your business,' she said loftily. 'But if you must know, I can't keep typing all the afternoon without stopping. It makes my wrists ache. I have to give myself a rest every now and then.'

'Oh, yeah? It's been really quiet in the shop too,' he said. 'We've had one customer in since dinner-time, and she was "only looking" . . . Anyhow, I'm glad the old man's gone out. It gives us the chance for a talk, don't it?'

'I'm afraid I can't spare the time. I must get on with my typing—'

'Get away – the typing can wait.' He perched on the corner of Mr Faber's desk, swinging his legs. 'I've got a little surprise for you.'

'What sort of surprise?'

'You'll see. I had a bit of luck last night. I happened to be walking past a jeweller's shop and when I looked in the window – guess what I saw?'

'The Koh-i-noor diamond?'

'Not exactly.' He took a small box from his inside pocket and opened it. 'What d'you think of that?'

She stared at it. 'Mummy's brooch! I don't understand . . .'

'No more did I – that's why I went in to ask about it. Of course I'd only seen it the once, that time I came to call and your Mum knocked the table over, but I helped pick the things up, and that's when I noticed it. So I said to myself: "There's a coincidence – they must be a matching pair" and I went into the shop to see how much they wanted for it, but—'

'But that's Mummy's brooch,' Babs told him. 'She lost it weeks ago. We looked everywhere . . . How on earth did it turn up in a jeweller's shop?'

'Let me finish,' he said. 'I thought at first it couldn't be the same one, because the bloke in the shop told me they're only imitation pearls – not worth more than a few quid.'

'I don't understand.' Babs was bewildered. 'It *is* the same one, I'd know it anywhere.'

'I asked the jeweller where he got it, and he told me some feller brought it in who worked on the dustcarts, and he'd found it in one of the rubbish bins somewhere near the Crystal Palace. That's when I twigged it must have got thrown out by mistake. Mind you, by rights he should have handed it in, or took it to the police – but there, that's human nature, isn't it? Finders keepers, as the saying goes.'

'Which jeweller was it?' Babs asked. 'I'll go and ask him—'

'No, I'd rather you didn't do that. It might lead to a lot of unpleasantness. I wouldn't want to make trouble for anyone – that's why I bought the brooch myself, so I could let you have it. Now you can give it back to your Mum, can't you, seeing she sets so much store by it. Least said, soonest mended, eh?'

'Well – yes, I suppose so.' Babs went to the hatstand in the corner, fumbling for her purse in her coat-pocket. 'How much did you pay for it?'

'No, no – don't bother about that. This will be my little present for your Mum.'

'Oh, I couldn't possibly let you! I must give you the money. How much?'

'Well, if you really want to know, it set me back three quid,' he told her.

She looked embarrassed. 'I'm afraid I haven't got that much on me.'

'Tell you what, let's go halves. Call it thirty bob, eh? My pleasure.'

'Oh, that's very nice of you.' She produced the coins from her purse. 'There . . . You must come round one evening, so we can thank you properly.'

'Ta very much,' he said. 'I'd really like that.'

Next morning, Babs reported that her mother had been overjoyed to see her brooch again, and that they would like him to come to supper at Belmont on Saturday evening. Once more, Ray put on his best suit, and arrived carrying a small bunch of spring flowers.

Muriel Glynn accepted the bouquet with amazement and delight.

'For me? Mr Duke, you really are too kind. Aggie dear, would you find a vase and put these in water? I don't know what I've done to deserve such generosity. First the brooch, and now these lovely flowers . . .'

'Glad I could help,' he assured her. 'Small world, eh? I just happened to be walking past the shop when I spotted the brooch in the window—'

'So Babs told me – though heaven only knows how it got into our dustbin.' Fondly, Muriel touched the brooch, now pinned to the bosom of her dress. 'As you see, now I have it back safe and sound, I shall never let it out of my sight again.'

Gerald joined them, announcing that supper was ready. 'Aunt Ethel's waiting to dish up, and I've just decanted the wine – so if you're ready . . .'

Babs began to help her mother up, but Ray stepped forward gallantly. 'Allow me, Mrs Glynn.' He offered Muriel his arm. 'My privilege.'

They made a stately progress along the landing to the dining room, which was dark and sombre, the stained-glass windows ornamented with various shields and heraldic designs.

'The central one is the DeWitt coat of arms,' Muriel told Ray, as she took the chair at the head of the table. 'We're rather proud of it.'

She insisted on Ray having the place of honour at her right hand, and a few moments later Ethel came in with a steaming soup tureen. Gerald circled the table, pouring a little wine into each glass, and they began their supper.

After such formal preparations, it was something of an anti-climax; lentil soup was followed by boiled bacon and cabbage, and dessert consisted of a handful of nuts and a plate of old, wrinkled apples – 'From our orchard,' Muriel explained. Even the wine was rough and raw but Ray, who had never tasted wine before, was impressed.

When Aggie and Ethel cleared away the dishes, he complimented them on the meal and thanked them for inviting him.

'It was the least we could do,' said Muriel. 'If it wasn't for you, my lovely brooch would have been lost for ever – and I treasure it so much.'

'Yes, I know, but . . .' He hesitated, then said bluntly: 'If you don't mind me saying so, I was a bit surprised when the jeweller said the pearls weren't real. I mean, being a present from your father and all that.'

Muriel smiled. 'Yes – I was surprised myself when Babs mentioned it, but afterwards of course I remembered. When Papa gave me the brooch, he said it was far too precious to wear every day, so he had it copied. The real pearls are safely locked away in a bank vault, with our other valuables. But I've had the brooch so long, I'd quite forgotten it was a copy – wasn't that silly of me?'

She turned her liquid violet eyes to the stained-glass windows, where the last glow of daylight was fading from the sky, and changed the subject.

'Oh, do look – this is my favourite time of day. The garden always looks at its best in the dusk – such a shame I can't go out to enjoy it. Babs, dear, I don't believe Mr Duke has visited our garden. Why don't you take him to see the daffodils, before it gets dark?'

There wasn't much to see. The daffodils were almost over – dry orange trumpets, twisted into the long grass; the lawn was a shaggy field, and the shrubbery had run wild. They strolled along the overgrown path of crazy paving to the trees that lined the boundary wall.

'That's the Crystal Palace grounds over there,' said Babs. 'I'm glad the sailors have moved out; they were so rude – they used to whistle and call out whenever they saw me.'

As they reached the end of the path, Ray said, 'Can't say I blame 'em. You're the sort of girl any chap would whistle at.'

'Don't be silly. It's getting cold – shall we go in?' She was about to go back to the house, but he put out an arm, blocking the way.

'Not just yet. I like it out here.'

'There's nothing more to see. Daphne used to look after the garden, but we're hoping to find another gardener soon.'

'I'm not that struck on gardens, myself. It was you I came out to see. Didn't you say you were going to thank me – properly?'

'Please, Ray. It will be dark soon. Let me pass—'

'In a minute. I brought back the old brooch, didn't I? I think I ought to get a reward for that.'

He was very close to her, and they were completely hidden among the bushes; no one could see them from the house. When he put his arms round her, she lifted her face to him and let him kiss her – a long, hungry kiss. Until this moment she had felt nothing for him, but now for the first time his passion was echoed by hers. The sudden wave of longing took her by surprise. Involuntarily, her hands clutched at his shoulders, and her mouth opened under his. It was thrilling – but it was frightening, too.

Struggling against her own instincts, she pulled away from him, saying breathlessly: 'There, that's it – that's your reward, and I hope you're satisfied . . . because it's all you're going to get.'

Then she dodged past him, walking quickly up the path and into the house.

In the weeks that followed she took care not to get into a situation where they would be alone together. One morning at the end of May, as Ray was turning round the sign on the shop door so that it said Closed For Lunch, Valerie Watkins tapped on the glass. Unwillingly, he opened the door again.

'Can't you see we're shut?' he asked. 'It's dinner-time.'

'I know that – is Babs here?'

'She's having her sandwiches in the office.'

'Oh good. Will you tell her I'd like a word with her?' She waited on the doorstep; a moment later Babs picked her way through the sofas and armchairs.

'Hello, Valerie. Ray said you wanted to see me?'

'That's right. How long have you got for lunch?'

'Just the hour – why?'

'Fine. Bring your sandwiches and let's go into the Palace grounds for a picnic. I haven't seen you for ages.'

'But the grounds aren't open to the public yet.'

'I work there now, don't I? I'll take you in with me.'

'Well, if you think it'll be all right . . .' Babs went to collect the salmon-and-shrimp paste sandwiches Auntie Ag had made her.

Ray, who had overheard their conversation, asked: 'All right if I come too?'

'The more the merrier.' Val was in a cheerful mood. 'Have you got some sandwiches as well?'

'No, I generally have a beer and some bread and cheese over at the pub.'

'Don't worry, I've got more than I need. I'll share mine with you,' Val told him.

So they walked to the end of Church Road, and crossed over to Crystal Palace Parade. Valerie showed her staff pass to the man at the gate, and he let them through.

'It's too good a day to stay indoors.' Val led the way to the main terrace. 'We've been so busy all the morning, it's nice to get out.'

But it was busy outdoors too. An army of gardeners were at work, weeding the flowerbeds, or cleaning out the huge ornamental fountains. Val found a shady spot under the trees, and threw herself down on the grass, remarking, 'Isn't it nice, watching other people working? It's simply frantic inside. Mr Buckland keeps everybody on their toes – morning, noon and night.'

'Who's Mr Buckland?'

'The General Manager – my boss. He works so hard himself, he expects everybody else to do the same.' Val opened her packet of sandwiches and offered it to Ray. 'Help yourself . . . and if you see a man in a grey homburg, just tell me and we'll duck out of sight. He's always on the go, patrolling the grounds, and if he catches anyone not working, he goes wild.'

'But it's your lunch-hour,' protested Babs. 'You're entitled to some time off.'

'He never stops, so he can't understand why lesser mortals have a weakness for little things like food and sleep.'

'What a slave-driver!' Babs was shocked. 'I wouldn't work for a man like that. You must be sorry you left the insurance company.'

'No fear! I wouldn't have missed this for worlds. I can't wait for the Gala opening; I spent last week sending out gilt-edged invitations to all the important people – cabinet ministers, generals, bishops – they'll all be here on the great day.'

'All the nobs, eh?' said Ray with his mouth full. 'Any chance of you slipping Babs and me a couple of tickets?'

'Not a hope; the whole place is going to be packed. Though I did manage to wangle some tickets for Ted and Daff – and Annie.'

Babs bridled. 'You mean Daphne's invited, and I'm not?'

'Oh, not indoors,' explained Val. 'There's going to be some rows of seats outside the main entrance for ex-servicemen and their families to watch the King and Queen arrive; I persuaded my boss to put Ted on the list. And they're inviting war-widows and people who lost their nearest and dearest, so that includes Mum as well, bless her. But later in the day, when the Royal Family and the bigwigs have gone, they're letting in the general public. I could get you in then, if you like.'

'I don't think I'll bother,' said Babs. 'I hate crowds.'

'How about you?' Ray asked Val. 'I suppose you'll be inside, with the high-and-mighty?'

'Well, yes – but I'm singing with the choir in the main hall. I should have a grandstand view of the opening ceremony.'

'Some people have all the luck,' sniffed Babs, taking a dainty bite of salmon-and-shrimp. 'What's your boss like, this Mr Buckland?'

'Oh, he's wonderful. Mind you, I wouldn't like to get on the wrong side of him. The other day he found some of the builders playing cards when they were supposed to be working, and he sacked them on the spot. But as long as you do your job, he's as nice as pie.'

'I meant – what does he look like?'

'Tall, well-built, good-looking – why?'

'I just wondered. And you share an office with him, do you?'

'Oh no, he's got his own office. The rest of us work in a little row of rabbit-hutches – the secretary, the accountant, the cashier and so on.'

'I thought you were his secretary?'

'Goodness, I'm just one of the dogsbodies. There are about eight of us altogether, doing the typing and filing and running errands.'

Babs polished off the last of her sandwiches and screwed up the paper bag. 'I shouldn't care for that. I'd sooner work for Mr Faber; it's just him and me in our office – that's so much nicer.'

'Well, yes – as long as you get on with him.'

'Of course I do; he's a charming man. Very quiet and polite – quite attractive in his own way.'

The two girls were so enthralled by this discussion, they had almost forgotten Ray was there; now he broke into the conversation.

'What d'you mean, attractive? Faber's an old man – he must be over forty.'

Babs turned her head, looking him up and down. 'Being attractive has nothing to do with how old you are – it's not a physical thing. Mr Faber's a real gentleman. That's what makes him attractive.'

Ray scrambled to his feet and began to walk away. Valerie called after him, 'You haven't finished your sandwiches! Where are you going?'

'To the pub!' He threw the words over his shoulder. 'I need a drink.'

The ninth of June turned out to be sunny. After a cloudy start, the sky cleared and by midday several of the men in the stands at the main entrance took off their coats, and some of the ladies put up parasols in case they should get sunburned.

'Royal weather,' said Kate Watkins.

Next to her, little Annie sat on her mother's lap, clutching a small Union Jack which they had bought from a street-hawker. Kate said,

"Scuse me, duck – can Nana have this a minute?' Taking the little flag, she started to fan herself vigorously. Annie was indignant, and began to wail.

'Here, have this instead, Ma,' said Ted. Val had given them a copy of the official programme before they set out; taking it from Daphne, he passed it to his mother. 'She won't give us any peace unless she's got her waver.'

'I was trying to read that,' Daphne objected mildly. 'What time are the King and Queen supposed to turn up? How much longer have we got to wait?'

'Hang on, something seems to be happening,' he said, standing up to get a better view.

Other people followed his example, and soon the whole crowd were on their feet. When the open barouche came into view along the Parade, they began to cheer, and by the time it drew up alongside the strip of red carpet, the noise was deafening.

King George dressed in naval uniform, and Queen Mary in powder-blue, stepped from the carriage, attended by an equerry and a lady-in-waiting. The Crystal Palace officials were lined up on the pavement, and one gentleman stepped forward, unwound a parchment scroll and began to read out a speech. Owing to the noisy enthusiasm of the crowd, not one word of it could be understood.

'Who's that?' Daphne yelled in Ted's ear.

'Search me,' he said, and grabbed the programme from his mother. 'It says here "*Loyal Address to Their Majesties – Sir Alfred Mond*".'

'Who's he when he's at home?'

'The Commissioner of Works, according to this.'

'And what does he do?'

'How the heck should I know?'

By now the crowd was growing impatient, and several people began calling for order. 'Quiet, please! Silence for His Majesty!'

A hush fell as the King's equerry handed him a sheet of paper. He unfolded it and began to read.

'It was with great satisfaction that I learned some seven years ago that the Crystal Palace and its grounds had been secured for the nation.'

'What's he mean?' whispered Kate, and Daphne replied under her breath: 'The Crystal Palace had gone bankrupt, then the Lord Mayor of London started a fund to buy it for the nation, before the land-grabbers could get their hands on it.'

Meanwhile, His Majesty continued: 'It would have been an irreparable loss to the capital of the Empire if this vast building and its beautiful site, intimately associated as they were with the history of the glorious reign of Queen Victoria, had ceased to be available for public use and enjoyment.'

'Then the war broke out, and it was closed down anyhow,' muttered Ted.

'Until today,' added Daphne.

As if he echoed her, the King went on, 'Today it is my agreeable duty to inaugurate at one and the same time the return of the Crystal Palace to the uses of peace – and its opening as a national possession; a place for education and recreation, and the promotion of industry, commerce and art . . .'

When he had finished his speech, he cut the ribbon, and the Royal Party moved on into the building.

As the ceremony was over, the crowd settled back on to the benches. Kate, who had shifted a little to one side in order to see past the picture hat of a woman in front, plumped down, much to her embarrassment, on to the lap of a strange gentleman.

'Oh, I beg your pardon,' she exclaimed, turning red. 'Clumsy of me!'

'Not at all, madam.' The gentleman raised his top hat. Several years older than Kate, he was dressed entirely in black, and wore a pair of gold pince-nez. 'It wasn't your fault – the stands are overcrowded.'

'Still, that's only to be expected,' she said, moving into the next vacant place. 'On such a happy occasion, I mean.'

'You call this a happy occasion?' he asked.

'Well, yes – don't you?'

He made no reply, but looked off into the distance, over the heads of the crowd. Feeling rebuffed, Kate edged further from him, and asked Ted: 'What happens next?'

'I dunno. I suppose we sit here and wait till they come out again.'

'And how long will that be?' said Daphne.

'Ask me another.' He shrugged, and glanced at the programme again. 'What's going on indoors?'

Inside, under the great glass roof, it was very warm indeed – and even more crowded. The building was decorated with hundreds of flags, and packed with four thousand people – a distinguished gathering of statesmen, high-ranking officers from the armed forces, church dignitaries, and leading members of the legal profession and the Civil Service.

From her vantage point high up in the Concert Hall, Valerie had an uninterrupted view of the Royal Box; as she watched, the Royal Standard broke, fluttering out, and the King and Queen appeared, taking their places. At once the conductor gave the signal, and the assembled musicians launched into the National Anthem – the massed bands of the Coldstreams and the Scots Guards, a full symphony orchestra, and the mighty Willis organ – all singing with one voice, beseeching God to save their gracious King.

The anthem was followed by a hymn: *Oh, God, our help in ages past* and a short religious ceremony. The Bishop of Southwark offered a prayer for the fallen, and the Archbishop of Canterbury gave thanks for peace. Then there was more music, and more speeches, and at last the ceremony was over.

It was strange to be talking of peace, Valerie thought, when so much of the Palace was filled with weapons of war. Twenty-four acres of floor-space had been allocated to the new Imperial War Museum; a lavish display, with three large sections of the building given over to the Army, Navy and Air Force. Their sombre exhibits – guns, tanks, model battleships – were in stark contrast to the potted palms and climbing ferns; eighteen-inch shells were piled up in a pyramid among Egyptian statues and mummy-cases, and a sea-plane which had flown in action at Jutland was perched above an ornamental pool of prize goldfish.

When the Royal Party had left, an inaugural luncheon was held for all the other distinguished visitors, and after that was cleared away, the doors were thrown open, for the first time in six years, to the general public.

'Isn't it beautiful?' said Kate, as they wandered up and down the aisles.

'Nice to see the old place again,' agreed Ted, with a wide-eyed Annie perched on his shoulders. 'Look at all the pretty flags, sweetheart.'

Daphne said nothing; the grim exhibits seemed out of place against the background of flowers and foliage and a riot of coloured bunting.

Turning a corner, they came across a party of schoolgirls walking two by two; one of the teachers in charge recognised Daphne, and they gathered around her.

'Miss Glynn – fancy seeing you! Oh sorry, it's Mrs Watkins now, isn't it?'

Some of the older girls remembered Daphne – 'You were teaching the Upper School when I was in the Juniors, miss' – and they all made a fuss of little Annie, who looked amazed to find herself the centre of so much attention.

'You must be so proud of her,' said the youngest teacher enviously. 'If I had to decide between teaching and having a family, I know which I'd choose.'

'Why should you have to choose?' asked Daphne. 'Why not do both?'

The teacher looked astonished. 'You don't mean you'll come back to school one day?'

Daphne looked quickly at Ted, but he had turned away. 'Well – I might,' she said.

A little later, Valerie found them at the end of the central nave, and exclaimed: 'I've been hunting high and low for you lot! Where have you been so far? What do you want to see next?'

Kate sighed. 'Between you and me, duck, what I really want is a sit-down and a nice cup of tea. I'm parched.'

'Let's all have tea,' suggested Val. 'There's a Lyons refreshment room along here. I expect Annie would like a fizzy lemon, wouldn't you, lovey?'

'We'll come and find you presently,' said Ted. 'Why don't you and Mum look after the infant for ten minutes? Daff and me want to do a bit more sightseeing first.'

So Valerie led her mother and her niece into the tea-room, but all the tables were taken. A waitress in a trim black dress and starched white apron told them: 'I'm afraid you'll have to share. This way, please.'

She took them to join a solitary man, nursing a pot of tea for one, and began, 'Excuse me, sir. Would you mind if—'

He rose to his feet. 'But we've already met. Please – you're very welcome.'

It was the man Kate had sat down upon, a few hours earlier. Afraid she might blush again, she demurred. 'Oh no, we wouldn't want to be a nuisance.'

'Not in the very least. What a dear little girl.'

So they all sat down; the waitress took their order and disappeared. They began to make polite conversation, saying how much they were enjoying the exhibition. Then the dear little girl, bored by all this grown-up talk, reached forward, clutching at the milk jug, which overturned, flooding the table and dripping on to the gentleman's knees.

Valerie jumped up. 'I'll get a cloth,' she offered, and rushed off, leaving Kate babbling apologies.

'There's no harm done.' The gentleman pulled out a handkerchief and dabbed at his trousers. 'Accidents will happen. This is your granddaughter, I take it?'

'Yes, this is Annie. Tell him you're sorry, there's a good girl.'

'There's nothing to be sorry about, I assure you. It makes a change for me to meet a young family. Perhaps you'll allow me to introduce myself. My name is Colpoys – William Colpoys.'

Out in the main hall, Ted and Daphne were walking round the exhibits. She was still very quiet, and at last he said, 'All right, let's have it – what's wrong? Why are you so down in the dumps?'

'Who says I'm down in the dumps?'

'It's written all over your face. I suppose it was meeting those girls from Carmichael Road that did it.'

'No, it wasn't. I was pleased to see them.'

'Come on, you know you're still hankering to go back to teaching.'

'That wasn't what upset me. It's all this—' She gestured helplessly at the guns, the shells, the armoured cars all round them. 'I liked the Crystal Palace the way it used to be.'

Under a glass showcase, a diorama showed a cross-section of the front-line trenches, demonstrating how the retreating enemy had planted booby traps in the dugouts. Laughing schoolboys were jostling to press a row of buttons; each one lit up a flash, representing a hidden land mine – they were having a wonderful time.

'It's only a game to them,' she said, 'but I can't help thinking – those used to be real bombs once. Real men got killed . . . You were there, you must know better than any of us. How can you bear it?'

'I told you, Daff,' he said. 'It wasn't all like that – we had some good times as well. There was the concert party – the troop shows – we had a lot of fun.'

'*Fun?*' She stared at him. 'Watching a concert party?'

He smiled sheepishly. 'I wasn't watching – I was in it.'

'What do you mean? I don't understand.'

'We put on our own shows behind the lines. We made up sketches and did a few skits. You know me, always making a fool of myself.'

'You never told me that.'

'No, well – I suppose it sounded a bit daft. But I used to enjoy going on stage, making the blokes laugh . . .'

He was looking past her now, gazing at another time, another place. She tried to make sense of what he had told her, but she felt completely lost. All at once, her husband had turned into someone she had never known. Suddenly, he was a stranger.

In the little office behind the furniture shop, Babs was seeing Mr Faber in a different light.

It was early-closing day. As a rule they had the afternoon off, but today Mr Faber had asked the staff to put in a few extra hours – and since he was paying them overtime, they had all agreed. Tubby Dingwall and Ray Duke were out in the yard, unloading a new delivery of furniture from the van and taking it into the stockroom at the back of the building, while Mr Faber and Babs brought the ledgers up to date, in time for next week's annual audit.

There wasn't enough room for the big old-fashioned account books on her little desk, so Babs was sitting at Mr Faber's desk, with the relevant files open around her.

Mr Faber hovered at her shoulder, checking the columns of figures as she turned the pages. It was so warm, he had taken off his jacket. Babs was wearing a thin summer dress with short sleeves, and he was very aware of her perfume, mingled with the soft, intimate smell of her body.

'What's that? A three or an eight?' he asked, bending over her to look more closely at the totals. As he leaned forward, her hair brushed against his face; instinctively, he drew back.

'I think it's an eight,' she said evenly.

He walked away, feeling the blood pounding in his veins, struggling to control his feelings. With an effort, he kept his voice steady as he said: 'I'm sorry to make you work on such a fine day. You must wish you were out enjoying the sunshine.'

'I don't mind,' she said. 'It's the same for all of us, isn't it? I expect you'd rather be at home with Mrs Faber, wouldn't you?'

He paused, then replied carefully, 'Not really. My wife lives in a little world of her own these days. I try to keep her company, as much as I can – but she doesn't seem to take much interest in anything any more.'

'Oh, I am sorry.' Babs glanced at him, but he had his back to her. She could not see his expression. 'How sad.'

'Yes, it is sad. Being an invalid cuts her off from everything; life must be very lonely for her.'

'For you too, I expect. What a shame you haven't any family.'

He swung round to face her. 'We had a daughter, but she had

meningitis. She died when she was nine years old . . . almost exactly ten years ago.'

Now it was Babs who looked away, unable to meet his eyes. 'How dreadful. I'd never have said, if I'd realised—'

'Not many people know; I don't like to talk about it. My wife broke down completely after that, and she's been – unwell – ever since.'

'I'm so sorry,' she said helplessly.

He took a step towards her. 'I remember you told me you're nineteen. If Margaret had lived, she would have been your age.' He hesitated, then went on: 'Perhaps you remind me of the daughter I lost.'

'I understand.' Babs moistened her lips with the tip of her tongue. 'I'm glad you told me.'

'By the way, I'd sooner you didn't mention this to anyone. I'd like to keep it a secret – between you and me.'

'All right.' She did not know what else to say, and added clumsily, 'P'raps we ought to get on with the books.' She turned the next page of the ledger, bowing her head; he stood close to her once more.

'The figures are so tiny, it's hard to make them out,' she said. 'That looks like a five, but it could be a six.'

He bent over her. 'Where? Show me.'

The smell of her youth and beauty filled his nostrils. She put her hand on his, guiding it down the page.

'There,' she said.

The moment she touched him, a shock of electricity passed between them. He put his other hand lightly upon her shoulder.

'It's not a six,' he said. 'It's a five.'

'Oh yes, so it is. Thank you.' She was breathing faster. His hand slid up her arm, making her tingle. 'It's a good job you're here – to put me right,' she whispered. 'I might have made a mistake otherwise.'

His fingertips slid on to her breast – stroking, exploring . . . She turned her head, looking up into his eyes, and then they kissed. This would be another secret between them.

But their secret was shared by someone else.

Alone in the stockroom, behind the office, Ray Duke was peeping through a crack in the wall, watching them.

At first he was angry. How dare the little bitch let that old man fiddle with her like that? She'd been so high-and-mighty when he tried it – and here she was, carrying on like some little tart . . . But

66

as he watched, he grew more and more excited. An insistent desire overwhelmed him – and it was made even more thrilling by another emotion, deeper and more passionate. Suddenly, he knew what he had to do. They were playing into his hands; he couldn't go wrong.

He clenched his fists and gritted his teeth to stop himself laughing out loud.

Chapter Four

'TIP OUT THE button box. I need all the pearl buttons you've got,' Ted told his mother. 'I've got to look like a regular Pearly King.'

Kate laughed. 'Fancy you doing a turn on the stage. Whatever would your Dad have said, I'd like to know?'

When the family discovered that Ted had taken part as a comedian in troop shows, Kate had been amused and astonished, but as Val pointed out: 'I don't know why you're so surprised. He's been larking about as long as I can remember.'

She had introduced her brother to Mr Barnaby Pine, one of the bass singers in her Choral Society, who organised amateur concert parties to raise funds for the Red Cross. It was Val too, who found a stack of old songs in a local junkshop and brought them home in triumph, helping Ted choose a comic cockney ballad to sing at his first appearance with Mr Pine's troupe.

His debut was to take place at an open-air performance next Saturday at Grange Wood, a public park in Thornton Heath, not far away. There was an ornamental bandstand in the grounds, and on fine evenings these summer shows attracted a loyal and appreciative following.

With only a few days to go, Ted was beginning to feel nervous. He kept going over the words of his song, hoping he would remember them when he stepped out on to the bandstand stage, to face the audience.

'What are you worried about?' Val asked him. 'You've done shows before, in France.'

'The blokes out there weren't fussy – they'd laugh at any old rubbish,' said Ted. 'These people are paying for their tickets.'

On the kitchen floor, Annie watched round-eyed as her father nursed an imaginary baby, feeding it from an imaginary bottle.

> *"E's got 'is muvver's blue eyes,*
> *Yer 'umble's beautiful thirst.*
> *Me an' the missus – er . . .'*

He ground to a halt.

Daphne supplied the missing words: 'Me and the missus is proud of 'im . . .'

'Oh yes. *Me an' the missus is proud of 'im – 'e's our first . . .'*

Sitting at the table, Kate and Daphne were sewing pearl buttons on to an old jacket, to transform Ted into a costermonger. He would have a little round billycock hat on the back of his head, and a spotted red handkerchief knotted like a choker round his throat.

'You'd better come and sit at the side of the stage in case I need prompting,' he told Daphne. 'You know the song better than me.'

'Don't be silly, you were word-perfect at breakfast-time,' she soothed him. 'You'll be all right. We can't all come and hold your hand.'

'It seems dreadful you're not going,' said Kate. 'Are you sure you wouldn't rather I stayed at home with Annie?'

'Of course not,' Daphne told her. 'You mustn't miss Ted's big night – you'll enjoy it.'

Val suggested, 'Why don't you bring Annie as well, then we can all go? It wouldn't hurt her to stay up late for once.'

'No, I don't think so. She's a bit young for that sort of thing,' said Daphne firmly. 'You can tell me about it afterwards.' She wouldn't admit that she felt scared at the thought of watching Ted perform in public; she would have suffered agonies of stage fright on his behalf.

'Well, I'm sure you'll have plenty more chances to see him,' Val told her. 'He's going to be a big success, and Mr Pine will make him the star of the show.'

'Oh, shut up!' said Ted uncomfortably. 'Blow being a star – I'll be happy as long as I get through without drying up.' He took a mouthful of beer, then began all over again:

> *"E's got 'is muvver's blue eyes,*
> *Yer 'umble's beautiful thirst . . .'*

*

Saturday was the busiest day of the week at Fabers Furnishings.

At the end of the afternoon, when Babs cashed up the takings, she was able to report that the shop had broken its own record. 'You're thirty-seven pounds up on last week.'

Mr Faber was delighted. 'That's excellent news!' He called through the open doorway to Ray and Tubby: 'A very good day's work – congratulations.'

'Any chance of a bonus?' asked Ray hopefully.

Mr Faber pretended not to hear him. 'Tubby, you take the keys. Lock the back doors and the yard gates, will you? Ray, you can fold up the front awning.'

When he had closed the office door, he said to Babs in a different tone, 'I've just had an idea. If you're not in any particular hurry, perhaps you'd let me buy you a drink on the way home?'

'Oh Mr Faber, that's ever so kind of you; another day I'd love to, but I'm afraid I can't this evening. I've promised to go out with my friend Valerie. I mustn't be late.'

His face fell. 'I'm sorry. Are you going somewhere special?'

'It's just an open-air concert in Grange Wood, only my brother-in-law's taking part, so I can't very well get out of it.'

'No, I suppose not.' He lowered his voice. 'If you only knew how much I hate Saturday nights – the thought of not seeing you until Monday . . . Sundays seem to go on for ever.'

'Oh, you are sweet.'

Shyly, he took her in his arms. 'My little girl.' He kissed her forehead, her cheeks, her lips. 'What would I do without you?'

She closed her eyes, enjoying the sensation, proud of her power to arouse him, but when he began to unbutton her dress she drew away.

'No, we mustn't. Somebody might come in.'

Helplessly, he let her go. She took her light summer coat from the hatstand and held it out to him. 'Mr Faber, would you be a dear?'

Obediently, he helped her into it. She leaned back for a moment, and he felt the pressure of her body against his.

'When we're alone, I wish you'd call me Walter,' he said.

'All right, then.' She blew him a kiss. 'I'll be here first thing on Monday morning – Walter.'

Then she opened the office door. He called after her: 'I hope you have a pleasant evening, Miss Glynn.'

'Thank you, Mr Faber.'

As she walked towards the door, Ray stepped out from behind one of the kitchen cabinets. 'Where are you off to, then?' he asked.

'I'd be very grateful if you'd mind your own business,' she said, and went out of the shop, her head in the air.

He watched her go, and smiled to himself.

The bandstand at Grange Wood was open on three sides, with a back wall of wooden planks; there were no curtains or any kind of scenery – just a simple platform, bare except for a few chairs and a piano that had seen better days.

In chilly weather, it would have been an ordeal for audience and performers alike, but this sunny midsummer evening, a large and enthusiastic crowd was assembling. In the third row of deckchairs, Valerie sat with her mother and Babs, waiting for the show to begin.

Conditions for the artistes were primitive; a single tent served as a dressing room for both men and women, separated by a curtain hung from a clothesline. A trestle table and a cracked mirror were provided for the men; after three years in the Army, Ted was not self-conscious about undressing in front of the others, but since the entrance to the tent was an open canvas flap, and there were members of the audience walking past outside, he climbed into his stage costume as quickly as possible.

'How are you feeling, my friend?' asked Mr Pine, a hearty man with a booming voice. 'Not nervous, I hope?'

'No, sir,' Ted lied. 'I'm fine.'

'Good, good – but you're looking a little pale.' Mr Pine peered closely at him. 'Good heavens, man, you're not wearing any make-up!'

'I beg your pardon?'

'Greasepaint! Eye-black – lipstick—'

Looking at him, Ted saw that his face was painted a rich, unnatural ochre; his eyes were vividly outlined, and his lips were carmine.

'I never bother with that stuff,' he said. 'In the troop shows, we didn't have any greasepaint – nothing but burnt cork for moustaches.'

'Well, you'll need some tonight! There are a dozen bright spotlights out there. If you don't put some colour on, you'll look like a ghost!'

Outside the tent, the pianist was beginning an overture, rattling off a snappy version of *Alexander's Ragtime Band*.

Barnaby Pine glanced at his watch. 'Come and sit yourself down, my friend. You won't be on for fifteen minutes or so; we've got plenty of time.' He threw a grubby towel round Ted's neck, and began to apply the basic groundwork. 'A mixture of number five and number nine – then we'll put in the highlights. Watch carefully, so you can do it yourself in future.'

Ted felt his last drops of courage oozing away. How could he walk out in front of a crowd of strangers, wearing paint and powder on his face? He'd be booed off the stage . . .

The concert began with a troupe of little girls from a local dancing academy who mounted a Rosebud Ballet, followed by a pair of duettists who promised one another the keys of heaven, and a brisk young conjuror who baffled the spectators with incomprehensible card tricks.

It was all very pleasant, but Babs found her attention wandering. She was thinking about Walter Faber, and wondering if he'd invite her to have a drink with him another time. Of course, they would have to go somewhere very discreet, well away from Anerley or Upper Norwood . . . She wondered what would happen after a drink or two. Would he take her somewhere else? Would he try to do anything that was really – shameful? She didn't mind him stroking and fondling her; it was rather a nice feeling, and there wasn't any harm in it – but he did get excited sometimes, and she had to be careful. After all, he was a married man, and it might be very awkward.

Valerie nudged her, pointing to the programme. 'Ted's on next.'

When he made his entrance, Babs was startled. He was dressed as a costermonger, with a funny round hat, a terrible red kerchief and no collar. He looked disgraceful. Worse still, when he began to sing, he put on a thick cockney accent, dropping his aitches. Worst of all, the audience was laughing at him . . .

> 'My old girl an' me, you know, got tied up a year ago;
> Our fust kid 'as come to town – a quid he cost us – money down!
> Shan't forget when I 'eard the news;
> I felt so 'appy, I went on the booze –
> Came 'ome rockin' abaht on me pins –
> I could see double, an' thought 'e was twins!'

She was horrified. He was making an exhibition of himself – and yet . . . He sang with so much charm and good humour, making the silly jokes with such obvious glee, it was no wonder the audience warmed to him. Babs had always had a secret admiration for her brother-in-law. She could never understand why – when he first met her and Daphne – her sister was the one he'd fallen for. It seemed so unfair . . .

And now here he was, with his boyish good looks and that lovable grin, nursing a make-believe baby and singing his way straight to the heart of every woman there.

> *'When Maria's wheeling 'is pram,*
> *Fol-de-rolled up so smart –*
> *There's a look on 'er chivvy what seems to say –*

He paused – a long, knowing pause – then winked:

> *''Ow's this for a start?'*

The applause broke over the stage in a huge wave; he threw back his head like a swimmer breaking the surface after a dive, with a look of joyful amazement. It was the beginning of a love affair between Ted Watkins and his audience that was to last for the rest of his life.

Daphne was putting Annie into her nightie when Ray knocked at the kitchen door.

'Oh, where's Mrs Watkins?' he asked. 'The other Mrs Watkins, I mean.'

'She's out this evening. Can I help at all?' said Daphne, and as Annie began to struggle, 'Come on, put your arms through the sleeves like a good girl.'

'I just came down to pay my rent, seeing it's the end of the week. But if it's not convenient, I can come back later.'

'Money's never inconvenient, Mr Duke,' she smiled. 'Leave it with me – I'll see she gets it.'

'OK then.' He put the money and the rentbook on the kitchen table. 'I can see you're busy, so don't bother about signing the book. I'll pick it up another time.'

'No, I'd better do it now, to keep things straight.' Daphne put her daughter down on the rug and found a pencil, then, checking the coins, she added: 'Oh – you've only paid for one week.'

He put on a puzzled expression. 'Yes, I pay by the week.'

'But don't you remember? Last week you said you were a bit short, so she let it run on. It's two weeks you owe her.'

'There now, it went clean out of my head. Trouble is, I'm still a bit pushed. Tell her I'll be all right by the end of the month. I'll settle up then.'

'Very well.' Daphne sighed; it wasn't the first time there had been problems over Ray Duke's payments. 'What's happening at the end of the month? Are you expecting to come into some money?'

'Sort of. Last time my mother wrote, she said Father was going to send me a cheque.'

'That's nice.' Slightly embarrassed, Daphne forced herself to go on. 'It's funny, we were saying the other day – all the time you've been here, I don't ever remember you getting any letters. I'm sure I'd have noticed one with an American stamp.'

He smiled, perfectly at ease. 'There's a reason for that. I have my correspondence sent to a Post Office box number. I like to collect it myself.'

'Really? Isn't that rather inconvenient – having to call in to see if anything's come for you?'

'It's no bother. Tell you the truth, I've had trouble in the past with letters going astray. Living in digs, I soon found out I had to be careful – some people can be dishonest.'

'I see.' Daphne signed the rentbook and handed it back. 'There – I've made a note that there's still one week outstanding.'

'Thanks for the reminder.' He glanced round the room as Daphne picked Annie up. 'So you're on your own tonight? The rest of the family out gallivanting, eh?'

'My husband's taking part in an open-air concert. Mrs Watkins and Valerie have gone to see the show.'

'Of course, I should have realised. Babs mentioned something.'

'Yes, she's gone with them,' Daphne said shortly.

'Very nice, if you like that sort of thing. She did say where it was, but I can't remember offhand—'

'Grange Wood. The other end of Church Road, going towards Thornton Heath. It's not far.'

'Oh, yes. Well, I mustn't hold you up. Anyway, I'm off out myself. I'll just say toodle-oo for now.'

Taking his rentbook, he went up the stairs, and Daphne heard the front door shut. She was glad he'd gone. For some reason she never felt entirely comfortable, alone in the house with Ray Duke.

The first half of the concert ended with a Grand Highland Scena; most of the company were in kilts, and the senior girls from the Penge Academy of Dance did an eightsome reel, followed by a rendition of *The Bluebells of Scotland* played by eight children with handbells. The applause was polite, but not overwhelming.

'Now there's a fifteen-minute interval,' said Daphne. 'We could get cups of tea at the kiosk, if you like.'

'I'll just sit here. I expect it'll mean queueing up,' said Kate. 'You can bring me one back.'

As they set off to the refreshment kiosk, Val said to Babs, 'Well? What did you think?'

'It's quite good, really. I liked the Scottish part.'

'Yes, but what did you think of Ted?' Val persisted. 'He was the best, wasn't he?'

Babs pursed her lips. 'I'm afraid I was rather disappointed. It wasn't what I'd been expecting. Why did he have to do a comic song? And that cockney accent – anyone who didn't know him might think he always talks like that. He's got a very pleasant voice – why couldn't he sing properly?'

'Because he's a funny man – he always has been,' Val told her. 'He likes making people laugh. In the second half, he's taking part in a sketch.'

'Oh dear. Why does he have to cheapen himself like that?'

'Honestly, Babs, you are the limit! There's no need to be so stuffy about it!' As they reached the kiosk, Val broke off, 'Oh lor'. Ma's quite right, there *is* a queue. Let's hope we shan't have to wait long.'

'I don't think I'll bother, actually,' said Babs. 'I hate having to line up like a lot of sheep. You get your teas if you want to; I'm going to stretch my legs.'

The daylight was fading now. As she walked away from the bright lights, away from the kiosk and the bandstand, the shadows gathered round her. Seeing Ted Watkins on the stage had disturbed her more than she would admit. It was as if he had stood there in the spotlight, stretching out his arms, asking for love.

The path became narrow, winding up a little hill among clumps of rhododendrons and laurel; suddenly she stopped, aware of someone behind her. When she looked back, she was surprised – and irritated. Ray Duke walked up to her, with an odd smile on his face.

'What are you doing here?' she asked. 'Have you been following me?'

'Yes, I have. I heard what you said to Valerie. You didn't think much of the show, then?'

She shrugged. 'It was all right. I didn't see you in the audience.'

'I haven't been here long. Like I said, it was you I came to see. I want to have a talk. I never see you nowadays.'

'What do you mean? We see each other every day!'

'You're always in the office. I'd begun to think you were keeping out of my way on purpose.'

'Don't be silly.' She tried to walk past him. 'I must get back – the show will be starting again.'

'You don't want to go back there. It's a load of rubbish.' He gripped her arm. 'I got things to say to you.'

'No. I must go—'

But he held her tightly. 'Important things – important to both of us. Let's find somewhere we can talk.'

'They'll wonder where I've got to.'

'Let them. You know how I feel about you. You're hot stuff, you are. You're driving me barmy . . . And I'm not the only one either, am I?'

She tried to break free. 'I don't know what you're talking about.'

'Oh yes, you do. "My little girl" – that's what he calls you.' He imitated Faber's gentle, yearning voice. '"I want you to call me Walter – when we're alone".'

She whirled round. 'You were listening!'

He saw the fear in her eyes; it was what he'd been waiting for. 'Course I was,' he said. 'Now then – you're coming with me.' He took her further into the woods; among the trees, it was already growing dark. He found a tiny clearing, and pulled her down beside him on the mossy earth.

'What do you want?' Her voice sounded thin and unreal. She was frightened, but she felt a strange excitement within her.

'I want you, Babs,' he said. 'Ever since I saw you, I've been crazy about you. I want you to be nice to me – like you're nice to him.'

He put his arms round her, forcing her down. It was like the last time he'd kissed her – her mouth opened under his and helplessly she found her body responding to his insistence. Only this time, it was different. His fingers were already at work upon her dress, pulling up her skirt . . .

'No! Please—' she tried to protest. 'You mustn't! I never—'

'Why not? This is what he does, isn't it?' he asked breathlessly, and then he laughed. 'Or p'raps he can't manage it any more. P'raps he's past it. He's no good to you, darling. He can't do it for you like I can.'

'Please stop. Please,' she said faintly.

He took no notice; she realised he was tugging at the buttons of his trousers. 'You want it really,' he grunted. 'You know you do.'

'No,' she whispered. 'No . . .'

But when she felt his legs thrusting between hers, his bare thighs hot and hard against her skin, nothing else mattered but that very moment – and giving herself up to the moment, she gave herself to him.

At ten o'clock Daphne heard the front door open, and the Watkins family came home in high spirits. Talking and laughing, they trooped into the kitchen, surrounding her.

'Ssh! Not so loud,' she warned them. 'You'll wake Annie.'

But they were too jubilant to care. 'You should have been there,' said Valerie. 'It was a triumph!'

'The show went off all right, then?' she asked.

'Oh yes, it was very good,' agreed Kate. 'You'd have been so proud of Ted – he was the best of the lot.'

'Get away with you.' Ted smacked his mother playfully, and told Daphne, 'I think she might be a bit prejudiced.'

'No, it's true,' said Val. 'Mr Pine says Ted's welcome to be in his shows any time he likes.'

'Oh, that's wonderful,' said Daphne. 'You didn't forget your words?'

'No, I think I made up a few bits of my own,' Ted grinned, shining with happiness.

'You should have seen him in the sketch – he even set the other actors off,' added Kate. 'They were laughing that much, they could hardly get the words out!'

Val chimed in: 'What about the part where you poured the ink into the wineglass and drank it by mistake?' and she started to giggle again at the thought of it.

Above the laughter, Daphne heard a familiar sound. Upstairs in her little bed, Annie had been woken by the sound of revelry, and was complaining bitterly about being left out.

'What did I tell you?' she exclaimed. 'I'll try to settle her down—'

But Ted was already on his way upstairs. 'Leave this to me! This is my big night – let's bring her down to join the party!'

Daphne groaned. 'It'll take hours to get her off again.' Then another thought struck her. 'You said you'd bring Babs back with you. Where is she?'

Val and Kate exchanged glances, and Val replied, 'She didn't stay for the second half. I think she had a headache coming on – she went home.'

But Babs hadn't gone straight home. It was nearly eleven before she returned to Belmont; on the way to her room, she met her brother on the first-floor landing.

'You're very late,' he said. 'I'm just off to bed. Mama's still up, by the way. She wants to see you.'

'Oh no.' Babs bit her lip. 'Couldn't the Aunts have put her to bed for once?'

'Auntie Eth did offer, but she wasn't having any. She'd made up her mind to sit up till you came in.' Glancing down, he noticed a muddy green patch on her skirt. 'Hello – you've been in the wars. Pulled through a hedge backwards, by the look of you!'

'I tripped over the root of a tree,' Babs said quickly. 'I'll just go and put on a dressing gown – tell Mummy I'll be down in two ticks.'

Slipping out of her dress, she examined her reflection closely in the mirror for any telltale signs; then she powdered her face and combed her hair before going to her mother's room.

'Wherever have you been, dear?' Muriel asked. 'I was so worried – I thought something must have happened to you.'

'No, nothing happened. I went to see Ted's concert, then I came home – that's all.'

'It must have been a very long concert. Did you enjoy it?'

'No, I didn't. It was very amateurish – and Ted's performance was disgraceful. I didn't stay to see him – I came away before it was over.'

'You don't mean to say it's still going on, at this time of night?'

'No.' She corrected herself. 'It upsets me so much, watching Ted make a fool of himself in public, that I went for a long walk to try and get over it.'

'I don't understand – why did it upset you? Didn't the audience like Ted? Did they throw things at him?'

'Oh no, nothing like that. They encouraged him, that was the trouble.' Under the pressure of conflicting emotions, Babs was working herself up. 'Valerie told me he was going to sing something, and I'd been looking forward to it, but he chose a very vulgar comic song. He was supposed to be a costermonger, whose wife had just had a baby. I'm only thankful Daphne wasn't there to see it. He did it all in a dreadful common voice, and some of the jokes were very suggestive . . . I've never been so ashamed in my whole life.'

*

On Monday morning Ted found it hard to come down to earth. After the heady excitement of Saturday, the streets of South London seemed particularly grey and bleak. It was like waking from a dream and facing reality again.

He caught his usual tram, trundling slowly to Camberwell. Mulligan's Pickles were produced in a small factory off the Peckham Road, a dank, dark building unchanged since Queen Victoria's reign.

He told himself that things could have been worse. He wouldn't like to work in the factory, with the smell of vinegar clinging to his clothes, his hair and his skin – and life wasn't much better in the packing department either, washing, filling and labelling an endless procession of glass jars.

As he clocked in at the staff entrance, he decided he was really lucky to be a traveller, out on the road all day. He went into the Sales Office to report for duty and pick up his list of calls. At least Monday was one of his easy days – Lewisham, Catford and Beckenham – not too far from home. Sometimes, if things went well, he even managed to snatch half an hour at midday to drop into Sackville Road and surprise Daff.

He collected his order book and sample case from Lilian Phipps, the Sales Manager's secretary. A sharp-tongued young woman, with hair dyed a bright, unlikely yellow, she was known among the travellers as 'Piccalilli Lil'. He was about to go out again when she called him.

'Oh, Mr Watkins – one moment, please.'

He turned back. 'Yes, Miss Phipps – what can I do for you?'

'One of your colleagues is off sick. Mrs Andrews telephoned us from the hospital. Her husband was involved in a traffic accident. Two motorcars collided, and he was knocked off his bicycle.'

'I'm sorry to hear that.' Ted didn't know Frank Andrews very well and didn't particularly like him – a pasty-faced man who never cracked a smile at Ted's jokes – but he didn't wish him any harm. 'Nothing serious, I hope?'

'A broken leg. He'll be off for some time, so until we can get his routes allocated, I've re-organised the rounds. Today he should have been doing Bromley and Elmers End – perhaps you'd take over his calls? They fit in with yours quite well. Here's his order book.'

With a heavy heart, Ted accepted it; instead of an easy day, he would have to work twice as hard. Not for the first time, he wished they could afford a telephone at Sackville Road. It would have been nice to let Daff know he wouldn't be home till late.

'No peace for the wicked,' he said, trying to make light of it. 'How long am I going to have to cover for him?'

'I couldn't say.' Miss Phipps lowered her voice. 'That will be up to Mr Henderson, naturally. We must wait and see what he decides.'

She always spoke of the Sales Manager in tones of reverence. Ted winked at her, saying cheerily: 'Fine – perhaps you'd let me know when you come down from Mount Sinai?'

Miss Phipps gasped, 'There's no need to be blasphemous!' – though whether she was referring to the Almighty or to Mr Henderson, Ted wasn't quite sure.

Another man's rounds took twice as long, because the addresses were unfamiliar, and he didn't know the most convenient buses or trams. As a rule, he took his time over his regulars. By now, most of the shopkeepers had become personal friends, and he made a point of enquiring after their wives, their ailing grandmothers, the cat's new kittens or the pet goldfish. And wherever he went, they always asked him for a story.

'Come on, Ted,' they'd say. 'What's the latest? Tell us a new one.'

So he'd sit on the edge of the counter and tell them the one about the cross-eyed policeman on point-duty – or the courting couple in the graveyard – or the grocery boy who sat on the bacon-slicer and got a little behind in his orders . . . It was good to make them laugh. It put them in a better mood, and they might add a few more items to next week's deliveries – a full order book could mean a rise at the end of the year.

And if it made them happier, even for a little while, the world would seem a friendlier place.

Ted took after his mother in that way. Kate Watkins enjoyed cheering people up; when she was out shopping she always stopped for a chat with anyone she recognised, waving and smiling to friends and neighbours – even to people she couldn't put a name to, if their faces seemed familiar.

As a result, it took her a long time to get round the shops, and today, when she realised it was nearly dinner-time and she hadn't even peeled the potatoes, she tried to hurry. When she came round the corner of the ironmongers, she walked slap into somebody coming out of the Post Office, and dropped her shopping-bag.

'Oops, my fault!' she exclaimed. 'Not looking where I was going.'

'Allow me.' The stranger stooped to pick up some scattered apples and oranges before they rolled into the gutter. Looking at her again, he added: 'It's Mrs Watkins, isn't it? We seem to be fated to run into one another.'

He wasn't a stranger at all, though she hadn't seen him since the Gala Opening Day at the Crystal Palace. He looked just the same – still wearing his top hat, his gold pince-nez and his sombre black suit.

'Well, I never!' she cried. 'Fancy meeting you, Mr Colpoys! Do you live round these parts?'

'Not far away, in Gipsy Hill – but I have an office in Anerley Road. I've been writing letters all the morning, and I ran out of stamps, so I came out to catch the midday post.'

'It's a small world, and no mistake,' she said, stuffing groceries back into her bag. 'We live just round the corner, in Sackville Road. How've you been keeping?'

'Pretty well, thank you. Though I'm glad the weather has turned cooler. I found the heatwave rather uncomfortable.'

'Oh yes, it was really too warm, wasn't it?' She couldn't help thinking he might have found it less oppressive if he hadn't been wearing a heavy winter suit. 'If I'd known you were a neighbour, I'd have asked you round for a cup of tea one afternoon, but I suppose you wouldn't have the time, working in an office all day?'

'Oh, I don't work all day. I've more or less retired now – I just call into the office for a couple of hours in the mornings . . . It keeps me busy.'

Something in his tone made Kate feel sorry for him; she suspected he might be rather lonely.

'Well, any time you fancy a cup of tea, don't forget where we are – number thirty-seven, Sackville Road,' she told him.

'That's very kind of you,' he said – then added, surprised at his own daring: 'It would be a great pleasure. Tell me when it's convenient to call, and I'll be glad to.'

'Would you really?' Kate was all smiles. 'No time like the present – how about this afternoon? Say four o'clock?'

'Four o'clock it shall be. Number thirty-seven – I'll be there!' he said.

After lunch Kate usually had a little nap, but there was no time for that today. She got out the carpet-sweeper and the dusters, and went over the sitting room, brushing and polishing everything. Then she set out the best tea service, and the Victoria sponge sandwich she'd made on Saturday – 'Good job I put it in a tin, it hasn't gone stale' – and cut watercress sandwiches into triangles.

Daphne laughed. 'Anybody'd think you were entertaining the

King! You don't even know the man – he might be dreadfully boring.'

'Don't be silly. You met him too – we sat next to him in the grandstand, don't you remember? He's very nice and polite, so I invited him to come to tea and he said he'd be glad to.' But when she heard the front-door knocker, her heart fluttered a little. It was true – she didn't really know the first thing about him.

Daphne answered the door and brought him into the sitting room.

He seemed rather shy, as if he regretted having accepted the invitation. Daphne took his hat and coat and went to hang them up. He and Kate sat on either side of the fireplace; as it was summer, there was a Japanese paper fan in the grate instead of a fire. A silence fell, and Kate struggled to think of something to say. Inevitably, they both spoke together.

'It's very overcast now, the weather—' she began, while he said: 'A pleasant room you have here—' They both laughed politely, and apologised at the same time.

When Daphne looked in, with Annie in her arms, Kate said, 'Perhaps we should have tea right away, dear?'

'I'll bring yours on a tray. Annie and I will have ours in the kitchen.'

'Oh no, you must come and join us!'

'No, thanks.' She looked at Annie. 'I heard what happened last time – I don't think Mr Colpoys would care for another milk-jug in his lap!'

He assured her that he'd completely forgotten the incident – which was untrue – but she wouldn't change her mind. When she had brought the tea, she left them alone together.

Kate plunged in bravely. 'What sort of business are you in, Mr Colpoys, if you don't mind me asking?'

He explained that he was the senior partner in a firm of solicitors – Colpoys & Son. Kate, who had only the haziest idea of what solicitors did, said, 'That must be ever so interesting.'

'It can be. Most of the time it's drudgery.'

'But you must enjoy it. You still go to the office every day, even though you're retired.'

'I go to the office because it gives me something to do. If it wasn't for that, I'd never meet anyone. I live alone, you see.'

'Oh, do you?' So she was right about him being lonely. 'You're not married?'

'I was – many years ago. My wife died in childbirth.'

'Oh, I'm so sorry. How dreadful . . .' Kate wished she hadn't asked. In an attempt to strike a more cheerful note, she said, 'I'm sure your son must be a comfort to you.'

'I have no son, either,' he said quietly.

'Oh, but I thought – Colpoys and Son . . .'

'I always hoped Jack would join me in the family business, but the fates decreed otherwise. Oh, he went up to University to study law, but then the war came and he enlisted immediately. He was killed in nineteen-fifteen – at Ypres.'

His eyes were filled with pain, and Kate did not stop to think; she went over to him and took his hand.

'I know what it's like,' she said. 'I lost my husband a few weeks after the war broke out. Mons, nineteen-fourteen.' Then she realised what she had done, and felt embarrassed. 'Excuse me,' she said, letting go of his hand. 'I shouldn't have—'

'Please, Mrs Watkins – don't apologise. It's good to meet someone who understands.'

To cover her confusion, she busied herself with second cups of tea. As she passed his cup to him, she added shyly: 'I'd never have mentioned it, if it hadn't been for the name of your firm – Colpoys and Son. I suppose it was your father's business, was it? And you're the son?'

He shook his head. 'No, I began the company. It was my dream that one day Jack and I would be partners. After he died, I changed the name on the brass plate – as a kind of memorial. I expect you think it was sentimental of me.'

'No, I don't – I think it's a very good idea. And I'm glad you told me.'

His face softened into a smile. 'I'm glad you asked.'

It was quite late when Ted finally arrived back at Mulligan's Pickles. It had been a long day, and something had cropped up which puzzled him. He found Miss Phipps putting on her hat and coat, about to go home.

'How did you get on?' she asked. 'It certainly took you long enough.'

'I had a lot of ground to cover.' He looked at the old-fashioned wall-clock. 'Ten past six. I don't suppose Mr Henderson's still here?'

'Yes, he is. He was only asking a few moments ago if you'd returned – he was hoping to see you.'

'Oh, good. I want to have a word with him myself.'

Miss Phipps ushered him into the holy of holies, saying in an awestruck whisper, 'Mr Watkins, sir. I'll be going now, if that's all right?'

'Perfectly all right, Miss Phipps – off you go.' The Sales Manager was a large man, with a cheroot smouldering at the corner of his mouth. 'Come in, Watkins. Take a pew.'

Rather surprised – sales representatives were not usually offered a chair in the Manager's office – Ted sat down.

'You've been covering for Andrews, I understand? Bad business, that. Those damn motors are becoming a public nuisance – always causing accidents.'

'Yes, sir.'

'Anyhow, you managed to get round all his regular calls, did you? No problems, I hope?'

'No sir, except . . . There is one thing needs sorting out.'

'Oh, yes? What's that?'

Ted opened Andrews' order book, turning the pages until he found what he was looking for.

'Here it is. A shop in Bromley – I had a talk with the chap who runs it, because it struck me he wasn't ordering many of our products, and I was hoping to persuade him to try some of our new range . . . but then we found we were talking at cross-purposes. He's got shelves full of our pickles – and they're selling very well. But according to the order book, Andrews had only managed to move a few jars every month. It doesn't make sense.'

Mr Henderson puffed at his cheroot for some time, studying the order book in silence. At last he said, 'Seems to have been a wee bit careless, our Mr Andrews. I'll make some enquiries.'

'I thought at first it was just a mistake, only as far as I can see, it's been going on for quite a while. There's probably some simple explanation, but—'

'Yes, I dare say. Still, I'm glad you keep your eyes open, Watkins. All right, leave it with me – I'll look into it.'

Ted didn't get home till well after seven.

'What time do you call this?' Daphne said. 'I did you a sausage toad for your tea, but it'll be like leather by now.'

He was so tired, he hadn't much appetite, though he tried manfully to get through it while Daphne went on to tell him about Kate's visitor.

'I couldn't help teasing her – I said she ought to be ashamed, picking up strange men in the street at her time of life. Still, I think he enjoyed his tea, and she's asked him to come again. His son was killed in the war. I should have guessed – Val told us most of the people in the grandstand had lost relatives in France.' Then, as Ted pushed his plate away: 'You don't really want it, do you?'

'It's not that – I keep thinking about Frank Andrews.' Briefly, Ted told her what he had discovered. 'I wish now I'd kept my trap shut. It's not going to be much fun for him if he comes out of hospital and finds himself in hot water with the boss.'

'Well, you had to say something, didn't you? If there's been some sort of mistake, the sooner they sort it out, the better.'

'Yes, but suppose it wasn't a mistake? Suppose Andrews has been fiddling the orders?'

'Cheating the company?'

'I don't see any other explanation. I believe he was selling the shop a big order each month and entering a small one – and pocketing the difference.'

'If that's true, you certainly did the right thing. You had to report it, didn't you?'

'I suppose so,' he said miserably. 'But I can't help feeling badly about it, all the same.'

He was still brooding over it next morning. However early he got up, he never seemed to have time for a proper breakfast, but swallowed a cup of tea and chewed a slice of toast on the run, while he polished his shoes and finished dressing.

When the post arrived, Daphne collected it from the front-door mat, leaving him to keep an eye on Annie, who sat in her high chair, eating bread and milk.

'You're getting more of it down your bib than in your mouth,' he told her. 'Do you want me to help you?'

But the little girl gripped her teaspoon firmly, protesting: 'No, Dadda – let go! Annie do it!'

When Daphne returned he said, 'She's spilled half of it, because she will do everything herself. Talk about stubborn . . . I wonder where she gets it from?' But Daphne wasn't listening; frowning, she tore open an envelope. 'What is it this time?' he asked. 'The gas bill, or the water rate?'

'It's from my mother – goodness knows what she wants.' She scanned the letter quickly, her face darkening. Then she tore it up, and dropped the pieces into the wastebin under the sink.

'Hey! What's wrong?' he asked.

'Nothing. It's a stupid letter – take no notice,' she said shortly. 'It's nothing.'

'It must have been something. What's she on about now?'

'It was about Saturday night – the show. Apparently my dear little sister went home and told her it was common and vulgar and indecent.'

'Oh, so that's it.' He smiled wryly. 'Let me guess – she's not accusing the Rosebud Ballet of being indecent, is she? Or claiming that the Highland dancers had no knickers under their kilts? It's yours truly she's getting at, isn't it? Go on – you might as well tell me.'

'You know what they're like. Babs was shocked because you did a cockney song and she told Mother there were some filthy double meanings in it.' Daphne put her arms round him, on the verge of tears. 'Oh Ted, I'm sorry.'

He hugged her. 'Don't take it to heart, Daff. Your family are all potty, one way or another – we know that. You mustn't let them get you down. Try to see the funny side.' He kissed her again, adding: 'I must run, or I'll be late for work. Cheer up, sweetheart. Look after your Mum, Annie! See you tonight.' Grabbing his hat and coat, he rushed out of the house to catch his tram.

He reached the factory and clocked in at the usual time, so he was quite surprised when Miss Phipps called him over, looking even more disapproving than usual. 'Mr Henderson wants you,' she said heavily. 'You're to go in.'

'Oh – right,' he said, and thought: 'Andrews again, poor devil. Still, he must have known what a risk he was running.'

Mr Henderson looked up, lighting a cheroot. This time he did not invite Ted to sit down.

'Ah, Watkins.' He blew out a cloud of smoke, shuffling some papers about on his desk.

'If it's about Frank Andrews, sir, I'm very sorry if I—'

Mr Henderson raised a flabby hand to silence him. 'This has nothing to do with Andrews. I looked into that matter last night after you'd gone. It was a clerical error in the Accounts Department; I soon sorted it out. But thanks for bringing it to my notice so promptly. The sooner these little mistakes get cleared up, the better.'

'Yes, I suppose so.' Ted was puzzled but relieved. 'Then, if it's not about Andrews—'

'It's about you, Watkins. I'm sorry to say I've had some serious criticisms of you, from the retailers you deal with. They say you're over-familiar – enquiring about their private lives, prying into personal matters. People don't appreciate it, you see.'

'I don't understand.'

'And making jokes. They say you waste a lot of time trying to tell funny stories – they don't find that amusing. They're busy men, Watkins, with work to do – they don't like you showing off. These are grocers' shops we're dealing with, not music halls.'

'Yes, but I thought— they all seemed to like—'

He cut in again. 'I'm afraid not. As I say, we've had a great many complaints, and in view of that I'm afraid we have no alternative but to let you go.' Picking up a typed letter, he passed it across the desk. 'This is to terminate your employment officially. Take it to the cashier and you'll be paid a month's salary in lieu of notice. And if I might give you a word of advice? When you start looking for another job, *don't* try to be too clever, Watkins. Like I say – people don't appreciate it.'

Chapter Five

TED TORE OPEN the envelope and tipped the contents out on to the kitchen table – notes, silver and coppers.

'There you are,' he said. 'A month's housekeeping – and you'd better make it last, 'cos Gawd only knows where the next lot's coming from.'

Kate and Daphne looked at him, unable to believe their ears.

'You don't mean it!' exclaimed Kate. 'They gave you the sack, just because you told a few jokes?'

Little Annie stood on tiptoe, clinging to the edge of the table and looking wide-eyed at this unexpected treasure trove. 'Money,' she said, deeply impressed, then added immediately: 'Will you buy me a chocky bar?'

'Not now, love. Mum and Dad have got things to talk about.' Still trying to make sense of it, Daphne turned to Kate. 'Could you take her upstairs for a bit?'

'Well yes, all right.' Kate picked up her granddaughter: 'Upsy-daisy, ducks, come with Nan.'

Annie struggled fiercely. 'It's not my bedtime yet. It's not *fair*!'

Still protesting, the little girl was whisked away, and Daphne shut the door firmly, then turned to face Ted. 'The jokes were just an excuse to get rid of you, weren't they? It was because you discovered that chap Andrews had been taking money from the firm.'

'Serves me right – I should've kept my trap shut.'

'No!' Daphne was stung to anger. 'You had to report it – how can they punish you for that? It's not right!'

Even in the midst of gloom, Ted managed the ghost of a smile. 'You sound just like Annie – *It's not fair!*'

'No, it's not. And it doesn't make sense, either.'

Ted slumped on to the sofa. 'I've been thinking about it all the way home. I reckon Henderson was in on it as well. They must have cooked it up between them – a smart way to make a few extra quid. That's why he couldn't wait to get shot of me.'

'You're not going to let them get away with it, are you? You can report Henderson as well – go over his head, ask to see the Managing Director.'

'What's the use?' Ted leaned back against the wall. 'By the time they check up, Henderson will have altered the books – he'll cover his tracks somehow. Then it'll just be my word against his, and who do you think they'll listen to?'

'But you can't leave it like this. You've done nothing wrong!'

'It wouldn't do any good, love. Besides, I was fed up with the damn job anyway. I never want to see another jar of pickles as long as I live . . . Tomorrow morning I'll start looking round for something else.'

Sitting beside him, Daphne took his hand. 'It's not going to be that easy, you know. Didn't you see the latest figures? Nearly two and a half million unemployed.'

'I'll find something, don't you worry. There's always an opening for a smart lad!' He put his arm round her shoulders, pulling her closer. 'That crook Henderson – who does he think he is, telling me people don't like my jokes? He'll laugh on the other side of his face, when I'm topping the bill at the Lewisham Hippodrome!'

Daphne smiled at him with a mixture of exasperation and love. 'Yes, Ted, that's all very well, but seriously . . .'

He smiled back at her, but when she looked into his eyes, she saw that he was perfectly serious.

In the weeks that followed, she bought the local papers and scoured them for possible vacancies, but without success. More often than not, by the time Ted followed them up, he found the posts had already been filled.

In those that were still vacant, some 'previous experience' was an advantage, and Ted had no experience except one year as a commercial traveller and three in the Army. The reference given him when he left Mulligan's was brief and not over-enthusiastic, and the first thing any prospective employer asked was: 'Why did you leave the last job?' – a question Ted found difficult to answer.

So the weeks turned into months, and summer deepened into autumn, and as he was still out of work, Ted had to sign on and draw the dole each week. He didn't like it, but with no other source of income, he had no choice.

Kate didn't like it either. Throughout her married life, Eddie Watkins had never been forced to draw the dole, and she couldn't help thinking of it as something shameful, to be concealed from the neighbours and never mentioned, but since her widow's pension and the paltry rent paid her by Ray Duke were not enough to support the family, she had to swallow her pride and accept it.

Daphne continued to search through the Situations Vacant columns, and sometimes Ted went after other, mysterious jobs, but he always came home empty-handed and unsmiling.

One evening, in a sudden fit of frustration, he smacked his fist into his palm, and burst out: 'I was so *near* it today, I know I was! I almost struck lucky.'

She asked him what sort of job he'd been after, and at first he wouldn't tell her. At last, a little shamefaced, he admitted that he had been visiting all the variety theatres in South London, trying to see the manager at each one and ask for an audition.

'You mean you're still thinking about that?' asked Daphne.

'Why not? I know I can do it,' he told her. 'Don't you think I can?'

'Yes, but you don't get on in the theatre by knocking on doors and asking for work, do you? It's not like that; you've got to build up a reputation.'

'I've got a reputation, haven't I? I make people laugh! Ask anybody who's seen the concert party.'

Since he had been unemployed, Ted had performed more frequently in Mr Barnaby Pine's concerts, appearing on bandstands and at garden fêtes, in church halls and parish rooms – polishing his skills, and learning his craft.

'But they're just amateur shows.' Daphne tried to bring him down to earth. 'They're not like real theatres.'

'You needn't remind me,' he retorted. 'Nine times out of ten, as soon as they hear I'm not a professional, they won't even see me. But today was different. Today the Manager of the Brixton Empress asked me up to his office. He sat there in his swivel chair and said: "Right you are, young man. Go ahead – make me laugh." And I did. I told him a few stories, and he laughed so hard, I could hear the chair creaking. I thought I'd hit the bulls-eye at last. When I'd finished, he even gave me a whisky and soda. He told me I was a darn sight better than some of the acts he books every week, but he couldn't use me 'cos I'm not a pro. "Come and see me when you've had some professional experience, and I'll give you a job," he said. I asked him how I'm supposed to get experience if nobody's going to take a chance on me, but he just laughed again. "Ah, that's the catch!" he said – but he wished me luck. I tell you Daff, I nearly made it.'

She put her arms round him; he looked so desperate and so determined, it almost broke her heart. She knew he was wasting his time, but how could she tell him that?

During these unhappy weeks, she was grateful that her mother didn't know Ted was out of work. It would have been one more black mark for the Watkins household; a granddaughter of Montague DeWitt – married to a man who couldn't even hold down a job in a pickle factory? She would never have heard the last of it.

Since the night of Ted's début at Grange Wood, and Muriel's letter, Daphne had not been in touch with the family at Belmont. Her mother had not written again, and Babs had not shown her face at Sackville Road.

It was Annie's fourth birthday that broke the ice. A large package came by post, containing a Dutch doll with jointed wooden limbs, dressed in a blue-and-white gingham dress and a sunbonnet. Annie fell in love with it and carried it everywhere, showing it off proudly to everyone she met.

'Annie's baby,' she explained. 'From Annie's Granny.'

'I expect Aunt Aggie made the clothes – she's always enjoyed dressing dolls,' Daphne told Valerie. 'And they put in a birthday card with it, signed by the whole family.'

Underneath the signatures, Muriel had scrawled: '*Ask your Mummy why we haven't seen you for such a long time – has she forgotten us?*'

'I suppose I'll have to go and thank them now,' sighed Daphne. 'But I'm not looking forward to it. Perhaps I should take Annie round to tea on Saturday afternoon.'

When the furniture shop closed at one o'clock, Walter Faber put on his coat and his bowler hat, about to leave the office. A sudden thought occurred to him, and he asked Babs: 'Have you brought sandwiches for your lunch, Miss Glynn? I know you generally do.'

'Yes, Mr Faber – cheese and tomato, and an apple,' said Babs.

'Ah . . . I was about to go to the White Swan as usual, but I wondered – as it's such a fine day, perhaps you might like to bring your lunch with you, and we could go for a stroll in Crystal Palace Gardens? The days are getting shorter now; we may not have many more opportunities.'

'It's very kind of you, Mr Faber. Another time I'd be only too glad,' Babs told him. 'But I've got to finish typing the new sale catalogue and check it through before I send it out. I'll never catch the afternoon post if I don't work through my lunch-hour.'

'You're too conscientious, Miss Glynn. I'm sure a breath of air would do you good.' Mr Faber closed the door and lowered his voice. 'Babs, dear, we've hardly had any time together lately. The catalogue can wait. I must see you—'

She smiled regretfully. 'Thanks all the same, Walter – I'd really rather finish it now. We can go for a walk another time, can't we?'

He seemed to shrink a little. 'Just as you wish, of course.' Then he turned and went without another word.

In the shop, Ray opened the front door and locked it carefully after Mr Faber, then marched back to the office, whistling. He entered without knocking, and kissed Babs on the nape of her neck.

'That's my girl,' he said, running his hand lightly down her spine. 'That's got Weary Wally out of the way.'

'Poor Mr Faber – you mustn't be nasty about him.'

'What d'you mean – "*Poor Mr Faber*"? He's just a dirty old man, trying to touch you up. It's time he realised you're not interested in him.' His fingers caressed the curve of her thigh. 'I've got a surprise for you.' Taking her arm, he led her out of the office.

'What sort of surprise? Where are we going?'

'To the stockroom.'

'I shouldn't – I've got this typing to finish. I told Mr Faber—'

'Yes, I heard you – and he said the catalogue can wait. You're coming with me.' Ray took her into the stockroom and shut the door, then produced a flat cardboard box. 'Present for you,' he said.

'Ooh – whatever is it?' She took the lid off; under a sheet of tissue-paper, she found a pair of knickers, trimmed with lace and silk ribbon.

'Pretty, eh? It's to make up for them you had on last week, when we went to the pictures – the ones that got a bit torn.'

She frowned. 'They weren't "a bit" torn – you were so rough, I was really cross.'

'I said I was sorry, didn't I? Don't you like them?'

'They must have been very expensive.' She took them from the box, her eyes glowing. 'I must say, they're very nice. D'you think they'll fit me?'

'We'll soon find out, won't we? Go on – try 'em on.'

'What, now? Oh, I couldn't! Somebody might come in.'

'Don't be daft. The doors are locked, Wally's in The Swan and Tubby's out with the van, doing a delivery round Streatham. We got the place all to ourselves . . . I want to see you wearing them.'

'Well, all right then, but you mustn't be naughty.'

Slowly, she began to undress. Aware of the effect this had upon him, she felt a thrill of excitement as she unfastened her suspenders and rolled down her stockings. Modestly, she slipped out of her drawers, then sat on a pile of mattresses, stepping into the smart lacy knickers. Provocatively, she pulled up her skirt.

'Well? How do I look?'

'Bloody marvellous.' His voice was thick with desire as he moved towards her. 'Now it's my turn.'

'No, Ray. I told you – you mustn't—'

But he tumbled her on to her back, throwing himself across her. 'Fair do's,' he breathed. 'You put 'em on – I take 'em off.'

Laughing, she put up a show of protest, but very soon they were both naked, rolling together on the springing, bouncing mattresses.

When it was over, she clung to him, still tingling in the afterglow of their passion. 'If Walter ever found out, he'd kill us,' she whispered.

'Forget about him,' purred Ray, rubbing himself against her like a cat. 'It's me you love, isn't it?'

'You know I do.'

'I want to hear you say it. Go on, tell me.'

'I love you, Ray.'

'That's my girl.' He held her tightly. 'When am I going to see you again? How about Saturday afternoon? How about us going for a walk in the woods, eh?'

'I can't go out on Saturday. My sister's bringing Annie round to tea – I've promised Mummy I'll be there.'

He put his hand beneath her chin, turning her face to him. 'You won't go telling anybody else about us, will you? If they found out, they'd put a stop to it. That's why nobody must ever know.'

When Walter Faber came back from lunch, Ray unlocked the front door for him, smiling politely and smoothing down his hair. In the office, Babs was busy at her typewriter. Mr Faber hung up his hat and coat.

'How are you getting on?' he asked. 'Nearly finished?'

'I'm afraid not. It's taking longer than I thought. I kept making mistakes, and having to start all over again.'

His eye fell on the paper bag beside her, containing her sandwiches and an apple – untouched.

'You haven't had your lunch.'

'No, I didn't feel like it. I've got rather a headache – I expect that's why I was making mistakes.'

Standing behind her, Walter lifted his hand, longing to stroke her hair and smooth away the pain – but the office door was open. Sadly, he let his hand drop to his side.

'I'll find you an aspirin,' he said.

The van smelled of apples and earth and cabbages; it was a pungent smell, but Alf Gunn and his son had stopped noticing it. As they drove down Herne Hill, Alf suddenly clutched Steve's arm:

'*Watch out!*'

An early-morning traveller, hurrying to catch his train to the City, had stepped off the kerb in front of them. Steve slammed on the brakes, bringing the van to a squealing halt.

'Damn fool!' he said. 'Why can't he look where he's going?'

'Why can't you keep your eyes open?' his father reprimanded him. 'You almost ran into him – what's the matter with you? You're half-asleep!'

'No, I'm not,' said Steve, letting in the clutch. The van lurched forward, trundling on. 'I was thinking about something else.'

'What time did you get home this morning?' his father wanted to know. 'You were out half the night – you knew very well we'd got an early start.'

It was still dark when they had set out on their trip to Covent Garden, to load up with fresh supplies of fruit and vegetables. Now it was nearly eight o'clock, and the streets were already busy with traffic.

'I wasn't that late, Dad,' muttered Steve. 'I was in by midnight.'

'Beats me why you spend so much time out of the house,' Alf grumbled. 'Where do you get to, I'd like to know?'

'Nowhere special. It was early-closing day. I can do as I please on my half-day, can't I? I was out with some of my pals.' He knew he should have told his father the truth – he would have to, sooner or later – but this wasn't the right moment. Perhaps Dad might be in a better mood after they'd had their breakfast.

When they got back to Upper Norwood, the two men unloaded the van in the backyard, carrying crates and sacks indoors. By the time they went upstairs Mrs Gunn greeted them accusingly.

'You're very late. That tea's been made half an hour – don't blame me if it's stewed.'

'Couldn't help it, Mum – there's a lot of traffic about.' Steve took his place at the kitchen table, next to his young brother, and helped himself to a slice of toast. 'I'm starving.'

Alf sat at the head of the table, glancing at the empty chair beside him. 'Where's the old man? Not up yet?'

'Your father's having a lie-in this morning; he says he had a bad night. I told him he ought to see the doctor, but you know what he's like, he won't listen.' Freda Gunn turned to her youngest child. 'Tony, if you don't want that bit of toast, stop messing it about, you'll get crumbs all over the table. If you've had enough, you can go and ask Grandad if he'd like another cup of tea. Alfred – look what you're doing, you've dripped egg down the front of that pullover. Get it off this minute, and I'll rinse it through before it dries on.'

Obediently, Alf took off his jacket and dragged the pullover over his head. Freda Gunn was a tiny woman, not much more than half the size of her husband and her eldest son, but she kept the menfolk in their place. Down in the shop, Alfred might be the boss, but up in the flat nobody dared question Freda's authority.

About to leave the table, Tony remembered something, and turned eagerly to his big brother: 'Hey, Steve – I saw you yesterday!'

'So what?' Steve attacked his fried egg. 'I saw you as well, pie-face. We see each other every day, don't we?'

'I don't mean indoors!' The seven-year-old boy struggled to explain. 'I was coming home from school along Anerley Road, and I saw you and another chap riding a – ow!' He broke off with a smothered yelp. 'What did you kick me for?'

'Shut up, can't you?' Steve glared at him, but the damage was done.

'Riding a motorbike?' Alf broke in sharply. 'Is that what you were going to say?'

Caught in the crossfire, Tony looked from his father to his brother, at a loss. 'P'raps it was somebody else,' he said lamely.

'It's OK, Tone,' said Steve. 'Yes, Dad, we were trying out somebody's motorbike. Is that a crime?'

'You've been larking about with those young rips from the garage again, haven't you?' Alf's face was turning red. 'I thought I told you to stay away from them. They're riffraff, that's what they are!'

'You don't even know them—'

'I know as much as I want to know!'

'*Be quiet!*' Freda tapped a teaspoon against her cup; immediately, they fell silent. 'That's quite enough of that . . . Alf – finish your egg before it gets cold. Steve – don't answer your father back. Tony –

didn't I tell you to go and see if Grandad wants another cup? What are you waiting for?'

When breakfast was over, the men went downstairs to open the shop and get ready for customers. Alf asked Steve to bring in another box of Bramleys, and he did as he was told, in stony silence.

Alf grunted, 'Thanks,' and went outside to set up the fruit-stall on the pavement.

Tony ran downstairs, swinging his school-bag, while his mother called after him from the landing, 'If you're late for the register, don't blame me!'

On his way through the shop, Tony mumbled awkwardly, 'Sorry, Steve. I never thought about Dad – you know, about the motorbike.'

His big brother pulled a face at him. 'Try thinking another time, eh?'

'Yeah . . .' Very daring, Tony asked: 'Can I have a ride on the pillion?'

'No, you can't!' Steve aimed a punch at the small boy's head. 'Now scoot, you cheeky little beggar!'

Grinning, Tony fled as his father came in. Having had time to cool down, Alf was ready to make amends, addressing Steve in a more friendly tone. 'Should be a good match, Saturday – eh?'

Opening a box of cookers, Steve asked, 'Sorry, Dad – what's that?'

'The match next Saturday – Palace versus Sheffield. It should be pretty good.' Then, seeing the expression on Steve's face, Alf added, 'You hadn't forgotten? You are coming?'

Of course he'd forgotten; he'd arranged to go round to the garage again on Saturday afternoon, but to say so now would be asking for trouble. Steve turned away, polishing the apples on his sleeve, and lied: 'I hadn't forgotten. I'll be there.'

When the first customer walked in, Alf was busy at the back of the shop, so Steve had to serve her.

'Good morning,' said Valerie.

Steve scarcely glanced at her, and grunted – an indeterminate noise that might have meant anything. Valerie persevered: 'I'd like a couple of bananas, please.'

He said nothing, but snapped two off and wrapped them in news-paper.

She tried again: 'How's everything going? I haven't been in lately – how are the racing cars?'

He didn't seem to hear, but took her money without a word.

'Thank you.' She lingered for one more try. 'I seem to remember you used to be very keen on motor-racing.'

96

'Yes,' he said shortly. 'What about it?'

She drew back. 'Nothing. I was only asking.'

'Sorry, I'm rather busy this morning.' With that, he turned his back on her and began to rip open a crate of cabbages.

'Thank you,' said Valerie again. 'Good morning.' She walked out of the shop, furious with him, and with herself.

For some time now, she had been avoiding Gunns. Steve had been so pleasant, and he had such a friendly smile; as a sensible girl, she realised that after Eric there was always the danger of becoming involved with someone else on the rebound. And yet – she had had the impression that Steve rather liked her, too.

So today she had allowed herself to call in and buy something, and this was the result. Last time, he had been so nice; today he couldn't even be bothered to speak to her.

'Let that be a lesson to you, my girl,' she told herself. 'Just because he smiled at you once or twice, you let your imagination run riot!'

She walked on to the Crystal Palace, showing her pass to the man on duty at the gate. The sun was still shining, but the day didn't seem quite as cheerful. At home things weren't very cheerful either. Mum never said much about Ted being on the dole, but Val knew she was worried sick about it. And although Daff and Ted tried to pretend everything was all right, that didn't fool anyone. She felt sorry for both of them. Daphne being so loyal, trying to help Ted find another job – and Ted himself, tramping round the streets, hunting for work, secretly hoping that he'd get his big chance on the stage one day . . .

She was still thinking about him when Mr Buckland came into the office with a roll of paper. It was the proof copy of a poster, advertising a concert next month: the famous singer, Carrie Tubb, supported by a company of talented artistes, would be appearing in the Concert Hall as part of the South London Co-Operative Festival.

'I've made one or two minor corrections,' Mr Buckland told her. 'This has to go to the printers as soon as possible – I want two hundred and fifty copies by Friday.'

'Yes, sir.' As he started to leave, she added suddenly, 'Excuse me, sir, could I ask you something?'

'Will this take long?' He pulled the gold watch from his waistcoat pocket and glanced at it. 'I have an appointment in ten minutes.'

'No, sir, not long. I just wanted to ask you – about my brother.'

Henry Buckland was a busy man, but he listened patiently as Val told him how talented Ted was, and how he deserved to be given a chance. When she paused for breath, he asked: 'You say he performs with Barnaby Pine's concert party? You should suggest that Mr Pine might care to hire our theatre for a few performances. I like to encourage local groups, and the booking fees are not unreasonable.'

'No, sir, I know that, but . . .' Val tried to explain that now Ted had had some success as an amateur, he wanted to turn professional. 'That's why, seeing this concert next month – I mean, you often have professionals, here, so I wondered whether—'

'My dear girl, I couldn't take that responsibility. I haven't even met your brother. I know nothing about his talent as a performer.'

'I'm sure he'd be pleased to come and audition, any time you like.'

Henry Buckland shook his head. 'I don't book the artistes. I leave that side of it to an agent – Mr Thring. He's had forty years' experience. I never involve myself directly with the performers . . . I'm sorry.'

He threw her a little nod by way of apology, and was about to go when he saw the disappointment in her face. On the spur of the moment, he added: 'If you like, I could have a word with Thring about your brother. I can't promise it will do any good, but he might be able to advise him.' Then he took out his watch once more. 'I don't want to rush you, but the printers are waiting.'

On Saturday afternoon, Steve Gunn accompanied his father to 'The Nest' – the football ground opposite Selhurst railway station, which had been the home of the Crystal Palace team for the past three years.

As Alf had said, it was an important match, and the streets were thronged with men and boys moving steadily in one direction, towards the entrance gates.

'They'll have a good crowd, by the look of it,' said Alf. 'Beats me why they couldn't move the games back to the Palace. What's wrong with the pitch there, I'd like to know? I went to all the big matches when I was your age. They used to hold the Cup Final there—'

'Yes, Dad, you told me,' said Steve, trying not to sound impatient.

'I know the Club had to move out during the war, when the Navy took the place over, but what's to stop them moving back now? The team's still called "Crystal Palace" – they should be playing there.'

As they approached the stadium, he cocked his head on one side and they heard the deep-throated roar of the spectators; the unmistakable sound of a football crowd, awesome as a mighty waterfall, or a roll of thunder.

'By God, the game's started!' exclaimed Alf, and broke into a run.

At the ticket-office, he complained: 'What the heck are they up to? Kick-off's not till three o'clock!'

The man on the gate said, 'Seemingly they started five minutes before time, to let the Wednesday team catch their train back to Sheffield.'

Alf cursed under his breath as they hurried into the stand; all around them, indignant spectators were still pouring into the ground, while on the pitch the game was already in full swing.

It got the match off to an uneasy start, and for some time the players seemed uncertain – circling one another like boxers looking for an opening.

'It's their left wing that's the trouble.' Alf glowered at the field in disgust. 'They've no attack. Look at Wood – what's he think he's doing?'

'Last season you though he was a marvel,' Steve reminded his father.

'I said he was patchy – strong one minute and disappointing the next . . .' Then, as the players pressed forward, Alf yelled: 'Shoot, man! Use your feet, can't you? Naaah – the man's useless. He's what I call a selfish player – never gives anything to his partner. Mind you, what can you expect? They've never had a proper team since they moved away from the Palace ground.'

On the field, the Yorkshire players were beginning to assert themselves, and the crowd seemed to sense that a goal was in the offing. When Price, Wednesday's Captain, moved his forwards into position, the ball flickered to and fro between them, until after twenty minutes' play, McIntyre dodged Rhodes, the Palace Captain, and scored the first goal.

They followed this success with another, and the Palace supporters groaned and catcalled; their team seemed to be totally disorganised.

'What's wrong with 'em? A load of big Jessies, that's what they are!' Taking a deep breath, Alf yelled: 'Put your backs into it, can't you?'

Whether or not it was his clarion call that rallied them, they certainly began to recover. The crowd went wild when Conner, a local lad, hooked the ball over the head of the Sheffield goalie and into the net. And that wasn't the end of it: as soon as play resumed, Conner broke through the centre – a Yorkshireman tripped him near the penalty mark, and a free kick was awarded.

Palace's Jones took the kick, completely deceiving the defence; instead of shooting for goal, he passed to Conner again – and before the Wednesday team realised what was happening, Conner had scored his second goal within minutes.

When the half-time whistle blew, Alf Gunn threw his arm round Steve's shoulders. 'What did I tell you? They're a fine team!'

Seeing his father in such a good mood, Steven began: 'Dad, I've got something to tell you. It's about the garage – Wright's Motors. They've offered me a job.'

'What?' The light went out of Alf's eyes, as if he had turned off a switch. 'What sort of job?'

'Mechanic – in their workshop. They'll train me; I'll get my qualifications, and the money's good. They want me to start on Monday week – and I've said yes . . .'

The sun continued to shine down; at Belmont, Gerald and Babs carried a folding table and a teatray into the garden. Even Muriel left the house, leaning heavily on Daphne, to enjoy the golden weather.

'Such a perfect afternoon,' she said. 'An Indian summer.'

Little Annie, who had been picking daisies from the overgrown lawn, looked up with interest. 'Like cowboys and Indians?' she asked.

The grown-ups laughed gently. 'Isn't she bright?' said Aunt Ethel. 'Fancy knowing about cowboys, at her age!'

'I took her with me to Carmichael Road the other day,' said Daphne. 'They let us borrow some storybooks from the Mixed Infants.'

Her mother looked very disapproving. 'Do you think that's wise? She might pick up all sorts of germs. You don't know who's had those books.'

'I don't think there's much risk,' said Daphne. 'Annie really enjoys books – she's beginning to read quite well.'

'Already?' Muriel was astonished. 'But she's only four years old!'

'That's what comes of having a teacher for a mother,' said Gerald. 'I suppose she'll be doing multiplication and long division next?'

'We can do adding up and taking away, can't we, lovey?' Daphne pointed at a plate of iced buns on the table. 'There were six cakes there just now, and you've had one – so how many are there left?'

'Five,' replied Annie promptly, and when Ethel patted her on the head, she added hopefully: 'And if I have another one, there'll be four.'

Gerald told her she was a little monkey, and gave her another bun.

'You shouldn't spoil her,' Muriel scolded him. 'If she has too many sweet things, she'll make herself ill.'

'I don't think one more will hurt her,' said Aggie, sitting on the grass beside her great-niece. 'Shall we make a daisy-chain? Let Auntie Ag show you how.'

Muriel turned back to Daphne. 'It's so good to see you both – it's been such an age. How are you all getting on in that funny little house of yours? You must tell me all your news.'

Daphne helped herself to a cucumber sandwich, before replying. 'I don't think there's much to tell. We jog along, the same as ever.'

'Not quite the same, surely?' Muriel asked. 'I understand your husband's out of work now.'

For a moment, Daphne was taken aback; then she saw that Babs, busily refilling the teapot with hot water, looked rather pink. Of course – Ray Duke must have known Ted had stopped going to work, and he would have told Babs.

'Oh, you heard about that?' she said briskly. 'Yes, he's not at Mulligan's any more.'

To her surprise, her mother leaned across and squeezed her hand. 'I was so pleased, dear. I never really felt happy about him selling pickles. I'm sure he can find a much nicer job, if he puts his mind to it.'

'Yes, I hope so.' Casting about for a fresh subject, Daphne's eye fell upon the doll's pram which Annie had insisted on wheeling all the way from Sackville Road. 'How do you like Annie's new pram? She had it for her birthday, and now she takes your Dutch doll everywhere she goes.'

Overhearing this, Annie scattered a handful of daisies and scrambled to her feet. 'Can I take Baby for a walk, Mum? You said we could walk in the park. Please, can we?'

'Later on, love, on our way home. We're having tea with Grandma and the Aunties and Uncle Gerry now.'

'They can come as well, can't they? We can all go to the park!' Annie ran to her grandmother, tugging at her and trying to drag her to her feet. 'You will come for a walk with Baby, won't you, Grandma? Please?'

Muriel was about to refuse, but there was something so flattering about the child's determination, she allowed herself to be cajoled.

'Why not?' she said, levering herself up from the canvas chair. 'After all, it's a lovely day – we should make the most of it. Daphne, dear, give me your arm. We won't go too far, will we? The doctor says I must never get overtired.'

In the end they all made a little expedition to the park – the one area of the Crystal Palace grounds that the public were free to enter without any charge. It was quite an occasion, since Muriel hardly ever left the house, and the outing seemed to be doing her good.

Then, as they turned a bend in the path, Muriel gripped Daphne's arm very tightly, and stood stock still.

'What is it, Mother?' Daphne asked. 'Aren't you feeling well?'

Muriel did not reply. Her sisters clustered helplessly round her, and Ethel cawed, 'Find her a chair – she's going to faint. Someone fetch a glass of water!'

Gerry muttered, 'Good Lord, of all the rotten luck . . .'

Following his gaze, Daphne saw her father coming towards them. Harry Glynn was taking a stroll in the afternoon sunshine, with Miss Preece on his arm. She would have gone to meet him, but her mother's grip was like a vice.

'Don't leave me. Don't speak to him,' Muriel gasped.

Harry too stopped in his tracks. 'Hello, Daffie,' he grunted. 'Well, well – quite a surprise, eh?'

Annie ran to her grandfather, trundling the doll's pram over the uneven path. Whenever he dropped in at Sackville Road, she always gave him a warm welcome.

'Grandpa! Grandpa, have you seen my baby? This is Baby, in her new pram!'

In spite of his arthritis, Harry stooped to kiss his granddaughter, then admired the pram and its contents.

'Your baby, d'you say? Very handsome, I'm sure.' He straightened up. 'That must be nice, having a baby of your own.' Screwing up his eyes, he cast a searching look over the little group. 'Babs – Gerald – I hope you're well? Ethel and Aggie – good to see you. And you too, Muriel, of course.'

Muriel bit her lip and continued to look away, cutting him dead.

Stiffly, he raised his shapeless tweed hat, then passed on, saying to his companion: 'Small world, eh? Never know who you'll run into, these days.'

Daphne could feel her mother shaking with anger. As soon as the enemy was out of earshot, she burst out: 'That dreadful man – how dare he speak to me? And that painted creature with him – did you see her dyed hair?'

Daphne said quickly, 'Annie, I'm going home with Grandma now. Why don't you and Auntie Babs take Baby as far as the lake and back? We'll see you presently.'

She and Gerald helped their mother along the path, while the Aunts clucked and whispered behind them.

'How *dare* he?' Muriel repeated. 'Glorying in his wickedness. Flaunting his mistress without a scrap of shame—'

'That's his landlady, Mother, Miss Preece.'

'Oh yes, he can't keep his hands off women – any women!' Muriel was still highly indignant. 'Did you hear what he said to little Annie? *"It must be nice to have a baby"*. I shudder to think how many unwanted babies he's brought into the world – love-children, that's what they call them. I call them children of lust!'

Aggie gave a little moan. 'So terrible for you, meeting him suddenly like that.'

'It can't have been exactly pleasant for him, either,' said Daphne.

The afternoon had also turned out unhappily at the Selhurst football ground; after the excitement of the first half, no more goals were scored. When the whistle blew, the score remained unchanged, with two goals to each side, and the spectators went home unsatisfied.

Alf Gunn was in a black mood and scarcely said a word. Once or twice Steve tried to start a conversation, commenting on various players, but his father said nothing. He tried to throw in some more information about the new job – the prospects, the annual fortnight's holiday, the extra pay for overtime – but Alf didn't seem to hear.

When they got back to Church Road, Alf tore off his cap and his coat and flung them angrily into the armchair, saying to Freda: 'Our son's leaving us, Mother! What d'you think he's going to do, eh? Chucking up his job here in the shop, that's what. He wants to go and get covered in muck and grease at that precious garage. Leaving us in the lurch, he is – but of course he doesn't give a damn about that!'

'Language!' said Freda sharply, putting down her knitting. 'Not in front of the boy, if you don't mind.'

At the table, Tony had been filling in the outlines of cows and horses in his *Big Magic Farmyard Painting Book*; now he sat staring at his brother, while the paintbrush dripped on the page, unnoticed.

'Is this true, Steven?' asked Freda.

He told his mother about the new job, as simply as he could. When he had finished, she said: 'Well, they do say there's money to be made in motorcars, and if that's what you want . . .' She addressed her husband. 'Alfred, he's a grown man, and it's up to him to do what suits him best. We can manage without him. I know it'll leave you short-handed in the shop, but I can do some of his work – and I'm sure Grandad will help out whenever he's feeling up to it.'

'That's all well and good – but what about Covent Garden? Who's going to drive the van?' grumbled Alfred. 'I can't do it. I'm too old a dog to learn new tricks.'

'I can still drive the van,' Steve cut in. 'If we make an early start, I should get back here by eight, then I'll be at the garage by half-past. I offered to work late to make up the extra time, and Mr Wright said that would be OK.'

'So that's that.' Alf knocked his hat and coat on to the floor and flung himself into the armchair. 'You work and slave for your kids all your life, and this is the thanks you get – walking out and leaving you! First Julie takes herself off, Up West, and we hardly ever see her, and now it's Steve. I suppose we'll be left on our own one of these days!'

'Don't talk so silly, Alfred. You know as well as I do, you were very proud of Julie when she got that job in Oxford Street. This could be a good opportunity for Steve, too. And don't go throwing your clothes on the floor, setting the boys a bad example. Just you pick them up this minute!'

Alf did as he was told, and went to hang his hat and coat on the hall-stand. When he came back, he ignored Steve, talking across him to Tony. 'How about coming with me next Saturday, to watch the Palace play at Selhurst? How would you like that, son?'

A smile spread across Tony's face. 'Not half!'

By the time they got home to Sackville Road, Annie was very tired, so Daphne undressed her and bathed her right away, putting her to bed a little earlier than usual.

When she went down to the kitchen, she found Ted, Kate and Valerie looking at her expectantly. She began to tell them about the tea-party at Belmont, and the awkward encounter in the park – but they weren't really listening.

'Ted's had some good news,' said Kate. 'Wait till you hear!'

'What sort of news?' She turned to him eagerly: 'A job?'

'Not exactly.' Ted didn't want to sound too excited, and he turned to Valerie. 'You tell her.'

So she reported that Mr Buckland had talked to the theatrical agent, P. P. Thring, about Edward Watkins, the up-and-coming amateur comedian – and Mr Thring had telephoned Valerie at the Crystal Palace to ask for more details.

'I must have said the right thing,' she finished, 'because he's asked Ted to go and see him at his office on Monday morning!'

'Oh, Ted!' Daphne hugged him. 'It sounds as if your luck's turned at last. Well, you deserve it.'

'Hold your horses!' he laughed. 'It might come to nothing. Maybe he won't like the look of me.'

'How could anyone not like you? I'm sure he'll get you some work,' Daphne told him. 'This is the chance you've been waiting for.'

'I hope so.' Ted was trying not to count his chickens. 'But we can't expect miracles. Even if he gives me some work, it won't be a regular income. It'll probably be just the odd date here and there.'

'Yes, I know, but it doesn't matter.' Daphne faced the others. 'If Ted's going to make a name for himself on the stage, there's only one thing for it. I shall go back to teaching.'

They all looked at her, and then Ted repeated blankly, 'Teaching? But what about Annie?'

'I'll only do half-days at first, and take Annie with me. She can go into the Mixed Infants.'

'But the school won't take her till she's five—' began Valerie.

'I talked it over with the Head. Annie can sit in with the first class – she's every bit as bright as the five-year-olds.' With her arms round Ted, she smiled up at him. 'You, me, and Annie . . . we'll all start work together.'

Ted didn't have much to say for the rest of the evening, but when they went to bed and turned off the light, he cuddled up to her as he always did, then said quietly, 'So you're going back to teaching. You had it all planned.'

'Well, yes.' There was a tone in his voice that Daphne had never heard before. 'You don't mind, do you?'

'I wish we'd talked it over first, instead of you fixing things without telling me.'

'It isn't fixed – not yet. I just wanted to find out if it would be possible, and it is.'

'It sounded pretty fixed to me. Anyhow, you've got what you wanted.'

'And so have you! The chance to go on the stage!' She held him closer. 'This way, we both get what we want. It makes everything possible – don't you see?'

'Yes, I see. You're very clever. But I always knew that.'

'Ted, don't be cross,' she whispered. 'Everything's going to be all right, I promise.'

Then she kissed him, and soon his body began to respond to hers, moving smoothly into the familiar patterns of love – and after that everything was all right . . . Or very nearly.

Chapter Six

P. P. THRING'S OFFICE was not imposing – two rooms above a pawnbroker's shop in Kennington Road. The outer room was small, presided over by a formidable lady who wore steel-rimmed glasses and had her hair knotted into a tight bun. She sat at a small desk behind an old-fashioned typewriter, and when Ted climbed the stairs and walked in, she said severely: 'Name, please!'

'Ted Watkins. I've got an appointment with Mr Thring.'

'It's the first I've heard of it.' She eyed him narrowly over the top of her glasses. 'Who made the appointment?'

'My sister Valerie fixed it up on the phone with Mr Thring. She works at the Crystal Palace.'

'Fancy . . .' She rose majestically and opened a communicating door to the inner office. 'Do you know anything about a Ted Watkins?' she asked.

'Never heard of him,' croaked a hoarse voice.

'He says you arranged an appointment through his sister – works at the Crystal Palace, he says.'

'Oh, wait – it's coming back to me now . . .'

'You've been using the telephone behind my back, haven't you? Well, don't do it again!' The dragon returned, saying curtly, 'He'll see you. Go on in.'

Ted entered the inner sanctum. The walls were covered with theatrical photographs and out-of-date posters; behind a much larger desk P. P. Thring was wreathed in a cloud of cigarette smoke. He was probably in his middle sixties, but looked like an ageing toad – squat and bald, with several chins, and myopic eyes magnified by the thickest glasses Ted had ever seen.

'Come in, old man, come in. Sit down. I talked to your sister the other day, didn't I? Seemed like a nice girl – married, I suppose?'

'No, not so far. She's only twenty.'

'Aha, still a chance for me, eh?' Mr Thring cackled, rubbing his hands. 'She told me you want to be a comedian – right?'

'No, sir – I'm a comedian already. But I want to make a living at it.'

'Don't we all, old man, don't we all?' Mr Thring squinted at him. 'Let's have a good look at you. Tell me a joke.'

Although Ted had been preparing a few funny stories on the way, running through them in his head on top of a tram sailing down Brixton Hill, this sudden command was disconcerting, but he pulled himself together and began.

'Have you heard the one about the ship's captain who was invited to take his crew to a vicarage tea-party?'

Mr Thring nodded. 'I've heard all the jokes there are – but don't let that stop you. Tell it to me anyhow.'

Still more disconcerted, Ted launched into the anecdote, using different voices for the vicar, and the vicar's wife, and the ship's captain, working up to the pay-off line as the Captain roared at his crew: '. . . And the first man who tells him – back on the ship!'

He waited for the laugh. There wasn't one. Mr Thring nodded, without even cracking a smile.

'Very nice, old man, very comical. What else do you do? Sing? Dance?'

'I haven't done much dancing. I can shuffle a bit – but I've got a pretty good voice. I do some of the Albert Chevalier numbers – costermonger ballads, that sort of thing.'

'Right you are.' Wheezing, the little man hoisted himself out of his chair and crossed the room. 'Follow me.' He passed through the outer office, saying over his shoulder, 'You, too, Bessie. He needs an accompanist.'

The dragon left her desk, joining them without comment as they proceeded down the stairs. She locked the street door behind them, leaving a card hanging on the knocker, bearing the words *Back In Five Minutes*.

'Where are we going, Mr Thring?' asked Ted, falling into step beside the little man.

'To find a piano, of course – no room for one in the office. Don't stand on ceremony, old man. Call me Percy, everybody does.'

The ill-assorted trio crossed the road, and to Ted's surprise Percy

107

Thring pushed open a side door at The Horns public house. It was nowhere near opening-time, but the two barmen inside greeted the little man casually.

'We have an arrangement, you see, for the use of the piano,' Percy explained. 'Right, Bessie – tinkle the ivories.'

The dragon seated herself at the battered upright, saying to Ted, 'I don't suppose you've brought your music?'

'No. I didn't think—'

'Ah, well, I dare say I'll pick it up. What are you going to delight us with?'

Remembering his first success at Grange Wood, Ted fell back on *How's This For A Start?*, and Bessie followed the melody pretty well. The two barmen got on with their work, ignoring the entertainment. Clearly, this was a common occurrence.

Ted went on to sing another old favourite, *Boiled Beef And Carrots* – and when he had finished, Percy Thring said, 'That's enough. Thanks, Bessie, you'd better go back and mind the phone. Sir Oswald Stoll may be ringing up to book some acts for the Coliseum.'

Bessie left without a word, and as soon as she had gone Percy signalled to one of the barmen. 'Just going into the back room, Nobby. Bring us my usual, and another for my friend while you're about it.'

When they were settled into what seemed to be the landlord's private office, he winked at Ted over his whisky-and-water. 'This is another little arrangement we have. I'm what you might call a regular.' He raised his glass. 'Down the hatch!' Refreshed, he rewarded Ted with a benign smile, like a cockney Buddha. 'So – you're aiming to be the greatest comedian in the world, eh?'

'I wouldn't say that,' Ted began modestly.

'Good, because you'll never be that till he pops off, which God forbid. He was in here a few weeks ago – did you know that?'

'Who?'

'The greatest in the world – Charlie Chaplin, of course. Came over from Hollywood on a trip to London – didn't you see it in the papers? Staying at the Ritz, he was. The crowds practically mobbed him in Piccadilly – stopped the traffic! – but he gave 'em the slip, nipping out the back way, and took a cab over the river to visit his old haunts. He came from these parts, you know. Number Three, Pownall Terrace, that's where he lived with his Ma, and when she was put into the asylum, he went to live with his Dad, at two hundred and eighty-seven, Kennington Road . . . I happened to be looking out of the window that afternoon, and I saw him walk past. Nobody else recognised him without his bowler hat and his little moustache, but I'd seen him when he was on tour with Fred Karno, years ago. I've never forgotten it.'

He wasn't looking at Ted any more, but gazing into a misty past where everything had brighter colour and sharper outlines than the blurred world around him.

'I told Bessie I was popping out for a few minutes, and I went after him. I guessed where he was going; this pub had been one of his regular haunts in the old days. Of course, it was a bit different then . . . When I came in, I saw him standing at the bar, with a drink in his hand, gazing around – looking a bit sad, I thought, to see how it had changed. Afterwards, when he went out, I followed him down the road, and he stopped outside the Kennington Road School, peering through the railings at the playground. That's where he used to go, when he was a nipper.'

'Did you speak to him?' asked Ted.

'How could I? He doesn't know me from Adam. What could you say to a man like that? He's the greatest – don't you think so?'

Ted hesitated. 'I think he's a great clown – acrobat, almost. But that's not my line. I use my voice – singing songs, or just talking to people. I could never be like him.'

'No – and nobody else will be, neither. Still, that's not to say you shouldn't take a whack at it, eh?' Percy Thring's manner changed; suddenly he was brisk and businesslike. 'I'll give you a trial, old man. Peckham Working Men's Club – Smoking Concert, Friday week. Give 'em ten minutes – two or three numbers – and I'll try to squeeze a guinea out of 'em. All right?'

All right? Ted didn't care about the money. Even though he would have to pay the agent ten per cent commission out of his guinea, he was more than satisfied. It was his first professional engagement; he'd have done it for half-a-crown.

Walter Faber glanced at his watch. Babs was not at her desk – through the office door he could see her at the far end of the shop, with Ray Duke. They were talking quietly – and then they began laughing together. It was unbearable.

He raised his voice, calling: 'Miss Glynn! Would you mind?'

Babs stopped laughing and returned to the office, putting on a serious expression – but her face was flushed, and her eyes sparkled.

'I'm afraid I have to go out,' he told her.

'Oh, yes?' She looked surprised; he hadn't mentioned this before.

'I should have told you. Mrs Faber has been suffering some gastric pain, and I called the doctor before I left home this morning. It was particularly unfortunate that it should happen on a Friday – it's always difficult to get any medical advice at the weekend – but he finally agreed to come and see her at half-past four. I must be with her.'

'I understand.' Babs tried to look concerned. 'Somebody's got to be there, to let him in.'

'It isn't that – our housekeeper could let him in – but I'm anxious to speak to the doctor myself. I'm concerned about my wife's health, naturally.'

'Of course, you must be. If there's anything at all I can do—'

'It's very good of you; everything is under control. But I doubt if I shall be able to get back here before the shop shuts. In the usual way, I'd ask Mr Dingwall to lock up for me, but as it happens he isn't here either.'

There had been some problems with the furniture van, which had broken down during a delivery round. Tubby Dingwall had driven it over to the garage for a thorough overhaul, and Mr Faber had told him to take the rest of the afternoon off.

'So I must ask you to lock up for me.' He took the keyring from his pocket and put it on the desk. 'I'm sure you can manage it – you've seen me do it often enough. Go round the whole place, to make sure all the lights are switched off, then lock and bolt the front door – and lock the back door when you leave.' He paused for a moment, then added: 'You might ask Duke to go round with you, to check everything. Two heads are better than one, they say.

'Yes, Mr Faber – all right. We'll do that.'

He took his coat from the peg, and began to put it on. As he turned away, shrugging into the sleeves, she could not see his face, and his voice was flat and expressionless as he remarked: 'You and young Duke appear to be getting on quite well. I'm glad of that. Good staff relationships are very important.'

She did not know what to say, but remembered to ask, 'Excuse me, what shall I do with the keys afterwards? Do you want me to drop them in at your house, on my way home?'

He faced her with a courteous smile. 'I wouldn't want to take you out of your way. You can keep the keys overnight, as long as you make sure you're here bright and early tomorrow, to open up.'

'Oh, yes, I'll be here, I promise.'

'I'm sure I can trust you, Miss Glynn.' He wished her a pleasant evening, then left the shop, throwing a 'Good night,' at Ray on his way out.

As soon as he had gone, Ray came rushing into the office, asking what was going on. When Babs told him, Ray looked thoughtful.

'Funny thing, him asking you to do the locking-up. I wonder why he didn't ask me?' Then he broke off, as some customers entered the shop. For the rest of the afternoon, they were kept busy. Most of the shoppers had a good look round, but left without buying anything, although Ray did manage to sell a pair of Lloyd Loom basket chairs, painted eau-de-nil.

Well before half-past five, be began to pull down the blinds, then joined Babs on a final tour of the premises, bolting and locking the doors. At one minute past the half-hour, they were outside the shop, walking along Church Road, when Ray exclaimed suddenly: 'Bloody hell! I think I left the light on in the stockroom.'

'I don't think so. I'm almost sure you switched it off—'

'I meant to, but I was talking to you when we came out, and I might have overlooked it. I'd better make sure.'

'I'll come with you,' said Babs, fishing in her handbag for the keys.

'Don't bother – give 'em to me. You walk on, and I'll catch you up.'

He took the keys and broke into a run; moments later, he let himself in through the back door – but he did not to go the stockroom. Instead, he went straight to the toilet; the little side window was firmly shut, and he opened it slightly. Then he went out, locked the back door again, and ran as fast as he could, catching up with Babs at the top of Anerley Hill.

'You were right,' he said breathlessly, handing back the keyring, and she put it into her bag. 'I had turned the light out. Still, better safe than sorry, eh?'

For some reason, Babs gave an involuntary shiver, and he glanced at her. 'What's up? Feeling the cold, are you?' He slipped his arm round her waist. 'I bet I could warm you up . . .'

'Don't, Ray!' She pulled away from him. 'Someone might see.'

'I can't help it – I like holding you close to me.' An idea flashed into his mind. 'What are you doing tonight?'

'Nothing special – why?'

'How about you and me going dancing? There's a Friday-night hop at the Palace – then I could hold you in my arms all the evening.'

★

'What's the time?' asked Ted, combing his hair at the mirror above the kitchen sink.

Daphne was folding up his stage costume – the costermonger's jacket with the pearl buttons – and putting it into an attaché case, together with his make-up tin, his billycock hat, and the spotted red handkerchief.

She smiled. 'You asked me that five minutes ago. It was six o'clock then, and now it's five past.'

'All right, Clara Clever. Only I mustn't be late.' He turned to her. 'How do I look? Is this collar all right?'

'It's fine. What are you so anxious about? The audience won't see you like that, will they? You'll change when you get there.'

'There's the other artistes – I want to make a good impression.'

'I told you, you look fine.' She closed the attaché case and gave it to him. 'There you are.'

'Did you put in my music? For the pianist?'

'Of course I did – don't worry.' She kissed him. 'You're going to be a big success tonight, I just know it.'

'I hope you're right. I wish you were going to be there – it would make me feel a lot better. But being a Smoking Concert, it's a men-only night.'

'You can tell me about it when you get back. I'll sit up for you.'

The door opened, and Valerie came into the kitchen, wearing her hat and coat. 'Still here?' she greeted her brother. 'I hoped I'd catch you, to wish you luck.'

'I'm going to need it,' muttered Ted. 'Percy Thring said he'll be there. If I make a mess of it, I'll never get another chance.'

'You'll be all right – stop fussing!' She straightened his tie. 'Are you ready? I'll walk with you to the bus-stop – keep you company.'

'Why? Where are you going?'

'Only as far as the Palace. There's a dance on, and the girl who takes the tickets went down with 'flu, so I told Mr Buckland I'd fill in for her.'

'You've just done a full day's work for that man!' protested Daphne. 'You let him take advantage of your good nature.'

'I don't. I volunteered . . . We owe him a favour. If it wasn't for Henry Buckland and Percy Thring, Ted wouldn't be starting his new career.'

'Starting or finishing – one or the other.' Ted picked up the attaché case. 'Do you think I ought to say good night to Annie first?'

'Don't you dare!' said Daphne. 'Your Mum's bathing her – you'll get soapsuds all over your best suit. Off you go, and good luck.'

So Ted and Val went out together, and Daphne heard the front door bang. Left alone, she sank into a chair, relieved that she didn't have to keep smiling any longer – and grateful that they hadn't noticed she was shaking. Shutting her eyes, she sent up a silent prayer, asking God to accompany her husband to the Peckham Working Men's Smoking Concert tonight, and beseeching Him to grant Ted a little miracle.

The dance at the Palace began at seven o'clock; when Ray and Babs arrived, the band was playing a cheerful waltz called *I'm Forever Blowing Bubbles*, but there were not many couples circling the floor.

Babs was startled to find herself face to face with Val, on duty at the door. She tore their tickets in half, saying cheerily, 'Look who's here!' Embarrassed, Babs hoped Val would not jump to any conclusions about seeing them together, but if anything, Ray seemed to be rather pleased.

'Yes, we felt like having a fling,' he said. 'Pity there aren't more people here, though. It looks half dead.'

'Oh, it'll fill up later,' Val told him. 'It's early yet.'

'Let's show 'em how it's done,' Ray said to Babs. 'May I have the pleasure?'

He held out his arms, and she allowed herself to be swept on to the floor. He was a good dancer, and she began to relax; as they waltzed together, he started to sing along with the band:

> *'They fly so high – nearly reach the sky,*
> *Then like my dreams, they fade and die . . .'*

A few miles away, in Peckham, Ted was singing a different song.

'Me an' the Missus is proud of 'im, 'e's our first . . .' He broke off, seeing the pitying smile on the pianist's face. 'It used to be a very popular number – don't you know it?'

The stage at the Working Men's Club was small, and the dressing room behind it even smaller. Half a dozen men were crowded together, changing their clothes and slapping on greasepaint. A friendly conjuror had told Ted they could think themselves lucky. His wife, who assisted him on the stage, handing him his props, was upstairs sharing a broom-cupboard with a soprano and a pair of ragtime dancers called The Twin Tornados.

The pianist raised his voice above the hubbub. 'Yes, I know the number,' he said. 'And by the end of the evening the audience will know it too – they'll have heard it twice.'

Ted frowned. 'What do you mean?'

'See the chap at the other end of the room, changing his trousers? That's Mr Gus Elen.'

Ted stared at the short, sad-faced man, who looked like an elderly monkey. 'Gus Elen? I saw him at the Penge Empire when I was a kid . . . I'd never have recognised him.'

'Wait till you see him got up in his Pearly King outfit – he's a different man then. And he's giving us some of the old favourites tonight – *Down The Road, If It Wasn't For The Houses In Between* and *How's This For A Start?* You'd better think again, old boy. What other numbers have you got?'

'I haven't got any others.' With his hopes crashing around him, Ted put the sheet-music back in his attaché case. 'Well, I have – but they're all the same sort of thing.'

'Pity about that.' The pianist smiled acidly. 'You'll just have to do something else, won't you? Do you juggle at all? Know any cardtricks?

Ted watched Gus Elen putting on a tailcoat, covered in gleaming buttons, and was glad he hadn't changed into his own pearly jacket.

'No,' he said. 'I don't do anything like that.'

For two pins he'd have picked up his bag, and gone home.

By nine o'clock, Valerie had finished work. There wouldn't be any more admissions now – latecomers weren't allowed in after nine, to insure against drunks turning up at closing time and making a nuisance of themselves. So now she was free to go.

Leaving the central hall, she began to walk down the long, echoing transept – like a cathedral nave crossed with a conservatory. Halfway along, a buffet served light refreshments near Follett Osler's Fountain: twenty-seven feet high, a fantasy of cascades and shining crystal, it had been built for the Great Exhibition of 1851 in Hyde Park and transported intact when the Palace was moved to South London.

A solitary figure stood beside it, gazing into the flowing water.

'Hello, again – all on your own?' said Valerie. 'Where's Ray?'

'I don't know. I've been looking everywhere for him,' said Babs.

'Perhaps he's in the whatsit,' Val suggested.

'Don't be silly. He's been gone half an hour at least. He'd have been back long ago if he was in there.'

'Not if he's got himself locked in. Would you like me to send in one of the attendants?'

'No!' Babs reddened angrily. 'He told me he was going outside. He said it was too warm indoors – he wanted a breath of air. I went out to see if I could find him, but it's so dark and there are so many steps, I was afraid I might fall and hurt myself.'

'I'll go and scout around for him if you like,' said Val. 'I know my way pretty well by now.'

'Would you?' Babs was pathetically grateful. 'I feel such a fool, stuck here by myself.'

On her way out into the grounds, Valerie couldn't help thinking that Ray Duke might have gone to look for more entertaining company; young men frequently wandered off among the bushes in search of adventure – anxious mothers were always warning their daughters about the perils they might meet in the shrubbery.

After the warmth of the building, the night air struck cold and she thrust her hands into her coat pockets. A shaft of light from the building picked out a young man with a girl on his arm – he looked familiar, and then she realised it was Steve, from the greengrocers. She didn't recognise the girl, but she only saw them for a moment before they disappeared.

So that was the kind of person he was. Obviously his morals were as bad as his temper . . . Depressed and obscurely angry, she began to wish she hadn't offered to look for Ray, but she could hardly give up the search so quickly. Following the path that led to the Maze, she walked on, away from the lights and the sound of the band, into the darkness.

Somewhere in Peckham, Ted stood in the wings at the side of the stage, watching the two Tornados; identical twins, they were bright, buxom girls, and they finished their routine with an energetic buck-and-wing – arms whirling like windmills, feet tapping, hips swaying and bosoms bouncing in unison. The all-male audience at the Smoking Concert responded with enthusiasm, stamping the floor and banging beer mugs on the tables. At the end, they shouted for more, and the girls rushed on again and again to acknowledge the applause.

Making their final exit, flushed and laughing, they told Ted as they passed him: 'Lovely audience, dear – all yours.'

With a sneer, the pianist struck up a few bars of *For He's A Jolly Good Fellow*, and nodded to Ted, signalling him to make his entrance. The stage was the smallest he'd ever seen, but when he stepped out from the safe shelter of the wings, it looked as big as the Albert Hall. It seemed to take forever to reach the centre; he stood there, caught in the crossed beams of two spotlights. When the pianist stopped playing, a sullen silence fell. He had never felt so terrified.

He knew what this audience wanted – pretty girls, kicking up their legs. They didn't know who the hell he was, and they didn't want to; their lack of interest rolled toward him across the footlights like a thick, damp fog.

The situation was hopeless – and the sheer hopelessness of it suddenly struck him as so ludicrous, he couldn't help grinning.

'Hello,' he said. 'I'm Ted Watkins. You don't know me and I don't know you – and here we are, stuck with each other for the next ten minutes . . . It's a funny old world, isn't it?'

Amazingly, the silence was broken by someone at the back of the room, who snorted with laughter. Ted responded gratefully.

'There you are,' he said. 'That's what I mean – you've got to laugh, haven't you? It's like what happened to a pal of mine the other day . . .'

Then he was off. He told them the one about the plumber and the lady who got her toe stuck in the bath-tap, he told them the one about the two gladiators going into the arena to fight a lion, he told them the one about the princess who kissed a frog and got a big surprise . . . for ten minutes he kept up a continuous stream of stories, each one flowing into the next, creating a little world of comic characters – lovely ladies and saucy plumbers, ancient Romans and moth-eaten lions, princes and princesses and croaking frogs – captivating the audience, leading them from one absurd climax to another, and all the time holding them in the palm of his hand.

When he had finished, they didn't want to let him go, but while they were still rocking with laughter, he grinned once more and said: 'I've got to be going now. It's been nice meeting you – we mustn't leave it so long next time.'

When he walked off the stage, he was surprised to find that the wings were crowded; during the past ten minutes, the other artistes had drifted in to watch him. As they gathered round Ted, congratulating him, Gus Elen shook his hand.

'Nice work, son – you'll do!'

It certainly was a funny old world.

Valerie was cold and tired and fed up. There was no sign of Ray; the moon had gone behind a cloud, so it was hard to see where she was going. She felt angry with herself. Why ever had she offered to come and search for him in the first place? She decided to take one last look along the path that led to the lake; if he wasn't there either, she would give up.

The path was narrow, under overhanging trees, and she couldn't see a thing. She knew this was a favourite spot for courting couples – she could hear smothered giggles and whispers in the undergrowth. Feeling very foolish, she stepped off the path, hoping to take a short cut through the bushes that would bring her out beside the lake, but soon realised she had lost her way; confused, she stumbled through the darkness with leaves and twigs slapping at her face, and hit her head on a low branch. Her foot slipped on a soft patch of mud that gave way beneath her, and losing her balance she fell headlong – landing with a splash in black, icy water.

In a blind panic, she scrambled to her feet, gasping and choking and spitting out a mouthful of brackish water – and at the same moment she heard a second splash as someone else jumped in.

A pair of strong arms picked her up, and a man's voice said, 'Don't worry, you're safe now. I've got you.'

She began to struggle in his arms, spluttering: 'I can manage! Put me down!'

Ignoring this, her rescuer carried her on to dry land, through the bushes and back to the path, where he set her on her feet again.

'How are you feeling?' he asked.

'A bit wet, otherwise all right,' she said through chattering teeth. 'It's very good of you, but there was no need. The water's not deep – I wasn't in any danger.'

'You're in danger of catching pneumonia,' he told her. 'We've got to get you back to the Palace. What you need is a change of clothes and a hot drink.'

'I'm all right, I tell you!' she snapped. 'I can manage perfectly well, thank you.'

He took no notice, but threw off his overcoat and made her put it on; with one arm around her shoulders, he marched her firmly back towards the Palace. Val tried to break free, telling him she would rather die of pneumonia than humiliation in front of strangers, but he wouldn't listen.

'Don't talk so daft,' he said. 'Why can't you do as you're told?'

By now they were closer to the building, touched by a faint spill of light from the windows, and they looked at each other for the first time.

'Here – I know you, don't I?' said Steve Gunn.

'Yes,' said Valerie. 'And if you don't let me go home, I'll never come into your shop again as long as I live.'

A smile lit up those huge, dark eyes. 'All right then, I'll walk you home,' he said. 'Where d'you live?'

She told him, and as they headed for the exit gate, he asked: 'Didn't you have anyone with you? You weren't all on your own, surely?'

'Yes, I was. I wasn't at the dance – I work here, in the office.'

'Oh, I see.' Then he thought for a moment. 'So what were you doing down by the lake, crashing about in the bushes all by yourself?'

'I don't think that's any business of yours,' she said with as much dignity as she could muster, then spoiled it by adding: 'I won't ask what *you* were doing. That was fairly obvious.'

'What do you mean by that?'

'I happened to see you earlier, going into the shrubbery – with a friend.'

'Oh, her. Yes, but we had a bit of a misunderstanding, and she went off with another bloke. I was wandering around by myself when I heard you screaming for help.'

'I did not scream for help! I might have called out when I fell in. It was rather a shock—'

'I bet it was.' He let her go first through the turnstile, then added: 'Now I've told you what I was doing there, I think you ought to tell me what you were up to. That's only fair.'

'If you must know, I was looking for a friend. Well, not so much a friend of mine, actually – the friend of a friend. He took her to the dance, and then he went off and left her high and dry.'

'High and dry?' Steve Gunn threw her a sidelong glance. 'Some people have all the luck, don't they?'

Val looked down at her sodden skirt and shoes, leaving a trail of puddles on the pavement, and she found herself smiling. 'You know very well what I mean. Poor girl, I felt sorry for her being stood up like that, so I offered to go and look for him.'

Still with his arm around her, Steve led her across the road at the end of Crystal Palace Parade, and they set off down the hill in the direction of Sackville Road.

'But you didn't manage to find him?' he asked.

'No, I didn't. He'd vanished into thin air. I can't imagine what's happened to him.'

At that moment, Ray Duke was not much more than a hundred yards away from them, going through Mr Faber's desk. The beam of light from his pocket torch shone upon the black japanned cashbox, as he lifted it out. It was locked, of course – he had known that it would be – but that didn't matter. He could easily prise it open with a chisel from Tubby Dingwall's toolkit.

Carefully, he laid the torch down – he could not risk switching on the overhead light; it might be visible to a passing copper on his beat.

Ray's heart was pounding, but he wasn't scared; everything had gone so smoothly, he felt a kind of elation. It had been so easy to slip away, getting out of the grounds by shinning over the wall. Nobody had seen him as he raced along Church Road and down the alley to the backyard. The toilet window was just as he had left it – he pulled it open and climbed through. It was a tight squeeze, but he managed it. And now here he was, with the cashbox in his hands. Soon – very soon now – he would be a rich man . . .

The electric light snapped on – so bright, he was momentarily dazzled. Spinning round, he screwed up his eyes against the glare.

Walter Faber was standing in the office doorway, his hand still on the light-switch.

'I've been waiting for you,' he said, his voice carefully under control. 'I knew you'd come, sooner or later . . . Where is she?'

Ray's thrill of elation had gone. Fear and anger clawed at his guts. His mouth was dry, and he had to lick his lips before he could speak. 'Where's who?' he asked huskily.

'Miss Glynn, of course. You brought her here, didn't you? I guessed as much. "Canoodling" – isn't that what you call it?'

Staring at him, Ray whispered, 'I don't know what you're talking about.'

'Don't lie to me. I've seen the state of those mattresses after you've been messing about with her in the stockroom. I'm not a complete fool, you know.' He glanced over his shoulder. 'What have you done with her? I was in the stockroom, waiting for you to turn up. *Where is she?*'

'She – she's not here . . .' The words came out thickly, as if Ray's tongue were too big for his mouth. 'I come here – *came* here – on my own.'

'What?' For the first time, Faber noticed the cashbox in front of him, and understood. 'Good God . . . So it wasn't pleasure you were after this time – it was money, was it? Did you persaude the girl to give you the keys, or did you take them from her by force?'

'I haven't got your bloody keys.' Ray tried to think straight, his head whirling. 'How did you get in? Did she give 'em to you? Did she go round to your house, after all? What's she been saying to you, the little bitch!'

Angrily, Faber took a step towards him. 'No, she didn't come to my house – she didn't bring me the keys. You don't really imagine there's only one set of keys to this place, do you? So – you admit you and the girl planned this together?'

'No, we never! I got in on my own, through the back window. It wasn't fastened properly. I helped Babs lock up, and after I got home I thought we might've left that window open, so – so I came back to make sure. And then I climbed in – just to see everything was all right.'

'And I suppose you were just looking for the cashbox, to make sure it hadn't been stolen? You filthy little liar.' Faber crossed the room and picked up the telephone. 'I'm going to call the police,' he said, as he waited for the operator at the exchange to answer. 'I'm going to hand you over to the authorities.'

A shrill voice in his ear said, 'Number, please.'

He began to say, 'Connect me with the local police station—' but at the same moment Ray interrupted him.

'I wouldn't, if I was you. Not unless you want everybody to know.'

Distracted, Faber looked at Ray. 'What do you mean?'

'You tell the police, and I'll tell 'em about you – you and Babs. About how you put your hand up her skirt, and how you pulled down her knickers and touched her up—'

The operator was saying impatiently, 'I can't hear you, sir. What number do you require?'

'I – er—' Walter Faber cleared his throat. 'Hold on a moment, please.' He put his hand over the mouthpiece, saying to Ray: 'I don't know what you're talking about.'

'You've been interfering with that young lady – she told me all about it. If you make trouble for me, it's all going to come out in court. And I'll make sure your missus gets to hear about it too – you and your goings-on. Babs will back me up. She don't want any more to do with you.'

Walter Faber uncovered the mouthpiece, then said quietly, 'I'm sorry . . . Sorry you've been troubled.' Slowly, he replaced the receiver.

Chapter Seven

VALERIE SNEEZED – AGAIN.

'What did I tell you?' exclaimed Kate. 'I knew it – you're coming down with 'flu. They say there's a lot of it about.'

'I'll be fine, Mum,' Valerie told her, fumbling for her handkerchief.

'Drink this,' said Daphne, who had made her a hot lemon drink.

When Val came home, cold and bedraggled, Kate had insisted on running her a hot bath immediately, and now she was sitting by the kitchen fire, telling them the story of her adventure and feeling the warmth creep back into her bones.

'But who was the young man?' asked Kate. 'I don't know him – where does he come from?'

'You do know him, Mum. Steve Gunn – he works at the greengrocers. You've seen him hundreds of times.'

'And what was he doing, prowling round the lake in the dark?' Her mother wouldn't be satisfied until she had all the details. 'Have you been meeting him on the quiet, without telling us?'

'Of course not! I've never even spoken to him, except when I've been into the shop. I lost my way and fell in the lake – he helped me out and offered to see me home. He wouldn't take no for an answer.'

'Why didn't you ask him in? You should have offered him a cup of tea.'

'I did ask, but he said no. I think he felt a bit embarrassed.'

Kate pounced at once. 'What was he embarrassed about? Is he ashamed to face us, or what?'

'I expect he felt awkward about coming in,' suggested Daphne. 'He always seems very pleasant, but he doesn't have much to say for himself.'

'That's right, he – he—' Valerie wrinkled her nose, gazed into space, and sneezed again. 'Oh, lor'. I *am* catching a cold.'

'It's a pity you haven't got something stronger than hot lemon,' said her mother. 'When Dad was alive, we always used to keep a quarter of brandy in the house, for emergencies.'

'I believe Ted's got a drop of scotch somewhere.' Daphne foraged in the larder and came back with a half-bottle of Johnny Walker. 'There's only a couple of mouthfuls left, but you're very welcome to it.' She emptied the dregs into Valerie's cup. Val drank it, then shuddered.

'Ugh. I hate the taste, but if it's good for colds . . .' Yawning, she stood up. 'I suppose I ought to go to bed. I meant to stay up till Ted gets home, but—'

'Don't you worry about Ted. I'll be here to congratulate him when he comes in,' said Daphne. 'Or cheer him up, if necessary.'

'We'll go on up, then,' said Kate. 'Come along, duck. I've put a hot bottle in your bed, so you'll be snug as a bug in a rug.'

'You'll have to go round to Gunns in the morning and thank your knight in shining armour for his gallant rescue,' said Daphne, as they left the kitchen.

'Perhaps I should.' Val paused, with her hand on the banister-rail. 'Yes, I think you're right – I'll do that.'

Daphne smiled to herself as the door shut behind them; then she took Val's place, settling herself in the fireside chair with a book – a battered copy of *The Mill On The Floss* – but she found it hard to concentrate, and her eyelids drooped.

When Ted walked in later, she woke with a start; the book slipped from her hand, falling to the floor.

'Oh, you made me jump!' she said, rubbing her eyes.

'I woke you up, you mean! It's late – you should be in bed.'

'I told you I'd wait up.' When she kissed him, she knew at once that he had been drinking. 'Well, go on, tell me – what happened?'

'I don't where to begin.'

'Begin at the beginning – "*Once upon a time . . .*"'

He laughed and sat in the chair, taking her on his lap as if she were a child. 'Right, then. Once upon a time, there was this young comic who was scared to death . . .' He told her about Gus Elen, and the terrible discovery that he was about to perform some of the great man's numbers. 'So in the end, I told them a few stories instead, and they seemed to like them.'

'So they didn't throw pennies at you?'

'No. I asked them to chuck their old five-pound notes instead . . . Tell the truth, it went down pretty well. The other artistes slapped me on the back, and Mr Elen told me I should go a long way. Timbuctoo, I think he said.'

'He didn't!'

'No, he didn't. They were all very nice to me, and old Percy Thring bought me a drink and told me I'd done well. Of course, he'd heard all my stories before, but he enjoyed the way I told them. He says he can find me plenty of work. So I bought him a drink and I think we may have got through one or two more, before they chucked us out. Then I caught the late bus up Lordship Lane as far as Forest Hill, and walked the rest of the way. Which is why I'm a bit late . . . I wouldn't say no to a nightcap now. I think there's a drop of Johnny Walker left—'

'There was, only I gave it to Val – sorry.'

'You did what?'

'She fell in the lake tonight. Mum was afraid she might catch a cold, so she made her have a hot bath, and I gave her a lemon drink with the last of your whisky.'

He peered at her mistily, bemused by this spate of information. 'Ah . . . In that case, we might as well go to bed.' They stood up, and he retrieved her book from the floor, with some difficulty. 'You've been reading.'

'I was – only I fell asleep. I was a bit tired.'

'You're not going to sleep as soon as we get into bed, are you? I don't want you to go to sleep yet.'

'Oh, I expect I'll manage to keep awake for a while . . . I'm sorry about the whisky – you deserve a celebration.' She hugged him. 'So is it going to be fame and fortune for the great Ted Watkins from now on?'

'I don't know about that. Percy says it'll take time to build me up.'

'But he did say he'd get you some work?'

'He's got me a date already. The week before Christmas – a regimental dinner at Aldershot. The money's very good – he's doubled my fee already! I'm getting two guineas next time.'

'Oh, that's nice.'

They looked at each other and began to laugh, and Ted said, 'I think I'd better start looking round for a day job, to keep me going.'

'We'll manage,' she told him firmly. 'I'll be able to help out as well. That's why I was reading *Mill On The Floss*. I'm going to be teaching it to the Sixth Form. I start at Carmichael Road again next week.'

'Oh.' He managed to smile. 'Congratulations all round, then.'

Linking their arms, they began to climb the stairs. On the half-landing, he stopped, looking puzzled.

'Hang on,' he said. 'What was Val doing by the lake anyway?'

Next morning, Babs overslept, which got the day off to a bad start. She knew she had to get to the shop with the keys before anyone else, and this meant she had no time for breakfast, so she felt cold and hungry.

This was all the more aggravating, because when she arrived at Church Road, the shop door was open and Mr Faber was sitting in the office.

'Good morning!' she said, handing over the keys, and began to take off her coat. 'If I'd known you'd be here, I wouldn't have bothered to rush. How did you get in?'

'I remembered I had a spare set of keys,' he replied smoothly. 'Don't trouble to take your things off – shut the door. I want to talk to you.'

Mystified, she snatched a quick look round the shop before shutting the door, but there was nobody in sight.

'Where are the others?' she asked.

'There's nobody else here, Miss Glynn. Please sit down.'

Then she knew it was serious. Whenever they were alone together, he called her Babs. Miss Glynn meant trouble.

'Is there something wrong?'

'I'm sorry to have to tell you that Ray Duke isn't here; he won't be coming in today, or any other day. I have had to dismiss him.' He chose his words carefully. 'Perhaps you know why?'

She felt a pang of guilt. He must have found out about her and Ray carrying on, but she wasn't going to admit anything.

'No, how should I know?' she said, wide-eyed. 'What's happened?'

'I came back to the shop last night, and found Duke here. He was about to break open the cashbox when I caught him.'

For a moment, Babs was lost for words. This was the last thing she had expected, but at least it had nothing to do with her – except . . .

Her thoughts racing, she asked: 'But how did he get in? I'd got the keys.'

'Exactly. I thought he might have taken them from you, or that you had given them to him.'

'No! Why would I do such a thing?'

'You might have had some private reason . . . But when I taxed him with it, he said he didn't have any keys; he told me he found the toilet window open and climbed in. Surely you checked that all the doors and windows were fastened before you left?'

'Yes. The little window was properly shut, I know it was.' But even as she spoke, she remembered how Ray had borrowed the keys and dashed back to the shop. He could have opened the window then.

Her face reflected these changing thoughts, and Mr Faber asked: 'Are you certain it was closed?'

'Well, I thought it was . . . I suppose it can't have been,' she finished lamely.

'Unless he persuaded you to leave it open for him?'

'Of course not!' exclaimed Babs indignantly. 'You know I wouldn't do a thing like that!'

'Perhaps I don't know you as well as I thought,' he said sadly. 'It took me some time to realise that you and Duke were engaging in immoral behaviour when you were alone here. There were certain – indications – in the stockroom. That's why I came back last night, to find out if my suspicions were correct.'

'Is that why you left the keys with me?' She stared at him with a kind of horror. 'You did it on purpose, didn't you? Setting a trap to catch us. You wanted to find us here – together!'

'That's not true!' he burst out, in a spasm of disgust. 'It's the very last thing I wanted. I've never been so disappointed in anyone – I could never have believed it of you.'

Anger blazed up in her. 'Don't speak to me like that! You needn't be so high-and-mighty. You couldn't wait to get your hands on me, could you? Taking advantage of me – and you'd have done a lot more, if I'd let you . . .'

'*Don't* – don't say that. This is unendurable.' The words seemed to choke him. He tried to control himself, and took a deep, shuddering breath before saying: 'I have to tell you – I can't continue to employ you, Miss Glynn. I shall pay you a full month's wages, but I must ask you to leave now – at once.'

'That's not fair!' She stood up. 'I didn't have anything to do with last night – I never knew about the cashbox! You can't sack me for that!'

'That isn't the reason.' Now the truth poured out of him in great gasps. 'It's because you told him – what happened between us. I thought those times we shared were – were something beautiful, but you turned them into a filthy joke, to laugh about behind my back.'

She looked away, saying sullenly, 'That's no reason for kicking me out. I haven't committed any crime, have I?' Trying to justify herself, she began to plead with him. 'Besides, it'll all be different now, won't it? Now Ray's gone, it'll be just the two of us. We can be like we were before. Walter – please . . .'

He opened the desk drawer and took out a small brown wage-packet. Holding it out to her he said, so quietly, it was almost a whisper: 'Do you really think we could go on working together – after this?'

She realised he was right; it was impossible. Without a word, she took the money and left the office. As she walked down the aisle between the dining-tables and the three-piece suites, he said softly, 'Goodbye, Babs,' but she pretended not to hear.

She walked quickly along Church Road, wondering what she would say to the family at Belmont. Wrestling with this problem, she did not notice the figure lurking in the side alley. A hand caught her arm, and she gasped.

'It's all right,' said Ray. 'It's only me.'

'You!' She turned on him, unleashing the full force of her anger. 'Don't you dare speak to me – I don't ever want to see you again!'

'I got to talk to you,' he said. 'It's important.'

'Get away from me, do you hear? I've a good mind to call the police!'

'Don't be daft. That's what he wanted to do – old Weary Wally – but I soon talked him out of it. But I suppose you know he's given me the boot?'

'Yes, I know, and I'm glad – it's no more than you deserve. You're a rotten devil, and because of you I've got the sack as well!'

'Sorry about that, but it's all the more reason for us to stick together. We're in the same boat, you and me – that's why I've got to talk to you.'

'I won't listen to you, you're nothing but a cheap little crook. Why should I believe a word you say?'

'Because I only did it for your sake, that's why. I did it for us, Babs, because I love you.'

'What?'

'Look, we can't talk here – let's have a cup of tea, eh? There's a caff in Westow Street what opens early for breakfast. I'll buy you a bacon sandwich. How about that?'

A mixture of hunger and curiosity drove her to accept the invitation. If they had looked back as they turned the corner into Westow Street, they might have seen Valerie walking along Church Road, on her way to work. Val, with other things on her mind, did not notice them either; passing the furniture shop, she turned into the greengrocers next door.

It was still early, and she was the first customer. Mr Gunn welcomed her cordially.

'Morning, Miss. What can we do for you?'

She looked round, but there was no sign of Steve. A little angular woman in a shapeless grey jersey and a green cotton apron seemed to have taken his place.

'Oh, I don't actually want to buy anything. I was hoping I might see—' She tried to make light of it. 'Never mind. I'll look in again, another time.'

'No need for that, Miss,' said Mr Gunn. 'If you tell me what you're after, I might be able to help.'

'Really, it's nothing important.' Then, since he seemed unwilling to let her go, she added: 'I was expecting your son to be here . . . Steve.'

The little woman looked up sharply. 'Steve? What about him?'

'I just wanted a word with him. Perhaps he'll be here later.'

'Not in the shop, he won't.' Freda Gunn came closer, for a good look at Valerie. 'Our son doesn't work here any longer.'

Alf chimed in: 'That's right. He's gone off to get his hands dirty, working in a garage. Left us in the lurch.'

'Alfred!' Freda shot him a stern look. 'Steven's hoping to better himself – mad about cars, he is. Can I pass on any message?'

'Well . . .' Wishing she'd never started all this, Valerie said, 'Just tell him I came in to say thank you.'

'Thank you?' Freda and Alf exchanged glances. 'What for?'

Again Val tried to laugh it off. 'I'm Valerie Watkins. I'm the one he pulled out of the lake last night.'

Light dawned at last. 'So *that's* it!' cried Freda. 'I couldn't help wondering. He came home with his boots full of water and his trousers soaking – he said he'd walked into a pond by mistake!'

'He pulled you out?' Alf stared at Val. 'Well, I'm blowed. Fancy him not telling us.'

'I'm very glad you came in.' Freda shook Valerie's hand. 'Very good of you – there's not many girls would have bothered . . . I tell you what – if you want to thank him yourself, why don't you pop round tomorrow afternoon, about four o'clock, say? He'll be here then – we can all have a nice cup of tea.'

'I don't want to put you to any trouble.' Valerie backed towards the door.

'No trouble, dear. I'm sure he'll be pleased to see you, and we'll be looking forward to it.' She dug her husband in the ribs. 'Won't we, Alfred?'

'Eh? Oh, yes,' he echoed her. 'Looking forward to it.'

Freda called after Val, 'Four o'clock tomorrow, Miss Watkins – don't forget!'

The café in Westow Street was hardly a romantic setting; small and airless, it reeked of frying fat, and the tea-urn on the counter kept up a sinister accompaniment of bubbling and gurgling, occasionally spitting out jets of scalding steam. The tables were cramped, covered with oilcloth that bore the rings left by other people's mugs of tea; even at this early hour, the place was bursting with life.

Ray picked a table near the window, as far as possible from the other customers; there was a boisterous group at the back of the room – three lorry-drivers and a window-cleaner, exchanging bawdy anecdotes and hooting with laughter. The background of noise prevented Ray and Babs from being overheard by anyone else and, since the front windows were misted with condensation, they could not be seen by passers-by.

Facing one another over the crumbs of their bacon sandwiches, they were alone in their private world.

'I did it for you,' Ray said again. 'Because I love you, and you love me. Don't you understand?'

'No, I don't love you. How could I, after what you've done?'

'All right, it was wrong of me, I see that now. Only I haven't much money put by, and old Faber's got more than his fair share. I was just trying to even things up a bit.'

Babs stared at him, dismayed. 'You're not one of those – what do they call them? – like in Russia. You're not a *communist*, are you?'

'Course not!' Ray was visibly shocked. 'What do you take me for?'

'I don't know. I don't know what to think . . . I used to think I loved you – but not after last night.'

'Babs – listen. OK, I made a mistake and I'm sorry about that, but it doesn't change how I feel about you, or the way you feel about me.' Under the table, he rubbed his leg against hers. 'Remember the good times we had together? It could never be like that with anyone else. We belong together, you and me – you know that.'

At his touch, she felt the same thrill, the same magic beginning to spread through her. She tried to fight against it, arguing: 'But I can't trust you any more!'

'You got to trust me. I want to do right by you, Babs – I want us to be together for always. That's why I was trying to get some money, so I'd have something to offer you – a home of our own, don't you see? I want to marry you.'

No one had ever proposed to her before. Gazing into his eyes, Babs felt dizzy with excitement. Her body yearned for him, and her heart beat faster at the thought of marriage – a white wedding, a never-ending honeymoon, where they would live happily ever after . . .

The rosy dream shattered as the café manageress appeared, removing their greasy plates and giving the table a cursory wipe with a damp rag. 'Will you be wanting anythink more?' she asked.

Ray shook his head impatiently. 'No, nothing. We're OK.'

She looked meaningly at the untouched mugs in front of them, and muttered, 'Don't let your tea get cold, will you?'

As she moved away, the door opened and a gust of cold air blew in from the street. The newcomer was a middle-aged woman with a harassed expression. She gave the manageress a nervous smile and began hurriedly: 'I'm sorry to bother you, Gladys, but could you oblige me with a pint of milk? My boy came home unexpectedly, late last night, and I've run right out. I've not got enough for his breakfast. Would you mind? I'll give it you back as soon as the milkman's been.'

The manageress sighed heavily and went off to the back kitchen. Looking round, the woman recognised Babs and squeezed out another uncertain smile. 'Good morning, Miss Glynn. You're out and about early.'

Babs nodded, tight-lipped. When the woman had taken her bottle of milk and disappeared, she said under her breath, 'She would have to come in and see me with you. I just hope she won't go round telling everybody.'

'Why? Who is she?'

'That's Mrs Bywaters. She's got the millinery shop over the road – I've bought things there once or twice.'

'What does it matter?' Ray asked. 'She's nobody.'

But the spell had been broken. Babs looked at Ray, then said, 'I'm sorry. It was a lovely idea, but I couldn't marry you.'

'Why not? I'd make you happy. I love you so much—'

'I know, but I couldn't possibly. My family wouldn't like it.'

'Your Mum likes me – you said she does.'

'Not as a son-in-law. Mummy's got such big ideas. She's set her heart on me marrying someone – you know, grand . . . Someone with a title and pots of money. I'm really sorry.'

He scowled. 'I'll have pots of money one day – you wait and see.'

'You mean, when you come into your legacy? When you're twenty-one?'

'That's right.' He brightened up a little. 'Only a another year or so to wait. Mummy will feel different about me then, eh?'

'She might . . . but until then—'

'Until then, we can be engaged, can't we? I'll buy you a ring!'

'That would be nice.' She was beginning to feel dreamy again. 'But the family wouldn't understand.'

'All right, then, we won't tell them. It'll be a secret engagement – how about that?'

Her face softened. 'Well, perhaps. We'll see.' Under the table, she felt his hand groping for her knee. A tremor of pleasure ran through her, but she pushed his hand firmly away. 'No, Ray, we've got to be sensible.'

'That's right, we must make some plans. For a start, we're both out of work.' A thought struck him. 'What are your family going to say when they find out you've been sacked?'

'I shall say Mr Faber was very nasty to me, so I gave in my notice. They won't be surprised; it's happened before.'

'But we've got to earn some cash, haven't we? And I've got to find somewhere to live. I can't pay rent to the Watkinses with nothing coming in.'

'Couldn't you send a letter to Hollywood?' she suggested.

'Hollywood?' For a moment he couldn't think what she meant, then he added quickly, 'Oh, you mean my parents?'

'Of course. If you explain, they'll send some money to tide you over, won't they?'

'Well, they would, of course – only I can't get in touch with them right now. They're travelling at the moment – on location for a new movie. It'll be some time before they're back in California.'

'Oh dear. Then we'll have to think of something else.' Babs sipped her tea. The manageress was quite right – it was cold.

'There is one thing,' Ray said. 'If you were to tell your Mummy old man Faber had been trying to interfere with you—'

Babs recoiled. 'Oh no, I couldn't possibly!'

'Why not? It's what he did, isn't it? We could say I caught him at it, and I punched him on the jaw! That would explain why you had to quit the job, and why he booted me out as well! And it's all true – practically.'

'But I don't see what that's got to do with—'

'Wait a bit, I haven't finished yet. That would explain why I had to give up my digs at Sackville Road, on account of being short of cash – and your Mum would be so grateful, she might agree to me moving into Belmont for a while.'

'Moving in?'

'Why not? Daphne's old room must be empty. I bet if you were to ask her nicely, she'd say yes. You can tell her we're both looking for better jobs; she'll understand I can't afford much rent at the moment, till I'm earning again.' With a snicker of laughter, he added: 'Is Daphne's room anywhere near yours, by any chance?'

'Yes, it's next door to mine, but—'

'Fancy . . . That's what I call really convenient.' He took her hand. 'I mean, seeing that we're secretly engaged to be married one day, what would be the harm?'

'Oh, Ray.' She caught her breath. 'It does sound lovely, but I don't know . . .'

Teasingly, he tickled her palm with his middle finger: 'I do,' he said. 'You leave it to me.'

Saturdays were always busy at Fabers Furnishings, and today Tubby Dingwall had been run off his feet dealing with customers, taking orders, and promising delivery as soon as the van was back on the road again.

It wouldn't have been so bad if the boss had taken a turn in the shop now and then, but he seemed to be chained to his desk. Every time Tubby had to go into the office for a catalogue, or to check a delivery date, Walter Faber didn't appear to be doing anything at all. He was just sitting there, gazing at nothing, with a strange look on his face.

Some time around midday, there was a bit of a breathing-space, and Tubby took the opportunity to have a word with him.

'I sold two more of them pickled-oak chairs,' he reported. 'That makes five altogether this week.'

'Very good.' His employer spoke tonelessly, and Tubby realised he wasn't even listening.

'Excuse me for asking, sir, but are you feeling all right?'

'I'm perfectly well, thank you. Why?'

'I thought you looked a bit, I dunno, sort of done up.'

'I'm a little tired, that's all.'

'Yeah, I'm a bit tired myself. Been on the go all morning, I have.' Tubby ventured to ask, 'Do you think you'll be able to help out for a bit, if we get another rush on?'

'Oh yes, call me if you need me.'

About to leave, Tubby lingered to say: 'Seems a pity we're short-handed of a Saturday. The other two both got some time off, have they?'

'No.' Faber selected a broad-nibbed pen; dipping it into Indian ink, he began to write something on a piece of card, as he went on. 'Mr Duke and Miss Glynn won't be working here in future. They've left us.'

'Oh, why's that?'

'I had to dispense with their services. They turned out to be unsatisfactory.' He finished writing, then handed the card to Tubby. 'Put this in the window, would you?'

The message was brief – just two words: *Help wanted.*

On Sunday afternoon, Val was getting ready to go out. Dissatisfied with the reflection in her mirror, she went downstairs in search of Daphne.

'Can I borrow your pink scarf?' she asked. 'Just for the afternoon?'

'Yes, of course.' Daphne put down her book and went to find it. 'Where are you off to?'

'Nowhere special, only this black outfit is so gloomy, I look as if I were going to a funeral. Thanks, Daff – you're a pal.' Knotting the pink scarf round her throat, she surveyed the result in the looking-glass over the sink. 'I hate myself in black – it makes me look so washed-out.'

'Then why are you wearing it?'

'Because it's my best! Except for my green, and that's too thin for this weather.' She glanced at the clock: 'Nearly four – I must be on my way.'

Intrigued, Daphne asked: 'Why are you in your Sunday best if you're not going anywhere special? Come on, what's all the mystery?'

'It's no mystery. I'm going to have tea with Mr and Mrs Gunn.'

'Oh, of course – Sir Galahad's parents. I was forgetting. He'll be there too, I suppose?'

'How should I know?' Val tried to sound offhand. 'I wish I'd never said I'd go, only they were so pressing it would have been rude to say no. But I shan't stay long.'

'That's right, hurry back and tell me all about it. I'm on my own this afternoon. Ted's taken Annie up on the hill, to fly her kite.'

Val looked surprised. 'Without you?'

'Yes. I packed them off so I'd have some time to prepare my first lessons for tomorrow. You'd think I'd be used to teaching by now – I did it long enough – but I still feel nervous about starting again. And now I'm getting sick of my own company.'

'You can always go up and talk to Mum if you're feeling lonely.'

'Oh, I daren't – she's getting herself ready for her beau! Didn't you know Mr Colpoys is coming to tea? Anyhow, good luck with the Gunns!'

Val pulled a face. 'It'll probably be very boring.'

But it wasn't.

The side door at the shop was opened by a small boy – a miniature version of Steve. 'Hello,' he said. 'Are you Miss Watkins? I'm Tony – Steve's my brother.'

He led the way upstairs; the front room was quite large, but it seemed to be full of people. Mrs Gunn dropped her knitting and got up, holding out her hand.

'Miss Watkins, nice to see you. You know my husband – and now you've met Tony, our youngest. He's only seven, but very bright for his age.'

'Mum!' Tony protested. 'I'll be eight soon!'

Ignoring this, Freda Gunn continued: 'I expect you're surprised at the difference in their ages. There's nearly fourteen years between him and Steve.'

Alfred took Val's hand, pumping it vigorously. 'That's right,' he said. 'We thought we'd finished after Julie and Steve – first a girl and then a boy, as the old song goes – but then young Tony suddenly popped up. Quite a surprise for us, I can tell you!'

'Alfred!' Freda glared at him, then led Valerie on to meet a handsome brunette in her early twenties. 'I don't believe you've met Julie? She's our eldest – two years older than Steven. Julie's one of the Catering Supervisors for Messrs. Joseph Lyons, at their big tea-shop in Oxford Street.'

'Mum, I've told you a million times, I'm only a glorified waitress.'

Julie smiled as she shook Val's hand. At first sight she seemed rather forbidding – very well-groomed, with immaculate hair and make-up, and rather cold and hard – but when she smiled, her face lit up and she became beautiful.

'The pay's good, but that's because we have to work all the hours God sends,' she explained. 'We do different shifts, that's the trouble – first thing in the morning, or last thing at night. So I don't often get home, except now and then of a Sunday.'

'I suppose you have to live near your work?' Valerie asked.

'Yes. Me and three of the girls share a flat, off Charlotte Street. It's not too bad, I suppose, but there's no place like home.'

In an armchair by the fire, an elderly gentleman cleared his throat noisily, and Freda Gunn exclaimed: 'All right, Grandad, we haven't forgotten you. This is Alfred's father – Jack Gunn. He's a bit deaf, I'm afraid, so you'll have to speak up.'

Valerie shook hands yet again. The old man nodded and smiled affably, then turned to Freda, asking at the top of his voice, 'Who did you say she was?'

'You must excuse him, he doesn't realise he's shouting.' Freda took a deep breath. 'This is Miss Watkins, Grandad. We told you about her!'

'Never seen her before in my life!' he bellowed, still bobbing and smiling at the same time.

'I've seen you, Mr Gunn!' said Valerie, as loudly as she could. 'At the Crystal Palace – you play the cornet in the brass band, don't you?'

'What's that? Does she want me to play for her?' The old man began to struggle to his feet. 'I'll give her a tune if that's what she wants—'

'Not now, Grandad. After tea, perhaps.' Freda pushed him back into his chair, saying to Val, 'Steve told us you work at the Palace. That must be interesting.'

'Yes, it is – and I've seen Mr Gunn with the band, playing at the firework displays.'

Vaguely aware he was being discussed, Jack Gunn beckoned his son and roared, 'What's she saying about me? Who is she, anyway?'

'It's Miss Watkins, Dad – the girl Steve saved from drowning!' Alf bellowed at his father.

'Dad, for God's sake! How many more times?' exclaimed Steve. He emerged from the darkest corner of the room, looking extremely uncomfortable. He did not shake hands with Valerie, but asked gruffly: 'How are you feeling? Recovered from your little dip, have you?'

'I'm fine. I thought I'd caught a cold, but it didn't come to anything.'

Reaching up to her tall son, Freda tapped him on the shoulder. 'Don't let me hear you taking the name of the Lord in vain, especially when we've got company. Now then, shall we sit down to tea?'

Everyone made a move, and for the first time Val saw the tea-table in all its glory. She had expected a cup of tea and perhaps a biscuit or a slice of cake, but this was another matter.

The large round table, spread with a lace cloth, was covered with plates and dishes piled high with food of every kind. There were biscuits, certainly, and two kinds of cake – Madeira and Dundee – fairy-cakes and buns with pink icing; there was watercress and a jug of celery, and various sandwiches cut into dainty triangles – some of them with mustard-and-cress peeping out at the sides; there was a vast mixed salad in a cut-glass bowl, topped with circles of hard-boiled egg, a plate of cold meats – sliced ham, tongue and beef – and a pyramid of sausage-rolls. It was a high tea; the highest Valerie had ever seen.

'Goodness!' she gasped, torn between admiration and dismay. 'When you asked me to tea, I thought you meant just – tea.'

'We generally have a bit of a spread on Sundays,' Freda smiled.

'Specially if we've got visitors,' added Tony.

'Don't talk so silly!' Freda slapped his hand as he reached for an iced bun. 'And don't *pick*! This is a special occasion; it's not every day your brother saves somebody's life. Alfred – will you say grace, please?'

Seated next to Valerie, Steve threw her an accusing look, as his father closed his eyes, folded his hands and began: 'For what we are about to receive, may the Lord make us truly thankful.'

Kate held out a plate of scones. 'Would you care for another?'

'Oh no, I've done very well,' said Mr Colpoys. 'I couldn't eat anything more.' Then he added, 'Although, I wonder if I might ask a favour?'

'Another cup of tea?'

'Not even that. I was about to say, would you think it very rude of me to ask if I could smoke a pipe?'

'Not at all! I'll fetch you an ashtray.'

'You're sure you don't mind?'

'I want you to make yourself at home. Will you need some matches?'

'Thank you, no.' He pulled out an old-fashioned lighter, and a tobacco pouch. 'I always feel a smoke rounds off a good meal – and this has been a special treat for me, because I'm particularly fond of scones. My wife used to make them when we were first married. It's pleasant to be reminded of the old days.'

'It must be lonely for you.' Kate spoke sympathetically. 'I count my blessings, having my family living here with me.'

'Yes, you're fortunate in that respect. The worst thing about living alone is that it makes one so dull. I'm sure I talk too much.'

'What a thing to say! You're not dull!'

'No, I mean it. Solitary people don't get much chance to talk, so when they meet a friend, they can't stop. And what's even worse, sometimes I find I'm talking to myself. If I become too self-centred and eccentric, you must tell me frankly. I shan't be offended.'

'I don't think you're eccentric at all.' There was a tap at the door, and she broke off. 'That'll be Daphne, with more hot water for the pot. Come in, dear!'

But it wasn't Daphne. Ray entered the room, and looked uneasily at the stranger.

'Sorry – I didn't know you had company,' he said.

'That's all right. Come in, Mr Duke. I don't think you know Mr Colpoys?' She turned to him. 'This is Mr Duke, the young man who has the bed-sitting room on the top floor.'

They shook hands, then Ray turned to Kate. 'That's what I looked in to tell you. I won't be needing the room any more after today.'

Kate was taken aback. 'You're not thinking of leaving us?'

''Fraid so. Not that I want to, mind – I can't afford it any longer.'

Disconcerted by this, in front of a guest, Kate said awkwardly, 'Oh dear, I don't think it's an unreasonable rent for—'

'I'm not saying that. But at present I'm rather pushed for cash.' He put a handful of coins on the tea-table.

Still more flustered, Kate tried to forestall him, saying, 'Perhaps we could talk about it later.'

'Can't do that, I'm afraid. I've just been packing my things, and I'm clearing out now. You'll find that's the amount owing, up to today. That'll leave us square.'

'But why?' she began.

'I'm sorry to say I've had a spot of unpleasantness at work. Matter of fact, I've been dismissed.'

'At the furniture shop? Oh, I'm sorry.'

'I'm not. I couldn't have stuck it much longer, working for that man. He's no gentleman.'

Ray was enjoying himself. He told them how Mr Faber had made improper advances to Babs, and how he'd arrived in the nick of time to defend her, how he'd attacked Faber ('I just saw red, I couldn't help myself – I simply went for him, hammer and tongs!') – and was sacked on the spot. He explained that Babs had given in her notice and walked out in sympathy.

'I feel sort of responsible in a way,' he concluded. 'After all, it was me got her the job in the first place. Course, I'd never have suggested it if I'd realised what sort of man Faber was. Did you know he's a German? According to Mr Dingwall what works there, his family came over from Berlin years ago. He was nearly locked up during the war, along with the rest of the Huns.'

Amazed by these revelations, Kate said, 'How dreadful! But what will you do? Where are you going to live?'

'Lucky for me, Babs came to my rescue. She asked me round to Belmont last night, and when we explained the situation, Mrs Glynn kindly invited me to go and stay there, till I get fixed up somewhere else . . . So in the end, it's turned out not too bad, really.'

'No, really. I couldn't eat another mouthful!' Valerie pushed her plate away. 'It's all delicious, but I had a big dinner.'

'I don't know, you young girls are all the same.' Freda made a reproachful clicking noise. 'Julie's just as bad – don't eat enough to feed a gnat, you don't! And as for you, Steve . . .' She turned on him accusingly. 'It's not like you to pick at your food. What's happened to your appetite?'

'I wasn't hungry,' he replied curtly. 'I told you I couldn't stop long – I've promised to meet somebody.'

'Manners!' his mother scolded him. 'You can't walk out in the middle of tea when we've got a guest!'

Throughout the meal, Steve had hardly spoken. Valerie had been very aware of him, sitting next to her with a face like thunder. Now she broke in. 'Actually, I ought to be making a move as well. They'll be wondering what's become of me at home.'

'What a shame. Grandad was going to play his cornet for you.'

'What's that?' the old man leaned forward, cupping his ear. 'Would she like *Roses of Picardy*?'

'Another time that would be lovely,' Valerie told him, as loudly as she dared, then pushed back her chair. 'It's been such a nice afternoon,

Mrs Gunn. Thank you very much for asking me, but I really must be going.'

'Well, if you must . . . Tony, fetch Miss Watkins' hat and coat.'

Steve stood up as well. 'If you're going to Sackville Road, I might as well come with you. I'm going that way.'

Alfred Gunn wagged a roguish finger. 'Don't take her round the lake, this time!'

Steve scowled at his father, and helped Val into her coat. She assured old Mr Gunn that the next time she came, she would positively insist on hearing *Roses of Picardy*.

As soon as they were out in the street, Steve asked her: 'Did you really have to go? Or were you just saying that?'

'Well, sort of.' Stealing a glance at him, she added, 'I thought you looked as if you wanted to get away.'

'True enough, I did.' Then he turned on her, adding resentfully, 'But why did you have to tell them that rubbish about me saving your life?'

'I never said that!'

'That's what they told me. According to Mum, you said I rescued you from drowning!'

'I said you pulled me out of the water! I admit I didn't mention the water was only a couple of feet deep – I'd have felt such a fool . . . But I never said a word about drowning.'

'Well, they managed to turn it into a big rescue. I shouldn't wonder if they send off to get me a gold medal. Mind you,' he added darkly, 'I know what they were up to.'

'What do you mean?'

'I told them I'd arranged to meet somebody else this afternoon, and they fixed all this so I couldn't go. They said it would look bad if I wasn't there when you turned up.'

Holding her head high, Valerie remarked, 'I didn't realise you were hoping to see someone else. I'm sorry if I ruined your afternoon.'

'No, it's not that. I'm meeting this bloke from the garage where I work: he's teaching me how to strip down an engine, in his spare time. I've only just started there, and I've got a heck of a lot to learn.'

Valerie relaxed. As they continued down Anerley Hill, she said, 'Oh well, I still think it was very good of you to jump in and rescue me. I mean, I *could* have been drowning – I can't swim.'

'Can't you?'

'No, I can't. We didn't go for seaside holidays when I was little.'

'No more did we. We never had holidays, 'cos Dad couldn't leave the shop. I learned to swim at Dartmouth Road Baths.' He stopped walking, and looked at her. 'You should learn, too.' Then he added: 'I could teach you, if you want.'

'At the Baths?'

He smiled shyly. 'Yes – if you'd like to.'

She looked up at him, and smiled back. 'Yes, I think I would like to. Thank you, Steve.'

Chapter Eight

WHEN RAY MOVED into Belmont, the family made him welcome. They were so grateful for his timely intervention at the furniture shop. If he hadn't arrived at the crucial moment, when that dreadful man behaved so disgracefully – well, it didn't bear thinking about.

'Anything like that upsets me so much,' said Muriel, clasping Ray's hand. 'The very thought makes me ill – physically ill. We must never mention it again.'

'That's right, old dear. Let's look on the bright side,' agreed Gerald. 'Put it all behind us, eh?'

'Let's hope that you and Babs have better luck in your next situation.' Aunt Ethel cocked her head on one side, regarding Ray with a beady eye. 'Have you begun to make any plans, Mr Duke?'

'Nothing definite,' replied Ray. 'But I've got one or two irons in the fire. I don't intend to be out of work for long, and as soon as I'm earning again I'll pay a proper rent for my room, don't you worry.'

'It's not a question of money, Mr Duke,' Muriel intervened. 'This is our home, not a hotel. We look on you as our guest.'

'But a paying guest, Mu dear,' Ethel pointed out. 'We have to be practical. The bills must be paid, and since Babs isn't drawing any wages either—'

Muriel gave her sister a chilly smile. 'If you'd be good enough to let me finish, Ethel. I'm sure Mr Duke will make a contribution to the household expenses when his situation improves.'

'And glad to do it, Mrs Glynn, believe you me,' said Ray. 'I shan't be comfortable till I'm paying my whack.'

'I'm sure you're going to be happy here.' Muriel patted his hand. 'It must be so difficult for you, alone in London while your father and mother are overseas. Babs tells me they're such busy people – in America, she said – isn't that wonderful? But we shall do our best to make you feel at home. If there's anything you want, just say the word.'

'I hope your bed's properly aired.' Aunt Aggie looked anxious. 'It hasn't been slept in since Daphne left. Perhaps you'd like a hotty-botty?'

Stunned, Ray asked: 'A what?'

Babs tried not to catch his eye. 'Auntie Ag means a hot-water bottle.'

'Oh, I don't think I'll bother, ta. I'm pretty warm, as a rule.'

At the end of the evening they went off to bed. Babs escorted Ray to the door of Daphne's old room and said, 'I hope you have a good night.'

'I hope so too,' he said, adding under his breath, 'come inside, and I'm sure I shall.'

'Stop it!' she whispered. 'Don't be so wicked.' Then, in her normal voice: 'You know where the bathroom is, don't you? Well, good night. I'll see you in the morning.'

He went in and began to undress. It was a pretty room; the flowered wallpaper and lace curtains were rather feminine, perhaps, but he wasn't going to grumble about that. The jug and basin on the washstand were decorated with rosebuds, and there were fluffy pink towels on the towel-horse. He'd struck lucky this time and no mistake.

Five minutes later he tapped gently on Babs' door, and slipped inside without waiting for an invitation. She sat up in bed immediately.

'Ray, is that you?' she whispered.

'Who did you expect – Rudolph Valentino?' Shutting the door carefully, he approached the bed. 'Move over, can't you? Give us a bit of room.'

'But suppose somebody saw you!'

'Nobody saw me; I made sure of that.'

He tugged at the bedclothes, but Babs hung on to them, protesting: 'Somebody might see you on the way out!'

'I'll explain I'd been to the bathroom and I opened the wrong door. It's easy to make a mistake when you're in a strange house.'

'Oh, you are awful.' She was already weakening. 'Whatever would Mummy say if she found out?' She heard him slip off his dressing gown; even in the darkness, she could tell that he was naked.

'It was your Mummy who put the idea in my head. "If there's anything you want, just say the word". And you know what the word is, don't you?'

'No, Ray. Don't say it—'

'*I want my hotty-botty!*'

With that he threw himself on to the bed, and stifled her giggles by rolling on top of her.

Daphne had tried to tell Annie what going to school would be like, and at first the four-year-old girl seemed very thrilled by the idea.

Being an only child, the thought of having other children to play with was very attractive, and everything her mother told her about school – the running and skipping games in the playground, the plasticine and the sand-tray, the books to be read and pictures to be painted – made it sound like a kind of wonderland.

But this morning, dressed her in her grey jersey and skirt and her school hat and coat, Annie seemed to be having second thoughts. 'I will like it, won't I?' she asked doubtfully.

'Of course you will.'

'And you're coming with me, aren't you?'

'I'll walk to school with you, but when we get there, a nice lady called Miss Bonny will be looking after you in the Infants class. I have to go to another part of the school, to teach some of the big girls.'

'Yes . . .' Annie turned to her father, finishing his breakfast at the kitchen table. 'And if I don't like it, I can come home, and you can look after me instead, can't you?'

Ted buttered a finger of toast and spread some of Kate's home-made jam on it. 'Here – shut your eyes and open your mouth, and see what the good Lord sends you!' he said, then popped it into her mouth, adding: 'Only I shan't be at home, love. I've got to go and look for a job. But I'll try to be here this afternoon, then you can tell me what a good time you've had at school – how's that?'

Annie chewed thoughtfully, then nodded. 'All right,' she said at last.

She and Daphne set off, hand in hand, and Daphne kept up a flow of conversation, pointing out any stray cats or dogs they passed, and encouraging Annie to wave at the window-cleaner on his bike. Annie was unusually quiet. Daphne hoped with all her heart that the experiment was not going to be a failure – whatever happened, she couldn't change the plan now. The Head was relying on her; she had to teach three different classes before the dinner break – and she was down on the staff rota to take Morning Assembly.

When they reached the school, Annie stared with round eyes at the crowd of children tearing around the playground, whooping and shrieking, and tugged at her mother's sleeve. Daphne had to stoop down to hear what she was saying.

'Do I have to?' asked Annie, in a small voice.

Daphne gave her a kiss, and said, 'Come on – let's go in and say hello to Miss Bonny.'

The First Form classroom was a cheerful place. Not only were the walls covered with paintings, but the Christmas decorations had gone up already, and the coloured paper-chains and pleated bells looked very festive. As it was a bleak morning, a small fire was burning in the grate.

A few steps into the room, Annie stopped, looking round at everything – at the rows of desks with their little benches, at the blackboard, and at the sand-tray, which had been turned into a farmyard with model cows, pigs and horses.

Miss Bonny, a cosy, greying lady in a mauve overall, came to meet them. 'So this is Annie,' she said, bending down to shake hands. 'I'm very pleased to meet you.'

Annie made a great effort to be grown-up. 'How do you do?' she said. Then, advancing to the centre of the room, she added graciously: 'You've got a nice room . . . And a very nice fire.'

'Thank you, Annie. I hope you'll enjoy your first day here.'

'I'll try,' she said.

Daphne kissed her once more, then hurried to the staff-room, hoping for the best. With so much on her mind, she found it hard to concentrate, and when she entered the main hall, stepping on to the platform, the rows of faces below her looked like a blur. As a newcomer, she introduced herself to the assembled pupils.

'You may be surprised to know that I was a girl at this school myself, and I came into this hall every morning for prayers, just as you are doing now. Some of you might even remember seeing me, because when I became a teacher I came back again. But that was a few years ago, and you would have been in the Infants or the Juniors then.'

Saying this reminded her of Annie, in the First Form, and she felt a stab of anxiety. She tried to pull herself together. 'Now, let's start our days as we always do, with the Lord's Prayer. Close your eyes, please.'

She began to recite the prayer, but her thoughts were with Annie. She had looked so small, beside all the other children in the playground.

'. . . Give us this day our daily bread, and—'

Then she stopped; her mind felt as if it had frozen. She could not think what she had just said, or what she should say next. Complete blankness overwhelmed her. How could she possibly forget the words of the most famous prayer of all? She racked her brains, but no inspiration came.

Somewhere, somebody coughed; someone else sniggered, and people began shuffling their feet.

'Quiet, please.' Daphne looked helplessly at the sea of faces; they were opening their eyes now, staring at her. She struggled to regain control of the situation, and improvised rapidly.

'There is a girl talking in this room. I cannot continue until I have absolute silence . . . I am waiting.'

They all held their breath. Daphne went on waiting until, at last, an idea occurred to her.

'You know, it's not much good listening to the prayer unless we think what the words mean. Let's go back to the beginning and start again – and this time I want you to recite the Lord's prayer with me. Are you ready? *Our Father, Which Art in Heaven—*'

They all joined in; the familiar cadences rolled on like a river, flowing through the hall, and came to an end with no further interruption. Daphne sent up an extra prayer of her own – a prayer of gratitude.

She had a lot to be thankful for. When she collected her daughter at dinner-time, Miss Bonny told her: 'She was good as gold – and she can read better than a good many of the class, who are nearly a year older. It was a pleasure to have her with us.'

Glowing with pride, Daphne took Annie home – a very different Annie, who skipped along the pavement, swinging on her hand and chanting a new song she had just learned:

'All things bright and beautiful, all creatures great and small;
All things wise and wonderful, the Lord God made them all.'

That evening, when Annie was tucked up in bed, Daphne confessed to Ted, 'All the same, I still feel badly about this morning.'

'Why? You told me she got on very well.'

'But I felt so ashamed when I forgot the words during prayers. It made me realise how long it is since we went to church. And it's the same with Annie. I taught her the alphabet and her numbers, but I never taught her *All Things Bright and Beautiful*.'

He brushed this aside. 'She'll soon catch up.'

'You don't understand. It suddenly struck me that I only pray when things go wrong – when I need something. The rest of the time, I forget God altogether. Do you know the last time I said a prayer? That evening when you did your first show, at Peckham. I asked God if He would spare us a miracle that night.'

'Well, He certainly did. He came up trumps, and I'm very grateful.'

'So am I – and it's about time we said thank you. That's why I decided. Next Sunday we're going to church – all of us.'

'Mum and Val as well?'

'I expect your Mum will be glad to. She told me she went every week, when your Dad was alive.'

Ted groaned. 'We all did – Matins and Evensong – and us kids got packed off to Sunday School in the afternoon as well, to give them a bit of peace. We had a real basinful of church in those days, Val and me.'

'Well, I'll go and ask Val—' She stood up, then sat down again. 'No, I can't. I remember now, she's gone to the Baths . . . She's learning to swim.'

Valerie was very frightened.

It wasn't the Dartmouth Road swimming bath that frightened her, though that was alarming enough. The high arched roof threw back endless echoes, so each splash – each shout from the other swimmers – seemed to be a continuous roar in the background.

The smell was off-putting, too; the chlorine crept into her nose and made her eyes sting. As she squeezed herself into a bathing costume, in the damp, draughty cubicle, she wished she'd never agreed to come for a swimming lesson.

It wasn't even that she was afraid of the water, or the possibility of drowning. More than any of these things, she was frightened of looking silly in her navy-blue woollen costume.

She had borrowed it from Daphne, and Daphne was rather slimmer than she was. She felt ashamed to go out and face Steve; terrified that he would think she looked ridiculous – and plain – and fat . . .

But she knew he was waiting for her – she couldn't hide in the cubicle any longer. Taking a deep breath, she went out to meet him, wishing she were dead.

He was standing by the steps, at the shallow end. He looked very different without his clothes on – bigger, and more muscular – and more handsome. He also looked uncomfortable; he must feel ashamed to be seen with such a hideous lump of a girl. It never occurred to her that he, too, might be feeling shy.

He forced a smile. 'So there you are,' he said.

'Yes.' She tried to smile back. 'Here I am.'

'All ready, then? Shall we make a start?'

She wanted to say: 'No, let's not – let's forget the whole thing and go home.' But she heard herself reply in a high, bright voice, 'Yes. I'm looking forward to it.'

He jumped into the water, throwing up a wave that splashed over her legs and feet. It felt very cold, and she began to shiver.

'I don't have to jump in as well, do I?' she asked.

'No. Come down the steps – I'll help you.'

'It's all right, I can manage.'

The steps were made of wood, well-worn and slippery. She began to climb down backwards, one step at a time, feeling the icy water creeping up around her thighs. Then she lost her footing on the bottom step.

She fell backwards, and Steve caught her in his arms. That felt very strange; she hardly knew him yet here they were – almost naked, their bodies close together as the cold, hostile water sloshed around them.

'Sorry, stupid of me,' she muttered breathlessly.

'That's all right.' He sounded breathless too. 'We may as well begin.'

He started to explain the principles of swimming, assuring her that as long as she remained calm and confident, she would be perfectly safe in the water. As long as the lungs were full of air, it was impossible for the human body to sink.

She didn't believe it. After all, if people couldn't sink, why did anyone ever drown? But her teeth were beginning to chatter, and she was in no state to argue with him. She merely nodded, trying to look calm and confident.

Then he put his hands on her waist, and encouraged her to lift her feet from the bottom of the bath. Numb with fear, she obeyed, and found that her legs floated up until she was lying in the water.

'It's all right, I won't let you go,' he said. 'Now then – stretch your arms out in front of you, then slowly force them apart – push the water away. One, two, three – *push* . . .!'

She tried to do as she was told, and for a while they continued like that; he walked slowly backwards and forwards across the pool, supporting her, and she pretended to swim. But she was so clumsy, and so nervous, she kept bumping against him. His body felt hard and strong, and she hated herself for being so feeble.

Steve was hating himself too, cursing his own body. Touching her soft, smooth skin, he was becoming excited; the feel of her body aroused him, and he was horribly embarrassed – afraid that she would notice – afraid she would never speak to him again . . . He tried to control himself, but finally blurted out abruptly: 'I think we should stop now. I expect you've had enough.'

Without thinking, he let go of her.

At once she panicked, dropping through the water like a stone. Instinctively, she clung to him, her legs threshing, her arms gripping him tightly, hanging on to him. In a tangle of arms and legs, they apologised together.

'Sorry – I'm sorry – my fault—'

As soon as her feet touched the bottom of the pool, she pulled away, blushing and mortified. 'It's no good, I'm useless. I'll never learn.'

'Don't be silly – you're doing very well.'

'No, I'm not. I know what you think – I'm too fat and stupid!'

'I don't. I think you're—' he contradicted her before he could stop himself '—Beautiful.'

And in that moment, the Dartmouth Road Baths ceased to exist. The other swimmers disappeared – the cold and the humiliation didn't matter. They stood waist-deep in water, face to face, and the whole world changed.

When they spoke again, their words didn't matter either.

'We – we'd better get out,' mumbled Steve. 'Don't want you catching cold.'

'No, all right.'

'Meet you at the exit in ten minutes – all right?'

'I'll be as quick as I can.'

When Daphne suggested that Val and Kate might like to come to All Saints on Sunday morning, Kate agreed at once.

'It will be nice to go to church again. I seem to have got out of the habit, somehow.'

Val hesitated. 'I would, only – I've sort of promised to do something else.'

'Oh? Where are you off to?'

'Just out – with Steve.'

Daphne smiled. 'Another lesson? You must be very keen on swimming.'

'Well, yes, I am – but not on Sunday. He's asked me to go for a day in the country, on his bike.'

'He's got a tandem?'

'No, a motorbike. He says I can ride on the pillion.'

One of the first things Steve had done when he began work at Wright's, was to buy himself a second-hand motorbike; the garage was letting him pay for it in instalments out of his wages, and it was his pride and joy.

'Well, you be careful,' Daphne warned her. 'And let's hope it keeps fine for you.'

So the little party went to church without Valerie.

They all enjoyed the service in different ways. Annie found it very exciting – the flowers, the coloured glass in the windows, the voices of the choir and the booming notes of the organ. Kate remembered all the times she had sat in the same pew with her husband, and the good times they had known together.

When Ted was a small boy, he had been a chorister, singing at Matins and Evensong week in and week out – but as soon as his voice broke and he left the choir, he had become a very infrequent worshipper. But he still enjoyed the music, joining enthusiastically in the hymns with his strong, clear baritone.

Daphne prayed, giving thanks for all the good things that had come their way – the beginning of Ted's theatrical career, and her own return to teaching – and the continuing good health of the whole family, in spite of the 'flu that was going round.

She prayed too that Ted would find a day job, to help out between engagements. Her own salary at Carmichael Road was a help, of course, but a little extra money would still be welcome, and although they never talked about it, she felt sure Ted would be happier if he could contribute to their finances regularly.

On the way home, they passed Fabers Furnishings, and Daphne stopped to look at the notice in the window.

'Help Wanted,' she read aloud. 'How about that, Ted? It might be worth trying.'

'Working for Faber?' Ted grimaced. 'That could be a bit awkward.'

Kate looked shocked. 'Oh no, you can't have anything to do with a man like that.'

'A man like what?' asked Annie, interested. 'What man?'

Kate said repressively, 'Little pitchers have long ears. Never you mind, duck, he's not worth talking about.'

'Yes, but we only know one side of the story,' Daphne persisted. 'Babs does get rather carried away sometimes . . . And if it's a salesman he's looking for, he won't find anyone better than Ted.'

'I suppose I could give it a try.' Ted sounded doubtful. 'Maybe I'll drop in and see him tomorrow.'

On Monday morning, he called on Mr Faber. He admitted that he'd had no experience of selling furniture, but felt sure he could learn.

Walter Faber noted that he had a pleasant appearance and a friendly manner, and guessed the customers would take to him. They discussed wages and came to an agreement – Ted would start work as a salesman in a week's time.

As he jotted down Ted's details, he frowned slightly, and asked: 'Your address is thirty-seven Sackville Road? Surely that's where—?'

'Yes, Ray Duke was our lodger. He's left us now.'

Mr Faber seemed to shrink back in his chair, before continuing in a muffled tone: 'And, if I'm not mistaken, your wife and Miss Glynn—?'

'Babs is my wife's sister.'

A pulse beat in Faber's temple. He could not look at Ted as he said quietly, 'I don't know what you have been told by Miss Glynn or Mr Duke, but if there might be any difficulty—'

'I don't see any difficulty myself,' Ted told him. 'As my wife said, there are two sides to every story, and that's nothing to do with me. The question is – do you want me to work for you? Will I be able to do a good job here? And I hope I can.'

Walter Faber looked up; their eyes met. 'Thank you, Mr Watkins,' he said. 'I hope so too.'

When Daphne and Annie got home from school that afternoon, Ted greeted them cheerfully. 'How about a kiss for the new furniture salesman? I start on Monday.'

Annie didn't understand, but she knew Mum and Dad were happy, so she kissed them both.

Daphne hugged Ted. 'I asked God if He could manage one more miracle – and this is the result. He didn't keep us waiting long, did He?'

*

Val's outing, on the back of Steve's bike, had been a complete success; to her surprise, she wasn't scared. After the first few moments of breathless excitement, she soon got used to sitting behind him, her knees digging into his thighs and her arms around his waist, whizzing along the suburban streets.

They left the built-up areas, and rode on through West Wickham to Westerham, then stopped for a picnic on the short, springy turf of the North Downs. The winter landscape was bright and clear in the crisp winter afternoon, but they did not feel any chill in the air.

When the picnic was finished, they sat on, side by side, and he put his arm round her shoulders. There was nobody in sight; they had the whole world to themselves – and then he kissed her.

Afterwards, he said, 'I believe I'm in love with you. I hope you don't mind.'

'Of course I don't mind. I think I've been in love with you for a long time, only I never knew it till now.'

'That's all right then,' he said seriously, and added: 'So – what are we going to do about it?'

'I don't know.' She couldn't be serious at a moment like this. She wanted to laugh, to shout or sing, and she explained joyfully: 'I can't think straight. Do we have to do anything about it? I want it to go on like this, for ever.'

'Yes, but people who love each other usually get married, don't they?' He was happy too, but his happiness was shot through with frustration. 'I'd marry you tomorrow if I could, but I haven't got any money. I'm going to start saving, but it'll take quite a while.'

'I don't care. I'll start saving too – and we can wait, can't we? It's worth waiting for.'

The next Sunday they went out again. This time he took a more ambitious route, through Croydon and Purley, across Walton Heath. He wouldn't tell her where they were going, saying he wanted it to be a surprise. At last he stopped, and parked the bike at the side of a narrow lane overhung with trees.

'Let's walk a bit,' he said, shouldering the knapsack that contained their picnic.

He led the way along a path that twisted through the bushes, and she wondered where he was taking her, but she trusted him completely. At last he pushed aside a screen of branches – and they stepped out into the sky.

'I bet you thought Crystal Palace was high up, didn't you?' he said. 'How about this, then?'

She sometimes dreamed that she was flying through the air, floating high above the ground, looking down on it. Now the dream had become real.

'The world must look like this from an aeroplane,' she said.

They were at the top of Box Hill; the ground seemed to drop away at their feet, and far below her she saw tiny buildings – a farm, a cluster of houses, a road with one or two miniature cars driving along, and a toy train puffing white steam as it cut through the patchwork of woods and fields. Further off, a mist shrouded the view, but she could see a ghostly line of hills, stretching away into eternity.

They found a bench and had their picnic, marvelling at the panorama, but Box Hill has always been popular with Londoners, and this time Steve and Val were not alone. Sightseers passed to and fro, admiring the view.

When they had finished their picnic, Steve suggested it might be less crowded if they went for a stroll in the woods, but they could find no privacy. Once, thinking they were alone in a secluded spot, he took Val in his arms – and was rudely interrupted by a man saying indignantly: 'Look where you're going, can't you? You nearly trod on her handbag!'

Recoiling, they found they were almost on top of a pair of lovers, locked in an embrace in the undergrowth.

'Come on,' said Steve. 'Let's go.'

To make matters worse, the mist, which had been gradually closing in, turned to a drizzle and the drizzle became a downpour. After that, they turned tail and headed for home, driving through a steady deluge that continued all the way to the Crystal Palace.

When they arrived, wringing wet, Steve was in a black mood; Val tried to cheer him up, but without success.

'Don't try and pretend,' he grumbled. 'You know as well as I do it's been a blooming awful day. I suppose you'll want to go home now?'

'I don't have to. We've still got this evening, haven't we?' she asked.

'What can you do, on a Sunday?' he burst out angrily: on the Sabbath, all places of entertainment were closed. 'If it had been a Saturday, we could have gone to the pictures. You're welcome to come round to our place if you want, but the family will be there. It's not as if I'd got a room of my own – I still share with Tony.'

'Anyway, I don't expect your Mum and Dad would be very keen

on us shutting ourselves up in your bedroom,' Val pointed out. 'There must be *something* we can do.'

'I know what I ought to do,' he said. 'I should give the bike a good going-over. It's had a real soaking and it's covered in mud – it needs a proper overhaul and a clean and polish. But what would you do, while I'm working on it?'

'Couldn't I help?' suggested Val.

He stared at her, unable to believe his ears. 'Do you mean that?'

'Why not?'

His face lit up. 'I thought you were one in a thousand – now I know you're one in a million!' he told her. 'All right, then – we'll clean the bike together!'

Freda Gunn looked scandalised when they told her what they were going to do. 'Oh no, Valerie,' she said. 'You don't want to go out in the shed with that messy old bike. Why don't you stay here and talk to me instead?'

'That would be nice, but I'd like to make myself useful,' Val explained tactfully.

'I could teach you to knit, if you want?' Freda indicated the shapeless grey mass of wool that hung from her needles. 'This is going to be a cardigan for Grandad. I could show you how to do the cuffs and the pockets.'

Vaguely aware that he was being discussed, Grandad sat up in his armchair and asked hopefully: 'Has she come to hear *Roses of Picardy*?'

'Not just now. Later on, I'd love to!' Val told him, as loudly as she could without actually shouting. 'Would you explain to him, Mrs Gunn? We'll come upstairs as soon as the bike's finished. Excuse us, won't you?'

Then she hurried down to the backyard, and held the shed door open for Steve while he wheeled his bike in, patting it lovingly as if it were a champion racehorse.

It turned out to be a long job. Most of the time, Val couldn't even understand what Steve was talking about; he kept rattling off words like 'carburettor' and 'throttle' and 'plugs', and expecting her to know what they meant. And it wasn't a very cosy place to spend the evening; the shed was cold and draughty, and smelled overpoweringly of the onions that were also stored there.

But she was with Steve, and he was like a schoolboy showing off his latest toy – as happy as a lark, unscrewing bits and pieces here and there, pouring out a stream of technical jargon, and occasionally giving her the odd nut or bolt to hold, or some mysterious metal object which she had to wipe carefully with an oily rag. She was determined not to let him know that she was bored and tired and decidedly chilly. When he saw she was shivering, he was immediately contrite.

'You must be frozen, after getting drenched this afternoon. You should have stayed upstairs in the warm, with Mum.'

'I'd rather be here with you,' she said truthfully. 'I've never been any good at knitting.'

'Neither has she.' He grinned. 'Dear old Mum. She loves her knitting, but she's always dropping stitches or getting the pattern wrong, so the things she makes come out funny sizes – pullovers with arms so long they hang over your hands, or else they're so tight they nearly choke you. You'd better prepare for the worst – she's taken a real shine to you, and she's making you a twin-set for your birthday. Goodness only knows what you'll do with it!'

'I'll wear it, of course,' said Val bravely. 'Whatever it's like.'

'She's already bought the wool,' he warned her. 'Two colours – purple and orange.'

'Never mind. It's very kind of her, and—' Val broke off, sniffing the air. 'Can you smell something?'

He sniffed too. 'Only petrol – and onions.'

'Besides that. I thought I could smell something burning.'

Steve looked at the kerosene lamp that hung from a bracket on the wall. By now it was dark outside, and the lamp was the only light in the shed.

'Nothing wrong with that,' he said. 'Nothing's burning in here.'

'Outside, perhaps?'

Outside, the smell of burning was stronger. Steve glanced up at the back windows; there was no sign of fire there – but now they could hear the crackle of flames.

'Next door,' he said. 'The furniture shop!'

Dragging a large wooden crate to the wall, he scrambled up to look over into the adjoining yard.

'My God!' he exclaimed. 'It's the stockroom at the back. There's a window broken, and I can see the flames inside—'

'Telephone for the Fire Brigade!' Val urged him.

'We haven't got a phone, but there's one over the road. You go up and warn the others. Tell them to get ready to leave, in case the fire spreads.'

He ran indoors, through the shop and out into the street, leaving Val to break the news to his family. It took a few moments to make them understand, and even after she had explained, their reactions were confused.

'I must go down and shift them onions,' said Alfred. 'If the shed catches light, we'll lose the perishing lot.'

'Can I come too, Dad?' Tony jumped up gleefully. 'Can I see the fire?'

Recognising Valerie, old Jack Gunn greeted her happily, picking up his cornet and saying, 'Yes, I'm all ready. I've got it right here—'

He put the instrument to his lips, and launched into the opening bars of *Roses of Picardy*.

Freda took charge, cutting through the hubbub with a voice like the crack of a whip.

'Not now, Grandad! The shop next door's on fire! Tony, get your hat and coat, we may be going out. Alfred, stay where you are. If the building catches fire, we'll have more to worry about than a load of onions. Get the money and the insurance policy and the box with our birth certificates while I put your father into his overcoat. Oh, for goodness sake, Grandad, do stop playing that thing!'

After that, everything happened very quickly. Freda began to pack up their most valuable possessions – not forgetting her knitting-bag and the unfinished cardigan – and Steven came back, having used a neighbour's telephone to call the brigade.

The Fire Station was in Crystal Palace Parade, and the engine arrived within minutes, pulled by a team of white horses. The firemen ran out the hose through the alley into Faber's yard, and broke into the stockroom.

By this time the fire had taken hold and was raging furiously, with a sound like distant thunder. The furniture and upholstery were ablaze in a sea of flame and thick black smoke. Out in the street, the Gunn family stood huddled on the pavement by the engine; like the horses, they waited patiently.

Suddenly Steve pointed. 'Look at that!'

Inside Fabers' shop, a dull yellow glow rose and fell, flickering on the drawn blinds. The fire was spreading fast.

For the next half-hour, the brigade fought the flames, and gradually brought them under control. At last the Chief Officer came along the alley, taking off his helmet and mopping the perspiration from his face.

'Looks like we're winning,' he told Alf Gunn. 'I don't think you've got anything to worry about, next door. We're just damping it down.'

'Can I go in now?' asked a man's voice.

Walter Faber stepped forward from the crowd of onlookers; a neighbour had phoned him, and he had been standing in the shadows, watching helplessly. He introduced himself to the Officer, and asked again: 'May I go in and see the damage?'

'Not for the moment, sir. I must ask you to wait, in case it flares up again. I'm afraid you're in for a shock when you see it. There's not a great deal left.'

'Have you found out how it started?' Faber asked. 'A short-circuit in the wiring, perhaps?'

'No, sir. By the looks of it, somebody broke a window at the back. I imagine they chucked in a can of petrol, and some burning rags.'

'You mean it was started deliberately?'

'More than likely. Do you have any idea who might be responsible? Somebody with a grudge against you, perhaps?'

'No.' Walter Faber cleared his throat. 'No – I've no idea.'

Alf Gunn put his hand on Faber's shoulder and said gruffly: 'Let us know if there's anything we can do to help. If there's anything you think of – bang on our door, any time.' Then he moved away, following his family indoors.

As soon as they were upstairs, Freda packed Tony off to bed, telling him he'd had quite enough excitement for one night, then she tried to explain to her father-in-law that the house was not going to burn down after all.

'Glad to hear it,' he said cheerfully. 'That's something to celebrate, eh? Would you like me to—'

'Not tonight, Grandad,' said Freda firmly. 'It's time you were getting ready for bed as well. I'm going to make us all a nice cup of cocoa. Valerie – I expect you could do with one.'

'I think I'd rather go home, thanks all the same.' Something in her voice made Steve look at her; he saw she was trembling.

'What's the matter?' he asked.

'Nothing. It's just – I've always been terrified of fire . . .'

'But it's over now – there's nothing to be afraid of,' he told her.

'I know, I'm just being silly. I'll be all right when I get home.'

He put his arm round her. 'You don't think I'm going to let you walk back there on your own, do you?' So they went off to Sackville Road together; when they got there, she asked if he'd come in with her.

'You can help me tell them what happened. I'm sorry to be so silly, but I can't stop shaking.' She took him down to the kitchen and

155

introduced him to her mother, and to Daphne and Ted. Between them, they told the family about the fire.

Kate shook her head. 'I can't say I like Mr Faber, after what he did, but it's a dreadful thing to happen to anyone. I wonder if he's insured?'

'Bound to be,' said Steve. 'But it's going to hit him hard. It'll be a long while till he gets the shop repaired and ready for business.'

Daphne looked at Ted, and sighed. 'I'm so sorry, love . . .'

'Can't be helped.' He threw her a wry smile. 'Isn't this what they call an Act of God?'

Catching the unspoken message, Valerie exclaimed: 'Oh no, I forgot!' She told Steve; 'Ted had just got a job as Faber's new salesman.'

I was due to start work tomorrow.' Ted shrugged. 'Oh well, back to the Labour Exchange.'

They went on talking about the fire for some time, and Daphne noticed that Steve Gunn was very silent. She assumed he must be feeling a little awkward among strangers, but when the conversation flagged, he broke in and asked: 'Have you always been a furniture salesman, Mr Watkins?'

Ted chuckled. 'I wish you'd call me Ted. When people say "Mr Watkins", I always think they're talking about my Dad! You're Steve – I'm Ted – and she's Daff, all right?'

For the first time that evening, Steve smiled. 'OK Ted, thanks.'

'And to answer your question – I've never sold furniture in my life. My last job was selling pickles, and I try to sell a few laughs as well from time to time.'

'Yes, Valerie told me – but I was wondering if you might be interested in selling cars.'

'I'll sell anything that's going, if I get the chance. Piccalilli or pantechnicons, it's all the same to me . . . Why?'

'I work at Wright's Motors and they're looking for a salesman in the showroom. Would you like me to have a word with the Manager?'

'I'd be delighted! Mind you, you'll have to tell him I don't know the first thing about cars – I can't even drive! – but I'm a quick learner.'

Steve sent a message the following day; Mr Wright would be interviewing prospective salesmen on Friday afternoon, and he'd be happy to see Mr Watkins at four o'clock if he'd care to come along.

'I'll sponge and press your best suit,' said Daphne. 'You see? You weren't meant to get that job at Faber's – this proves it. God had a better job lined up for you.'

Ted teased her, 'You'll be telling me next this is the little miracle you asked for.'

'Of course it is – and this is the job you're going to get!'

But she had not taken into account the 'flu epidemic which was still going round. By Thursday, Ted had retired to bed with a high temperature.

Like many healthy people who sail through life with nothing but the occasional cough or cold, illness hit him hard, and he resented it. When Daphne poured out his medicine, he was feeling very sorry for himself.

'Talk about bad luck!' he croaked, slumped back on the pillows, flushed and sweaty. 'Why can't things go right for once? It's about time I had a stroke of luck!'

'Don't say that – you've had plenty of luck. Now swallow this, and you'll feel better.'

'Call this luck? Losing two jobs in one week? I haven't got a hope of going for that interview tomorrow. You'd better ask Val to tell her boyfriend God's decided otherwise.'

'She can say you're not well, and ask Steve to make another appointment for you next week.'

'What's the use? The way I feel at the moment, I don't suppose I'll ever work again – and I don't much care, either!'

On her way home from school, Daphne had bought an evening paper, in an attempt to take Ted's mind off his troubles – but the headline depressed him still further.

It said simply: *Marie Lloyd dies*.

'I can't believe it.' Ted stared at the page; all he could see was that cheeky, heart-shaped face – the tiny gap between her front teeth, like a child – and the twinkle in her eye which wasn't childish at all. 'Our Marie – she's always been the same, as long as I can remember. Did you ever see her?'

'We were never allowed to go to a music hall,' Daphne reminded him. 'But I've heard my father talk about her.'

'Everybody talked about her. She was one of the best . . . and now she's gone.' He tried to focus on the blurred newsprint. 'Fifty-two, it says here – that's no age, is it? She was working a few nights ago, at the Edmonton Empire. After the first house they called a doctor, and he tried to make her go home, but she wouldn't listen; she played the second house, though she could hardly stand. Her last number was

One of the Ruins that Cromwell Knocked About a Bit, where she played an old drunk, staggering round the stage – only this time she wasn't acting. When she fell down, the audience shrieked – they thought it was all part of the act . . . Of course she'd been a sick woman for some time, and those husbands of hers didn't help, either. The last one, the jockey, he got through most of her money . . .'

Daphne sat on the edge of the bed and put her hand over his, saying, 'I suppose the stage is rather a chancy business.'

After a moment he went on, 'I still can't believe she's gone. The night I worked with Gus Elen, he was talking about Marie. He said: "She's done some silly things in her time, but I'll say this for her – she's got a heart as big as Waterloo Station". And now she's gone.'

He turned to Daphne, with the ghost of a smile. 'Yes, it's a chancy business. Up one day, down and out the next. But once you walk out on that stage, you've got to go on – till the curtain comes down.'

The same week, another news item gripped the nation. A man called Percy Thompson had been found dead at his home in Manor Park. The police took Mrs Thompson into custody and charged her with murder, along with her young lover and accomplice, Frederick Bywaters. Day by day, everyone followed the story as it unfolded – nowhere with closer interest than in Upper Norwood.

Babs and Ray were on their way to the newsagents in Westow Hill, hoping there might be some fresh details in the late editions.

'You must remember her,' Babs was saying impatiently. 'That morning in the café, she came in and you asked me who she was.'

Ray tried to recall the woman's face. 'You said she ran a millinery shop or something.'

'That's right – *that* was Florence Bywaters. It's her son Freddie that's accused of murder! The police went to her flat and searched his room, looking for clues. Poor woman, she must be feeling so dreadful.'

'D'you mean to say he lives there? Over the shop?'

'Yes, when he was home on leave. He's a sailor; he would have been off to the Far East in a few days, but the police arrested him before the ship sailed.'

'So he nearly got away with it.' Ray's eyes shone with a strange, faraway look. 'Poor sod.'

'Ray, please! You know I hate it when you swear,' said Babs primly.

He ignored her protest. 'Come on, let's go round to Westow Street and see if there's anything going on. Maybe the police are still searching. Anyway, it'll be a bit of fun.'

'Not much fun for Mrs Bywaters – or Edith Thompson,' sighed Babs, but she let him drag her along. 'I know it's awful, but I can't help thinking he must have loved her very much, to kill that man for her sake.'

'Either that or he'd got his eye on the old geezer's money. I mean – if he thought she was going to be a wealthy widow—'

Babs was horrified. 'That's horrible! Do you really think so?'

'Well, it's only human nature, isn't it?' Ray shot her a sidelong glance. 'Don't tell me it hadn't crossed your mind now and again. Come on, be honest. That's the reason you said you couldn't marry me, isn't it? 'Cos you thought I was after your money?'

She stared at him incredulously. 'What gave you that idea? I haven't got any money.'

'Well, maybe not at the moment, but you've got a rich family.'

Babs began to laugh. 'Don't be silly, we're not rich! Oh, Mummy likes to pretend we're frightfully well off, but she spent everything Grandfather DeWitt left her ages ago. You must have noticed the house is practically falling down – we can't afford to have it done up. Do you really imagine we'd go out to work if we didn't have to?' She laughed again. 'What a joke – we haven't got a bean!'

If it was a joke, Ray did not find it funny. They walked on to Westow Road in an uneasy silence. As they reached the corner, they nearly collided with Val and Steve, on their way to Church Road. Babs eyed Steve with interest as Val introduced them.

'I've been dying to meet you,' she said. 'Valerie's told me so much about you.'

'How do you do,' he said, shaking hands. He nodded at Ray, who grunted. Having worked in neighbouring shops, they already knew one another, but there was no love lost between them.

'I suppose you've heard the news?' Val asked. 'Isn't it terrible?'

'No, what? Something about Bywaters?' Babs asked eagerly.

'Oh no. I meant the news about Ted – such bad luck. First the fire at Mr Faber's shop – but of course you know about that—'

Ray smirked. 'Unlucky for Faber, wasn't it? I wonder how it happened?'

'But what's that got to do with Ted?' asked Babs.

Val told them that Ted was going to start work there; she went on to explain about the interview tomorrow afternoon at Wright's Garage, and how he had gone down with 'flu.

'Sorry to hear that,' said Ray. 'Give him my regards, won't you? Tell him I hope his luck changes soon.'

By Monday, Ted was feeling well enough to get up and stagger round to the garage. He told Daphne it was worth a try. At least he could apologise for not turning up last Friday, and if by any chance Mr Wright hadn't picked anyone for the job, he might still strike lucky.

At the end of the afternoon, when she brought Annie home from school, Daphne asked him: 'Well? What did he say?'

Ted shook his head. 'He was very decent about it – said he'd bear me in mind if they get another vacancy, but apparently someone else turned up on Friday with a good line of sales-talk . . . Your friend and mine – Raymond Duke.'

'Oh no!' exclaimed Daphne. 'How did that happen?'

'Ask me another.' Ted grinned. 'So much for your little miracle.'

Chapter Nine

THE WORKSHOP AT Wright's was closed on Saturday afternoons, so Steve had a free half-day. He'd arranged to pick Val up on his bike at two o'clock, but she sent a message to say that she had to do some overtime at her office and wasn't sure when she'd get away, so she would come and meet him at Church Road instead.

It was nearly half-past three by the time she got there. The shop was crowded with customers, buying early new potatoes and spring greens for tomorrow's Sunday roast, and Alf waved cheerily while Freda called to her, 'He's in the sitting room. Go on up!'

Upstairs, Val was surprised to find Steve on his own. 'Sorry I'm late,' she said, looking round. 'Where is everybody?'

'Grandad's at a band practice, for the concert on Easter Sunday, and Tony's out playing football with his pals.' He took her in his arms. 'We've got the place to ourselves for once.'

He began to kiss her – and to her embarrassment and Steve's dismay, she found she was crying.

'Hey, what's wrong?' he asked.

'Nothing, really,' she sobbed. 'But I've had such a terrible week.'

He steered her to the sofa, where she cuddled up beside him, her head on his shoulder. 'Tell me about it,' he said.

She tried to explain. Ever since Monday, things had been difficult. Mr Buckland wasn't his usual sunny self, and when the General Manager was in a bad mood, it affected everyone.

'I've never known him so short-tempered. Nobody could do anything right,' said Val. 'He walked past one of the maintenance men who was banging a nail into a wall – he'd been told to put up a shelf in one of the offices – and Mr Buckland simply exploded with rage and yelled: "*What do you think you're doing? How dare you knock holes in my Palace?*" I thought he was going to sack the poor man on the spot. When he explained, Mr Buckland simmered down a bit and said: "Oh well, I suppose you'd better get on with it. Only try not to kick up such an infernal racket, d'you hear?" And he shut himself in his office, and slammed the door so hard, it was like a bomb going off.'

Ten minutes later, Val had taken Mr Buckland his afternoon tea. She had knocked gingerly at his door, then getting no reply, she had tried again, a little more loudly.

'Who the devil's that?' he shouted, so she went in. 'What are you trying to do – break the door down?'

'I'm sorry, sir, you didn't hear me the first time. I've brought your tea.'

'Surely you know how to knock at the door by now, young woman?' he snapped. 'Not too quietly, but not too loudly, either. There is such a thing as a happy medium.'

As she reported this to Steve, he reacted indignantly. 'I think I'll have a few words to say to Mr Henry Buckland! He can't treat my Valerie like that!'

Val said hastily, 'Oh no, that would only make things worse. Besides, he did apologise afterwards.'

Possibly Mr Buckland had realised from the look on Val's face that he had gone too far. As she was about to hurry from the room, he called her back.

'I spoke hastily – forgive me. I've had a good many problems to deal with recently. For instance, this new Wembley Stadium is going to hit us hard.'

Before the war, there had been a great exhibition at the Crystal Palace – the Festival of Empire. Specially built pavilions were put up in the grounds, to represent each of the countries taking part, filled with examples of art, handicrafts and industry from Canada and Australia, from India, South Africa and the rest.

The Festival had run from May to October 1911, and it had been a big success. After the war, plans were made to hold a similar exhibition – and Mr Buckland assumed that the Palace would be the site of an even more lavish display.

His hopes were dashed when it was decided that the new exhibition was to be on a larger scale – too large for the limited space at the Palace. An area of north-west London had been chosen; land at Wembley had been purchased, and huge permanent buildings were being erected there. The greatest of these structures was the Wembley Stadium, already completed a year ahead of the exhibition.

To rub salt into Mr Buckland's wounds, it would be open for the first time next month, as the venue for an important football match – Bolton Wanderers versus West Ham United – in order to give the public an opportunity to inspect the vast sports arena.

'You realise what this means? There's no hope of staging any major events here now,' Henry Buckland told Valerie. 'Apparently the Cup Final will always be held at Wembley in future.'

Val explained to Steve: 'That's why he's been so ratty lately. The Palace is his pride and joy, and he'd pinned his hopes on putting on a really big show.'

'They say the old place doesn't make as much money as it used to,' said Steve. 'Is that true?'

'Nobody ever talks about things like that in our office, but when you see the long faces in the Accounts Department, you can't help wondering.' She sniffed, and fumbled for her little lace handkerchief.

Steve pulled out his own handkerchief, saying: 'Here, take mine. Go on, have a good blow.'

'Mum taught me you shouldn't blow on a borrowed hanky.' Val smiled through her tears. 'I'll take it home and wash it out for you.'

'Don't be daft. Are you feeling any more cheerful yet?'

'A bit, only I haven't told you the worst part. Did you hear what happened yesterday? As if things weren't bad enough already, the building caught fire.'

'Yes, one of the chaps at work mentioned something. I don't understand, though. The Palace is built of glass and metal girders – how can a place like that catch on fire?'

'There's lots of wood as well – the floors and the offices and so on. They say it did five thousand pounds' worth of damage.'

'Blimey . . . How did it happen?'

'It was in one of the staff locker-rooms. Smoking's forbidden in there, but they think it was probably a cigarette-end that started it.' She gripped his hand. 'It's frightening.'

He realised she was still very tense, and asked, 'But you weren't in any danger?'

'No – it happened just after midnight. When I arrived for work this morning it was such a mess. Some of the iron girders holding up the gallery had cracked in the heat; they're still being shored up. The smell of burning made me feel sick. I kept thinking of that fire you

163

had, next door. You know I'm silly about fire. It just terrifies me.' At the memory of it, she began to tremble, and he kissed her again.

'Don't take on so. Now it's happened, you can stop worrying. They say lightning never strikes twice in the same place, so you're safe now. The Palace won't catch fire again.'

He was still kissing her when the door opened, and Freda exclaimed: 'Oh! Sorry, I'm sure – only we've had a bit of a lull downstairs, so I was wondering if Valerie might fancy a cup of tea.'

Pulling herself together, Val wiped her eyes, saying, 'Thank you, that would be very nice.'

'She's a bit upset,' Steve explained. 'They had a fire at the Palace.'

'I know, isn't it shocking? There must be some maniac going round, setting light to places. Some people are funny like that. They can't be trusted near a box of matches.'

'Oh, I think it was probably an accident—' Val began.

'But you can't be sure, can you? You hear such dreadful things.' Then Freda added: 'Steve, be a good boy and put the kettle on for me, eh? I want to have a word with Valerie.'

When he went off to the kitchen, Freda produced a cardboard box, saying, 'I've got a little something for you, dear.' It had *Carlsbad Plums* printed on the side, but she said, 'Take no notice of that – it was the only box I could find. Go on, open it.'

Val took the lid off. Inside, under a sheet of tissue-paper, she found a large piece of knitting, in alternate bands of orange and purple.

'*Oh* – how lovely,' she said helplessly. 'It's the twinset Steve told me about.'

'The bad boy – it was supposed to be a secret! Only it's not a twin-set. I had a little difficulty with the pattern, so in the end I turned it into a dress. Hold it up so I can see if the size is right.'

Val obeyed. It was much too long and almost shapeless, but she said that it was beautiful, and told Freda she shouldn't have gone to so much trouble.

'No trouble, dear, I enjoy doing it. Besides, Alfred and me are both very fond of you. I wanted you to have something special . . . We're so glad Steve's picked such a lovely girl.' Awkwardly, she went on: 'I hope you don't mind me asking, but has he said anything?'

'I'm sorry?' Val was confused.

'About future plans. Dates – choosing a ring – anything like that?'

'Oh no. Well, we haven't known each other very long.'

'Quite long enough. His Dad says he'll be a fool if he lets you slip through his fingers.' She broke off. 'He's coming back – don't say anything, will you?'

As the door opened, and Steve came in with a tea-tray, Freda continued quickly, 'Hold the dress up and let him see how you look. Don't the colours suit her?'

That evening, they went to the Electra, to see Douglas Fairbanks in *Robin Hood.* As they queued up at the box office, Steve asked her: 'How about if I get us a double ticket for one of the Lovers' Knots?'

These were seats built for two, designed for courting couples. Val felt a little nervous, but she couldn't help admiring Steve's boldness.

'All right, if you like,' she said.

As the lights went down he whispered in her ear, 'I've never dared ask till now, but tonight – well, it's what we are, isn't it? A courting couple?'

Val had been looking forward to the film, but after the first ten minutes she lost interest; the Lovers' Knot made it difficult to follow the story.

As they walked back to Sackville Road together, their arms round one another, she said softly, 'I do love you. I've never been so happy.'

'Yes,' he said. 'I'm happy too, only—'

He was silent for so long, she asked: 'What is it? What were you going to say?'

'Oh, it's just I get impatient sometimes. What was Mum on about this afternoon, when she sent me off to the kitchen? It must have been something about me. What did she say?'

'She was very kind.' Val had to tell him the truth. 'She asked if we'd made any plans.'

'She would. Why can't she mind her own business?'

'She didn't mean to be nosy – she just wants us both to be happy.'

'That's what I want too. It's what I want more than anything in the world – to ask you to marry me – but I've only got a few quid in my Post Office savings.'

'Couldn't we rent a little flat? Even one room – we could manage.'

'I wouldn't ask you to do that – you deserve better. If I rent a decent place, I'll have to put down six months in advance; that's what I'm saving up for. Only by the time I've paid the instalments on my bike each week, there's not all that much left – and I have to give Mum something for the housekeeping . . . I'm beginning to wish I'd never bought the damn bike.'

'You know you don't mean that.' Val thought hard. 'I'm sure my

Mum would help, but she's only got her pension now. Do you suppose if you were to speak to your Dad, perhaps he—'

'No!' The word came out more angrily than he intended. 'Sorry, I didn't mean to bark, but I can't ask Dad. He's never really got over me leaving the shop. I can't go back now and ask him for money – I've got to do this on my own somehow.'

She put her face up to him, and they kissed. 'Don't worry, we'll manage somehow,' she whispered. 'We'll just have to be patient a bit longer.'

At midday, the staff of Wright's Motors went to the pub over the road, leaving the two youngest recruits to keep the premises open for business. As a rule, lunch-times were very quiet. Steve was able to carry on doing repair jobs without interruption, but for Ray, a deserted salesroom soon became boring, so he drifted into the workshop for a chat.

'I'm a bit busy,' muttered Steve, his head and shoulders under the open bonnet of a smart little roadster.

'Yeah, I can see that.' Ray perched on the end of the work-bench, swinging his legs and striking a match to light his cigarette.

Steve emerged long enough to snap: 'Put that out! What are you trying to do – start a fire?'

Ray gave a snicker of amusement. 'It might liven things up.' But he pinched out the cigarette-end carefully and put it back in the packet to smoke later. 'You're down in the dumps today – what's up? Fallen out with the lovely Valerie?'

'No!' Steve scowled. 'What gave you that idea? We're fine.'

'Well, you don't look it. I thought you must've had a row.'

'Nothing of the kind.' Steve straightened up again. In a way, it was a relief to be able to talk to someone else about the problem – even someone he didn't much like. 'She's the girl for me. I want to get married and settle down, but till I've got some money saved up, there's not much chance.'

'So that's it.' Ray studied him thoughtfully. 'I know what you mean. I've been thinking about getting hitched myself, only I'm flat broke – and Babs isn't much better off. I used to think her family must be rolling in money, living in that big house, but seemingly the house is pretty well all they've got left.'

'Mmmm. Anyhow, I must get on.' Steve went on working.

Ray threw him a sideways look, and remarked: 'Ah well, look on the bright side, eh? Easter next weekend – and we've got the day off on Monday. Tell you what, why don't we go along to the Palace, the four of us? There's going to be a funfair in the grounds – and seeing as how Val and Babs are such friends, we could have a real good time. What d'you say?'

Steve hesitated; he knew how Val felt about their ex-lodger, but it was true that she enjoyed Babs' company.

'I suppose I could ask her,' he said. 'Matter of fact, we were thinking of going to the fair anyhow. Val's brother is doing a turn at the Palace theatre, Monday night, so we've fixed up with Daff to go to the show.'

'All the better!' Ray was immediately enthusiastic. 'Get 'em to put by a couple of extra tickets for us – free seats, of course?'

'I don't know.' Steve was getting impatient. 'I'll have a word with Val, but I must get on with this now. The job's promised for two o'clock.'

So he asked Val, and Val asked Daphne – and Daphne had an idea. Ever since the Grange Wood Concert Party, there had been a coolness between her and the family at Belmont where Ted's stage career was concerned, but if Babs were coming to the show . . . Daphne saw the possibility of a reconciliation.

That night, as she slipped into her nightdress, she told Ted: 'I had a brainwave. I suggested that Babs ought to bring Mother along as well. You could get her a complimentary seat, couldn't you?'

'What – Her Majesty in person? She wouldn't cross the road to see me – she'd sooner watch a public execution.' Climbing into bed, Ted chuckled at the thought. 'Unless it was me for the chop! In that case she'd probably pay for her own ticket.'

Daphne smiled. 'Mother's not that bad! And you did say this particular show was going to be something special. A lot of famous stars, you told me – she'd enjoy that.'

'Yes, it's a good line-up. Percy must have pulled a few strings, to get me included. I think it was on account of me living just round the corner; they don't have to pay travelling expenses . . . But you're wasting your time, inviting Mummy. I'll bet you anything she won't come.'

'Bet you half-a-crown she does.'

The following evening, Daphne reported that Ted owed her two shillings and sixpence. Not only were Ray and Babs bringing Muriel Glynn; they had requested extra tickets for Gerald, Aunt Ethel *and* Aunt Aggie!

Ted groaned. 'Gawd – that'll put the kibosh on the evening!'

Not to be outdone, he invited his mother to join the party but Kate, who still felt rather awkward about Ted's in-laws, said she'd rather come another time. After all, someone had to stay behind and look after little Annie, as the concert wouldn't finish until long after her bedtime.

The funfair, of course, was open all day, and Ray and Babs arranged to meet Val and Steve at three o'clock, in the North Tower Gardens.

As they lined up to go through the turnstiles, Ray said resentfully, 'Of course Val got in on her staff pass – and I s'pose she took Steve in as her guest. All right for some, isn't it? Why couldn't she have fixed up free passes for us as well?'

'It's only sixpence to go in,' Babs pointed out. 'And we're getting free seats for the concert – we mustn't grumble.'

The two couples met at the North Tower Gardens, as arranged – and set off at once to sample all the fun of the fair. By mid-afternoon, the grounds were thronged with people, and they kept getting separated in the crowd, losing each other, then coming together again.

There was a boating-lake in the shadow of the North Tower, and the girls wanted to take a boat out and sail round sedately, but the young men wouldn't hear of it. There was a more exciting way to take to the water.

Against their will, Val and Babs allowed themselves to be persuaded, and the foursome paid for admission to the giant Water Chute. They climbed an enclosed stairway, and came out on a small platform at the top of a steep incline; an attendant hurried them into a boat and sent them on their way.

The boat bobbed along placidly for a few yards, then tipped over the edge of a sharp drop, thundering down in a continual cascade of water. The girls screamed, clinging on to their partners – which was the whole point of the exercise – and shut their eyes as the tiny craft splashed down in the lake below, sending up a great wave on either side, like the wings of a swan.

Gasping and giggling, they scrambled out on to dry land once more, and Ray said: 'That was a bit of all right, eh? How about another go?'

But Babs and Val decided that once was enough, and Steve said there was another sideshow they ought to try.

Sir Hiram Maxim, the American inventor, had installed his Captive Flying Machine in the Palace grounds; for as long as he could remember, Steve had wanted to go up in an aeroplane. If he couldn't achieve the real thing, this might be a good substitute.

The girls were apprehensive, but again they were overruled. Steve paid for the tickets and they went inside a wooden building, then out on to a raised platform where the flying-boats hung, waiting for passengers.

Even Steve and Ray felt slightly nervous, though they would have died rather than admit it. They climbed into one of the flying boats – long and pointed, with four rows of seats; each boat held twelve or more passengers – then held on tightly as the whole contraption began to revolve like a gigantic roundabout – slowly at first, but soon gathering speed.

As it moved faster and faster, the flying-boats swung out on the ends of their cables, under the pull of centrifugal force, until they were whizzing round so fast, the grounds – the spectators – the Crystal Palace on the crest of the hill – all swam together in one continuous blur. The world seemed to tilt on its axis, because they were flying at an angle of forty-five degrees, and the support cables stretched out horizontally.

Babs buried her face in Ray's shoulder; Val gripped Steve very hard, convinced that she was about to be killed. At any moment their flying-boat would be flung off into space, crashing into smithereens . . .

But the cables stood up to the strain, and gradually the machine slowed down until the flying-boats came to a halt beside the platform once more.

Babs slapped Ray playfully as they reeled down the steps. 'You beast, scaring me like that! I'm not going on any more rides with you, Raymond Duke!'

Val agreed. 'Let's try something more restful, something that doesn't go up and down!'

In the end they settled for a glimpse of the future. Gypsy Zara promised to tell fortunes with the aid of cards and palmistry.

The young men said it was a waste of money, but the girls insisted that it was time they were allowed to have their own way. Besides, a notice announced that any couples consulting Madame Zara would be given a specially reduced rate – two for the price of one.

That settled it; Val linked her arm through Steve's, and they entered the booth together.

It was only a tent; sunlight glowed strangely through the walls, and there was a smell of warm canvas and trampled grass and oriental joss-sticks, which were burning smokily in a brass vase.

Madame Zara greeted them pleasantly; she had deep-set, hooded eyes, and a few wisps of brightly hennaed hair escaped from the gaudy bandanna knotted round her head. She asked them to be seated, and instructed them to shuffle and deal half a dozen cards each, face down. Turning the cards up one by one, she began her prediction: they were going to be happy, they were an ideal couple, they would be married and have a large family.

Then she asked them to hold out their hands, palms upward, scrutinising the creases, the little mounds and valleys, comparing and considering their life-lines, their head-lines and heart-lines. At last she said: 'Life will not be all roses. I see problems ahead – deception – a long separation. But if you remain true to one another, these obstacles can be overcome, and you will reach a deep and lasting happiness. Take care, have courage. Above all, you must never doubt, but have faith always. That will be two shillings, please.'

Dismissed, they left the tent, making way for Ray and Babs.

There was a change in the atmosphere. Madame Zara stared at them both for a long moment, then asked: 'Why have you come to me?'

Babs looked uncertainly at Ray, who guffawed and replied, 'We thought it might be a bit of a laugh.'

Madame Zara drew herself up. 'I'm sorry, I can't help you. You may leave now; there will be no charge.'

Babs interjected quickly, 'Oh no, Madame – he's only joking. We want to know what's in store for us, don't we, Ray?'

Ray shrugged. 'If you say so. OK – carry on, Missus.'

Madame Zara seemed unwilling to continue, but Babs pleaded with her, and at last she said grudgingly, 'Very well. But there's something here I do not understand – the psychic force is very powerful. Before we cut the cards, I should like to see your hands, please.'

Under her direction, they placed their hands on the table, and she examined their palms.

For a while, nothing happened; no one spoke or moved, and Babs held her breath. It was very quiet inside the tent. The noise of the crowds and the music of a brass band in the distance seemed to be part of another world, remote and unreal, as they waited for the fortune-teller to speak. But she said nothing. She uttered a strange sound – a kind of groan – then slipped sideways, toppling from her chair on to the trodden grass.

'She's ill!' Babs dropped to her knees beside her.

Ray said, 'Naah – she's fainted. It's stuffy in here, not enough air.'

Babs interrupted him. 'Look at her face. She's gone a nasty colour.'

Madame Zara's complexion was greenish-yellow, with mottled patches round her nose and mouth. Helplessly, Babs shook her, saying: 'It's all right. Wake up, Madame. You'll be all right. Ray, don't stand there staring – fetch a doctor!'

But the fortune-teller opened her eyes, and drew a long, shuddering breath. Between them, they helped her up and settled her in her chair again.

'How are you feeling?' asked Babs. 'Shall we take you out into the fresh air? Would you like us to call a doctor?'

'No, I'm quite well. You may go – I shall recover in a moment.'

'But we can't just go and leave you like this—'

'I'm perfectly all right.' The lady spoke sharply. 'Just go!'

They began to back away, fumbling for the tent-flap, but Ray lingered to ask, 'What was it you saw, when you read our palms?'

Lifting her head, she looked straight at him – and he saw terror in her eyes. But all she said was, 'Nothing – I saw nothing. Please leave me alone.'

There was no more to be said. They ducked under the tent-flap and hurried across to rejoin their friends. Babs started to tell them what had happened, but Steve broke in, pointing. 'Look!' he said.

They saw Madame Zara, still very pale, emerging from the tent. She turned round the sign that said *Now Open*, so that it read *Closed*.

'I knew she was ill,' said Babs.

'We should never have wasted our money on her in the first place,' scoffed Ray. 'It's all baloney.'

'I rather liked her,' said Val. 'She told us some interesting things, didn't she, Steve?'

'Like what?' Babs was curious. 'What did she say? Go on, tell us.'

Val shook her head. 'You'd only laugh,' she said.

Ten minutes later someone else lifted the tent-flap and entered the fortune-teller's booth – but Madame Zara was no longer Madame Zara.

'Hello, old dear,' said Harry Glynn. 'You've shut up shop early, haven't you?'

'Yes,' said Miss Preece flatly. 'I thought I would.'

'Business a bit slow?' he asked. 'Not enough clients?'

'It's not that. I was doing nicely, until . . .' His landlady stood up, pulling on her outdoor coat. Without her bright bandanna headscarf, she looked much older and very tired.

'Until what?' The old man knitted his brows. 'You haven't had any trouble, I hope? No bother from the police?'

'No – I had a dizzy spell. Something I'd eaten, I expect. Would you be kind enough to give me your arm? I think I'd like to go home now.'

She leaned on him – and at his touch, something like an electric shock ran through her. Appalled, she stared at him then broke away, exclaiming quickly, 'It's all right. I can manage, thank you.'

But she could not take her eyes from him; shadowed and sombre, her gaze seemed to pierce him through and through.

'Gad, woman – what's wrong now?' he asked. 'Why are you looking at me like that?'

'It's nothing . . . Just something I saw in someone's hands. Nothing of any importance.'

She dodged past him, out of the tent, and he had to hobble more quickly than usual on the way home, in order to keep up with her.

Ted was right; the list of artistes that evening was very impressive. As a newcomer, he had a comparatively humble place in the running order, appearing early in the bill.

The show opened with The Sunshine Babes from a local dancing school, and they were followed by a young couple who produced musical sounds from a bizarre collection of instruments, including handbells and musical glasses; the young lady rubbed her finger round the rim of eight glasses filled to different depths with coloured liquids, conjuring up some haunting bell-like notes. Finally her partner whistled *Humoresque* while she accompanied him with a violin bow on the blade of an ordinary saw, gripped between her knees.

The audience in the Crystal Palace Theatre was enthralled, and for an encore the two artistes played *Killarney* on penny-whistles and danced an Irish jig at the same time.

In the auditorium, Daphne was not enjoying the show. This would be the first time she had seen Ted perform in public, and she was sick with nerves. She felt as though she would soon be stepping out on to the stage herself – her stomach turned to lead at the thought.

To polite applause, Ted Watkins strolled on and introduced himself. He told the ladies they were a very handsome lot – then added that he had to say that because he'd probably be running into them all tomorrow morning, going round the shops. He admitted he was a local lad, born and brought up in Norwood – and they welcomed him with a delighted roar as one of their own. Effortlessly, he began to weave his web of stories, sliding from one ridiculous tale to another, inviting them to enter his world of comic fantasy – and they followed him willingly.

There was no doubt that he was a big hit, but even then Daphne could not relax. When he disappeared in a storm of applause, she breathed a sigh of relief, wiping the palms of her hands on her handkerchief. Why couldn't she just sit back and enjoy his performance, like everyone else? She would never know the answer to that – she never dared tell him how much she suffered, each time he walked out on a stage.

The other members of the family were loud in their approval, and when the lights went up, Muriel patted Daphne's hand. 'Edward was very good, dear, and perfectly respectable. I shall tell him so. He's done nothing he need be ashamed of.'

In the interval, Gerald offered to fetch ice-creams for the ladies, while Ray nudged Steve and said, 'How about you'n me nipping out to the bar for a pint?'

Steve looked at Val, who said, 'I'll stay here and have an ice. Don't be too long, will you? They ring a bell when it's time to come back.'

The bar was crowded, thick with smoke and raucous with noisy chatter. There were very few ladies to be seen, and if Muriel had been there, she would have described those present as 'very unladylike'.

In these predominantly masculine surroundings, Steve pushed his way through to a quiet corner, where Ray had bagged a table, without spilling a drop from the two pint mugs he was carrying.

'Well done, old man – bottoms up!' said Ray. After his first gulp of beer, he began: 'I've been thinking about what you were telling me the other day – about needing to raise a bit of cash, to get spliced – and I've got an idea. I wonder if you'd be interested in coming in on it with me?'

Steve was puzzled; Ray had never been particularly friendly until now.

'What sort of idea?' he asked. 'And why me?'

'Well, seeing Babs is Valerie's sister-in-law, it seems like we might be related by marriage, one of these days. I believe in keeping this sort of thing in the family, don't you?'

Steve shrugged. 'What have you got in mind, exactly?'

'I'd sooner not go into details; I'm still working on it. But one thing I do know – I'm going to need a car. Trouble is, I don't drive. Mr Wright's keen for me to learn – he says he's going to teach me, but that won't happen overnight, will it? I need someone to drive me now. Well, next Friday, to be exact.'

'I haven't got a car,' said Steve. 'Only the motorbike.'

'That's no good – I need a fast car. You could get hold of one, couldn't you? Borrow one from the workshop for half an hour?'

'I dunno . . . I'm not supposed to drive customers' cars.'

'You have to take 'em out on a test run when you do a repair job, don't you? Before you deliver them to the customers?'

'Yes, I suppose so, but . . . what time of day were you thinking of?'

'Half-past two, after all the others come back from the pub. I thought that'd suit both of us, seeing we take a late dinner-hour.'

'How far would we have to go?'

'Only to Penge. It'll only take half an hour. Are you interested?'

'I might be,' said Steve cautiously. The interval bell shrilled, and he stood up. 'Let's talk about it later – the second half's starting.'

But Ray stayed where he was. 'I'd sooner talk now – we might not get another chance on our own like this. What's it matter if we're a few minutes late going back? These old-fashioned turns give me the pip. I'd sooner go to the flicks any day . . . Sit yourself down – what do you say to another drink? On me this time.'

Steve allowed himself to be persuaded. Over the second beer he said, 'You still haven't told me what it's about. How do we make our money?'

Ray tapped the side of his nose. 'You leave that to me. I'll pay you a fair whack if you get me there and back – that's all you need bother about.'

'But I've got to know what I'm letting myself in for.'

'You're going to be my chauffeur for half an hour, that's all – and I'll give you a very generous tip! How does a tenner appeal to you?'

'Ten quid?' Steve's eyes widened; he hadn't been expecting anything like that for half an hour's work. 'It sounds OK, but I wouldn't want to get mixed up in anything – you know, not quite right . . .'

Ray laughed. 'Don't trouble yourself about that. Keep your mind on that ten quid – and no questions asked! What d'you say – yes or no?'

Steve realised there must be something shady about the proposition, to make Ray so secretive, but the idea of ten pounds in his pocket seemed to bring his wedding day that much nearer – and that would please Valerie.

There didn't seem to be any harm in driving Ray to Penge. After all, if someone hired a taxi, the cab-driver didn't ask what his passenger was doing at the end of the journey, did he?

'All right. Half-past two, Friday. I'll have a car for you.'

They shook hands on it and finished their drinks, then went back into the theatre, treading on people's toes as they squeezed along the row, murmuring, 'Sorry. 'Scuse me – sorry. Beg pardon – sorry . . .'

The programme ended with two star performers. Miss Florrie Ford came on, leading the audience through a medley of old favourites like *Down At The Old Bull And Bush, Hello, Hello, Who's Your Lady-Friend?* and *Oh, Oh, Antonio.*

Florrie was florid, fair, and – though nobody could call her fat – generously proportioned. The audience sang and applauded lustily, but they reached still greater heights of enthusiasm when the last artiste came on: the 'Prime Minister of Mirth' – Mr George Robey.

In the collarless jacket that was his trademark, with the little bowler and those thick black eyebrows raised in an expression of permanently shocked surprise, he sang a couple of comic songs, finishing with: *I Stopped – And I Looked – And I Listened*, rolling out the naughtily suggestive lyrics in a fruity, upper-class voice that dared the audience to misinterpret them. At every big laugh, he would pause in pained dismay, saying sternly: 'Desist, if you please – kindly desist!' Or, when he felt they had really gone too far, the magisterial reproof: 'I'm *surprised* at you. I didn't come here to be laughed at!'

Daphne wasn't sure if her mother would like this, but when she looked along the row she saw that Muriel was weeping with laughter. At last Robey beckoned Florrie Ford to join him in a duet which was not saucy at all but openly and shamelessly sentimental – a final chorus of his most popular song:

> *'If you were the only girl in the world
> And I were the only boy . . .'*

Afterwards, when the applause finally died away, the family picked up their hats and coats and waited for Ted to come round from the dressing room to meet them. He had taken off his make-up in a hurry, and Daphne noticed he still had a smudge of highly coloured greasepaint at his temples, and a heavy black rim under his eyelashes.

She kissed him. 'You were marvellous,' she said tenderly. 'The whole show was marvellous. We all enjoyed it.'

Ted kissed Val too, and Babs gave him a swift peck on the cheek. He shook hands with the Aunts and with Gerald – then he reached his mother-in-law, still sitting regally at the end of the row of seats.

She held out both hands to him, drawing his face down to her for a kiss. 'I must congratulate you on a most enjoyable evening,' she said. 'And with such excellent colleagues, too. Miss Ford has a very powerful voice, of course, though she is rather too much the rough diamond for my taste – but Mr Robey is quite splendid . . . Of course, he's a real gentleman – his brother is a High Court Judge, I believe. There's no disguising quality like that, is there? But you were very good too, Edward. I was pleasantly surprised. I can't understand why you go on performing in suburban theatres and open-air bandstands – you really should go straight to the Palladium, my dear. You must see the manager there, and insist that he puts you in a concert as soon as possible.'

Ted managed to keep a straight face. 'I'll try that,' he said solemnly. 'And I'll let you know what sort of answer I get – if it's repeatable.'

Later that night, Harry Glynn left his bed and pulled on a ragged old dressing gown, sticking his feet into a pair of carpet slippers with holes in the toes.

He couldn't sleep; he was worried about his landlady, and wondered if she were sickening for something. She had been behaving strangely all day – closing up the fortune-telling booth in the middle of a Bank Holiday afternoon, then taking herself off to her room as soon as they got home. Clearly, she was upset about something, but she wouldn't tell him what was wrong.

She had gone to bed without any supper, and he had been forced to make himself some cheese on toast. It gave him indigestion, and when he went to bed himself, he had been unable to sleep.

Shuffling quietly across the landing, so as not to wake the other lodgers, he turned the handle of Miss Preece's door. It was locked – and that was unusual, too. She must have been awake, because when he knocked softly, she said at once: 'Who's there?'

'It's me – Harry. I want to talk to you. What's wrong?'

'I told you, nothing's wrong. I just want to be left in peace.'

'I know something's up – you might as well tell me. Unlock this door.'

'Certainly not! Go back to bed – you'll disturb the whole house.'

'Tell me what's bothering you, and I'll go.'

'I don't want to talk to you, that's all. I just want to be by myself, to think things over.'

'What sort of things?'

A tiny pause – and then he caught her reply, so quiet, he could hardly make out the words. 'The usual things – a matter of life and death, that's all. Good night, Mr Glynn.'

And she refused to say another word.

'Auntie Eth?' Gerald put his head round the office door. 'It's nearly twenty to three.'

It was Friday afternoon. By midday on a Friday, Ethel DeWitt always had the Estate Agency's accounts made up, and the books balanced.

'Dear me, is it that late?' She lifted her beady eyes from the columns of figures in her ledger. 'I've been chasing a missing half-crown that's hidden itself. Someone's made a mistake, and it certainly wasn't me!'

'You'd better buck up, or you'll miss the bank,' Gerald warned her.

'Don't worry, I'll be there in five minutes.'

He helped her into her coat and she pulled on a shapeless felt hat. It was slightly askew, but she didn't bother to look in the mirror. She had long since given up bothering about her personal appearance.

At fifty-nine years of age, Ethel hardly ever thought of herself as a woman. She was just a person – gender was irrelevant. She took pride in herself as an efficient book-keeper, and one of the family's breadwinners; it was her meticulous accounting and her professional efficiency that marked her out, not her sex.

Picking up the leather bag, she said to her nephew, 'I'll be as quick as I can, but don't let anyone touch the cash entry slips. Leave them as they are – I'll find that half-crown when I get back.'

Then she set off, through the front office and into the street, turning right and right again, on her way to the bank. It was a journey she had made every Friday for twenty-odd years; she could have walked there in her sleep. Slightly flustered, she scolded herself for not having kept an eye on the time. The bank shut its doors at three o'clock sharp – whatever happened, she mustn't be late. People said you could set your watch by Ethel DeWitt.

She quickened her pace as she entered the alley that led through to the High Street. The bag seemed heavier than usual, but then they'd had a very good week. Deposits had been put down on several properties, in addition to the usual weekly payments for rented accommodation. Most were paid in cash, and a good many of them were in coin.

The twitten, as local people called it, was a narrow, dog-legged passage with a sharp bend at the halfway point. At this time of day, it was generally deserted, and Ethel was surprised when she turned the corner to find a man in the shadow of the wall, his hands up to his head. For a moment she thought he was about to raise his hat, and felt he must be someone she knew – then she realised that he was tying a scarf around the lower part of his face.

Ray's fingers slipped as he fumbled with the knot. The silly bitch was walking so fast, she'd taken him off-guard. Well, that would have to do. He stepped forward, blocking her path, and grabbed the leather bag.

'Let go!' she squawked. 'Let go this minute, do you hear?'

Ray hadn't expected her to resist. He thought she would be so frightened she would let go of the bag at once, like that other old biddy, long ago – but Ethel hung on stubbornly and began to call out in a high, piercing tone: '*Help! Police! Help me!*'

Ray tugged harder, beginning to panic. Stupid old woman! Why didn't she let go? And why the hell couldn't she stop yelling?

He pulled hard, wrenching the bag from her hands, and staggered back. The sudden movement loosened the scarf, which slipped – and although the brim of his hat was pulled well down, he saw the recognition in her eyes.

Wielding the heavy bag like a weapon, he swung it high, beating her about the head again and again. She uttered a hoarse cry and collapsed under the rain of blows. He heard the crack as her skull struck the cobblestones, then she lay still, with her eyes closed.

There was a moment of silence, broken only by a rasping noise that he gradually realised was the sound of his own breathing – shallow and frantic – and he began to run.

At the far end of the twitten, on the corner of Penge High Street, Steve sat in the car and waited. He heard the sound of running feet, and glanced over his shoulder. When he saw Ray racing towards him, he leaned over to open the passenger door; he guessed that something had gone badly wrong.

'What's up?' he began, as Ray scrambled into the car.

'Shut up!' panted Ray. 'Just drive, will you? Go on – fast!'

The engine roared into life, and the car leaped forward. 'Where to?' Steve asked. 'Back to the garage?'

'Don't be so bloody stupid. Get away from here – anywhere!'

'What's happened?' Steve was unable to make any sense of all this. 'Where did you get the bag? What's it got in it?'

'Never you mind – I got to think.'

Ray found it hard to marshal his thoughts. He kept remembering the way the old girl had looked, lying there on the ground – and the sickening noise her head had made when it hit the stones. He felt sure she was dead. What the hell was he going to do?

They drove in silence for a while, until Steve said: 'Look, we can't keep driving round like this. If we don't get back to work pretty sharpish, there'll be trouble.'

'Yeah.' Ray made up his mind. 'OK – let's go back. And for Christ's sake don't say a blind word about this. You ain't seen nothing – you don't know nothing!'

'That's true enough.' Steve was far from happy about the situation, but he swung the wheel and turned the car back towards Anerley and Wright's Motors.

They got back in record time, and Ray put the leather bag inside his locker in the staff washroom, before smoothing down his hair and going into the saleroom.

Luck was with him. Mr Wright was occupied with a customer, and nobody seemed to notice he was a few minutes late back. He began to breathe more easily. Maybe it was going to be all right, after all.

At the end of the afternoon, Ray hung back until everyone else had been to the staff-room. As soon as he was sure he wouldn't be disturbed, he went to his locker, then shut himself up in the toilet cubicle to examine the leather bag. It had a brass fastening, which was locked; he pulled out a pocket-knife and prised the lock open.

To his disappointment, the bag contained more cheques than cash. He put these back, and counted the rest. It came to nearly three hundred pounds altogether, in coins and banknotes. Ah well, it wasn't a bad haul. He stowed the money away carefully in his pockets, then put on his hat, coat and scarf, tucked the bag under his coat, and left the building.

He was disconcerted to find Steve outside, waiting for him.

'Don't be stupid,' he said out of the corner of his mouth, walking on without slackening his pace. 'We mustn't be seen together – it's too risky.'

'But we've got to talk,' Steve began urgently. 'You've got to come clean with me. What's this all about?'

'The less you know, the better. Just keep out of my way for the next few days – understand? I'll settle up later.'

With that, he turned the corner of the street, hoping that Steve wouldn't lose his nerve and start shooting his mouth off. This wasn't his usual route; he was going to Belmont by way of Penge. Remembering how he had taken the phoney brooch back to Mrs Glynn, he had worked out what seemed to be a foolproof plan.

When he let himself in at the front door, Babs was coming downstairs. She ran down the last few steps, holding out her arms to him as if she were seeking comfort.

'Oh Ray, something dreadful's happened,' she exclaimed, 'and you're so much later than usual!'

'Yes, I had to stay on a bit at work.' About to put his arms round her, he put down the leather bag – and her face changed.

'That's Aunt Ethel's bag,' she said. 'Where did you get it?'

'So it *is* hers – I thought so.' It was a relief to be able to rattle off the story he had worked out on his way home. 'I found it in the street, in the gutter. I came home through Penge; matter of fact, I was hoping the florists would still be open, 'cos I wanted to buy you some flowers, only by the time I got there the damn shop was shut . . . Anyhow, I was coming along the High Street when I noticed the bag. I knew I'd seen it before – she often brings it home on Fridays after work, doesn't she? – so I picked it up to be on the safe side, and brought it with me. Good job I spotted it. I'll just pop up and give it to her—'

'You can't – she's not there.'

Babs took him upstairs, explaining how Gerald had come home early, to break the bad news. Apparently poor Auntie Eth had gone to the bank after lunch as usual, and when she didn't return, they were worried about her. Then a policeman arrived, saying that Miss DeWitt had been found in a nearby alley. She'd been taken to the Norwood and District Hospital and—

Ray broke in sharply. 'The hospital? You mean – she's not dead?'

'No, but her skull's fractured, and it's touch and go whether she'll recover. Ray, are you all right?'

He had changed colour, and was swaying slightly, but he fought to keep his voice steady as he replied. 'I'm OK. I thought you meant she was dead when they found her.'

'No. There's still hope, thank goodness. We're waiting for news.

You'd better come and see Mummy; you can imagine what a state she's in. Gerry and Auntie Ag are with her, but she's terribly upset.'

'Yeah, of course. Well, I can give the bag to Gerry. He'll be able to take it back to the office.'

They went into the drawing room, and Ray had to tell his story again. On seeing the leather bag, Muriel burst into tears, and Aggie fluttered round with handkerchiefs and smelling-salts. Ray tried to pass the bag over, but Gerald refused to take it.

'You'll have to hand it in at the police station,' he said. 'I won't touch it – it might have fingerprints on it.'

'Oh, d'you think so?' Ray looked taken aback. 'I hadn't thought of that. I wiped it when I picked it up, 'cos it had some mud on it . . . I s'pose it'll have *my* fingerprints all over it now.'

'All you've got to do is tell them where you found it,' Gerry said. 'It will be needed as evidence. You might even be called as a witness.'

'You mean, if they catch the thief?' Babs asked.

Gerry threw a sidelong glance at his mother. 'Or if – you know what I mean – if anything should happen to Auntie Eth.'

This brought on another flood of Muriel's tears, and Gerry tried to calm her down, telling Ray, 'You'd better nip round to the station as soon as poss. They'll need all the information they can get.'

Ray was reluctant to visit the police station, but could find no good reason to refuse. He turned to Babs. 'You wouldn't come with me, would you? I'll feel a bit awkward on my own – I shan't know what to say.'

'Just tell them what you told us,' she said. 'I'll come with you if you like – wait till I get my things on.'

But there was no need to go to the police. While Ray waited for Babs, the doorbell clanged, and a few moments later she returned, followed by a uniformed police sergeant.

'Mummy, this is Sergeant—I'm sorry, I've forgotten your name?'

'Anderson, Miss.'

'Sergeant Anderson, of course. He's got some good news for us.'

The sergeant cleared his throat and reported that he had been at Miss DeWitt's when the lady regained consciousness. She was still in a serious condition, but the doctor said he had every reason to hope she would make a good recovery.

Ray blurted out, 'Did she – did she say anything?'

The sergeant turned and looked at him. 'Just a few words . . . Might I ask your name, sir? Are you a member of the family?'

Babs introduced Ray, explaining that he was a guest in the house, and adding: 'Funnily enough, we were just on our way to the police station, so you've saved us a journey. Give Sergeant Anderson the bag, Ray.'

Ray handed it over, mumbling something about picking it up in the street on his way home. The sergeant looked inside the bag, then said, 'I shall have to ask you to accompany me to the station, Mr Duke. We shall require you to make a statement, describing exactly when and where you came across this article.'

'But I've told you already,' Ray protested. 'I don't know anything.'

'You may be able to help us in the investigation, sir,' continued the officer. He looked Ray up and down, then asked: 'Would you be good enough to turn out your pockets, sir? Everything you're carrying – on this table, if you please.'

Ray was about to argue, but something in the sergeant's manner stopped him. Slowly, he did as he was told. On the table, a pathetic pile of objects mounted: a grubby handkerchief, a crumpled cigarette packet, a matchbox, a penknife and handfuls of coins – coppers and silver, and several golden guineas. Then, reluctantly, he pulled out a thick wad of banknotes.

'May I ask where you got this money, sir?' asked Sergeant Anderson.

'I went to the bank, dinner-time. I was drawing out my savings.'

'But you told us you had no money—' Muriel began reproachfully, until a look from Gerald silenced her.

'I take it you were wearing these same clothes, earlier in the day?' the sergeant went on.

'I'm not sure. I can't remember—' Ray began to stammer. 'Look here, I – I'm a bit tired – I've had a busy day. I'll come round to the police station presently.'

'No sir, I'd like you to come with me right away, please.'

'I keep telling you – I don't know nothing—'

'I'm sorry, Mr Duke, I must insist. We have an eye-witness who saw a young man running out of the alley immediately after the incident, answering to your description. He jumped into a car and drove off.'

The family stared at Ray. He tried to laugh, without success. 'This is bloody silly – they've got me mixed up with someone else. I've never driven a car in my life. It couldn't have been me!'

'I didn't say you were the driver, Mr Duke; you were the passenger. But I must ask you to tell me the driver's name.'

Ray's face, shining with sweat, took on a hunted expression and his mouth worked several times, soundlessly, before he managed to say: 'It was Steve – Steve Gunn. He works at the garage . . . It was his idea in the first place – he talked me into it.'

Chapter Ten

IT WAS VERY quiet in the flat above the greengrocery shop. The only sounds were the rustle of Alfred's evening paper, and the clicking of Freda's knitting needles. Occasionally Grandad would stir in his sleep and mutter something unintelligible. At the centre table, Steve and Tony were playing a game of Snakes and Ladders; the dice rattled in the eggcup, and Tony repeated under his breath: 'One, two, three, four,' as he moved his counter over the correct number of squares.

This peaceful scene was broken by the sound of the bell at the side door, downstairs. Freda looked up. 'Who can that be?'

Alf cocked an eye above the top of his newspaper. 'Could be somebody for you, Steve. Valerie, perhaps?'

'She didn't say she was coming round tonight.' Steve rolled the dice. 'Two . . .' He moved his counter on two squares, landing on a winding serpent that took him back down, almost to square one. 'That's a fat lot of help.'

The bell rang again, and old Jack Gunn opened his eyes. 'What's that? Is it time to get up?'

'It's the door, Grandad!' Freda told him loudly. 'Tony – run down and see who it is.'

'Mum!' he protested. 'We're in the middle of a game, and it's my go!'

'Well, I'm turning a heel; this sock might come out a funny shape.' She looked pointedly at her husband. '*Somebody's* got to answer it . . .'

Wearily, Alf put aside his paper and left the room. Tony threw the dice again, and exclaimed: 'It's a six – I'm going up a ladder!'

'Ssh! I'm trying to hear.' Freda listened to the low rumble of men's voices on the floor below, then footsteps climbing the stairs. Alf returned, followed by two men – a uniformed police constable and a man in a raincoat.

'It's the police,' said Alf. 'They want to talk to Steve.'

Steve looked up: 'Me?'

Tony stared at the strangers, gazing from one face to the other. Grandad, wide awake by now, asked: 'Have we got visitors?'

The plain-clothes inspector introduced himself, then glanced at Tony and asked: 'Is there another room we could use, Mr Gunn? It might make things easier.'

Slowly, Steve rose to his feet, but Freda interrupted. Dropping her knitting, she went straight to the inspector, saying angrily: 'What d'you think you're up to? Walking in here as if you owned the place . . . If you've got something to say to my son, you can say it in front of us. We've got no secrets.'

'I thought you might prefer this young man to be out of the way.' The inspector nodded in Tony's direction.

'Tony – into the kitchen,' Alfred said heavily. 'Quick march, and no arguing.'

Fearfully, the boy obeyed. As soon as the door closed behind him, the inspector turned to Steve. 'You are Mr Steven Gunn?'

'Yes. What's this all about?'

'I have to ask you – where were you at two fifty-three this afternoon?'

Steve's expression changed. 'So that's it,' he said. 'It's to do with the car, is it?'

Freda broke in again. 'What car? What are you talking about?'

'If you don't mind, Mrs Gunn . . .' The inspector did not speak in a loud or threatening tone, but his look reduced her to silence. Then he addressed Steve again. 'Were you driving a black sports car – with the registration number BG 177?'

'That's right,' said Steve.

'I must ask you to accompany me to the police station, sir. You may bring a bag with a spare shirt, socks, and a change of underclothes.'

Now it was Alf's turn to interrupt. 'What's going on?'

'I'm sorry, sir – I think your son understands. Steven Gunn, you are not obliged to say anything, but I must warn you that anything you say will be taken down and may be later used in evidence.'

'No, this isn't right! Stop them, Alfred!' Freda tried to intervene, but her husband held her back.

Steve's voice was not much more than a whisper as he said, 'Don't worry, Mum. I'll just up and get my things.' When he left the room, the constable went with him.

Grandad struggled out of his chair. 'Did he say something about an arrest? What's the boy done?'

'Nothing, Grandad. It's a mistake,' said Freda fiercely.

The kitchen door opened, and Tony stood there, his eyes wide with shock. 'It's not true, is it, Mum? You won't let them take him away, will you?'

With his arm around Freda, Alf answered for her. 'They just want to ask Steve some questions, son. Nothing for you to bother about – and you shouldn't go listening at keyholes, neither.'

'Why are they taking him in?' Grandad wanted to know. 'What's it all about, eh?'

'Not now, Dad – we'll talk about it presently. Why don't you go upstairs and have a lie-down?'

Muttering to himself, old Jack took himself off, huffing and puffing as he made his way up to the top floor. A moment later, Steve came back with the constable, carrying his case.

'I'm ready now.' He kissed his mother, and put his hand on his father's shoulder. 'It'll sort itself out – don't worry.' He turned to Tony. 'See you soon, Tone. Oh – Valerie will have to know about this. Will you tell her for me?'

The constable held the door open, and they took Steve downstairs. The front door banged, and the police car drove off.

'I could go and tell Valerie now, couldn't I?' Tony said in a small voice. 'I know where she lives – Sackville Road.'

'No.' His mother shook her head. 'You're not to tell her – we're not telling anybody. It's a mistake.'

'But Steve said—'

'It's just a mistake, that's all. Now be a good boy and get on with whatever you were doing. It'll be all right.'

'I can't play Snakes and Ladders by myself!' he burst out, with a sob in his voice. 'Why did they have to take him away? When I was winning, too.'

The tears rolled down his cheeks as he packed up the board and put the coloured counters back in the box. A strain of music floated down from the top floor; Grandad was trying to comfort himself with an old favourite. They all remembered the familiar words:

> *Oh, God, our help in ages past*
> *Our hope for years to come . . .*

*

That evening, there was a film show on at the Palace in the small cinema. As they were short-staffed again, Valerie was helping out as an usherette, showing the audience to their seats. When they had taken their places, she closed the doors and went across to the lady in the Box Office.

'Will you be needing me any more tonight?' she asked.

'No thanks, dear. I've only got to cash up, then I'll be off home myself. Thanks for your help – I hope it didn't spoil your evening?'

'No, I wasn't doing anything special. I'm going home to wash my hair and have an early night. My friend's taking me out tomorrow.'

As she began to put on her coat, the cashier said, 'Excuse me for asking, but I don't think I've seen you in that dress before, have I? Is it new?'

Valerie hesitated for a split second before answering. 'It was made for me by a lady I know.'

'Ah . . . I thought it didn't look like one you got from a shop.' The cashier tried to find something complimentary to say, and finally hit upon: 'Nice bright colours . . .'

Val made her way out of the building. It was coming on to rain, and she wished she'd brought her umbrella. At the top of Anerley Hill, it was pelting down so hard, she stopped under a shop awning. Two middle-aged women were already sheltering there; she knew them by sight, and listened idly to their conversation.

'. . . I saw the car waiting outside the shop – two policemen, there were. They arrested him in the flat upstairs, and took him off with them.'

'Whatever had he done?'

'I couldn't say for sure, but I heard somebody say it was murder – or attempted murder. Mind you, it's his mother I feel sorry for.'

'That poor woman. What she must be suffering . . .' Then she noticed Valerie, and nudged her friend. They both stopped talking, exchanging a meaning look.

Val couldn't understand it. Surely they weren't still going on about Mrs Bywaters' son? But Freddy Bywaters wasn't arrested in his mother's flat . . . It had been a great sensation at the time, but that was months ago and he'd been hanged for murder – there was no doubt about it.

Aware that the women were still staring at her, she felt suddenly uncomfortable. As the rain seemed to be easing off, she decided to brave it, and hurried down the hill. When she got home, she ran down to the basement, pulling off her mac and calling, 'It's coming down cats and dogs! I tried to run between the drops, but I'll have to dry my coat in front of the—'

Entering the kitchen, she stopped short. Babs was there, talking to Daphne, and as they turned towards her, she felt afraid. They were looking at her like the two women up the hill – half-embarrassed, half-pitying.

'Hello, Babs,' she said uncertainly. 'This is a surprise.'

Daphne tried to smile. 'Babs called round to see you. I said you might be rather late, but she decided to wait anyway.'

'Why? What's the matter?'

Daphne took Val's mackintosh from her and spread it out on a clothes-horse in front of the kitchen range, where it began to steam gently.

'I've got something to tell you,' Babs said. 'It's about Steve.'

Daphne broke in, saying to Val, 'I'm going to sit with your Mum for a while. I'll leave Babs to explain.' On her way to the door, she put her arms round Val and hugged her, before leaving the room.

'Something about Steve?' Val turned to Babs. 'Is he ill? Has there been an accident?'

Babs told her as much as she knew – and what she didn't know, she guessed. Valerie groped blindly for a kitchen chair and sank into it. When Babs had finished she said in a shaky voice, 'In a way, I knew already. I heard two women gossiping – they said somebody had been arrested, and I thought they were talking about Bywaters again. They said something about murder – but your Auntie's going to be all right, isn't she?'

'That's what they said at the hospital, but it was touch and go. She could have been killed. It's no thanks to those brutes that she wasn't.'

'But Steve's not like that! He'd never do such a thing!'

'How do you know? I didn't think Ray was like that, either. Wicked – that's what they are. Thank God we found out before it was too late.'

Val screwed up her eyes, finding it hard to focus on Babs. 'What do you mean, too late?'

'Ray wanted to marry me. And you and Steve were planning to get married too, weren't you? We've had a lucky escape.'

'No!' Val shrank back. 'No, I can't believe it – not Steve.'

'You've got to face the facts. They're two of a kind; they must have been planning this for ages – plotting it together.'

'But Steve didn't even like Ray. He told me so!'

'Don't you see? That was part of the scheme, to stop us getting suspicious. They pretended they didn't get on, and all the time they were working it out – laughing at us behind our backs.' As Babs grew angrier, her voice rose. 'And we believed them! Serves us right for being so stupid.'

Val sat quite still, staring at nothing. She could see nothing now but deception and pretence and bitter disillusion.

'I trusted Steve,' she said slowly. 'I thought I knew what sort of person he was, but he wasn't real . . . None of it was real.'

Was this what they meant by heartbreak, she wondered? But she didn't feel any pain; she felt nothing but blankness – a great emptiness. In a moment, part of her life had been taken from her – gone for ever, leaving nothing in its place.

'Are you all right?' Babs asked her.

'Yes, I'm all right.'

'Well, you don't look it.' Babs peered at her more closely. 'It's probably that awful dress. I don't know why you go on wearing it.'

'I don't know either.' Slowly, Val stood up. 'You're quite right – I won't wear it again.'

Once a month, Mr Colpoys called round to visit Mrs Watkins. It had become a regular event – on the second Sunday, he came to tea, and Kate made him a special cake.

This week, she was full of the shocking news about the attack on Daphne's Auntie, and how Valerie's young man had turned out to be a thorough bad lot, along with their ex-lodger.

'I believe you met him once – young Mr Duke? It makes my blood run cold to think of him living here. We might all have been murdered in our beds . . . Well, they're both locked up now, waiting till the case goes to court. It's been a dreadful blow for Val, I can tell you.'

'I'm sorry to hear that.' Mr Colpoys polished his pince-nez, and replaced them carefully on his nose. 'But I can't say I'm surprised. There's so much crime and violence about. Youngsters have no moral fibre nowadays.'

'I expect it's the war,' said Kate, cutting a slice of home-made Madeira. 'When they were growing up, their fathers were off in France, fighting – and so many of them never came back. It must make a difference.'

'It seems to me that's all the more reason why this modern generation should have some respect for law and order. They ought to look back to those brave men who gave their lives for our country, and try to be worthy of their glorious memory.'

His voice trembled a little; too late, Kate remembered that he always got upset when the war was mentioned.

'Have a slice of Madeira,' she said. 'I want you to give me your honest opinion. I put a little grated lemon-peel in the mixture, for a change, so you must tell me what you think.'

Mr Colpoys sampled the cake thoughtfully, then relaxed into a smile. 'Better than ever, dear lady. You've surpassed yourself.'

Outside, the sun broke through the clouds, and the sitting room was suddenly filled with light.

It was a typical April day. Walking slowly up Anerley Hill, Harry Glynn glanced at the clouds and wondered if he had been rash to come out in such uncertain weather. If the rain brought on his arthritis again, his hands might be too painful to hold a brush, and he had to finish his latest painting – spring flowerbeds in Kelsey Park – and sell it damn soon, or he wouldn't be able to pay this month's rent. He still owed Miss Preece for last month.

Not that she had said anything about that. She seemed to be avoiding him, which wasn't like her at all.

He had been racking his brains to think what he could have done to annoy her, but he couldn't remember anything in particular. It wasn't like the time she caught him undressing the silly girl who'd been modelling for the Roman slave . . . He'd explained he was only adjusting her toga, but Miss Preece didn't believe him. And he'd been very good about not smoking his pipe in bed too, ever since he set fire to the sheets, so it couldn't be that.

But there was a definite coolness between them, and it was very unsettling. He missed their little chats together – especially the cosy talks they used to have sometimes in her bedroom, late at night, lying there in the darkness . . . Absorbed in these reflections, he crossed the road without looking where he was going.

He walked straight into a boy on a bike, freewheeling down the hill. The cycle went over with a crash, its wheels spinning in the air, and the boy picked himself up, unhurt but highly indignant, telling Harry to keep his perishing eyes skinned another time! Bruised and battered, Harry scrambled to his feet, finding a three-cornered tear in his left trouser-leg. His knee was painful; he had a nasty graze, oozing blood.

He had intended to walk up to Crystal Palace Parade, but now he changed his mind. Sackville Road was just round the corner – he would drop in on Daphne instead and ask for first aid, running repairs and, if possible, a little refreshment.

Arriving at Number 37, he hobbled up the front steps and rang the bell.

Kate opened the door. She began to explain – Ted and Daphne had gone out for a Sunday-afternoon walk with Annie.

Harry grimaced. 'Just my luck. I was involved in a small catastrophe – d'you mind if I come in and sit down for a few moments?'

Glancing down, Kate exclaimed, 'Oh dear, you're bleeding! Whatever's happened?'

While he explained, she took charge of the situation, helping him down the stairs, fetching her dressing gown and a spare pair of trousers, and telling him to get undressed while she boiled a kettle. In passing, she looked into the sitting room, asking Mr Colpoys to excuse her for a few minutes, as she was dealing with an emergency, then returned to the kitchen.

She found Harry sitting by the fire, his bony knees sticking out of the floral-patterned dressing gown, not in the least embarrassed. He winced once or twice while Kate bathed his knee and dabbed some iodine on the graze; then she offered him the spare pair of trousers.

'You'd better slip these on – they belonged to Mr Watkins. I don't know why I've kept them, really. They should have gone to the Church jumble – and they're too big for Ted. Still, they'll come in useful now. You can't go home in those. Have you got someone who can mend them for you?'

'As a rule, my landlady's very good about things like that,' Harry said, 'but she's not been quite herself lately . . . However, I dare say I could manage it. Can you lend me a needle and thread?' He looked at Kate hopefully, and she sighed.

'You'd better leave them. I'll see to it . . . How are you feeling? Do you need any help, or can you manage to get into these trousers by yourself?' She held them out and he struggled to his feet, beginning to unfasten the dressing gown.

In the doorway, Mr Colpoys cleared his throat, saying with dismay, 'I beg your pardon. I came down to enquire if I could be of any assistance. Please excuse me—'

Kate began hastily, 'Oh no, thank you, we can manage. Let me introduce you. Mr Colpoys – Mr Glynn.'

Still trouserless, with the flowered dressing gown flapping round his knees, Harry hobbled across to shake Mr Colpoys by the hand, saying heartily, 'You see before you the victim of a minor traffic accident, sir, and this good lady's son is married to my daughter. We are related by marriage, in a manner of speaking. Despite appearances, I assure you there has been no impropriety of any kind.'

Suddenly the situation struck Kate as so absurd, she started to giggle. Blushing, Mr Colpoys retreated to the sitting room above, and resumed his tea, but somehow, the lemon Madeira cake didn't taste quite the same.

When the front door slammed, Muriel Glynn sat up at once and asked in an agonised whisper, 'Who's that? There's someone in the house!'

Babs tried to soothe her. 'It'll only be Aggie, back from the shops. Don't worry.'

'Are you sure? I keep thinking it might be that dreadful man again. He's still got a front-door key, you know. Suppose he walked in here? We'd be completely at his mercy!'

'Do try to calm down, Mummy. He won't come back; he's been remanded – and I'm sure he'll be sent to prison for a very long time. You mustn't upset yourself.'

A few moments later, Auntie Aggie came in, smiling brightly and carrying a heavy shopping-basket, reciting: 'Home again, home again, jiggety-jig!' She handed Babs the shopping-list and a leather purse. 'I think I got everything you wanted.'

'Oh, good. Shall we check the list together?' Babs began to tick off the items as Aggie unpacked the basket: tea, coffee, sugar, flour, lamb cutlets, tinned peaches. 'All safe and sound,' she said kindly. 'You've done very well, Auntie.'

'I try to do my best,' said Aggie, beaming with pleasure.

Babs was about to re-pack the basket when she said suddenly, 'Just a minute – there's something else here.' She pulled out a packet of birdseed, reading the label aloud: 'Chirpy-Cheeps for your canary. What's this?'

Aunt Aggie's smile faltered. 'Oh dear, how did that get in the basket?'

'I think you must have put it there, Auntie. Why did you do that?'

'I can't remember – I thought it looked rather nice. Such a pretty picture, don't you think? That dear little canary—'

'But we haven't got a canary,' Babs reminded her.

'I know, but perhaps we could buy one.' Aggie's voice trailed off. 'A surprise for poor Ethel, when she comes out of hospital.'

'Auntie, tell me the truth,' said Babs. 'Did you pay for these Chirpy-Cheeps?'

Aggie's face crumpled. 'Don't be cross with me.'

'You've done it again!' Muriel broke in, outraged. 'After all your promises, too. If you go on stealing, the police will come and take you away as well! You're no better than that horrible man – a common thief!'

Agnes began to cry – wrenching, tormented sobs, shaking her frail body. 'I didn't mean to, Mu, really I didn't! I must have picked it up by accident. I forgot to pay for it . . .'

Babs stood up. 'Don't keep on at her, Mummy, it only makes things worse. Never mind, Auntie Ag – try not to do it again. I'll take this back to the shop and explain it was a mistake. Now dry your eyes and go down to the kitchen; it's time to get the supper ready.'

Agnes was flustered and tremulous for the rest of the afternoon. Supper, when it finally arrived, was almost uneatable, and when they had cleared away, Babs suggested that her aunt might like to go to bed and have a nice rest.

Plaiting trembling fingers, Aggie asked, 'What about the washing-up?'

'Don't worry about that,' said Babs. 'Gerry can help me.'

'I say, I've been slaving away at the office all day!' her brother protested. 'I'm having to do Eth's job now, you know, as well as mine.'

'Yes, it's made extra work for all of us, but it won't kill you to wield a teacloth, will it?'

Working side by side at the kitchen sink, Babs told her brother about Auntie Ag's latest lapse.

'I'm pretty sure she didn't know she'd done it. Of course Mummy scolded her, and that finished her off – floods of tears and solemn promises never to be naughty again.'

'Poor old Aggie.' Gerald polished a dinner-plate. 'I suppose Ethel being in hospital has unsettled her. It's probably a delayed reaction.'

'Perhaps. But Mummy's right – if she goes shoplifting every time something upsets her, she'll get arrested herself one of these days.'

'Maybe we shouldn't let her go to the shops? Wouldn't she be better off at home, doing the housework?'

'But she *enjoys* shopping – and it's good for her to get out of the house sometimes. Anyway, who else is there? I've got enough on my hands as it is, taking care of Mummy, though I ought to start job-hunting again. With Ethel out of action, we're going to need another salary coming in.'

'Have you started looking through the Situations Vacant?'

'Not yet. I mentioned it to Valerie; I hoped she'd put in a word for me at the Palace, but she said they can't take on any more staff.'

'I suppose I might talk old man Hawkins into giving me a rise, now I'm doing two people's work. I'd say that deserves a bit extra, wouldn't you? Mind you, there's no knowing how long Aunt Eth's going to be off sick. Once she gets out of hospital, she'll probably want to go back to work.'

'At her age? I doubt it. Anyhow, it'll be some time before they let her out. You haven't seen her lately.'

'I thought she was making a good recovery?'

'So she is, but it's bound to take time. And when she comes home, she'll probably be like Mummy, a permanent invalid. She's still very weak.'

'Does she ever talk about what happened?' asked Gerry. 'Does she remember anything about it?'

'No. They say it's often like that after a bad shock – it seems to blot out the memory. It's funny in a way – Ray Duke confessed because he thought she'd recognised him, but she doesn't remember a thing about it.'

'Still, they've got his confession now – and there were eye-witnesses who saw them making their getaway, him and Steve Gunn. I'd say it's an open-and-shut case.'

'I hope they get life sentences,' said Babs vindictively, pouring away the washing-up water. 'Aunt Ag's not the only one suffering from after-effects. I've been to see Valerie once or twice, and she's still in a terrible state. It hit her very hard. She thought she was in love with Steve.'

'I thought you were in love with Duke, but you seem to have got over it pretty well.'

Babs repudiated this. 'I was never in love with him. He amused me for a while, but I never really fell for him – not head-over-heels, like Val. I'm worried about her, Gerry; she shouldn't have to suffer like that.'

'It's rotten bad luck she ever got mixed up with him.'

'I was thinking – couldn't you take her out once or twice, make a fuss of her? You told me once you liked her – it might make all the difference. I happen to know she rather admires you, as a matter of fact.'

'Does she, by jove?' Brightening up, Gerry stroked his moustache. 'Yes, Val's a good sort. I'll think about it.'

*

The case of the two young offenders was heard at the Central London Criminal Court some weeks later. Babs persuaded Gerry to take her to the hearing, and he asked Mr Hawkins at the Estate Agency for a day off. He hoped he might see Valerie in court, but she stayed away, trying to put the whole thing out of her mind. She wanted no more to do with Steve Gunn; she didn't want to see him ever again.

Since Ray and Steve had admitted their guilt at the preliminary hearing, the magistrates had passed them over to the Central Criminal Court for sentencing. They had spent the intervening weeks at a remand prison, but had been kept apart there, so they had no chance to confer.

When Steve was taken into the courtroom, he saw Ray for the first time since the afternoon of the crime – but Ray would not look at him.

Steve could not understand this, but then he had scarcely understood anything that had happened since he was arrested. Time had passed slowly and meaninglessly; he had been shuffled from place to place, among hostile strangers, like an awkward, unwanted parcel. He had felt cold and hungry and very unhappy, but he could blame no one but himself. He knew he had done wrong in agreeing to help Ray, and now he had to take his punishment. He hoped it would not last much longer.

Looking round the courtroom, he saw some faces he recognised in the public gallery; his father and mother were there, and his sister Julie, sitting in the front row. They smiled and waved, and he tried to smile back. In another row he caught a glimpse of Babs Glynn, together with a moustached young man he did not know . . . but he could not see the face he was looking for.

He longed for news of Val, but had heard nothing. At first he hoped she would write to him, but when no letter arrived he assumed she was not permitted to correspond with him. He searched the crowd of faces in the gallery in vain; perhaps the ordeal would have been too much for her to bear.

There was a sudden flurry of activity, as a gentleman in a black gown told them all to rise, and a very old man in a red robe and an extraordinary white wig took his place behind a desk, high up against the back wall. When the old man sat down, everyone else was allowed to sit down too.

Steve tried to concentrate on what was being said, but there were so many strangers there, saying complicated things, it was hard to make out what was going on. The police inspector who arrested him was in the witness box, answering questions about the circumstances of the crime. He discovered that Ray was being charged with robbery with violence, and he himself was charged as an accessory, aid and accomplice . . . Well, that was no more than the truth.

One after the other, two posh-sounding gentlemen asked the inspector a lot of pointless questions about the events of Friday, 6 April, 1923, when Miss Ethel DeWitt was robbed and assaulted – pointless, since they appeared to know all the answers to their questions already.

Then a doctor entered the witness box; he described in detail the number of blows Miss DeWitt had suffered, the state of her injuries, and her present medical prognosis.

The voices droned on, like flies buzzing at a windowpane. It seemed somehow dreamlike and unreal that these complete strangers should concern themselves so intimately with things that had happened weeks ago, when none of them had been anywhere near – and that these strangers should be helping the Judge to decide what would happen to Steve and Ray.

At last it was the Judge's turn, and that was even more unreal. He must have been very old, because his voice was thin and quavery. Articulating each syllable with an effort, he addressed the prisoners, asking: 'Is there anything you wish to say before I pass sentence upon you?'

Steve shook his head and muttered 'No, sir' – but suddenly Ray stood up.

'Yes, Your Lordship. If you please, I just want to tell you I wouldn't never have done it if it hadn't been for this chap Steve Gunn, Your Lordship. It was all his idea. He got it planned, and then he left me to do the dirty work while he stayed and waited in the car – and I want to say I'm truly sorry for what I done and I wish I hadn't let him talk me into it and if you give me another chance, I swear I'll never get into trouble again, so help me, God!'

Steve almost laughed – it was so ridiculous, he could hardly believe his ears – but then he realised what Ray was trying to do, and a wave of anger flooded over him; a hot, sickening rage rose like bile, nearly choking him.

'You lying sod!' he shouted, launching himself upon Ray, and the two young men grappled furiously before they were dragged apart.

'*Silence! Silence in court!*'

Strong hands grabbed Steve, twisting his arms behind his back, and he stood helpless and panting as the Judge reprimanded him for this outburst.

Then the tired, elderly voice continued: 'This court has taken pains to investigate the histories of both offenders, and I am satisfied that the facts the witnesses have presented to us are accurate in every respect. The prisoner Gunn comes from a good, respectable family, and he has no previous criminal record – which makes it all the more reprehensible that he should have transgressed in this manner. The prisoner Duke however, has no known family, having been a foundling, brought up in an orphange, and he has been in trouble as a juvenile on two previous occasions.'

In the gallery, Babs pursed her lips. So that had been another lie. Those stories about his wealthy parents in Hollywood were fairy tales. She hated herself for having been taken in by them.

The Judge's voice was becoming more and more faint, and he paused to take a sip of water from the carafe upon the desk before concluding.

'Under these circumstances, I have no alternative but to commit you, Steven Gunn, to prison for a term of three years, in the hope that this may give you pause to reflect upon the error of your ways. Raymond Duke – there is no doubt in my mind that you were the ringleader and instigator of this most unpleasant and callous crime, and I therefore commit you to prison for five years, with hard labour. You may take them down.'

There was a moment of silence, then the sound of a woman sobbing, as Freda Gunn broke down and wept on her husband's shoulder.

Steve did not look up; he could not bear to see his mother's grief. Numb with shock, all he could think was: 'Thank God Val isn't here. It would have broken her heart.'

The same evening, Gerry Glynn called at Sackville Road. Daphne opened the front door, and when she took him downstairs, he told her what had happened in court.

'So Gunn got three years and Duke got five,' he finished, 'and I can't say I'm sorry. They brought it on themselves, didn't they?'

'I know. All the same, it's a terrible thing to happen. How has Babs taken it?'

'Pretty well, considering. We must be thankful things between her and Duke never went any further. How's Valerie? Is she here?'

'No, she's working late. She offered to do some overtime, to take her mind off things. She's going through a bad patch.'

'I know. Babs said I ought to come and break the news to her.'

Daphne glanced at the clock. 'I'm expecting her back any time now. Do you want to wait?'

'Perhaps if I walk up to the Palace, I might meet her on the way?'

As he turned to go, Daphne put a hand on her brother's arm. 'Gerry – be careful how you break it to her.'

'What d'you take me for? I'm not a complete idiot.'

He walked slowly up the hill; the sun had gone down and the street-lamps had just come on. In the distance he saw Val coming towards him, moving from one little pool of lamplight to the next, in and out of the shadows.

He went up to meet her, raising his hat. 'Hello, Valerie. Daphne said I might run into you.'

She looked at him in surprise, then her face changed. 'Is it – something about Steve?' As they walked on, he took her arm; her face was in shadow again, but he could feel the tension within her, tight as a coiled spring. 'You were in court today, weren't you? With Babs?'

'Yes – she thought you'd want to know.'

'I don't want to know!' The words burst from her. 'I don't want to hear anything about him.' But her voice wavered, and she added, 'Except – just tell me – what happened to him? Was he sent to prison?'

'He was. Duke got five years – Steve Gunn got three, because he was just an accomplice.'

'I don't want to hear any more.' She gripped his arm tightly. 'Can we talk about something else, please?'

When they reached the Sackville Arms, he said, 'Come on, I'll buy you a brandy. It'll steady your nerves.'

'My nerves are quite steady, thank you,' said Val, but she let him take her into the saloon. The brandy was warming, and she began to relax.

In the public bar, someone was playing the piano – a popular song that was all the rage – *Who's Sorry Now?*

They listened for a moment, and then Valerie said, 'There's no point in being sorry. It was a bad mistake, but now it's over. I must put it behind me and start again.'

'You're very wise,' Gerry told her. 'Yes, you must look ahead, and think of other things.'

They went on chatting for a long time. Val found him easy to talk to; he was gentle and understanding. Until this evening, she had never really got to know him, though she had always thought of him as friendly and pleasant. But tonight he seemed to be something more than that.

When he left her at the front door of Number 37, he asked if she would care to go to the pictures next week. She agreed at once, and the following Saturday they went to see the new Greta Garbo film.

After that they went on meeting regularly. As spring turned to summer, and the evenings grew longer, he began to take her further afield – bus-rides into the country, or trips to the West End – they went to the theatre, applauding Jack Buchanan in *Battling Butler*, and a clever young man named Noël Coward in *London Calling*.

She looked forward to their weekly outings. One evening they went to a dance at the Trocadero, and afterwards they sat on the top deck of the bus to Crystal Palace, in the back seat; since they had been dancing together all the evening, it seemed quite natural for him to put his arm around her.

It seemed equally inevitable when he kissed her.

As soon as their lips met, she remembered Steve – so vividly, it was like a stab of pain – yet Gerry's kisses were sweet and tender, very different from the overwhelming passion she had known with Steve.

But she mustn't think of that. She would not let herself remember . . . From the day he walked out of her life, she had never cried over Steve; she had shut him out, closing the door on him and turning the key. No regrets – no tears . . . Until now.

She found she was weeping helplessly. The tears ran down her cheeks, and Gerry was kind and consoling, drying her eyes and murmuring, 'It's all right. You don't have to say anything. I understand.'

He held her in his arms until the bus reached Crystal Palace Parade, where they got off. When it drove away into the night, he continued to hold her, whispering, 'My dearest girl, I love you very much. This may not be the right time and place, but I have to ask you – will you marry me?'

BOOK TWO

1925–1928

Chapter Eleven

THE DAWN CHORUS woke Valerie. She opened her eyes and lay on her back, listening to the birds. For a moment, she did not know where she was; even after all this time, she could not get used to waking up in a different room, with the light streaming through the windows on the wrong side of the bed. Then she remembered. Of course, this was her home now.

She went on lying there, listening to the birdsong and the slow, heavy breathing of the man beside her. She guessed that he had his mouth open; the noise he was making was something between a groan and a snore.

When she turned her head, there he was on the pillow, his lips parted and the hairs on the edge of his moustache stirring with each long exhalation – dear Gerry. She wondered if he would remember what day it was.

As she studied him, he opened his eyes; their faces only a few inches apart. Drowsily smiling, he said, 'Good morning. What time is it?'

'I don't know. Early, anyway. Go back to sleep.'

He closed his eyes, burrowing deeply into the pillows. 'Good night.'

She moved closer, kissing his forehead. 'Happy anniversary,' she murmured.

He frowned. 'You what?'

'Happy anniversary,' she reminded him. 'Our first.'

'Oh, so it is. I hadn't forgotten.'

Of course he hadn't. He was such a good husband – everyone said so.

'I thought I'd take you out to supper this evening,' he went on. 'A decent meal – a bottle of bubbly. How about the dear old Troc? You'd like that, wouldn't you?'

'That would be lovely.'

Satisfied, he settled back to sleep, still smiling.

Dear Gerry – always so good to her. Some husbands never bothered about anniversaries; some men would consider it sufficient to thrust a bunch of flowers at their wives when they came home from work, before asking: 'What's for supper?' – but Gerald wasn't like that. Tonight he would take her out, dancing and dining at the Trocadero. She was a lucky girl. Looking back over the past year, Valerie could hardly believe her good luck.

She had got to know Gerry just when she needed a friend – someone to take her mind off her problems and help her forget her unhappiness. He had been a shoulder to cry on, a partner on the dance-floor, a companion on trips into the country or visits to the West End. Always there, always reliable – dear, dependable Gerry.

And when he kissed her for the first time, that was wonderful, too. He was so understanding, never demanding more than she felt able to give. It seemed extraordinary, in retrospect, that the first time he asked her to marry him, she had refused him. And the second time – and the third.

Each time she did so, she felt guilty. He was so nice, she didn't want to hurt him – but when she tried to explain, he wouldn't let her.

'No, it's too soon. I must be patient, I realise that,' he said. 'I understand exactly how you feel.'

Everyone else was sympathetic too, but they all seemed to think he was the ideal husband for Valerie. They made such a perfect couple, didn't they? Where else would she ever find such a kind, considerate man?

Babs told Val she must be mad to turn him down. 'It's a marvellous arrangement! My sister's married to your brother, now *my* brother wants to marry *you* – my best friend. You've got to change your mind and say yes – you simply must!'

Daphne and Ted also seemed to be in favour of the idea, and when Gerry came round to tea at Sackville Road, he made such a fuss of Kate – bringing her a huge bunch of tulips, and complimenting her on the home-made cake – Mrs Watkins was completely bowled over.

'Anyone can see how much he loves you,' she told Val. 'I don't know how you can refuse him. Don't you feel anything for him at all?'

'Of course I do. I feel very grateful and very flattered, and – I don't know . . .' Val shook her head, unable to define her feelings. He was everything she could possibly want in a husband – and yet . . .

She might never have made up her mind, if it hadn't been for an unexpected visitor.

One Saturday afternoon at the beginning of December, Gerry had arranged to take her up to Oxford Street to do some Christmas shopping; she had been complaining that she could never find anything in the shops at Sydenham or Penge, so he suggested they should make an expedition to Selfridges.

He promised to call for her at half-past two, and when the front-door knocker banged at twenty past, Val called out to her mother: 'He's early! It's a good job I'm all ready.' She pulled on her hat and coat and ran to open the door – then gasped, clinging on to it for support.

The young man standing outside on the top step wasn't Gerry; it was Eric Blatchley – Eric, whom she had not seen since that New Year's Eve when he sent a polite letter to explain that he would not be seeing her again as he had become engaged to someone called Brenda, whom he had met when he moved to Raynes Park.

'Hello, Valerie,' he said. 'I hoped I'd find you at home – how are you?'

She shook hands automatically, at a loss for words. 'Eric – hello. What are you doing here?'

'I happened to be in the district, so I thought I'd call on the off-chance. How have you been keeping? You're looking very well.'

'Thank you.' She struggled to think of something to say. 'I'm sorry I can't ask you in, but I'm just on my way out – Christmas shopping.'

'Oh, I see.' Eric didn't seem to be in any hurry to leave; rooted to the doorstep, he prolonged the conversation. 'How are all the family? I hope Mrs Watkins is well?'

'She's fine, thanks. And how's your – um – Brenda?'

He reddened slightly. 'Of course, you wouldn't know. That's all off – I don't see Brenda any more.'

'Oh? I thought you were engaged?'

'So we were, for nearly a year. It didn't work out, I'm afraid. In the end, she married somebody else.' Eric cleared his throat. 'That's one of the reasons I decided to look in today. If you're not too busy, I was hoping I might take you out for tea somewhere?'

She stepped back, her hand still on the door. 'Oh no, I'm sorry. I told you, I'm going shopping.'

'I could carry the parcels,' he suggested eagerly.

She thought what a silly young man he was – and how silly he looked, with those bulging eyes and sticking-out ears. How could she ever have imagined she loved him? Retreating, she was about to close the door, when Gerry appeared, looking over Eric's shoulder, and saying with a frown: 'Hello – what's going on here?'

Confused and embarrassed, Valerie felt impelled to carry the situation off calmly, and explained a little too quickly.

'I don't believe you've met. This is Eric Blatchley, who used to be a friend of mind – I mean, we worked in the same office before he moved to Raynes Park. Eric, this is Gerald Glynn—'

'How do you do?'

'Pleased to meet you.'

Awkwardly, the two men shook hands, and then to her own astonishment, Valerie heard herself saying in a clear, confident voice: 'Gerald Glynn is my fiancé. We're going to be married.'

Eric congratulated Gerry, made his excuses, and departed as quickly as possible, and Gerry, torn between amusement and delight, stepped into the hall and embraced Valerie.

'I knew it! I knew you'd see it my way, sooner or later.'

She couldn't explain; she could only apologise for taking him by surprise. 'I'm sorry,' she babbled, 'I don't know what came over me, springing it on you like that. What do we do now? I don't suppose you still feel like going Christmas shopping?'

'Christmas shopping be damned!' guffawed Gerry. 'We're going shopping for an engagement ring, before you change your mind!'

When they broke the news to their respective families, everyone was delighted at the prospect of another link between the Glynns and the Watkinses.

Kate kissed her son-in-law-to-be and said she'd felt certain from the beginning that he and Val would hit it off. She just knew they were going to be very happy.

At Belmont, the Aunts took turns to kiss Valerie, and Babs hugged her, exclaiming: 'What did I tell you? Everything turned out for the best in the end, didn't it?'

Muriel gave Val a peck on the cheek, telling her she was a dear little thing, then presented her with a silver bangle she had not been able to wear on her pudgy wrists for the last fifteen years, and welcomed her into the bosom of the family, adding graciously, 'Try to remember you're one of us now, Valerie – never forget that.'

The wedding date was fixed for the last Saturday in April – and then a problem arose. Gerry had taken it for granted that Val would move into Belmont with his family. He was quite surprised when she explained, as politely as she could, that she didn't feel this would be the best plan.

'But why not?' He was puzzled. 'It's not as if you were going to be at home all day. Aggie and Eth will do the cooking and cleaning and all that, while we're both at work.'

For Valerie had made it clear from the outset that she did not want to give up her job in the Crystal Palace office, and Gerald did not have any objections. It would be useful to have an extra salary coming in every week; so far, Babs had not been successful in finding herself another post.

'But that's all the more reason for us to stay here,' he told Val. 'You wouldn't have time for housekeeping if we had a place of our own.'

'I'll manage,' Val told him firmly. 'I'll find the time, don't worry.'

So he made some enquiries at his office, and old Mr Hawkins suggested that Gerald and his bride might care to move into the 'show flat' in a grand new block at the top of Westwood Hill, only a few hundred yards from the Crystal Palace.

Westwood Court had been erected by Crabbe & Carter Ltd, a firm of speculative builders who had bought up a few shabby mid-Victorian houses at the top of Sydenham Hill, razed them to the ground, and put a blankly anonymous red-brick box in their place. A large hoarding faced the main road, with an artist's impression of a fairy-tale castle, tucked among tree-tops and fleecy clouds, where carefree couples and cherubic children pointed gleefully at the panorama of the rolling Surrey downs beneath them. As their slogan, they had coined the phrase: *Halfway to Heaven*.

The prices were not cheap, but since Gerry and Val were taking over a flat that was already decorated, with kitchen and bathroom equipment built in, it would not cost a great deal to furnish it – and as Hawkins & Company were the sole agents for the property, they were able to arrange a mortgage on very favourable terms.

All the same, their problems were not over. Some questions remained: where would they spend the honeymoon? And – before that – where should they get married?

It had to be a church wedding: on this point, Muriel and Kate were in agreement. They wouldn't consider any hole-and-corner arrangement in a registrer's office, without hymns or prayers; nice people didn't do such things. It had to be a church – but which one?

The Glynns had never been regular churchgoers, although Muriel explained to visitors that the thing which caused her most suffering in her present condition was the fact that she was not strong enough to attend the house of God every Sunday. Ethel and Aggie had been infrequent worshippers, because Aggie's behaviour was rather unpredictable; she sometimes felt compelled to begin a loud conversation during the sermon, and although she liked to join in the hymns, there had been an unfortunate occasion when the choir were halfway through *There Is A Green Hill Far Away*, and Aggie launched into *Ten Green Bottles*.

Since she came out of hospital, Ethel had started going to church again, but usually to early-morning Eucharist, and always by herself.

So the Glynn family had no strong attachment to any particular church, whereas the Watkins family had never gone anywhere but All Saints – so that settled that, and Valerie introduced Gerald to the vicar, who agreed to publish the banns of marriage on three successive Sundays.

It was a white wedding, of course. Kate and Valerie went shopping in Croydon and found a very nice off-white dress in the week of the Blue-Pencil Sales at Kennards – ankle-length, in art silk, with a tiny pattern of flowers woven in, so Kate said she could wear it for dances later on – and with a headdress and a veil, and long white gloves, it would be just the thing for walking down the aisle.

That left the biggest problem of all. Where would they hold the wedding reception? Traditionally, the wedding breakfast was the responsibility of the bride's family – and a wedding breakfast could run into a lot of money.

They held a family conference at Sackville Road. Ted was working pretty frequently by this time, but his fees seldom rose above five or six guineas, and Daphne provided the only regular income for their part of the family. Val had her weekly pay-packet too, of course, but after she and Daphne had settled up with Kate for their weekly bed and board, no one had much cash left for entertaining.

'We'll have to plan it carefully,' Kate decided. 'I'm sure we can make enough sandwiches and fairy-cakes and jellies. It'll be what they call a fork luncheon.'

'I've never tried eating jelly with a fork,' said Ted. 'Should be interesting.'

Daphne kicked him under the table. 'If you can't take this seriously, you'd better go and play with Annie in the garden.'

'I'm perfectly serious.' He defended himself. 'I can see us running out of money if we're not careful – and what about the wedding cake? They don't give them away with a pound of tea, do they?'

'I expect we can make the wedding cake, if we put our minds to it.' Kate tried to sound confident. 'Daff's a dab hand with icing. The only thing is – how big will it have to be?'

Daphne turned to Val. 'Have you and Gerry worked out how many people will be coming?'

'I'm afraid it's rather a long list,' Valerie admitted. 'Gerry seems to know such a lot of people – there are aunties and uncles and long-lost cousins rolling up from all over the place. I think it adds up to somewhere between fifty and sixty people.'

They looked at one another in a stunned silence. Kate said faintly, 'Fifty or sixty? Where are we going to put them all?'

'I suppose we could split them up into small groups. Some upstairs in the sitting room, some down here . . .' Val began doubtfully.

Kate was horrified. 'You can't have wedding-guests in the *kitchen*!'

'Perhaps you could give them numbers and let them in, ten at a time,' said Ted. 'The rest can wait outside in the garden, till they hear their numbers called – as long as the weather keeps fine, of course.'

Daphne turned on her husband, taking a deep breath, but Val said, 'No – Ted's right, we can't possibly hold the reception here, there isn't room. We shall have to hire a hall.'

'And how much is that going to cost?' asked Kate. 'Could we afford it?'

Val had an idea. 'There's the refreshment rooms at the Palace, and the restaurant – I could talk to Mr Buckland. He might let us have special rates, seeing I'm on the staff.'

The following morning when she took him his coffee, she picked what she hoped would be a good moment and raised the subject. '. . . About fifty or sixty altogether,' she explained. 'And I was wondering – could we hire one of the refreshment rooms for a couple of hours? How much would it cost?'

Mr Buckland chewed the ends of his moustache. 'I can't tell you right away – I shall have to discuss it with the catering manager. What's the date of the wedding?'

'April the twenty-sixth. It's a Saturday.'

He blew out his cheeks. 'I think you'd better sit down. This is more difficult than I thought. Does it have to be a Saturday?'

'Well, weddings generally are, aren't they? During the week, everyone's working.'

'Quite. As you know, the weekends are our busiest time; that's when the restaurant and the bars and the refreshment rooms make their money. It would be impossible to close any of those areas to the public – at least, not without charging you a great deal of money for the privilege! I don't imagine you'd be very keen on that?'

'Well, no. To be perfectly honest, we couldn't afford very much.'

'I understand. And I'm very sorry I can't help. I like the idea of you holding your wedding reception at the Crystal Palace; I only wish I could have obliged, but the interests of the Palace have to come first – always.'

'I know.' Crestfallen, she turned to go. 'I'm sorry to have bothered you.'

As she reached the door, he stopped her. 'One moment – a thought occurs to me. You're expecting fifty or sixty guests, you say. How would you feel about holding your reception at Rockhills?'

After the Crystal Palace was transported from Hyde Park to Sydenham, Rockhills had been built at the corner of the Palace grounds by the original architect, Sir Joseph Paxton. In due course, when Henry Buckland left his post as Manager of the Royal Spa at Harrogate, he moved into Paxton's old residence and made his home there.

'It's fairly commodious,' he continued. 'And while my daughters have been growing up, we've given several parties. If the weather is clement, we can always open the French windows, and let the guests stroll in the garden.'

'You really mean it?' Valerie stared at him. 'Your own house – on our wedding day?'

Mr Buckland smiled. 'I'd been wondering what to give you as a wedding present, my dear. How would you like to have a wedding reception – with the sincere good wishes of the Buckland family?'

Gerry had begun to snore again. As quietly as possible, Valerie slipped out of bed and tiptoed to the windows. Pushing back the curtain, she looked out across the little patch of grass and the flowering cherries – across the West Hill, to the tiled roofs and chimneypots of Rockhills, gleaming in the morning sunlight, half-hidden among the trees.

One year ago, she had felt so horribly nervous.

It would have been intimidating in any case, to visit Mr Buckland's house; to enter it on the arm of her husband, immediately after their wedding, was terrifying.

All through the marriage service, she found herself thinking about the ordeal ahead. By comparison, the ceremony seemed almost insignificant, and she had to force herself to concentrate on the vicar's words, and the exchange of vows.

Her white veil blurred everything. Nothing seemed clearly defined, until Gerald slipped the ring on her finger, and the final blessing was spoken. Even then, when he lifted the veil to kiss her, she couldn't believe that they were man and wife; it seemed like make-believe – as if they were on a stage, acting their parts in an old, familiar play.

They posed for a group photograph outside the church, then scrambled into the hired car under a storm of confetti and rice. As they drove away, Gerry kissed her again and asked: 'How does it feel to be Mrs Glynn?' – and that was unreal, too.

When they arrived at Rockhills, Mr Buckland was waiting to welcome them, and Valerie met Mrs Buckland for the first time, together with their daughters – Irene, aged twelve, and Chrystal, aged eight.

Very soon, the other guests began to arrive, and she had to stand beside Gerry at the head of a receiving line, shaking hands with a long queue of people, many of whom she had never set eyes on before, accepting their good wishes and congratulations, and repeating over and over again: 'Thank you so much. Very kind . . . So glad you could come.'

In the flowing stream of faces, a few stood out. Her mother, of course, followed by Daphne and Ted, and little Annie in her best party frock – then Babs, with Muriel leaning heavily on her arm, supported by Aggie and Ethel.

The procession seemed endless, and although after twenty minutes a few latecomers and stragglers were still scurrying up the gravel drive, Mr Buckland announced that a cold collation was being served in the dining room.

Still rigid with fear, Valerie could hardly swallow more than a mouthful. In her nervousness she kept taking sips of champagne until Gerry murmured in her ear: 'Steady on, old dear. Mustn't get squiffy, must we?'

Perhaps he was right. Perhaps it was the champagne that made her feel so light-headed, as if she were standing outside herself – a dispassionate observer, watching the whole scene from a distance. The speeches and the telegrams seemed to be irrelevant. Even when the Best Man – an old schoolmate of Gerry's, whom she scarcely knew – ploughed through a series of faintly risqué jokes, Valerie felt as if it had nothing to do with her at all.

With Gerry's hand closing upon hers, they cut the cake together, and then Mrs Buckland took her up to a spare bedroom, where she was able to change out of her finery into a 'going-away' dress. She told herself that the worst part was over – yet she still felt frightened, and had to nerve herself up to go back to the reception.

By that time, most of the guests had drifted into the garden. It was a pleasant afternoon, and she lost count of the number of times someone recited: 'Happy is the bride the sun shines on . . .'

On the south wall of the house, a fine old wisteria was coming into bloom, and in the warm air the scent was sweet and heady. Val found Gerry's aunts sitting on a bench beneath the blossoms, enjoying their little outing.

'Such a beautiful house – and such a lovely garden,' said Aggie. 'You wouldn't remember, Valerie, but our garden used to be like this, once upon a time – isn't that right, Ethel?'

'Ah, but in those days Daphne was still living at Belmont. She had green fingers,' Ethel said. 'Perhaps, now I have more time to spare, I might try my hand at gardening.'

'I could help, couldn't I?' began Aggie – then added: 'The trouble is, I never know which are weeds and which are flowers. They look the same to me.'

'Quite right, dear.' Ethel patted her sister's hand. 'I'm sure they are the same, in God's eyes. Perhaps we should leave our garden as it is, and let Him do what He likes with it.'

Not for the first time, Valerie reflected how much Ethel had changed during her spell in hospital. Her sharp features had softened. Looking up at Val with her head on one side, she was no longer a parrot but a little pouter pigeon, cooing, 'You're very pretty, my dear – and Gerald's a lucky young man. I'm sure you're going to be very happy.'

Aggie leaned forward to say in a whisper, 'May we ask where you're going for your honeymoon? Or is it a secret?'

'Oh, we're not going far.' Val felt as if she were reciting a lesson she had learned by heart. 'Only to London. Gerald's booked a room at one of the big hotels – I don't know which one. It's just a long weekend, really, before we both go back to work.'

'Fancy!' Aggie clasped her hands. 'We've never stayed in a hotel, have we, Ethel? But of course, we've never been on a honeymoon either.'

Through the French windows, Valerie heard someone saying loudly: 'Sorry to arrive late – unavoidably detained. Accidents will happen, even at the best of times. Well, where's the bride and groom?'

Aggie gasped, 'That sounds like – but it can't be! He wouldn't dare . . .'

When they despatched the invitations, Valerie asked Gerald what he would do about his father. From the day Harry Glynn walked out of Belmont, Gerald had hardly spoken to the old man, and never thought of sending him an invitation, but since he had taken to visiting her mother at Sackville Road, Val had met Mr Glynn several times, and insisted that he must be asked to the wedding.

Reluctantly, Gerry had agreed, but said: 'You know he's cut himself off from the family. I shouldn't think for a moment he'll come.'

But he had.

Excusing herself, Valerie hurried indoors, where she found Harry Glynn talking to Mr Buckland – who was looking slightly bemused.

'What did you say yer name was, old boy? Buckley? Never heard of you – which side of the family do you come from?'

Valerie performed the introductions, and Harry insisted on kissing the bride.

'I've just been telling your friend Mr Buckley,' he explained, 'I'm sorry to turn up so late, but I wanted to look my best this morning – determined to do you proud, eh? – then I had a spot of bother with my shirt. I put it down on top of my paintbox, and got a couple of smudges on it. Burnt Umber and Ultramarine all down the front – blasted nuisance. I tried to get them out with a spot of turps, but it stank to high heaven, so I had to wash it out, and then the damn thing wouldn't dry in time, so in the end I had to wear this one instead.'

He was wearing his best black suit, more appropriate for a funeral than a wedding, and it did not quite go with his red-and-blue checked flannel shirt.

Valerie assured him he looked very smart, and asked if he'd had any lunch. She was about to lead him into the dining room, where the remains of the meal had not yet been cleared, when they came face to face with another couple in the doorway – Babs, with her mother on her arm.

Mr and Mrs Glynn gazed at one another in frozen silence, until

Harry said affably: 'How do, old lady? How's the world treating you, eh?'

Muriel drew herself up and turned to her daughter. 'I did not come here to be insulted by hooligans,' she said. 'Take me home at once.'

'Touchy as ever, I see,' said Harry. 'Indigestion, I dare say. You want to watch that – it can be nasty at your age.'

On their way to the front door, Babs and Muriel ignored this completely, and Valerie broke in, saying: 'Help yourself to some food, Mr Glynn, while I go and find Gerald. I know he'll be pleased to see you.'

She found Gerry in Mr Buckland's smoking-room, playing billiards with the Best Man. When she explained the situation, Gerry groaned.

'I knew it was a mistake to invite the old devil. Oh lor', I suppose I'll have to go and speak to him.'

In the dining room, Mr Glynn was tucking into a plate of game pie and addressing Mr Buckland with his mouth full.

'So you're the chappie who runs the Crystal Palace? Interesting job – but if you don't mind my saying so, there's one or two things you could do to liven the place up. I've always felt what you really need is an exhibition of paintings – you don't mind me mentioning it, do you? Paintings by local artists – that would create a lot of interest. If you like, I could bring round a selection of my work for you to have a look at.'

Trapped in his own home, Mr Buckland wore a hunted look. Kate Watkins, walking by at this moment, took in the situation at a glance.

'Now then, Mr Glynn,' she said firmly. 'I'm sure Mr Buckland doesn't want to be bothered with business this afternoon . . . Oh look, here's Gerald come to see you! Why don't you bring your plate outside and we'll find a nice quiet corner of the garden where we can sit and have a chat – how about that?'

Valerie watched as her mother led them away and tried to apologise to Mr Buckland.

'Good heavens – there's no need for any apology, Miss Watkins,' he assured her, then corrected himself: 'I beg your pardon – Mrs Glynn, I should say. We shall have to get used to your new name, shan't we? Now, if you'll excuse me, I must have a word with Mrs Buckland . . .'

He slipped away, leaving Valerie not knowing whether to laugh or cry, but her overwhelming feeling was one of sheer panic.

'*Mrs Glynn*' . . . The words sounded like a death-knell.

★

When they left Rockhills, there was no car waiting to take them off on their honeymoon. As Gerald said, it was only a few minutes' walk to the station, and it would be a shocking extravagance. Val agreed – though it seemed odd to be walking along Crystal Palace Parade, carrying suitcases.

There were two railway stations at the Crystal Palace; the first one, halfway up Anerley Hill, had been built in 1854 to coincide with the opening of the Palace when it was transported from Hyde Park. Eventually this became known as 'Crystal Palace Low Level', for in 1865 a much grander station was opened, near the main exhibition building. Like a baronial castle, with towers at each corner, the 'High Level' station dominated the west side of Crystal Palace Parade, with an Italianate arcade underneath the busy main road, giving direct access to the Palace grounds.

On her wedding day, Val didn't notice the grandeur of the architecture; she was too busy climbing aboard the train, helping Gerald to put their bags up on the luggage-rack, and flopping back against the buttoned upholstery as the steam-engine pulled out.

'Pity we didn't put the wedding off for a couple of months!' Gerry said playfully, as the train gathered speed.

'Why? What do you mean?' Val asked anxiously.

'They're going to change over to electric trains on this line in July – quicker, cleaner, and no danger of getting cinders in your eye.'

'Oh, I see.' Val tried to smile, and wondered how he could be so unconcerned. All she could think about was the ordeal that lay ahead of them. 'How long before we get there?' she asked.

'Not long – only about twenty minutes.'

Didn't Gerry feel anxious at all? Surely it must be a daunting prospect for him too, this leap in the dark, this exploration into the unknown . . . But then – perhaps it wouldn't be unknown territory for him.

It hadn't occurred to her until now, and as Gerry watched the telegraph poles flashing by, she studied his profile. Could he have experimented already, with some other girl?

Of course. That was what young men did, wasn't it? 'Sowing their wild oats'. The thought of Gerry in bed with another woman was somehow chilling, yet she supposed she should feel grateful. At least if he knew what he was about, they wouldn't both be incompetent bunglers, making fools of themselves.

Not that Valerie was totally ignorant. She had talked to her mother about it once, some years ago, although they didn't really get down to brass tacks. Afterwards, Kate left a little booklet in Val's bedroom. It contained some disconcerting diagrams, looking more like problems in geometry than anything that could be described as 'making love'. Later, there had been long discussions with other girls at school – enlightening and alarming in equal parts.

They had giggled, and shuddered, and Val had said: 'No, but honestly! People couldn't *really* . . . Could they?'

Tonight, she was going to find out.

When they alighted from the train at Victoria, they walked straight into their hotel, alongside the station. Valerie was impressed by the foyer, and the dignified hall-porter who snapped his fingers, whereupon a uniformed pageboy instantly rushed forward to take their luggage, and ushered them into the lift.

Their room was high up at the back of the building; from a small window, Val looked down upon the vaulted glass roofs above the platforms. Inevitably, they reminded her of the Crystal Palace, and she felt a pang of homesickness. She would have given anything to be back there, safe and sound.

Gerald tipped the pageboy, and they unpacked their bags, laying out nightclothes and dressing gowns, and putting their spongebags on the washstand. A discreet printed notice informed them that they should: *Ring the bell to summon a chambermaid when requiring hot water* and that *Bathrooms and other facilities are to be found at the end of the corridor.*

'Do you want to have a bath and change before supper?' Gerry asked.

'Perhaps that would be a good idea.' She took a change of clothes, and set off in search of the bathroom.

The water was not very hot, and she was not tempted to lie back and soak. She dried herself swiftly, peering at her reflection in the blotchy mirror on the wall, and wondered what Gerry would think of her body when he saw it for the first time. Then she put on her evening dress, and returned to the bedroom; she was surprised to find that Gerry had already changed into a dinner-jacket and a bow tie.

'Aren't you going to have a bath?' she asked.

'I had one this morning,' he said casually. 'How about a drink before supper? Do you fancy a snifter?'

'Not just now, thanks. Later, perhaps.'

'Well, I'm going to nip down to the bar. Come and join me when you feel like it.'

Then he disappeared. She stood looking out across the station roofs, and wished she had never been born. For a moment she considered packing her bag again and making her escape. She could go home and explain to Mum that the whole thing had been a silly mistake, couldn't she?

No, of course she couldn't. Hopelessly, she sat at the dressing table, combing her hair, and putting on face-powder and lipstick – taking enormous care over it, in order to make the job last as long as possible.

Finally, with a cold, dead feeling at the pit of her stomach, she went off to the lift, which lurched and clanked down to the ground floor.

She found Gerry in the bar. He was rather flushed, and he laughed a little more loudly than usual as he said, 'Well, old dear. Name your poison!'

She asked for a lemonade, which he ordered, together with another whisky and soda.

Through an open doorway, she could hear dance-music. Gerry said this was the reason he'd chosen this particular hotel – they had a decent floor in the restaurant, so they could trip the light fantastic after supper.

During the meal, they shared a bottle of white wine, and Gerry insisted on ordering brandies with the coffee. Val had never tasted brandy before, and didn't really like the taste, but she told him it was very nice.

After that, they fox-trotted to an American tune that was all the rage. In Gerry's arms, Val twirled and swayed until her head was swimming, while one of the musicians put down his saxophone and sang the refrain:

> 'It had to be you . . . It had to be you . . .
> I wandered around, and finally found a somebody who . . .'

'That's how it was,' she thought. 'I was wandering around and finally found someone – and it had to be Gerry. Who else could it have been?'

As soon as she asked herself the question, a picture came into her mind – a motorbike parked under some trees, a steep hill, a view of rolling downs that seemed to stretch on and on until they melted into sky . . . And a young man standing close beside her, his arm around her waist – strong, passionate, with large, dark eyes . . .

She mustn't let herself think about that. She was Mrs Gerald Glynn now; and she was about to go to bed with her husband.

After a charleston and a tango, Gerry asked: 'Have you had enough?'

'Yes, I think so. I am feeling a bit tired,' she told him.

'I'm not surprised – it's been a long day. How about an early night?'

So they went up to their room, where they took it in turn to go along the corridor to the bathroom and 'other facilities'. When Gerry came back, he was wearing his pyjamas and dressing gown; Valerie was sitting up in bed in her brand-new nightdress, trying to stop shivering.

'I'll put the light out, shall I?' he asked, and pressed the switch without waiting for an answer.

She heard him taking off the dressing gown; the bed rocked as he climbed in beside her.

'How are you feeling?' he said – and his voice sounded alarmingly close.

'I'm all right,' she lied. 'I'm fine.'

'A little nervous, perhaps?' She could hear that he was smiling. 'Don't worry – I'll be very gentle.'

He kissed her, and then began to undress her, taking off her nightie. She did not resist; she felt as if she were a hospital patient, being prepared for an operation. Defenceless, she lay on her back and waited.

'There's nothing to be afraid of,' he whispered. 'Just leave it to me – you don't have to do anything.'

Having undressed her, he drew away, and she realised he was taking some sort of precaution; then he wriggled out of his pyjamas. When he touched her, his naked body was hot against hers.

They began to embrace; it seemed extraordinary – intimate, yet somehow impersonal. He kissed and fondled her, and for a while that was rather pleasant, but when she began to enjoy it, he became more excited, and as he grew excited, he became impatient, and the whole thing became rather violent – then painful – then reached a sudden climax that left Gerry moaning with pleasure, all passion spent.

'*There!*' he gasped, when he could speak. 'Not too bad, was it?'

'No,' she said politely. 'It was very nice. Thank you.'

'It'll be better next time,' he said. 'When we get to know each other.'

Then he gave her a last, approving kiss, told her she was a good girl, rolled over – and fell fast asleep.

Val did not sleep much that night. She was still awake when she heard the whistle and rumble of the first trains pulling into the station below, and saw the glimmer of dawn through the window – and realised that married life had begun.

Now, a year later, she turned away from the window of their smart modern flat – 'Halfway to Heaven' – and looked at the sleeping figure in the bed.

Since their honeymoon, Gerry's lovemaking had become a set routine which took place once a week on Saturday nights, and the procedure never varied.

The words and music of last year's popular song were still jingling through her brain:

> . . . A somebody who
> Could make me be blue, could make me be true
> Even be glad, just to be sad – thinking of you . . .

Only it wasn't Gerry she was thinking of.

When the honeymoon was over, and they took up residence at Westwood Court, their days soon fell into a regular pattern. She resumed her job at the Crystal Palace, and learned to become a practical housewife in her spare time, cooking supper in the evenings, doing her housework at weekends, fitting in the shopping during her lunch-break or on her way to work.

There was one shop she no longer visited. When she needed fruit or vegetables, she made a detour all the way down Anerley Hill; she did not call in at the greengrocers in Church Road any more, but took the long way round, by Westow Hill and Westow Street, to avoid passing Gunn & Son and risk being seen through the shop window.

Once or twice she had run into members of the family. Grandad still played his cornet with the Palace brass band, but he was getting short-sighted now, as well as deaf, and never recognised her. One evening, when Gerry took her to a film at the Electra and the lights went up at the end of the programme, she discovered young Tony Gunn sitting in the same row. He turned red, and pretended not to see her, ducking out through a different exit.

When the new Woolworths opened in Upper Norwood, she had

gone along to see if their claim to sell 'nothing over sixpence' was true – and found herself face to face with Steve's mother and his sister Julie. It had been embarrassing for all of them. Julie recovered first, flashing an automatic smile and saying, 'Good afternoon.' Freda echoed the greeting a second later, but could not manage the smile – and they passed on before Valerie could think of anything to say.

But the most difficult meeting had taken place last Sunday.

Val had not given up her membership of the Penge and District Choral Society, and on Sunday mornings she still went to choir-practice in the small Concert Room at the Palace.

It was a lovely spring day; strolling along Crystal Palace Parade, she saw the Gunn family walking towards her – Alfred and Freda arm in arm, accompanied by Grandad and Tony. There was no side street to offer an escape route, and Val could not turn back and run for cover. Putting on a bright, fixed smile, she went on, and as they approached her she said, 'Good morning. Lovely day, isn't it?'

Alf raised his hat, but did not speak; Freda muttered something unintelligible – and old Jack Gunn asked loudly: 'Who's that pretty girl? Is she a customer?'

'Not now, Grandad!' snapped Freda, and they swept on without pausing.

Blushing, Valerie quickened her pace. A moment later, she heard the sound of running footsteps, and turned to find Tony racing after her. He had grown several inches in the past year – he must be eleven by now, and looking more like his brother every day. But he still sounded like a child as he blurted out: 'Why don't you ever send Steve a letter? He's very unhappy 'cos you don't write to him, and it's not fair.'

Several yards away, the family had stopped and were looking back. His mother called out shrilly: 'Tony! Come here this minute!'

The boy's courage failed him; he hung his head and retreated to join the others. Freda grabbed his wrist and hauled him along the road, scolding him.

Val turned away, her heart pounding. She could see Steve so clearly in her mind's eye.

'He's very unhappy 'cos you don't write to him . . .'

Now, as she stood at the bedroom window, she conjured up Steve's physical presence – his smile, his voice, the touch of his hand, the sight and sound and smell of him – as real and vivid as ever.

Impulsively, she went back to the bed and threw her arms round Gerald. Startled out of sleep, he was astonished to find her cuddling him, unbuttoning his pyjamas, running her hands over his body, stroking and caressing him—

'Hey – what the devil?' he mumbled. 'What's this in aid of?'

'Happy anniversary,' she said, and kissed him fiercely.

Chapter Twelve

'BURNT,' SAID MURIEL. 'These cakes are burnt, so don't try to pretend they're not!'

'Cheer up, Aunt Ag,' said Daphne. 'King Alfred had the same problem.'

Aggie's mouth quivered. 'I was going to take them out at four o'clock, but the kitchen clock must have stopped, because when I noticed the smell of burning, it still said ten past three. They're only a little scorched, Mu; if you cut off the black bits, they'll be quite nice inside.'

'They're disgusting, Agnes. Take them straight to the dustbin.' Muriel pushed her plate away so violently, it toppled off the edge of the tea-table and smashed on the floor, and she blamed that on Aggie too. 'Now look what you've made me do,' she said.

Aggie burst into tears and Ethel helped her from the room.

'Don't upset yourself, Mummy,' said Babs. 'I'll fetch the dustpan and brush.'

Seven-year-old Annie had been watching this scene, wide-eyed, and now Daphne said to her: 'You can help to clear up the pieces, can't you, love?'

So Annie went off to the kitchen with her Auntie Babs, leaving Daphne and Muriel together. As soon as the door shut, Daphne said to her mother, 'Do you have to be so unkind? Aggie can't help it, and you only make things worse when you bully her.'

'How dare you speak to me like that?' Muriel glared. 'Just because you're a teacher, that doesn't give you the right to lecture me. I'm not one of your wretched pupils.'

'No, my wretched pupils wouldn't behave so badly.' Daphne

relented, pulling her chair a little closer and taking her mother's hands in hers. 'I know it's hard for you, being stuck indoors all day long, but taking it out on poor old Ag doesn't help, does it?'

Muriel tossed her head. 'Perhaps I was hasty, but you don't know what it's like, being cooped up with Agnes and Ethel, day in and day out. Sometimes I think I shall finish up as mad as they are.'

'It's a shame you don't get out more often. It's a nice warm afternoon – we could have had tea in the garden—'

'Have you seen the garden? It's a wilderness! It's gone to rack and ruin since you deserted us. If only you could come round more often, to do a little pruning, and mow the lawn.'

'I wish I could, but I've got my own home to look after. I hardly ever have time to help in the garden there. When we came out today, I left them all arguing about who was going to cut the hedge.' She paused, realising that she had said too much, and Muriel picked this up at once.

'"Them all"? Who do you mean? I thought Edward was performing at one of his concerts this afternoon?'

'Yes – he's got an open-air show at Streatham Common. I meant Valerie and some friends. Mrs Watkins is giving a little tea-party.'

'Very nice for her.' Muriel pursed her lips. 'I only wish I had friends and neighbours I could call upon to help with our garden. As for the state of the house, you can see for yourself. Since Babs has been going out to work it's turned into a pigsty.'

Babs had found a job at last. Gerry convinced old Mr Hawkins that the Estate Agency accounts were too much for one person to handle, and persuaded him to take Babs on as an office junior.

Daphne ventured to say, 'I've been meaning to talk to you about that. Don't you think it would be a good idea to put this house up for sale, and move into something a little smaller?'

Muriel recoiled. '*Sell this house?* Have you taken leave of your senses?'

'You said yourself, Aggie and Ethel can't manage it. It would solve all your problems. You'd probably get a good price for it—'

'It's out of the question! This is our family home – my father's house, your grandfather's . . . DeWitts have been living here for three generations.'

Babs returned with Annie, who set to work, sweeping up cake-crumbs and pieces of broken china, and Muriel turned to Babs bitterly.

'Do you know what Daphne has suggested? We should sell this

house and move into some little box! Have you ever heard anything so outrageous?'

Babs sided with her mother. 'Oh Daphne, how could you!'

'I'm trying to be practical. It would save so much money—'

'You mean, a little terraced house, like Sackville Road?' Babs reproved her. 'Can you imagine Mummy living somewhere like that?'

Daphne realised she was wasting her breath. 'Oh well, we'll talk about it another time.' She turned to Annie. 'You've made a good job of that.'

'Hasn't she just?' Muriel was all smiles again. 'You're Granny's little helper, aren't you, darling? I wish you lived here all the time – you'd make this house neat and tidy for me, wouldn't you? You might even be able to keep the garden in order as well!'

Annie said cheerfully, 'Yes, I like gardening. I help my other Grandma sometimes.'

'Your other Grandma is a very lucky woman,' said Muriel. 'She has so many kind people to help her.'

'Oh yes,' Annie chattered on. 'I was going to help her cut the hedge this afternoon, but we had to come here instead. Now Grandma's got Grandpa Glynn and the other gentleman to do it for her.'

Muriel's smile curdled, as she rounded on Daphne. 'I hadn't realised *that man* was a regular visitor at your house?'

'He sometimes comes to tea with Mrs Watkins.' Daphne indicated Annie, who was hanging on every word. 'Do you think we might change the subject?'

'I have no wish to talk about that person, I can assure you. Of course I knew Mrs Watkins invited him to Gerald's wedding. I suppose I might have guessed – he always did have a weakness for the lower classes.'

'Thank you for tea, Mother.' Daphne stood up, with a bright smile. 'Run and find your coat, Annie – it's time we went home.'

As it happened, Harry Glynn was not helping to cut the hedge.

'It's my arthritis, you see. I haven't got the full use of my elbows,' he explained, when Kate offered him the shears. 'But I'm sure Colpoys will oblige – isn't that right, old man?'

'I shall do my best,' said Mr Colpoys, taking off his pince-nez.

'You are kind,' said Kate, handing him the shears. 'Then I can get on with weeding the lawn. These daisies pop up everywhere – they don't seem to know when they're not wanted.'

'I have known people like that,' muttered Colpoys, lighting his pipe. Then he felt ashamed of himself, and hoped nobody had heard him.

Kate was already getting to work with a little pointed trowel, digging out the daisy-roots, while Valerie sprayed the greenfly on the rambling roses at the bottom of the garden.

'That's what I like to see,' smiled Harry. 'Everyone hard at work.'

'And how are you going to occupy yourself?' asked Mr Colpoys, gripping his pipe between his teeth, and snipping away with the shears.

'I think I'll follow your example.' Harry pulled out a battered old briar. 'Could you spare me a pipeful of tobacco, old man?'

Grimly, Mr Colpoys handed over his tobacco pouch and Harry filled his pipe, then, producing a sketchbook and a pencil from his pocket, he said, 'I think I'll try a spot of drawing – that's more my style.'

Under his hand, the pencil took on a life of its own. It hovered, dashed in a line here and there, added a soft smudge of shadow, and gradually a recognisable likeness appeared on the blank page: Kate Watkins, sitting on the grass, her face shadowed under a broad-brimmed sun-hat, weeding daisies.

At the end of the garden, Valerie heard the two old men sparring and thought how tiresome they were. She was beginning to wish she hadn't come round to Sackville Road this afternoon. Ever since dinner-time she had been feeling restless. While Gerry was carving the half-leg of lamb she suggested they might go for a walk this afternoon, as it was such a nice day.

'Sorry, no can do,' he said casually. 'I've got to meet a chap over at Blackheath at four – didn't I tell you?'

'No, you didn't. Can't I come with you? We could have a walk on Blackheath Common, couldn't we?'

'Not really. It's a business chat – well, it might be. I met him when we sold him his house. Interesting bloke – he's got a job with the BBC.'

'Blackheath Borough Council?'

Gerry laughed. 'A cut above that, old dear. It's the British Broadcasting Company – he works in their office at Savoy Hill. Quite an important sort of chap; he seems to think he might be able to find a place for me in the BBC.'

Valerie was astonished. 'Doing what?'

'I don't know exactly. That's what we're going to talk about.'

'You mean, you're thinking of giving up your job with Hawkins and Company and going into broadcasting? But wouldn't that be a huge gamble? We don't know anything about it – it may be just a nine-day wonder.'

'It's been going for a few years. According to this chappie, they've got ten million listeners already. From what I gather, it could become really big business – and I'd be getting in on the ground floor.'

Valerie couldn't understand what all the fuss was about. The wireless might be all right in its way, for old people and invalids who had to stay indoors all day, but it wasn't her idea of fun. When she wanted to be entertained, she'd rather go to the pictures, or a theatre – or the Crystal Palace! – not sit at home with a pair of headphones jammed over her ears, twiddling a silly thing called a 'cat's-whisker'.

'All right, you go and see your BBC friend if you want to,' she said. 'I'll walk round to Sackville Road and have tea with Mum.'

She'd forgotten it was Mum's day to entertain Mr Colpoys – and as so often happened these days, Mr Glynn had dropped in as well. Val had been on the point of leaving, saying she'd come back when Mum wasn't so busy, but Kate begged her to stay and give a hand with the garden.

So here she was, bored and uncomfortable, feeling like a fish out of water – though she had to admit that if she'd stayed at home, she would probably have felt the same. She tried to analyse the mood she was in; all the week she'd been fidgety, unable to settle.

There was nothing wrong with Westwood Court; it was quite a nice flat, perfectly comfortable and convenient to run. And her sense of insecurity had nothing to do with Gerry. True, she didn't much like the idea of him giving up a steady job and chasing after this BBC thing, whatever it might be – but she had been on edge all the week, long before broadcasting had been mentioned.

All the week . . . ever since last Sunday, when she ran into the Gunns. She had tried to put the incident out of her mind, but it was there all the time, gnawing away at her. She shook her head, like a dog emerging from a pond, and made an effort to concentrate on the rambling roses, attacking them with the spray as if she could wipe out her own troublesome thoughts as well as the greenfly.

Kate stood up, mopping her brow. 'This is warm work,' she said. 'I'm going to get a glass of lemonade – would anyone else care for some?'

'That sounds very nice,' said Mr Colpoys, still clipping.

'You're doing wonders with that hedge,' Kate told him. 'It's looking very trim already.'

'It's not straight,' said Harry, as he went on sketching.

'It looks all right to me,' said Kate.

Mr Colpoys stepped back. 'I can't see anything wrong with it,' he said.

'I can,' Harry told him. 'Comes of being an artist, you know. I've got an eye for that sort of thing.'

Glancing over his shoulder, Kate exclaimed, 'Oh, I say! That's me – doing the lawn! Oh, Mr Colpoys – Valerie – do come and look. You can tell it's me, can't you?'

It was extraordinarily lifelike. Harry had caught her perfectly – not just Kate's physical appearance, but the warmth of her personality, the turn of her head, the sunshine on the grass – they were all there, captured in a few strokes of the pencil.

'It's lovely,' said Valerie, and Mr Colpoys murmured reluctantly, 'Yes indeed, very skilful.'

'Comes of having a good sitter,' said Harry jovially. 'You ought to call at my studio one day, Mrs Watkins, and let me work it up into a full-scale portrait – in oils.'

Kate laughed, though she was secretly flattered. 'Me? I'm no oil-painting! The very idea!'

Mr Colpoys frowned at Harry. 'Are you serious?'

'Why not?' Harry grinned at him. 'Perhaps you might like to buy it – I'd let you have it at a special price!'

'No, really. I couldn't possibly!' spluttered Mr Colpoys. 'Excuse me, I must get on with that hedge.'

Suddenly Val couldn't bear it any longer – the hot afternoon, the two old men bickering, while curiosity drew her like a magnet . . .

'I've got to go now, Mum,' she said. 'I'm not sure what time Gerry will be coming home, and he'll be wanting his tea when he gets in.'

She grabbed her hat, and fled – and at the top of the hill she turned into Church Road and rang the bell at the greengrocers' shop.

When Tony opened the door, several emotions chased each other across his face: surprise, anger, hope – a glow of happiness. But all he said was, 'Hello. Come in.'

She followed him upstairs, not knowing quite why she was there, or what she would say; she only knew that she had to come. When they walked into the sitting room, Tony said, 'It's Valerie, Mum. She's come about Steve.'

Val gasped. 'I never said that! That's not why—'

'Isn't it?' Tony stared at her. 'What else did you come for?'

Freda was sitting in the bay window, where the afternoon sun threw a golden light upon her. She had been working on a garment in stripes of red and blue, and Val felt guilty, thinking of the woollen dress that had hung in her wardrobe for over two years. Freda put down her knitting.

'Good afternoon,' she said. 'What can I do for you?'

Her voice gave nothing away, but Val sensed antagonism behind the polite, defensive barrier.

'I happened to be passing, and I thought—' Words failed her, and she corrected herself. 'No, that's not true. I've been thinking about this ever since last Sunday, when Tony said about writing a letter . . .'

'Are you going to write to him?' Tony's face lit up. 'Blimey – he won't half be pleased!'

'Tony, go to your room,' said Freda. 'And don't use bad language.'

'Blimey's not bad language. I want to know what she's going to do—'

'Blimey means "God blind me", and I won't have you saying such things. Go upstairs and read a book, and don't come down till I call you.'

Grumbling, he obeyed. Freda pulled up a chair, saying formally, 'Won't you sit down, Miss Watkins?' Then her face changed. 'I'm sorry, my mistake. You're Mrs Glynn now, aren't you?'

'Yes.' Val sank into the chair gratefully, for her knees were shaking. 'It's been a long time.'

'Since my son went to prison?' Still the same measured tone. 'One year, ten months – almost to the day.'

'I meant – since the last time I was here.'

'It comes to the same thing. Why have you come, after all this time?'

'I wanted to know how you were getting on,' said Val lamely. 'I mean – the whole family.'

'You can see we haven't changed much. Grandad's at the Palace, playing in the band. Mr Gunn's out as well – at Brixton.'

'Brixton?'

'That's where Steve is, didn't you know? They have visiting on Sunday afternoons, and we take it in turns. Alfred goes one week, and I go the next. Grandad's too old to go, and Tony's too young.'

'And how is . . .' She had to swallow, and begin again. 'How is

Steve?' She could not remember when she had last said his name out loud.

'He's pretty well, considering.' There was a pause, and then Freda asked: 'Is that all you wanted to know?'

'No. Tony said something about me writing to Steve. He said Steve was unhappy because I hadn't written.'

'How did you expect him to feel?' Freda's eyes flashed suddenly. 'When they put him inside, he was in love with you – he wanted to marry you. And he hasn't had a word from you, from that day to this.'

Val bent her head. 'I'm sorry, but I couldn't. I wouldn't have known what to . . .' She broke off, trying to breathe deeply. 'What I mean is, it was all over – for me, anyhow. I thought it must be over for him too.'

'Why was it over?'

'Well, you know – after what he did.' Now it was Val's turn to feel a spark of indignation; she'd done nothing to be ashamed of, had she? 'Because of what happened. Knocking down the old lady – hitting her—'

'Steve didn't do that!' Freda's voice was clear and strong. 'That's the other one; he's the villain – not our Steve. All Steve did was drive the car.'

'But he knew what was going on. They'd planned it together—'

'He knew nothing! He was paid to drive there and pick up that other devil. He didn't know what was going on till the police took him.'

'But they said he was an accessory – that's what they called him. They said he was guilty.'

'Then they were wrong.' Freda leaned forward, gripping Val's wrists. 'Look me in the eyes. Do you really believe Steve would do such a thing? You know him as well as anyone – he loved you and I think you loved him. Can you see him agreeing to a thing like that?'

'No.' The word came out in a whisper – but it was the truth.

'Thank you – that's all I wanted to know. He did wrong, I'm not denying that. Well, he's paying for it now, and I think he's paying too high a price. He'll get through it all right – I'm sure of that – but he'll get through it easier if you'd give him some help.'

'You mean – a letter?'

Freda studied her, then said quietly, 'A visit would be better.'

Val felt the blood rush through her veins, washing over her like a waterfall, and thought she was going to faint. 'But – but they wouldn't let me, would they?'

'You and him was going to be married. Who's got a better right to visit him? I'm sure we could fix it, if you'd say yes.'

'I don't know. I'm not sure.' Val put a hand to her head, trying to clear her thoughts and steady herself. A question occurred to her. 'Does he know – about me being married?'

'No sense leaving him in a fool's paradise. I told him myself; Alf couldn't do it.'

Val nerved herself to ask, 'What did he say?'

'Not much. It wasn't what he said – it was how he looked. But it didn't change nothing. He always asks after you, every week – if we've seen you, if we've heard anything . . . So – will you go and visit him?'

'I don't know. It wouldn't be right, would it? Not the way things are now. What could I say to him? Don't you think it would upset him?'

'He's upset already, with you not going. I think he'd rather see you.'

Val didn't know what to say. Finally she murmured, 'I'll have to think about it. I'd have to talk it over with my husband, in any case.' But even as she said it, she knew she would never do that.

'All right – you think it over. But remember what I said.'

When Val rose to go, Freda stood up too, indicating the knitting she had been working on. 'It's going to be a football jersey for young Tony. He's in the Junior Team now, doing very well, too, for his age.' As they walked towards the door, she remarked: 'That's a pretty dress – new, is it? I don't suppose you ever wear the one I gave you, nowadays?'

'Well, it's been so warm lately. Perhaps in the autumn.'

'Perhaps,' said Freda. 'Anyhow, thanks for coming round. I'll tell Steve I've seen you; he'll be glad to know.'

'Oh no, you'd better not. In case . . . Well, you know.'

'I'll tell him, all the same. Even to hear you've been round here – that'll be better than nothing.'

That evening, as Daphne was supervising Annie's bath, the front door slammed and Ted called out: 'Daff? I'm home! Where are you?'

'Upstairs!' she called back. 'Annie's in the bath.'

He ran up the stairs two at a time, and burst in, flushed and excited.

'Hello, love.' He perched on the edge of the tub and chucked his daughter under the chin. 'Hello, Tufty.'

'I've asked you not to call me that,' said Annie, with dignity. 'I can't help having sticking-up hair, can I?'

'Sorry, Tufty.' He dabbled his hand in the water, then stroked Annie's head, smoothing out the rebellious hair. 'There – flat as a pancake.'

'Now you've made her hair all wet!' Daphne protested. 'It'll have to be dry before she can go to bed.'

'I don't mind,' said Annie, and asked eagerly, 'Can I stay up till nine o'clock? Gracie Payne in my class is nine, and she stays up till nine o'clock every night – and I'm going to be nine very soon.'

'So that's why Gracie Payne always has dark rings under her eyes,' said Daphne. 'You can sit up and read your book till your hair's dry, then it's off to sleep with you, my lady – and no arguments.'

'Anyway, she can't go to bed yet,' added Ted. 'We've got a visitor.'

Daphne groaned. 'Why didn't you say? The house is a mess, and so am I.' Looking at herself in the steamy mirror, she dabbed at her hair. 'Who have you brought home this time?'

'It's all right – it's only Percy.'

'Percy? Mr Thring?' Daphne had never met Ted's agent, but he was a very important person in their lives. 'I'll have to go and change – you might have warned me.'

'I didn't know myself till he turned up at Streatham Common. He motored down from Kennington to see the show and give me some good news – then he drove me back here afterwards. Take your time. There's some beer in the larder – I'll give him a drink while we're waiting.'

Ten minutes later, Daphne entered the sitting room in her best dress and a cloud of perfume that Ted had given her last Christmas, which she saved for special occasions. Annie, in her nightie, shook hands with Mr Thring.

'So you're Miss Annie Watkins, eh? I've heard a lot about you!' wheezed Percy, blinking owlishly through his pebble-glass spectacles. He turned to Daphne. 'Mrs Watkins – this is a very great pleasure.'

'How do you do, Mr Thring?' said Daphne. 'It was good of you to drive Ted home after the show.'

'Well, what's the use of having a motor if you can't do a pal a good turn, that's what I say.'

'And that's why we're a bit late,' Ted added. 'Percy got lost a couple of times.'

'On the way from Streatham?' Daphne was puzzled. 'Didn't you tell Mr Thring the short cuts?'

'He tried,' chuckled Percy, then had a coughing fit and thumped his chest. 'But I don't like people giving me directions – it only confuses me. I follow the sun; in the morning it's east, in the evenings it's west – that's good enough for me.'

Annie thought for a moment. 'How do you manage when it's dark?'

'Night-times, I stop and ask.' He took off his spectacles and polished them on the end of his tie. 'Still, we made pretty good time. We'd have got here sooner, if I hadn't driven up on the pavement to avoid a nasty accident.'

'Oh dear,' said Daphne. 'Nothing serious, I hope?'

'No. Damn great Airedale dog ran out in the road, slap in front of me. People don't keep their animals under proper control.'

'Quite right – except it wasn't an Airedale, it was a boy on a scooter,' said Ted.

'There you go again – confusing me with details . . .' Percy replaced his glasses and plumped heavily into the armchair. 'Now then, are you going to break the news to your good lady, or shall I?'

In the end, they told her together. Another of Percy's artistes – a comedy dancer and contortionist ('Dudley Dubblo – the Double-Jointed Scream!') – had been forced to cancel an engagement at very short notice, as the law had finally caught up with him for theft, fraud, tax evasion and failure to pay maintenance for the wife and family he had abandoned. As a result, Dudley would be unable to perform at the New Cross Empire tomorrow, since he would be appearing elsewhere.

Percy glanced sideways at little Annie. 'At His Majesty's Pleasure, as they say. I suppose you might call it a Command Performance.'

'So Ted's going on instead, tomorrow night?' asked Daphne.

'Twice nightly – tomorrow, and all the week,' Percy nodded. 'And a very nice spot too, opening the second half.'

Ted broke in. 'If I go down well, Percy says there could be a lot more dates to follow.'

'Dudley Dubblo's broken his contract, you see,' said Percy. 'This could be the start of a whole new career for your husband, my dear. The bill-posters will be going round first thing in the morning, sticking slips over the hoardings.'

'He's changing my name as well. I'm going to be Watt instead of Watkins from now on,' exclaimed Ted.

'That's my idea. It's got more punch, somehow.' Percy pointed at an imaginary poster, following the words with his forefinger: '"*Ted Watt – the 100-Watt Comedian!*" – what d'you think? You must come along – I'll put out a pair of comps on Friday.'

Daphne frowned. 'Comps?'

'Complimentary tickets,' Ted explained. 'You could bring Val, to keep you company.'

'Can I come?' asked Annie. 'Do they let you in if you're nearly nine?'

'Not this time, love,' Daphne told her. 'You'll have to stay and look after Grandma. I'll take you to see Daddy on the stage very soon, I promise. This time it's Auntie Val's turn.'

Valerie was happy to go to New Cross; she would have been at a loose end otherwise, since Gerry was going to Savoy Hill after work on Friday, to discuss the possible job.

During the interval, she and Daphne did not go to the bar – only a certain type of woman went to the bar unescorted – but remained in their complimentary seats, at the front of the dress circle, while Val poured out some of her troubles.

'Gerry still doesn't know what sort of job they're offering him. He doesn't think it's book-keeping – which is just as well, because he's never really liked doing the accounts at Hawkins and Company. Aunt Ethel had a good head for figures; I don't think Gerry has . . . But what else could it be? He doesn't know the first thing about broadcasting.'

'I don't suppose many people do,' said Daphne. 'Everybody must have to start from scratch. And Gerry's never been afraid of taking on a challenge; he did lots of different jobs before he went into estate agency.' She ticked them off on her fingers. 'He started as an office-boy with the *Beckenham and Penge Advertiser*, hoping to become a reporter, but he didn't last long – I think it was a bit too hectic for him. Then he worked in a bookshop, but he said there was no money in it, so he did a few months as a door-to-door salesman, selling encyclopaedias – but that didn't suit him either. He got taken on as a temporary postman one Christmas, but he hated starting work in the middle of the night – so in the end he finished up at Hawkins'. It's been quite a varied career.'

'Isn't that typical?' Val sank back into her seat. 'That's what I mean. Ever since I've known Gerry, he's never said a word about those other jobs – he never tells me anything!'

'Well, they weren't much to boast about,' said Daphne. 'In fact, the job at Hawkins' is the only one he's ever stuck at.'

'All the same, he might have told me.' Val was still aggrieved. 'And Hawkins' is a steady job, with good prospects. Why does he want to throw it up, all of a sudden?'

'He's probably bored – I expect the BBC sounds more exciting. Perhaps he's feeling restless.'

'Restless? Yes, I can understand that.' Val looked away, gazing down at the stalls below, already filling up again; an interval bell was ringing. 'It's a big decision to make, all the same.'

'How much are the BBC offering him?' asked Daphne.

'How should I know? He never tells me things like that – I don't even know what he earns now. I tell you, he keeps me in the dark.'

Daphne looked shocked. 'Don't you ever discuss things?'

'Never. He decides what he's going to do – he doesn't ask my opinion.'

'Yes, he's always been like that. Perhaps it comes from growing up as the only boy in a house full of women. He keeps his thoughts to himself.'

'He certainly does.' In the orchestra pit, the musicians were filing in to take their places, and Val tried to sound more cheerful. 'The show's starting again.'

'What else were you going to tell me?' Daphne asked her. 'You said you wanted to pour out all your troubles – was there something else?'

The footlights sprang into life, sending a brilliant glow over the red stage curtains as the house-lights dimmed.

'No, not really,' said Val.

When she left Freda Gunn, she had promised to think over what she had said. Since then she had thought of very little else, and now she had made up her mind, but she wouldn't tell Daphne that. At the side of the proscenium arch, a small box lit up, with the figure '8' picked out in electric bulbs.

She consulted her programme. '"*Number Eight: Ted Watt – the 100-Watt Comedian*". Here we go!'

The curtain rose, the band struck up *How's This For A Start?* and Ted strolled on, grinning at the audience in a friendly way.

'Hello,' he said. 'Fancy seeing you, of all people! It's a funny old world, isn't it?'

Daphne's stomach tightened; she dug her nails into the palms of her hands, suffering agonies on his behalf. After all the Working

Men's Clubs and open-air bandstands, this was the first time Ted had ever walked out on to a real stage, in a proper theatre – but he stood there, as easy and confident as if he were at home. And Daphne realised, with a little shock of recognition, that he was.

His act only lasted ten or twelve minutes, but he scored another hit. The audience loved him, and when he walked off with a cheery wave, they didn't want to let him go. It was only when the band-leader struck up the music for the following turn, and the Flying Bozzini Brothers shot out of the wings on roller-skates, that they settled down to watch the rest of the show.

After the curtain fell, and everyone stood to attention for the National Anthem, Val asked, 'Are we going round to his dressing room?'

'No, we can't, because he's sharing with the roller-skaters. We're to go to the pub opposite the stage door, and he'll meet us in the snug.'

'In the what?'

'It's a room at the back, where they go for a drink after the show. It's a good job you're here; I'd never dare go in there by myself.'

'Perhaps he'll be waiting for us – he's had plenty of time to change.'

But he wasn't there. The snug was crowded with several of the other performers – dancers and singers and jugglers and clowns, looking very different without their costumes and make-up. Yet they still had an indefinable something that marked them out at once as 'theatricals'; they talked a little louder and laughed a little longer than other people.

Bravely, Daphne and Val pushed through to the bar and ordered two port and lemons, then they squeezed into a corner with their drinks, while the tide of exuberant gaiety and gossip washed around them.

'. . . Only two calls, though she tried to milk another one. I told her she was pushing her luck, but she wouldn't listen. When she walked out the third time, there wasn't a ripple, and she died the death.'

'Reminds me of old Maggie Whatsit – I never can remember her other name, something foreign it was – she always said she had Russian connections, but I know for a fact the family came from Cardiff. You know who I mean – she used to do Gems From The Opera – and one night she was out there, dying on her feet, and there were some drunks in front, who started giving her the bird. She struggled on, taking no notice, then some bloke in the gods yells out:

"*Shut up and give the old cow a chance!*" And Maggie turns round, looking like a duchess, and says: "*Thank you – I'm glad to know there's one gentleman here tonight*".'

Val nudged Daphne, under cover of the general hubbub. 'Somebody's talking about Ted.'

Daphne listened. A fat, florid man was saying, 'Yes, the new lad's quite promising. I notice the laughs have been building all the week – he's a good second-half opener. Better than poor old Dudley, in some ways.'

His companion agreed, adding: 'All the same, I was sorry to hear about Dud's spot of trouble. He's had bad luck lately – one damn thing after another – and all on account of his ex-wife. What a bitch, squeezing him for every penny.'

'Some women are like that. Ever since she found out about him and the girl in Leeds – what was she, an exotic dancer? Didn't she do a routine with a snake?'

'She did a routine with old Dud, anyhow . . .'

They roared with laughter, and Daphne hated them. She hated them all, with their stupid jokes and innuendoes, their loud voices and loud clothes.

'Here comes Ted,' said Val, as he came through the swing doors.

At once a crowd of colleagues surrounded him, offering to buy him a drink. When he joined his wife and sister, a brimming pint mug in his hand, he was shining with happiness.

'Sorry about that,' he said. 'Got waylaid – how did you like the show?'

'Very much,' said Val. 'You were the best.'

'Not so loud!' He winked. 'They might think you were biased.' Turning to Daphne, he planted a beery kiss on her lips. 'Well, sweetheart? What did you think?'

'You were very good,' she told him.

'This is only the beginning,' he said. 'Sorry I was a bit slow coming round, but being a Friday – it's the night the ghost walks.'

Val stared. 'A ghost? Where?'

He laughed. 'Just a saying. Friday nights are when the pay-packets come round. And I had a personal message from the management tucked inside mine. They're offering me a contract – eight weeks guaranteed, plus a rise in salary. How's that for a start? – to coin a phrase.'

They were interrupted by one of the chorus-girls, who kissed Ted on the cheek, saying: 'I'm really pleased for you, Ted – we all are. You deserve it.'

Smiling, Ted said, 'Thanks, Maisie. Let me introduce you. This is Daphne, my wife, and my sister Val. This is Maisie. You saw her doing her high kicks earlier on – third from the right!'

Unabashed, Maisie shook hands. 'Nice to meet you – were you in front tonight?. You must be ever so proud of him.'

Gradually, the others joined them, and Daphne and Val were introduced again and again, shaking hands with more people than they could ever remember. It was nearly closing-time when they left the pub, and they caught the last train back from New Cross, through Brockley and Honor Oak.

There was nobody else in the third-class compartment; Daphne and Ted sat on one side, with Val opposite. They were all tired, and for a while nobody spoke, then Daphne broke the silence.

'You never finished telling us about the new contract.'

'Oh, didn't I?' Ted tried to remember. 'I thought I did.'

'You said it was eight weeks – that doesn't mean eight more weeks at New Cross, does it?'

'You never play more than one week, in variety. This is eight weeks round the circuit – Brixton, Shepherds Bush, Hackney – then Coventry and Nottingham and – I can't remember them all. The usual sort of tour.'

'So what did you say?'

'I said yes, please! What did you expect me to say?'

'You could have said you wanted to talk it over with me first.'

He put his arm round her. 'I knew you'd say the same. This is the best break I've ever had – I'd be crazy to turn it down.'

'I see.'

Across the carriage, Val was watching them, and Daphne looked away quickly. They travelled on in silence, except for the steady rhythm of the train-wheels drumming on the rails.

Later, when they were in bed, Daphne raised the subject again. 'Is that what you want?' she asked. 'To go away on tour for eight weeks, leaving me and Annie at home?'

'I won't be away for eight weeks. Around London, I'll get home every night after the show. It's only when we do the provincial towns I'll be away. Do you mind?'

'Of course I mind! I'll miss you – Annie will miss you. I'd have thought you might miss us, too.'

In the darkness, he moved closer. 'I'll miss you like hell, but that's the way things are, in the business. You have to expect it.'

He began to embrace her, but she pulled away, saying, 'I don't have to like it.'

He drew her towards him. 'If it bothers you that much, why not come with me, you and Annie? I'll find us some decent digs—'

'How could we do that? I've got my job, too, although you've never really taken that seriously, have you?'

'Couldn't you ask for some time off? Just a few weeks?'

'You know I can't. There's Annie to think of as well – we can't take her out of school.' Daphne choked back a sob. 'I don't want you to go. I love you!'

'And I love you, sweetheart – you and Annie.' His hands roamed over her, stroking, soothing, reassuring. 'Of course I do. If it means that much to you, I won't go. I haven't signed anything – I'll turn it down. I'll go on doing the concert parties and the shows in the park. I'll stay with you.'

'Would you really? Oh, Ted.' She flung her arms round him, and joy and unhappiness and guilt mingled with her tears, as they made love.

At the beginning of June, Valerie's visiting order came through. The following Sunday, she carried it with her when she caught the bus to Brixton.

She hadn't told anyone about it, outside the Gunn family. Gerald had begun his new job at Savoy Hill, and as he worked for the Director of Programmes, and the programmes went out every day of the year, he had to work one weekend in three. This Sunday he would be on duty all day, until the transmitter went off the air at half-past ten.

So Gerald was safely out of the way, and she didn't have to make up any lies . . . But that didn't ease her conscience.

As she travelled down Brixton Hill, she felt ashamed, as if she were about to commit a crime. She told herself this was silly. She was going to visit Steve because she felt sorry for him – that was the only reason.

When she got off the bus she began to walk up a long, straight avenue of trees, among other young women going in the same direction – women with children and push-chairs, older people with scared, set faces – and she felt very frightened.

She was tempted to turn round and go home again, but she

couldn't do that. Freda had told Steve last Sunday, so he was expecting her. It would be cruel to disappoint him. And – deep down – she knew she could not turn back. She must see him again; something more than pity had brought her here.

Sick at heart, she entered the prison with the other visitors. They sat for what seemed an eternity in a bare, ugly waiting room. At last they were allowed in, a few at a time. Mercifully, Val's name was among the first to be called. In a kind of nightmare, she stood up and followed the uniformed officer as he unlocked a door and led the way along an echoing corridor smelling of carbolic and cabbage-water.

The visiting room had tiled walls, and worn linoleum on the floor. Three tables were set out across the room, each with a single bentwood chair on either side. At the centre table, Steve sat waiting for her.

He looked different. His hair was shorter and he'd lost weight; his face, which used to be so full of life, seemed guarded, hiding his emotions. He wore a drab cloth jacket, shabby and patched as if it had been worn by a hundred other men before him. His face was pale, and he did not even smile . . . Yes, he looked very different.

Yet she would have known him anywhere; even in a crowd, she could have picked him out at once. It was his eyes – those big, dark eyes, fixed upon her. She could feel his gaze on her skin, like sunburn.

She sat down. Embarrassed, she glanced round the room. The other couples were intent on one another – no one was looking at her. Nobody except Steve.

The officer on duty, realising she was a newcomer, came over and told her quietly, 'Please keep both hands on top of the table at all times, miss.'

'I'm sorry.' She obeyed nervously, trying to smile at Steve. 'Hello,' she said.

'Hello, Val. Thanks for coming.'

His voice hadn't changed. It was just the way she remembered it – the way she had heard it in her mind, since he went away.

She managed to ask, 'How are you?'

'Not so bad. How are you?'

'Oh, I'm fine,' she said.

'How's your family? Daphne and Ted, and your Mum?'

'They're fine too.'

'And – your husband? Is he all right?'

'Yes. He's working today. He has to work some weekends.'

'Did he mind about you coming to see me?'

'No.' Then she found she couldn't lie to him. 'I didn't tell him.'

There was a pause while Steve considered this, then he asked, 'What's he like? I never met him, did I?'

'I don't think so. He's – very nice. He's been very good to me.'

Another pause, then: 'Do you love him?'

She could feel her heart beating as she replied, 'I told you – he's very good to me. A very good husband.' She looked down at her hands; his were clenched into fists upon the table-top, a few inches away, yet the distance between them seemed enormous.

She heard him say, 'Mum told you, didn't she, how it happened? I never knew about the old lady – till afterwards.'

'Yes, she told me.'

'I've only got another year to go. Less than that, if I get some time knocked off.' He stammered, stumbling over the words. 'You know I – I still love you. You do know that?'

She lifted her head, looking into his face; his eyes were bigger than ever, and she felt as if he could see into the depths of her mind and her heart and her soul. Gazing across the table, they entered one another through their eyes – until she could not bear it a moment longer.

Standing up, she pushed back her chair. 'I'm sorry – I can't stay,' she said. 'I've got to go.'

She had been afraid he would ask her if she still loved him too, but he did not need to ask. He had seen the answer already.

'I'm sorry,' she repeated helplessly. 'Goodbye, Steve.'

The duty officer stared in surprise as he opened the door for her, and she walked through it without looking back. She knew now that she should not have come – and that she must never see Steve again.

Chapter Thirteen

1926 WAS A year of industrial unrest. In March, the coal miners refused to accept a wages cut; in April, a national coal strike began – and by the beginning of May, a major crisis seemed to be unavoidable.

On Monday, 3 May, when Val came home to Westwood Court after work, she heard their new telephone ringing inside the flat as she put her key in the lock. Wrenching the key round, she thought for a moment that the lock wasn't going to turn, but then the door flew open and she stumbled into the hall.

The telephone was still ringing as she picked it up, putting the receiver to her ear and bringing her lips close to the mouthpiece.

'Hello?' she began anxiously.

'You're supposed to announce the number first,' said a tinny voice that she could hardly recognise as Gerry's. 'They tell us not to say hello.'

'Why not?' Val asked.

'So the caller knows he hasn't got a wrong number.'

'But you knew it was me, didn't you?'

'Yes, I did, but—'

'Then it didn't make any difference, did it?' Val pointed out.

Gerry sighed, and began again. 'I'm ringing to tell you not to bother about supper for me. I'm not sure what time I'll get home.'

'Oh, why's that?'

'We've been asked to stay on duty in case of a National Emergency. They're expecting a bulletin from Downing Street.'

'What sort of bulletin?'

'I'm not supposed to tell you this, but it's almost certain the Trades Union Congress are going to call out all their workers for a General

Strike, and Mr Reith has told us to stand by. I may have to stay here all night.'

'Oh, I see. Will you ring up again and let me know?'

'I can't promise – I'll probably be too busy. But you can always turn on our wireless and listen in; we'll interrupt the programmes as soon as there's any further news.'

After she had replaced the telephone receiver on its little hook, Val switched on the wireless set.

This was Gerry's pride and joy. As soon as he was taken on to the BBC's permanent staff, he had bought a crystal set, but that was very unreliable, and the earphones were uncomfortable. When the new Marconi three-valve model came out, with its own loudspeaker, Gerry had bought one – it cost nearly thirty pounds, which Val considered wildly extravagant – so she could listen to her husband over the airwaves.

The Director of Programmes had decided that Gerald Glynn's voice was ideally suited to broadcasting, and in between his office work, he stood in for any of the regular announcers when they were off-duty, to introduce programmes or read the news bulletins.

Though the Marconi was the latest model, it took a long time to warm up; the three valves glowed sluggishly, then slowly brightened until they gave out enough light to read the small print in a newspaper. If there were a General Strike, there wouldn't be any newspapers – and then Great Britain would have to rely on the British Broadcasting Company as its only source of information.

The loudspeaker whistled in a menacing way. Gerry had explained that this was called 'oscillation', and that it was perfectly harmless, but Val still found it rather alarming, and her fingers trembled as she tuned in the signal from the Daventry transmitter.

At last she heard a small string orchestra playing a pizzicato piece called *The Grasshoppers' Dance*. Oh well, no news was good news. At ten o'clock, there was the usual time signal, followed by a general news bulletin in which the announcer reminded listeners of the Prime Minister's recent message to the nation: '*Keep steady . . . Remember that peace on earth comes to all men of goodwill.*'

Val didn't quite understand what Mr Baldwin had meant by this, but it seemed vaguely encouraging, so after fifteen minutes of *Folk Tunes of the British Isles* played by the Band of the Royal Air Force, she switched off the set and went to bed.

That night, the transmitters stayed on the air later than usual; it was nearly midnight when a duty-announcer told the nation that negotiations between the Government and the TUC had broken down, and the first General Strike in British history had begun.

Before the Strike, the BBC were not allowed to broadcast news earlier than seven in the evening, as Fleet Street was afraid this would cut down the sale of newspapers. In the emergency, the Government relaxed this rule, and news bulletins were put out at frequent intervals all day.

The offices and studios at Savoy Hill were in a state of siege, guarded by police, in case militant strikers tried to break in and sabotage the programmes; the BBC staff – including Gerald – worked round the clock, snatching a few hours of sleep on camp beds. Val did not see her husband for several days, though she occasionally heard his voice.

In the outside world, life went on – with difficulty.

There was no public transport, until well-meaning volunteers – students, stockbrokers and other professional men – learned to drive trams, trains and buses. Even so, a great many people had to walk to work each day.

The distribution of food was a problem, but the Government organised fleets of vans and lorries to carry butter, flour, meat and other vital supplies all over the country, although there was a widespread fear that the food would run out.

On Wednesday morning, Miss Preece was coming home after a weary expedition round the Penge shops, grateful to have got hold of some bread, cheese and milk, when she met her next-door neighbour pushing a perambulator.

Since Mrs Winthrop was a widow, well into her fifties, Miss Preece greeted her with astonishment. 'Oh, are you looking after somebody's baby?'

'Er, yes.' Mrs Winthrop seemed uncomfortable, and tried to pass on, but Miss Preece planted herself in front of the pram.

'Do let me see the little dear.' She peeped under the hood, then straightened up. 'I thought as much. You're hoarding, aren't you?'

The perambulator was stuffed with goods – sacks of potatoes, packets of sugar, pats of butter and pots of jam.

'Mind yer own business!' Mrs Winthrop gobbled like a turkey. 'How dare you? Take your hands off me pram!'

'Don't you know they've asked us not to buy more than we need? That way there'll be fair shares all round. Think yourself lucky I don't report you to the police!' exclaimed Miss Preece.

'Rubbish!' Mrs Winthrop spat out the words. 'This Strike could go on for months. We got to do something, or we'll finish up starving to death. I'm surprised you ain't seen that in yer crystal ball!'

She manoeuvred the pram through her front gate, calling spitefully over her shoulder: 'Blooming fortune-teller! I'm a law-abiding citizen, I am!'

When Miss Preece went indoors Harry came to meet her, wearing a disreputable old pair of canvas trousers and a filthy vest with streaks of paint all over it, in every colour of the rainbow.

'What's going on? What was Old Mother Winthrop yelling about?'

Miss Preece told him. 'She's been buying up half the food in Penge by the looks of it. When I told her what I thought of her, she turned ugly.'

'Not her – she was born that way,' grunted Harry. 'Leave her to me. I'll give her a piece of my mind—'

He was about to go and have it out with the lady there and then, but Miss Preece stopped him. 'No, don't. It wouldn't do any good.'

'I'm not letting her insult you like that. You need someone to speak up for you, my girl!'

'*I am not your girl!*' Miss Preece faced him squarely. 'I don't need your help, Mr Glynn. Anyway, I'd be ashamed for her to see you in that state – you look like an old tramp!'

And she marched into her kitchen, shutting the door in Harry's face.

To everyone's surprise, life went on much the same as usual. There were some unpleasant scenes – several confrontations between strikers and strike-breakers – but by and large there was very little violence. There was enough food to go round; nobody starved, and although the public grumbled at the daily inconveniences, on the whole they put up with them.

On Saturday afternoon, Val invited Daphne to bring Annie round to tea at Westwood Court, saying she had a surprise for her.

'What sort of surprise?' asked Annie, as soon they arrived.

'If I told you, it wouldn't be a surprise, would it?' Val smiled. 'You wait and see.'

'Is it a present or something?'

'Annie! You mustn't ask questions like that – it's not polite,' her mother told her.

'Sit down, and I'll bring in the tea,' said Val. 'I was lucky when I went round the shops yesterday. I got some icing sugar, so last night I made us a cake.'

'Is that it?' Annie's face fell. 'Is that the surprise?'

'No, it isn't — the cake's an extra,' Val assured her, and Annie brightened up again.

As they took their places at the tea-table, Daphne passed on the latest news about Ted. 'Percy Thring's got him a very good contract — a ten-week summer season at Broadstairs, in a concert party.'

Val looked at her in surprise. 'Ten weeks in Broadstairs? That's down in Kent somewhere, isn't it?'

'Yes, near Margate. What's wrong with that?'

'I thought you hated the idea of Ted going away. Last year, when he was offered that tour, you made him turn it down.'

'I didn't make him — he turned it down himself. He realised how lonely we'd be without him, didn't he, Annie?'

But Annie wasn't listening; peeping inquisitively round the room, she was looking for the mysterious surprise.

'Well, there was a lot of fuss about it, I know that.' Val began to pour the tea, passing a cup to Daphne.

Percy Thring had been far from pleased when Ted rejected the tour, and his dragon secretary, Bessie, had told Ted that he was not only ungrateful, he was a damn fool! When Ted explained that it didn't suit him in his present situation, Percy had calmed down a little, and they reached a compromise. Ted agreed to play the suburban London dates, and Percy found another act to take over the rest of the tour, in the provinces. But a certain coolness remained between Ted and his agent for several months.

One day, when Ted dropped into the office, Percy was out and Bessie gave him a stern lecture, telling him he must never let such an opportunity slip through his fingers again.

'If you're going to get anywhere in this business, you've got to put the business first. Your private life has to come second,' she said severely. 'That's always been my motto, and I recommend you to follow it.'

Ted looked across the desk at the plain elderly spinster, with her grey hair scraped up into a bun and her steel-rimmed glasses, and she added dryly, 'Oh, I know what you're thinking — but I've had my chances, believe you me. Only I preferred to stay and work for Mr Thring. We've been together for thirty years now, and I've never regretted it.'

Something in her tone made Ted say suddenly: 'You're really fond of Percy, aren't you?'

Bessie lowered her eyes; it was as if a shutter had come down, guarding her privacy. 'I respect Mr Thring. He's been very good to me – I've no complaints.'

'Well, there you are. You chose to stay with Percy, like I've chosen to stay with Daphne. It comes to the same thing, doesn't it?'

'Perhaps.' Her expression softened. 'But if you take my advice, you'll find a way to juggle your career and your private life at the same time. It's a good trick, if you can do it – and you'll never be happy if you don't.'

Now, with the start of the summer season looming up, it seemed that Ted would be able to follow Bessie's advice.

'Don't you understand?' Daphne asked Val. 'A seaside concert party isn't like touring around the country – it's ten weeks in one place. As soon as school breaks up, Annie and I will be able to go with him.'

'Staying at the seaside – for the whole summer? Won't that cost a fortune?'

'Ted's got the address of a good boarding house; they do breakfast and an evening meal, and we'll have a picnic on the beach during the day. It's really very reasonable.'

'Sounds wonderful,' said Val enviously. 'Aren't you the lucky ones? Can you pop me in your suitcase and take me with you?'

'We haven't got a big enough suitcase,' said Annie – and the two women laughed.

'Only joking, love – I couldn't go away all the summer – Uncle Gerry wouldn't like it. And neither would Mr Buckland. I only get two weeks' holiday from the Crystal Palace.' Then an afterthought occurred to her. 'You said ten weeks – but you don't get that long for school holidays, do you?'

'Not quite. Ted will have to go off on his own before the end of term,' Daphne admitted. 'But that won't be too hard. He'll be so busy rehearsing and getting the show on at the start of the season, he wouldn't have much time with us anyway. We can manage without Dad for a few weeks, can't we, Annie?'

Val said no more, but she couldn't help wondering why Daphne seemed happy to accept a few weeks without Ted this summer, when last year the very thought of being separated from him had been unbearable. Changing the subject, she brought out the cake, covered with pink icing and decorated with chocolate drops. Annie's eyes grew round at the sight of it.

'This must be your lucky day!' Val teased her gently. 'An iced cake *and* a surprise. Oh, that reminds me, I must keep an eye on the time.'

She glanced at the clock on the mantelpiece. 'We mustn't miss it, whatever we do.'

When tea was over, and Annie had finished her second slice of cake, Daphne offered to help clear away and wash up, but Val said, 'No, we'll leave that till later. The surprise comes next.'

She switched on the wireless, and Annie said flatly, 'Oh, we're going to listen to *Children's Hour*.'

She had been allowed to hear the programme once or twice before, and though she enjoyed the odd sensation of hearing invisible people talking to her, she felt slightly let down; it was no longer a novelty.

'That's it, isn't it?' She asked. 'The surprise?'

'Not quite – but you're getting warmer,' said Val. 'Now shush! – and listen.'

Somewhere a piano tinkled out a tune called *Country Gardens*, and then a very posh lady said, 'And now, children, it's time for today's birthday greetings – and here to read them out we have a new Uncle for you – Uncle Gee-Gee. Come along, Gee-Gee. Who are the lucky children with birthdays today?'

'Thank you, Auntie Sophie, and hello children. This is Uncle Gee-Gee speaking,' drawled a familiar voice. 'And the first name on our list today is little Marigold Chilcott, who lives at Muswell Hill.'

Annie sat bolt upright, as she recognised the voice. 'It's Uncle Gerry!' she exclaimed. 'Why did she call him Uncle Gee-Gee? That's silly – he's not a horse.'

Daphne broke in: 'I didn't know Gerry was working on *Children's Hour*,' she said. 'Has he stopped being an announcer?'

'No, he's only standing in for somebody who's off sick. They all have made-up names, Annie. They call him Gee-Gee because it's his initials – G. G. for Gerald Glynn.'

The loudspeaker voice continued: '. . . Mummy and Daddy say many happy returns of the day, Margaret – and I believe that if you look in the cupboard under the stairs, you might find a very special parcel waiting for you! Now, who have we got next? Oh, my goodness – it's Peter and Patricia Howard from Sevenoaks – and you're both seven today, so what does that make you? Come on, all together now—'

A chorus of male and female voices in the studio called out in unison, 'Hello, *twins*!'

Gerry went on, working his way through a long list, finishing at last: 'Well, that's all for today, children, except I have one message for a little girl who hasn't got a birthday till next September, but she's a special friend of mine, so I'm going to say a quick hello to Annie Watkins, in Upper Norwood. Hello, Annie – and goodbye to you all!'

'Thank you, Uncle Gee-Gee,' said Auntie Sophie coldly. 'And now it's time for a little more music.'

Val switched off the set, saying, 'That's enough of that! Well, were you surprised, Annie?'

Annie was still staring at the wireless. 'That was me!' she gasped. 'He was talking to *me*! Can I come another day? Will he do it again?'

But it never happened again. At the end of the programme, Gerald was reprimanded for sending a personal message to a member of his family. Such unprofessional behaviour could not be tolerated, and Uncle Gee-Gee was never invited to appear with the Uncles and Aunties in *Children's Hour* again.

Annie was delighted, however, and went home in a glow of happiness. There was something magical about being talked to by a box in the corner of a room. It would have been even better if some other friends or family could have heard it too, but wireless sets were few and far between in South London.

Certainly Grandpa Glynn had not heard it; even if he could have afforded a wireless set, he would have scorned such newfangled rubbish. In any case, as Gerald went on the air, Harry was just leaving Miss Preece's house, on his way out for an evening stroll, calling in at a nearby pub on the way back.

When he opened the front door, he found a young lady walking up the path – a pretty young lady, in a summer dress of green and yellow, made of some light material that fluttered in the evening breeze.

'Hello, my dear!' he saluted her cheerfully, taking his pipe out of his mouth. 'What can I do for you?'

'Is this where Miss Preece lives?' the young lady asked.

'That's right, she's the householder – I'm one of her paying guests. What name shall I say?'

'My name's Robinson, but she doesn't know me. I heard about her through a friend.'

'Really?' Harry examined her carefully; she was an extremely attractive creature. 'And what have you heard about Miss Preece?'

'My friend told me she used to read fortunes sometimes. Does she still do it?'

'As a matter of fact, she does. Are you keen on that kind of thing?'

Miss Robinson seemed ill at ease. 'Yes I am, rather,' she said. 'I was hoping to make an appointment – do you think I could?'

'I'm sure you could. I'll go and call her.' He turned, and found Miss Preece standing behind him in the open doorway. 'Ah, there you are. Talk of the devil – beg pardon, I didn't mean that. This is Miss Robinson, who wishes to consult you. I said I felt sure you'd give her a reading – cards, palms, crystal – whatever she wants.'

'Oh yes?' Miss Preece looked the newcomer over. 'Who sent you, Miss Robinson?'

'A friend of mine – Miss Birkett. She used to live nearby, only she's moved now. You did a reading for her.'

'Birkett . . . I don't recall the name,' said Miss Preece dubiously. 'I never see clients except on personal recommendation.'

'But this is personal! She told me about you and . . .' The girl lowered her voice. 'I'm having some private problems – I need your advice. You will see me, won't you?'

'Certainly she will!' said Harry. 'The young lady's upset, Miss Preece. You can't refuse when someone's in need of help, can you?'

'Well, if it's a personal recommendation.' Miss Preece was weakening. 'But I haven't got time now. You'll have to come round next week. How about Wednesday evening – will that suit you?' Miss Robinson murmured her grateful thanks, and disappeared. Miss Preece turned on Harry accusingly. 'You didn't ought to talk to strangers about my gifts – that's strictly private. It could lead to unpleasantness.'

'Nonsense! Slip of a girl like that – how could I turn her away?'

'I'm sure you couldn't!' Miss Preece sniffed. 'Any young girl can twist you round her little finger. You ought to be ashamed of yourself . . . You'll be getting me into trouble one of these days!'

Harry winked, and patted her bottom. 'Chance'd be a fine thing.'

'How dare you!' Miss Preece glared. 'Sometimes you forget yourself, Mr Glynn!'

Harry sighed, and wandered off down the path. At the gate, he turned and called, 'I don't suppose you'd fancy a quick one at the Golden Lion?'

The slam of the front door was the only reply.

'No, I thought not,' he said sadly, and went on his way.

Soon after one o'clock on Wednesday afternoon, the BBC's Chief Announcer, Stuart Hibberd, came into the office where Gerald was on duty.

'Get on to Downing Street,' he said curtly. 'Quick as you can.'

Gerald knew better than to ask questions, but did as he was told. When the telephone operator at the exchange said, 'Number, please?' Gerald told her: 'This is the BBC at Savoy Hill. Put me through to Number ten, Downing Street, please – the direct line.'

There was a short pause, then the operator said, 'I'm sorry, that line is engaged. Would you like to try again later?'

'This is very urgent,' said Gerald. 'I'll hold on.'

He explained to Mr Hibberd, who tossed a sheet of typescript on to the desk, muttering impatiently, 'If they don't hurry up, the news bulletin will be over. I thought Mr Reith would be pleased to have this so quickly.'

In the adjoining studio, the General Manager himself was broadcasting the one o'clock news to the nation. During the crisis, Mr Reith had taken turns with the other announcers to read the regular bulletins.

Stuart Hibberd indicated the typed page, telling Gerry, 'This came through on the ticker-tape soon after he'd gone on the air, so I had it copied out at once, and put it on the table in front of him.'

'Is it a big story?'

'The biggest. The General Strike is over . . . But the Great Man just glanced at it, scribbled a pencilled note in the margin – "Get this confirmed by Downing Street" – then handed it back to me, while he went on reading. I've heard of Scottish caution, but this takes the biscuit!'

When the operator put the call through, Gerald passed the telephone over. Moments later, Mr Hibberd took the page back to Mr Reith, with the word '*Confirmed*' written across the top – and the news was broadcast to the listening millions.

That evening, when Gerry arrived home, he presented Valerie with a bottle of champagne and told her to get out the glasses.

'To celebrate the end of the Strike?' she asked. 'How wonderful!'

'Not only that – I've had some good news of my own,' he told her.

He had been summoned by the Director of Programmes, and entered his Chief's office with a feeling of trepidation, wondering what he had done wrong this time.

'I have received a confidential memorandum about you from the Head of *Children's Hour*, Mr Glynn. I gather you overstepped the mark when you were reading out the kiddies' birthday list?'

'Yes, sir. I'm sorry. He's already told me I won't be asked to take part in children's programmes again.'

'He was quite right to admonish you – we can't run any risk where children are concerned. If everyone went on the air and told the little dears the first thing that came into their head – well, the imagination boggles.'

'Yes, sir. I really am most frightfully sorry.'

'Never mind; all is not lost. Since you appear to have the ability to think quickly and work without a script, I am considering the possibility of sending you to a different department – Outside Broadcasting. We are about to extend the scope of our OBs, to cover more sporting fixtures and public events, like royal weddings, the Opening of Parliament, Armistice Day and so on – and I think you might be the man for the job. I'm sending you off on a short tour round the regional studios; it will be necessary for you to get acquainted with them all, since OBs may be transmitted from anywhere in the country. Bearing this in mind, I want you to hold yourself in readiness to be sent out of London at any time.'

Relating this to Val as they sipped their champagne, Gerry added, 'He told me to pack a suitcase, spongebag and toothbrush, and keep them in the office, since I could be sent off at very short notice.'

Val thought fast. 'And that might happen during the summer?'

'Any time, apparently, there's no knowing.' He drained his glass. 'It'll make a change to get out of London. I'm looking forward to it.'

'Yes, I see.' Val began again. 'I was just thinking – I've got a couple of weeks' holiday due to me, and Daff and Annie are going to Broadstairs with Ted. I suppose, if you're not here, I could go with them, couldn't I?'

Refilling his glass, Gerry shook his head. 'Hardly. I've no way of knowing when I'll be sent out of town. You might fix up a trip to Broadstairs while I was still at Savoy Hill.'

'Well, would that matter?'

'Of course it would! It would mean I'd come home in the evening, tired and hungry, and there'd be no supper on the table. Sorry, old dear, I'm afraid it's out of the question. Are you ready for some more bubbly?'

'No, I've still got some left.' Val looked into her glass. The liquid seemed flat – the sparkle had gone out of it.

Half a mile away at the bottom of the hill, Miss Preece was laying out the playing cards, one by one. Though it was still daylight outside, the window was thickly curtained, and the shaded gasolier above the centre table threw a pool of yellow light on the cards, which were face down.

'Now then,' she said. 'Turn them up one at a time, please, starting with the one nearest you.'

Miss Robinson did so; it was the five of diamonds.

'A good beginning,' said Miss Preece.

'What does it mean?' asked the girl, in a half-whisper.

'A small sum of money – or it could be a present. Something to wear, perhaps . . . Have you got a birthday soon?'

'No, my birthday was at the end of March.'

'Aries – fancy. Turn the next card, please.'

It was the same suit; the three of diamonds, this time.

'You will receive news of an absent friend,' said Miss Preece. 'Are you expecting a letter?'

'No. Perhaps it's Miss Birkett – the one I told you about. I haven't heard from her lately.'

'Strange, I don't remember the name – but then I see so many people.'

'Do you give lots of readings? They keep you busy, I expect?'

Miss Preece shrugged. 'It comes and goes. Another card, please.'

'Spades this time – the six of spades.'

'That could mean a quarrel, or an estrangement – or the separation of friends. Perhaps when you parted from your friend Miss Birkett you weren't on the best of terms?'

'I wouldn't say that. She got a job in Weston-Super-Mare, and we sort of lost touch, that's all.'

Miss Preece sucked her teeth, then said, 'I think you said you needed advice about a personal problem. If you were to tell me about that, it might be easier. You have to know what you're looking for, in the cards. You must tell the cards what it is you want to know.'

'It – it's about a gentleman friend. I don't know whether I should trust him, or not.'

'Ah, I knew trust came into this somehow – I could sense a lack of trust. Would you mind showing me your hands, please?'

Miss Robinson held out both hands, palm uppermost, and Miss Preece studied them in silence for some time.

'I'm getting strong vibrations I don't understand,' she said eventually, 'vibrations of power – danger, even. There's something you haven't told me. I can't help you if you're holding something back. I get the impression that you wish you hadn't come to consult me.'

'Yes, that's true.' Miss Robinson withdrew her hands. 'Did you say the fee would be five bob?' She stood up and put a handful of

252

coins on the table. 'There's your money. You needn't tell me any more; I've found out everything I needed.'

'What do you mean?' asked Miss Preece, but the girl began speaking rapidly, as if she wanted to get this over as soon as possible.

'I have to inform you that I am a policewoman serving in this Division, and I must warn you that you are breaking the law. It is my duty to report you for infringing the Vagrancy Act of 1824—'

'Vagrancy? What do you mean? I'm not a vagrant – this is my house—' Miss Preece slumped back in her chair, as the policewoman continued.

'. . . For pretending or professing to tell fortunes, by palmistry or other means, and for accepting money for such activities . . .'

The colour had left Miss Preece's face. Her dyed hair and carmine lips stood out hideously against her greenish pallor.

'You wouldn't – you're not going to arrest me?'

'I'm sorry, madam. I must put in a report to my superior officers. You will be hearing from the authorities in the near future . . . Good evening.'

And the young woman left the house. There were times when she did not enjoy her job, and this evening she did not feel proud of herself.

From his studio, Harry heard Miss Preece crying – deep wails of grief. He burst into the parlour, saying, 'Good Gad, woman, what's wrong with you? What's happened?'

Between her anguished sobs, she told him the story, ending, 'It was her, of course – that cow next door. She threatened to do it, and now she has. Put the police on to me, she did – and now they're going to lock me up. Oh Harry, whatever shall I do?'

He put his arms round her, patting her on the shoulder and saying gently, 'There, there, don't take on so. They won't do anything to you – I won't let them. Leave it to me, old girl. Never you fear, I'll sort this out somehow.'

But though he spoke confidently, for once Harry Glynn was a worried man.

On Sunday afternoon, Mr Colpoys was expected at Sackville Road. Before he arrived, Kate Watkins went down to the kitchen to speak to Daphne, and to Val, who had called in to collect Annie and take her out for a walk.

'Excuse me interrupting, but I was wondering . . .' She threw a meaning look at Annie and lowered her voice. 'It's rather awkward. Could I have a word with you, Daff – privately?'

Annie was immediately interested. 'Is it about me? Can I listen?'

'No, duck, it's nothing to do with you. I want to talk to your Mum in private.'

'Can Auntie Val stay?'

'Yes, if she wants to. That's different.'

'Why is it different?' Annie wasn't going to give in that easily. 'Why can she stay and I can't?'

Daphne took charge of the situation. 'You heard what Nana said – and I've got something for you to do. I want you to go into the garden and pick one leaf from every kind of plant you can find – just one leaf, no more.'

'Why?' asked Annie suspiciously.

'It's for your scrapbook. You can make a map of the garden, and we'll press the leaves and stick them in to show where you found them growing, so you must remember where they all came from. And if you find more than twenty different kinds, you might even get a little prize – how's that?'

Annie cheered up and set off on her quest. Val watched her go, then turned to Kate. 'You can tell she's a teacher, can't you?'

'Oh, shut up!' protested Daphne, halfway between amusement and indignation.'That's a rotten thing to say.' She addressed Kate. 'Anyway, it worked. So what's the problem?'

Looking rather pink, Kate said, 'You know Mr Colpoys is coming round this afternoon?'

'I should just think I do. You've been on the go ever since daybreak, polishing the silver, making cakes, sweeping the stairs and cleaning the windows, sponging the leaves of the aspidistra—'

'Oh, you do exaggerate! But – I don't know if you've noticed – your Dad sometimes drops in of a Sunday, when Mr Colpoys is here.'

'Yes, I had noticed.'

'And I don't think Mr Colpoys is any too pleased about it. So I was wondering whether—'

She hesitated, and Val threw in: 'You want Daff to say you're out, is that it? Asking her to tell lies, just so you and your boyfriend can have a tête-à-tête without any interruptions. I'm surprised at you, Mum!'

'Don't you be so cheeky – I don't want her to say anything of the sort. Only I was thinking, Daff, if your Dad should happen to turn up, p'raps you could give him a cuppa and keep him down here with you – would you mind? I don't like to ask, only he seems to make Mr Colpoys rather uncomfortable for some reason.'

Daphne sighed. 'I'll try, but I can't make any promises. My father has a knack of getting his own way.'

'Well, do your best, there's a dear.' All smiles again, Kate returned to the sitting room, to await her visitor.

Since Annie was still out in the garden, Val began to tell Daphne about Gerald's new job on OBs. 'That's what they call Outside Broadcasts,' she explained.

When Daphne realised that Gerry would be travelling round the country during the next few months, she suggested again that Val should come with them to Broadstairs, but Val shook her head.

'I thought of that, but Gerry said no. He wants me to stay at home, so I'll be there if he needs me.'

For a moment there was silence in the kitchen, and then Daphne began quietly, 'Val, can I ask you something? It's been on my mind once or twice lately, only I wasn't sure if I should say anything. It's about Steve Gunn.'

Val looked at her swiftly. 'What about him?'

'It occurred to me, he'll be due for release soon, won't he? It's almost three years now since—'

'I know it is.' Val bent her head, then repeated flatly, 'Well, what about him?'

'I couldn't help wondering – won't it make things difficult for you when he comes out? I mean, he'll probably go back to his family, to the shop in Church Road.'

'Why should that make things difficult?'

'Well, you were both very close, before – before things went wrong. If you happen to see him, it might be upsetting for you, mightn't it?'

'I shan't see him – that was all over a long time ago.'

'Don't you ever think about him now?'

When Val looked up her face was blank; all expression had gone from it. 'No, I never think of him at all,' she said.

Then they heard Annie running in from the garden, and Val welcomed the interruption, grateful she would not have to tell any more lies.

Triumphantly, Annie burst in, laying out thirty-one different varieties of leaf on the table, and was rewarded with a chocolate biscuit as her prize.

Val took her off for a walk in the park, to visit the prehistoric monsters, posed in startling tableaux around the islands in the lake – and shortly afterwards Mr Colpoys arrived to take tea with Mrs Watkins.

Half an hour later, Harry Glynn knocked at the front door.

Daphne let him in, took his arm, and led him firmly downstairs, saying; 'Ted's out – he's working over in Sutton this evening, and Val and Annie have gone for a walk, so I'll be glad of your company, Father. Come and sit down while I make us a pot of tea.'

But Harry refused the chair she offered him, scratching his head and saying awkwardly, 'Very good of you, my girl, but I was hoping to go up and see your mother-in-law. She is in, I hope?'

'Yes, she is, but she's got somebody with her, as a matter of fact. Sit down, and let me cut you a slice of lemon-curd tart.'

'Thanks all the same, m'dear – some other time, perhaps. Do you happen to know – is Mr Colpoys with her?'

'Well, yes. Perhaps you should wait till he's gone.'

'But it's old Colpoys I want to talk to. I need his professional advice, on a legal problem.'

Daphne looked at him in despair. 'What have you done this time?'

'Good lord, it's not me – perish the thought! It's my landlady, Miss Preece. She's got into a spot of bother with the police, in point of fact. Do you think you could slip up and tell Colpoys I'd like a word with him? Tell him he's the only thing standing between the old girl and Holloway. And you'd better stay out of the way. I shall have to talk frankly to him, man to man. If he seems reluctant, offer him a slice of lemon-curd tart – that should do the trick.'

Too dazed to argue, Daphne went up to the sitting room and passed on the message. Mr Colpoys had no alternative but to answer the call for help.

'Oh dear, it's very worrying.' Kate turned to Daphne, as the door shut behind him. 'What's it all about – do you know?'

'No idea – he wouldn't tell me. In fact I'm under instructions to keep out of the way, so he can talk to Mr Colpoys in confidence. I suppose I should think myself lucky he didn't send *me* to collect thirty-one different leaves from the garden!'

In the basement, Harry settled Mr Colpoys in the best chair, then started to explain the nature of Miss Preece's crime.

'The poor creature's off her head with worry. I'm no expert on legal matters, that's why I thought of you. After all, we've become good friends over the last year or two, haven't we? I felt sure I could turn to you in this time of trouble – I knew you wouldn't let me down. I'll go through the facts slowly and clearly, in case you want to take notes. Shall I begin at the beginning?'

Mr Colpoys, who had never considered Harry Glynn to be a friend, opened and shut his mouth several times, before saying: 'Yes . . . Thank you. Please carry on.'

As Daphne said, her father had a knack of getting his own way.

On Monday evening, Mr Colpoys arrived at Miss Preece's house, and Harry introduced her to the old gentleman. She ushered them into the front parlour. Today the curtains were open. There were no shaded lights or incense-burners, and no sign of a crystal ball or a pack of cards.

They sat stiffly round the central table, and she clasped her hands tightly. 'Well?' she said. 'Have you any news?'

Mr Colpoys cleared his throat, eyeing her over his gold pince-nez.

'This afternoon I called in at Division Police Headquarters, and spoke to the Inspector,' he said. 'I explained that I was representing you unofficially, and he detailed the possible charges against you. You understand that by telling fortunes, you have been breaking the law?'

'I've sometimes had a booth at the funfair—' she began, but he silenced her with a magisterial forefinger.

'Sideshows of that nature are considered to be a feature of fairground entertainment; as long as they are clearly intended for amusement only, the authorities do not normally take proceedings in such cases. Likewise, telling fortunes for friends and acquaintances in the privacy of your home is not in itself an illegal activity.'

'Well, that's what I've been doing—'

'I think not. You have been performing this service for strangers, encouraging them to believe that you can predict the future and receiving payment for so doing, in direct contravention of the law. Under the Vagrancy Act, for deceiving and imposing upon His Majesty's subjects, you could be liable to imprisonment for a period of time not exceeding three calendar months—'

Miss Preece tried to speak, but Mr Colpoys continued to recite the archaic phraseology.

'Not only that, you could also be liable under the Fraudulent Mediums Act, as a person with intent to deceive, exercising powers of telepathy, clairvoyance or such powers aforementioned. If it can be proved that money was paid in respect of such services, anyone found guilty of these offences could be liable to a fine not exceeding the statutory maximum of—'

This time Miss Preece managed to break in, and her voice cracked as she exclaimed: 'They're going to send me to prison and fine me *as well*?'

'I did not say that.' Mr Colpoys took off his pince-nez; without them, his expression was less severe. 'I'm acquainting you with the possible penalties. However, this afternoon I spoke on your behalf, and explained that this was the first time you had ever been charged with any such offences. That is the truth, isn't it?'

'Oh yes, sir. I've never been in any trouble before.'

'That is what I told the Inspector. I also told him that when I explained the situation to you, I felt sure you would not break the law again. Is that correct?'

'Yes, sir. I mean no, I won't.'

'Very good. In view of this, the police are prepared to let the matter drop, without preferring charges.'

Miss Preece stared at him. 'You mean that's the end of it? No fine – no three months?'

'Provided you behave yourself in future.'

Miss Preece staggered to her feet, thanking him profusely. She hugged Mr Glynn, with tears of joy streaming down her face, leaving trails of eye-black on her cheeks, then she turned to Mr Colpoys and seemed as if she might embrace him as well. He sidestepped diplomatically, backing into the hall and waving aside her expressions of gratitude.

'Think nothing of it, madam,' he said, making for the front door. 'Only too glad to be of assistance. Good evening, Miss Preece – Mr Glynn.'

'Many thanks, old boy!' Harry caught up with him on the doorstep, thumping him heartily between the shoulderblades. 'And if you're ever in any trouble yourself, don't hesitate to call round. I'll do the same for you any time. After all, that's what pals are for – eh?'

Later that night, after a festive supper of cold pork, pink blancmange and Stilton cheese, washed down with pints of beer and a halfbottle of sherry, Harry Glynn wound up the celebrations in Miss Preece's bedroom.

Lying beside him, drowsily contented, she said, 'So it's all over. Thank you, Harry. If it hadn't been for you and Mr Colpoys, it doesn't bear thinking about.'

'Then don't think about it. It's over, and we're back together again

– that's all that matters.' He slipped his arm around her companionably, then added, 'I'd begun to think I'd lost you for good, old girl. It's been a long time since you and me were on these terms, eh?'

In the darkness, she nestled up against him. 'I'm sorry about that. It was a sort of feeling I had – you know how I get those feelings sometimes. I was frightened. I was afraid to let you get – too close.'

'I don't understand. I thought I'd done something to annoy you.'

'It wasn't that. It was on account of that young chap – what was his name? Duke, was it? The one who attacked your sister-in-law and got sent to gaol. I met him once, that Bank Holiday Monday when he came to the fair with your daughter. I read his palm that afternoon, and I could see it there, plain as pikestaff. I could see death . . . And when I took his hand, I could *feel* death – I could smell it, even. I swear to you, I was never closer to death than I was at that moment, Harry. I was holding death in my hand.'

'But Ethel didn't die. Oh, I know that young ruffian knocked her about, but she recovered—'

'I don't mean *her* death. But he will be the bringer of death – more than one death. I've never been so frightened of anything as I was that day . . . And I was afraid of you, as well.'

'But why me?'

'It's hard to explain. That Mr Colpoys – he didn't believe I had the gift. He was polite enough, but I could see what he thought – another old fraud, that's what he believed. And it's true I can't always see things clear, and sometimes I have to make things up – I can't tell when the vibrations will come through. But they came through that day – so strong, they terrified me.'

'When you touched the boy's hand?'

'Yes, then – but after he'd gone – that was the worst part of all, because you came into the tent, and when you put your hand on me. I felt it again – just the same. The same coldness of death, like it had come from that boy – only this time it came through you, Harry. That's when I knew you and him must be linked, somehow, so then I was afraid of you as well.'

'But I don't even know the blackguard. He had nothing to do with me!'

'Oh yes, he had. I'm sorry, Harry, don't ask me to explain it 'cos I can't tell you any more. I only know you and him are mixed up together somehow – and that boy carries evil with him, everywhere he goes. Evil – and misery. And death . . .'

Chapter Fourteen

AUGUST WAS VERY hot that year.

South London sweltered under a heatwave, and although the inhabitants of Upper Norwood were grateful for an occasional breeze on the windy heights of Crystal Palace, it was never really cool; heat rose from the pavements, sticky and oppressive. People who could afford a holiday made expeditions to the coast, flinging themselves into the sea like lemmings – and those who were hard up tried to escape for a day trip to Brighton or Margate or Southend.

As soon as Carmichael Road School broke up, Daphne and Annie had gone to join Ted at Broadstairs, so Kate was living alone at Sackville Road. Valerie went round to visit her mother as often as she could, making excuses to drop in for a cup of tea, or join her on shopping trips.

'I don't like to think of you being here all by yourself,' she said, as they were getting ready to go out one Saturday afternoon.

'Bless you, it doesn't bother me! What have I got to be afraid of? Nobody's going to break in – they know there's nothing here worth stealing,' said Kate. 'I quite enjoy having the place to myself for a change.'

'All the same, why don't you go down to stay with Daff and Ted for a week or so? The sea air would do you good.'

'I'll think about it, but I don't really fancy all that travelling.'

'It's not far; you can get a coach from the Crooked Billet in Penge that takes you all the way. And I know they'd be glad to have you. Daff said there's a spare bed in Annie's room.'

'Perhaps we could both go?'

'It'd be a bit of a squeeze – it's only a single bed! Anyway, I can't. Gerry wouldn't like it if I left him on his own.'

As they set off up Anerley Hill, to do the weekly shopping, Kate asked, 'Where is Gerald this afternoon? At home, or out watching cricket?'

'He's on duty. I'm not expecting him back till this evening.'

'He works such long hours – he leaves you alone too much.'

'Oh, I'm used to it. Besides, he enjoys the job so much. I've never known him so happy.'

As they turned into Church Road, Kate asked quietly, 'How about you, duck? Are you happy?'

'Of course I am. Do I look miserable?'

'No, but I sometimes wonder . . . You and Gerald – you're both so busy, both going out to work – you don't seem to spend a lot of time together.'

'Well, we're very happy. We understand one another,' Val told her. 'I couldn't wish for a better husband.'

'That's all right, then.' Kate changed the subject, hunting for her shopping-list. 'Let's see, what have I got to get? Back rashers, a packet of Rich Tea biscuits – oh, and half a pound of tomatoes, if they're—' She broke off; Valerie had stopped dead and was staring across the road. 'What's the matter?' said Kate. 'What are you looking at?'

Valerie asked quietly, 'Do you see the notice in the shop window?'

'Which one? Oh, yes.' Kate screwed up her eyes, reading aloud: "*Welcome home, Steve*" . . . Oh – I hadn't realised.'

'Neither had I. Let's cut through to Westow Hill – do you mind?'

'But I want to get some tomatoes. It won't take a minute.'

'I'm not going in there, Mum. I'm sorry – I couldn't.'

'All right.' Kate squeezed Val's hand. 'You wait here. I'll just pop in – I won't be two ticks.'

Valerie turned away, looking into a newsagent's window at the titles of the magazines and the headlines on the evening papers – but the words ran into a blur. All she could think of was the Gunn family, welcoming their son home from prison. Perhaps he was in the shop now, or upstairs in the sitting room, looking out over the road. Perhaps he had already seen her . . .

She shut her eyes, pressing her forehead against the cool plate glass. She had known this would happen one day, but had not expected it so soon.

After what seemed like a lifetime, she heard her mother's voice, softly concerned. 'Valerie, are you all right?'

'I'm fine.' She forced herself to smile. 'Let's go on.' Walking along the road, she asked. 'Did you get what you wanted?'

'The tomatoes – oh, yes. It was Mrs Gunn who served me.'

'Did you see anyone else?'

'Her husband was in the shop as well. They know me, of course – I've been going to Gunns for a good many years now. I mentioned the notice in the window, and she said: "We're not ashamed of our boy, you know. We're just thankful he'll soon be home again".'

'Soon? He's not there now?'

'Not yet. He's coming out on Monday, she said. I asked her to give him our best wishes.'

'Oh Mum, you shouldn't have!'

'Why not? He's taken his punishment. She asked after you – she said she hoped they might be seeing you, one of these days.'

With her heart pounding, Val tried to speak calmly. 'You didn't tell her I was waiting across the road?'

'Of course I didn't. I think I said something about the weather. That's all – nothing for you to be embarrassed about.'

It was nearly seven o'clock when Val got back to Westwood Court. She found Gerry already there, sitting in an armchair, stripped down to his shirt and underpants, reading the sports results. He greeted her jovially.

'Hello, stranger. I was beginning to think you'd run off with the milkman! Where have you been? I'm starving.'

'Sorry, but you could have helped yourself to some bread and cheese.'

'I didn't want to spoil my supper. What are we having?'

'Cold ham and salad. It's too hot to start cooking.'

'Yes, it's been a regular scorcher, hasn't it? It was stifling in the studio; that's why I'm cooling off – I opened all the windows as soon as I got in.' When he held out his arms, she stooped to kiss him, and he pulled her into a clumsy embrace. He smelled of beer and sweat, and his hands were clammy. She extricated herself, and he complained playfully, 'Oh, lor'. Is it too hot for that, too?'

'I've been trudging round the shops with Mum – it was a bit tiring.'

'I bet it was.' He stood up. 'Tell you what, if you don't feel like cooking, why don't we go out somewhere? Give ourselves a little celebration?'

'Why, what are we celebrating?'

'It's more of a farewell, actually. I won't be here after the weekend; they're packing me off to Scotland. I've got to catch the night train to Glasgow tomorrow. I'll be away all next week.'

She caught her breath. 'Oh, will you?' There was no air in the room. She felt as if the walls were closing in, trapping her . . . She gripped his hands tightly. 'Take me with you, Gerry! I'll explain to Mr Buckland, they owe me some time off. Let me come to Scotland as well.'

'Sorry, old dear. This is a business trip, not a holiday. The powers-that-be wouldn't take too kindly to me dragging you along. It's only a week – you can go and stay with your mother if you feel lonely.' He broke away, adding, 'If we're going out, I'd better put on my best bib and tucker.'

She followed him into the bedroom. 'I don't want to stay in London if you're not here, Gerry. I know – I'll go and stay with Ted and Daphne. They keep asking me.'

'Righty-ho, if that's what you want.' He took a clean shirt from the chest of drawers and selected a tie. 'But you will come and see me off tomorrow night, won't you?'

'If you want me to. And I'll telephone Broadstairs, and tell them to expect me some time on Monday. It'll be a good chance for me to get away.'

On Monday morning, Freda Gunn could not keep still for a moment.

She had spent most of Sunday cleaning the house – dusting, sweeping, making sure everything was in apple-pie order for Steve's homecoming. Even now, when the cushions had been plumped up a dozen times, when every fold of the curtains was hanging symmetrically and every ornament on the mantelpiece sparkling, she could not stop flitting from place to place, straightening a picture-frame, or polishing an apple in the fruit-bowl.

The only untidy object in the sitting room was her father-in-law. Jack Gunn sat in his favourite chair, in his vest and trousers with his braces dangling and no shoes on his feet, reading the newspaper.

'Oh Dad, I do wish you'd go up and finish getting dressed,' Freda told him. 'They'll be here soon. You might at least put your shirt on!'

'Our Steve won't worry his head about whether I'm wearing a shirt or not,' grumbled the old man. 'They won't be here till nearly dinner-time, you said so. I don't know why Alf didn't take you with him . . . Running round here like a blue-arsed fly.'

'Language!' Freda glared at him. 'Steve wouldn't have liked it if me and Alfred had both gone to meet him. He doesn't want a lot of people fussing . . . And I was afraid it might upset me. I didn't want to break down and make an exhibition of myself in front of everybody, did I? He wouldn't thank me for that!' She went and fetched Jack's shoes from the kitchen, then knelt beside his chair, lacing them up for him in spite of his protests.

'Let me alone! I can do that – I'm not an invalid!'

'No, but if you go stooping down, you might bring on one of your funny turns. Stop arguing, Grandad.'

'The boy generally helps me. Where is young Tony?'

'He asked if he could go out and play football with his pals, so I said yes. Well, it's better than having him hanging round all the morning, getting in everyone's way.'

Frowning, Jack said: 'Hang on, who's minding the shop? Somebody ought to be downstairs, serving the customers.'

Freda stood up, explaining patiently, 'I did *tell* you, Dad. The shop's shut today. We've got enough to think about, with Steve coming home. We didn't want to be bothered with anything else.'

'You shut the shop – on a Monday? That's not right. People expect to go shopping Mondays. They'll be wanting fresh veg after the weekend.'

'It won't hurt them to go without for one day. It's only once in a blue moon.'

The sound of the street doorbell made her jump, and she put her hand to her heart. 'Whoever's that?'

'Must be Alf and Steve, back already.'

'It can't be! They weren't letting him out till eleven; and Alf's not been gone above half an hour.' She rushed to the window, peering down into the street. 'It's our Julie!' she gasped.

'Come to welcome her brother home, has she? Good girl.'

'Yes, but she's not on her own. There's two other girls with her – friends from the Corner House, I suppose. Oh dear, what did she have to go and do that for? We don't want a lot of strangers here.'

The bell pealed again, and she hurried to the stairs, saying as she passed the old man, 'Now will you go and get dressed? We can't have you looking like that in front of company – letting the family down.'

Jack struggled to his feet and trudged up to the attic, leaving his newspaper in a crumpled heap on the floor. When Freda returned to the sitting-room, she scooped it up without pausing for breath.

'Do come in, won't you? This is a nice surprise. Oh, just look how Grandad's left this room, he is the limit, he really is! Sit down and I'll put the kettle on. Well, Julie, aren't you going to introduce your friends?'

'I'm trying to, if you'll let me get a word in edgeways! These are two of the girls I work with – the ones who share the flat. This is Marguerite, only we all call her Margie, and Eve – or Evie – whichever you like, she's not fussy.'

They were a little older than Julie, but they were all looking lovely in their summer dresses – sweet-pea colours of pink, mauve and blue, with the latest short hairstyles and short skirts to match.

Margie and Eve told Freda they were very pleased to meet her, and she rushed around, bustling in and out of the kitchen, making a pot of tea, putting a lace cloth on the table, setting out a plate of biscuits, and asking if they took milk and sugar.

When tea was ready, they all sat round the table.

'Well, this is nice!' said Freda. 'I've heard Julie speak of you so many times, but I never dreamed I'd be meeting you like this.' She gave Julie a meaning look, 'Today of all days.'

'You mean because of Steve getting out of gaol? Well, that's why we're here – to give him a hero's welcome!'

Freda smiled nervously. 'Oh dear, I hope Julie explained to you. Steve didn't really do anything wrong – he got led astray, in a manner of speaking. It was more of a misunderstanding than anything else.'

'Yes, Julie told us.' Margie smiled back. 'It was really bad luck for him. We told her to wish him all the best, from us.'

'So Julie said, why didn't we come down and wish him luck in person?' chimed in Eve.

'It just so happens, we're all three off-duty today. We don't have to go in to work till tonight,' added Julie. 'So I thought – why not? It's a lovely day for an outing, and better than being cooped up in London.'

'You're going to be here all day?' asked Freda, trying to keep her smile in place.

'I hope you don't think we're intruding?' asked Eve. 'You must tell us if we're in the way. We can easily nip off by ourselves, can't we, Margie?'

'Not at all,' said Freda valiantly, with another agonised look at

Julie. 'The only thing is, because I wasn't expecting visitors, I'm not sure if there'll be enough to go round at dinner-time.'

Julie brushed this aside. 'We don't eat much. Appetites like birds, these two. What are you going to have, anyhow?'

'It only cold meat and salad,' Freda admitted. 'I thought, this weather . . .'

'But that's perfect!' exclaimed Julie. She pointed to a wicker basket she had brought with her. 'We've got a pork pie and some bottles of beer, and some strawberries. I thought we could all go across to the Palace and have a picnic. Wouldn't that be nice?'

By the time Grandad came downstairs in his best suit, Julie and Freda had re-packed the picnic basket. Jack was introduced to the girls; beaming with delight at finding himself surrounded by such charming young ladies, he went straight back to the attic to fetch his cornet.

Julie sighed, 'It's going to be a bit of a crowd, isn't it? Steve might feel awkward if he walks in and finds us all here. Where did you say Tony's gone?'

'He's in the Palace grounds, playing football – why?'

'Tell you what – we'll take Grandad and the picnic and go over and find him. Then you'll have Steve to yourself for a while when Dad brings him in, and when he feels like it, you can bring him over the road. How's that?'

At midday, when Steve came home with his father, the flat was empty except for Freda – sitting in her usual place by the window, trying to knit. When they walked in, she stuck the needles back in the ball of wool, saying, 'That's enough of that. I kept dropping stitches – my fingers are all thumbs today. How are you, son?'

He was wearing the clothes he had on when they arrested him, but he had filled out since then. The jacket looked uncomfortably tight across the shoulders.

Freda stood up, and he took her in his arms. For a moment, nobody said anything. At last she let him go, whispering, 'It's good to have you back.'

He found it hard to speak. 'I saw the notice you put in the shop window. Thanks.'

He looked round; the flat seemed bigger than he'd remembered. After Brixton, it was quiet, and very peaceful. He kept a grip on himself. He'd have looked pretty stupid – a grown man, crying like a kid.

'Where is everybody?' he asked. 'Where's young Tone?'

'Over at the Palace. He went across to play football – it was better for him to have something to do, than sit round here waiting. And Julie's there too – isn't that nice? – and Grandad. We're all going to have a picnic – that was her idea. And some other friends as well.'

'Friends?' Steve held his breath. 'Who?'

'Nobody you know. From the Corner House – the ones who share her flat. They seem very nice girls . . . Do you feel like going over to meet them?'

'In a minute. This is all – a bit strange.' Steve looked out of the window. 'It's funny – nothing's changed, but it's all different, somehow.' Without turning round, he added: 'I don't suppose you've seen Valerie?'

'Not lately. Her mother was in – which day was it, Alfred? Saturday, wasn't it? She saw the notice in the window, and came in to ask after you. She said to give you her good wishes – hers, and Valerie's.'

'That's nice.' He did not move; Freda could only see the back of his head. At last he said, 'Is there any beer in the larder? I could do with a drink, before we go out.'

When they entered the Crystal Palace grounds, the rest of the family were nowhere to be seen. Although it was a weekday, a great many people had come out to enjoy the continuing heatwave; the open terraces were thronged with visitors, and children, making the most of the school holidays, scampered in and out of the crowd, begging to be taken to the funfair.

Steve remembered the last time he had visited the fair – the water-chute, the flying-boats, the fortune-teller; his memories tormented him, but he could not put them out of his mind.

'I can't see Julie, can you?' said Freda. 'And where's Grandad?'

'They won't be up here,' said Steve. 'Too many people – no room for a picnic. They'll have gone down to the lake, I bet.'

On the way down the green slope of the hill, they passed a group of lads kicking a ball about. Steve glanced at them idly – then stopped, and looked again. One of the boys stopped too. He had been about to intercept a shot for the goal, but the ball passed within a yard of him, rolling easily between the two piles of folded jackets which did duty as the goal-mouth.

His team-mates yelled at him, but Tony Gunn took no notice. He began to run towards his brother, the game completely forgotten.

When they were only a few feet apart, Tony slowed down. Steve walked forward to meet him; they looked at one another uncertainly.

'Blimey, you've grown!' said Steve huskily, then opened his arms wide.

Tony hung back, smiling sheepishly. 'Hello, Steve,' he said.

'Sorry, I suppose you're too big for that kind of thing,' apologised Steve, and held out his hand instead.

Tony came towards him – and the moment their hands touched, they fell on one another, hugging, laughing, lightly punching each other.

'You were still a nipper when I went away,' said Steve. 'Look at you now – practically a man. How old are you – eleven?'

'Twelve,' Tony corrected him. 'I'm catching up with you!'

With one arm round Tony's shoulders. Steve asked, 'Where's the rest of the family?'

'Down at the boating-lake. They wanted me to stay with them till you came, but I didn't like to. All those girls – I wouldn't know what to say to them.'

'You'll learn, don't worry,' Steve grinned, as they set off down the path again. He called back to his parents, who followed them: 'They're by the lake – what did I tell you?'

The picnic was a great success. It was too hot to sit in the sun, so the girls had found a cooler spot in the shade of some willows. Grandad was comfortably settled with his back against a tree-stump, and Julie was setting out food on cardboard plates. When she saw Steve, she jumped up and ran to meet him – and another reunion took place.

Then Steve embraced his grandfather, and Julie introduced her friends, while Alfred made himself useful, pouring the beer into paper cups.

'Here's to you, my son – a long life and a happy one!' he said, and they all drank Steve's health.

When the last crumbs of pork pie had been eaten, and the last bottle emptied, Julie said, 'Who wants to come for a walk through the Maze? How about you, Mum?'

'No thanks, dear – too much like hard work.' Freda opened her bag and pulled out the knitting she had been engaged upon earlier. 'I'm quite happy to stay put.'

'You're never going to start on that!' exclaimed Julie. 'This is supposed to be a holiday!'

'All right, it's a holiday, but I can't sit here, doing nothing. I'll just watch the rest of you enjoying yourselves. What are you going to do?'

'We could play football,' suggested Tony, but Julie overruled him.

'In this weather? Not likely! Why don't we take a boat out? It'll be my treat. Come on, girls – who's for a life on the ocean wave?'

Eve smiled at Steve under her long eyelashes. 'Are you coming with us?'

'Oh, I dunno,' he muttered. 'I might stay here and talk to Mum and Dad, or something.'

'I was counting on you to row the boat!' said Julie. 'All right – how about you, Tony? Will you be our strong man?'

Tony felt very grown-up as he helped the three girls into the rowing-boat. As Margie stepped in, the boat rocked a little, and she squealed.

'Help! Who's going to save me if I drown?'

'You won't drown,' Eve told her. 'If you ask him nicely, Steve will jump in and rescue you, won't you, Steve?'

Julie saw her brother's face, and said quickly, 'Give it a rest, you two. Why don't you sit down and shut up?'

Freda remembered the night when Valerie tumbled into the lake, and glanced quickly at her son, but said nothing.

He stood up, remarking, 'I think I'm going to stretch my legs after all that food and drink. Give myself a chance to walk off my dinner.'

'Where are you going, Steve?' called Tony, from the boat. 'Do you want me to come with you?'

'No – you stay where you are. I feel like being on my own for a while. See you later.' With that, he turned away, making his way up the hill once more, to the huge edifice of steel and glass that shone dazzlingly in the sunlight.

The blood was racing through his veins, and he was breathing fast – taking swift, shallow breaths, as if he could not get enough oxygen.

Inside the building, under the green shade of the indoor shrubs and overhanging palm trees, it was much cooler, and the crystal fountain made a refreshing sound as drops of water fell, glittering, into the basin – but he could still feel the sweat trickling down his brow.

He knew where he was going – this was where they had met sometimes, after she finished work. He pushed through the door marked: Private – Staff Only, and walked into the offices.

A stranger sat at a desk, clattering a typewriter; a girl in a trim white blouse and a black skirt, who looked over her shoulder as Steve came into the room.

'Can I help you?' she said.

'Well, yes please. I'm looking for Valerie Watkins. I mean, Mrs Valerie Glynn.'

'I'm afraid she isn't here.'

This was a setback he had not expected; he had been so sure he would find her at her desk.

'Oh, I see. Thank you,' he said politely. 'She's gone out, has she? Will she be long?'

'No, I mean she's away all this week – on holiday.'

The disappointment hit him with a sledgehammer blow. 'On holiday,' he repeated stupidly. 'Do you mean – is she at home?'

'No, she's gone to the seaside. She won't be back till next Monday – a week today. Would you like to leave a message? Who shall I say called?'

'Never mind, it doesn't matter. I'm just a friend.' He did not seem to be able to think clearly, and stammered: 'I – I suppose she's gone away with – with Mr Glynn?'

'No, she's gone to stay with her family. Her brother's on the stage – he's in a concert party, at Broadstairs.'

'Ted – yes, I know him, too. Well, thanks anyway. Sorry to have bothered you.'

He walked out – out of the office, out of the great glass building, back into the fierce sunlight, where the heat hit him like a punch in the face, and all he could think was: 'She's gone away.'

He could not face the family yet, and spent some time roaming through the park like a lost soul, seeing nothing and hearing nothing except two words, pounding in his brain like a drumbeat: '*She's gone . . . She's gone . . . She's gone . . .*'

By the time he got back to the lake, the sun was going down and the western sky was streaked with orange and red; high on the hill behind him, it was reflected in the walls of glass, making the Crystal Palace look as if it were on fire.

Still propped up against his tree-stump, Grandad had his cornet to his lips, playing a soft, muted tribute to the end of a golden day; a slow, melancholy waltz.

Steve looked around him. 'Where's Julie and her friends?' he asked his mother. 'Where's Tone?'

'They're still out on the lake,' Freda told him. 'Julie paid for a couple of hours . . . Throwing her money about, as usual.'

He saw them – a misty silhouette coming out of the sunset, rowing slowly towards the landing-stage, as the boatman called through a megaphone: 'Come in, number seventeen – your time is up.'

The boat moved at a leisurely pace, hardly making a ripple on the lake. As it went gliding past, Julie waved lazily to Steve – Margie seemed to be asleep, and Eve trailed one hand through the water. Tony rowed on, taking his time, lifting the oars after each stroke as a cascade of tiny drops punctuated the calm, flat surface.

Steve watched them go by, aching with loneliness.

When the boating party came ashore, they seemed to be in a kind of trance, somewhere between sleeping and waking; moving like a dancer, Julie hummed the melody her grandfather was playing.

'That's a pretty tune,' said Freda. 'What's it called?'

By way of reply, Julie sang a few words:

> *'I'll be loving you – always.*
> *With a love that's true – always . . .'*

Opening her eyes, Margie sighed, putting her hands on Steve's shoulders.

'I don't want to go back to town,' she said. 'Marry me, and take me away from London – let's stay here for ever and ever.'

'Oh no, you don't!' Firmly, Julie removed her. 'Take your grubby paws off my brother. We've got to catch the puffer-train and go back to work.' Quoting some long-forgotten melodrama, she declaimed: 'Collect your bead-bags, girls – we are approaching the wicked city.' She stood on tiptoe and planted a kiss on her brother's cheek. 'It's good to see you home again, Steve.'

The family waved them goodbye at the Low Level station, and as the train pulled out, Steve could hear the three girls singing together:

> *'Not for just an hour,*
> *Not for just a day,*
> *Not for just a year – but always . . .'*

Later that evening, after Tony had gone to bed, Steve said: 'I think I'll have an early night myself, Mum, if you don't mind. I'm feeling all in. I'm not used to so much exercise.'

'Well, you've done a lot today. At any rate, you'll have a good night's rest.'

'It'll seem funny to be sleeping in my own bed again, with proper sheets and a decent pillow.'

Freda kissed him good night, then said, 'Sleep as long as you like. You can have a lie-in tomorrow.'

'I won't do that.' Steve cleared his throat, adding casually, 'I want to make an early start in the morning. Don't think I'm being ungrateful, will you, but all this is a bit hard to take at first. I need to spend some time on my own, for a few days. So I decided I'd have a little holiday – make the most of the weather, somewhere down at the seaside. I hope you don't mind.'

'That's a good castle,' said Daphne.

The sandcastle had a turret at each corner, made with an upturned tin bucket, and a shallow moat running all the way round it, dug out with a wooden spade. It even had an archway opening into the courtyard, carefully moulded by Annie, who had poked her fingers through the wall of dampened sand, fearful that the whole creation might collapse into a shapeless heap; it was a moment of triumph when she withdrew her hand and the archway remained intact.

'It's not finished yet,' she told her mother, picking up the bucket. 'I've got to put some water in the moat – can I go and get some?'

'But it won't stay in the moat.' Daphne tried to dissuade her. 'It will only soak away into the sand.'

'Oh go on, let me – it might stay for a little while,' Annie cajoled. 'Can I, Mum – please?'

Daphne sighed. 'You can try if you like, but don't blame me if it's no good. Don't go too far into the sea, and try not to get your knickers wet!' She watched Annie trotting happily down to the sea as it foamed over flat, shining sands.

'You fuss too much,' said Valerie, stretched out sleepily in a deckchair. 'She can't come to much harm paddling, it's so shallow.'

'She could be knocked down by a wave and swept out to sea,' said Daphne. 'Then you'd have to go in and rescue her.'

'Thanks very much,' said Val, without opening her eyes. 'Why me?'

'Because you're the one who can swim. You know, you should give her some swimming-lessons while you're here – she'd be so thrilled. Did you bring your bathing-costume?'

'No. I haven't been swimming for years – I've probably lost the knack.'

'Isn't it like riding a bicycle – one of those things you never forget? You ought to take it up again – you used to enjoy swimming.'

'I can see I'm not going to be allowed to have a nap.' Valerie sat up. 'Yes, I used to go swimming, and now I don't. Any more questions?'

Remembering who had taught Val to swim, Daphne said, 'No, no more questions.' She greeted Annie, who came running up the beach, slopping water over the edge of the toy bucket. 'Careful, you're spilling it!'

'Fuss, fuss, fuss,' said Val. 'Plenty more where that came from.'

Annie tipped the water into the moat, where it vanished instantly, leaving nothing but a furrow of dark, damp sand; she looked up at her mother, daring her to say, 'I told you so.'

Val said quickly, 'Let's dig a channel down to the sea. When the tide comes in, it will fill up the moat.' She dropped to her knees beside Annie and they set to work, scooping out a deep gulley leading to the water's edge.

'Don't be too long,' Daphne warned them. 'The show starts at three – if the weather doesn't break.' She looked up at the sky; no longer blue, it was thick with a heat-haze. Then she said to Val, 'You do know they don't change the programme till Thursday? Are you sure you want to sit through it again?'

'Of course I do,' said Val, as she went on digging. 'We always like watching Dad, don't we, Annie?'

Daphne said nothing; even here, where the atmosphere was so free and easy, she still felt nervous for Ted.

The concert party performed twice daily, on an al fresco stage at the top of the beach, backed up against the wall of the promenade. Facing the stage, rows of deckchairs were set out in wide semi-circles; already, the audience were beginning to take their places and a boy in a peaked cap was going along the rows, collecting threepence a time and tearing tickets off a perforated roll.

Many more people would drift across to join them when the show began, sitting on the sands or standing at the back; without chairs, they were able to enjoy the show for nothing.

Somebody rang a handbell, as a signal that the performance was about to begin; Val and Annie abandoned their digging and took their places. The ticket-collector gave them their free tickets. 'Afternoon, Mrs Watt,' he said. 'Come to see your hubby again, have you?'

Daphne smiled politely. Since Ted had adopted his new stage-name, she had got used to being called Mrs Watt, though she still resented it a little. It somehow implied that she had no identity of her own.

As they sat in their deckchairs – not too near the front, because

273

Daphne didn't like to catch Ted's eye – Val glanced at her and asked: 'What's the matter? Are you all right?'

'I'm fine,' said Daphne. 'I just feel as if I'm starting a headache. It's very close, isn't it? There must be thunder about.'

Then a piano played an arresting introduction, with a lot of loud-pedal work, and Annie nudged her auntie, whispering, 'It's going to begin . . .'

The front curtains parted, whisking back to reveal a small stage with a permanent backdrop – a stylised sunburst, its rays painted in alternating stripes of metallic gold and silver. To one side, a jolly lady with peroxide-blonde curls thumped away at a little upright piano, and the other artistes rushed on from the wings, singing to the tune of *California, Here I come.*

> *'Hello, people – how d'you do?*
> *We're so glad to welcome you.'*

There were seven of them, including the pianist; three men and four women, dressed in Pierrot costumes with black-and-white pom-poms and little pointed hats. Annie said excitedly: 'There he is! There's Dad!'

Ted was in the middle of the line, singing and dancing with gusto. He spotted the family at once, and though his broad, infectious grin embraced the whole audience, he gave Val a conspiratorial wink.

She began to relax; she was determined to enjoy this holiday. Soon she would be able to forget about London and Upper Norwood – and Steve.

At the back of the town, a charabanc had just pulled up in the coach park. The driver climbed down from his cab to open the doors, and the passengers began to exercise their cramped muscles. As they stepped out of the coach, the driver announced: 'For them what's going back to London this evening, you've got just three hours here. You've got to be back at the coach by six-fifteen. I'll be setting off sharp at half-past, and I won't hang about!'

Steve stepped down on the sticky tarmac, and the driver asked him: 'Are you going back tonight, son? Or stopping here?'

'I don't know – I might stay,' said Steve. 'I haven't decided yet.'

He had no luggage with him; he had made no plans. He didn't know what he was expecting or hoping. He only knew that he had no choice – he had to see Valerie.

He did not even know where she was staying, but he knew he

would find her. When he walked out of the coach-park, he came face to face with a poster advertising: *Sunshine Follies – laughter, song and dance. Twice daily at three p.m. and seven p.m. – weather permitting.*

He walked through the little seaside town, looking for a theatre, but could only see a small cinema. Undaunted, he went into the foyer and enquired: 'Can you tell me the way to the theatre? The *Sunshine Follies?*'

The woman in the ticket-booth said, 'It's not a theatre – it's only a fit-up on the beach. Keep straight on till you get to the harbour; you can't miss it.'

He did not really understand, but he followed her instructions. The road was lined with identical boarding houses, with cards in the front windows advertising Bed and Breakfast.

It was strange to think that Valerie was staying at one of them, but he couldn't start knocking on doors at random, asking for her. Better to go to the theatre – or the 'fit-up', whatever that might be – and ask there. They would know where Ted Watkins and his family were staying.

The boarding houses gave way to some imposing, expensive hotels, and a sprinkling of little shops selling buckets and spades, shrimping-nets and water-wings, and confectioners' windows stacked with bright pink rock, every piece stamped with the words *Broadstairs* all the way through.

He could see the glitter of the sea just ahead, and smelled the pungent, evocative mixture of salt and fish and seaweed – and he quickened the pace. He came out on to the promenade; there was the pier and the harbour – and there was the beach, crowded with holiday-makers. He heard the sound of a piano, and a girl's voice singing:

> *'Hello – hello – who's your lady-friend?*
> *Who's the little girlie by your side?'*

Steve ran down the stone steps leading to the beach, then saw the little stage below the wall, and the Pierrot Company performing for their audience; sixty or seventy men, women and children were sitting in rows, and others standing around them, watching the show – but he picked out Valerie immediately.

She sat looking up at the stage, her face alight with happiness, and he felt a stab of anger: what right had she to feel happy, without him? But the spasm of jealousy did not last. As he studied her profile, the curve of her cheek, the tilt of her chin, every other emotion was swept away in an overwhelming flood of love.

He saw Daphne sitting beside her, and a little girl he did not know at first, then realised with a shock that she must be Val's niece – little Annie, grown beyond all recognition in three years. Three years . . . it seemed like a lifetime, but at this moment he was not angry or frustrated or impatient. He felt as if he could stand here for ever, watching Valerie, never asking for any more happiness in this world.

Now the entire company was lining up for a closing chorus, inviting the audience to join in:

> *'Dear old pals, jolly old pals,*
> *Clinging together in all sorts of weather . . .'*

On the stage, one or two of the artistes looked up anxiously at the sky, and Ted called to the audience, 'Don't worry. If it starts to rain, you can all get under my umbrella!'

And he produced a tiny paper parasol from his sleeve, opening it and holding it above his head, which made them all laugh as they sang, '. . . *Give me the friendship of dear old pals!*'

Then the curtains swished together, amid a burst of applause.

Steve thought this was the end of the show, and expected Val to stand up; when the audience stayed where they were, he realised it must be the interval.

An ice-cream man wheeled his barrow up to the crowd, selling cornets and wafers, and some of the children began to pester their parents. Steve had been wondering how to approach Valerie, and this gave him an idea. Fumbling for change in his pocket, he purchased three ice-cream cornets, then made his way cautiously along the rows of deckchairs. When he reached them, he took a deep breath, and said, 'How about an ice cream?'

Daphne looked up and began to say, 'No, thank you, we—'

She stopped short, and Annie exclaimed happily: 'I've seen you before!'

'That's right,' said Steve. 'Hello Annie, have an ice cream.'

Daphne pulled herself together. 'Hello, Steve,' she said. 'This is a surprise.'

'Yes. I thought p'raps you'd like an ice?'

Not knowing what else to do, Daphne took them from him, and handed one to her daughter, murmuring, 'That's very kind. Say thank you, Annie. Val – would you—?'

Valerie was very pale; she'd heard his voice, but she had not even looked at him. Turning her head away, she said, 'No—I don't want one.'

'Can I have yours?' asked Annie quickly.

'If you like,' said Val. Amazed and delighted, Annie clutched two cornets, one in each hand.

'I've got to talk to you, Val,' said Steve.

She began to say, 'No, I don't think so—' but she knew he would not go away. Annie, licking two ice creams alternately, was fascinated by their conversation, and one or two people nearby were listening too.

She stood up. 'We can't talk here. Excuse me, Daff.'

As she stepped past her, Daphne asked, 'Val, are you sure?'

'It's all right, I won't be long. Back in a minute.' She led the way along the row, and Steve followed her.

Moving through the crowd as if she were in a dream, she walked on towards the sea – not so far now, because the tide was starting to come in. Already, water was flowing into the channel she and Annie had been digging, filling the moat round the castle. When she reached the water's edge, she turned and faced him at last.

'What are you doing here?' she asked.

'I got out yesterday,' he said. 'I thought you knew. I went to your office, and they told me you were here, on holiday, so I came down on the coach today.'

'But why? Why did you do that?'

'You know why,' he said.

Looking into his eyes, she felt as if she were falling – falling towards him. With an effort, she averted her face, staring at the waves – breaking, rolling in, retreating.

'No, I don't know. Why did you follow me here?'

'Because I love you.'

Looking at the sea, she saw flecks – rings – appearing on the surface, and felt the first drops of rain upon her hands and face as she forced herself to say, 'That's impossible. Everything's changed – I'm married now.'

'But we still love each other. Nothing can change that.'

Further up the beach, there was a flurry of activity. People were running for shelter, huddling together beneath the promenade wall. The men of the Pierrot Company, pulling mackintoshes over their costumes, were helping to pack up deckchairs; the matinée had been abandoned.

Val turned upon Steve fiercely, as raindrops streamed down her face. 'How could you do this? It's all over – don't you understand that? Why can't you leave me alone?'

A rumble of thunder and a flash of lightning threw the holiday-makers into a panic. Val flinched and turned away from him, starting to run – running blindly, to escape from the storm – to escape from Steve.

Within a few moments, he was the only person left on the beach. There was a deafening thunderclap, and the rain began to come down in torrents, but he stayed where he was. A few yards away, Annie's sandcastle, overtaken by the tide and battered by the downpour, collapsed in ruins.

With his wet clothes clinging to him, Steve lifted his head, driven by the pain within, howling her name.

'*Valerie!*' he shouted. '*Valerie!*'

But the storm swept away his cry; there was no one to hear him.

Chapter Fifteen

NEW! THRILLING! DIRT-TRACK RACING – *Saturday next, at the Crystal Palace!*

Steve was outside the shop, arranging a display of cauliflowers on the stall along the pavement, but he paused to study this advertisement.

It was a flyposter, pasted on to the whitewashed window of the vacant shop next door. Some people said the shop had a jinx on it; it had been standing empty for a long time now. After the fire, Fabers Furnishings had been restored and redecorated, but the shop had never really been successful again; it was as if the heart had gone out of it – or perhaps it was the shopkeeper who had lost heart. Either way, the business failed. Walter Faber had to sell up and move away. Since then it had been rented out to several different ventures – a café, a fancy goods store, a second-hand clothes shop – but none of them had prospered, and now it was empty again.

The poster stood out against the blank, lifeless window – a vivid impression in crimson and black of a motorcycle scorching round a bend, the rider, head down in goggles and helmet, plunging toward a curve in the track.

Looking at the picture, Steve could almost hear the roar of the engine, and imagined the power carrying him away, faster and faster . . .

'Excuse me,' said Mrs Watkins.

He woke from his daydream. 'Sorry – I was miles away.'

Kate was looking at the poster too. 'You used to have a motorbike yourself, didn't you?'

'Yeah, I did – once.' He stood back to let her enter the shop. 'What can we do for you today?'

'Two pounds of potatoes, please.'

Freda Gunn, serving someone at the far end of the shop, called out, 'Morning, Mrs Watkins. Nice day!'

'Yes, almost like summer, isn't it?'

It was the middle of May; Steve had been home for nearly nine months. Without much hope, he had gone to Wright's Motors, asking if they would take him back, and was told they made it a policy never to employ anyone with a police record. They also refused to give him a reference, so his chances of finding other work in that line were slender. Times were hard everywhere; unemployment was a problem all over the country.

In the end he had agreed to go back to his old job, helping out in the family shop. He didn't like it, but it was better than going on the dole. So here he was, setting out cauliflowers and weighing out potatoes – back where he started . . . With one big difference.

As Kate put the potatoes into her shopping-bag, he asked, 'How's Valerie?'

'Oh, she's keeping busy, as usual. They're expecting the dirt-track racing to bring more people to the Palace – and that means more work for Val.'

'I suppose so . . . Give her my regards when you see her, will you?'

'Yes, all right. You're keeping well, are you?'

'Me? I'm fine.' How could he tell her? He woke up each morning with a feeling of dread at the pit of his stomach, as if some terrible disaster were about to happen – and as he came to, he realised that the disaster had already occurred. With no prospect of happiness, he went on automatically, living from one day to the next; without hope, without Valerie, he was only half-alive.

'I'm fine,' he repeated, and followed Mrs Watkins out of the shop, to finish arranging cauliflowers in the trays outside. Again the advertisement caught his eye: *Saturday, 21st May, 1927 – Grand Opening of the New Dirt-Track Season.*

The Crystal Palace had made one attempt at motorcycle racing the previous year – 'Path Racing', they called it – over a mile of track, marked out on the gravel paths, starting at the Penge gates, up the hill, past the fairground to the Italian terraces, beside the lake and back again. This year they were putting the whole thing on a professional basis, with teams of riders and a properly constructed dirt-track.

Steve was still gazing at the poster when his mother joined him in the doorway.

'I expect you'd like to go and see that, wouldn't you?' Freda said.

'Watching's not the same as riding – anyhow, I'll be working – Saturday afternoon, Dad will be taking Tony to the football. I'll be here in the shop, with you.'

'You don't have to,' she said softly. 'I'll get Grandad to give me a hand. We can manage without you for once. You go and watch those noisy old bikes – it'll make a change for you'.

Freda was right; the motorbikes were noisy.

On Saturday, Daphne took Annie round to Belmont, to have tea with her family, and almost as soon as they arrived, they were startled by the sound of the bikes revving up. As it was a warm day, the sitting-room windows were wide open, and the noise was very loud. Muriel put her hands over her ears.

'What is it?' she asked fretfully. 'What's happening?'

Daphne explained, 'It's the dirt-track racing, Mother. This is the first day of the season.'

'Such an ugly name, too. What a terrible din – somebody ought to do something about it.'

Babs got up and closed the windows; the noise was still audible, though a little less distracting. 'There, that's better, isn't it?' she asked.

'A little better,' Muriel admitted grudgingly. 'Except there's no air in the room – we shall all suffocate.'

'Perhaps if you took your cardigan off, you'd be more comfy,' suggested Babs. 'Let me help you.'

Slightly mollified, Muriel allowed Babs to remove her cardigan and hang it over a chair. Turning her attention to her granddaughter, she said, 'Goodness gracious, how you've grown, Annie! It's a long time since you came to visit your poor old Grandmama. You must ask Mummy to bring you to see me more often!'

'It's not that long, actually—' Daphne began, but Muriel was deaf to the interruption.

'Anyway, I'm very glad you're here now. And you look so nice and cool – where did you get that pretty frock? I believe your Mummy's been spoiling you again!'

'It was a present from Ted's mum,' said Daphne. 'She made it herself.'

'How kind of Mrs Watkins,' said Muriel, setting her teeth into a smile. 'I only wish I could make pretty things for you to wear, but my poor old hands can't hold a needle these days.' Then her sadly sweet expression changed to fury as a speeding motorbike, coming close to the boundary wall, rocketed past in a burst of sound. 'Really, this is intolerable! Telephone the police, Babs – they must put a stop to it!'

'The police won't do anything. They're not breaking the law,' Babs pointed out.

'They're disturbing the peace, and that's a crime, isn't it? Upsetting elderly people and frightening little children,' snapped Muriel. She turned to Annie again. 'You're frightened, aren't you, darling?'

'No, I'm not, Grandma,' said Annie. 'Can I go and watch the races?'

'Certainly not!' Muriel glared at her, then rounded on Babs again. 'You must complain to the authorities – what's the name of that man we met at Gerald's wedding? Henry somebody? He's in charge, isn't he? Go and speak to him at once. Tell him the residents are getting up a petition. Say that unless this horrible din is silenced, I shall send a stiff letter to our Member of Parliament!'

Babs, who had been hoping to see some of the racing herself, said, 'I don't know whether I'll be able to find Mr Buckland, but I'll try.'

As she was about to leave, Daphne suggested: 'Why not take Annie with you? She'd like to see what's going on.'

'All right. Come on, my love – let's go!'

All smiles, Annie went out – with Babs, swinging on her hand and calling, 'Bye-bye, Grandma. Bye-bye, Mum!'

As the door shut, Muriel sighed. 'I do wish you wouldn't let her call you that. It sounds so common. "Mummy" is much nicer.'

'All the girls at school call their parents Mum and Dad. I don't want Annie to feel different from the others.'

'But she is different, dear. She's growing up to be a young lady,' said Muriel. 'You must never forget that. Such a shame she had to wear that home-made dress.'

'I thought you said it was pretty?'

'I could hardly say anything else, could I? I didn't want to hurt the child's feelings, but of course I could tell at a glance.' An idea crossed her mind. 'As a matter of fact, I'd been thinking of giving the little darling a present myself. If I give you the money, could you buy her

282

a sunhat, from me? It's very dangerous for a child to get the hot sun on the back of her neck. You must buy her a hat with a big brim, and pink ribbons to tie it under her chin – perhaps some little pink rosebuds round the crown . . . She'll look so sweet.' Muriel began to search the table of knick-knacks beside her armchair. 'Now let me see, what have I done with my purse?'

Out on the dirt-track, the noise was deafening.

Babs and Annie stood hand in hand, breathless with excitement as the bikes came flashing round the banked curve one after another, heading straight towards them, up a steep incline and at the very last moment, skidding round a hairpin bend before disappearing over the crest of the hill. As each rider approached the sharp turn, he threw his bike sideways at an alarming angle, planting one boot into the track, sending up a cloud of dust and a shower of cinders before spinning round the corner.

The smell of hot metal, petrol and exhaust fumes was overpowering; the whine of the engines and the scream of skidding tyres melted into a heart-stopping climax of excitement, as Annie clutched Babs' hand and shouted at the top of her voice: 'Isn't it *wonderful*?'

When the last bike had passed, there was a short respite while they waited for the next onslaught, and Babs had a chance to collect her thoughts and look about her. By chance, they had hit on an excellent vantage point, far from the crowds at the finishing-line. They had this isolated corner almost to themselves, but they were not completely alone. A few yards away, a young man and a boy waited for the next thrilling instalment.

The young man looked round, and gave a brief nod of recognition. 'Hello, Babs,' he said. 'Hello, Annie. Enjoying the fun?'

Babs recoiled indignantly. 'Don't you dare speak to me! I don't want anything to do with you!'

'No harm in passing the time of day,' said Steve reasonably. 'I don't think you've met my brother. This is Tony – Tony, this is Annie Watkins and her Auntie Babs.'

Babs tugged at Annie's hand. 'Come along, we're going. We don't know that man.'

Annie hung back. 'I do. I saw him at the seaside last year – with Auntie Val.'

'What?' Babs stared at her – then at Steve. 'Is this true?'

Glancing at his brother, Steve said, 'Tone – why don't you take

Annie to the refreshment tent, and buy her a bar of chocolate?' He dug in his pocket. 'Get one for yourself as well.'

Babs tried to stop them, but Annie had already slipped away. 'No, Annie. Wait!'

'She won't come to any harm; Tony will look after her.'

Babs was torn between anger and curiosity. She detested Steve, but she had to find out what Annie meant. 'All right,' she said. 'Only come straight back; we're not stopping.'

Tony took Annie's hand. Four years older and a head taller than the little girl, he looked quite grown-up beside her as they walked away. Impatiently, Babs tackled Steve.

'Tell me the truth – have you been seeing Valerie? Meeting in secret?'

He answered wryly, 'Not often. I wish I had – but I haven't.'

'What do you mean? Don't you know she's a married woman now?'

'Yes, married to your brother. But I met her all the same, last summer. Just the once.'

'When she was on holiday?'

'That's right. I saw her at Broadstairs.'

'You must be mad – both of you. What happened?'

'I don't think that's any of your business, do you? But if you're so interested, you'd better ask Val about it—'

His words were drowned as another bike flashed into view, tearing up the steep slope. Even though she was desperate to hear more, Babs broke off and watched as a single rider, in a dashing scarlet jacket, came hurtling towards them. When he got to the hairpin bend, he tried to save a few precious moments; instead of reducing speed like the others, using one foot as a brake, he attempted to fling the bike round by brute force, hauling it back on course before it hit the dirt.

But he misjudged the timing by a split second, and the bike slewed under him across the track, throwing him off; they heard the hollow thud as his crash-helmet struck a rock – and he lay very still. The motorcycle engine coughed and died; after the ear-splitting noise, the silence was terrifying. For an instant nothing moved, except one wheel of the bike, still spinning – then Babs and Steve ran forward together. Steve dropped to his knees, unbuckling the helmet and lifting it off gently. The man's head lolled sideways, and Steve examined him carefully.

'He'll be OK – he's only stunned,' he said. 'Keep an eye on him. I'll shift the bike before the next bloke runs into it.'

Babs knelt beside the unconscious man. He was dark-haired and sun-tanned – very good-looking, in a rugged way. A strand of black hair had fallen across his face, and she pushed it back, instinctively stroking his forehead.

His eyelids fluttered, and he looked up into her face. He frowned at her for a moment, then smiled.

'Hello, gorgeous,' he said. 'Where did you spring from?'

She had a ridiculous urge to go on stroking his face, but managed to control herself.

'You had a crash,' she said. 'You hit your head. How do you feel?'

'Bloody awful,' he replied. 'But all the better for seeing you.'

'Do you think you can sit up?' Putting her arm around him, she helped him into a sitting position, taking his weight against her breast.

'I thought for a minute I'd died and gone to heaven, with an angel looking after me,' he said, appraising her openly. 'What's your name, darling?'

Before she could reply, Steve came over to join them, wheeling the bike.

'The front suspension's taken a beating,' he said, 'But I think I can straighten it out if I can get hold of a tool-box. Are you all right?'

'Yes, I think so.' The rider grimaced, trying to focus. 'Who's your friend, Steve? Aren't you going to introduce us?'

Steve turned to Babs, and grinned. 'Babs Glynn – Roger Kirkwood. Only don't get the wrong idea – he carries on like this with every girl he meets – *and* he's a married man!'

Babs felt her cheeks flaming as she retorted, 'Don't be impertinent. You really are disgusting—' She broke off as two men in overalls came running up the hill. They helped Kirkwood to his feet and insisted on taking him to the First Aid tent, in spite of his protests.

Hot on their heels, Steve's brother returned with Annie, both gazing at the overturned bike.

'What happened?' asked Tony. 'Was it an accident?'

'Come along, Annie.' Babs grabbed her niece. 'We're going.'

Still clutching half a bar of chocolate, Annie tried to say, 'Thank you' to Steve, but Babs interrupted.

'Don't speak to him – he's nothing to do with us.'

As they set off towards the park gates, Steve shouted after them: 'Next time you see Valerie, give her my love!'

*

'Tea's ready!'

Aunt Ethel held the sitting-room door open and Aunt Aggie wheeled in the tea-trolley.

'Where's Babs?' Ethel looked around. 'And where's Annie? Are they in the garden?'

'Shall I go and call them?' offered Aggie.

'No, they're not in the garden,' said Muriel, in a measured tone. 'I'm very glad the child isn't here, Agnes, I have something to say to you.'

Aggie's smile died. 'What's the matter, Mu? Is there something wrong?'

Daphne tried to intervene: 'Don't, Mother, please,' but there was no stopping Muriel now.

'Will you be good enough to tell me where my purse is, Agnes?' she said.

Aggie looked bewildered. 'I haven't seen your purse. Isn't it here?'

'If it were here, I wouldn't be asking you about it, would I?' Muriel's voice hardened. 'Come along – let's not waste time.'

'But I don't know anything about your purse,' protested Aggie. 'Really I don't.'

'It was here, beside me, an hour ago – and now it has vanished.'

Ethel chimed in: 'I expect you've mislaid it somewhere, Muriel. I'm quite sure Aggie had nothing to do with it, she's been with me in the kitchen, cutting bread and butter and getting tea ready. Where did you have it last?'

'The last time I saw it was when Agnes brought me my medicine, after lunch.' Muriel pointed to the empty medicine-glass on her side-table. 'The purse was there then, and now it isn't.'

Ethel looked at Aggie. 'Are you sure you didn't move it, dear? Perhaps you tidied it away somewhere safe – try to remember.'

'No, I never touched it.' Aggie was crying now; tears trickling down her cheeks, and her nose was dripping. 'I swear I didn't – really and truly, I didn't!'

'Mother, for goodness sake.' Daphne stood up. 'There's no need for this. Your purse is bound to turn up presently.'

'No doubt – and we know where, don't we? In Agnes's bedroom, along with all the other things she's stolen.' Muriel was working herself up into a state of righteous indignation. 'As if I didn't have enough to put up with. I'm a helpless invalid, and my own sister steals from me . . . I've tried to be patient, Agnes. I've warned you again and again, but this time you've gone too far. I'm going to call the doctor and have you put away!'

With a little wail, Aggie ran out of the room, and they heard her stumbling up the stairs, sobbing. Ethel and Daphne turned reproachfully to Muriel; she tossed her head.

'It's high time somebody took a firm line. You're too soft with her, and it only makes her worse. She needs to be taught a lesson! In a few minutes she'll come back with the purse, pretending she found it lying on the stairs, and begging to be forgiven.'

'Mother, don't you understand?' said Daphne. 'She can't help it! As often as not, she doesn't even remember when she takes something. She doesn't do it deliberately.'

'So you say.' Muriel sniffed – then another metallic crescendo from the dirt-track distracted her, and she threw up her hands. 'There they go again – why doesn't Babs stop them? It's not right that a woman in my condition shuld have to suffer like this. It's not fair!'

Steve found Roger Kirkwood outside the First Aid tent, sitting on one folding chair, his feet up on another. He wheeled Roger's motorbike off the path on to a patch of grass, and kicked down the forked rest to prop it up.

'There you are, mate,' he said. 'Good as new – well, nearly.'

The champion rider glanced at the machine and grunted; 'Thanks for bringing it in. Not that it's going to be much use to me. They say I mustn't drive today, in case I get dizzy spells. What a load of horseshit.'

Steve eyed the bandage round his head. 'How are you feeling?' he asked.

'My head feels like it's splitting in half, otherwise I'm OK. They say I'll have a dome the size of St Paul's by tomorrow.'

'You were lucky; your helmet took the worst of it. You must have a good solid skull – it wasn't even grazed.'

'How do you know that?'

Steve laughed. 'I was there when you took that spill. I took your helmet off to see what the damage was. You were out to the world, but not for long.'

'That's right, I remember now – you and the little blonde. She's your girlfriend, is she?'

'She wouldn't thank you for saying that! No, she's just – a friend of someone I used to know.'

Roger Kirkwood raised an eyebrow. 'Interesting . . . What did you say her name was?'

'Babs – Babs Glynn. Why d'you ask?'

'You wouldn't happen to know her address? I might drop her a line – thank her for doing her ministering angel stuff. Girls like it if you write 'em a letter.'

'I don't know exactly where she lives. It's one of those houses over there, in Crystal Palace Park Road – I don't know the number.'

'Oh well, it was just an idea.' Roger dismissed it, then stood up with an effort and walked over to examine the bike. 'What did you mean when you said it was "nearly" OK?'

'The front suspension was a real mess when I picked it up.'

Roger peered at it. 'Yes. Looks like someone's done a pretty good job on it, though.'

'I did what I could – borrowed some tools from the lads on the track. It will need a proper repair job before the next race-meeting, but at least you'll get it home in one piece.'

'Of course, I was forgetting – you used to be a mechanic, didn't you?'

'Yes, I worked in a garage. I had a bike of my own, in those days.'

'What do you do now?'

'I work for my Dad – he's got a greengrocer's shop.'

Roger straightened up, squinting at him. 'Hang on, I think I'm still a bit dizzy – I'd better sit down. Pull up that other chair, and tell me what the hell you're talking about.'

So Steve told him the whole story, and when he had finished, Roger Kirkwood fumbled inside his jacket and pulled out a card, saying, 'I don't ride bikes for a living – it's only a kind of hobby. Speed – that's the thing I'm crazy about – bikes, cars, but mostly airplanes. That's my line; I work as a pilot at Croydon Aerodrome, so I know the chap who runs their workshop. They've been rushed off their feet lately. There's a hell of a lot of aircraft going in and out of Croydon these days, and it's getting busier all the time. If you're interested, give me a ring. My number's on the card.'

When Babs brought Annie in, Muriel scolded her.

'Wherever have you been? I suppose you realise the tea is completely stewed by now? We didn't like to start without you. Ethel, dear, you'd better throw this away and make a fresh pot.'

Ethel took the teapot and went out without a word.

'I can't imagine what took you so long,' Muriel continued. 'And whoever you spoke to, it hasn't done the slightest bit of good. The noise of those dreadful machines has been going on all the time, louder than ever.'

'I'm sorry, I wasn't able to speak to anyone. I only saw the men in charge of the motorbikes – the riders and the engineers—'

'You should have demanded to see someone in authority!'

'I never had the chance. While we were watching one of the races, there was an accident. A man got thrown off his bike – we had to try and help him.'

Daphne looked anxiously at her daughter. 'Was he badly hurt?'

'No, I don't think so, but some other people came and took him to the First Aid tent.'

'There, you see? It's not just a nuisance, it's highly dangerous. It must be stopped!' exclaimed Muriel.

'And we saw somebody else, didn't we?' Annie joined the conversation. 'I don't know his name, but I saw him before, with—'

Babs interrupted her quickly. 'Yes, it was very embarrassing. Do you remember that young man who used to work at the garage with Ray Duke? Steve Gunn – he was there too, and he was being very impertinent, so we came away.' Changing the subject, she asked: 'Where's Auntie Ag?'

'Agnes has gone up to her room.' With a meaning glance in Annie's direction, Muriel lowered her voice. 'I'm afraid she became rather hysterical – you know what she's like.'

Daphne tried to explain as tactfully as possible. 'Mother lost her purse, and she thought Auntie Ag might have come across it. It think perhaps the noise was getting on everyone's nerves—'

Muriel bridled. 'Nothing of the kind! Agnes has been up to her old tricks again. I had to speak to her severely.'

'You haven't lost your purse, Mummy.' Babs stood up. 'It's in your cardigan – I hung it up for you.' It was still on the back of a chair, and she produced the purse from one of the pockets. 'There you are.'

There was a moment of silence, and then Daphne said, 'Well, Mother? Are you going to apologise to Aggie?'

Muriel's face was expressionless. 'Certainly not – why should I? It was a natural assumption. You'd better go and tell her the purse has been found. Ask her if she'd like to come down and have some tea. Tell her she's forgiven, and we'll say no more about it.'

A few moments later, Daphne tapped on the door of Aggie's room, and a muffled voice said, 'Come in.'

She opened the door; Aggie was lying curled up on her bed, her hand over her mouth. She had stopped crying, but her face was still blotched with tears. Daphne sat on the edge of the bed and hugged her.

'It's alright, darling,' she said. 'There's nothing to worry about. Mother found her wretched purse; it was in her cardigan all the time. She told me to tell you you're forgiven.'

Aggie smiled with relief. 'Oh, I'm so glad.'

'You're *glad*? If I were you, I'd be simply furious! The way she carried on, accusing you—'

'Well, we all make mistakes, don't we? And I know I do silly things sometimes,' she added tremulously. 'Then I forget what I've done. It was understandable, really.'

'It doesn't give her the right to bully you! When she's in one of those moods, I wish you'd turn round and tell her to shut up.'

'Oh, I couldn't! It would only make things worse.' Aggie sighed. 'When she loses her temper, she shouts at me, and I can't bear it.'

'Why not shout back at her? You know we're all very fond of you – we'd back you up. Just try and stand up to her sometimes. It would do you both the world of good.'

Babs did not sleep soundly that night.

Two things had combined to upset her. First, Steve Gunn's mocking reference to his meeting with Valerie, last summer. He had said they only met once, but she wasn't sure she believed him. If he and Val had embarked on a secret affair, he would hardly admit it, would he? There was something in the way Steve had called out: '*Give her my love*' which made her suspicious.

And then there was her own extraordinary encounter with the motorcyclist. It was the first time she had been close to any man since Ray went to prison, and the physical contact had been disturbing. He was so full of life – strong and powerful, and good-looking – and after she had gone to bed, the thought of him kept her awake. She recalled the sound of his voice, the way he had looked at her, the feel of his smooth, warm face beneath her hand . . .

Babs had always found men attractive. Ever since she was a schoolgirl, she had been involved in various flirtations – and sometimes she had gone a little further than that, though she had never given herself completely to any man until she met Ray.

The outcome of that relationship had frightened her badly. She realised she had been playing with fire, and resolved never to get into such a dangerous situation again. Since then, she had given up flirting. Apart from her colleagues at Hawkins Estate Agency, she hardly spoke to any men at all, and tried to put such thoughts out of her head . . . Until this brief, unsettling exchange with Roger Kirkwood. Now, in a rush of excitement, a cavalcade of forbidden images tumbled though her mind, leaving her shaken and breathless – and angry.

During these long months, while she had been living her dull, drab life, had Valerie been deceiving her husband – carrying on with Steve while Gerry was out of the way?

Babs was determined to know the truth.

She was tempted to go to Westwood Court and have it out with Val right away – but it was a Sunday morning, and Gerry might be there. Then she remembered that Valerie often went to All Saints on Sundays, and since Gerry was not a regular worshipper, she usually went on her own.

Babs made up her mind. This morning, she would go to church.

Valerie was pleased to see her, and they sat in the same pew, joining in the hymns together. The last one was an old favourite; they had sung it at Valerie's wedding.

> *Love divine, all loves excelling.*
> *Joy of heav'n, to earth come down . . .*

Afterwards, as the organ played the out-voluntary, they left the church, shaking hands with the vicar in the porch, then strolled back towards Crystal Palace.

'This is a nice surprise,' said Val. 'You don't often come to All Saints, do you?'

'Not often. I hoped I might see you.'

Walking along Church Road, Valerie said, 'I generally go the long way round, by Westow Hill. Do you mind?'

Babs looked at her. 'You don't like walking past that shop?'

'I suppose it's silly, but . . . you do understand, don't you?

'I thought I did,' replied Babs. 'Until yesterday.'

'What do you mean? What happened yesterday?'

'I met Steve Gunn. We had a little talk.'

Valerie turned to face her. 'You talked to him? What did he say?'

There was a bench under some trees in Westow Street, and Babs said, 'Perhaps we'd better sit down.'

Sitting beside her, she told Valerie how she had come across Steve and his brother at the dirt-track racing, and how Steve had insisted on striking up a conversation – and that Annie had remembered a day last summer when he had gone down to Broadstairs.

'He told me he only met you once, but I couldn't be sure. Have you gone on seeing hm since then?'

'No!' Val was indignant. 'That's an awful thing to say!'

'Well, I didn't know, did I? You never told me you'd met him at all – why did you keep it a secret?'

'I was embarrassed, that's why! It happened as soon as he got out of prison; he found out where I was, and he followed me there.'

'What for?'

'Well, he – he wanted to tell me he still loved me.'

'So what did you say to him?'

'I was very upset – naturally. I told him I was married, and I said I never wanted to see him again. And I never have, except once or twice from a distance – at the other end of the street, or from the top of a bus. But I've taken care to keep out of his way. That's why I never go by the shop. It's all over now; it was over a long while ago.'

'Yesterday he said: "If you see Valerie, give her my love". . .'

Val caught her breath, then forced herself to say: 'You should have told him he can keep his love. I don't want it.'

May had been warm and sunny, but June came in like a wet blanket. The rain poured down from a muggy grey sky, and people sheltering under shop-awnings muttered sarcastically: 'Flaming June . . .'

As the raindrops chased each other down the windowpanes, Babs sat in the back office at Hawkins and Company, typing out a prospectus for another new property.

Semi-detached, in good position, two minutes from Southern Railway. Two recep., three beds, kit. and bath—

Absorbed, she heard the door open behind her.

'Ah, Miss Glynn. If I might interrupt you?'

She did not turn her head, but went on typing. 'Yes, sir. I'm just finishing this.'

Old Mr Hawkins had brought in a potential customer. 'This gentleman wishes to put his house on the market. Perhaps you'd take down the details and explain the procedure? This is our Miss Glynn. I'm sure she will give you every assistance, Mister – er – I'm sorry, what was the name again?'

'My name is Faber . . . Walter Faber.' When Babs looked up, he smiled tentatively. 'Miss Glynn and I are old friends,' he said. 'We used to work together at one time.'

'Really? What a coincidence. In that case, you'll know that she is extremely efficient; you are in very good hands.' And Mr Hawkins left them together, shutting the door behind him.

'May I take your waterproof, Mr Faber? Let me hang it up to dry.' Babs helped him off with his raincoat, hanging it on a peg behind the door. 'Not a very nice day, I'm afraid. Won't you sit down?'

'Thank you. You're looking very well.'

'Yes, I am. I hope you are, too? And how is Mrs Faber?' Too late, she realised that he was dressed in black, and wore a black tie. 'Oh, I'm so sorry—'

'Mrs Faber passed away nearly two months ago. I think it was a happy release for her.'

'But a terrible loss for you, I'm sure.'

'Yes, that's true – and a great upheaval. Among other things, it means I have to sell my house. I'm looking for a small flat, which will be easier to manage.'

'I expect we can find you something suitable. But to begin with, may I take down the particulars of your house?'

They faced one another across the desk, and she began to make notes. As Walter talked, she studied his face. She had not seen him since she left the furniture shop, four years ago, but he looked more than four years older.

He described the house as well as he could, then added, 'I imagine you'll want to come and see round the property, to check the details?'

'I expect Mr Hawkins will come and look at it, or one of the senior members of the staff will make an appointment.'

'You won't be coming to look at it yourself?'

'I don't think so.'

'I see.' He bit his fingernail, then said: 'As a matter of fact, I have a confession to make – I knew you worked here. When I decided to sell my house, I started looking round the estate agents. One afternoon, I caught a glimpse of you, through the shop window, and it seemed as if – I don't know – as if it was meant to happen. It gave me the chance to speak to you again.'

He put one hand lightly on hers, and a tiny thrill of electricity passed between them as he continued, 'I hope you don't mind me saying this. I saw the item about Duke in the local paper. It must have been a shock for you.'

She lowered her eyes. 'You were quite right about him. He was a bad lot – I know that now.'

'I was very sorry. Not for him – for you.'

She withdrew her hand. 'We'd better get on. If you're interested in finding a flat, I can give you some prospectuses—'

'Thank you.' He hesitated, then began again. 'I wonder – would you have supper with me, one evening? I'll find a quiet restaurant, where we can talk . . . That is, if you'd like to?'

As she looked at him, he suddenly seemed much younger – shy and sincere. With a glow of happiness, she replied, 'Thank you, Walter. Yes, I'd like that.'

There was to be a National Band Festival at the end of the month, and naturally the Crystal Palace Brass Band were taking part. In preparation for the event, they were putting in extra rehearsals, and when Val left her office one evening, she saw the musicians arriving, on their way to the Concert Room.

One of the attendants called to her as she walked through the south transept, on her way out of the building. 'Could you spare a minute? This gentleman was asking for you.'

It was old Jack Gunn, his cornet tucked under his arm. He peered at her short-sightedly. 'Valerie – is that you, girl?'

'Hello, Mr Gunn. What can I do for you?'

'Young Steve asked me to look out for you. He said I might catch you after work – we got extra rehearsals this week, you see, for the Festival.'

'Yes, I see.' Aware that the attendant was listening, she tried to cut the conversation short, but it was impossible to hurry old Jack.

'In the general way, we only practise once a week, but we've got these damn test-pieces to do. The buggers make 'em difficult on purpose – triple-tonguing, they put in – all that fluttery business. I don't hold with it meself . . . it's not proper music, to my way of thinking.'

'I'm afraid I can't stop. I'm just on my way home—'

'Steve asked me to give you this, very particular, before you go. He said as he couldn't send it through the post, in case of it falling into the wrong hands. Here you are.'

He produced an envelope from his pocket and held it out to her; the sight of Steve's handwriting made her heart turn over. Still very conscious that the attendant was listening, she drew old Jack down a side aisle, out of earshot.

'I'm sorry, I think you'd better keep the letter,' she said gently. 'I don't want it.'

'But you got to! Very insistent, he was. "*Make sure she gets it*," he told me. "*Give it to her, nobody else – it's important*," he said . . . You got to read it.'

She could not argue. Slipping it into her handbag, she said, 'Very well, thank you. But I really have to go now – excuse me.'

All the way home, she walked very quickly, as if she were running away from something, or from someone.

She was confused by conflicting emotions. She felt angry, certainly. It was unfair of Steve to use his grandfather as a messenger – he must have guessed she would not disappoint the old man by refusing to accept the letter. Yet she understood why he had not sent it to Westwood Court. He wouldn't want the letter to be picked up from the doormat by Gerry – and if he had sent it to the Crystal Palace, there would have been the risk of someone else opening it, along with the rest of the office mail. And he could not deliver it to her in person; she had told him very clearly that she did not want to see him again.

Well, she had accepted the letter – but that didn't mean she had to read it. She could throw it away unopened, couldn't she?

When she got home, the flat was empty; Gerry had said he might have to work late.

She took the envelope from her bag and studied it. Steve's handwriting made her pulse skip a beat. She hadn't seen it for years, but she would have known it anywhere; it was as much a part of him as his voice or his smile. She knew, too, that she should destroy the letter unread, yet among all these emotions at war within her, one of the strongest was a desperate curiosity. Without even stopping to take off her hat and coat, she tore open the envelope.

Dear Valerie,

A few weeks ago, I met Babs and talked to her. She was not pleased to see me, but then I did not expect her to be. I don't care much what she thinks of me, but she had Annie with her, and Annie remembered me from last summer, and said so.

It strikes me now that Babs might have said something to you later. She could have tried to stir up some trouble – that's why I'm writing to you.

This was true, but it was not the whole truth. Steve had also remembered something Roger Kirkwood had said to him, on the same occasion: 'Girls like it if you write 'em a letter.'

Val turned the page and read on.

If anything I said to Babs has made things more difficult for you, I just want to tell you I am sorry. You know I would never do anything to hurt you. And although it is a bit late to say so, I want you to know that I am sorry I came to Broadstairs that time, and upset you.

I didn't stop to think. I wanted to see you and to be with you – it was stupid and selfish, I see that now, and I don't blame you for being angry.

So I am writing this to try and put things right. I hope you will forgive me, and that one day we will meet again and talk – as friends, if we cannot be anything else. I still miss you, and I would sooner have your friendship, if that is all there is for us, than face the rest of my life without ever seeing you again.

One more thing I should tell you. Through a chap I met who works at Croydon Airport, I have now got fixed up in the workshop there as an aircraft mechanic. It is an interesting job, with good prospects; it keeps me busy and gives me plenty to think about. At present I am still living at Church Road, but travelling to Croydon every day takes up a lot of time and I have started looking for digs in Waddon, and hope to make a move before long.

If you ever feel like dropping me a line to tell me how you are getting along, you can always write care of Mum and Dad. They will forward any letters addressed to me without opening them. It would be nice to hear from you, and to know you are all right.

Your friend, Steve.

When she had finished reading the letter, she turned it over and started again from the beginning; altogether she must have read it three or four times. At last she replaced it in the envelope and put it away carefully in the top drawer of the chest of drawers, underneath her stockings and underclothes.

Then she sat down with a writing-pad on her lap, and tried to compose a reply.

She started the letter several times, but abandoned each one after a few sentences, afraid of saying too much – afraid Steve might misinterpret her words. It was hard to find the right tone; neither too encouraging nor too dismissive, too cool or too affectionate.

Finally she gave up, and tore the unfinished attempted into tiny scraps, then flushed them down the lavatory.

For several weeks Steve waited hopefully, but he never received a reply to his letter.

Chapter Sixteen

'SIT DOWN, BOTH of you,' said Val. 'I'm going to bring in the soup.'

Daphne and Ted took their places on either side of the dining table, and Daphne said; 'Isn't this nice? A real family party.'

'Val suggested we should take you to the Talbot Arms, but I persuaded her to cook something at home instead.' Gerald sat in the carving-chair at the head of the table. 'It's much more cosy and peaceful. We don't want waitresses breathing down our necks, do we?'

'Depends on the waitresses,' said Ted – then, as Daphne shot him a stern look, 'Only joking, sweetheart. Take no notice.'

Val brought in a steaming soup-tureen, and announced, 'It's mushroom, and it's out of a tin, so there! That's the worst of being at work all day, I don't get much time for proper cooking on weekdays.'

It was a Thursday evening, and she and Gerald had invited Ted and Daphne to supper at Westwood Court.

'The trouble is, weekends are awkward for Ted,' Daphne explained, and he chimed in:

'As a rule, Saturdays and Sundays are the only nights when I do go out to work!'

'Then I'm glad we picked this evening,' said Gerald, 'because I had a particular reason for asking you round here.' He wiped a few drops of soup from his moustache with the edge of his napkin. 'I wanted to know – how would you feel about coming along to do an audition for the BBC?'

'What – me? On the wireless?' Ted was taken aback. 'I never really thought about it.'

'Well, think about it now, old man,' Gerald urged him. 'Our

Variety Department are always on the lookout for new talent. We're broadcasting vaudeville shows every week now, and we can't keep on trotting out the same old names all the time. Why don't you let me put your name forward? After all, what have you got to lose? If they don't like you, there's no harm done, and if you happen to strike lucky, it could be another string to your bow, so to speak.'

'I think that's a wonderful idea,' said Daphne. 'Much better than having to go out on some horrible tour. It's worth trying, isn't it?'

'I suppose so.' Ted still sounded doubtful. 'Where would the audition be? Do you hire a theatre, or what?'

'No, they hold auditions at our studios, in Savoy Hill – not only for variety artistes, but dramatic actors and actresses as well. If you're interested, I can certainly drop a word in the right ear.'

'Well – thanks very much, Gerry. I'll try not to let you down.'

When Val brought in the main course – a roasted half-leg of lamb – she asked after the rest of the family. 'And how's my lovely Annie? It'll be her birthday in a week or two, won't it? What does she want for her present?'

'She hasn't made up her mind yet, but you'll be getting an invitation to her party,' Daphne told her. 'That's if she's forgiven you. She was quite indignant she wasn't included this evening.'

'Nobody else would have got a word in, if she'd been with us,' said Ted. 'Talk about a chatterbox – I can't think where she gets it from.'

'I can,' said Daphne pointedly, and turned to Gerry. 'If it's a quiet, peaceful family gathering you're after, don't come round to our house.' She was interrupted by a ring at the doorbell.

'Now what?' exclaimed Val. 'Start carving, Gerry – I'll see who it is.'

She went out of the little dining room, and returned a moment later, followed by a uniformed police constable.

'Begging your pardon for the intrusion,' he began, 'but we're going through all the flats, making enquiries. You haven't had any unexpected visitors this evening?'

'No. This is my sister and her husband, and I assure you they were invited.' Gerald introduced Daphne and Ted. 'What's it all about, officer?'

'We've had a report of an attempted break-in on these premises, half an hour ago, and it's possible the intruder may be still in the building. If I might just take a look around?'

With Gerald's permission, the constable made a quick tour of the flat, looking into every room; there was no sign of any uninvited guest.

'Right, sir. Thanks for your help. Sorry for the inconvenience,' he said, making his way out.

'Now then – where had we got to?' Gerald asked, taking his seat again.

'You'd just started carving, I know that,' said Val, 'What were we talking about?'

Ted smiled. 'Something about a peaceful family gathering, wasn't it?'

'It all seems so unbelievable, anyone breaking in here,' said Val.

'There are a lot of unsavoury characters about these days,' said Gerry, wielding the carving-knife. He turned to Valerie. 'Perhaps it was that friend of yours, Steven Gunn. He's at large in the district again, I hear. I shouldn't be surprised if he's turning his hand to burglary now.'

'Don't be ridiculous!' said Val, so sharply that they all looked at her. 'Steve Gunn wouldn't do such a thing. He's not that kind of person.'

'He was an accessory to robbery, and one thing can lead to another—'

'Just because he was sent to prison, that doesn't mean he was guilty. I don't believe he had anything to do with . . .' Her voice trailed away, and she asked, 'How do you know he's out of prison? Have you seen him?'

'No, I'm happy to say I haven't. I meant to tell you – Babs said she'd run into him a few weeks ago. She warned us to keep our eyes open.'

'I never heard such rubbish!' snapped Val. 'For goodness sake let's talk about something else. Daphne – Ted – help yourselves to greens and potatoes before everything's stone cold.'

Later on, when they were drinking coffee in the sitting room, the policeman returned to put their minds at rest.

'I thought you'd like to know. We found the chap we were looking for, hiding up on the roof, and he'll be spending the night in the cells, so there's no reason for anyone to feel alarmed.'

Valerie's voice sounded strained as she asked, 'Who was he, do you know? I mean – where did he come from?'

'He's not a local lad, if that's what you mean. Comes from Bermondsey way. Been out of work for a year – no job and no prospects – half-starved, by the look of him. Well, I'll wish you good night, ladies and gentlemen.'

'Poor devil,' muttered Ted, as the front door closed again. He had not forgotten what it felt like to be out of work.

This time it was Daphne who changed the subject. 'How was Babs when you saw her? She hasn't been near us lately, has she, Ted?'

'She's kept pretty busy at the office,' said Gerry. 'I asked her to come round and join us tonight, but she wasn't free. Apparently she's putting in some overtime. The house-property market must be doing a roaring trade!'

At that moment, Babs *was* discussing the property market – but she was not in the office.

In the grillroom at the Talbot Arms – an old-established hotel in Dulwich – Babs was dining with Walter Faber, and they were talking about his proposed move.

'Only a small flat; just one bedroom will be enough,' he told her, as they finished the meal.

'One bedroom?' Babs queried this. 'What about your housekeeper?'

'I don't employ a housekeeper any more,' he said. 'After the funeral I had to let her go. Well, it wouldn't have done, would it – a widower and a single woman, living under the same roof. You know how people talk.'

'But how have you been managing since then – on your own?'

'Pretty well. There's a woman who comes in once a week to keep the place clean; I make my own meals, and I usually eat out at midday.'

' I see . . . so you only want one bedroom. That may be more difficult,' Babs warned him.

'Oh? I should have thought it would make things easier.'

'At Hawkins and Company we tend to concentrate on the better class of apartment. One-bedroom flats are in the lower price-range; only one step above bed-sitting rooms, quite honestly.'

'Well, perhaps I could consider a two-bedroom flat. I suppose it might be convenient, if I ever have a guest to stay.'

'That's right. And at other times it can be used as a boxroom, to store luggage or furniture.' Considering, she put her head on one side, and he thought he had never seen her look so lovely. 'I expect, moving from a whole house, you'll have rather a lot of furniture?'

'More than I need really. I've accumulated a good many handsome

301

pieces over the years; it's hard to decide what to keep and what to get rid of.'

'Yes – and it's not always easy to sell second-hand furniture, though I suppose you must have some good contacts in the trade?' She leaned forward confidentially. 'I hope you don't think I'm being inquisitive, but I know you gave up your shop in Church Road. I couldn't help wondering – have you taken other premises? In another district, perhaps?'

'I couldn't face the strain of setting up my own business again, and the capital outlay would have been crippling. I had all the expenses of my wife's illness, you see – doctor's bills, hospital fees and so on . . . I decided I'd be better off working for some larger establishment, and I was lucky enough to be taken on as a department manager at a local store.'

'Oh, yes? Which one?'

'Catchpolls, at Sydenham. I'm in charge of furnishing fabrics.'

'Catchpolls? But that's where I—'

'You were in the accounts department at one time – I hadn't forgotten. You'll think I'm silly, but it pleased me to know you had worked there too. It seemed to be a link between us.' Feeling he had gone to far, he indicated the coffee-pot. 'Would you care for a second cup?' he suggested.

'Thank you.' As he took her cup, their fingers touched and she smiled back at him. 'Shall we get down to business? You were talking about the furniture you want to keep. Could you give me some idea how many pieces you plan to take with you, then I'll know how much space you're going to need, when I'm looking out some possible addresses.'

Handing her the coffee, he asked: 'Could you do me a favour? Most of my stuff is rather old-fashioned, and it occurred to me – if you'd be kind enough to visit the house, you might help me decide what to throw out, and what to hang on to. Or would that be asking too much?'

'I'll be only too glad to help. When were you thinking of?'

He took the plunge. 'If you're not in any particular hurry, how about this evening?'

Half an hour later, he unlocked the front door, and Babs walked in.

She was impressed. The house wasn't as large as Belmont – only on two floors, but in a much better state of repair, and decorated with great care. The furniture was a little dated, but everything had been chosen with excellent taste.

Walter went ahead, switching on lights in every room and drawing the curtains at all the windows. She guessed he did not want passers-by to see him escorting a young lady through the house.

The doors and windows were all tightly shut, yet Babs felt a sudden chill; when she shivered, Walter was immediately concerned.

'I hope you're not in a draught? Let me switch on the gas fire.'

'Please don't bother. I mustn't stay long; my family will be wondering what's become of me.'

'Of course, your poor mother. Forgive me, I should have asked – I hope she's keeping well?'

'She has good days and bad days – you know how it is.'

'Yes, I do know.' His eyes clouded for a moment, then he said; 'Well, now you've seen the ground floor, shall we take a look upstairs?'

There were three bedrooms. The housekeeper had slept in the smallest; the biggest, looking over the garden at the back of the house, held a double bed. The room had no character – no feeling of personality coloured it in any way. On the dressing-table, a matching set of hand-mirror, brush and comb lay beside a cut-glass bottle of cologne; there was a thin film of dust over everything.

Walter led the way to the remaining bedroom, at the front; a masculine room, it smelled of bay-rum and shaving-soap, and there was a tweed jacket on a hanger, a trouser-press in one corner, and a narrow single bed. He crossed the room to close the curtains, saying flatly, 'This is where I sleep.'

'I suppose when your wife became so ill, she had to have a room of her own.'

Over his shoulder, Walter said in the same level tone, 'My wife was an invalid for a long time. We had separate rooms for most of our married life.'

Babs went closer to him, putting her hand on his sleeve. He turned to face her – and then she was in his arms.

'Thank God,' he said, and his voice was thick with emotion. 'I didn't know whether you – I didn't dare hope . . . Thank God I've found you again.' He kissed her hungrily, his hands gripping her like a drowning man clinging to a lifebelt.

She had been half-expecting him to make some move. When he suggested they should go upstairs, she was prepared for it, though she did not know how she would respond. When he embraced her, she did not have time to stop and think – her own responses frightened her a little. She returned his kisses with a passion which left her breathless.

It had been so long since any man had touched her, but it wasn't only his masculinity that excited her, it was the feeling of being wanted – of being loved. It was as if she saw herself through his eyes, the object of his desire; through him, she found herself desirable.

She had to remain in command. She knew she had complete power over him, and she must not lose control.

Gently, she held him at arms length, whispering, 'Dear Walter, we mustn't. Not here, not now. You said yourself, people will talk, and it is getting late. I have to go.'

'When can I see you again? he asked urgently.

'Soon – very soon. I'll telephone you from the office. I shall have some flats for you to inspect anyway. Perhaps I can persuade Mr Hawkins to let me take you to see them.'

'I hope so. I'm relying on you to help me make the right choice,' he said, kissing her once more.

'Goodbye, Walter dear,' she said, breaking away from him. 'Thank you for a wonderful evening – I really enjoyed it.'

Gerald was as good as his word. Ted received a letter requesting him to attend an audition at Savoy Hill, and a few days later made his way to the studios, in a narrow street off the Embankment.

Daphne had insisted that he wore his best suit, and although he pointed out that the BBC were interested in his voice, not what he looked like, she tied his tie for him and polished his shoes before she would let him go.

When he entered the studios, he was introduced to half a dozen people – all of them very earnest and intense; the men with spectacles and beards, the ladies with short-cropped hair or plaits coiled into snail-shells over each ear. They told him where to stand, warned him not to touch the mike (this seemed to be their pet name for the microphone – a strange object like an oversized meat-safe) and instructed him not to speak until the green light went on. Then they all trooped out of the studio and left him alone.

He could still see them through a glass wall, looking like fish in an aquarium, and he gave them a friendly wave. They ignored him, and talked among themselves for several minutes; he could not hear them, but he could see their mouths opening and closing – looking more like fish than ever. It was so absurd, he forgot to be nervous, and tried not to laugh.

When the green light shone, he allowed himself a chuckle as he said: 'Well, I dunno – it's a funny old world, isn't it? This is me, Ted Watt, speaking to you over the airwaves. I can't see you and you can't see me – so I'd better start by telling you that I'm tall, dark, amazingly handsome, and a terrible liar . . . Mind you, I never think of myself as a liar, though it's true that I tell stories. Like the story about the Scotsman who bought a lot of day-old chicks, because he heard they were going cheep . . .'

And he began to create a pattern of nonsense, weaving each absurdity seamlessly into the next. It was rather eerie, telling jokes in a soundproof room with no response but silence, but he could see the people behind the glass wall, no longer earnestly serious but smiling – giggling – enjoying themselves. That helped a lot.

When he had finished, the Head of Variety told him he'd done very well, adding as an afterthought, 'Though I think you'd better cut the one about the Scotsman. Mr Reith might not like it.'

But that didn't seem to matter. They told him he would hear from them very shortly, and a month later he was summoned back to make his first broadcast.

He was called for ten-thirty in the morning, though the show was not due to go on the air until eight in the evening, and sent along to Studio 1 for a rehearsal. The producer – a harassed young man with receding hair and a Fair Isle jersey, explained that it would be a mainly musical programme, and that Ted was the only speaking performer. The others were all singers and musicians, accompanied by a small orchestra.

He introduced Ted to his fellow artistes: there was a plump Italian tenor, a Welsh harpist, a pair of twins who played duets on two pianos, and an Austrian soprano. He forgot most of their names immediately, but the red-haired soprano smiled at him so sweetly, and looked so pretty, he had no difficulty in remembering that she was called Marta – Marta Linden.

As they shook hands, she said in her soft, continental accent, 'You will have to be most patient with me if I make foolish mistakes, please. This is my very first time.'

'Same here,' Ted told her. 'It's my first broadcast as well. Cheer up! If we get stage-fright, we can hold hands – the audience will never know!'

She laughed, and it was only later in the morning that the producer took Ted aside and explained that, far from being a beginner, Fraulein Linden was a world-famous star of Viennese operetta, and had broadcast all over Europe. This just happened to be her English début.

Ted felt embarrassed, and was relieved to find that she didn't seem to have taken offence. She made a point of coming over to chat to him when there was a break in the rehearsal – and she smiled as sweetly as ever.

There were a good many breaks during the rehearsal; the producer had problems in placing the artistes at the correct distance from the mike, and getting the correct sound-balance for the various instruments of the orchestra. He had particular trouble with Ted. As he was the only performer on the show unaccompanied by music, his voice created an echo in the large studio, which they tried to baffle – at first by putting screens round him, and when that failed, draping the screens with fire-blankets.

By the end of the afternoon, the sound engineer was still unsatisfied with the result, and not long before they went on the air, the producer called Ted in to the control-room and said, 'I'm afraid we're going to have to change the setup again.'

'Don't tell me – you want me to put on feathers and war paint when I go into my wigwam?' Ted tried to make light of it, but he couldn't help wondering how he would be able to give a perfomance under these conditions.

Unamused, the producer answered, 'We've decided not to have you in Studio 1 at all; the sound quality's all wrong. I'm putting you into Studio 1A, with the duty announcer.'

Studio 1A was not much bigger than a bathroom; just large enough to hold a small table with a microphone on it, and one chair. Seated in the chair was Ted's brother-in-law.

'Sorry about this, Gerald,' the producer began, 'but we're getting a nasty echo in there, so Ted's coming in here to share your mike. Let me introduce you—Gerald Glynn – Ted Watts.'

'We have met,' said Gerry, with a courteous bow.

'That's right,' Ted told the producer. 'I've been sleeping with his sister for the past ten years.'

Seeing that the producer was speechless, Gerry hastened to explain. He welcomed Ted to the tiny studio, which was normally used by the announcers who linked the various programmes throughout the day.

The producer apologised for the fact that there was no room for a second chair, but added: 'After Gerald's made the opening announcement, he'll be pushing off, so you'll be able to sit down.'

'You mean I'll be in here all by myself?' asked Ted.

'Yes, it will give you a much better acoustic. We'll flash the green light when you're on air.'

He gave Ted some last-minute instructions and then hurried away, while Gerry prepared to make his next announcement.

Ted said, 'I didn't expect to see you. I thought you were away doing outside broadcasts these days?'

'Yes, I generally cover the sporting events, but there was nothing doing today so I got shunted back to town, to fill in for one of my colleagues who's on leave, lucky swine.' Gerry looked at the clock, watching the second-hand sweeping slowly round. 'Not long now – two minutes to go.'

Ted felt panic welling up inside him. Everything was so different from what he had been expecting, he was hopelessly out of his depth. Apart from a small glass panel in the door, there was no window in the tiny room; he couldn't even see the producer, or his fellow artistes in the big studio – nothing but the blank, hostile wall in front of him.

'How the hell can I crack jokes when I haven't got an audience?' he asked. 'I need a few friendly faces to play to.'

'You mustn't think of it like that, old man,' said Gerry, 'You're not performing to a few dozen people in the park now, you know; you're broadcasting to the whole country. Ten million men and women are sitting by their wireless sets, listening to you – they're your audience!'

He put on a pair of headphones, saying casually, 'Well, this is it. Fifteen seconds to go . . . .'

As the second-hand reached the hour, the green light flashed, and he continued smoothly: 'Good evening, listeners. It's eight o'clock – time for this week's *Variety Parade* – and we are privileged tonight to introduce the celebrated Austrian soprano, Fraulein Marta Linden, supported by a team of popular entertainers . . . Ladies and gentlemen – welcome to *Variety Parade!*'

The green light went out, and Gerry removed the headphones, passing them over to Ted and saying, 'You might as well listen to the rest of the show, then you'll know when they're getting near your spot. Have the chair, old boy; I'm off for a cup of tea – and the best of luck!'

And he went out, leaving Ted on his own. Putting on the

headphones, he could hear the orchestra playing the opening music, and he felt as if he were alone in the world.

For the first time in his life, he was paralysed by fear. The idea of cracking gags in this suffocating little box, playing to a blank wall, reduced him to a jelly; the thought of faceless millions listening all over the country turned his bowels to water. He wanted to tear off the headphones and run out of the building, running as far and as fast as he could —

But he had to stay there; somehow, he had to get through the next half-hour. He tried to think – tried to cudgel his brain and make it work.

If he couldn't *see* his audience, he would have to imagine them. He shut his eyes and tried to visualise one or two people – real people . . . Daphne would be listening, he knew that; she and Annie and Kate had gone round to Valerie's flat to listen to the broadcast. He tried to picture them – and then, over the headphones, he heard the voice of Marta Linden, pure and sparkling as a crystal stream bubbling over pebbles. She was singing *Vilia* – from *The Merry Widow*, wasn't it? Her carefree voice soothed him, reminding him of the way she had smiled.

When the song came to an end, the green light went on, and Ted pictured that enchanting smile. Smiling back, he began confidently: 'Hello, how are you keeping? Ted Watt's the name, and I'm very glad to meet you. It's a funny old world, isn't it?'

Later that evening, in a handy pub along the Strand, he celebrated his first broadcast, then caught the last train home from Charing Cross. By the time he let himself into the house at Sackville Road, he expected to find Daff in bed and asleep. But when he went into the kitchen, she jumped up and ran to meet him, kissing him and saying: 'Don't make a sound, you'll wake Annie. I couldn't sleep – I had to wait up till you got home. You were marvellous, we all thought so – and I was so proud of you. What was it like? Did you enjoy it?'

'Before it started, I was terrified. . .I've never been so scared. I kept thinking: "How can I tell jokes to ten million people?" Then at the last moment I decided to think about just one person, and play it all to her—' He broke off, cursing himself for having had too much to drink. Why did he say 'her'? But it was all right; Daff was looking happier than ever.

'You were thinking of me, all the time?' She hugged him again. 'Oh Ted, I do love you.'

That night was a turning point in Ted's career. The BBC were delighted by the number of letters they received; the audience had enjoyed the new, unknown comedian, and wanted to hear him again. Within weeks, Ted was booked for a Saturday-night Variety programme, and his popularity went on building steadily.

And it wasn't only the listeners who liked him.

At the end of September, Percy Thring had some good news for Ted. One of the big touring managements was planning a production of *Cinderella* next Christmas at the Gaiety Theatre in Hastings, and Ted had been asked to play Buttons. The principals were all invited to go to the manager's office in Charing Cross Road, to sign their contracts and have their photographs taken.

Ted broke the news to Daphne. It would mean being away from home for six or seven weeks, from late December until early February, but for some of that time Carmichael Road School would be on holiday, so Daff and Annie could join him in Hastings.

Daphne wasn't keen on spending Christmas among strangers, in a boarding house, but she knew it was an important step up the ladder for Ted, and she mustn't stand in his way. Annie was overjoyed at the prospect of another trip to the seaside, and Daphne had to explain that she wouldn't be able to paddle or build sandcastles in the middle of winter – but Annie didn't care; it was something new and exciting, and she could hardly wait.

One Monday morning, Percy picked Ted up in his new Baby Austin and drove him to Charing Cross Road. Peering through the windscreen, Percy grumbled continuously about the traffic, which was becoming more impossible every day. As they scraped between a tram, a furniture pantechnicon and a brewer's dray, Ted closed his eyes and wondered what a tall thin Baby Austin would look like.

When they reached the West End, Percy couldn't find anywhere to park the car, and finally left it with two wheels up on the pavement, partially blocking Denmark Street, while they went into the manager's office.

Ted knew he would not be the star of the show; he was introduced to Ronnie Rivers and Lew Lake, a well-known slapstick double act – *Rivers and Lake – Always a Big Splash!* – who were playing the Ugly Sisters and topping the bill. Their low comedy routines, involving pails of whitewash, broken crockery and a cake-baking scene complete with bags of flour and real eggs, were ancient and traditional, but still reduced audiences to hysteria. Ted's gentle, zany patter would provide a welcome change of pace.

He shook hands with the two ageing clowns, and found they were rather quiet and shy in private life, unlike the frenzied buffoons they became on stage. They also had a habit of finishing each other's sentences.

'We caught your turn the other night, on the—'

'—on the wireless. We both thought you were—

'—very good indeed. We said to ourselves, "*That lad's going to go—*"'

'—*go a long way*. That's right, we did. Very glad to be—'

'—to be working with you . . . Specially when we heard that you—'

'—you were specially asked for. Yes . . .'

Puzzled, Ted said: 'You mean – asked for by the manager?'

'No, *she's* the one who asked—'

'—asked him to sign you—'

'—up!'

Then the door opened and Cinderella walked in; not in rags, but wearing a fur coat, her pretty face half-hidden under a matching fur hat.

'Good afternoon, Mr Watt. How nice to meet you again,' said Marta Linden.

An agreeable glow spread through Ted as the manager explained that it was Fraulein Linden who had suggested he should play opposite her.

'Since she heard you on the air, she felt sure you would work very well together. Now, will you all gather round the desk and sign your contracts, please, so we can get a group photo?'

Ted stood next to Marta Linden, and when the photographer asked them to move in a little closer, he slipped his arm round her shoulders. She turned and looked into his eyes as the photographer said: 'Hold it, please. Nobody move – nice and still now . . .'

For a long moment, they smiled at one another – and Ted decided that he was going to enjoy Christmas very much indeed.

On Thursday, Valerie was working late.

Mr Buckland always stayed on until the end of the evening on a Thursday, because it was the busiest night of the week. Throughout the summer and autumn, there was the long-established tradition of a 'Brock's Benefit' every Thursday night.

A few years after the Palace moved to Sydenham Hill, a firework display was held as a special attraction, thrown open to firework manufacturers who competed with one another to provide the most spectacular show. The contest was won by Charles Thomas Brock, and as a result he and his family continued to produce regular pyrotechnic displays for more than sixty years.

'Brock's Benefit Nights' had become famous all over the country; huge crowds gathered on fine Thursdays throughout the summer season, so a number of the Palace staff remained on duty.

The offices were not manned as a rule, but today Val had offered to put in some overtime. Mr Buckland took care to collect items from all the newspapers – national, as well as local – which carried stories concerning the Palace; these press-cuttings were kept in a file and from time to time transferred to a series of scrapbooks.

Keeping the scrapbooks up to date was one of Val's jobs, but this summer she had been so busy, she had let the cuttings file get out of hand. When Gerald told her that he would be on the evening duty roster at Savoy Hill, she welcomed the opportunity to tackle the scrapbooks without interruption.

Now the scissors and paste-pot were at her elbow, the bulging file of cuttings was open on the desk – she had even remembered to bring a packet of sandwiches and a thermos of coffee to keep her going.

Unfortunately, things didn't work out the way she'd planned.

Before every firework display, the Crystal Palace Brass Band played a concert of popular pieces to entertain the crowds on the terraces, until the sun went down and it was time to light the blue touchpaper; the first thing Val noticed was that the band did not strike up at the advertised time. It was almost a quarter of an hour later before she heard a rousing selection from *Chu Chin Chow*, and she wondered why; the bandmaster was a stickler for punctuality as a rule.

Soon after this there was a knock at the door and one of the attendants appeared. 'Excuse me, Mrs Glynn – could I trouble you?'

'Yes, of course. Why were the band so late in starting?' she asked. 'Was there a problem?'

'Sort of, yes. One of 'em was took ill, just as the bandmaster raised his baton. Keeled over and fell off his chair, he did, clutching his heart and groaning. Me and one of the trombones picked him up and lugged him off to the gardeners' shed. That's where he is now.'

'Oh dear, do you think it's serious? Should I phone for a doctor?'

'I think it's a heart attack, only he won't let nobody send for a doctor. That's why I wondered if you'd have a word with him.'

'But I'm not a nurse. I haven't even done first aid.'

'No, but he might listen to you, on account of you being a personal friend. It's old Mr Gunn, you see. I remembered that other time, when he asked to speak to you.'

Val's heart sank. 'I wouldn't call myself a friend, exactly. I used to know the family at one time . . . I'd much better get a doctor—' She put her hand on the telephone, but he stopped her.

'I told you – he don't want no doctor, wouldn't hear of it – and he's gone a very nasty colour. Why don't you come and see if you can talk some sense into him?'

And so, reluctantly, she went. By now the band had embarked on the overture to *Zampa*, and though they were one man short, the musicians were blowing up a storm. Inside the gardeners' shed, it was quite hard to hear what Jack Gunn was saying.

'Who's that? Valerie? Come closer, I can't shout. Glad to see you, girl.' He forced out the words with difficulty. 'Had a bit of trouble with the old ticker. Thought I was a goner for a minute.' Lying on a tarpaulin, propped up against some sacks of loam, he looked very far from well. His face was grey, and Val could see he was in pain.

'I really think we should get a doctor—'

'No! I told that other bloke – the one in the brass buttons – I don't want no doctors. They'll only send me off to hospital, and once you go in one of them places, you never get out no more. I want to go home. You can see about it, can't you?'

'Do you want me to telephone your family?'

'Not Alfred. Don't speak to him, nor Freda – they'll just go working theirselves up, sending for ambulances and Gawd knows what. I want you to talk to young Steve. Tell him to come and fetch me; he'll see me right.'

'Oh, but hasn't he moved out to Waddon, to be near the airport?'

'Not yet, he ain't, He's not found any decent digs. Ring him at home, there's a good girl.'

She could not argue. Back in her office, she looked up the number in the directory. How strange – she had known it by heart at one time.

'Hello?' It was Freda who answered. When the telephone rang she was always the first to pick it up. 'This is Freda Gunn speaking, who's that?'

'It's Valerie – Valerie Glynn. I'm sorry to bother you, but could I speak to Steve? Is he there?'

Freda sounded astonished. 'Yes, he's here. Hold on.'

There was a long pause, then at last she heard Steve's voice. 'Hello – Valerie?'

She gripped the edge of the desk, determined to speak calmly. 'I wouldn't have rung, only your Grandad's been taken ill. I'm afraid it's a heart attack, but he won't see a doctor. He wants you to come and take him home. He doesn't want your parents to know; he's afraid of upsetting them.'

There was another silence, and she had to ask: 'Steve, are you still there? Did you hear what I said?'

'Yes – it's OK. Tell him I'll come right away. Thanks for phoning.'

Then he rang off. She put down the phone and sank into her chair. She would have to go and pass Steve's message on to the old man, but she wouldn't stay with him. Steve would be here in a matter of minutes; by then she would be back at her desk. Whatever happened, she would not see Steve.

'Well – what do you think?' asked Babs.

It was the third flat they had visited. Two of them had been previously occupied – darker patches on faded wallpaper showed where pictures had hung or a sideboard had stood – but this flat was brand new. The walls had no covering but lining-paper, and the woodwork was unpainted, waiting for a purchaser to make his own choice of decoration.

'It's very pleasant,' said Walter. 'Light and spacious.'

'How do you feel about it, compared to the others?'

"I don't know. After a while, one lot of empty rooms begins to look pretty much like another.'

'You must have some preference, surely?'

Babs tried to sound reasonable, though she was growing rather cross. When she left the office, armed with various keys, they had set off to tour the available properties. She had been looking forward to this evening, but hadn't realised it would take so long – and Walter seemed different, somehow. Last time they met, she had been aware of the tension within him – the hidden passion, just below the surface. This time, it was rather boring.

He was behaving impeccably, treating her with the utmost respect, taking care never to come too close to her. Was he growing tired of her already?

Since there were no chairs, she perched on a windowsill, pulling her skirt a little higher as she crossed her knees.

'If you hate these flats, tell me what's wrong so I can look for something different. Tell me exactly what you want.'

'You know what I want,' he said. Their eyes met for a moment, and he looked away. 'Two bedrooms, one reception room, kitchen and bath.'

In that moment she felt a spark of excitement leap across the gap between them, and her spirits rose as she went on; 'You must be frank. If this isn't your style, you must say.'

'I like them all, in different ways. It's hard to choose.' He crossed the room to join her by the window. 'This one has a good view, over the trees. Why don't you tell me what you think? Which one would *you* choose?'

'It's not up to me, is it? My opinion doesn't matter.'

'It matters to me. You've got to like the flat too.'

'Why? What do you mean?'

He did not look directly at her, but went on gazing over the treetops in the gathering twilight, as he replied. 'Because I hope – in time – we might both live here.'

'Walter!' She gasped. 'I never dreamed – never for a minute—'

He put his hands on her shoulders and looked into her face. 'You know how I feel about you. The dearest wish of my heart is that one day, when the time is right, you might be willing to marry me.'

She did not know what to say. Marrying Walter was something she had never seriously considered. For one thing, he was twice her age – though she still found him quite attractive. It was a shame he didn't have his own business any longer, but he must be pretty well off. She felt sure that Mrs Walter Faber would never want for any little luxuries.

'You've taken my breath away,' she said. 'I never expected—'

'Does the idea horrify you? I know I'm fifty-three, and you're only twenty-six. Perhaps the thought disgusts you?'

'You know that's not true!' Putting her arms around him, she pulled him towards her. 'I'm very fond of you. I think you're a lovely man – handsome, exciting – only . . .'

When she hesitated, he prompted her gently. 'Only, you don't love me. Is that it?'

'I'm not sure. I only know I can't give you an answer now. It's too soon after your bereavement. Much too soon.'

'Of course – we'd have to wait for a year at least. That's what I meant when I said I hoped you might live here – in time.'

She kissed him lightly; but when he began to fondle her, she drew back.

'Not yet, Walter. You must give me time to decide. Time to think it over – and get to know each other better. And meanwhile, about the flat – if you really want to know, this is the one I like best.'

'So do I. You'd like living on the top floor?'

'It's not just that. It's because nobody else has ever lived here. I'd never want to move into a place where other people had been – I'd sooner make a fresh start.'

'My darling girl.' He patted her cheek. 'You're right, of course. That's what we both need – a fresh start.'

'But we mustn't rush into anything.' She slipped from his embrace. 'And I ought to be going. Will you be very sweet and see me home?'

'You can't go yet – the night is young!' He was still on a wave of elation. 'We ought to go somewhere to celebrate – somewhere special.'

'Walter, please don't take anything for granted. I haven't said yes.'

'You haven't said no, either. That's something to celebrate, isn't it? Come on – where shall we go?'

Back in the office, Valerie tried to get on with her work, but she could not put her mind to it. She had not made much impression upon the file of press-cuttings, and to make matters worse, she had knocked over the paste-pot. That wasted another ten minutes, cleaning up the top of the desk.

She kept thinking about old Mr Gunn – he had looked very ill – and wondering what was happening. Had Steve arrived to collect his grandfather? Suppose he were too ill to be moved? She half-expected the attendant to return and ask her to send for an ambulance.

As she trimmed the cuttings, to fit into the scrapbook, the door opened behind her, and a draught sent them fluttering to the floor. She did not pick them up – she did not even turn her head; without looking round, she knew who had come into the office.

'Hello, Val,' he said.

With an effort, she stood and faced him, and saw that he was looking fitter. His prison pallor had gone, he was suntanned and clear-eyed – but when their eyes met, she looked away.

'How is he?' she asked. 'Should I call a doctor?'

'No, he'll be OK. I brought Tony with me, in case it took two of us to get the old feller home, but I needn't have worried. By the time we got here, he was feeling a lot better. He had a big tea before he set out for the band concert, and he must have eaten it too fast – it was probably heartburn. Anyhow, Tony's taken him home to bed, to be on the safe side.'

'That's a relief. I was really worried.' She began to pick up the scattered cuttings; she would not look at him again.

'I'm sorry I put you to so much trouble,' he said.

'No trouble.' She continued to tidy up her desk. 'You'll have to excuse me, I must get on. Good night.'

Instead of leaving, he shut the door and came a few steps nearer. 'There's something else I want you to know. This wasn't a put-up job. I wasn't trying to trick you into ringing up, if that's what you thought.'

She whirled round indignantly. 'I didn't think anything of the sort! I could see he was ill – he looked dreadful. If I'd thought that, I wouldn't have phoned, would I?'

'I wasn't sure. After the letter I sent you last time . . . You never wrote back. I suppose you were angry?'

'It wasn't that so much. I would have answered it, but there didn't seem to be anything to say.' In a softer tone, she added: 'It was a nice letter – I was glad you sent it.'

After a moment, he said, 'You don't know what it means, talking to you like this. We can still be friends, can't we?'

By now the tension between them was unbearable, and she blurted out: 'I'm sorry, Steve, I can't stop. I've got to go home.'

'I suppose he's waiting for you, your husband?'

'No, Gerry's working late too, that's why I—' She answered without thinking, and regretted it immediately. She should have said that Gerry was waiting for her, but she had never lied to Steve. 'I must be on my way,' she finished lamely.

Overhead, a series of explosions ripped through the night air; she jumped nervously and said, 'The fireworks have started, it's getting late. I really must go.'

'Well, if you must. I'll walk back with you, part of the way. We don't have to talk about – you know – what happened. We can watch the fireworks. When was the last time you saw one of Brock's Benefits?'

She tried to smile. 'I can't remember. They happen every week – I take them for granted now.'

'We might as well take a look, on the way out.'

She knew she must not stay in the office with him – out on the terraces, among the crowds, it would be easier. As soon as they reached the gates, they'd go their separate ways, and that would be that.

'All right.' She began to put her coat on and he made a move to help her, but she edged away, saying. 'Thanks, I can manage.'

Leaving the office, she locked the door and they walked through the darkened building – a great cathedral of glass, illuminated by occasional coloured starbursts high above them in the night sky.

Out on the top terrace, they lingered for a few moments to watch the spectacle; the batteries of Roman candles and the giant Catherine wheels and, as a grand climax, a pyrotechnic version of the Battle of Jutland, complete with replicas of warships firing shells at each other, until one of the ships, outlined in a thousand shining sparklers, tilted and submerged slowly under a sea of golden rain, to tumultuous applause.

The night air was growing chilly. 'We'd better go,' Val said, 'before we get caught up in the crowds.' The display hadn't quite finished, but they did not wait for the grand finale – set-piece portraits of the King and Queen, glittering in red, white and blue fire – and set off towards the exit on Crystal Palace Parade.

Making conversation, Val enquired after Steve's family, and sent her regards to his parents. In turn, he wanted to know about Daphne and Ted, and she told him Ted was going to be in a pantomime at Christmas. As they approached the gates, they realised something was wrong. Ahead of them, through the railings, there was a lot of commotion going on. They heard confused shouting, and saw the glow of torchlight on angry faces.

One of the ground staff hurried towards them. Recognising Val, he said: 'You can't get out that way, Mrs Glynn. It's some sort of protest – a couple of hundred unemployed chaps with banners and flaming torches, making a nuisance of themselves.'

'But I've got to get through. I'm going home,' said Val.

'This exit is closed. We're sending everybody to the Anerley Road Gates.'

So they had to retrace their steps. The firework display was over, and attendants directed the spectators toward other exits; they were swept along with the crowds.

At night, the paths were popular with courting couples, and Val was aware of shadowy figures, half-hidden in the shrubbery. Determined to keep the conversation going, she asked Steve how he was enjoying his job at the airport and he told her about the new airliners, carrying passengers to places all over the world.

'It must be very interesting,' she began, then stopped as she heard a voice piercing the darkness – a voice that was all too familiar.

'It's been a lovely evening, Walter. I can't remember the last time I came to see the fireworks.'

Looking back, Val saw Babs – accompanied by a man she recognised with surprise as Walter Faber. If Babs saw her here, with Steve . . .

Tugging at his arm, she drew him off the path and under the trees, saying urgently, 'It's Babs. I don't want her to see us.' She buried her face in his shoulder and he put his arms round her, holding her tightly.

After a moment, he said, 'It's all right – she's gone.'

'Thank you. I'm sorry about that, but—'

Then she looked up into his face – and there were no more words. The years fell away. They were together, in each other's arms, as if they had never been apart. She never knew how long they stayed there. They did not speak, but kissed one another again and again, trying to make up for all the time that had been lost.

When they could speak, Steve said, 'Nothing's changed. We love each other – nothing else matters.'

But Val shook her head: 'No, we can't. We mustn't – this is terribly wrong.' Summoning all her strength, she pulled away from him. 'No, Steve, don't say any more. Don't try to stop me. You must let me go!'

Then she turned and ran from him, running down the path and into the crowd – running away from her only hope of happiness.

Chapter Seventeen

WHEN THE CURTAIN fell for the tenth and last time, Ted turned to Marta, who was standing beside him in the line-up across the stage, and said with a grin: 'I think they like us . . .'

Breathlessly, she flung her arms round him and kissed him. 'We are a big success – did I not tell you?'

As the line broke up and the artistes moved offstage, talking and laughing, Ronnie Rivers and Lew Lake began to grumble.

'They're still applauding – still calling—'

'—still calling for us. We could have taken ten more—'

'—ten more curtains. What's the matter with the—'

'—with the stage-manager?'

From his corner, the stage-manager growled at them. 'I'm doing you a favour! Any more calls, and you'd never have got to the pub before turning-out time!'

There was no doubt about it; the opening night of *Cinderella* had been a triumph.

Still smiling, Ted went off to his dressing room – and that was very satisfactory too. For the first time in his career, he had a room all to himself. Ronnie and Lew shared the Number One dressing room; the Principal Boy, who had played Drury Lane in her younger days, had Number Two. Marta was in Number Three, and Ted had been given Number Four. It was small, but for the run of the panto it belonged to him and no one else.

From the first day of rehearsals, in a dance studio off the Tottenham Court Road, everything had gone smoothly. Ted had no difficulty in learning his lines, though he had never been in a 'book show' before; most of his scenes were with Marta and she made it all seem easy.

There had been one awkward moment. During the kitchen scene, before the Fairy Godmother arrived to transform Cinderella and send her off to the ball, Buttons and Cinders had a song-and-dance number together, and as soon as they began to work on it, a balding man with a little goatee beard appeared from nowhere and took charge of the rehearsal. He seemed to be very hard on Marta, and kept stopping the pianist, telling Marta she was taking it too fast, or too slowly, phrasing it wrongly, and even singing off the note.

When he turned away to have a discussion with the pianist, Ted muttered, 'Who the hell does he think he is? What's it got to do with him?'

Marta stared at him in amazement. 'My God, I was forgetting – you have never met. How stupid I am!'

She dragged Ted over to the piano. 'Franz, *liebchen* – I must introduce you to Mr Watt. Ted, this is Franz Neumann, who is our musical director – and also my husband.'

Cool and self-possessed, Herr Neumann clasped Ted's hand, assuring him that it was a great pleasure to make his acquaintance – and the rehearsal went on as before.

Afterwards, while Ronnie and Lew were running through one of their routines, Ted said to Marta, 'I never knew you were married. It's a good job you mentioned it. I was just going to tell him to shut his face and stop picking on you!'

Marta laughed. 'You are very sweet . . . Don't worry, Franz is always strict with me when we rehearse. It is because he wants everything I do to be quite perfect. I know that, so I do not mind.'

Ted said nothing; he was still recovering from shock. How could anyone as young and fresh as Marta be married to that disagreeable old man?

As if she were reading his thoughts, Marta explained: 'Franz was my first singing teacher. He picked me out of the chorus in Vienna and gave me private coaching. He made me a star – and then he married me!'

So that was that. From then on, Ted's attitude towards Marta was a little different – a little more cautious – but her attitude to him didn't change at all. She was as friendly as ever, and she continued to flirt with him.

But she had never kissed him, until tonight.

Ted was still thinking about that as he wiped the greasepaint from his face, still whistling *Sometimes I'm Happy* – the duet they sang together in the show – when there was a knock at the door of the dressing room.

'You can come in – I'm decent!' he called out.

The door opened, and Daphne entered the room, hand in hand with Annie.

'The man at the stage door said it would be all right for us to come and find you,' said Daphne, while Annie jumped up and down.

'I saw you, Dad – I saw you!' she exclaimed.

'We both saw you – and we thought you were very good.' Daphne kissed him carefully on the lips, since his face was smothered in cold cream. 'It's the best thing I've ever seen you do.'

'Except I wanted you to marry Cinderella at the end. I think it's horrid the way she went off with that rotten old Prince Charming – and he isn't even a man, he's a lady!' Annie complained indignantly.

There was another knock at the door, and Marta swept in, wrapped in an oriental kimono, her titian hair tied up in a scarf. 'Are you coming across for a drink at the – oh, I beg your pardon. I did not know you had visitors.'

Ted introduced them. They all shook hands, and Daphne said, 'We thought it was a very good show, didn't we Annie? Only she wanted Cinderella to go off with Buttons at the end.'

Marta laughed, and told Annie, 'But that would never do! Buttons can't go away with anyone else. He must go home with you and your Mama, mustn't he?' She smiled at Daphne. 'Forgive me, please. I came in to ask if Ted was going for a drink with the others. I am sorry to have interrupted you.'

As she turned to leave, Ted looked at Daphne wistfully. 'I suppose we couldn't look in at the pub, just for a quick one? As it's the first night?'

Daphne's heart sank, but she managed to smile. 'I don't really see how. What about Annie?'

'No, of course not, it's impossible,' Marta chimed in. 'You can't take your daughter to a public house! Besides, it's late – she has to go to bed, I'm sure.'

Ted looked so crestfallen, Daphne couldn't bear to spoil his big night. She said quickly, 'You go with them. I'll take Annie home.'

He brightened up at once. 'Are you sure? I don't have to—'

'No, do go. You'll enjoy it.'

When she had put Annie to bed, still complaining that life was not fair, Daphne got undressed and climbed into the old-fashioned bedstead with brass knobs at all four corners. She tried to read for a while, but soon let the book drop; it had been a long day and she was very tired, but she couldn't settle until Ted came back . . . Of course he wouldn't stop at one drink; she knew that.

A few streets away, she heard a steam-engine whistling; she hoped the trains wouldn't run all night and keep her awake. When she had arrived with Annie that morning, Ted wasn't able to meet them at the station. There was a final dress rehearsal before tonight's opening, and so she had to carry her own suitcase through the rain. She had been grateful then that the boarding house was so near, though she couldn't help feeling disappointed that it was in the middle of the town.

Ted had told her that the other principals in the company were staying at the Queen's Hotel on the promenade – but that was very expensive, and he'd chosen a homely boarding house instead to save money. Daphne was glad he was being sensible, but she still wished they could have had a view of the sea from their bedroom.

She felt confused and unhappy, and she didn't really know why.

She had enjoyed the pantomime more than she had expected; she felt less embarrassed than usual, watching Ted on stage – perhaps because he was playing a character in a story, not just being himself. His scenes with Cinderella were particularly good. The Austrian girl had a lovely voice, and her duet with Ted was really delightful. Daphne remembered the words of the song:

> *Sometimes I'm happy – sometimes I'm blue.*
> *My disposition – depends on you . . .*

And yet . . . There was something in the way they had sung and danced together – the way they looked at one another – that made her uncomfortable.

> *Sometimes I love you – sometimes I hate you*
> *And when I hate you – it's 'cos I love you . . .*

And she remembered Annie saying, '*I wanted you to marry Cinderella at the end . . .*'

She gave herself a mental slap, telling herself not to be ridiculous. Ted had told her weeks ago that Marta was married to the orchestra conductor, and she knew perfectly well that she had no earthly reason to feel jealous, and yet . . .

With the song still tinkling through her head, she must have drifted

322

off to sleep, because the next thing she knew Ted was getting into bed beside her. When he kissed her, she smiled drowsily.

'Just a quick one? Only one?'

'Or two – or three,' he admitted. 'Tell you the truth, the landlord asked us into his private room at closing time, for a nightcap. It was quite cosy. You'd have liked it.'

'Never mind.' She kissed him again. 'You're here now, and so am I.'

'Oh, Marta made me promise to tell you. She and Franz are giving a party at the Queen's on Christmas Day. She asked me to tell you you're specially invited – and we're to take Annie as well.'

'A party – on Christmas Day?'

It would have been a free day together. This year, Christmas was on a Sunday.

'Well, it's the only night we're not working . . . Starting at half-past seven, she said.'

'And going on till when?'

'Goodness knows. But we can take Annie for a couple of hours, can't we? Everyone will be there – I think we ought to go.'

'I suppose we have to.' She sighed. 'But I wish we didn't.'

'Why? I thought it was very good of her to ask all three of us. You liked her when you met her tonight, didn't you?'

'Yes, she seems very nice. It's just, I'm not very good at parties – and all these theatre people . . . They live in a little world of their own. I shan't know what to talk about.'

'You can talk to me and Annie. Anyhow, we needn't stay long – and I bet you'll enjoy it when you get there.'

She cuddled up to him. 'I'd rather stay here – with you.'

On Christmas Eve, in the tiny kitchen of the Westwood Court flat, Valerie was decorating an iced cake. She had made the rich fruit cake several weeks earlier, and she was very proud of it; it had been kept in a closed tin to 'ripen', and as it was generously laced with brandy, whenever she took off the lid to admire her handiwork, it smelled delicious. This week, she had iced it – first a layer of marzipan, then a covering of soft icing. She never liked the traditional icing, and complained that it was like eating plaster of Paris – she always expected to break a tooth on it . . . It also reminded her of her wedding day, though she did not mention that.

She circled the cake with a red ribbon and a bow, then added some

tiny figures – a snowman, a baby Eskimo, a polar bear – wreathed
with imitation holly-leaves and berries.

As she was working, she heard the telephone ringing in the hall.
Gerry would answer it – it was bound to be for him anyway.

When the cake was decorated to her satisfaction, it was to go back
in its tin; tomorrow they would take it with them to Sackville Road.

Kate had invited Gerry and Val to have Christmas dinner with her
at midday; since Ted and Daphne and Annie were away, she would
have been on her own otherwise. Val had offered to help cook the
dinner, but Kate wouldn't hear of it, so she was providing the
Christmas cake instead. She was just adding the finishing touch – a
tiny Santa Claus driving his sleigh – when Gerry opened the kitchen
door.

'Oh, don't look – you mustn't see it till tomorrow!' Val tried to
shield the cake from him. 'I want it to be a surprise.'

He gave a yelp of laughter. 'Don't be silly, darling, it's only a cake.
Anyway, I've just had a surprise, I shan't be here tomorrow.'

'What do you mean? Why not?'

'That was the office. I've got to be on duty.'

'Oh no, on Christmas Day?'

He grimaced. 'I can't say I'm exactly overjoyed at the prospect,
either. Still, I suppose someone's got to do it.'

'But you shouldn't be working this weekend. You said you weren't
on duty again till Tuesday.'

'That's how it was on the roster, but now Charlie's got 'flu – taken
to his bed with a raging temperature, poor chap. So I've got to take
his place.'

'All day at Savoy Hill? How will you get there? There won't be
any trains—'

'That's all right. They're sending a car to pick me up at nine a.m.
And I'm not working at Savoy Hill; I'm going to Eastbourne. Charlie
was going to do the announcements for a concert at the Grand Hotel
tomorrow night – Albert Sandler and his Orchestra – and I've got to
stand in for him.'

'Well, I think it's a shame. All that way, for one stupid programme.
I hope they're bringing you home by car afterwards?'

'That's the general idea, though God only knows when I'll get back
– not till the wee small hours, I imagine. Still, at least you're spending
the day with your mother. It would have been a miserable Christmas
for you otherwise.'

Val turned away and began to pack the cake into its box. She was

324

resigned to a miserable Christmas by now. Every year since her marriage, it had been something of a disappointment. At home in the old days, the Watkins family made a big occasion of it, even when they were hard up. She remembered one year soon after Dad was killed, when they made it a rule that all the presents they gave each other must come from the Penny Bazaar; on Christmas morning there was a pile of brightly coloured packages round the little tree – tiny gimcrack toys, a matchbox containing a ruby ring made of glass, a tin trumpet, a paper fan, a miniature candlestick . . . Every gift chosen with care and given with love.

Gerald never really enjoyed Christmas. Val found it difficult to buy suitable presents for him, because he seemed to have everything already. If she asked him what he wanted, he always said: 'I could do with some new shirts. Plain white, with stiff collars, to wear to the office – nothing fancy.'

And every year he bought her a new dress, but as he couldn't choose one without her, it was never a surprise. He didn't enjoy going round the shops either, so in the end he simply gave her a cheque and sent her off by herself to buy her own Christmas present – and there was nothing to look forward to.

On Christmas morning, although she had packed up his new shirts in shiny paper with gold ribbons, he tore the wrappings off straight away, checked the shirts to make sure they were the right size, then kissed her on the cheek, saying: 'Very nice, old dear – just what I wanted.'

Valerie had bought her new dress a month ago and put it away in the wardrobe until today; now she took it out and tried it on, twirling a little to show it off for Gerry's approval.

Again, one quick glance was sufficient. 'Yes, darling, very nice. It suits you.' He looked at his watch. 'The car should be here any minute. Give my love to your mother. By the way, I bought a bottle of champagne as my contribution to the feast. You'd better take it with you – think of me while you're drinking it.' There was a ring at the doorbell, and he pulled on his overcoat. 'That'll be my driver. Have a nice day! I'll be home some time after midnight, so don't wait up.'

One last peck on the cheek, and he was gone. It was just like any other morning, really, not like Christmas at all.

Later, when she joined her mother at All Saints, her spirits began to revive. Shoulder to shoulder, they sang all the old familiar carols, and the Christmas magic began to work. When the service ended and they came out of church, they were surprised to find that a few scattered flakes of snow were falling.

'Well, I suppose it's seasonable,' said Kate. 'It's not often we get a white Christmas – I wonder if it will lie?'

'I shouldn't think so. After all the rain we've had lately, the ground must be very wet, though they did say on the weather forecast last night that it was going to turn a lot colder.'

Val was carrying a shopping-bag containing the cake tin, the champagne, and some gifts for her mother. It was quite heavy, and when she transferred it from one hand to the other, Kate asked, 'Why did you bring that to church with you? You could have let Gerald carry it. He'll be coming round to Sackville Road later on, won't he?'

So then Val had to explain about his sudden departure for Eastbourne, and her mother's face fell.

'Oh, but I've got a roast capon waiting for us in the oven. How are we going to eat that all on our own? And the Christmas pudding – it's big enough for half a dozen people at least!'

'I know. I'm sorry, but Gerry didn't have any choice. His boss told him he had to go to work – so he went. Never mind, Mum. It'll be nice and cosy – just the two of us.'

They both made an effort to pretend they were enjoying their Christmas dinner, but it all seemed a little unreal. Kate was determined to keep up all the traditions and made Val pull a couple of crackers and wear a paper hat, though she did draw the line at opening the champagne.

'Oh no, it'd be wasted. We'd never get through a whole bottle!' she protested. 'You know what I'm like – one glass and I'd be tipsyloola. Why don't you save it for New Year's Eve? If Gerald's not working then . . . Go on – take it back with you and keep it for another time.'

Val had to agree that this made sense, but she insisted on unpacking the Christmas cake. They could have a slice each with their tea; then she would cut it in half and take some home, so Gerry could have a piece tomorrow.

'All right, then,' Kate agreed reluctantly. 'But I don't like to think of you going back and spending the evening all by yourself.'

The original plan had been that Gerry and Val would have a quiet evening at home, listening to the wireless – listening, in fact, to the very concert Gerry would now be announcing. And Kate had invited a friend to supper.

'Of course you'd be more than welcome to stay here and keep us company,' she explained, slightly red-faced. 'Only – well, it's Mr Colpoys I've asked round, 'cos he lives on his own – and he's rather shy. You do understand, don't you?'

'I wouldn't dream of barging in on you and your boyfriend,' Val teased her. 'I'll have a nice evening at home. I'll listen to Gerry and the concert from Eastbourne – and he'll be coming home afterwards, so don't you worry about me.

After tea, she helped her mother with the washing-up, then set off once more. The snow had persisted, and now it was coming down in big, soft flakes. Though the pavements were wet and shining, snow had begun to lie on the rooftops, on hedges and trees. Val had to tread carefully because the paving-slabs were slippery and she was still carrying the champagne in her shopping-bag, so the journey back to Westwood Court took longer than usual. By the time she entered the building she was cold and tired and damp.

She stepped out of the lift on the second floor, walked along the corridor and turned the corner – and there, outside the front door of her flat, was Steve Gunn. His coat was white with snow, and he was stooping to put a large bunch of flowers on the mat. Shamefaced, he straightened up.

'I didn't think you'd be here,' he began, defensively. 'Your Mum told my Mum you were spending the day with her – you and your husband . . .' He looked past her, expecting to see Gerald following. 'Isn't he with you?'

'No, he's not,' said Val, trying to pull herself together. 'But that's no business of yours – and it doesn't give you the right to—'

She broke off. Somewhere around the corner, she heard a door opening. She didn't want anyone to see her here with Steve, who was still clutching the enormous bouquet of bronze mophead chrysanthemums. Swiftly, she unlocked the front door, and practically pushed him into the flat.

'Come in,' she said. '*Quickly*, for goodness sake!'

Shutting the door behind her, she took off her hat and coat, hanging them up on the pegs in the hall. Steve stood and looked at her helplessly, then tried to put the flowers into her hands.

'Happy Christmas,' he said.

'I don't want them!' She rejected the offering. 'What on earth were you thinking of? You shouldn't have come here. You've no right—'

'I know I haven't. But I couldn't let Christmas go by without – well, *something* . . . I thought you'd be out. I was going to leave them

327

on the step. I didn't put in a card or anything – I knew you'd guess who they came from.'

Suddenly Val's turbulent emotions swelled up in a burst of anger. 'And what if I did? What was I expected to do about them? How was I supposed to explain them to Gerald?'

He took a step back, shocked by the intensity of her attack. 'I don't know. You didn't have to explain, did you? You could have pretended they'd been left for somebody else – by mistake.'

'Oh yes, it was a mistake – my mistake! I should never have talked to you that night. I should never have encouraged you.' Without warning, her anger faded, leaving her close to tears. 'I asked you to let me go. To leave me alone . . . Why didn't you do that?'

'Because I couldn't,' he said – so quietly, she could hardly make out the words.

The flowers in their paper sheath were trembling, and a few bronze petals drifted to the floor; she realised that he was shivering.

'I'm sorry,' she said wearily. 'You'd better take off that wet coat. I'll light the fire.'

'But – he'll be coming in, any minute—'

'No, he won't. Not for a while . . . Here, give me those before they shed all over the carpet.'

Taking the flowers, she led the way into the sitting room and put a match to the gas fire. It popped and roared, and the little blue flames budded and blossomed into warmth.

She found a vase, and put the chrysanthemums on the sideboard; their colour lit a second fire in the room, and the flat became a more welcoming place.

She told him about the change of plan, explaining that Gerry had been called back in an emergency; he would not be home till late. Then she said, 'I'm going to make some tea. Would you like a cup?'

His face lit up with happiness, and her heart went out to him, but she steeled herself and continued, 'Just one cup of tea, then you'll have to go.'

'But you said he won't be home till late—'

'That's got nothing to do with it. You shouldn't be here. It's not right – you know that. And I shouldn't have brought you in but – seeing it's Christmas . . . Just one cup, that's all.'

In Hastings, Ted's family were getting ready to go to the Queen's Hotel.

Annie was wearing her party dress – pink, with white organdie

328

frills at the neck and the cuffs. Ted was in his best suit – navy-blue, enlivened for the occasion by a very dashing red tie. He had been given it at breakfast-time by his daughter, who had saved up her pocket money to buy it. Daphne had tried to steer her on to a more conventional choice, but Annie's mind was made up. When Ted opened his Christmas presents, he told her it was very smart indeed. He wouldn't dream of going to the party in any other tie.

Now they sat and waited as patiently as possible while Daphne finished doing her hair. She studied her reflection in the dressing-table mirror without enthusiasm.

'I look like an old hag,' she said. 'But it's no use complaining. I must learn to put up with it.'

'Your mother's fishing for compliments again,' Ted told Annie. 'We both know she looks beautiful, and she knows it as well, but she wants to hear it all over again. One, two, three—'

In unison, he and Annie chorused loudly: '*You – look – beautiful!*'

Daphne laughed, despite herself. 'All right,' she said. 'Let's get it over. Let's go to this beastly party.'

They were halfway down the stairs when the boarding-house landlady came out of her front parlour, saying: 'Oh, there you are. Just on your way out, too – what a mercy I caught you. There's a telephone call for you, Mrs Watt, from your brother.'

'From Gerry?' Daphne looked at Ted. 'You don't think something's happened to Mother?'

'Your mother's as tough as an old boot. He's probably ringing to wish you a Merry Whatsit and a Happy New Thingummy.'

The landlady ushered Daphne into the parlour and passed her the phone; she put the receiver to her ear. 'Hello, Gerry? Daphne speaking.'

A few minutes later she rejoined Ted and Annie in the hall. 'Well, that's a surprise. He's not at home, he's in Eastbourne.' She explained the sudden emergency over the broadcast, and went on to add: 'It's been snowing hard all day. It took them ages to drive down, and now they've had reports that some of the roads over the Downs are completely blocked, so they can't risk driving back to London tonight. If they broke down there'd be no garages open, so they're not going back to town until tomorrow, in daylight.'

'Poor old Val – she'll be worried to death.' Ted frowned. 'Has he told her?'

'Not yet. He rang here first to see if we can give him a bed for the night. Eastbourne's only about fifteen miles away, and they say the coast road isn't too bad.'

'Why can't he stay in Eastbourne – at the Grand?'

'They're full up because of the holiday weekend. Anyway, he said he'd sooner come to us than spend Christmas night with a lot of strangers. I've asked our landlady, and she says she'll make up a camp bed for him in Annie's room, so I told her I'll stay and help—'

'What about the party?' asked Ted. 'It's half-past seven already.'

'We've got to go to the party!' Annie was appalled. 'You *promised*!'

'Gerry won't be here for hours yet,' Ted pointed out. 'There's heaps of time – and Marta will be expecting us. Come on, let's go.'

When they had drunk their tea, there was still plenty left in the pot, so they both had second cups. Then Val remembered the Christmas cake in its tin, and lifted it from her shopping-bag, along with the champagne. She put the bottle on the sideboard and took out two plates, then proceeded to cut two slices of cake. When she told Steve she had made it herself, he said it was the best Christmas cake he'd ever tasted.

They were still feeling inhibited by their unexpected meeting, confining their conversation to safe, impersonal topics and hardly daring to look at one another except in swift, sidelong glances. When the telephone rang, they both started guiltily, and Val answered it.

'Oh – hello, Gerry,' she said.

Steve hung his head, feeling like a criminal. Val turned her back, unable to face him and talk to her husband at the same time.

'What do you mean – what sort of problem? So where are you now? And how far is Hastings? I see . . . Yes, well – it can't be helped. Give Daff and Ted my love – and a kiss for Annie. Goodbye, Gerry – good night.'

When she hung up, she covered her face in her hands. For a few moments there was silence, except for the roar of the gas fire, then Steve asked: 'What's the matter?'

She lowered her hands and folded them in her lap, twisting her wedding ring round and round as she explained what had happened.

'So he's not coming back till tomorrow?' Steve said.

'No. I think you'd better go. Go now – please. Right away.'

But he did not move. Gently, he said, 'There's no hurry, is there? I was hoping there might be some tea left in the pot.'

'It'll be stewed by this time.'

'I don't care.'

'You really should go—'

'I don't care about that, either.'

She tried to breathe slowly and deeply, wishing that her heart would stop beating so fast.

'Anyway, I've got to listen to Gerry's broadcast in half an hour.' Then she stood up and went over to the sideboard, lifting the teapot lid. 'There's half a cup each, I should think – and that's all. After that . . .'

She left the sentence unfinished. The tea was lukewarm, and tasted bitter, but they drank it anyway. Now there seemed to be nothing left to talk about; they had run out of neutral subject-matter. At last, with a sense of relief, Val switched on the wireless and they caught the end of the previous programme. After the time signal, they heard Gerald's voice.

'Good evening. I am speaking to you from the Palm Court of the Grand Hotel, Eastbourne, where we are bringing our Christmas Day entertainment to a close with a concert performed by Mr Albert Sandler and his orchestra, together with Mr Sandler's guest artiste – the soprano, Miss Mavis Bennett.'

'Our programme begins with the Grand Fantasia from Gounod's *Faust*, and will be followed by the first of Miss Bennett's selection of songs; the aria *I am Thine*, with solo violin obbligato by Mr Albert Sandler—'

Abruptly, Val got up and switched the set off.

After a moment, Steve asked, 'What did you do that for?'

She moved round the room, plumping up cushions, collecting the empty cups and taking them back to the sideboard, giving herself little jobs to do and trying above all to keep her emotions under control. Over her shoulder, she answered him.

'It was somehow – disgusting. As if the three of us were here in the room together. I couldn't – I just couldn't bear it. I'm sorry. Do you want some more tea?' Automatically, she lifted the pot, then remembered. 'Stupid of me. Of course, we finished it.'

He indicated the bottle on the sideboard. 'How about a drop of champagne?' he suggested.

They looked at each other for an instant, then she picked up the bottle and held it out to him.

'Could you open it for me? I'll get some glasses.'

Kate's supper was more modest than her midday meal – home-made soup, cold chicken and salad, with a slice of Christmas cake to round it off, but her guest preferred a simple menu.

'A splendid repast,' said Mr Colpoys, pushing away his plate and wiping the crumbs from his lips. 'You have excelled yourself, Mrs Watkins.'

'Oh, it was nothing. I told you, it was Valerie who made the cake.'

'She has obviously inherited your talents,' he said. 'I congratulate both of you.'

'Would you care for another cup of coffee?'

'Thank you, no. If I have a second cup I shan't sleep tonight.' He stood up, adding: 'If you will permit me, I have something to give you – a little surprise.'

He went out of the kitchen for a few seconds, then returned with a parcel untidily wrapped in brown paper. 'You must forgive the packaging – I fear I have no skill in that department. But it comes with the season's greetings – and my very best wishes.'

'A present? Oh, Mr Colpoys, you shouldn't. I wasn't expecting . . . I'm sorry, I haven't got anything for you,' she apologised.

'You have given me so much already, dear lady; you provide boundless hospitality and excellent meals. And above all, you have given me your friendship, which I prize very highly.'

A little flustered, she smiled uncertainly. 'It's very good of you to say so, but it's been my pleasure. You shouldn't go spending your money on me.'

'I didn't buy this from a shop. It's rather more personal than that . . . I hope you like it.'

Kate cut the string and took off the brown paper. Inside she found a silk scarf, with intricate oriental designs – scrolls, flowers and leaves in brilliant colours, set off with a black fringe.

'It's beautiful,' she said, unfolding it. 'Wherever did it come from?'

'Originally from India, I believe, though I bought it in Paris, more than thirty years ago. I was on my honeymoon; my wife and I were strolling along one of the Boulevards when she saw it in a shop-window. She remarked how pretty it was, and I went straight in and bought it for her. I was young and impulsive in those days . . . Won't you put it on?'

'Oh, are you sure? I mean, if it belonged to your wife—'

'Please. I should like to see you wearing it.'

She draped it round her shoulders. 'Such lovely material. It's so soft, like a cobweb.'

'My wife said it was too fine for every day, and as a consequence she hardly ever wore it. It's been shut away in a drawer for a long time. I hope you will wear it more often.'

'I'll be proud to. Thank you very much.'

She was standing close to him, and without stopping to think she kissed him. To her surprise, he put his arms round her and returned the kiss; without passion, but with a deep affection that had been building slowly through the years.

They said no more. When he released her, she moved back to the table and poured herself another coffee; they did not refer to their moment of intimacy. Then she took the shawl off and folded it carefully, saying, 'I'll always treasure it. Thank you.'

Soon afterwards, he took his leave of her, and when he had gone she began to clear the table, thinking to herself: 'I don't suppose that will ever happen again – and I hope it doesn't. It didn't mean anything, I know that; it was only because I was wearing her shawl. All the same, it's not every day you get kissed by a gentleman, my girl. It's something to be proud of, at your age!'

Then she felt a little ashamed of herself. 'I suppose it was my fault really. I started it. Wouldn't Val be surprised if she knew? And Ted . . . Whatever would they think of their old Mum, carrying on as if she was a girl again? Well, I'm certainly not going to tell them. They'd both be very shocked.'

At the Queen's Hotel, the party was in full swing.

As it was Christmas Day, there were no evening meals served in the restaurant; the tables had been moved out and chairs lined the walls. A piano had been brought in, and Marta's husband provided an accompaniment to the party chatter. It was hard to recognise the tunes above the general hubbub; at the other end of the room Daphne sat beside Annie, and thought once again what a noisy crew these theatrical folk were.

Ted was somewhere at the heart of the crowd, talking and laughing with a dozen different people at once; clearly he was in his element.

The only other guests who did not seem to be entirely at home in this festive atmosphere were the two comics, Ronnie and Lew. They came and sat next to Daphne and Annie and struck up a quiet, if disjointed, conversation.

'Not quite your cup of tea, all this? We know how you—'

'—know how you feel. It's not our style either. We're not—'

'—not great party-goers. On our nights off, we generally—'

'—generally stay at home with a good book. People say we're not—'

'—not very sociable. But it wouldn't do if—'

'—if we were all alike, would it?'

Franz played a *glissade* down the piano keys, commanding silence, and called upon his wife to sing. To his accompaniment, Marta sang a little serenade; it was not in English, but Daphne knew what it meant from the amorous glances she cast at the men around her. Ted stood beside her, and she played up to him, turning her solo into a witty flirtation.

At the end there was a burst of applause; Daphne laughed and clapped her hands like all the others, and wished she were home in Sackville Road with Ted and Annie, safe and sound.

At the piano, Franz turned to Ted. 'Now it is your turn to sing for your supper, my friend. You are very smart in your dashing red tie – you are not a follower of the Communist Party, I hope?'

'No, sir. I'm the father of a daughter with a very striking taste in neckties,' Ted replied, waving at Annie down the length of the room, and everyone laughed.

'What did Daddy mean? What did he say about me?' Annie asked.

'He was just explaining that you'd given him that lovely tie,' Daphne told her quickly. 'He likes it very much.'

'And what is the proud Papa going to sing for us?' continued Franz.

Ted suggested *How's This For A Start?* – since he did not get a chance to include it in the pantomime – but Herr Neumann was not familiar with it, so after a brief discussion, Ted and Marta launched into an unrehearsed version of the popular number *Tea for Two*. It was more of a comic song than a love song – ridiculously simple and simply ridiculous – yet there was something very charming about the way they sang it, gazing at one another. This time, the applause was louder than ever.

Daphne stood up. 'I think we should make a move,' she told Annie. 'It's past your bedtime, young lady.'

Ignoring her daughter's protests, she said good night to Ronnie and Lew, and they threaded their way through the crowd until they reached Ted.

'It's getting late,' Daphne told him. 'And we don't know what time Gerry will get here. We must be there to meet him.'

Ted brushed this aside. 'Oh, he won't arrive for hours.'

'It's not only that. I really should get Annie to bed—'

'Maybe you're right. Tell you what – why don't you two go ahead? I'll stay for one more drink, then I'll catch you up. See you later, Tufty.'

'Oh, Daddy – not Tufty!' Annie scolded him. 'How many more times?'

Ted kissed her, then asked Daphne, 'You don't mind walking back to the digs without me, do you, sweetheart?'

'No, I don't mind,' she said.

It was still snowing hard. Along the promenade, there was a halo of whirling snowflakes around each street-lamp; as they walked back to the boarding-house, their feet left parallel tracks of black footprints in the snow, while Annie chattered eagerly.

'Mum, do you think there'll be enough for snowballing tomorrow? Can we make a snowman, Mum – can we?'

'We'll see.' Daphne lifted her face to the stinging flakes; they stung her skin like a swarm of bees, then melted on her cheeks, like tears.

In the hotel, they were playing party games; someone tied a blindfold over Ted's eyes, and willing hands spun him round till he was dizzy, then pushed him into a bout of Blind Man's Buff. It was a childish game – but tonight the players were not children.

Groping helplessly for someone he could take prisoner, Ted's hands closed upon a slim waist – soft, naked arms and smooth skin. He recognised the perfume at once, but pretended he did not.

'Give me a clue,' he said, and by way of a reply she kissed him full on the lips; a long kiss, which gave a promise of pleasures to come.

'Marta . . .' he said.

'How did you guess?' She tore off his blindfold, laughing. 'You must tie it upon me now. It is my turn, I think.'

Ted glanced back at the piano; Franz was still sitting there, nodding and smiling. It was only a game, after all.

By the time he returned to the boarding house it was nearly half-past eleven. In her dressing gown, Daphne was sitting up, reading a book.

'Sorry I'm a bit late,' he said. 'I got rather caught up.'

'Never mind – Gerry isn't here yet. How was the rest of the evening?'

'Not too bad. We played party games – it was a pity you couldn't stay.'

Then they heard a car drawing up, and went out to welcome Gerald.

Val and Steve were sitting at either end of the sofa, keeping an empty space between them. For a long time neither of them had said a word.

The champagne bottle stood upon a low table, with their empty glasses. Val stretched out a hand and lifted the bottle – but that was empty too.

'None left,' she said.

'Well . . .' Reluctantly, Steve stood up. 'I suppose I should be going.'

'Yes, I suppose so.' She replaced the bottle carefully. 'It's very peculiar. I feel – I don't know – not drunk . . . Just sort of peaceful, as if I were floating.'

Steve walked to the window and pushed aside the curtains.

'Is it still snowing?' she asked.

'No, it's stopped. Come and look.'

Moving slowly, she joined him at the window. The clouds had broken, and the moon shone down on an extraordinary scene. The trees, the grass, the roads had vanished; it was a frozen world, silent and unreal as the landscape of a dream. The streets were deserted, with no wheel-tracks or footprints to break that perfect whiteness.

'Deep and crisp and even,' said Val softly. 'It will take you a long time to walk home.'

'Yes, but I suppose I ought to go . . .'

She hesitated, then said, 'Yes – you ought to.'

They turned to one another at last.

'Do you want me to?' he asked.

'No,' she said.

And then they were in each other's arms, and they had no choice at all.

Kate began to wish she had followed the example of Mr Colpoys; if she had not had that last cup of coffee, perhaps she would have been able to get to sleep.

It had been a nice day – but odd, and unexpected. It was a pity Gerald had missed their Christmas dinner. Of course she had enjoyed her daughter's company, though there was something about Val nowadays that worried her. She seemed a little withdrawn; although she was as sweet and affectionate as ever, Kate felt she was holding something back, hiding her real feelings. It must make things difficult for her, Gerry being away so much.

Another anxiety nagged at her. Although she was fond of Mr Colpoys, she couldn't help wishing she hadn't kissed him. She hoped he wouldn't think she was throwing herself at him. He was a lonely man and she was sorry for him, but she didn't want him to get any wrong ideas – that would never do. She had had one happy marriage, and that was enough. She didn't want to upset the settled pattern of her life.

Before he left, Mr Colpoys seemed very concerned about her being alone in the house, and she had told him truthfully that it didn't bother her. Daphne and Annie would be home again in a week or so, and she never felt at all nervous about being on her own.

Never – until tonight.

For some reason her nerves were all on edge. She imagined she could hear someone moving about downstairs. A floorboard creaking – a tiny thud – the squeak of a hinge . . . But then the house often settled itself at night, like an old dog stirring in its sleep.

She turned over, trying to put these thoughts out of her mind, but sleep would not come.

Then – quite distinctly – she heard a door open and shut. That wasn't her imagination.

Moving quietly, she got out of bed, put on her dressing gown and slippers, then began to make her way cautiously down the stairs. She did not need any lights; she could find her way round the house blindfolded. Step by step, she went silently downstairs, until she saw a thread of light beneath the kitchen door. For a moment she felt very frightened – but she could not turn back now.

Screwing up her courage, she opened the door.

A man was sitting at the table with his back to her, helping himself to the remains of the cold chicken. At the sound of the door, he sprang up and swung round, gripping the carving-knife.

'Hello, Mrs Watkins,' said Ray Duke. 'Happy Christmas.'

Chapter Eighteen

KATE WAS VERY frightened indeed.

Everything she knew about Ray fell into her mind. She thought of the attack on Ethel Glynn, his five-year prison sentence, his dismissal from Fabers Furnishings, his general dishonesty and duplicity . . . Choking back her fear, she managed to stammer out: 'What – what are you doing here?'

'I let myself in – I'm sorry. I know it was wrong of me, but when I saw there were no lights on in the house, I realised you'd all gone to bed, and I didn't want to disturb anyone. So I went down the back alley and over the garden fence, and I'm afraid I tried the larder window. It was fastened, but I slipped in the blade of my penknife and slid it open. I hope you don't mind, only to tell you the truth I was getting pretty desperate.'

He had changed. Even his voice had altered – it was a little lower and a little softer than she remembered. He did not sound like a desperate man; he sounded sincere, and quietly confident.

'I didn't mean . . .' She tried again, struggling to find a way of framing the question. 'What I meant was, how did you get here? Aren't you supposed to be in – you know . . .?'

'In gaol?' He smiled at her, as if they were sharing a joke together. 'Yes, I was, till a couple of weeks ago.'

'You got away?' She was horrified. If he had escaped from prison, he was capable of anything.

Ray threw back his head and laughed, a whole-hearted laugh. 'Ah, now I understand! Don't worry, Mrs Watkins – I'm not on the run, if that's what you're thinking. It's all official and above-board. They let me out in time for Christmas – I was lucky, wasn't I? Yes, I got my sentence remitted – that's what they call it – on account of I'd seen the error of my ways and turned over a new leaf. They said I was a model prisoner.'

Then he saw that her eyes were fixed on the carving-knife in his hand, and he put it back on the table. 'Don't be afraid. I'm not here to rob you, or do you any mischief. You're the last person in the world I'd ever want to hurt. That's why I came here tonight, because I'd nowhere else to go. I was very cold – and tired – and near to starving. I didn't know where else to turn.'

Looking at him carefully, she saw he had lost weight; his face was thinner, with deep hollows below his cheekbones – and he was deathly pale, looking as if a puff of wind could blow him away. She stopped feeling afraid, and began to feel pity for him instead.

'You'd better finish your supper,' she said. 'I'll make you a hot drink.'

His voice was choked with emotion as he said, 'I knew I could rely on you. You were always good to me.'

When he had eaten all he wanted – and it wasn't much; he said that he didn't have a big appetite these days – she shovelled some more coal on the fire, which had been damped down for the night, and poked up a cheerful blaze in the grate. Then they sat on either side of the kitchen range, and he began to tell her his story.

'I've had plenty of time to think – and to repent. In some ways, a stretch inside was the best thing that ever happened to me; it made me take stock of myself. The prison chaplain was very helpful too. He lent me loads of books, and whenever he visited me we used to study the Bible together, taking it in turns to read aloud. It changed my whole life, Mrs Watkins.'

'And that's why they let you out?'

'I got a job in the prison library. Sundays, I helped in the Chapel, as a server. The librarian, the chaplain – even the Chief Warder – they all spoke up on my behalf, and the Governor recommended me for early release.'

'I'm very glad. So you were able to go home?'

'Home?' He laughed again, but this time there was no amusement in his laughter. 'Oh no, I never had any home. I'd nowhere to go back to.'

'But your mother and father—' Then she broke off, remembering that Ray's family background had turned out to be nothing but fantasies.

He said gently, 'I never knew my mother and father. I made all that up. The truth is, I was a foundling, brought up in an orphanage. I never had a family. My Mum and Dad gave me away – they didn't want me. That's why, when they opened the prison gates, I had nowhere to go.'

'That's dreadful. They turned you out, just like that?'

'Oh, I was given an address – a hostel for homeless men, in Deptford. But that was no good. Worse than prison, in a lot of ways.'

'Oh dear, why was that?'

Ray's eyes clouded. 'The men who stayed there were scum – the lowest of the low. They spent their money on drinking, or gambling, or women. When they realised I wasn't that sort, they made my life a misery, playing jokes on me – their idea of jokes, anyhow. I couldn't tell you some of the tricks they played – vile, filthy things. And they stole the little bit of cash I had – I was left with nothing. That's when I made up my mind to come back here, the only place I'd ever really felt at home.'

Settling back in his chair, he gazed around the cosy room.

'I was going to throw myself on your mercy and ask if you'd help me, but the weather got rough. The snow was thick, and my boots were letting in water – it took me longer than I thought to get here. Course, I don't have a watch any longer, so I didn't know how late it was, but when I saw the place was in darkness, I realised you'd all gone to bed.' He looked up at the ceiling. 'How are they all keeping? Valerie, Mr and Mrs Watkins, and their little girl? She must be – what? Seven? Eight, perhaps?'

'Annie was ten on her last birthday, in September.'

'Ah, bless her, doesn't time fly.' His smile softened his expression. 'They're all keeping well, are they? I hope I didn't wake anyone else, coming in like I did?'

'No.' Kate held her breath, wondering what she should say. She knew he was a criminal, a dangerous man – yet he had talked of his past with such remorse, and when he spoke of little Annie, he seemed so genuinely moved, he had touched her heart. 'As a matter of fact,' she blurted out, 'they're not here.'

'Not here?' He stared at her. 'Why – where are they?'

'Ted's got a job in a pantomime at Hastings – at the seaside, and Daphne and Annie have gone to spend Christmas with him. And – of course, you wouldn't know – Valerie doesn't live here now. She's married to Daphne's brother. They've got a nice flat at the top of

Westwood Hill. She was here today, as a matter of fact. We had our Christmas dinner together.'

'Well, well, times change . . .' He added casually: 'And who's up in the attic now? You've got yourself another lodger, I dare say?'

Again she hesitated, but it seemed silly to pretend. She wasn't afraid of him any more.

'No, I haven't. Annie sleeps in Val's old room. Now she's a big girl, she wants her own bedroom. But there's nobody in the attic.'

'Is that so?' He nodded thoughtfully; she saw something change behind his eyes. 'So you're all on your own? We've got the house to ourselves?'

Suddenly she thought she had made a terrible mistake, because he looked so strange – he wasn't smiling now.

'That's right,' she said, in a voice not much more than a whisper.

Slowly, he stood up and moved towards her, and she wanted to call for help – to run away – but she couldn't make a sound, and she couldn't move. Then she realised that he was holding out his hand.

'Thanks very much for the food and drink. I'm sorry I helped myself, and I'm very sorry to have broken in on you like this.'

Dazed, she shook his hand. 'What do you mean? Are you going?'

'Of course. If I'd known you were by yourself, I'd never have bothered you. It was a stupid thing to do – I'd no idea you were all alone. I'd been hoping that I might have—' He paused, then seemed to change his mind. 'Oh well, I'd better be on my way. Now I've got some food inside me, I'm not as cold as I was.'

'But where are you going to go?'

'I don't know. I'll find somewhere . . . Don't you worry about me.'

He started for the door, and she got up, following him and putting her hand on his arm.

'No, wait. You can't go out like that, it's freezing out there. What were you going to say, just now? You said you'd been hoping you might have something or other – and then you stopped. What was it?'

He shrugged apologetically. 'I'd been hoping you might let me spend the night on that sofa, if I wasn't in anyone's way, but that was when I thought you had your family at home. I couldn't expect you to take in a stranger when you're on your own – it wouldn't be right. Thanks again, Mrs Watkins – and good night.'

He was about to go, but she stopped him.

'You're not a stranger. And there's no need for you to sleep on the

341

sofa – it won't take two minutes to make up the bed in the attic. You can have your old room back.'

He stared at her, and she thought she saw tears shining in his eyes.

'Do you mean that? I won't be any trouble, I promise you. I just need a place to sleep for the night – or two nights, maybe. Just till I get myself sorted out.'

'That's all right, son. You stay as long as you want,' she said, and left the room.

'God bless you,' he said huskily, as the door closed behind her.

Now he was smiling again; a satisfied smile.

The first time, everything seemed to happen at once; when she looked back on it later, Val could never remember the details.

She had been determined not to go to bed with Steve, but as soon as they embraced, their desires took charge of them, and their bodies, aching with loneliness, would not be denied.

They kissed each other desperately, stroking, fondling, undressing one another; there was never a single moment when they took a conscious decision to go on – never a moment when they could have drawn back.

At some stage, Val remembered reaching out a hand to switch off the overhead light. Steve, nuzzling her ear, asked: 'Why did you do that?'

'I don't know,' she replied.

It had been an automatic action. Ever since her wedding night, she and Gerry had made love in the dark – she had never seen her husband naked.

Now, as their clothes dropped away, they sank to the floor, lying on the fur hearthrug before the gas fire, and there was light enough – the burning elements threw a soft glow over their entwined limbs. It wasn't like Gerry's lovemaking – it was wildly urgent, their need for each other thrusting them inexorably on to a climax that was swift and overwhelming, caught up by a force of nature like a tidal wave . . . All too soon it was over. The tide of passion ebbed, and they were left behind like two shipwrecked castaways on a beach, embracing one another and whispering foolish words of love.

Their energy spent, a longing for sleep overtook them.

'We should go to bed,' said Steve. Rousing himself, he picked Val up in his arms and began to carry her to the bedroom.

In the doorway, she felt a sudden chill of shame.

'No, we can't – not here,' she said. 'I couldn't . . .'

Steven turned on the light, and saw the two single beds, side by side.

'You don't sleep together?' he asked.

'We used to. When we were first married, we had a double bed – but Gerry said it kept him awake, so we changed it.' She did not tell Steve that over the last few years their tussles of love had become less and less frequent. When Gerry felt the need of physical gratification – which he called 'a very special occasion' – he pulled her into his bed. It never took long; she neither liked nor disliked it, but accepted it as part of the pattern that made up married life.

'This is my bed,' she told Steve, stripping back the bedclothes. 'Help me carry the mattress into the sitting room; we'll sleep there.'

Between them, they manoeuvered the mattress through the door and put it down by the hearthrug; Val fetched a sheet and two pillows.

'We shan't need a blanket; I'll turn the gas fire down low, that will keep us warm enough.'

They did not talk much; perhaps they both knew that words might be dangerous – and anyway, they were tired and needed some rest. She curled up in his arms, and he pulled the sheet over them; she rested upon his shoulder, and sleep came so swiftly, it took them by surprise.

The second time, it happened quite differently.

It must have been in the small hours, some time after midnight. In her dreams, Val seemed to be swimming in warm, clear water – it felt soft and sensual, with a deep excitement that flooded her body with joy. Waking, she realised that it was no dream – the joy continued and intensified as she found that Steve was caressing her – kissing her – running his lips over her skin, worshipping every part of her with his gentle hands and his wet, hungry mouth.

He had switched on a table-lamp; its yellow shade threw a golden sheen over their nakedness. They had no need of darkness to shelter them; they had nothing to hide, and they twisted and turned into ever-changing positions, feasting their eyes upon each other. Val had never seen anything as splendid – as strong, as perfect – as Steve's hard, muscular body.

They had no feeling of shame. It was as if a door had opened for them, and now they were free to explore one another, giving and taking happiness in a thousand ways, happiness they had never even imagined – discovering a new world of love together.

With his head in her lap, Steve groaned with agonised delight. 'No – stop. If you go on like that, I shall – I shall have to—'

In one swift movement they changed their positions yet again, and she was ready to take him. This time they reached a new peak of ecstasy and remained there, locked together in mutual joy, until they fell asleep once more.

And the third time was the best of all.

When Val woke, daylight was showing between the cracks of the curtains. She slipped out of Steve's arms and ran to the window. Outside, it was broad daylight, and the winter sun shone on sparkling whiteness, casting deep blue shadows. Fearfully, she glanced at the clock; it was nearly nine.

She dropped to her knees beside Steve, shaking him tenderly. 'You must wake up – it's getting late. Gerry will be coming home.'

He opened his eyes, smiling up at her. 'Didn't you say they wouldn't set off till after breakfast?'

'Yes, but—'

'And it'll take them three or four hours at least to get through the snow. There's no hurry – come back to bed.'

When he opened his arms to her, she could not resist, but let him draw her down on top of him, enjoying the warmth of his firm body, and the strong arms that held her tight.

'What are we going to do?' she whispered.

'You know what we're going to do.' She felt him move beneath her, and realised that he was ready for her again.

'Oh no, we shouldn't. We mustn't—' she began, but he pulled her close, stopping her mouth with his own.

This time there was no urgency; their bodies moved as one, and they took their time, making every touch, every stroke, a moment of glory. Val could not be sure if the thrills that swept through her were hers or his. She did not know where her body ended and his began; they had become one body – their transports of love became one love that seemed as if it would never end.

But at last it was over; they lay together without speaking, almost without breathing, afraid they might shatter this perfection they had found.

After a long silence, he said lazily, 'You asked me a question.' Her face was resting upon his chest, and she could feel his words vibrating beneath her cheek. 'You asked what we were going to do.'

'It was a stupid question,' she said. 'I know what we have to do.'

'So do I. You must ask for a divorce – then we can get married.'

'No, Steve, don't say that.' She closed her eyes, unable to watch the unhappiness that had to come. 'You mustn't ask me to do that.'

'What do you mean? You don't love him, do you?'

'Not the way I love you. I could never feel like this about anyone else.'

'Then there's only one thing we can do. I know it's going to be difficult for you, but it's the only—'

She pulled away, raising herself on one elbow, but she couldn't look him in the face. 'Don't you understand? I can never leave Gerry – it wouldn't be fair. I married him. I've sworn to love, honour and obey, till death us do part. I made a promise; I can't go back on it now.'

He sat up, frowning. 'What are you saying? If you really love me—'

'You know I do. But I can't do that to Gerry. I couldn't leave him.'

'But what about us? What's going to happen to you and me?'

She stood up and moved away, picking up her dressing gown.

'Nothing will happen to us. It's over, Steve, you've got to understand that. Last night was wrong – dreadfully wrong, but we couldn't help ourselves. Because of the snow – and the champagne – we felt as if we were the only two people left in the world. And it was the most wonderful – the most beautiful night of my life – but it was completely selfish, and it must never happen again. You've got to go back to your family; I've got to tidy up and get this place ready for Gerry. We've got to go on as we were before.'

He stood before her, naked and defenceless. 'You don't mean that. You can't expect me to let you go, to forget last night.'

Knotting the belt of her dressing-gown, she faced him at last, feeling as if her heart were torn in two.

'I don't want you to forget. We'll both remember it as long as we live; it was something special – something magic – and I'll never be sorry it happened. But that was the first time and the last time, Steve. It won't ever happen again.'

For a while, he tried to argue with her. He became angry, threatening to stay and confront Gerald Glynn when he got home, confessing everything – he would put an end to their loveless marriage.

Val told him that would be silly and cruel. Gerry had done nothing to hurt her. He had never shown her anything but kindness – they had no right to wreck his happiness. She had given Gerry her word; she could not break it.

345

Finally Steve had to agree. Perhaps he realised that if she had been the sort of girl who would break a vow without any compunction, he would not have loved her so much. He got dressed; they took the single mattress back into the bedroom, carrying it between them like a corpse – and they said goodbye.

He kissed her for the last time, then left the building, walking away through the crisp snow.

After he had gone, she threw her sheets and pillowcases into the laundry basket and re-made her bed; then she ran a bath. Afterwards she got dressed and put on an overall, then set to work to clean the flat. First the sitting room, then the bedroom – polishing furniture, sweeping carpets, washing the paintwork, scouring away any speck of dust Steve might have left behind, anything that might bear witness to the fact that he had ever been there.

When Gerry came home, some time in the early afternoon, she had not quite finished, and he asked in astonishment, 'What the hell are you up to?'

'I've started the spring-cleaning,' she told him. 'Shan't be long now.'

'Spring-cleaning – on Boxing Day? Good Lord, hadn't you got anything better to do?'

'No, I hadn't. Do you want something to eat? There's some cold meat in the pantry, or cheese and pickles.'

'No thanks. We stopped on the way and had some sandwiches . . . Though I wouldn't say no to a drink.'

Going to the sideboard, he raised an eyebrow at the vase of flowers. 'Hello – where did these come from?'

She had forgotten the chrysanthemums. Evading a direct reply, she said, 'Pretty, aren't they? I thought they brightened the place up.'

'Yes, very nice.' Losing interest, he opened the sideboard door, studying the array of bottles. 'Now then, what have we got here? I suppose you and your mother polished off the bubbly between you?'

'As a matter of fact, I brought it back with me. Mum didn't want any.'

'Didn't she? Good – where is it?'

'In the dustbin – empty. I opened it last night . . . Sorry.'

He chuckled. 'You got through a whole bottle – all by yourself? Poor old dear, it must have been a rotten Christmas for you – nothing to do but get quietly sozzled! Did you hear the broadcast?'

'I started to, but it made me feel so miserable, I turned it off.'

'Ah well, I'll make it up to you. Tell you what, why don't I take you out tonight? A spot of supper and some dancing – I'll ring up the dear old Troc and see if they're open. We'll have our Christmas celebration.' He gave her a knowing wink. 'A very special occasion, eh? How about that?'

At the end of the first week of January, Daphne and Annie came home. *Cinderella* had another three weeks to run, so Ted was staying on in Hastings, but the new term was about to begin at Carmichael Road School, and they had to return to London without him.

When they arrived at Sackville Road on Saturday afternoon, Kate was waiting at the front door.

'Did you have a good journey?' she asked.

'Not too bad, apart from the weather.' Daphne carried their suitcase in, glad to get in out of the rain. 'It's been like this ever since we left Hastings – cats and dogs all the way.'

'Mum says we look like a pair of drowned rats,' said Annie cheerfully. 'Do you think I look like a drowned rat?'

'I think you look like a little angel – it's lovely to see you.' Kate hugged her granddaughter. 'You'd better get out of those wet things before you catch cold.'

'I'll run a bath for her, presently,' said Daphne. 'But I'm dying for a cup of tea first, if you've got some on the go.'

'Val's boiling the kettle now,' Kate told her, leading the way down to the kitchen.

Valerie and Daphne greeted one another, and exchanged more comments on the weather.

'I don't suppose you heard the news on the wireless this morning?' Valerie said. 'There was terrible flooding all along the Thames. Some people were drowned and hundreds more had to leave their homes.'

'We can think ourselves lucky we're so high up here,' said Kate, pouring the tea. 'What is it they say on the posters – *Halfway to Heaven*?'

Valerie said flatly, 'Or *Halfway to Hell* – it depends which way you look at it.'

'Oh, for goodness sake!' Kate passed her a cup of tea. 'Get that down you, my girl, and stop moaning. You've been a proper old misery lately. I don't know what's wrong with you.'

Daphne eyed her sister-in-law curiously; she sensed a change in Val, but couldn't quite put her finger on it.

'How's the world been treating you?' she asked. 'How's Gerry?'

'He's fine, thanks,' said Val. 'Only he's working again this weekend, so I'm at a loose end, as usual.'

Suddenly Daphne realised what was different about her. Valerie, usually bubbling with good humour, had not smiled once since they came in.

'But everything's all right, is it?' she asked.

Val turned away. She wasn't halfway between heaven and hell – she was living in hell, day and night – a hell of her own making. Pretending she had nothing to hide; trying to do her duty, to be a good wife, to smother her guilt and her loneliness – and never able to put Steve out of her mind for a single moment.

She tried to answer Daphne's question. 'I told you, everything's fine. Why shouldn't it be?'

'I don't know. I just thought, from what Mum was saying—'

'It's the weather that's getting me down – take no notice!' Then she looked more closely at Daphne. 'Come to that, you don't seem particularly cheerful yourself. How's Ted – is he OK?'

'Yes, he's doing very well. The show's a big success.'

Daphne remembered her last glimpse of Ted this morning on the station platform, waving them goodbye as the train pulled out. Then she had seen him turn and walk away – back to the digs, or to the theatre, or to the Queen's Hotel . . . She wondered where he was now, and who he was with.

'But you're right, the weather's really depressing. And we didn't much like leaving Dad behind, did we, Annie?'

'No – and it's school next week. I think we ought to have stayed in Hastings, with Dad.' Annie looked reproachfully at her mother. 'You could have written a letter to the Headmistress and explained, couldn't you?'

'No, I couldn't.' Firmly, Daphne changed the subject. 'So what's been happening while we were away? I want to hear all the news.'

'Mum's got some exciting news for you – haven't you, Mum?' said Val. 'Go on, break it to her gently.'

'Oh, do leave off. All this fuss about nothing,' muttered Kate.

'Well, if you're not going to tell her, I will. Guess who's living here now – upstairs in his old room? Ray Duke.'

Daphne stared at her, then at Kate. 'You're not serious? I thought he was still—' she glanced at Annie '—out of circulation?'

'He was, until Christmas. Time off for good behaviour – that's a laugh. Then he had the nerve to come back here and ask Mum to put him up, and she fell for it. I told her, she needs her brains tested.'

Kate coloured slightly. 'That's not a very nice thing to say, is it? Annie, dear, why don't you run up to your bedroom for a minute, while I talk to your Mum? You'll find a little something on your bedside table – a bag of wine-gums and this week's *Rainbow* – a sort of coming-home present. Off you go, there's a dear.'

Annie, who had been growing bored with all this grown-up talk, set off at once, and Kate shut the door.

'I wish you wouldn't keep going on at me about it,' she told Val. 'This is my house – I can invite who I want, can't I?'

'It's Daff's home as well – and Ted's. They might have something to say about you bringing in criminals.'

'He's not a criminal! He knows he did wrong – he's paid the penalty and he's truly sorry. He goes to church now, and he's trying to lead an honest life. When he asked for help, I couldn't refuse him.'

'So she's letting him stay here – rent free! Would you believe it?'

'Just temporary, just till he gets some work and starts earning again. Then he must find somewhere else; he understands that.'

'And when's that going to be? The Labour Exchange is full of people looking for jobs. He could be on the dole for ages.'

'All the more reason to give him a helping hand. You can't say he isn't trying; he goes to the library every day, and reads all the adverts.' Kate looked at the clock. 'He generally comes in about five. He'll be home soon.'

'In that case I'm off.' Valerie stood up, collecting her raincoat and umbrella. 'Sorry I can't stop, Daff, but I don't want anything to do with Mr Duke. I'm giving him a wide berth, and if you've got any sense you'll do the same.'

After she had gone, Kate said sadly, 'I've never known her like this. If she'd only meet him, she'd see how he's changed – but she won't even speak to him. You don't think I've done wrong, do you?' she asked anxiously.

'Well, not having seen him, I can't really say. It's good of you to give him another chance. I just hope he won't let you down.'

'He won't. He's a changed man – you'll see.'

When Ray came home half an hour later, Daphne had to admit that he had improved. He shook hands politely, and said he was glad to meet her again. He told her how grateful he was to Mrs Watkins, and assured her that as soon as he found a job, he would pay the rent he owed.

'Nothing so far, but I'll keep on looking. And once I get fixed up,

349

I'll find some other lodgings, I won't be a burden on you any longer than I can help, I promise you.'

She studied him carefully. It was true – he had changed. He returned her gaze frankly, and spoke with quiet assurance.

'Well, I wish you luck,' she said.

'Thanks, I appreciate that.' He squared his shoulders. 'I need some luck this evening. I'm going to tackle the most difficult job of all.'

'What's that?'

'I'm going round to Belmont. Miss Ethel suffered on account of me, more than anyone . . . I've got to face her, somehow.'

Daphne and Kate looked at one another, and Kate began: 'Oh, I'm not sure. It might do more harm than good—'

'I must try and make amends, if I can. I've got her on my conscience. I can't rest till I've seen her.'

'Don't expect too much,' said Daphne. 'She may not want to see you.'

'I know – but I've prayed for guidance. I realise it's asking a lot, but I've got to try.'

The Glynn sisters had finished their high tea, and Aggie and Ethel were doing the washing-up when the doorbell rang.

'Babs must have forgotten her key,' twittered Aggie, wiping her hands on a towel. 'I'll let her in.'

'It won't be Babs – not yet. She said she wouldn't be home till late,' Ethel pointed out.

'Well, I'll go and see,' said Aggie, and trotted off.

She crossed the tiled floor of the front hall and opened the door; a figure stood in the shadows under the porch.

'Good evening, Miss Agnes. May I come in?'

His voice was pleasant and vaguely familiar; she moved back as he stepped into the light. Then she recognised him – but it was too late. He was already in the house, closing the door behind him.

'Mr Duke!' she gasped. 'What do you want?'

'I'd like to speak to your sister, Miss Ethel. I've come to apologise for all the pain and suffering I caused her. I hope she will see me.'

He smiled nicely, but her heart was fluttering, and her knees shook so much, she was afraid they would give way. She supported herself by gripping the back of a chair, and said nervously, 'Oh, I don't know. I wasn't expecting – I don't know what to say.' Her scattered thoughts whirled about like mice in a wheel. She had no idea what to do. She must ask someone else – she must speak to Muriel: Muriel always knew best. With a great effort, she managed to say, 'Sit here, please. I'll go and ask. I'll be as quick as I can.'

She would not go to the kitchen and tell Ethel; the shock might be too much for her. Instead, she hurried up the stairs and went straight to the sitting room, where she began breathlessly: 'Oh Mu, such a dreadful thing. That wicked man – he's downstairs. I opened the door and he walked straight in . . . Whatever shall I do?'

Muriel, who had been reading the *Ladies' Journal*, looked up irritably. 'I haven't the faintest idea what you're talking about. I do wish you'd think before you speak . . . What man?'

'Mr Duke – Raymond. He wants to see Ethel.'

Muriel turned the page. 'Ridiculous. He's in prison, and a good job too. You're talking nonsense again.'

'No, really, Muriel. It's true – he wants to see Ethel.'

'Well, tell him he can't. He must have escaped from prison. Send him away, then telephone for the police.'

'Oh, I couldn't. I'm so bad on the telephone—'

'Do as I tell you!' snapped Muriel. 'Turn him out – tell him if he doesn't leave this house immediately, he will be in serious trouble. You must take a firm line with him.'

Agnes, who had never taken a firm line about anything in her life, looked as if she might burst into tears. With quivering lips, she backed away to the door, gasping, 'Yes, Mu – very well. I'll do my best.'

Downstairs, Ethel came out into the hall, looking for her sister. 'What's going on, Aggie? You left me with all the washing-up. Who was that at the—' Then she saw Ray. 'Oh. Good evening.'

Everything depended on this moment; he was very apprehensive, but he wouldn't show it.'

'Good evening. I don't know if you'll remember me. My name is—'

'I remember you; you're Raymond Duke. You're the one who robbed me.'

'Yes. That's why I'm here. I committed a serious crime, and I was sent to prison. That was right and proper. But I've been very lucky.'

'Lucky?' She did not understand him. 'What do you mean?'

'I've had nearly five years to think over my wickedness, and now I mean to make a new life for myself, because I've seen the error of my ways. I have been blessed by God's loving mercy, and I intend to lead a Christian life from now on. But before I can do that, I must repent of my sins – and I do repent, from the bottom of my heart. I want to apologise for the harm I did you – and if you can find it in you to forgive me, I beg your forgiveness.'

Saying this, he knelt before her on the cold, slippery tiles, and bowed his head. She moved a little closer, looking down at him.

'Do you really mean that?' she asked.

'As God is my judge.'

Aggie, coming downstairs with quick nervous steps, stopped dead at the sight of them.

'Oh Ethel, I'm so sorry. I should never have let him in—'

'That's all right, dear. Raymond and I have had a little talk. He's sorry for what he did. Stand up, Raymond. I forgive you.'

He grabbed her hand and put it to his lips, murmuring, 'You're so good. It's more than I deserve – much more.'

'Please, let's say no more about it. And I do wish you'd get up; this is rather embarrassing.'

Aggie interrupted, 'But Ethel, Mu said I should send him away. Turn him out, she said.'

'Muriel doesn't always know what's best, Aggie. Come along, Raymond, let's go upstairs. We can explain to Muriel together.' She took his arm, and they began to climb the stairs, with Aggie following them doubtfully.

As they entered the sitting room, Muriel dropped her magazine in shock.

'What is the meaning of this? Agnes, I told you what to do. How dare you bring this ruffian into my house!'

'It may be your house, dear, but I'm the one he came to see,' Ethel reminded her. 'He's apologised for what he did, and I accepted his apology, so there's no more to be said. He's become a God-fearing young man, and he's going to lead a better life – I think the least we can do is give him a cup of tea. Have you had anything to eat, Raymond? Would you care for a sandwich?'

'Well, I am feeling a bit peckish, but I wouldn't want to put you to any trouble.'

'It's no trouble. We'll go to the kitchen, and see what we can find.'

Ethel shepherded Aggie out of the room, leaving Ray alone with Muriel.

'Is it all right if I sit down?' he asked.

Muriel said nothing, and he took advantage of this to pull up a small footstool, close beside her.

'I should have come to you first, I realise that, but I had to ask for

352

Miss Ethel's forgiveness. I couldn't rest till I'd done that . . . Now that's done, I must admit it was you I wanted to see, most of all.'

'What do you mean?' She glared at him suspiciously. 'I've a good mind to call the police.'

'That's up to you, of course, but you'll find that they're not bothered about me any more. I've paid my debt to society, Mrs Glynn. I'm a free man again . . . Free to tell you how much I owe you – more than I can ever repay.'

'What are you talking about? What do you owe me – how much?'

'I don't mean cash. It's the day I first came here I keep thinking about – and your kindness to me then. I'd never been in such a beautiful place before, and I'd never met anyone like you. You opened my eyes. You were so good and generous – so beautiful in every way – for the first time in my life, I knew I'd met a truly great lady.'

As she listened, her expression altered, but she said flatly, 'I don't know whether or not your eyes were opened, Mr Duke – all I know is that you attacked and robbed my sister.'

'Yes. I was so ignorant, I thought money was the key to it all. I was tempted to the worship of Mammon. I thought if I could lay my hands on some money, I could be like you. I was stupid, as well as sinful . . . but I've learned my lesson, thanks to you.'

'To me?'

'That was the worst punishment of all. I realised what a fool I was, to throw away your friendship for the sake of money. I've never forgotten you, and the things you said. You opened your house to me – you opened your heart to me – and I never realised the true value of those gifts until I lost them. That's why I want to say thank you. I've no right to come here like this, and I'll probably never see you again, but I'll always remember you with gratitude – and love.'

Muriel tried to speak, but there was a lump in her throat. She took Ray's hand, squeezing it between her own, too moved for words.

The door opened, and Ethel came in, wheeling a tea-trolley and saying, 'We've made you some bloater-paste sandwiches, and a pot of coffee.'

Muriel pulled herself together. 'No, Ethel – not coffee. Bring up a bottle of wine from the cellar, and four glasses.'

Later, as Ray pulled the cork and filled their glasses, he asked, 'Just the four glasses? Isn't Babs at home this evening?'

'I'm afraid not. She was invited out to supper by a friend,' said Muriel. 'I don't know what time she will be back.'

'Quite late, she said,' Ethel chimed in. 'But we'll tell her you were here, and next time you come round, I'm sure she'll be pleased to see you.'

'Thank you. Perhaps you'd give her my kind regards?'

He did not stay long after that. When the bottle was empty, he wished the three ladies a very good night and left the house, having done all he had hoped to do on his first visit.

It was after eleven when Babs returned. Walter Faber had escorted her home, and Muriel was sitting up, waiting to see them both. As she explained, 'I couldn't sleep until I knew my little girl was safe and sound. Of course, you always take good care of her, Mr Faber, but you know how mothers worry.'

'I understand perfectly, Mrs Glynn,' said Walter. 'Your feelings do you credit.'

'I hope you both had an enjoyable evening?' Muriel continued. 'We had an unexpected visitor, Babs. Mr Duke called in to see us – he sent you his regards.'

Babs said angrily, 'That man! After what he did – how he has the nerve . . . I thought he was still in prison.'

'He was released early, because he's a reformed character. He spoke so well – so sincerely – we were quite touched. He hoped he might have seen you, but I said I was sure that next time he calls, you'll be only too glad—'

Seeing the look on Walter's face, Babs turned on her mother vehemently.

'Mummy, how *could* you? Ray Duke's wicked, through and through – wicked and evil. I never want to see him again. Never, as long as I live!'

When Ted came back from Hastings at the end of January, he brought a bag full of presents – Annie said it was like Christmas all over again.

Her gift was a miniature sweet-shop, with little glass bottles full of hundreds-and-thousands, a tin scoop, and a set of scales to weigh them out into tiny paper bags. Daphne felt it was rather a babyish present for a ten-year-old, but she kept her opinion to herself – and anyway Annie loved it. There was a box of handkerchiefs with embroidered rosebuds in the corners for Kate, and a little bottle of expensive perfume for Daphne.

She unwound the gold wire, took out the stopper, sniffed, then said: 'Lovely. Thank you very much,' before replacing the stopper and putting it away.

Ted hadn't overlooked Valerie either. Kate said she would be coming round to tea later, so they put her present aside. It was an ivory paperknife with a tiny spy-glass in the handle; when you put it to your eye, you could see a view of Hastings Pier.

Annie asked, 'Is that all the presents? Isn't there one for Mr Duke?'

'No.' Ted's face darkened. 'He's still here, is he?'

'He hasn't managed to find any work yet,' said Kate, 'but he goes on looking. I'll say that for him, he never gives up.'

'Well, you know my opinion,' said Ted. 'I agree with Val – I think it's a pity you let him move in.'

Kate pretended not to hear, and began to fuss over the box of handkerchiefs. 'These are really lovely – I'm sure the embroidery's done by hand . . .' Clearly, the subject of Ray Duke was not open to discussion.

Ted turned to Daphne. 'Well, I've got some good news, anyway. Percy came down to see the last night of the panto, and he told me he's got another job fixed up for me in the spring – ten weeks' work, and second billing! How about that?'

Daphne was delighted for him. 'Oh, that's marvellous. In London?'

'Not exactly; it's a tour round the halls. Some of them are in the London area – one week at Croydon Empire, I can get home easily from there – and some of them are East and West London – Hackney, Shepherds Bush. That might be more difficult, it depends on the last trains . . . but with a bit of luck I should get home every night. After that, the dates are further afield, Coventry, Northampton, Norwich—'

Daphne's smile faded. 'So you'll be going away.'

'Cheer up, sweetheart. Ten weeks isn't that long. Like I said, I'll be living at home some of the time. This is a real opportunity for me: second billing, closing the first half – but it's even better than that. Marta's got top billing, so she'll have the closing spot on the bill – and guess what? At the end, when she takes her call, she wants me to come on and do a duet with her, as an encore – remember when we ad-libbed our way through *Tea For Two* at the party? It went down so well, she wants to work it up as her closing number – isn't that terrific? Almost as good as topping the bill myself . . .'

He broke off, because Daphne had got up without a word and walked out. With a quick, embarrassed smile at Kate and Annie, he left the room and went after her.

She was sitting on the bed, trying hard not to cry. He sat beside her, putting his arm round her.

'I thought you'd be pleased.'

'How could you think that?' she asked. 'You know how I feel about you going on tour, leaving me here while you travel all over the place.'

'But it's my job. I won't get very far if I never go anywhere except Lewisham Hippodrome – or the bandstand in Grange Park! When Percy told me, I was like a dog with two tails. It's the best break I ever had.'

She turned to him. 'Tell me something. That perfume you gave me – it's the kind Marta uses, isn't it?'

He stared at her, thrown off-balance. 'Yes, I believe it is. What's that got to do with anything?'

'Did you ask her what kind to buy?'

'I asked her advice – she knows about that sort of thing. Why, don't you like it?'

'I'm sure it suits her very well – but I don't happen to care for it.'

'Oh, come on. There's no need to get worked up about—' He stopped, frowning. 'Is that what's upsetting you? Is it because I'm going on tour with Marta?' He laughed suddenly. 'My God – you don't think there's anything going on between us, do you?'

She looked away unhappily. 'I didn't know, did I? I didn't know what to think. You seem to be getting very friendly with her.'

'Yes – because we work well together, that's all. Sometimes in this business, you get a kind of understanding, you find you can play off one another – and when that happens, it'd be stupid not to make the most of it. But that's as far as it goes. She's happily married – *I'm* happily married . . . I love you, Daff. You're the only woman in my life, you know that.'

He pulled her closer, kissing her, petting her, telling her how much he loved her – and she burst into tears.

'I'm sorry, I know I'm being stupid, but when you're away I start imagining things. I'm so afraid of losing you . . . I wish you didn't have to go on tour.'

Holding her tight, he said, 'If it means that much to you, I won't go.'

'No – you must. You said yourself, it's the best break you ever—'

'What does that matter? I can get other work. I'll do more broadcasts – I don't care what I do, as long as I make you happy. I'll tell Percy he can find somebody else. I'm going to stay at home – with you.'

*

It was one of the worst winters anyone could remember. After the snow at Christmas and the floods in January, February brought gale-force winds that swept across Britain, creating havoc and killing eleven people.

The Crystal Palace grounds suffered serious damage; carefully tended flowerbeds and shrubberies were laid waste, and many fine old trees uprooted.

Grim-faced, Henry Buckland toured the devastated park, then told the Head Groundsman it was imperative that the gardens must be tidied up and restored as far as possible in time for Easter. He allocated a special budget for the work and gave permission for extra temporary staff to be taken on.

The arrangements fell partly on Val's shoulders; when applicants for jobs came into the office, it was her responsibility to take their particulars, sending on any likely candidates to be interviewed.

Halfway through the first batch, she came face to face with Ray Duke.

Since he had been living at Sackville Road, she had kept out of his way. This was the first time they had seen one another, and she found it very disturbing, but she tried to remain calmly efficient, making notes in the file of applicants.

'Name . . . Raymond Duke,' she said, as she wrote the words. 'Address . . . I take it you're still at Sackville Road, for the moment, anyway?'

'Yes. Your mother has been very good to me.'

'I'm sure she has. And you're hoping to be taken on the ground staff? Did you see the advertisement in the paper?'

'No; your mother told me. She said I ought to try for it.'

'I see.' Val made another note, then asked, 'Do you have any previous experience as a gardener, working on the land?'

'No, but I'm willing to learn.'

'Very well; that will be all. If you like to wait outside, with the others, you'll be called in to see the Head Groundsman.'

He did not leave immediately, but asked, 'What are you going to tell him about me?'

She looked at him coolly. 'I shall give him these details, that's all.'

'You won't say I've been in gaol?' As she hesitated for a moment, he went on: 'It might go against me – and I really need this job. I'm desperate to make some money, so I can pay your mother something.'

She closed the file. 'I shan't say anything about you, one way or

357

the other. He'll have the facts you've given me. He might ask you what you've been doing lately – it's up to you what you tell him.'

Ray thought this over, then nodded. 'Thanks. Much obliged,' and he left the office.

He got the job. At the end of the afternoon, she passed him on her way out of the building. He was one of a small gang of men, clearing up fallen branches, sweeping leaves from the paths; their eyes met, and he smiled slightly – a conspiratorial smile.

She walked on angrily – angry with herself for allowing him to upset her. Meeting him again had brought back too many memories.

Trying to put these thoughts from her mind, she forced herself to concentrate on Gerry. He had said he would be leaving work early today, and she was planning to cook liver and bacon for supper – that was one of his favourites. Glancing at her watch, she realised that if he had caught the early train, he would be arriving at the High Level station in a few minutes. On a sudden impulse, she decided to go and meet him, and instead of leaving the Palace by the usual exit, she made a small detour, down a flight of steps to the subway beneath the main road, leading directly to the railway station.

The subway was a showplace in its own right; the vaulted roof, supported by ornate columns decorated with tiles, was vaguely ecclesiastic, resembling the crypt of a medieval church in Tuscany – deliberately so, since a leading Italian architect had been brought over to design it.

She paused, looking about her, remembering the trip to London with Gerald on their wedding day. Under the shadowy arches, she saw a figure coming towards her – a young man, who carried a small suitcase and had a heavy rucksack on his back.

Though she could not see his face from that distance, she knew him.

Steve walked towards her. His footsteps echoed eerily under the vaulted roof – there was no one else in sight.

'Hello,' he said. 'What are you doing here?'

'I've come to meet Gerry – he'll be here any minute. How are you?'

'Pretty well. It's a bit of luck, seeing you like this. I wouldn't have been able to tell you, otherwise. I'm going away.'

It was like a leaden hand, gripping her heart. 'Away – where?'

'I've been offered a new job, through someone at the airport. They're taking on aeronautic engineers at Cardington.'

'Where's that?'

'Bedfordshire. It's where the new airships are being developed. The money's good, and it'll give me a chance to travel – see the world. I'll be trained to navigate, too, joining the aircrews.'

She managed to say, 'You'll like that. How long are you going for?'

'If it works out, I'll probably stay there.' He added quietly, 'I thought it's probably better all round, moving out of London.'

'Yes, I suppose so.' She heard the thunder of an approaching train and the screech of wheels as it slowed, entering the station. 'That will be Gerry's train – I must go.'

'I'll come part of the way. My train goes from the other platform.'

They walked side by side, keeping a little space between them, until they reached the iron staircase leading down to the platforms. It branched left and right. He stopped and said: 'Well – I go this way. I'm glad I saw you.'

They looked hopelessly at one another. Below them, passengers were stepping out of the train. Val wondered if Steve would kiss her, and hoped he would not. He put out his hand, and she held it briefly.

'Goodbye,' he said, then turned and ran down the iron steps.

She stood there – without moving, without thinking – waiting for the pain to end.

A moment later Gerry greeted her. 'Hello, old dear. What a surprise!' He took her arm and they strolled towards the exit, as he asked: 'Who was that chap I saw you talking to, when I came up the stairs?'

'Just someone I used to know.'

He glanced at her, speculatively. 'I thought I knew the face. It was him, wasn't it? That blighter – what's-his-name – Gunn?'

'Yes. I happened to run into him. He's got a job, somewhere near Bedford. He's moving out of London.'

'Ah, so we shan't be seeing him again?' Gerry said cheerfully. 'Gone for good, eh?'

'Yes . . . Gone for good.'

Chapter Nineteen

IT HAPPENED ON a Saturday evening.

Ted was out, working; the South Norwood Branch of the British Legion were holding their Ladies' Night at the Stanley Halls, and Percy Thring was providing the cabaret. Ray Duke had gone over to the pub, Annie was tucked up in bed, and Kate was in the sitting room, listening to a radio version of *School For Scandal* on their splendid new Pye, with its loudspeaker tastefully hidden behind a fretwork emblem of the setting sun.

Daphne had the kitchen to herself. She had done the week's washing after breakfast this morning, then hung it out in the back garden. It had been a good drying day, so she was able to get on with the ironing; tomorrow they would all have clean clothes to wear to church.

She was prodding the nose of the iron around the buttons on one of Ted's shirts when she heard a knock at the front door. Crossly, she put the iron on top of the kitchen range to keep warm, and set off upstairs – meeting Kate coming out of the sitting room.

'It's all right, I know you're busy – I'll go,' Kate said, straightening her skirt and patting her hair, in case it might be Mr Colpoys.

'But you're listening to a play,' objected Daphne.

'It doesn't matter. They're all talking in such a funny way, I can't make head nor tail of it,' said Kate, opening the front door.

'Good evening, madam. I wonder if I might speak to—' began Percy Thring, then, squinting at Daphne hovering behind her mother-in-law, he gave her a cheery wave. 'Ah, there you are. I was hoping I might catch you.'

Daphne introduced them to one another. Percy shook Kate's hand, saying, 'A great pleasure, Mrs Watkins – a very great pleasure.' He turned to Daphne. 'Could I have a quick word – if I'm not putting you out at all?'

'Of course – if you don't mind coming downstairs. I'm in the middle of the ironing.'

Kate was scandalised. 'You can't take a gentleman like Mr Thring into the kitchen! You must have the sitting room – I'll turn off the wireless.'

Daphne smiled at Percy. 'You won't object to talking across the ironing-board, will you?'

'Not in the very least, I assure you.'

So Kate had to give way, and went back to her struggle with Sheridan, while Daphne led her visitor downstairs.

'Would you like a cup of tea? Or if you'd prefer something stronger, I believe there are some bottles of beer . . .'

'Nothing for me, ta.' Percy plumped himself into the armchair by the grate, making a vague gesture towards the ironing-board. 'Carry on – don't let me hold you up.'

Daphne tested the heat of the iron, holding it close to her cheek, then continued to press Ted's shirt, saying, 'Ted's at South Norwood, I'm afraid. Oh, but you know all about that.'

'Yes, I've just come from there. I like to make sure everything's under control. I waited till the cabaret began, then I came away, and as I happened to be driving this way, I decided to call in, on the off-chance. Mind if I smoke?'

'Not at all.' A little puzzled, she fetched him an ashtray. 'There's nothing wrong, is there?'

'Ta very much.' He lit his cigarette, blowing out a cloud of smoke. 'I wouldn't say *wrong*, exactly, but I had a chat with Ted while he was getting ready to go on. Quite frankly, I was hoping to persuade him to change his mind about that tour I'd fixed up for him.'

'I see.' Daphne plied the iron more briskly. 'Did you have any luck?'

'I can't say I did. And that worries me, my dear – it worries me a lot. This is the second time he's cried off at the last minute, when I've got a contract waiting to be signed. He's not doing himself any good, letting people down like this – and he's not doing me much good either.'

'Did he explain why he doesn't want to go out on tour?' Daphne asked.

'He told me he'd rather stay at home with his wife and family.

361

Well, I can understand that. If I was lucky enough to have a wife and family, I dare say I'd feel the same. But I've got to think of the lad's future – his career. Your husband's got a lot of talent, my dear – a big future – but the way he's carrying on now, he's going to throw it down the drain.'

'I suppose he told you it's all my fault? I'm the one who doesn't want him to leave home?'

Percy took off his thick glasses, polishing them on the end of his tie, breathing on the lenses and holding them up to the light. His eyes were screwed up, small and helpless; he appeared naked without his spectacles.

'He never said anything of the kind – I swear that on my mother's life. But I remember how excited he was when I first told him about the tour – and how miserable he looked when he came into my office and said he didn't want to do it. So I put two and two together – and the answer was you.'

Daphne said nothing, but went on thumping away at the ironing-board.

'It's between you and him, naturally, and I'm the last person to wish to come between man and wife – but let me just put this thought in your head. Ted's come a long way in the last couple of years; he's building up a big following. If he goes on like this, he could go right to the top – name up in lights, the Palladium, the Holborn Empire – all the Number Ones . . . But if he pulls back now, when everything's on the up and up, he'll never get any further. Worse than that; in a year or so he'll start slipping back. He'll finish up where he started, playing the bandstands and the working-men's clubs – and for the rest of his life he'll regret it. And if I may speak frankly, Daphne – you don't mind me calling you Daphne? – he's going to blame you for standing in his way.'

Flushed and angry, she turned to face him. 'We talked it over, and he feels the same as I do. We want to be together—'

Wreathed in smoke, Percy rose to his feet, warding off her arguments. 'Very well, I'll say no more. I've said my piece, and I hope you'll think it over. Don't bother to see me out, my dear. I can find my way.'

Ted did not get home till nearly midnight. She was still lying awake when he crawled cautiously into bed beside her.

'It's all right, I'm not asleep,' she said. 'How was your evening? How did the cabaret go?'

'Like a house on fire! The Branch Secretary asked me back for their Ladies' Night next year.'

'That's nice . . . but according to Percy, you could be starring at the Palladium by then.'

'What are you talking about? What's Percy got to do with it?'

When she told him about their conversation over the ironing-board, Ted was very angry. He threatened to go round to Percy's office on Monday morning and tell him what he could do with his bloody contracts. He'd get another agent – there were plenty more who'd be only too pleased to take him on.

'Not if you keep turning down the contracts they offer you.'

'It's only the touring! I don't have to do tours – I can make a big name right here in London, on the wireless. What right has Percy got to tell me how to run my life?'

'I don't know, but perhaps he's got a point. I believe he wants what's best for you.'

'He wants what's best for P. P. Thring. It's his precious ten per cent he's worried about.'

'Yes, that too. But what's best for Percy is best for Ted Watt as well. He's been building Ted Watt up to be a star. Well, Percy can have his Ted Watt and do what he likes with him – as long as I can keep my Ted Watkins. You go on tour – do whatever you want to – as long as you come home to me in between times, I don't care.'

'You don't mean that. You're just saying it.'

'I do mean it. I've been thinking – you're the best comedian I ever saw, and I want you to be the biggest star in the world. I was being stupid and jealous because of Marta Linden, but if you tell me she doesn't mean anything to you, and that you still love me best – that's all I need to know.'

He kissed her; she tasted the whisky, but she didn't mind. She shivered with expectation as he pulled off her nightdress and began to make love to her. Of course he loved her, just as she loved him – nothing would ever change that. She offered herself to him completely, giving him her body, her heart and her soul . . .

Silently, Ted cursed himself for having had one drink too many. It was true, it made you feel ready for it, but then it let you down. He tried hard to concentrate on Daphne, and give her the love she needed . . . A line from a song floated through his mind for no reason at all: *Tea for two, and two for tea – me for you and you for me . . .*

He would see Percy on Monday morning, and sign the contract.

Very soon he would begin rehearsals for the tour – rehearsing with Marta.

Fired by this thought, he was filled with a sudden, overwhelming excitement – and realised that it was going to be all right, after all.

On Sunday morning Ted and Daphne overslept. When they came down to breakfast, they found Kate already at the table, with Annie and Ray Duke.

'We started without you,' she explained. 'I thought you must have had a late night – that's why I let you both have a lie-in.'

Ted took a long swig of tea and said, 'Thanks, I needed that. Yes, it was a big night, last night. I hear you met my agent?'

'Just for a minute. Daff introduced us . . . It was quite a surprise, him turning up out of the blue like that, wasn't it?'

Ted grinned. 'And I bet you're dying to know what it was all about?'

'Certainly not,' said Kate primly. 'I wouldn't dream of asking – it's none of my business.'

'Never mind, we'll tell you anyway. We've had a long talk, and there's been a change of plan. Daff and me have decided it would be a good idea if I go on that music-hall tour after all.'

Kate looked uncertainly at Daphne. 'Oh, do you think so?'

'We both think so,' Daphne smiled. 'It's too good an offer to turn down.'

'Can we come and see you doing the tour?' asked Annie hopefully.

'I don't see why not, as long as I'm playing somewhere near. Of course, some of the time I'll be living in digs.' Ted sighed. 'That's the only drawback. I don't like the idea of being away from home, leaving you three ladies all by yourselves.'

Ray, who had been listening in silence, spoke up. 'They won't be by themselves,' he said. 'I'll keep an eye on them.'

Ted turned to look at him. 'You won't be here either,' he said.

Ray frowned. 'Why not?'

'Now, Ted, don't start that,' said Kate, but her son continued.

'You'll be moving out – wasn't that the arrangement? As soon as you got a job, and some money coming in, you were going to look for a place of your own. Isn't that what you told us, Mum?'

'Well, yes, but—'

'I've only got a temporary job at the Palace,' Ray protested. 'Nothing permanent.'

'Val tells me you'll be there right through the spring and summer

364

– they're the busiest months. That ought to be time enough to find yourself some lodgings, don't you think?'

'Well, I'll see what I can do,' muttered Ray. Scowling, he pushed back his chair and left the table.

When the door slammed, Kate said reproachfully, 'Oh Ted, you shouldn't have said that.'

'I'm sorry, Mum, but it's time somebody gave him a push, or he'll be here for ever. And I certainly don't fancy the idea of going away and leaving him in the house. I don't care what you say – I don't trust him.'

On the other side of the kitchen door, Ray stood listening, his face twisted with hate.

'You're going to be sorry about that, Mr Watkins,' he thought. 'One of these days – you'll be sorry.'

On Monday, Ted signed his new contract; as a result, Franz and Marta invited him to come and rehearse at their Chelsea flat on Friday at ten a.m.

Like many South Londoners, Ted regarded anywhere north of the river as a foreign country, and it took some time to find his way to the address he had been given.

From Victoria, he travelled by Underground to Sloane Square, then continued on foot along the King's Road. He turned off, looking for Sloane Avenue, but soon got lost in the maze of narrow streets and had to ask the way. A passing milkman with a horse and cart gave him directions; at the kerb, the horse waited patiently, gazing at Ted with a patronising air – he suspected it knew its way round Chelsea better than he did.

By the time he reached the Neumanns' flat, he was out of breath and late for his appointment. He began by apologising.

'Sorry, I took the wrong turning. This part of London's all new to me.'

'That's all right. Come in, let me take your coat,' said Marta, helping him off with his mackintosh. 'You must make yourself at home, please.'

A lock of hair had tumbled over his forehead, and she stroked it back. Her fingers lingered for a moment, as she smiled at him fondly.

'It is good to see you again. When Franz told me you had changed your mind, I was so happy – I cannot tell you! The tour would not have been the same without you.'

The flat was on the first floor of a red-brick mansion block, with spacious, high-ceilinged rooms. Marta led him into the living room; modern furniture was mixed with comfortable, old-fashioned pieces, and on the walls, there was a jumble of pictures – portraits in oils beside modern abstracts and Impressionist landscapes. Signed photos of famous actors and singers jostled for space on the overmantel. Everywhere there were huge vases of flowers; hothouse carnations and lilies made the air heavy with scent.

At the heart of the room stood a grand piano. Franz rose from the piano-stool to greet Ted, shaking his hand enthusiastically. 'It is good of you to come all this way. We appreciate it, don't we, my darling? We have both been looking forward so much to working with you.'

Without wasting any more time, they began to go through the number, trying it in various keys before settling on one that lay comfortably for both of them. Most of the song would be sung as two separate solos, but on the final chorus, when they sang together, Franz had arranged a duet in harmony. He played Ted his vocal line, teaching him phrase by phrase, for Ted did not read music, and had to learn everything by ear.

After they had run through the number several times, they worked out the basis of a simple dance routine, and before they knew it, it was midday. Ted was sorry when Franz looked at his watch and said, 'Alas, I have to leave you now. I have a luncheon engagement near Covent Garden at one o'clock, with an old colleague of mine from Vienna. But perhaps you and Marta should continue without me. It will be useful, I think, to run through it a few more times and fix it into your heads.'

'And after that we will have a little lunch together. There is plenty of food in the refrigerator – we can make ourselves a picnic!' said Marta, with her eyes sparkling.

Ted was impressed; it was the first time he had met anyone who owned a refrigerator.

When Franz had gone, they sang the number a couple more times. Marta sat at the piano. She was not an expert pianist, and her attempts to hammer out the accompaniment were not very successful. At last she closed the lid of the keyboard and swung round on the stool, laughing.

'I think it is better we go through it without the piano!' she said. 'We will try it once more – unaccompanied – and this time we shall see if we can remember the dance.'

As they sang, they managed to piece the steps together fairly well; at the end they did a fast double-chassée, ending with a pirouette from Marta, before she fell into Ted's arms, the way they had rehearsed it.

'Wonderful!' she smiled up at him, as he was holding her. 'You move very well.'

She remained in his arms and suddenly – unexpectedly – she kissed him. It was not a playful kiss, but a real one, full on the mouth. When he could speak, he asked: 'What was that for?'

'Nothing . . . I just felt like it.' She tossed back her red curls. 'Why do you look surprised? You're a very attractive man.'

'You're very attractive too,' he said, clumsily disengaging himself. 'Do you think we ought to run through the dance once more?'

'I think we've done enough work for one day,' she said softly. 'Don't you have a proverb about all work and no play?'

She kissed him again, and this time her hands began to move slowly down, deliberately arousing him. He was growing excited; he knew that this was more than a simple flirtation, and his body was responding to her already. He thought of Daff, but she was a long way away – and besides, this had nothing to do with love. It was only a kind of game – he wouldn't be seriously cheating Daphne, would he, if he let himself give way to temptation?

Struggling with his conscience, he said, 'We shouldn't be doing this.'

'We knew this was going to happen.' She breathed the words in his ear. 'I knew the first minute I saw you . . . It's what we both want, isn't it?'

'But what about Franz? He trusts us. It isn't right to take advantage of – of—'

Even as he spoke, his hands were stroking her breasts, and she purred with pleasure. 'Oh, my darling. Franz knows very well what we are doing. He knew it when he left us alone together – and he doesn't mind at all.'

He drew back, staring at her. 'But he loves you!'

'Yes. Dear Franz, he wants me to be happy, you see. He still loves me, even when I go with other men. He's a strange person – he doesn't care.'

Ted did not know whether he believed her or not, but he felt a sudden chill – a sense of shame. For the second time, he withdrew from her embrace.

'I'm sorry,' he said. 'I think I ought to go.'

'But why? We're about to have some lunch – I will open a bottle of wine. Of course you must stay!'

'I can't. You see, my wife's a strange person, too. She *does* care.'

Marta raised an eyebrow. 'Ah, what a pity. But please don't worry – I'm sure we can still work together very happily. Only next time we rehearse, I shall make sure that Franz stays with us all the time – then you won't be embarrassed, will you, my darling?'

Before the tour began, they had two more rehearsals at Sloane Avenue; Franz was present all the time, and under his guidance the duet took shape. The atmosphere was relaxed, and when they played their first date at Shepherds Bush, it went like clockwork and was the hit of the show.

Ted admired Marta's professional skill. She treated him exactly the same, though he thought he detected a gentle mockery behind her smile which had not been there before. On and offstage, she remained a perfect partner.

After Shepherds Bush, they had a week at the Croydon Empire. This was their nearest date to Upper Norwood, so Ted told Daphne she must come to the second house on Saturday night, and bring Annie.

'Couldn't we come to the first house?' she shrugged. 'Otherwise it makes it so late.'

'But then you'd have to go home on your own afterwards,' Ted pointed out. 'After the second house, we can all travel back together. It won't hurt Annie to stay up late for once. We'll make it a real family party. Let's see, how many tickets should I book? You, Annie, Mum – and Val wants to come.'

'She did say something about bringing Gerry, if he isn't working.'

'Oh right, then we'd better ask Babs as well. She'll be very hurt if she thinks she's been left out.'

'She might not want to. She seems to be going out with Walter Faber an awful lot these days. You don't suppose there's anything – you know – serious between them, do you?'

'Good Lord, no! He's old enough to be her father . . . Do you think we ought to invite him along too? No – I can't quite see him enjoying a night at the Croydon Empire, somehow.' Ted began to add up on his fingers. 'I make that six tickets altogether.'

At least the journey home from the theatre was easy enough. The Empire was only a stone's throw from West Croydon station, and from there Ted could catch a train to Anerley each night, and walk up the hill. As the show was twice nightly – six o'clock and eight-thirty – he had to get his costume and make-up off quickly in order to catch the last train, and he never got indoors before half-past eleven.

When he returned on Wednesday night, Daphne and Kate were still up – and so was Ray Duke, who was having a cup of cocoa before he went to bed.

'How did it go?' Daphne asked, as she always did.

'Fine. Audiences are picking up every night – word-of-mouth's getting around. By the time you come on Saturday, we should have the House Full boards out.'

'Oh, that reminds me – Val dropped in earlier. She says Gerry's working this weekend, after all – isn't is a shame? Will you be able to get rid of his ticket, do you think?'

'I might. Anyow, I persuaded the manager to let me have comps, so it won't cost us anything.'

Kate cleared her throat, then said anxiously, 'I do think it's a pity, though. I mean, without Gerald, we're going to be all women . . .'

'What's wrong with that?' asked Daphne, amused.

'Well, it's not very nice, is it?' Kate tried to explain. 'Women going out on their own, at night. I know you'll think I'm silly, but—'

Ray Duke broke in. 'If there's a free ticket going, I don't mind taking Gerald's place. I'll be the man of the party, if you like.'

They all looked at one another, and Daphne said carefully, 'It's very good of you to offer, but I don't think so. Thank you all the same.'

'Why not?' Ray challenged her. 'Is there any reason I shouldn't go?'

'It might be rather awkward. You see, Babs is coming with us, and – well, you know how she feels about meeting you.'

Ray began to argue. 'You can explain to her, can't you? I wouldn't do anything to upset her.'

Ted took charge of the situation. 'It's not only Babs – I feel the same way. Let's not beat about the bush. I've already asked you to find somewhere else to live. I want you out of this house – and I don't want you taking my family out on Saturday night. Is that clear enough?'

Ray bridled. 'I wouldn't do anything wrong. What sort of person d'you think I am?'

'You wouldn't like it if I told you,' Ted answered. 'Now why don't you toddle off to bed and leave us to sort this out for ourselves?'

'I see.' Ray put down his empty cocoa cup with a clatter. 'Thanks for telling me – thanks very much. Now I know where I stand.' Pale and tight-lipped, he rose from the table and walked out of the room.

Ted groaned. 'I know, Mum – don't tell me. I shouldn't have said anything . . . Well, I'm sorry, but he really gets my goat.'

'No, dear, you were probably right.' Kate sighed. 'It wouldn't have done, him coming with us – not with Babs there and everything. But I've had an idea. Don't take back the extra ticket. I know someone who might like to go. I'll ask Mr Colpoys; it will make a nice change for him.'

Marta had the closing spot on the bill. She looked lovelier than ever, in an emerald-green dress that set off her gorgeous red hair; from the front, it seemed to be quite plain, with a deep neckline that followed the curve of her breasts – but when she turned her back the audience gasped. Beneath the long shoulder-straps, it was cut so low, she seemed to be half-naked, her beautiful back exposed almost to the end of her spine.

Daphne, whose face was already set in an expression of polite interest, dug her fingernails into her palms, but she had to admit it – Marta Linden had star quality.

She sang a selection of well-contrasted songs – some old musical-comedy favourites, some recent hits, a brief serenade in German, from a Lehàr operetta – and the audience adored her.

Then, when it seemed that the show was about to end, she played her trump card. After her display of bravura technique, she changed her personality altogether. Slipping on a ridiculous frilly apron over that sophisticated gown, she became a shy young bride – and beckoned her equally shy young groom to join her on stage.

Bashfully, Ted stepped out from the wings, and held her hand; together, they launched into *Tea For Two*.

First she sang – then he sang – and then they went into their dance, demurely tapping their toes in time to that captivating rhythm, and miming the events of their newly-wed routine. Getting up in the morning, stretching and yawning – then she baked an imaginary cake in an imaginary oven and presented it to her delighted spouse, who carried it off in triumph, cutting it into imaginary slices and distrib-uting them among the musicians in the orchestra pit . . . Then they did another reprise in harmony – and at last the tempo quickened, and they began dancing faster and faster, until the whirlwind finish when she tumbled joyfully into his arms, and the audience went wild, stamping and shouting and demanding an encore.

In the front row of the dress circle, Daphne wore a bright smile as she joined in the applause.

Mr Colpoys turned to her, saying, 'Your husband is a first-class performer' – and Kate leaned across to add, 'That young woman's very good. They go well together, don't they?'

'Yes,' replied Daphne, through clenched teeth. 'Very well indeed.'

On a wooden bench at the back of the gallery, Ray Duke decided he had had enough. He never enjoyed these theatrical shows anyhow, and now that some of the cinemas were showing talking pictures, he couldn't understand why anyone wasted good money on rubbish like this. Soon after he moved into Sackville Road, he had been to see *The Jazz Singer* . . . Well, who'd bother to listen to Ted Watt, when they could go and hear Al Jolson?

Ignoring the applause, he slipped away, running down several flights of echoing stone stairs. He had come here for one reason and one reason only; up to now, the evening had been a dead loss – but it wasn't over yet.

A few minutes later, the audience began to stream out of the theatre, but the Watkins family party were not ready to leave. Ted had told them to go into the Stalls Bar and wait there for him; it stayed open after the show, so the artistes could drop in for a well-earned drink before they went home.

Mr Colpoys had not expected this, and he looked anxious. 'Oh dear, I told the driver to meet us outside the theatre at the end of the performance. If we're not there, he may think he's missed us.'

When Kate invited Mr Colpoys to join them, he had been a little anxious at first, since he disliked crowds, but once she had persuaded him that they would be quite a small party, he began to look forward to it.

The original plan had been to travel to West Croydon by tram, and come back with Ted on the last train, but when Kate explained this to Mr Colpoys, he put forward another suggestion.

'Why don't we hire a car to take us there and bring us back?' he asked. 'I hope you will allow me to foot the bill – it will be my contribution to the evening's entertainment.'

This was a great treat. When the chauffeur-driven Daimler picked them up at Sackville Road, several of the neighbours came out to see them off, and Kate said, 'I feel like we're the King and Queen!'

There was plenty of room in the limousine. One passenger sat next to the driver, and three in the luxurious back seat. Facing them were two folding seats, making space for six people altogether. On the return journey, Annie would sit on Ted's lap.

But Mr Colpoys had not allowed for any delay after the performance.

'Stupid of me – I should have realised that Mr Watkins needs time to wash and change.'

'And he might feel like a drink before we go,' Daphne added.

'Ah yes, quite.' Mr Colpoys fidgeted for a few moments, then said: 'I'd better have a word with the chauffeur. It would be very unfortunate if he went off without us.'

While he was gone, Valerie bought everyone a drink, and they sat round a little table, discussing the show.

'I thought Dad was best,' said Annie loyally, sipping a fizzy lemonade through a straw. 'But I liked the man who made animals out of balloons. It was clever, the way he did it without popping them.'

'And I thought the German girl was marvellous,' said Babs. 'She's got real style, hasn't she?'

'Hasn't she?' said Daphne bravely. 'Only she isn't German – she's Austrian, actually.'

'Well, it's the same thing, isn't it? Oh, here comes Mr Colpoys. Did you manage to find our driver?'

'I explained the situation, and he's promised to wait.' Mr Colpoys took his seat at the table and lit his pipe, looking round him with interest. 'I must say this is very jolly. Do you know, I can't remember the last time I set foot in a theatre?'

'Let me get you a drink,' said Valerie. 'What would you like?'

'Oh no, please, I'll get it.'

He half-rose from his seat, but Val insisted that this was her round, and he finally consented to have a cream sherry. She was on her way back from the bar, when a sudden loud noise made her jump.

'Sorry, I've spilled some,' she apologised, as she handed him the glass. 'Whatever's that terrible racket?'

It was an alarm bell. The barman announced to the customers: 'I'm sorry, ladies and gentleman, I must ask you to leave the building. That's the fire warning. Go out by the exit doors – as quick as you can.'

Dismayed, they all began to move uncertainly towards the door, and Babs asked the barman, 'What's happening?'

'Couldn't tell you, miss. It might be a false alarm – they do have fire-drills sometimes – but we've all got to go outside anyhow.'

'What a nuisance,' she grumbled, as they hurried through the nearest fire-exit.

It led into a narrow side alley, running from the main road to the stage door. One of the theatre attendants stood there, directing them towards the street – but Kate and Daphne did not obey him immediately. Further along the alley there was a row of windows; one of these had been smashed, and they could see smoke pouring out through the broken pane.

Daphne gasped; 'Are those the dressing rooms?'

'Yes, madam. Keep moving, please,' said the attendant. 'Don't block the alley, we're waiting for the fire brigade.'

'But my husband's in the show!' Daphne tried to explain. 'He must still be in there—'

She was about to push past the man, but he stopped her, saying: 'Sorry – I've got my orders. Move along, please – into the street.'

Kate was trembling, but she tried to speak calmly. 'Better do what he says, dear. We'll only be in the way.'

'Yes. Quite so.' Very agitated, Mr Colpoys took Daphne's arm. 'We can't do any good here. I think we should go and wait in the car.'

Valerie was already halfway along the alley, holding Annie's hand. Babs hurried after them, saying to Val, 'Are you all right? You look as if you're going to faint.'

'I can't help it, I'm silly about fire. Take no notice . . . Just make sure Daff's all right, will you?'

By now there were a lot of people coming out of the building, and in the confusion the little group became separated.

Daphne protested fiercely as Kate and Mr Colpoys tried to steer her through the crowd. 'No, I must go back. I must find Ted—'

Her voice was drowned by the strident clanging of a fire engine, then a uniformed fireman came racing along the alley, running out a hosepipe.

'Come away, Daff. Ted will be all right – and you've got Annie to think of,' Kate urged her. 'Leave it to the fire brigade. They know what to do.'

'Dear God – Annie!' Daphne looked round wildly. 'Where is she?'

By now there was chaos in the main road. Two fire engines were blocking the street, holding up traffic, and to add to the confusion more and more people were arriving all the time – Saturday-nig'.t revellers, out on the town, drawn to the scene as if by a magnet.

Unable to see the hired car, Mr Colpoys was afraid it might have gone, then he exclaimed with relief: 'No – there it is, on the other side of the road. Follow me!'

He led the way, but Daphne turned to Kate, asking: 'Where are the others? What's happened to them? I must find Annie . . .'

Annie was perfectly safe. Valerie had already found the car, and they were sitting in the back seat. Val put her arm round the frightened child and tried to conquer her own terror, speaking in a quiet, soothing tone. 'You're all right now, my love. There's nothing to worry about. Mum and Dad will be here soon, then we can all go home. It won't be long now.'

'But where are they?' Annie wanted to know. 'Where's Auntie Babs?'

'I don't know. She can't be far away – she was with us a minute ago.'

Outside the theatre, Babs struggled to make her way through the crowd. 'Let me pass, please. I must get through,' she begged, then choked back a scream as someone took hold of her, pulling her out of the mob and dragging her into a shop doorway.

'I've got you now,' said a man's voice; it was a voice she knew very well. 'You're OK now.'

She looked into Ray's eyes. He was smiling, and although she had sworn to have nothing to do with him – though she knew he was not to be trusted – her heart leaped with joy, and a sudden excitement swept through her.

'What are you doing here?' she asked breathlessly.

'Looking for you – what d'you think?' he retorted. 'That's the only reason I came here tonight, hoping I'd find you.' He held her close to him. 'You're shivering – are you cold?'

'No, I'm not. I was just a bit frightened, that's all.'

He pulled her closer still. 'You've no need to be frightened,' he said. 'Not now that I've got you.'

He was about to kiss her, but she averted her face, saying: 'I must go. I must find out if Ted's all right. They'll be waiting for me.'

'They can go without you,' said Ray. 'I'm taking you home.'

The fire was brought under control very quickly. When Ted joined the party in the Daimler his clothes were dishevelled, his face smudged with floating soot, but he was unhurt. Sitting in the back seat, he told them as much as he could.

'It began in my dressing room, of all places. I was taking my make-up off, and talking to Marta and Franz – he'd got a timetable, looking up the times of the trains, 'cos we're playing Coventry Hippodrome next week – and suddenly there was an almighty crash! Somebody out in the alley chucked a stone at the window. We were too startled to move. Almost at once, something came flying through the broken glass – it looked like a comet – a blaze of light, with a tail of sparks behind it. According to the firemen, it was a bit of old rag that had been set alight. It fell on a chair under the window; I'd left a shirt hanging over the back of it, and the evening paper – they burst into flames right away.'

Kate's hand flew to her mouth. 'How dreadful! What did you do?'

'We made matters worse, because Marta screamed and ran into the passage. Of course we rushed out after her, leaving the door wide open, so that set up a draught. In no time at all, the whole room was blazing.'

'You could have been killed,' said Daphne, then she saw Annie's face and added quickly, 'but you weren't. You're safe and well, so there's nothing to worry about.'

'It's a miracle nobody was hurt. If it had happened while I was onstage with Marta, nobody would have known and the whole theatre could have gone up in flames.'

Kate asked: 'But why would anybody want to do such a terrible thing?'

'Search me . . . I know some people think I'm a lousy comic, but that's taking criticism too far!' He tried to make light of it, but he was obviously shaken. Looking around him, he said, 'Hang on – where's Babs?'

Sitting next to the driver, Mr Colpoys turned round and explained. 'I spoke to her just now and she said we should go on without her. She'd met a friend, who was going to take her home. She said she'll call in and see you tomorrow.'

Val said, 'I wonder if it was Mr Faber? He might have a car . . . Oh well, you won't have to sit on Dad's lap after all, Annie.'

Annie snuggled closer to her father. 'I want to,' she said.

Babs and Ray were not travelling by car. Ray said he'd sooner go back to Crystal Palace by tram.

'But the train's much quicker,' Babs objected.

'The tram's more fun. Let's go up on the top deck.'

She began to argue. 'This time of night? We'll freeze to death!'

'I'll keep you warm,' he promised.

The old trams had no roof. On sunny days, the upper deck was popular with younger travellers – when it rained, a few hardy spirits still braved the elements, for there were tarpaulin covers which fastened across each double seat, clipping into place and covering the passengers up to their chins.

It was not raining tonight, but the April weather was uncertain, and the waterproof covers were still in place. They were the only passengers on the top deck, and Ray chose the seat at the back; he tucked the tarpaulin into position around them, as the tram set off, rattling over the points.

Babs knew what would happen; she knew she should have been firm, and insisted on travelling inside – or refused Ray's invitation altogether and gone home with the family by car – but how could she resist?

Everything conspired against her; the fire-alarm, the sense of panic, the relief when she heard Ted was safe – most of all, her own treacherous desire . . . She had tried to forget Ray and shut him out of her life. Now he was here, and her body ached for him.

Lurching onwards, its wheels singing on the rails, the tall tram clanked and juddered, sending metallic echoes flying through the deserted streets; and all the time Ray kept kissing her, his hands all over her – stroking, tickling, caressing – undressing her . . .

'No – stop—' she gasped. 'We can't – not here – not now—'

'Yes,' he said. 'Now.'

Overhead, the April sky was sprinkled with frosty stars, but she didn't feel the cold night air. Beneath the sheltering tarpaulin, the touch of his nakedness upon hers burned like fire – a fire that scorched and melted her – the fire she had been waiting for, all these years.

'Yes . . .' She whispered. 'Yes. *Now* . . .'

The following day, Babs sat in her bedroom composing a letter.

Belmont,
Crystal Palace Park Road

Sunday, 8 April, 1928

Dearest Walter,

This is a very difficult letter for me to write, as you have always been so kind and I do not want to hurt you. I only put pen to paper now, because there is no other way.

Some time ago, when you were making plans for the future, you told me that you hoped to include me in those plans, and you asked me a question. I did not give you my answer then, as I needed time to think.

Now I have reached a decision, and I am sorry to have to say that my answer must be no.

It is not just because of the difference in our ages, though that would have been a problem – and one that might have become worse as the years went by. It is because I have searched my conscience, and I must tell you frankly that although I am very fond of you, I do not love you in the way you love me. In the light of this, it would not be right for us to marry. I could never be the kind of wife you deserve.

I shall always be grateful for your goodness and generosity, and think of you with deep affection, but in time I believe you will agree I am doing the right thing. I am sure you will find someone more suitable, and I wish you every happiness.

Under these circumstances, I think it would be better for us not to meet again. Please do not try to see me or reply to this letter, as the result could only be painful to both of us.

With many thanks once again, and all good wishes,

Yours sincerely, Barbara Glynn (Babs).

She read it through, making minor corrections to spelling and punctuation, then put it into an envelope, stamped it, and took it along to the pillar box. It would not go till the first collection on Monday now, but that didn't matter; it wasn't particularly urgent.

Once that was out of the way, she felt quite light-hearted, and strolled on until she reached Sackville Road, where she found Valerie and Daphne in the kitchen.

'How's Ted?' she asked. 'He's all right, is he?'

'Yes, he had a good night's sleep, and today he's as bright as a button,' said Daphne. 'He's upstairs, packing. They're going up to Coventry this evening, because they've got a bandcall at the theatre first thing tomorrow. I'll run up and tell him you're here.'

'Don't bother, I'll see him presently.' Babs sat down, crossing her legs. 'I'm glad you're both here; I've got something to tell you.'

Valerie smiled. 'Would that be something to do with Mr Faber? You saw him last night, didn't you?'

'I did not!' Babs was astonished. 'What made you think that?'

'Mr Colpoys said you'd met a friend who was going to see you home and we thought it must be Walter Faber, didn't we, Daff?'

'It wasn't him. It was Ray . . . We came home together on the tram.'

'Ray Duke?' exclaimed Daphne. 'You met him in Croydon?'

'Wasn't it extraordinary? He'd been to see the show, and I bumped into him, in the middle of the fire engines and all that . . . And we had a talk.' Glancing across at Valerie, she broke off. 'What's the matter?'

Valerie's expression had changed. All at once she seemed to have grown older; her face was deeply lined as she said flatly, 'I don't believe it. After all the things you told us – how you never wanted to see him again, how he was wicked and evil—'

'Yes, I know what I said, but I was wrong, wasn't I? Mummy was right, and Aunt Eth. They told me he'd changed. They said if I met him, I'd see for myself. Well, last night I did meet him – and he has changed. He's learned his lesson, and he deserves a second chance.'

'What do you mean by that?'

'Is he upstairs? Yes, he's probably packing as well. When we got home to Belmont last night, Mummy was sitting up, waiting for me, like she always does. We talked it over, the three of us. So now he's moving back; I've been getting his room ready for him. Well, since Ted told him to clear out, it seems the best plan, don't you agree?' She stood up. 'I think I'll just go up and give him a hand.'

When Babs had gone, Valerie repeated slowly, 'I don't believe it. She *knows* what he's like – how can she be such a fool? Daff?'

Daphne, who had been lost in thought, looked up. 'I'm sorry, I was thinking about something else. Do you remember, when Walter Faber sacked Ray all those years ago – there was a fire at the furniture shop, soon afterwards? A fire that started with someone throwing lighted rags through a window?'

Val stared at her. 'You think – Ray Duke?'

'I don't know. But we do know he was at the theatre last night – *and* he had a row with Ted last week.'

For a long time, they sat and looked at one another.

That night, he lay in bed, in the little room with flowered wallpaper and lace curtains and the washbasin with rosebuds; he was feeling pretty good.

Rolling on to his back, he enjoyed the feel of cool, clean sheets against his skin. He hadn't bothered to put on pyjamas. Babs would be here any minute now; the old ladies had all retired to bed long ago. He chuckled with quiet satisfaction, stroking himself gently.

In the end, it had been so easy. He'd got Babs where he wanted her. Poor bitch, she'd been dying for it . . . Of course, he'd have to be careful. The old girls would turn nasty if they tumbled to what was going on – but as long as he minded his p's and q's and went to church now and again like a good boy, he'd have them eating out of his hand.

He'd been through a bloody awful time – five years of hell – he'd gone down deep in the shit, but he'd come up smelling of rosebuds. And what they said was true – it *had* taught him a lesson. He'd learned a lot during those five years; he'd learned to be more careful in future. This time he wasn't going to make any mistakes. This time he'd do it right.

He heard the sound of the door opening and closing, and the rustle of Babs' nightdress as she tiptoed across the carpet.

'Come on in, baby,' he said softly. 'I'm all ready for you.'

BOOK THREE

1930–1936

Chapter Twenty

STEVE GUNN WOKE up in total darkness. For a moment he could not think where he was, but then he recognised the continual drumming of the airship's engines, and heard the gongs sounding: that was the signal for the engines to go slow.

Switching on the light above his bunk, he looked at his watch. Nearly two in the morning – time for him to go forward and take his turn of duty. He struggled to his feet and pulled on his trousers, which wasn't easy – like all the crew's quarters on the R101, the two-berth cabin was small and cramped. The upper bunk was empty; he guessed that Savory would be glad to change places and get his head down for a few hours.

He made his way along the narrow, swaying passage. The vibrations coming up through the matting beneath his feet told him that the ship was rocking, struggling in a stormy wind.

In the after engine-car, Savory greeted him gloomily. 'What a night . . . Did you get any sleep at all?'

'Yes – why not? What's been going on?'

'Oh, just a headwind blowing great guns – they had the devil of a job to keep us on course. And as if that wasn't enough, one of the engines packed up in mid-Channel, but we got her going again. Gawd knows how you managed to sleep through that little lot!'

The lights flashed and dimmed, and Steve exclaimed, 'Hello! Now what's wrong?'

'They just reduced speed. That means cutting down electrical power all through the ship.'

'But can they keep the revs up? What's the oil-pressure?'

Then, without any warning, the engine-car seemed to roll over; the two men clutched at the wall to steady themselves.

'Christ almighty, she's going into a dive!'

As the airship dipped sharply, an emergency signal came through to reduce speed altogether, but before they could do anything, there was a sudden thud, sending a shudder through the entire ship.

'Blimey, we've landed!' gasped Steve.

They seemed to bounce, rising up again for a few seconds, then falling back. This time the impact was much harder, and above the din of alarm-bells and the roar of the engines, they heard the harsh metallic scream of tearing metal, and a series of deafening explosions.

Perhaps Steve hit his head, because he could not remember anything very clearly after that – only blinding flashes all around him, and then a great eruption of dazzling light and scorching heat as the fire leaped out at him from all sides, and the great airship turned to flame.

*

> 'Nearer, my God, to Thee, nearer to Thee.
> E'en though it be a cross that raiseth me;
> Still all my song shall be
> Nearer, my God, to Thee, nearer to Thee!'

The congregation sang the hymn lustily, with Annie's sweet, clear treble high above the others in the pew; beside Daphne, Val and Kate made up a little family group. Valerie rarely attended All Saints these days, and Daphne had been quite surprised to see her in church. She gave no explanation, simply saying with a quick, meaningless smile, 'Oh, I just felt like it, that's all.'

She seemed very tense, and Daphne guessed that something was wrong – perhaps Val's marriage was going through a difficult time – but she said nothing. It was none of her business, after all. If their roles had been reversed – if Val had asked about her relationship with Ted – she would have found such questions very hard to answer.

Kate was screwing up her eyes to peer at the hymnal; the print was so small, it was hard to make out the words.

> 'There let my way appear – steps unto Heav'n
> All that Thou sendest me, in mercy giv'n;
> Angels to beckon me – nearer, my God, to Thee . . .'

*

She realised that Val, at her side, was no longer singing, and glanced at her to see what was the matter. Val was staring straight ahead, her eyes fixed on the altar; her face was pale, and she looked very anxious.

'What's wrong, love?' Kate asked, under cover of the singing.

'Nothing, Mum. I'm fine.'

'Are you feeling faint? Do you think you ought to sit down?'

'Honestly, Mum, I'm perfectly all right,' snapped Val, then, realising she had spoken harshly, she added: 'It's this hymn. It's the one they sang on the *Titanic* before it went down. I've always hated it, ever since.'

Kate clicked her tongue sympathetically, and squeezed her hand.

Val bit her lip hard; if Mum was too nice to her, she might break down and make a fool of herself. She tried to concentrate on the service, but her mind kept going back to Steve.

Ever since she had read the news item in yesterday's paper, about the R101 going on its maiden voyage from Cardington, she had felt certain that he would be on board, as a member of the crew.

It had been bad enough last year; the papers were full of it then – that had been the R101's test flight, when the great ship took to the air for the first time, floating from Bedfordshire and circling over London, crossing the Thames. Val had stood outside the Crystal Palace with hundreds of other people, watching the silver ship sailing across the sky. She could remember the old-fashioned airships during the war – long and thin, like cigars, they had proved to be unwieldy and out of proportion – but the R101 was proudly curved, and seemed to be the perfect shape. Everyone else had exclaimed with admiration at the magnificent spectacle; nearly seven hundred and fifty feet long, yet it looked like a child's toy as it floated serenely overhead.

But Val had not cheered and laughed and waved like the others; an icy fear had gripped her. She could think of nothing but Steve, somewhere up there in the engine-car, and her heart nearly stopped beating as she imagined the mighty ship breaking up, crashing to earth . . . It wasn't safe – it couldn't possibly be safe . . .

Yet she had been worrying over nothing; the R101 had concluded her trial run without a hitch and returned safely to Cardington. A month later, she had set off on a more ambitious trip; a thousand-mile cruise over the whole of the British Isles, and that too had been a huge success.

And last night she had begun her first commercial voyage; across the Channel, across Europe, and further still – a round trip to Karachi and back again. All Val knew was that the airship had set off some time on Saturday evening; she did not know how far they would have travelled by now, only that she had hardly slept at all last night, and that she had been determined to come to church this morning and say a prayer for Steve's safe return.

That would have been a great comfort, if only the choir hadn't begun that particular hymn . . . *Steps unto Heaven*. She had found herself thinking of the *Titanic* and its victims, drowning in the icy waters of the Atlantic.

Somehow she managed to control herself, and kept back her tears; and at last the morning service ended.

As the choir filed out into the vestry and the organ played, the congregation made its way out of the church. Leaving the porch, Val came face to face with Ray Duke, and her heart missed another beat. For the last two years, she had done her best to avoid him. He was another unhappy link with the past, he was bad luck . . .

'Good morning, ladies,' he said, making a little bow.

'Good morning,' said Daphne, and tried to pass on without stopping.

'Morning, Mrs Watkins.' Ray put a hand out and touched Kate's arm. 'I wonder if you could spare me a minute of your valuable time?'

'I'm afraid we're in rather a hurry,' Daphne broke in. 'We've got to get home and see to the dinner, so if you don't mind—'

'Just a couple of minutes, Mrs Watkins?' wheedled Ray, ignoring Daphne and addressing Kate. 'I wouldn't trouble you if it wasn't important.'

'Well – yes, all right.' Kate threw a nervous look at Daphne. 'Perhaps you'd like to walk part of the way with us, Mr Duke? We can talk as we go.'

'Ta very much.' Ray offered his arm and Kate took it; they strolled together like old friends, and Daphne, Annie and Val were forced to fall in behind them.

'We don't often see you at All Saints, Mr Duke. It's not your regular place of worship, is it?' asked Kate.

'Oh, I come quite often, as a matter of fact – only I generally sit at the back and slip away as soon as the service is over. I'm not one to push myself forward,' he explained modestly. 'But this morning I'd been praying for guidance, and when I saw you coming down the aisle, it seemed like my prayers had been answered. You see, I've been very worried lately, and what I need is some good advice – and

I suddenly thought, you've always been so helpful in the past, you're the person I should ask.'

Daphne and Val exchanged glances; what was he up to this time?

Kate put their thoughts into words, but more kindly. 'Well, if I can be of any help, I'll be only too glad, but what's the trouble?'

'It's embarrassing to have to mention such a thing, but I'm afraid it's what you might call a financial problem,' he replied.

Kate began hastily, 'Oh no, I'm very sorry – I'm afraid I couldn't help you there—'

'No, no, don't misunderstand me, please. I'm not begging for money – perish the thought!' Ray gave a boyish laugh. 'My goodness, no! But I'm out of work again, you see, and I've no regular income. I try to pick up odd jobs here and there, but that's not enough to live on. That's why I need something permanent.'

Kate was perplexed. 'But I thought you were on the ground staff at the Palace?'

'So I was, and as Valerie knows—' he turned his head, giving Val a friendly smile, 'I was very grateful for the work, believe me. But it's what you might call seasonal. Well, that's understandable. You can't blame them – but it makes it hard for chaps like me to get through the winter. I've been looking round for some other post, but times being so hard, there aren't many vacancies. I asked Babs if she could put in a word for me at the Estate Agents, but she said it wouldn't do any good—'

'Hardly surprising, really,' said Daphne, rather sharply. 'Considering what happened the last time you had any dealings with Hawkins and Co.'

Kate was shocked. 'Daphne, really! That's not a very nice thing to say. After all this time, surely we can let bygones be bygones?'

'I doubt whether Hawkins and Co. would see it like that,' retorted Daphne.

'No, well, be that as it may . . .' Ray waved this aside, turning his attention to Kate once more. 'That's why I was wondering if you knew anyone who might need to take on extra staff? I'm ready to turn my hand to most things, and I'm not afraid of hard work.'

'I'm sorry, I really am,' said Kate. 'But I don't know anybody like that. I wish I did.'

'Ah. I hope you didn't mind me asking, did you? I thought it was worth a try. I'm determined to leave no stone unturned, as the saying goes. And if you should get any bright ideas, you'll let me know, won't you?' He stopped walking, and glanced at his watch. 'Well, I must love you and leave you – I'm going the other way. Very nice to have met you all. As for you, Annie, you get taller every time I see you. How old are you now?'

'Thirteen,' said Annie. 'In September.'

'My goodness – quite the young lady, eh?' He turned to Daphne. 'And I hope Ted's keeping well?'

'He's very well, as far as I know,' said Daphne coolly. 'He's away on tour again, at the moment.'

'We don't see him often,' Annie chipped in. 'But he sends us postcards from wherever he goes – and he talks to Mum on the telephone sometimes.'

'Yes, but it's not the same as having him at home, is it?' Ray wagged his head sadly at Daphne. 'I'm sure you miss him when he's away . . . Do give him my kind regards, if you happen to be speaking to him.' With that he raised his trilby politely and walked away down Westow Street.

'The nerve of that man!' exclaimed Valerie.

'You mustn't be hard on him; he was only being civil,' said Kate defensively.

Daphne said nothing; but she wished she had not mentioned that Ted was away. There had been a sly look in Ray's eye when he said, 'I'm sure you miss him' – and of course, he was right. Even after all this time, she still hated Ted going off on tour. Last week, the Aston Hippodrome, Birmingham – tomorrow he would be opening at the Opera House, Wakefield, but today . . . She didn't know where he was, or what he was doing.

A hundred and fifty miles away, Ted was travelling by train, somewhere between Birmingham and Wakefield. There was no direct connection – there hardly ever was. Today they would have to change at Sheffield, and they had already waited two hours for a connection at Crewe Junction. When they were on a Sunday train-call, they aways seemed to change at Crewe.

'What time will we get to Wakefield?' Ted asked.

Franz Neumann pulled a timetable from his pocket and tried to consult it, but gave up after a few moments, confessing that he was baffled. Jock Mackay, who partnered his brother Charlie and the lovely Doreen Dobbs, making up the Adagio dance trio known as Juan, Carlos and Dorita, held out a hand.

'Mind if I take a look? I'm mebbe more used to timetables.'

'By all means. I cannot make top or tail of it,' admitted Franz, passing it over.

For a time the carriage was silent. Several of the party were asleep, nodding off to the hypnotic rhythm of the wheels.

'Whatever time we arrive, we shall be late,' sighed Marta, cuddling a little closer to her husband, and smiling at Ted.

He sat facing her across the compartment. After a moment he looked away, watching the flat fields revolving past the windows, like a giant gramophone record on a turntable. Although he had been working with Marta for some time now, and had come to look upon her and Franz as good friends, he still felt uneasy when she smiled like that. Those mocking lips seemed to be amused by some unspoken thought – and her eyes hinted at a secret they shared . . .

Secretly, he still found her amazingly attractive – and she knew it.

On stage, they worked together as well as ever – better, really, since they knew one another so well by now, they were almost telepathic. He could sense the slightest shift in her mood and respond to it – picking up a line a shade quicker here, or lingering for an extra split-second there. On stage they made a perfect couple – charming, funny, romantic – and audiences flocked to see them. Of course they still did their own individual routines, and these were successful too, but the public came to see them together, and their duet was always the high-spot of the show.

Tea For Two had become hackneyed, replaced last year by *Tiptoe Through The Tulips*, and recently they had begun to work on a new number; in identical straw hats and matching bow ties, brandishing dapper walking-canes, they stepped out together to *The Sunny Side Of The Street*.

The tune ran insistently through Ted's brain. Automatically, he went over the moves in his head – hand to the brim of the straw, straighten the bow tie, jaunty salute and step off on the back foot—

'*Just direct your feet – to the sunny side of the street . . .*' Marta breathed the lyric so softly, he could only just catch the thread of sound. He stared at her, shocked and a little unnerved.

'How did you know I was thinking about that?' he asked.

Amused, she replied. 'You were tapping your toes, in tempo – and I recognised the rhythm.'

Franz chuckled. 'Such hard workers, both of you – you even rehearse in the train! Do you never take a rest?'

'Tonight,' said Marta firmly. 'Tonight we shall enjoy ourselves. Why don't we invite Ted to supper at our hotel – and we will not talk about the show at all. For once there will be no rehearsal – agreed?'

'Agreed!' Franz exclaimed happily. 'Ted, you will come to our hotel at nine o'clock – and we will give you the best dinner to be found in Wakefield! What do you say, my friend?'

Ted grinned. 'I say thanks very much. That'll be something to look forward to, provided we get to Wakefield before nine o'clock!'

Jock Mackay looked up triumphantly from the timetable. 'Ten past eight,' he announced. 'That's the time our train's supposed to get in.'

'Then I'll be at your hotel at nine sharp,' Ted told Franz. 'Which one is it?'

Offhand, Franz could not remember the name, but Marta said. 'I'm sure it will be the best, whichever it is. Jock – you know everything. Which is the best hotel in Wakefield?'

Jock looked dubious. 'Are you sure there is a best hotel in Wakefield?' he asked.

Gerald was in the sitting room, listening to the midday news bulletin, while Valerie was dishing up the Sunday dinner in their tiny kitchenette. She carried the tray into the dining room, calling out: 'Dinner's ready!'

'Just a tick, old dear, I'll be with you directly,' he replied.

She began to set out the lamb chops on the plates, adding generous helpings of mashed potato and cabbage, then called again: 'Buck up, Gerry! Don't let it get cold!'

Reluctantly, he switched off the set, and came in to join her. 'Sorry to keep you waiting. I wanted to hear the details – but they don't seem to know much yet.' He sat down, tucking his napkin into his waistcoat. 'They don't even know why it crashed.'

'Why what crashed?' she asked. But even as she said it, she knew. She had known ever since last night.

'The airship – the R101. Didn't you hear?' he said, and went on cutting up his lamb chop.

Time seemed to slow down; she watched as the point of his knife-blade eased the meat from the bone, and cut it again and again into smaller pieces. He pronged a fragment on his fork, and pressed some cabbage and potato on to it, then raised the forkful to his mouth, inch by inch. She went on watching as his lips parted; she noticed the way the hairs of his moustache quivered when he chewed.

With an effort, she forced herself to ask, 'What happened, exactly?'

'Well, as I say, it's all a bit of a mystery so far. Apparently the blooming thing came down for no reason at all – some time last night, they said.'

So it had happened last night – while she was lying awake, imagining such horrors.

'And—' she framed each word separately, with great care, 'was anyone hurt?'

Gerry laughed. 'That's a good one! A damn great airship makes a crash-landing, and you ask if anyone was hurt. They were all killed – well, nearly all of 'em. Fifty-four people on board, and forty-six of the poor devils done for.'

'Oh, God.' She remembered the hymn – the *Titanic* – and managed to say: 'I suppose it came down in the sea – and they drowned?'

'Good Lord, no. They'd got across the Channel by then. They crashed slap-bang into good old terra firma, somewhere near a place called Beauvais. Only eight people survived, and they were all injured in the fire.'

'*Fire?*' The word was almost a whisper.

'Yes, of course. Dammit, what d'you expect? A bloody great balloon, full of gas – down it comes – crash-bang-wallop – something strikes a spark, and the whole thing goes up in a sheet of flame. Nothing left except a lot of twisted metal and charred bodies.'

She thought she was going to faint. Somehow she managed to struggle to her feet and make for the door, as he asked. 'Hey, what's up? Where are you going?'

'Bedroom – have a lie-down. I'm not feeling well.'

'But you haven't touched your dinner—'

'*I don't want any dinner. . .!*' She hung on to the edge of the door, and tried to apologise. 'I'm sorry, I – I'm not hungry. I couldn't eat anything. You carry on. There – there's an apple pie in the oven.'

She went into the bedroom, shut the door, and threw herself face down on the bed.

Gerald looked mildly concerned, but did as he was told and carried on. The lamb chop was very tasty; if she really didn't want anything, he might as well polish off hers as well – it would be a pity to waste it.

Twenty minutes later, wiping his moustache, he entered the bedroom.

'Very good dinner,' he said kindly, patting her shoulder. 'And the apple pie was top-hole. How are you feeling now?'

'Not very good.' Her voice was muffled, her face buried in the pillow.

'Oh dear, sorry about that. I hope you get better soon. I'm afraid I can't stop – got to catch my train, y'know.'

She lifted her head. 'What? Where are you going?'

'Off to work, of course. I'm on duty for the rest of the day – I did tell you.' Then, as he saw the tearstains on her agonised face. 'I say – you've been crying. What's wrong?'

'Nothing. It's toothache – it's hurting rather. I can take an aspirin. I'll be all right.'

'Poor old thing – beastly for you. Anyway, I'd better push off. See you tonight.'

He went out, and when she heard the front door slam, she relaxed. She didn't have to try and hold back the tears any more. She went on crying – on and on – trying to let out her grief, trying to weep away the pain and the fear and the loss.

When she was too exhausted to cry any more, she got up and began to unmake her bed. Then, with some difficulty, she dragged the single mattress across the carpet, through the doorway and into the sitting room, where she laid it on the floor in front of the fireplace. It took a long time; it had been so much easier when there were two of them to carry it.

She drew the curtains and lit the gas fire, and lay on the mattress, and closed her eyes, and thought of him, and tried to believe that he was here beside her, holding her in his arms, but it was no good.

Steve had gone; and she was alone in the world.

'Terrible news about that airship, eh?' said Harry Glynn, with his mouth full of seed-cake.

'Oh yes, dreadful,' Kate agreed. 'We heard about it on the wireless, dinner-time. Those poor men – and poor women too.'

Harry looked surprised. 'I didn't know there were any women on board?'

'No, I meant the wives and mothers at home,' said Kate. 'I know how they must be feeling – I remember what it was like in the war.'

'It was worse in the war,' said Harry. 'They died in their thousands then. Slaughtered like cattle, and all for nothing.'

'I beg your pardon.' Mr Colpoys set down his cup very precisely, in the middle of the saucer. 'It was not for nothing. Those young men gave their lives in order to bring peace to the world, to stop the filthy Huns trampling over Europe—'

'I'm sorry, I don't agree. Don't see the sense in it, myself,' Harry grumbled. 'Whoever heard of a war bringing peace? As soon as they stop fighting, the Governments all sit back and start making plans for the next war. When did a war ever settle anything?'

'You can't be expected to understand.' Mr Colpoys glared at Harry over the top of his gold pince-nez. 'You did not lose a son in the war, so you don't know what you're talking about.'

Kate interrupted quickly. 'Mr Colpoys, would you care for another cup of tea? How about another slice of cake?'

He shook his head, too angry to reply.

It was one of his occasional Sunday afternoon visits, and once again Mr Glynn had dropped in, univited. Kate could never decide whether it was sheer bad luck when their visits coincided, or whether Harry Glynn had worked out which Sundays Mr Colpoys came to tea – but either way, it made life very difficult.

Trying to steer the two old men off this sensitive subject, she went on brightly: 'You'll never guess who I met this morning – young Mr Duke. Do you remember Raymond Duke, Mr Colpoys? He used to be my lodger, in the old days. I think you met him once or twice?'

'I did indeed,' said Mr Colpoys coldly. 'Not long before he was sent to prison for attempted robbery with violence, I believe?'

'Well, yes, but he's a different man now, different altogether,' Kate hastened to explain. 'Going to prison changed his whole life. He's turned over a new leaf – he even goes to church now. That's where we met him.'

'I'm glad to hear it,' said Mr Colpoys, but Harry Glynn broke in.

'Just because he goes to church, that doesn't mean he's a plaster saint,' he objected. 'There's plenty of so-called Christians no better than whited sepulchres. A load of hypocrites, I call 'em.'

'You're not a churchgoer yourself, are you, Mr Glynn?' asked Mr Colpoys, putting the tips of his fingers together. 'No, I thought not. So once again, you do not speak from personal experience, and therefore your views do not carry a great deal of weight.'

'I go to church sometimes – weddings and funerals and suchlike – though I admit I'm not what you'd call regular,' said Harry defensively. 'But I can tell you a thing or two about that young chap. He's a bad lot, through and through.'

'I didn't realise you knew him.' Kate tried to recollect. 'You didn't meet him here, surely?'

'I may have done. I've run across him at various times, various places . . . I won't say I know him well. The things he's done, I prefer to give him a wide berth.'

'But all that's in the past,' Kate argued. 'And I think it's so unfair to condemn him, just because he made some mistakes in his younger days. That's why he can't get a regular job, on account of people are prejudiced. They won't give him a second chance.' She repeated what Ray had said to her this morning, then added in a moment of inspiration. 'Oh, Mr Colpoys, I just thought – I suppose there aren't any vacancies going in your office, are there?'

'I couldn't say. Since my semi-retirement, I don't go in every day myself, and I leave all matters of staffing to the office manager.'

'But if you could just put in a word for Mr Duke. He's so keen to make a fresh start, I'm sure he wouldn't let you down.'

'That's easy enough to say, but leopards never change their spots,' Harry broke in. 'That chap's a wrong 'un, and if you want my opinion, you'll have nothing to do with him. If I were you, I wouldn't touch him with a barge-pole!'

'Quite frankly, Mr Glynn, I am not very interested in your opinion.' Mr Colpoys was becoming more and more irritated. 'You know next to nothing about the young man!'

'I know a darn sight more than you do!' Harry retorted vigorously. 'My landlady's a very good judge of character, and she says he's not to be trusted. There's something wicked and dangerous about him – she knows about things like that, 'cos she's got a kind of second sight.'

'I suppose you mean she claims to be a fortune-teller? Yes, I remember the lady perfectly; she was lucky not to find herself appearing in front of the magistrates,' snapped Mr Colpoys, knocking his pipe out in the ashtray.

'There's no need to take that tone,' growled Harry. 'I'm trying to give you fair warning, not to get mixed up with young Duke. I'm telling you for your own good—'

Mr Colpoys rose to his feet with dignity. 'I prefer to make my own decisions, thank you.' Turning his back on Harry, he addressed his hostess. 'Thank you once more for a very delightful afternoon, Mrs Watkins, and I look forward to seeing you again, under happier circumstances. In the meantime, you may tell Mr Duke to apply to my office. It's possible that there may be an opening for a junior clerk, and I will see to it that he is granted an interview.'

At the end of the afternoon, Kate came down to pour out her tale of woe to her daughter-in-law.

'Oh Daff, it was awful, it really was. Mr Colpoys and your Dad practically had a stand-up fight!'

Daphne smiled. 'They're a bit old for that sort of thing, aren't they? Still, you ought to feel flattered – two men fighting over you.'

'Don't be so daft. It wasn't about me – it was about Mr Duke.'

Daphne's smile disappeared. 'What about him?'

When Kate had told her story, Daphne said, 'I'm afraid I agree with Dad. You're too soft-hearted. You let Ray Duke talk you into things, and he's not to be trusted.'

'I said I'd help him if I could, and now he's going to get an interview – what's wrong with that? I did what I could for him.' Looking round the kitchen, she asked. 'Where's Annie? She's not gone out by herself, has she?'

'She went to tea with Mavis Hillyard, one of her school friends. The Hillyards don't live very far away, just off Oakfield Road, and she's promised to leave there by six, so she'll be home before dark.'

'Well, I just hope she is,' said Kate uneasily. 'There are some funny people about these days . . .'

At the same moment, Mavis Hillyard was saying: 'Oh, come on, Annie. Football's boring – and it's getting late. Mum will be wondering what's happened to us.'

'Just a couple more minutes. I want to see them score another goal,' said Annie.

The two girls had gone for a walk in the grounds of the Crystal Palace; there was a football match in progress on the playing-field, between two teams of local lads. One of the players – a good-looking sixteen-year-old – intercepted a pass, kicking the ball into touch; it rolled off the pitch and finished up almost at Annie's feet. As the teenage boy raced over, she kicked it back to him.

He grinned, and said, 'Thanks!'

'That's all right,' she said. 'You're Tony, aren't you?'

He stared at her. 'How do you know my name?' Then, looking at her carefully, he added: 'I've seen you before somewhere.'

'It was years ago. We were watching the motorbike races – and you bought me a bar of chocolate.'

'Oh yes, I remember now. The day Roger Kirkwood came off his bike—'

His team-mates were getting restless, and someone yelled, 'Dirty devil, getting off with young girls. Ought to be ashamed of yourself!'

'Shut your face!' Tony shouted pleasantly, then, to Annie: 'Anyhow, nice to see you. Goodbye now.' Dribbling the ball, he loped back to resume the game.

Mavis, who was very impressed but determined not to show it, said primly, 'You shouldn't talk to strangers – it's not safe.'

'He's not a stranger – I know him. He's sort of a friend of the family – that's why I was watching him.'

'Well, we can't stop any longer. Mum said not to be late for tea. Come on!'

As they walked away, down the path towards the Thicket Road gate, Annie kept looking back over her shoulder; Even at this distance, she could still pick out Tony's tall, athletic figure. He seemed to stand out from all the rest.

Fifteen minutes later, when the match ended, Tony's team had won by three goals to two. They ran off the pitch in high spirits, whooping and jeering at their opponents.

In the changing-hut, the toilet facilities consisted of one lavatory, one washbasin, and one shower-stall. As there was no hot water, most of the players preferred to wait till they got home and could run a hot bath, but Tony always took a shower.

When he emerged, Joe – the team captain – was waiting for him, and as Tony towelled himself dry, Joe offered him a cigarette.

'Have a fag – oh, sorry. You don't, do you?' As Tony began to get dressed he perched on one of the wooden benches, blowing out a cloud of smoke and saying: 'You played a great game, Tone. Carry on like that, they'll be signing you up for the Palace one of these days.'

'Get away with you!' Tony aimed a mock-punch at him. 'Pull the other one, eh?'

'No, honest – I mean it.' Dropping his voice, because the last players were still making their way out, Joe added: 'Between you and me, I wasn't sure you'd turn out this afternoon, but I was bloody glad when you did.'

'What d'you mean? I said I'd be here, didn't I?'

'Yes, but – you know, after what happened . . .' His voice trailed off awkwardly. 'I thought you mightn't feel like it.'

Tony frowned. 'What are you talking about?'

'Well, didn't you tell me once that your brother worked at that airship place? Or has he left there now?'

'No, he's still on the R101. He's one of the engineers, in the crew – why?'

'You mean to say you didn't hear it on the wireless, dinner-time?'

'We haven't got a wireless. What the hell are you on about?'

'Jesus – you really don't know.' Joe wasn't much older than Tony; at seventeen, he found emotional crises difficult to handle, and his face flushed as he blurted out: 'Sit down, mate. I've got to tell you something – and I don't know how . . .'

*

Valerie was afraid to listen to the news bulletin, yet she knew she must. She had to learn the details, even if it meant hearing Steve's name read out among the list of those who had been killed.

She made herself turn the set on, and sat rigidly, waiting for the valves to warm up. At last the loudspeaker crackled into life, and she heard Gerry's voice reading aloud.

'Yesterday evening, the airship R101 left Cardington on her first inter-continental flight to Karachi, carrying sixteen passengers and a crew of forty-eight. The flight began well, and at a quarter to eleven last night, the airship left the British coast near Hastings, crossing the Channel and reaching the Pointe de San Quentin in France at approximately thirty-five minutes past midnight.'

Somehow it made it seem worse, listening to the report of the accident in Gerry's impersonal, dispassionate tones.

'Keeping on a south-easterly course, heading towards Paris, the R101 remained in radio-communication with Croydon Airport, saying that the ship was behaving well, and that there was nothing untoward to report. She passed over Beauvais about two a.m., apparently flying unusually low, and a few miles south of the city the ship struck the crest of a low hill. Fire broke out immediately and within a few moments the R101 was engulfed in flame and completely destroyed.'

Valerie closed her eyes, clasping her hands tightly to try and keep them from shaking.'

'Most of those on board are presumed to have been killed instantly; among them were Lord Thomson, Secretary of State for Air, and Sir Sefton Brancker, the Director of Civil Aviation, together with the Director of Airship Development, and the designer of the airship. Of the fifty-four men on board, only eight are alive – all of them members of the crew. The survivors have been taken to the nearest hospital in Beauvais; several of them in a very critical condition.'

'His Majesty the King has sent a telegram to the Prime Minister to express his deep sympathy—'

Valerie turned off the wireless and stood up. Moving slowly and carefully she put on her hat and coat, and left the flat. It was late afternoon, and the sky outside was growing dark and looked as if it were threatening rain, but she did not bother about an umbrella. She had not far to go.

She walked to Upper Norwood and made her way to Church Road, then rang the bell of the flat over the greengrocers shop.

For a few moments nothing happened, and she rang again. There had to be somebody at home – they couldn't all be out, surely? Then she heard footsteps on the stairs, and the door was opened by Steve's father.

'Oh, it's you.' He stared at her, bemused, as if he couldn't understand what was happening.

'I had to come,' she said. 'I just heard the news—'

He interrupted her, saying heavily, 'You'd better come in' – and led the way upstairs.

Freda Gunn was sitting at the centre table, gazing blindly at the lace cloth. She looked up as Valerie entered the room, but her expression did not change.

'I'm sorry. I know I've no right to come here, but I heard the news on the wireless—' began Val.

'We haven't got a wireless set. We didn't know anything about it, until we had a telephone call . . . All the way from France, it was.' Freda's eyes were clouded with shock and bewilderment. 'When I picked up the phone, I thought at first it was a wrong number – we often get them. I couldn't make it out. There was this French chap ringing us up from some hospital – I've forgotten the name of the place—'

'Beauvais?' suggested Val.

'It might have been. I was in such a state, I don't really remember. He spoke quite good English, considering, but it was hard to make out all the words. He said there'd been a disaster – that's what he said, a great disaster. The airship had crashed and most of them on board was killed; only some were fortunate. A few had been taken to hospital, he said, but not many.'

'Eight, out of fifty-four,' said Val quietly. 'And they were all members of the crew. That's why I came to ask if you'd heard anything about Steve.'

'It was Steve that asked the Frenchman to telephone. He's got very bad burns on his hands and legs – but he's alive. He's going to be all right.'

Then she opened her arms to Valerie, and they embraced one another.

Alfred Gunn, hovering near the fireplace, cleared his throat and said huskily, 'You're the first person we've told. Dad's up in his room, having his afternoon nap, and Tony's out playing football.'

As he spoke, they heard the front door bang, and running footsteps on the stairs. Tony burst into the room, breathless and very pale.

'Mum – I just heard! Joe said it was on the wireless – he said the airship's crashed, and everybody was killed—'

'Not everybody, son,' said his father. 'Steve's in hospital. He'll be coming home as soon as he's fit to travel.'

Tony's legs seemed to give way under him, and he collapsed into a chair. The relief was so great, he began to cry, hiding his face with his hands, ashamed that anyone should see a sixteen-year-old man in tears.

But by now Freda and Val were crying, too – and laughing at themselves for being so silly, rejoicing over the little miracle that had turned their own tragedy into joy.

'He'll be so glad when he hears you came round,' sniffed Freda, fumbling for the handkerchief she kept tucked inside her sleeve. 'You still love him, don't you?'

'Yes.' Val couldn't pretend any longer. 'Of course I do.'

'Can I tell him you'll see him, when he comes home?'

She hesitated for a split second. At a moment like this, what else could she say?

'Of course I will,' she said.

It had been a pretty good supper, Ted thought, as the aged waiter in the grillroom cleared away the cheeseboard. Not a very good supper, and certainly not a perfect one – the roast chicken was overcooked and the potatoes were underdone – but for a small hotel in Wakefield, and on a Sunday night too, it wasn't too bad at all.

Marta tipped up her wineglass, letting the last drops trickle on to her tongue.

'I think the staff are becoming impatient,' she said. 'Perhaps it is time for us to leave.'

Looking round the room, Ted realised they were the last customers. He began folding his napkin, saying, 'Yes, it's getting late. I ought to be going myself.'

'Oh, not yet!' Franz wouldn't hear of it. 'We haven't had our coffee. No meal is complete without coffee.'

'But if they want to close up—'

'A little earlier, I requested them to serve coffee upstairs, in our room,' Franz told him. 'And I have a bottle of very good brandy there, to accompany it. Everything is arranged.'

They had already had a good deal to drink; cocktails in the bar beforehand, white and red wine with the meal. As they left the table, Ted had the pleasant sensation that he was floating a few inches above the ground. On their way out, the old waiter bowed and grovelled as Franz pressed a tip into his hand.

It was not a large hotel, but it had some pretensions to luxury; there was even an old-fashioned lift to save the guests the trouble of walking up the stairs. While they were clanking and rattling slowly up to the second floor. Franz suddenly exclaimed: 'My God – I almost forgot! I promised I would take the band-parts to the theatre. It will save time tomorrow if the band have their music all ready for them, in the pit.'

When they reached the bedroom, he went straight to a battered suitcase, marked with his initials, saying to Ted, 'You will forgive me if I slip away for ten or fifteen minutes? The theatre is not too far from here.'

'Will there be anyone there, this time of night?' asked Ted.

'Oh, certainly. The stage crew will be busy getting our scenery in and setting up for the week.'

'Tell you what – why don't I take the band-parts round for you?' Ted offered. 'That'll save you having to turn out. If I go now, I can drop them in on the way back to my digs.'

Franz shook his head. 'You are very kind, but I have to see to it myself. I must have a word with the stage manager, to explain a few important details. Besides, you can't possibly leave yet – you haven't had your coffee.' He pulled on his homburg and his overcoat with the velvet collar, then picked up the suitcase.

'I shall see you later, my dear,' he said cheerfully, as he went out. 'Marta will look after you.'

'I will do my best,' said Marta. As the door closed behind him, she turned to Ted. 'Sit down, my dear. Make yourself comfortable, please.'

'Well, OK – but I mustn't stay long.' Ted glanced around. 'Looks like there's only one armchair.'

'That's all right, I shall sit on the bed. But first I will pour you some coffee – and some brandy.'

The tray of coffee was already waiting on a side table, along with the brandy bottle. She poured two cups of coffee, then sighed. 'I am so sorry – it seems we must drink our brandy from the glasses in the bathroom. They are not very elegant, but that cannot be helped. Excuse me for one moment, while I fetch them.'

She went through a door at the other end of the room, shutting it behind her, and Ted sipped his coffee. It had been standing for some time and was not very hot, and it was probably made from coffee essence, but he drank it anyway. He noticed that there were only two cups on the tray; the waiter who brought it had made a mistake.

After a few minutes had passed, it struck him that Marta was taking rather a long time to fetch the glasses.

When she returned, he realised why; she had changed out of her dress and was now wearing a smart silk dressing gown. He also noticed that she had put on a little more perfume.

She poured two liberal measures of brandy into the two sturdy glasses, and passed one across to Ted. Clinking their glasses together, she said, 'I shall drink to you and you will drink to me. Long life and happiness to both of us.'

'And to Franz,' said Ted. 'Don't you think we really ought to wait for him?'

'No, I don't think so. He may be some time.'

Ted tried the brandy. Franz was right – it was very good, smooth but powerful. He felt a warm glow creeping through him.

'Only two glasses,' he said. 'By the way, I noticed there are only two coffee-cups as well.'

'That will be all right; don't worry about it.'

Marta settled herself on the floor, sitting on the carpet near his feet. She tossed back her red curls, smiling up at him above the rim of her glass, then rested one hand on his knee.

'Dearest Ted,' she said softly. 'I have been looking forward to this moment ever since the day I met you.'

He blinked, trying to clear his misty brain. 'Hey – just a minute,' he protested, half-laughing, but half-serious. We mustn't be silly. Franz will be coming back soon—'

'No, he won't. He won't be back for a long, long time.'

'Yes, but . . .' Her hand was sliding gently along his thigh, caressing him. 'This isn't right. He's your husband – and he's my friend.'

'Of course he is. That is why he has left us alone together. Don't you understand yet, my angel? He told you – everything has been arranged.'

She put down her glass, and began to unfasten her dressing gown. As it fell open, he saw that she was naked beneath it. A sudden surge of breathless excitement took him by surprise, and she murmured: 'Yes . . . You feel the same way. I knew you would.'

He struggled to control himself, but it was impossible, and he said, 'We shouldn't do this. It's all wrong—'

'How can it be wrong, when we want it so much? And it is what Franz wants for us, also.'

'But that's impossible—'

'Listen, my darling. Franz is my husband. I love him very much, and he loves me too – but not with a complete love, not like this.' She let the dressing gown slip down from her shoulders. 'I have to tell you a secret. He is not like other men; many years ago he was very ill, and now – sexually, he is a cripple. But he understands that I have my own needs, and he wants me to be happy. That is why he asked you to come here tonight, so you can make me happy.'

Kneeling up, she continued to arouse him; gently, skilfully, unbuttoning and undressing him.

'Don't you want me to be happy?' she whispered, leaning closer.

He reached out, taking her slim, beautiful body in his hands, stroking her breasts . . . Suddenly, everything seemed perfectly simple. Suddenly, it was wonderfully easy to make everyone happy . . .

Everyone except Daphne – and she would never know.

Chapter Twenty-one

ON FRIDAY AFTERNOON, Babs had to stay late at Hawkins & Co; there had been an error in the accounts, and nobody was allowed to go home until it had been tracked down and put right.

By the time the mistake was discovered – an elementary error in transferring a small amount of money from a client's account – Babs was tired and irritable. The discrepancy had been nothing whatever to do with her, and she resented it, like a child who has been unfairly kept in after school.

She left the office in a bad temper, without saying good night to anyone, and set off along the twitten that led through to the High Street. It was almost dark now, and there were no street-lamps in the narrow alleyway. She remembered that this was where Auntie Eth had been attacked and robbed, all those years ago, and she quickened her pace, imagining that she could hear someone coming after her . . .. She told herself it was just her imagination – or the echo of her own footsteps – then, as she turned the dog-leg corner at the halfway point, a hand reached out of the darkness and grabbed her.

She opened her mouth to scream, but he pulled her close to him, saying: 'I've been waiting bloody ages. What took you so long?'

It was Ray. She gave a sob of relief as he embraced her, then scolded him for giving her such a fright.

'I was planning to surprise you,' he said. 'That's why I came round to meet you after work, to tell you about this afternoon.'

'Oh, of course – your interview at the solicitors! I'd forgotten – how did you get on?'

'I got the job. I start Monday.'

'Oh Ray, that's marvellous – I'm so glad.'

'So am I.' He began to kiss her. His kisses were hard and demanding, his tongue thrusting between her lips and his hands groping her body.

'No, don't.' She tried to pull away from him. 'Someone might see . . .'

'The hell with them – the hell with everything. I love you, Babs – and you love me. Nothing can stop us now. Don't you understand what this means? I've got a decent job at last – now we can get married!'

He was pressing her back against the wall, trying to pull up her skirt. It was terrifying and shameful – he was being so rough, he was hurting her – and yet his ruthless excitement electrified her, sweeping her along with the intensity of his passion. She longed to say yes, she longed to give way to him – but knew she must not.

'No, not now – not here.' With a great effort of will, she managed to free herself. 'We must go home. You must tell Mummy your good news.'

'Ask for Mummy's blessing first, eh?' He laughed – a harsh, angry sound. 'You really enjoy working me up – teasing me, don't you? But I'll make you pay for it later tonight. Just you wait, my girl.'

When they got back to Belmont, they went straight to Muriel's sitting room and Babs began, 'Ray's got something to tell you, Mummy. Something wonderful.'

'That's right,' he said smugly. 'I went for a interview today, and I got the job. I start next week as junior clerk at Colpoys and Son.'

'Aren't you proud of him?' asked Babs, beaming. 'I know I am.'

Muriel said nothing for a moment, then she lifted her face to the young man. 'Come here, my boy. Come and kiss me.'

He pressed his lips to the heavily powdered and perfumed cheek that she offered him; her skin was bloodless, dry and papery as a withered leaf. He wanted to laugh or shout with triumph. It was all working out just the way he wanted it.

'I'm very pleased for you,' Muriel said, releasing him. 'I'm sure I wish you every success in your new career. Did you say Colpoys and Son?'

'Yes, it's a firm of solicitors in Anerley Road—'

'I know where it is. I have had dealings with them myself in the past, when I needed some legal advice.'

Ray exclaimed gleefully, 'So they're your solicitors too? Well, I'm jiggered. It's a small world and no mistake!'

'No, you misunderstand. I don't deal with them any longer. I'm afraid I transferred my business elsewhere. I found them rather unsatisfactory, and their fees seemed quite extortionate . . . but I believe they have a good reputation, and it's certainly an excellent opening for you. I hope you will make a success of it.'

'And it's got prospects too,' Babs prompted Ray. 'Go on, tell her.'

'Well, Mrs Glynn, they say if I work hard and study I can hope for promotion in the office. I dare say, with a bit of luck, I could even finish up as a solicitor myself one of these days!' he told her. 'So what I was wondering – what I want to ask – me and Babs are thinking about getting married, if that's all right with you?'

'Married?' Muriel Glynn opened her eyes very wide. 'I think it's a little early to start making plans like that, dear boy. After all, you are only a junior clerk at present – very junior.'

'But if he works really hard, and I know he will,' Babs held Ray's hand, 'he'll be a solicitor very soon.'

Squeezing Babs' hand meaningly, Ray smiled. 'Once I make up my mind to something, I always get what I want – in the end.'

'My dears, you're both very young, and I'm sure it takes years to qualify as a solicitor; anything legal is always so long-winded. Besides, after a time you might decide you're not cut out for it, and want to move on. No, no, it won't do. I really think you must be patient for a while. Before you can begin to think about marriage, you must have some money behind you. You must make a name for yourself.'

'Oh, but Mummy, we can still be engaged, can't we?' Babs pleaded. 'We want to go and choose a ring.'

'I don't approve of long engagements; they so often turn out to be a dreadful mistake. But I can see you've both set your hearts on it, so why don't we call it an "understanding"? Nothing official – no formal announcement – just an understanding that you intend to marry one day. How about that?'

Babs smiled at Ray, breathless with love and hope and sexual desire. He smiled back, trying to look suitably grateful, but he felt sick at heart. Damn the old cow – damn her to hell. What right had she got to put a damper on things? Nobody had the right to stand in his way.

Annie Watkins and Mavis Hillyard stood by the playing-fields, watching the match in a cold November drizzle.

For several weeks now, they had been coming here regularly. Mavis didn't really enjoy football, though she was secretly proud to share a little reflected glory, since Tony always stopped to chat to them after the match, but as she did not understand the finer points of the game, most of the time she was bored and miserable – and today she was getting wet as well.

'Oh, come on, it's freezing out here,' she said, tugging at Annie's arm. 'We'll catch awful colds if we stay.'

'You go, if you want to,' Annie said, never taking her eyes off Tony. 'I'll wait till the whistle goes.'

'You're potty, you are,' grumbled Mavis. 'Standing about, getting soaked to the skin.'

'I'm not the only one.' Annie pointed out a large man on the opposite side of the pitch, his raincoat collar turned well up, and the rain dripping off the brim of his trilby. 'Did you see how the two captains talked to him at half-time? I bet he's somebody important.'

He was. After the match, he followed the footballers into the changing-shed. He congratulated several players, and told them they were all very promising – but Tony Gunn was the person he had come to see. Before he left, he gave him a printed card.

'There's my name and phone number at Selhurst.' The Crystal Palace Football Club had left their old home at 'The Nest' six years earlier, and moved to more spacious quarters at Selhurst Park. 'Give me a ring one day next week,' he said, 'and I'll fix up for you to come round for a trial turnout – OK?'

'OK, sir!' Tony grinned broadly, his hair plastered to his head and rivulets of muddy rainwater trickling down his face. 'Thanks – thanks very much!'

As soon as the talent scout had gone, the others gathered round Tony, pleased for him, but more than a little envious.

'You lucky devil. Jammy bastard – tuppence to talk to you now, I s'pose?'

'It's only a trial,' muttered Tony, as he got undressed, ready for his shower. 'Maybe they'll kick me out. I probably won't be good enough for them to take me on.'

But deep down he knew he was good enough. For years, it had been his dream that one day he would become a professional footballer and play for the Palace – and now that dream was going to come true. When the shock of the ice-cold water hit him, he hardly noticed it; inside, he was glowing with happiness.

One of his team-mates, pulling on a pair of trousers, yelled at him through the splash and hiss of the water: 'Better get a move on, Tone. I see your girlfriend's out there waiting for you!'

There was a general guffaw. They thought it was a great joke that Tony's thirteen-year-old fan never missed a match when he was playing.

'Are you going to take her to the pictures tonight?' asked somebody.

'When you sit on the back row, does she sit on your lap?'

'You want to watch out – you can get locked up, interfering with schoolkids!'

'Well, he's got to make do with a little 'un,' shouted a ribald voice. 'He's only got a little 'un himself!'

Red-faced and furious, Tony turned off the shower, hastily covering himself with a towel. Joe, the Captain, tried to intervene.

'You're a dirty lot of buggers. Give over, can't you? Take no notice of 'em, Tony.'

When the other players drifted out, Joe hung on for a few minutes, to have a quiet word with him.

'They don't mean anything by it, you know,' he said. 'They're probably a bit jealous, that's all, on account of you getting chosen for a trial.'

'It's not that. They've been going on about me and that kid for weeks now. I can't help it if she hangs about waiting for me, can I?' said Tony, peering into the single cracked looking-glass as he knotted his tie. 'Why do they have to pick on me all the time?'

'Well, they think it's funny you haven't got a girl of your own yet,' Joe said uncomfortably. 'A proper girlfriend – you know what I mean.'

Tony scowled at his murky reflection. 'I don't know any girls like that. I reckon girls don't take much of a shine to me.'

'Just you wait till you begin playing at Selhurst Park – they'll come buzzing round you like wasps round a jam-pot then,' said Joe. 'And I'm really glad for you, mate – you deserve it.'

He was about to leave when he remembered to ask: 'Oh, how's that brother of yours getting along? Have you heard any more from France?'

'He'll be coming back to England soon now, either this week or next.'

'Oh, that's good news. I bet your family will be glad to have him back home again.'

'He won't be living at home right away. They're sending him to some sort of nursing home place first, down in Surrey, for – what do they call it? – convalescence. But it's not too far away – somewhere near Reigate. We'll be able to go and visit him there.'

'Oh well. That's a step in the right direction, anyhow. Home for Christmas, p'raps?'

'Yeah – hope so.'

Tony was the last to leave the changing-shed, and he switched off the lights and locked up, shouldering the bag containing his shirt and shorts and muddy boots. Walking along the path in the steady drizzle, he saw two small, damp figures waiting for him under the trees, and his heart sank.

'Hullo, Tony,' said Annie, with a huge smile. 'It was a good game this afternoon.'

'Yes, very good,' Mavis echoed politely. 'We enjoyed it, didn't we, Annie?'

Suddenly Tony felt angry. Fifteen minutes ago he had been feeling so good – his wishes were all about to come true – and here were these two silly schoolgirls, hanging around and embarrassing him in front of his pals, and spoiling it all . . . He made up his mind to put a stop to it.

'Thanks,' he said shortly. 'But – look here – I'd rather you didn't keep coming to watch the game every week.'

'Why not?' Annie was taken aback. 'Why shouldn't we? We're allowed to, aren't we? What's wrong with watching?'

'Well, there's nothing wrong, exactly – but what I mean is, I'd sooner you didn't wait around afterwards like this. I'm very busy, see. I haven't got time to stop and talk to you, and I'd sooner you didn't, that's all. Besides, I may not be coming here myself much longer. I'm going to be very busy from now on . . . That's all – goodbye.'

And he walked on, taking long strides, anxious to get away. The stricken look on Annie's face was something he wanted to try and forget as soon as possible.

'Well!' exclaimed Mavis indignantly. 'What's the matter with him, all of a sudden?'

'I don't know,' said Annie.

'I call that very rude. If that's the way he feels, he needn't worry – we won't be coming here again, will we? I wish we'd gone home at half-time, like I wanted. Oh well, let's go and have some tea and get warmed up.'

Annie hung back. 'No – thanks all the same. I won't come to tea today, if you don't mind.'

'But Mum's expecting you. She's made a Bakewell tart—'

'I'm sorry. Tell her – I'm not feeling very well. I think you were probably right. I believe I am catching a cold after all.'

When Annie got home, her mother greeted her with surprise.

'I thought it was your turn to go to tea at the Hillyards this week?'

'I didn't feel like it.' Annie sniffed. 'I said I thought I'd got a cold coming on.'

'Oh, have you?' Studying her more closely, Daphne said, 'You've been crying.'

'No, I haven't. Well – only a little bit.'

'Did you have a row with Mavis?'

'No, I didn't. It was nothing to do with Mavis. It was – because of him. He was horrible to us.'

Daphne stiffened. 'Who was? Who are you talking about?'

'This boy who plays football. He's very nice as a rule, he always talks to us after the match. Only today he said he didn't want to see us any more. He says he's too busy . . . Why did he have to be so nasty all of a sudden?'

'I don't know, my duck.' Daphne put her arms round her daughter and hugged her. 'But men are like that, sometimes. You might as well get used to it.'

At Christmas, Ted was away from home again. He had another pantomime engagement – playing Idle Jack in *Dick Whittington*, at the Manchester Hippodrome. But this year he did not suggest that Daphne and Annie should go up to stay with him during the school holidays. After all, as he pointed out, Manchester was a long way away, and it wasn't as if it were the seaside; there would be nothing for them to do during the day. It would be far better for them to stay at home and save money.

Daphne agreed that this was very sensible, then asked casually who else would be appearing in the pantomime?

Ted told her, 'Nobody you know – oh, except Marta. She's playing Principal Boy this year.'

'Marta Linden – playing a boy?' Daphne considered the idea. 'Funny – I can't imagine it, somehow.'

It was not a very happy Christmas for anyone. Even at the flat above the greengrocers – although the Gunns were relieved to know that Steve was back in England, making a good recovery at the convalescent home, his absence cast a shadow over the family circle. They made an expedition by bus and train to visit him at Reigate, and he seemed pretty cheerful in spite of the bandages, but they didn't like him being so far from home.

On Boxing Day, Valerie met Freda in the street quite by chance, and heard the latest news. Freda suggested she might like to go and visit Steve, but Val said she couldn't do that – the journey there and back would take up most of a day, and it would be impossible to explain to Gerald.

Freda sighed. 'Yes, I suppose you're right . . . Still, Steve won't be there much longer; they'll be letting him come home soon. You'll be able to see him then, won't you?'

Valerie nodded. 'I hope so – if I can.' She added, awkwardly, 'Next time you speak to him, give him my love.'

1931 began with celebrations at the Crystal Palace offices; in the New Year Honours List, it was announced that Henry Buckland was to be awarded a knighthood in recognition of the sterling work he had done since taking up his appointment as General Manager.

The Crystal Palace trustees immediately made plans for a special banquet to mark the occasion, and Valerie was kept busy, sending out invitations to Sir Henry's friends and colleagues.

One morning in January, she was at her desk when one of typists came in, saying, 'There's a lady outside, asking to see you.'

'Oh?' Valerie looked up from the stack of envelopes she had been addressing. 'What does she want?'

'She didn't say – and she wouldn't give me her name. She says it's a personal matter.'

Perplexed, Valerie went out into the main exhibition hall and found Freda sitting on a bench, nursing her shopping basket. Suddenly sick with fear, Val sat down beside her.

'What's happened?' she asked. 'It's not – bad news?'

'No, dear – just the opposite.' Smiling, Freda patted her hand. 'I couldn't phone, in case they might be listening on the switchboard, but I knew you'd want to know. Steve's home. He came back last night.'

Relief broke over her like a wave, and for a moment Val couldn't speak. Clasping Freda's hand, she finally managed to say, 'How is he?'

'He's fine – looking very well. They say he's still got to take things easy for a week or so, but he's doing nicely.' She glanced at Val hopefully. 'I don't suppose you could pop in, after work? He'd be so glad to see you.'

'I wish I could, but I'd better not. If anyone saw me going in – well, you know how people talk.'

'Yes, that's what Steve thought. I told him I'd come and give you the news, but he guessed you wouldn't be able to call round to the shop. So he said, how would it be if he was to take a walk one afternoon, here in the park? Suppose next Sunday afternoon he happened to be strolling round, near the Maze – at three o'clock, say? Do you think you might happen to be there, sort of accidentally on purpose like?'

Val took a deep breath. 'Tell him – I'll be there,' she said.

On Sunday morning she went to church, and tried to pray. She knew she would be putting herself into temptation by meeting Steve, but she couldn't refuse to see him. More than anything in the world, she wanted to be close to him, to hear his voice, to look into his eyes – to be with him once more.

And it was all so easy. Gerry was out all day, on duty at Savoy Hill, and when she slipped away from Westwood Court at a quarter to three, nobody saw her – the streets were deserted.

There had been a heavy frost on Saturday night, and at dawn London shivered under an iron-hard crust of ice. The temperature stayed below zero all day, and even by the afternoon, very few people were venturing out; when she went through the staff entrance, she found the grounds were almost empty. A handful of children were playing, using an icy path as a slide, and in the distance she could see a few hardy young men kicking a ball around the playing-fields. Apart from them, she was alone in a frozen world – deserted, still and silent.

She walked carefully towards the fishermen's lake; there was nobody about, for the fish were imprisoned under grey glass – too thick for anglers, too thin for skaters.

When she reached the Maze, that was almost deserted too, for it was closed for the winter, the entrance barred by a padlocked gate and the hornbeam hedges a wilderness of leafless twigs – but Steve was already there, waiting for her.

She stopped and looked at him. For a moment, he did not move; they stared across an empty stretch of white, crystallised grass. It was over three years since the last time they met, and they were a little shy of one another.

Then he smiled. 'Hello,' he said.

'Hello,' she said, and walked on until they stood facing one another, at arm's length; they both kept their hands stuffed deep into their pockets, and did not touch.

'How are you?' she asked.

'I'm fine,' he said. 'The scars on my legs are healing nicely, and my hands are getting better all the time.'

'Tell me what happened,' she said.

Side by side, they walked round the outer circle of the Maze, and he tried to describe the night of the crash. It had happened nearly three months ago, and he had told this story so many times, to so many people, he found it hard to distinguish what he remembered from what he had learned afterwards.

He remembered the airship tipping forward, dropping nose-first towards the ground, and the double impact; and he remembered the fire.

'I never saw anything like it. I couldn't have imagined anything so – so . . .' He was at a loss for words. 'It wasn't just frightening, it was much more than that. It was like the end of the world – a different sort of thing altogether. Like being alive and dead at the same time.'

'But you got out safely – you were one of the lucky ones.'

'I'll never know why. One minute I was in the engine-car with old Savory – and the next moment we were both in this fire. It was all round us, and the flames made more noise than a furnace going full blast – roaring so hard, I couldn't hear him and he couldn't hear me. I threw myself at the wall – the outer fabric cover – trying to break through, but it was too tough. I must have slipped and fallen, because I ended up on the floor – only it wasn't the floor any longer, it was cold and wet. I suddenly realised I was lying on grass – cool, damp grass – I couldn't believe it. I looked up at Savory, and he pointed to the wall; in one place, the fabric was already burning, so it had started to tear – a long, jagged rip that came right down to the ground, where I was. But we couldn't get out that way, because the walls were nothing but flames. We both thought we were done for . . . and that's when it happened.'

'What happened?'

'I don't know what you'd call it – I call it a blooming miracle. The service water-tanks for the engine, up above, must have burst. A great downpour of cold water landed on top of us, flooding the car, and for half a minute it put out the flames. It didn't last, of course – there was too much blazing gas for that – but it gave us just enough time to push through the torn place in the fabric – and there we were

. . . outside, in the dark, and the cold night air. I can tell you I never tasted anything so good in all my life.'

She said nothing, but her hand slipped through his arm and she held on to him tightly. As they continued to walk, he told her the rest of the story in fragments; how they had run into Disley, the wireless-operator, who was wandering around in the undergrowth on the hillside, half-dazed. Disley had had a lucky escape too, but he insisted on finding a telephone and calling the Air Ministry in London before he would consent to being given first aid.

Teams of rescue workers were already hurrying to the scene of the crash, and the handful of survivors were taken to safety. None of them realised the full extent of their injuries until they reached the hospital.

Steve had a vague memory of his last view of the wreckage – the outline of curved steel girders, silhouetted on the horizon, like the unfinished roof of a huge railway station. At one end, the tail of the airship was faintly recognisable, with the remains of the observer's cockpit hanging in space, high above the ground; from its framework, a few rags and strips of fabric were still fluttering in the breeze. He could not remember seeing any other movement, or any sign of life.

'Oh, Steve . . . When you think – if you hadn't got out in time . . .' She broke off, unable to pursue this thought.

'Yes, but I'm here now, and so are you – thank God for that,' he said.

'What will you do?' she wanted to know. 'When you're fit enough to go back to work?'

He shrugged. 'There's no work for me at Cardington. Seems like this has knocked out any ideas of building airships, once and for all.'

'I'm glad of that anyway,' she said quietly. 'So – what happens now?'

'They say they'll take me back in my old job, at Croydon Airport. For the time being, I'll go on living at home . . . near you.'

For several minutes they went on walking in silence, through the bare winter trees; two solitary figures, moving like ghosts through a frozen wilderness. They had left the Maze behind, and the ice-bound lake, and there was no one in sight. At last they stopped walking, and turned to face one another.

'What's to become of us, Val?' he asked.

'I don't know,' she said.

'But – what sort of future have we got? What are we going to do?'

'Nothing. How can there be any future for us?'

'There has to be a future,' he said.

He took his hands from his pockets. For the first time she saw the clumsy grey mittens his mother had knitted, over the thick white bandages. She opened her arms to him – and as soon as they kissed one another, their future was settled. Somehow, some day, they would be together; there was no doubt about that – no doubt at all.

But although there was no one near them in the park, they were not quite alone.

On the other side of the boundary wall, the neighbouring houses commanded a view of the park – a clearer view now than in summer, for there were no leaves on the branches to screen the young lovers.

Standing at his bedroom window in Crystal Palace Park Road, Ray Duke saw them embracing, and he went on watching them as they walked off up the hill, with their arms round one another.

When he turned away from the window, he was smiling.

At last Tony's dream was about to come true.

After his interview at Selhurst Park, and the trial game, he was taken on – together with half a dozen other promising lads – and given a job with Crystal Palace Football Club.

It wasn't much of a job; the work consisted of helping the groundsmen to keep the pitch in good condition, cleaning up litter after every match, sweeping out and cleaning the dressing rooms, repainting and decorating as required – acting, in short, as a general handyman and dogsbody. But it also included training sessions with the Coach three times a week, and if Tony came up to expectations, a possible place among the Reserves.

One of these fine days, if everything went well, he would be running out on to the field himself; he would be a member of the team.

When he told Joe about his lucky break, Joe said they ought to go out and celebrate. 'But not here. If we go in any of the local pubs, you can bet your boots some nosy parker will kick us out for being under age. Why don't we go Up West, and paint the town red? How soon do you start work at Selhurst?'

'First thing Monday.'

'And after that you'll be in training. We'd better go out on Saturday night. Tell you what – can you rake up some cash between now and Saturday?' Joe winked at Tony. 'We might make a night of it, and pick up a couple of girls – what d'you say?'

'Yeah, why not?'

The idea was terrifying, but it was very exciting too. Tony decided that it was now or never; this would be his chance to prove himself a man. Once he'd been with a girl, they could never make fun of him again, or taunt him for messing about with schoolkids . . . He had nearly four pounds saved up in a tin money-box at home – that should be enough, shouldn't it?

So on Saturday they caught a bus all the way to the West End. It was a lot cheaper than the train-fare and there was an all-night service, running once an hour, to bring them home.

When they jumped off the bus at Trafalgar Square, they headed straight for Piccadilly Circus; everyone knew it was the hub of the world, and the place to have some fun. For a time they wandered around, looking in shop windows, and gazing wistfully at Eros, aiming his arrow into the heart of the passing crowds.

Now and again they saw a pair of likely-looking girls, and started to follow them. Once or twice they said, 'Good evening' and tried to strike up a conversation – but the girls tossed their heads scornfully or, worse still, laughed at them and told them to run home to their Mums . . .

So they went into a Shaftesbury Avenue pub instead. Joe spoke in his deepest tones, and ordered two pints of beer; the barmaid gave him a sharp look, but served him without comment. Then they squeezed into a corner alcove and sipped their beer, and took stock of the dismal situation.

'Don't know what's the matter with those daft women,' grumbled Joe.

'Perhaps they think we're under age, as well,' said Tony.

'Naaah – just a lot of stuck-up tarts, that's what they are,' said Joe. He took another swig, then wiped the foam thoughtfully from his upper lip. 'Mind you, there's always that . . .'

'There's always what?' asked Tony.

'Tarts. How much money have you got on you?'

'Nearly four quid.'

'And I've got a fiver. It was a Christmas present, only I haven't spent it yet. Nine quid – I bet we could get ourselves a couple of beauties for that.' They looked at one another, and he added uncertainly, 'How about it, then?'

'I'm game if you are.' Tony felt very scared, but he wouldn't admit it. 'Have you ever done this before?'

'Heaps of times.' Joe buried his face in his tankard. 'Nothing to it.'

They had two more beers – Joe said it was to give Tony some

Dutch courage, because it was his first time – and then went out in search of adventure.

Halfway along Frith Street, a young woman was standing under a street-lamp.

'Hello, boys,' she said.

'Hello,' said Tony. Joe said nothing.

'Well, you're a bright pair, I must say! You've both got faces like a wet week,' she said cheerfully. 'What's the matter – fed up, far from home, and nowhere to go?'

'Something like that,' said Tony. Joe still said nothing.

'How'd you like to come with me?' she asked. 'I've got a nice flat, just round the corner.'

Tony took a deep breath. 'How much?' he said.

'We can settle that later. It's not going to cost you a lot, I promise. I've taken a fancy to you, darling.'

'What about my pal?' said Tony.

'I can do a special price for the two of you – one at a time, mind, no funny business. Bargain rates tonight, seeing it's my birthday.'

'Well, all right.' Taking a closer look at her under the yellow glare of the gaslight, Tony saw that she wasn't as young as all that – she must have been in her thirties at least – but she had a jolly smile, and he wasn't going to miss this perfect opportunity. 'OK – we'll come with you, won't we, Joe?'

At last Joe broke his silence, backing away. In the lamplight his face had turned a greenish colour.

'No – not me. Sorry, Tony – I just remembered something . . . Got to get home – promised I wouldn't be late. Be seeing you!' With that, he turned and fled, disappearing into the night.

Tony nearly lost his nerve; for two pins he would have taken to his heels and followed him, but the young woman took a firm grip on his arm.

'Good riddance,' she said. 'I could tell at a glance, he wouldn't have been any fun. But I know you and me are going to have a good time. My name's Lindy – what's yours?'

'Tony,' he mumbled.

'Well, Tony – you come along with me. It's not far, only a couple of minutes' walk.'

He allowed her to lead him through Soho; they walked a long way, and the journey took a great deal longer than two minutes. She steered him across Oxford Street, into a rabbit warren of narrow alleys and courts somewhere behind Charlotte Street, and Tony asked: 'Is it much further?'

'No, we're nearly there. Just round the next corner, up three flights of stairs, and there we are – home sweet home!'

The top-floor flat took him by surprise. Lindy led him into a homely sitting room, furnished with solid, comfortable armchairs and a matching sofa. A fire burned invitingly in the grate, and another young woman was sitting beside it, reading the *Evening News*.

She looked up and smiled as they came in – totally unembarrassed, though she was dressed in nothing but a flimsy petticoat, and one of her shoulder-straps had slipped, exposing a rose-nippled breast.

Tony caught his breath, standing transfixed in the doorway, and Lindy said with a laugh: 'What's the matter, darling? First time you've seen a lady's titty-follol? Come on in. Take your coat off, and let's get comfy.'

But he stayed where he was, staring at the half-naked girl, and blurted out: 'I know you. I've seen you before.'

She shook her head. 'No, dear, I don't think so. I've got a very good memory for faces; I'm sure you've never been here before.'

'Not here – somewhere else. You're Margie.'

She frowned slightly. 'Yes – that's right, but I don't remember you. Remind me, where was it?'

'At the Crystal Palace. We went on the lake. I rowed the boat—'

As he said this, an inner door opened, and another middle-aged woman came into the room, wearing a black lace negligée.

'Sounds like we've got company,' began Julie pleasantly. Then as she saw him: 'Oh, my God – *Tony*.'

Lindy stared from one horrified face to another, totally mystified. 'What the hell's going on?'

Julie began to talk very quickly. 'Tony – it's all right, I can explain. Come and sit down. Where are you going? No, Tony – come back!'

But he was already tearing down the staircase; he flung himself down three flights, desperate to escape from this nightmare. Julie grabbed a coat from behind the door and threw it round her shoulders as she set off in pursuit of her young brother.

She nearly caught him at Tottenham Court Road, but he was too quick for her, and rushed headlong into the traffic. A taxi coming round the corner slammed on its brakes and skidded sideways – there was a squeal of tyres, a sickening crunch, and then Julie screamed . . . Tony was lying on the road, under the wheels.

It was nearly midnight when she telephoned home; to her relief, Steve picked up the phone.

'Thank God it's you,' she said. 'Sorry to ring so late – where's Mum and Dad? Have they gone to bed?'

'Yes. I said I'd wait up for young Tony; he's gone out on the razzle tonight. He's going to get what-for from Dad in the morning!'

'He won't be there in the morning. There's been an accident, but you can tell them Tony's all right. I've been looking after him.'

'What? I don't understand. Is Tony there? Let me speak to him—'

'He was here earlier, but he's in hospital now. Like you said, he'd been out on the razzle and – he got knocked down in the street. I was with him when it happened. I called an ambulance—'

She could not go on; Steve could hear that she was trying not to cry.

'What are you saying? My God, he's dead, isn't he? That's what you're trying to tell me—'

'No, he's going to be all right.' Somehow she managed to get the words out. 'Only there's something else, something I've got to tell you – but not now, not on the phone. Can you come here tomorrow morning? If I give you the address, will you be able to find it?'

'I dare say. I'll bring Mum with me – she'll want to visit Tony in the hospital—'

'No! Whatever happens, you mustn't bring her here. Make some excuse; tell her she can visit him later on, when he's feeling better. Say anything – but you've got to come here by yourself, Steve. I've got to talk to you.'

'Well, I don't know – it's going to be hard to persuade her.'

'For Christ's sake, this is important!' Again, Steve could hear the sob in her voice. 'I'll explain when I see you. Please – I'm begging you . . .'

'All right. Where do you live?'

It was nearly midday before he found the address, and climbed the three flights of stairs to the top·floor. The other occupants of the flat were still fast asleep, so he and Julie had the sitting room to themselves.

She looked haggard, drained from lack of sleep. Dressed in a severe grey skirt and jacket, she sat at the table and poured Steve a cup of coffee. Then, without looking at him, she began to tell him the whole story, slowly and clearly; she had had plenty of time to go over it in her head, during her wakeful night.

When she had finished, he had one hand over his face, shielding his eyes. Breaking the silence, she asked: 'Aren't you going to say anything?'

'After all that, I don't know what to say. I used to think you were doing so well, catering supervisor – whatever you call it.'

'I was a waitress, nothing more than that. The pay was lousy, and I worked my fingers to the bone. After a year or so, I swore I'd sooner die than spend the rest of my life waiting on tables. So – me and the girls, we got together and rented this place, and I've been my own boss ever since. Oh, I'm not proud of myself, but I'm not exactly ashamed either. We charge the going rate – we don't cheat the clients, or steal from them – and we keep ourselves clean. There are worse ways to earn a living.'

'But now – now the truth's come out,' Steve began awkwardly, 'what are you going to do?'

'That's up to you, isn't it? You and Tony. You can go home and tell Mum and Dad if you want – and break their hearts. Or you can shut your trap and we'll cook up some sort of story between us, to keep them happy. Something like – Tony had a few drinks – he stepped off the kerb without looking – I happened to be on my way home from work at the Corner House . . . How about that?'

Steve scratched his head, and muttered unhappily, 'Oh hell, I'll say whatever you like, but it all depends on Tony, doesn't it?'

They visited him together, in the Men's Orthopaedic Ward at University College Hospital.

His right leg was in plaster from hip to toes, hanging from a system of wires and pulleys, and he lay there, looking up at his brother and sister, with no expression on his face. They had brought him some flowers and chocolates and magazines, but he only glanced at them without much interest.

Carefully, Steve tried to explain the situation. Julie held his hand, saying, 'I'm not asking for my sake, Tony. It's for Mum and Dad – if they find out, I'm afraid of what it might do to them.'

Tony turned his head away and sighed. 'We're both in the same boat, I reckon. If they found out why I'd gone to your flat – if they guessed what I was doing there, they wouldn't like that, either. Don't worry, I won't tell them anything.'

'Thanks, Tony.' Leaning over the bed, Julie kissed him, but he did not respond, and she asked him, 'So – What are we going to say, then? We must work it out.'

'Say what you like, I don't care . . .' He did not look at her, but went on staring at the screens round his bed, boxing him in. 'I don't care about anything, any more.'

On another Sunday afternoon, a few weeks later, Annie went to the playing-fields again. She had gone alone this time, without telling anyone; she did not even want Mavis to know that she had disobeyed Tony Gunn's request that she should stay away from the football matches. She couldn't help it – she had to see him. If she stayed well out of sight among the trees, nobody would know she was there.

But as soon as the two teams ran out on to the pitch, she knew that Tony wasn't there either. He had said he was going to be busy, but where had he gone? She was determined to find out.

Throughout the match, she waited as patiently as possible for the final whistle; and she went on waiting after the players had gone off to change. She watched and waited until she saw the last man leave the shed; she knew he was Tony's team captain – she had seen them talking and walking together. Greatly daring, she stepped out of her hiding-place and addressed him.

'Excuse me,' she began. 'Can you tell me where Tony Gunn is?'

Joe stared at her. 'You're the kid who used to come and watch him every week, aren't you?'

'Yes, he happens to be an old friend of mine,' she replied with dignity. 'And I want to know where he is now.'

'You heard about the accident, did you?'

'*What accident?*'

'He was knocked down by a car. Broke his right leg – fractured in three places.'

'No . . .' She spoke in a whisper. 'I didn't know. Is he in hospital?'

'He was, but he came home yesterday. He's doing pretty well, really, except—' Joe hesitated, wondering how much he should say to the girl.

'Except what? Please – tell me.'

'Well . . . His leg didn't heal up properly. He'll be able to walk all right, but he'll have a bit of a limp. Rotten luck, just when he'd been signed up by the Palace. Of course, that's out of the question now.'

For a moment Annie stood and looked at him, then she said politely, 'Thank you for telling me. Good afternoon.'

She walked away through the gathering dusk, quickly and purpose-fully, leaving the park by the Anerley Gate; turning right up the hill, she made straight for Church Road. She knew where Tony lived. She had seen him there once or twice when she had gone shopping with her Nan, buying fruit and vegetables.

As it was a Sunday, the shop was shut. Taking a deep breath, she was about to ring at the side door when it opened, and old Jack Gunn came out, wrapped in a thick overcoat and a variety of hand-knitted mufflers, carrying a leather case that was the same shape as the cornet inside it.

'Hello!' he said, squinting at her in surprise. 'Who are you?'

'I'm Annie Watkins. Somebody told me about Tony. I'd like to see him, if you don't mind.'

'Watkins? Oh yes, of course – Valerie's family. Tony's upstairs in the sitting room. You can find your way, can't you? I'm off out myself. Got band practice this evening – mustn't miss that.'

He held the door open for her. Nervously, she began to climb the stairs, and he called after her: 'You'll find your auntie up there already. So long!' – and he shut the front door after her as he went out.

At the top of the stairs, Annie heard voices, and followed the sound. Walking into the living room, she found Tony lying on a sofa near the window, with a rug over his legs. Mr and Mrs Gunn were there, and Tony's brother Steve – and so was Valerie.

Annie began to explain once more that she had only just heard about Tony's accident, when Valerie stood up, saying brightly, 'So did I – great minds think alike! Still, I've got to be going now. Goodbye, Tony, I'm glad to see you looking so well. I'm sure you'll get better in no time, now you're home again. Sorry I can't stop.'

'That's OK – thanks for the flowers and the books,' he said flatly.

Valerie said her goodbyes to Freda and Alfred and turned to Steve, as if she were about to shake hands, but he stood up too, helping her on with her coat. 'I'll walk along with you,' he said. 'See you home.'

'Oh no, don't bother. There's no need.'

'No bother at all. The walk will do me good.'

'Well, if you're sure.' Val gave Annie a kiss. 'Don't stay too long, love. Tony has to get all the rest he can; we mustn't tire him out.'

Then she went off with Steve. Freda stood up too, giving her husband a meaning look and saying; 'I'll put the kettle on – I expect we could all do with a cuppa. You can come and help me, Alfred.'

'It doesn't take two of us to fill the kettle,' he grumbled.

'I shall need a new packet of tea, and it's on the top shelf in the larder. You can fetch it down for me,' she said, giving him a nudge. 'Oh, do come *on*, Alfred!'

Protesting, he allowed himself to be dragged away, and Tony and Annie were left together. She pulled up a chair to sit by him.

'I'm sorry, I came straight here,' she said. 'I didn't bring you anything.'

'I didn't expect you to. What are you doing here, anyway?'

'I was in the park, watching the football. I know you asked me not to, but I thought – well, it's a free country, why shouldn't I? Then I saw you weren't there, and afterwards I talked to the Captain, and he told me about the accident, and about you coming out of hospital, and all that.'

'Pity he couldn't keep his big mouth shut,' said Tony sourly.

'He wouldn't have told me if I hadn't asked,' said Annie, trying to be fair. Then she went on: 'He told me about your bad leg – and not playing football for Crystal Palace—'

Tony interrupted her. 'I don't really want to talk about it, if you don't mind.'

'No, of course not. Except I just wanted to tell you – I'm very sorry,' she said in a small voice.

'So am I,' he said.

'I know.'

'In fact, when they told me, I wished the taxi-driver had made a better job of it and finished me off,' he added harshly. 'If you really want to know, I wished I were dead.'

'I do know,' she said.

He turned on her angrily. 'How the hell can you know? You don't know what it feels like—'

'I can imagine. If it was me, I'd wish I was dead, too.' Tentatively, she put her hand lightly on his arm. 'Only I'm glad you're not,' she said.

He looked down at her hand on his sleeve – and then he looked at her – and then he smiled. It wasn't much of a smile, but it wasn't too bad, considering he was out of practice.

By now it was quite dark outside. Valerie and Steve were walking along Crystal Palace Parade, side by side, leaving a discreet distance between them. Instinctively they kept close to the wall, as far as possible from the lamp-posts at the pavement's edge.

'Will Annie tell anyone she saw you with me?' asked Steve.

'She might.'

'If she does, what will you say?'

'I'll tell them what I told her. I'd heard about Tony, and I felt I ought to go round to ask after him, being a friend of the family.'

'You don't think people are going to be suspicious?'

'I don't know. Oh Steve, this is the part I hate most. It spoils everything, having to pretend, having to tell lies and cover up all the time. Perhaps we should stop seeing one another.'

Appalled, he looked at her. 'You don't mean that?'

'Yes, I do. This is all wrong – it's going to cause nothing but misery for all of us – you and me, and Gerald too. Sometimes I think it would be better to end it: say goodbye and never see each other again.'

'We can't do that.' They stopped walking, and he pulled her close to him in the shadows. 'We love one another . . .'

'Please, let me go. It's getting awfully late and Gerry will be wanting his supper.'

'Damn Gerry! Can't you stop thinking about him for once, and think about me, for a change? About *us*?'

'I never think of anything else . . . but this is exactly what I mean – something always happens to spoil it. Being with you is wonderful, but we always seem to finish up by having an argument.' She shook him off. 'I'm sorry, I must go home.'

'Not yet,' he pleaded. 'I can't let you go like this. Come and have a drink first; the pubs will be open soon.'

'But suppose we should meet anyone?'

'There's a little pub in Cawnpore Street – the Railway Bell. Nobody knows us there. Come on, just one drink – ten more minutes.'

So they retraced their steps to Westow Hill, then turned down Gipsy Hill and into the peaceful, secluded grove, incongruously named after a forgotten Indian massacre. It was not an area they knew. The Railway Bell had a good reputation, but neither of them had ever been there before, so it would be neutral territory – somewhere safe.

As the pub had only just opened, it was almost empty, but the Saloon was warm and welcoming; in one corner, a burly man sat smoking a pipe. Val picked a small table at the far end, while Steve ordered the drinks.

He was just sitting down, raising his glass and saying, 'Cheers, Val. Good luck—' when Ray Duke sauntered in from the Public Bar, beyond the partition.

'I thought I knew that voice,' he said. 'Well, well, this is a surprise. Aren't you going to buy an old pal a drink, Steve?'

Steve squared his shoulders, setting his back against the wall. 'You're no pal of mine. You never were.'

Trying to avert a row, Val broke in quickly, 'Anyway, we're not stopping. I'm late already—'

'I bet.' Ray lifted the corner of his lip in a mocking smile. 'Mustn't keep Gerald waiting, must you?' He pulled up a chair and sat down, facing them across the table. 'Nice to see you both after all this time – together again.'

Steve clenched his fists under the table, struggling to keep his voice steady as he said, 'I don't remember asking you to join us. Why don't you push off?'

'No, Steve. Ray's quite right,' said Valerie, still trying to carry off the situation lightly. 'I promised Gerry I wouldn't be late.' She forced herself to smile at Ray. 'Only I happened to run into Steve a few minutes ago, and as we hadn't seen each other for such a long time, he asked me to come and have a drink, so—'

Ray laughed. 'Don't give me that! You've been seeing each other on the sly for God knows how long. Going for walks together in the park—'

Valerie felt herself blushing as she lied to him. 'That's not true. Whatever gave you that idea?'

'I saw you there, with my very own eyes. I saw you hugging and kissing – oh, don't worry, I haven't told anyone. I didn't even tell Babs . . . It can be our little secret, eh?' He threw Steve a calculating glance and said, 'I think you ought to buy me that drink, after all. Speaking as a pal, it'd be worth your while.'

Anger was building up inside Steve, about to explode, but he managed to ask, 'And what do you mean by that?'

'Well . . . a friendship like ours is a valuable thing, isn't it? I reckon we could put quite a high price on it. I mean to say, if Gerry ever found out about the way you two are carrying on—'

He never finished the sentence, because Steve jumped to his feet, overturning the table. The drinks went flying, and Ray's chair crashed to the floor. Steve flung himself on top of Ray, attacking him with the bitter fury he had been nursing for years, hitting him again and again, the blows thudding home relentlessly.

Val screamed, 'Stop! You'll kill him!'

Deafened by rage, he did not hear her – and if he had, he might not have listened. At this moment he wanted nothing more than to get rid of this creature who had ruined his life once, and was threatening to do so again.

The customer in the corner called for help, and two young potboys rushed in from the Public; it took all three of them to drag Steve on to his feet. The moment Ray could scramble free, he made his escape, out of the pub and away up the road, running for dear life.

Eventually, when Steve had calmed down and apologised to the landlord, and paid for the breakages, he and Val left the pub.

'I thought you'd gone off your head,' she told him.

'I couldn't help it,' he said. 'The thought of him, stirring up trouble for us, all over again . . . Do you suppose he'll tell Gerald?'

'I don't know, and I don't care. It doesn't matter anyway. I can't stand this any longer.' She moved closer to him. 'Put your arms round me – help me get my courage up. I'm going to tell Gerry myself when I get home. I'm going to ask him for a divorce.'

'Thank God,' he said; and they stopped walking, so he could kiss her. After a moment, he added: 'I'll come with you – we'll both talk to him.'

'Not this time, Steve. This is something I've got to do on my own.'

That evening, when Annie was in bed, Daphne went up to say goodnight to her. This was always one of the best moments of the day – they were relaxed and easy, enjoying each other's company. Tonight, when Daphne sat on the end of the bed, she had a feeling that her daughter wanted to tell her something.

Ever since she came home, Annie had been bursting to pour out the dreadful news about Tony, but she wasn't quite sure whether Mum would approve of her going visiting without an invitation. But now she felt she must take that risk – she had to tell someone, or burst.

'You know that boy I told you about? The one who used to play football on Sundays?'

Secretly rather amused, Daphne said, 'Yes – what about him? Have you seen him again?'

So Annie told her everything, from the moment she spoke to the team's Captain, right up to her final goodbyes, after a cup of tea and a bourbon biscuit provided by Mrs Gunn.

'They were very nice to me – the whole family – and they didn't mind a bit about me going there without being asked,' she said firmly. 'Tony must have been pleased to see me, 'cos he said I can go again if I like.' A tiny wrinkle furrowed her brow as she added, 'He says I make him laugh . . .'

'Well, I don't think that's such a bad thing,' said Daphne. 'He must be feeling very low at the moment. If you can cheer him up, that's something to be proud of.' Then she asked, 'When you said "the whole family", was Tony's brother there, as well?'

'Steve? Yes, he was at first, only he went quite soon, because he was taking Auntie Valerie home. I didn't see him again after that.'

Daphne stared at Annie. 'Valerie was there? You didn't say.'

'Oh, didn't I? Yes, she'd just heard about poor Tony, so she went round to visit him too – wasn't that funny? "Great minds think alike" – that's what she said.'

'And Steve took her home?' With her mind racing, Daphne stood up and moved to the door. 'Yes, I see . . .'

'Aren't you going to kiss me good night?' asked Annie.

'Oh yes, of course. Sorry, love – fancy me forgetting that!' Daphne returned and bent down to kiss her, repeating as she did every evening: 'Night-night, sleep tight. Hope the bugs don't bite . . .'

Annie looked up into her mother's face. 'What's the matter? You're not cross with me, are you?'

'No, of course I'm not. I was just thinking about – something else, that's all.'

When they had finished supper, Val usually cleared the table and did the washing-up, but tonight she left the dirty dishes where they were. Gerry pushed back his chair and lit a cigarette, about to return to the sitting room, but Val stopped him. Gripping her hands tightly in her lap, she said, 'Don't go for a minute, Gerry. I want to talk to you.'

'Can't it wait, old dear? There's a concert I want to listen to.'

'I'm afraid it can't wait. Please sit down; it is important.'

'Oh, really?' He returned to his chair. 'Very well – fire away.'

She took a deep breath and began to tell him the whole story. How Steve had been unjustly punished, all those years ago. How Ray had involved him in a crime he knew nothing about . . . How she had visited him in prison, secretly – and how they had met again since his release.

'I have fought against it, Gerry – really I have. I tried to tell him it was all over. I said I never wanted to see him again – I even tried to convince myself, but it was no good. I still love him; I've always loved him. I'm very sorry, but I can't keep pretending. I've never been a proper wife to you, I know that. I did try, but the truth is – I don't love you enough . . . not the way I love him.'

When she stopped speaking, the room was so quiet, she could hear the clock ticking on the mantelpiece. For some time, Gerald had been staring at his dessert-plate, which still had fragments of stewed apple and custard clinging to it. Now he lifted his head, gazing over Val's shoulder at a picture of bluebells in the beechwoods.

'Why are you telling me all this?' he asked.

'Because I've been living a lie, and I can't bear it any longer. I want you to divorce me, Gerry.'

Then he looked straight at her, and his eyes were cold with anger and contempt.

'Don't be so bloody stupid,' he said. 'You're my wife. I asked you to marry me, and you agreed – nobody forced you to. We have a contract, and I expect you to honour that contract.'

'But our marriage isn't working, Gerry – that's why I want to break the contract. I'm no good to you as a wife—'

'That's for me to decide, not you. I refuse to release you from your obligations. There will be no divorce, and you will not see the man again. That's all I have to say; now I'm going to listen to the wireless. You'd better get on with the washing-up.'

Chapter Twenty-two

'OUCH! THAT STINGS!' exclaimed Ray.

'I did warn you,' Babs told him. 'But it'll help to heal the cuts and grazes.'

'You poor thing,' said Ethel, while Aggie made little moans of sympathy in the background.

They were in the kitchen, and Babs – who sometimes had visions of herself all in white, as a second Florence Nightingale – was doing her best to give Ray first aid. When he staggered in, breathless and bleeding, with a black eye that was already beginning to close up, the ladies of Belmont had reacted with shock and dismay, and while Babs dabbed him with iodine, they all talked at once.

'Whatever have you done to yourself?'

'Was it an accident?'

'There are too many dangerous drivers on the road these days. Did you take the number of the car?'

'Give me a chance to get my breath back,' he gasped, still trying to decide how much to tell them. 'I'll explain it to you later.'

When Babs had attended to his cuts and bruises, and done her best to tidy him up, they returned to the sitting room, where Muriel sat waiting impatiently.

'Will someone be kind enough to tell me what has happened?' she demanded.

They gave the wounded hero the best chair; he looked round the circle of anxious, concerned faces, and began to feel better.

'I'll tell you,' he said. 'It wasn't an accident – I was set on by a gang of youths. I suppose it was my own fault for going into a public house in the first place, but I'd been walking home after church – I told you I was going to Evensong, didn't I, Babs? – and I was feeling a bit tired, so I thought a cooling drink might be refreshing. I should have known better; I won't be going in there again.'

'You say a gang attacked you?' asked Muriel. 'But why? What had you done?'

'Nothing. I was keeping myself to myself, until one of them recognised me.'

'You mean to say it was someone who knew you?'

'Oh yes, and I knew him too – at least I used to, in the bad old days. It was Steve Gunn – remember him? The chap who talked me into breaking the law – the one who managed to shift all the blame on to me.'

They all looked suitably horrified, and Babs said: 'I've noticed him hanging round the streets myself once or twice. But why did he attack you, all of a sudden?'

'I couldn't tell you, I'm sure. When he spoke to me, I was perfectly civil. I even offered to buy him a drink, and then they all went for me, hammer and tongs. Three of them, there were. I did my best to defend myself, but they were too much for me.'

'That's outrageous!' snorted Muriel. 'Didn't anyone intervene?'

'I think everybody was taken by surprise – I know I was. But then the landlord appeared and when he started yelling they let go of me. That's how I managed to get away. I think they'd have killed me if he hadn't walked in.'

'So there were witnesses?' Babs asked. 'You must report it to the police. They ought to be arrested—'

'Oh no,' Ray broke in quickly. 'I wouldn't want that – it wouldn't be a very gentlemanly thing to do. You see, they had a young lady with them. If it all comes to court, she'd have to be involved – and I wouldn't want that,' he said nobly.

'Why ever not? If she's the sort of woman who hangs around ruffians like that, it's no more than she deserves,' said Muriel, with righteous indignation.

'Yes, but – oh dear, I was hoping I wouldn't have to tell you this. The trouble is, I know her,' said Ray. 'We all know her.'

'Who are you talking about?'

'Valerie . . . our Valerie – Gerald's wife.' Ray hung his head. 'Now you see why I was hoping I could hush it up, but I suppose the truth had to come out in the end.'

'*Valerie?*' Babs stared at him incredulously. 'You mean – she was there – with Steve?'

'Well, yes. She used to go with him, years ago, didn't she? And seemingly, since he came out of prison, that's all started up again.'

'Oh no, surely not,' began Ethel. 'Valerie seems to be such a nice girl. I'm sure she wouldn't—'

Babs interrupted: 'But if Valerie was there, what did she do when they started the fight? Didn't she try to stop them?'

'No, she didn't. I think she was enjoying herself,' said Ray sadly. 'I heard her laughing.'

There was a stunned silence, broken by Muriel, who said bitterly, 'I never liked her. I've always been afraid something like this would happen; right from the beginning, when Gerald told me he was going to marry her, I had my doubts. It's always a mistake to marry out of one's own class. And I speak from experience. I made the same mistake, and I've regretted it all my life, as you well know.'

Babs was still trying to come to terms with the shocking revelation. 'Do you suppose Gerry knows – about her and Steve?' she asked Ray.

'I doubt it. I believe that's why Steve went for me – because I'd seen him and Val together. He was afraid I might tell Gerry. It was a warning to me to keep my mouth shut.'

'What a wicked, wicked man,' said Ethel. 'And as for Valerie, I'd never have believed it of her.'

'If Gerry doesn't know, somebody ought to tell him,' said Babs, and she looked at Ray. 'Do you think, since you're the one who saw them—?'

'Oh no, don't ask me that.' Ray hung his head. 'I couldn't bring myself to do such a thing. I wouldn't want to make trouble for anyone.'

Valerie was in the bedroom, going through the chest of drawers, finding and folding various items of clothing; she had taken down a suitcase from the top of the wardrobe, and now she was going to start packing.

Ever since supper, Gerald had shut himself up in the lounge, and she gathered that he had been making phone-calls. She couldn't imagine who he was talking to; it seemed unlikely that he would be complaining to any of his friends or family about his wife's disgraceful behaviour, but anyway she didn't much care. She was simply relieved that he was keeping out of her way.

Suddenly she heard him calling her.

'Valerie? Would you come in here for a few minutes, please? I want to talk to you.'

Surprised, and more than a little wary, she went in to the lounge. He was standing in front of the fender, warming his backside by the gas fire.

'I've been thinking over what you told me earlier on,' he said, 'and trying to make some plans for the future. I've also been talking to one or two friends and business colleagues.'

'You were telling them about me, were you?'

'Certainly not! You know I wouldn't dream of discussing our private affairs with anyone else. Though in a sense it concerns you – it concerns both of us.'

'Go on.'

'I had to decide what to do for the best, and it strikes me that the best possible thing for us to do would be to move away from London for a while.'

She looked at him blankly. 'What do you mean?'

'Do I have to put it in words of one syllable? I'd have thought it was pretty obvious: as long as we go on living in this part of London, you're liable to go on seeing the bloody man. Even if you give me your word that you won't have any more to do with him, there's still the risk of you running into him accidentally . . . And the sort of fellow he is, I shouldn't be surprised if he tried to pester you. So the best thing we can do is move – as far away as possible.'

She tried to stem the flow of words. 'There's no need for that—' but he was in full flood.

'Oddly enough, I had an offer of another job recently. I didn't mention it at the time, because I never considered it seriously. I've always been pretty happy with the BBC, and I was looking forward to moving into Broadcasting House – that's what they're going to call the new building, when it's finished. However, that's out of the question now. I shall hand in my official resignation tomorrow morning.'

'But why? You don't have to—'

'As I say, someone approached me the other day, asking if I'd be interested in a post with a new company that's being set up. They're planning to broadcast regular programmes on a commercial basis – rather like magazine publishing, really – all paid for by advertising. Various manufacturers – Ovaltine, Palmolive, Shredded Wheat – will be sponsoring programmes, and they're already recruiting certain key members of staff. And I was invited to join them.'

Val's head was spinning. 'I'm sorry, I don't know what you're talking about.'

'They're offering good money, but I said no. Well, I didn't want to leave the dear old BBC – and it means living abroad, as well. Under British law they're not allowed to run a commercial radio station in this country, so they're going to operate from Luxembourg, and beam the programmes across the Channel to British listeners. Originally I turned it down, but tonight it seemed to me it would be the ideal solution, so I've been making a few phone-calls, and I've told them I've changed my mind . . . We're moving to Luxembourg.'

'I wish you'd listen. There's no need – you haven't got to move.'

He shook his head. 'No, I think it'll be for the best. Quite apart from anything else, it gives us a chance to make a new start, in a new country. We'll begin all over again, Valerie. I'll do my best to forget the past, and I hope I can rely on you to do all you can to—'

'Gerry – why can't I make you understand? We can't begin again, it's too late for that. I'm sorry, it's no good. I don't love you, and I'm not coming to Luxembourg.'

'But I've already told them – it's all fixed. As soon as I've worked out my notice, we're going to pack up and go to—'

'You go if you want to. Perhaps you're right – perhaps that will be best. As you say, we won't run the risk of meeting each other accidentally, in the street.'

He began to redden with anger. 'If you think I'm going to let you carry on living here, you're making a big mistake. First thing tomorrow I'm putting this flat on the market!'

'I don't want this flat. I've started packing already; I'm moving out tonight.' She walked over to the telephone. 'I only have to make one phone-call, and then I'll be out of your way.'

As she picked up the receiver, he took two strides across the room. 'If you're going to telephone your fancy-man—'

She faced him without flinching. 'I'm doing nothing of the kind. I'm leaving you, Gerry – and I'm doing it in the traditional way. I'm going home to Mother.'

Now that Ted Watt was a minor stage star, he had installed a telephone at Sackville Road; when he was at home, it was useful to be able to keep in touch with his agent, and when he was away on tour – and he often was – it helped him to keep in touch with his wife and family.

When the phone rang, Daphne answered it eagerly. 'Hello, Ted? I was hoping you'd ring—'

'It isn't Ted, it's me.'

'Oh, Val. Hello. What can I do for you?'

'It was really Mum I wanted to speak to – is she there?'

'She's upstairs, getting ready for bed, I think. Shall I call her?'

'No, don't bother – you'll do. I just wanted to tell you I'm on my way. I'm coming home to stay for a while . . . I've been talking it over with Gerry, and – well, we're splitting up. If you can give me a bed, I'll be very grateful.'

Daphne felt a sick fear churning her stomach; so it was true, after all. 'But why?' she asked. 'What's wrong?'

'I'll explain later. I'll be there very soon. 'Bye for now.'

She was about to hang up when Gerry took the phone from her, saying: 'Let me speak to her. Daphne? Val's talking rubbish. We've just had a little disagreement, that's all. We'll soon sort things out.'

'How can you say that?' asked Valerie wearily. 'You know it's not true . . . I'm going to finish packing.'

She left the room, and Gerald continued confidentially: 'Perhaps it will help clear the air if she comes to you for a few nights. Try to talk some sense into her, for heaven's sake.'

'I'll do my best,' said Daphne.

He replaced the receiver, and almost immediately the telephone-bell rang. Startled, he picked it up, and from the bedroom Valerie heard him saying: 'Hello? Gerald Glynn speaking. Oh, hello Babs – yes?. . . What do you mean – what sort of thing?'

Then there was a long pause, and eventually he said heavily, 'Thank you, Babs. As a matter of fact, I already knew about it, but thanks for telling me anyway. Actually, I'm glad you rang; I was going to call you tomorrow, at your office . . . Yes, I've decided to give up this flat, and I should like Hawkins and Co. to put it on the market for me as soon as possible.'

Kate came downstairs in her dressing gown and said to Daphne, 'I thought I'd make myself a cup of cocoa, to help me get off to sleep. I heard the phone go just now – was it Ted ringing up?'

'No,' said Daphne shortly. 'It was Valerie. She's coming round.'

'Coming here? At this time of night?' Kate looked bewildered, then she saw that Daphne was sorting through a pile of newly ironed washing, picking out single sheets and pillowcases, and broke off to ask: 'What are you doing?'

'I'm going to make up a bed for her. She'll have to have the attic.'

'Whatever do you mean? Why is she coming here?'

'I don't know the ins and outs of it. According to Gerry, they've

433

had some sort of tiff, and she wants to move out for a while. She asked if we'd put her up for a few nights.'

'Oh, but that's dreadful . . .' Kate felt a sudden chill. She sat down in the armchair beside the kitchen range, which had been banked up for the night, but still gave out a comfortably warm glow. 'Val shouldn't do that. I know every couple has falling-outs sometimes, but you must never let the sun go down on your anger. How can they make it up again unless they stay together?'

'She doesn't seem to think they will make it up. She says she's leaving him.'

'Silly girl – she can be so headstrong sometimes. Come on, I'll give you a hand to make the bed up. I just hope the mattress is properly aired – that room hasn't been slept in for ever so long.'

They went upstairs quietly, so as not to wake Annie; it didn't take long to make the bed, and by the time Valerie arrived they were back in the kitchen and Kate was pouring out three cups of cocoa.

'Here, get this inside you, my girl.' She pushed one across the table to Valerie. 'I've put the sugar in already – just give it a stir. Well, now – what's this all about?'

'Didn't Daff tell you? I've left Gerald – it's all over.'

'What nonsense! You might think so now, but when you wake up tomorrow you'll feel quite different about it. Just because you and him have had a few words, that doesn't mean—'

'Mum – I do know what I'm talking about. And whatever Gerry may say, this isn't just a "little tiff" – the marriage is over. I've told him I want a divorce.'

'Oh, no!' Kate was very shocked. 'You don't mean to say Gerald agreed to that?'

'No, he said he wouldn't give me one.'

'Well, there you are then.'

'But we're separating, anyway. He's already spoken to Babs, and told her he wants her to sell the flat for him – he's giving up his job at the BBC, and he's going to move to Luxembourg. According to him, they're starting up a new radio station out there.'

'I see.' Kate frowned. 'That does seem a big step to take – going to live in a foreign country. Where is Luxembourg, anyhow? Is it a long way away?'

'Not that far,' said Daphne. 'Somewhere in between France and Belgium and Germany.'

'Oh dear, it'd be a terrible upheaval, I do see that,' sighed Kate. 'Fancy Gerald giving up his BBC job, just when he seemed to be so well settled, too. I can understand you not wanting to go, my duck – all the same, you surely don't have to break up your marriage just because of it?'

Slowly, Valerie went on stirring her cocoa, staring down into the cup.

'It's not only that,' she said at last. 'Our marriage has been falling apart for years – I should never have married him in the first place. We've always had – problems . . .'

'What sort of problems?' Kate wanted to know.

'Oh – various things. Look, Mum, I'm feeling very tired. Can we talk about it some other time? I just want to try and get some sleep – all right?'

'All right.' Kate stood up, gently patting her daughter's shoulder. 'You have a good night's rest, and I dare say you and Gerald will sort something out in the end. Good night, love, sleep well.' She went out of the room, and they heard her climbing the stairs, more slowly than usual.

'It's come as a shock to her,' Daphne said quietly. 'You mustn't blame her if she can't take it all in yet – her generation were brought up to believe that marriage lasts for ever.'

'Well, some marriages don't.' Val glanced at Daphne curiously. 'And what do you think? Is it a big shock for you as well?'

'Not exactly . . . You've been seeing seeing Steve again, haven't you?'

'So Annie told you.' Val sighed. 'I thought she probably would.'

'And that's why you want a divorce, is it?'

'We love each other – he wants to marry me. He's a good man, Daff.'

'Gerald's a good man, in his own way. He's been a good husband to you.'

'Perhaps I've never been a very good wife . . . I was in love with Steve long before Gerry asked me to marry him, only I was too proud to admit it. I could never be happy with anyone else.'

'You think that now, but it's only because you've been married for so long. You're feeling restless, so you start imagining things . . . Imagining what it would be like, married to Steve—'

'I don't have to imagine it. I know.'

Daphne's expression, which had been full of pity, suddenly froze. 'You mean, you and Steve—?'

'Yes, we have.' Val lifted her head, meeting Daphne's accusing

435

gaze. 'Not often, only once or twice. It seemed to happen so naturally. We never meant to – we just couldn't help it.'

'Of course you could help it.' Daphne's voice was low, but as cold as ice. 'You're a married woman, committing adultery – how could you do it? Aren't you even ashamed?'

'No, I'm not. I'm sorry if I've hurt Gerry, but at least it's all out in the open now – we don't have to lie and pretend any more. Daff, don't look at me like that. You don't know what it means, being tied to the wrong man. It's all right for you – you and Ted are happily married.'

'Are we?' Daphne stood up, automatically collecting the empty cups and saucers.

'Of course you are – everybody knows that.' Then, sensing the meaning behind Daphne's words, she asked: 'Well, you are happy, aren't you?' Getting no reply, she pressed on, astonished. 'You don't mean that Ted . . .?' She stopped, and began again. 'He isn't—?'

Angrily, Daphne turned on her. 'I mean Ted's away so much these days, I hardly ever see him – that's what I mean! Would you call that a happy marriage?'

Babs let herself into Ray's bedroom, shutting the door carefully and silently behind her.

'Are you awake?' she whispered.

'Course I am,' he said. 'I've been waiting for you. What took you so long?'

'I had to calm Mummy down for ages before I finally got her off to sleep. All that stuff about Gerry and Valerie really upset her. It upset me too.'

'Why, were you surprised? I wasn't. Valerie Watkins is nothing but a little tart – you must have known that. And Steve Gunn's a proper villain. Always was, always will be.'

'Then he's the one who led her astray, because Valerie never used to be like that. She was my best friend.' Babs pulled off her nightie and slipped into bed beside him. 'I'd never have dreamed anyone could change so much.'

'Well, now you know. If you ask me, Gerald should think himself bloody lucky to be shot of her.'

'Yes, but it's so horrible for him. What he must be going through now, all on his own . . . Somebody should have gone round there tonight. We really ought to be with him now.'

'Sorry, sweetie – I don't fancy three in a bed myself.'

'Don't be so wicked! Poor Gerry, I don't believe you're a bit sorry for him.'

'Well, you all keep going on about "poor Gerry" – how about "poor Ray" for a change? I'm the one that got beaten up, aren't I?'

'Yes, of course. Poor you . . . Let me kiss it and make it all better.'

She threw her arms round him, and he yelped with pain. 'Careful! I'm covered in bruises, remember? Go easy, can't you?'

'Oh, I'm sorry. I was forgetting . . . forgive me?' She planted a chaste kiss on his brow, and began to stroke him gently. 'How dare Steve Gunn take it out on you, just because he's got a guilty conscience. I think you were very brave. I just wish there was some way I could make it up to you . . .'

She knew what he enjoyed, and went on caressing him, deliberately trying to arouse him, but for once his mind was on other things.

'There is one way,' he said softly.

'How? Tell me.'

'You could marry me.'

'What?' She hadn't been expecting this, and it took her completely off-guard. 'But we can't. You know we can't!'

'Why can't we? If you love me, like you say you do—'

'You know what Mummy said.'

'It's not your mother I want to marry – it's you. We don't even have to tell her. Why don't we nip off quietly and get married in secret, at the register office?'

'Ohhh.' Suddenly it seemed very tempting. 'That would be marvellous, only—'

'Only what? Nobody else need know – and then you'd be mine, always, and I'd be the happiest man in the world.'

'Oh Ray, you're so sweet. I'll think about it.'

'What is there to think about? You've only got to say the word and we'll go and get spliced tomorrow!'

'It's not as simple as that. You have to give three weeks' notice or something. There's all the paperwork to be done – forms to fill up. They'd need our birth certificates and everything—'

'Are you sure? Birth certificates? Oh, blimey . . .'

'Ray! You know I don't like it when you say things like that.'

He wasn't listening. He turned away from her, momentarily cast down. 'I haven't got a birth certificate. I told you – I was brought up in an orphanage.'

'But they must have had all your papers. Didn't they hand them over when you left?'

'They don't do that. You're not allowed to know who your parents were – they never tell you.'

'Oh, that does seem unfair. But there must be some way you could find out. You could go to Somerset House and ask them to look up the register of births for the day you were born. They'll have it in their records – "Raymond Duke, somewhere in South London, born on the—"'

'That's no good,' he muttered. 'It won't be under that name anyhow.'

'Why not?'

"Cos it's not my real name, that's why not. I changed it when I left the orphanage.'

'Whatever for?'

'Because I didn't like my old name, did I? All the other kids used to make fun of me on account of my name, so I changed it. I thought "Duke" sounded better. It's got a bit of class about it, don't you think?'

'So what's your real name?'

'Never you mind – I hate my real name.'

'Oh, don't be silly. If we're going to be married, I'll have to know sooner or later – it'll be on the marriage certificate. Go on, tell me.'

'You'll only laugh.'

'I won't, I promise I won't. It's still Raymond, is it? I mean, that's your proper name? Or did you change that as well?'

'No, Raymond's OK – it's the other part I didn't like. According to the orphanage, when they took me in I was—' he hesitated, then confessed under his breath: '—Raymond Potts. They used to call me Potty.'

At once she began to giggle, and he turned on her furiously. 'There! I knew you would – and it's not funny, d'you hear? Damn you, you stupid bitch! It's not *funny* – not *funny*!'

He repeated the words again and again, smacking her buttocks hard at each repetition, making her cry out.

'Ow! You're hurting – *ow*! Stop it. I'm not laughing, really I'm not. Please stop!'

And yet a part of her didn't want him to stop. The stinging blows upon her naked skin were exquisitely painful, but they were strangely exciting too; when at last he stopped punishing her, she found she was tingling all over.

'You are a brute,' she panted. 'You've made me really sore . . .'

'Shut your face,' he grunted, and rolled on top of her, pinning her down. 'You'll be a lot sorer by the time I've done with you.'

*

A few days later, when Daphne and Annie came home from school, they found Kate getting tea ready. Annie rushed upstairs to change out of her school uniform, and Kate turned to Daphne.

'Oh, there's a letter for you,' she remarked. 'It came by the second post. I put it up on the mantelpiece.'

'Thanks.' Daphne glanced at it; the handwriting was all too familiar. 'It's from my mother – working herself up into a state over Gerald, no doubt.'

'Well, you can't blame her. Such a dreadful thing to happen,' said Kate sadly, as she went on cutting bread and butter. 'I mean, Val's my daughter and I'm very fond of her – I always will be – but even so, it's hard to excuse the way she's been carrying on.'

Daphne tore open the envelope and unfolded the letter, written in Muriel's big, florid script.

Dear Daphne,

By now you must know about the outcome of Gerald's unhappy marriage, since I understand that his wife has seen fit to move back into your house. Words cannot express my feelings at this tragedy – my heart bleeds for my son, and I cannot bring myself to tell you my opinion of the young woman who still bears our family name – the name she has dragged down to the gutter.

I realise that you had nothing to do with your sister-in-law's misconduct, and I am sure you are as disgusted as I am that you are now forced to live under the same roof with such a person. I would only urge you to try and make other arrangements; I hope you can prevail upon your husband to find you alternative accommodation in the very near future.

You must understand that after this terrible shock, I really cannot maintain any communication with the Watkins family. Naturally, I assume that your husband had no knowledge of his sister's activities, but for the time being I feel it would create embarrassment on both sides if we were to meet. Please explain that this is not a reflection on him in any way.

Of course it goes without saying that you and my darling grand-daughter will always be welcome here at any time; this is your real home, after all.

With much love, your affectionate Mother.

Daphne dropped the letter into the grate and watched the paper curl up and burn.

'What did she have to say?' asked Kate.

'Nothing much. It's more or less what I expected. She's so upset, she isn't making a lot of sense.'

'Poor woman, I feel so sorry for her. Well, for everybody, really. I just keep hoping that now Val's come home, she'll have a chance to think again and come to her senses.'

There was a knock at the front door, and Annie, on her way downstairs, called out, 'It's all right – I'll see who it is.'

A few moments later they heard voices in the hall, then the kitchen door opened and Annie came in, all smiles. Steve Gunn followed her into the room.

'Hello,' he said awkwardly. 'It was really Val I came to see. I should have realised she wouldn't be home from work yet.'

'I told him she won't be long,' Annie chimed in. 'I said he must come in and wait.'

Kate stood up, addressing Annie briskly. 'Now then, lovey – you can go to the sitting room, and listen to the wireless for a bit, while we have a little talk. You'll be just in time for *Children's Hour*.'

'Oh, Nan,' Annie protested. 'I'm not a child any more!'

'Never you mind. You still enjoy *Toytown* and Larry the Lamb, you know you do, so run along, there's a dear.'

Annie went out of the room with her head held high, deeply affronted, and Kate turned to Steve.

'You shouldn't have come here,' she said. 'I'm sorry – I don't mean to be rude, but you must see it isn't right.'

'But I've got to talk to Val,' he began. 'There are things we've got to settle—'

'How did you know she was here?' Daphne asked.

'Annie's called in to visit Tony a few times, since he's been laid up. She told him, and he told me.'

Kate bit her lip. 'She shouldn't have said anything – but of course, she wasn't to know. You've no right to come here, pestering Val. As if things weren't bad enough already, without that. You must go, right this minute, before she comes home.'

He stood his ground. 'I don't think you understand. Val's going to get a divorce, and then we're going to be married.'

'Oh, no, I don't know what she's been telling you, but that's not true. There's no question of any divorce,' said Kate.

'She asked Gerald to divorce her, but he refused,' explained Daphne. 'I think he's still hoping for some sort of reconciliation.'

'That's impossible. Their marriage is over.'

While they were arguing, they did not hear Valerie coming down the stairs. When she entered the kitchen they all fell silent.

As soon as she saw Steve, Val had eyes for on one else; he held out his arms to her, and her face lit up. They came together in the middle of that shabby kitchen, embracing one another as if they were the last two people left on earth.

Kate took a step towards them, but Daphne put a hand on her arm, restraining her.

When Val could speak, she asked Steve: 'What are you doing here?'

'I had to see you, didn't I? We've got a lot to talk about,' he told her.

'There's nothing to talk about!' Kate broke in sharply. 'I told you – it's all over. You must leave this house.'

Steve never stopped looking at Valerie as he said, 'They tell me your husband won't agree to a divorce.'

'That's right. But in the end, he'll have to. Sooner or later, he'll let me go – we've just got to be patient.'

'I can't do that.' Steve spoke softly, but with absolute assurance; his mind was made up. 'I've been looking for somewhere to live, and I've found a place for us in Sydenham. It's pretty small – only two rooms, and we'll have to share a bathroom with the tenants on the top floor – but it's clean, and we'll be together.'

Now it was Daphne's turn to interrupt. 'Steve, you heard what she said! She can't marry you unless Gerald changes his mind, and until he does, you'll just have to wait.'

'We've waited too long already,' he said, then continued in the same steady tone, 'I've paid a month's rent in advance. We can move in right away – tonight, if you're willing.'

'*No!*' Kate was horrified. 'Val – don't listen to him!'

But something of Steve's quiet certainty had rubbed off on Valerie. Looking into his eyes, she said simply, 'I'll go upstairs and get ready. It won't take me long. Most of my things are still in the suitcase. Wait for me.'

When she left the room, Kate confronted Steve angrily. 'How could you? You're ruining that girl's life. You don't seem to realise what you're doing!'

'We know what we're doing,' he said. 'Don't worry about Val – I'll take good care of her. Try to be happy for us, if you can.'

Desperately, Kate turned to her daughter-in-law. 'Daff, say something. We can't let Val go like this. Aren't you going to try and stop them?'

Daphne shook her head, looking away unhappily.

'I can't,' she said at last. 'I wouldn't know how.'

It was a shocking thing to happen. Young men and women who deliberately flouted the rules of decency and good conduct by living together – 'living in sin', as it was called – could not be accepted in polite society.

Their families tried to hush it up as far as possible, but the rumours soon began to buzz around, and Kate was agonisingly aware of other people giving her curious looks when she was out shopping.

She stopped buying her vegetables from Gunns; she could not bring herself to speak to Steve's parents, with this shared secret lying so heavily between them. It hit Freda Gunn very hard too. If anything, she was relieved as the weeks passed by without any sign of Kate Watkins dropping in for a few pounds of potatoes, or a couple of cooking apples. Knowing what they knew, they could not have met one another's eyes.

They were not the only women to be devastated by the scandal. The news had aggravated Muriel Glynn's nervous disorders so severely, she took to her bed; she seemed to be in a state of shock, and had to be waited on hand and foot by Ethel and Aggie. When she came home from work, Babs spent a lot of time sitting at her mother's bedside, reading aloud to her, coaxing her to have a little more milk-pudding, or to drink up the last drop of medicine – fussing over her and cosseting her.

'It's the shame of it,' Muriel complained, lying back against her pillows with her eyes closed. 'That young woman has brought shame upon our family.'

'I don't suppose she calls herself Glynn any more,' said Babs, trying to look on the bright side. 'If she's got any sense, she'll pretend she and Steve Gunn are married.'

'Whatever she may call herself, legally, morally, and in every possible way, she is Mrs Gerald Glynn.' Muriel shook her head sorrowfully. 'Nothing can change that.'

'Well, if I were Gerry, I'd let her have a divorce. I'd be only too glad to get rid of her,' said Babs.

'You know you don't mean that, dear. It's quite out of the question. There has never been a divorce in our family – it's the good name of the DeWitts I'm thinking of, naturally. Heaven knows I've never had any reason to feel loyalty towards the name of *Glynn* – but even after all the trials and tribulations I suffered at that man's hands, I never once thought of seeking a divorce. The DeWitts are above such things. We are separated; I have to content myself with that.'

'I suppose she could change her name to Gunn without getting married,' said Babs thoughtfully. 'There's a thing called a deed poll, isn't there?'

'So I believe, but I can't say I know much about it. However, even if she changes her name by some sort of legal trickery, in the eyes of the Archbishop of Canterbury, she will always be a Glynn.'

But Babs was continuing her own train of thought. 'It never struck me till now. I wonder how you go about changing your name? I must talk to Ray. He works in a lawyer's office, he could possibly find out.'

Muriel opened her eyes. 'Why are you so interested?'

'Oh, it's just that Ray might want to change his name some time,' Babs answered vaguely. 'I'm quite surprised he never thought of it before.'

'But why on earth should he do such a thing?'

'It's silly, really.' Babs shrugged her shoulders. 'He told me once that Duke isn't his real name. He began calling himself Duke when he came out of the orphanage, because they all made fun of him, so he called himself Ray Duke instead.'

'I don't follow you. What was wrong with his own name?'

'It's rather a joke, only he gets very cross if you laugh about it. Officially, he is really called Raymond Potts – well, you can see why he wanted to change it, can't you? I wouldn't fancy being Barbara Potts – can you imagine? I'd sooner be Barbara Duke, so if it's just a matter of having one of those deed-poll things, I don't see why he shouldn't change it once and for all. I mean, suppose we have a family of our own one day? It wouldn't be very nice for our children, would it?' She giggled, despite herself. 'Ray said the other boys used to call him Potty!'

'*Stop it! Stop it at once!*'

Muriel's voice sounded hoarse and unnatural. Babs turned and stared at her.

'Mummy, what is it? What's wrong?'

There was something in her mother's expression that puzzled her –

a hunted look in her eyes, a tenseness round the mouth that she had never seen before – but she could not interpret it.

'Nothing's wrong.' Muriel spoke in the same strained tone, choosing her words carefully. 'You must understand – there's no question of you marrying that young man! I can't possibly allow it.'

'But you said we could have an understanding. You said one day, when he's established himself and saved some money—'

'No, it's quite impossible. Now I've had time to think it over, I realise I was wrong. It would be completely unsuitable. I don't want to hear you mention it again.'

'But I thought you liked Ray!'

'I have nothing against him personally, but you must try to put the idea out of your mind – do you hear? He's not the right man for you, and he never will be.'

Clearly, there was no point in arguing. Babs changed the subject, and finally succeeded in calming her mother, sitting with her until she began to drift off to sleep. When she returned to the drawing room, she found Ray seated at the little card-table, laying out a hand of Patience.

'You were a long time,' he said. 'Being difficult again, was she?'

'Very.' Babs pulled up a chair and sat beside him. 'Red seven on black eight.'

'It's all right – I can see it for myself, thanks. What's got into her tonight?'

'Goodness only knows.' Babs hadn't meant to tell him, but now she suddenly burst out: 'As a matter of fact, it was about you. You see, I'd been talking to her about this idea I had—'

She told him her brainwave, that he should change his name legally to Duke instead of Potts – and he rounded on her furiously.

'Why did you have to bring that up?'

'Why not? I told her they'd been horrible to you at the orphanage, and I said I agreed with you. I'd much rather be called Mrs Duke than—'

'Yes, all right!' he snapped. 'So what did she say to that!'

'She said there was no question of us getting married anyway. She said she wouldn't allow it.'

'That's rubbish – she couldn't stop us.'

'I know, but she got very worked up about it. She said I'd got to put you out of my mind – you're not the right man for me – that sort of thing . . . I'm sure she doesn't really mean it. You know how she is when she gets a bee in her bonnet – she'll have forgotten all about it by tomorrow.' Looking at the cards over his shoulder, she leaned forward again, pointing: 'Black ten on red knave.'

'*Don't tell me* . . .!' But he made the move anyway, then stood up. 'Excuse me, would you?'

She assumed he was going to the lavatory, but it was nearly a quarter of an hour before he came back.

'Are you all right?' she asked.

'Yes – why shouldn't I be?'

'Well, you were such a long time, I thought perhaps you weren't well.' She studied him more closely. 'And you look a bit pale. Do you think it was something you had for supper?'

'I'm perfectly OK.' He sat down. 'I didn't go to the WC if that's what you're thinking. I went to have a word with darling Mummy.'

'Oh no. She was just beginning to doze off when I left her. You don't mean to say you went and woke her up?'

'Why shouldn't I? She'd been passing remarks about me behind my back – I'd got a right to find out what she meant by it. So I walked into her bedroom, and touched her on the shoulder, and she sat up right away, almost as if she'd been waiting for me.'

'Oh Ray, you shouldn't have. Now I'll have to go and settle her down all over again.' As Babs got up from the table, she noticed that he was beginning to turn up the cards again, one by one, and said: 'You're not allowed to do that.'

'I can if I want to. It's my game.'

'But you've been through the pack once already – it's cheating.'

'So what? If it doesn't come out the first time, I keep on till it does come out.'

'That's against the rules!'

'Losing is against the rules. It's winning that matters.'

She gave up and moved away, about to leave the room. With her hand on the door, she turned back to ask: 'By the way, what did Mummy have to say when you asked her? About us, I mean?'

'She told me what she told you. It wouldn't be a suitable match. I wasn't the right sort of person to marry her beloved daughter.'

'I'm sorry, Ray, she can be such a snob sometimes. I should never have reminded her that you were brought up in an orphanage.'

'I don't think it was that. It was my name she didn't like. She came right out with it – it was the first thing she asked me. "*Is it true that your real name is Potts?*" And when I said yes it was, she didn't want to know anything else. I got the feeling she'd heard the name before somewhere. She looked as if—'

He paused, and she prompted him. 'As if what?'

'As if she'd heard something about me – only she wouldn't say what.'

'But that doesn't make sense. What could she possibly have heard about you?'

'I don't know, but I can tell you one thing – I'm going to find out.'

Chapter Twenty-three

DAYS TURNED INTO weeks, and weeks into months, but Ray never stopped puzzling over Muriel Glynn's curious reaction when she learned his real name.

He broached the subject again, more than once, but she told him flatly that she had no idea what he was talking about. Of course she had never heard the name before. It meant nothing to her – nothing whatever.

He would not give up that easily. He asked Ethel and Aggie. Surely, if Muriel knew of some secret connected with his surname, her sisters would know it too? When he tackled Ethel, she shook her head, saying she was totally ignorant of anyone by that name, and he sensed that she was speaking the truth.

When he tried to talk to Aggie about it, she looked terrified. As he continued to question her she burst into tears, and he thought he was on to something at last – but she only whimpered: 'I may have heard the name, I can't really remember. I forget so many things these days – you won't be cross with me, will you, Raymond? It's not my fault if my memory plays tricks on me, is it?'

He realised that he had drawn a blank again; Aggie was feeling guilty for no better reason than that she was unable to answer his questions.

Even then he still persisted, coming back to the mystery time and time again, until Babs grew quite impatient with him.

'Why can't you just drop the whole thing?' she said. 'What difference does it make, anyway? Even if Mummy remembers the name, it's not important, is it?'

'I think it is. She heard it somewhere, I'm sure of that – and it must

447

be important, because of the way she looked at me . . . As if it was the name of somebody famous – my name.'

They were side by side in his bed, and Ray was lying on his back, staring up at the ceiling, as he mused, 'It can't be anything smart, like a hero. If he was as famous as all that, we'd have heard of him too.'

Anxious to wind up this tiresome conversation, Babs suggested flippantly, 'Perhaps Mr Potts wasn't famous at all. Perhaps he was *in*famous, and that's why she's trying to hush it up!'

Ray wasn't quite sure what 'infamous' meant, and she had to explain it to him, already regretting her little attempt at a joke – Ray could be so touchy sometimes . . . To her surprise, he didn't seem in the least offended, but looked rather pleased, rolling over and whispering in her ear, 'Yeah, maybe that's the answer. Maybe he was a well-known cat-burglar, or a jewel-thief – or even a mass-murderer? "Potts the Poisoner" – how about that?'

Chuckling throatily, he began to make love to her, as if this thought had aroused a sudden passion in him.

Time rolled by, moons rose and set, and the world described another circle in space – and Ray said no more to Babs about a romantic elopement or a secret marriage. Perhaps he had other things on his mind.

In a two-roomed flat on a first floor in Sydenham, marriage was never mentioned either.

'Penny for 'em,' said Steve, one summer evening.

He had not been home from work very long; they were always busy at Croydon these days, with more and more cargo-planes and airliners coming through every day – each plane needing to be serviced, re-fuelled and overhauled before taking off again.

When he got home, Steve always took off his overalls and put on an old towelling dressing gown, then shut himself into the bathroom – which they shared with Mr and Mrs Pilling from the top flat – and had a quick sluice-down all over. Afterwards, on a warm evening like this, he often sat in his vest and pants, reading the sports pages at the back of the evening paper, while Val, nestling on a cushion at his feet, made herself useful by darning his socks . . . And sometimes she let the mending fall, and just went on sitting there, gazing into space – lost in thought.

Now he put aside his paper. 'Penny for 'em,' he repeated.

'Mmm? Oh, I wasn't thinking of anything special.' She smiled up at him. 'I was just daydreaming.'

'What were you dreaming about?'

'Us . . . How happy we are.'

'Yes, we are happy, aren't we?' He searched her face, needing some reassurance.

'You know we are.' She rested her head in his lap, and he stroked her hair. 'The two happiest people in the world.'

'Sometimes I feel as if we're the *only* people in the world,' he said.

Since they had moved into their tiny flat, they had not seen many friends. Val went home to Sackville Road once a week, and Steve made frequent trips to the greengrocers in Church Road – but they never made such trips together, and never embarrassed their families by visiting them as a couple. By the same token, none of their relatives ever called in at the little two-roomed flat. The Watkinses and the Gunns did not exactly condemn them for the step they had taken, but they could not condone it either.

'We never seem to see anyone else,' he continued gently.

'That's the way I like it,' she told him.

'Are you sure? You wouldn't like to get out more – to the pictures, perhaps, or to a dance?'

'Of course not. I'm perfectly happy the way we are, truly I am.' Putting up a hand to touch his face, she said, 'Why, what makes you ask?'

'I only wondered. Tonight, when I was coming up the stairs, I heard you'd got the wireless on – a dance-band was playing – and as soon as I opened the door, you switched it off.'

'I wasn't really listening properly. It was just a bit of music, for company. I don't need it now you're home.' She stood up. 'Are you ready for supper? It's only cold meat pie and salad, 'cos it's been such a hot day.'

'That'll be fine.'

'And you'd better put some clothes on, make yourself decent. Suppose somebody was to come in, and find you sitting in your knickers, eating your supper!'

'Who d'you think's going to come in?'

But he pulled on a pair of trousers and a jersey while she went into the tiny cupboard they called a kitchen and laid out pie and salad on two plates. While he was waiting, Steve idly stretched out a hand to the wireless set and switched it on again. After a moment it warmed up, and he heard some more dance-music playing. When it came to an end, a man's voice said: 'That was *Smoke Gets in Your Eyes* – the latest record by Carroll Gibbons and his Savoy Orpheans. You are listening to the *Amami Melody Hour Programme*, brought to you by the makers of Amami Shampoo. Remember – Friday Night is Amami Night!'

Then he realised that the set was tuned in to Radio Luxembourg – and the voice was the voice of Gerald Glynn.

Without a word, Val came back and put the plates on the table; then she turned the set off again, and they sat down.

'You still miss him, don't you?' Steve asked.

'No, I don't. I sometimes switch on Luxembourg because it's easy to listen to. It's the music I like, not the announcements in between.'

'Look at me, Val,' he said. She faced him across the table, and he went on, 'You're unhappy about something. I've known it for weeks – and now I can see it in your eyes. Tell me what's wrong.'

'There's nothing wrong.' She tried to eat some salad, but he sat there looking at her, waiting, and at last she couldn't stand it any longer and put down her knife and fork. 'All right. You'll think I'm being very stupid, but if you really want to know, I've been thinking about my job at the office – about the Crystal Palace, and Sir Henry.'

'Your boss?' He stared at her, astonished. This was the very last thing he had expected. 'What about him?'

'He's been in such a funny mood lately. The attendance figures are going down, and they should go up in the summer. I suppose it must be worrying him – and when Sir Henry worries, we all worry.'

He relaxed a little. 'So that's really all it is? Nothing else on your mind at all?'

'Nothing else.'

Slightly reassured, he began to tuck into his meat pie. Though he was still not absolutely certain he believed her.

'Another cup of tea, Babs dear?' asked Aunt Ethel.

'I can make you another piece of toast, if you like,' said Aunt Aggie. 'It won't take a moment.'

'No, really, I must go. I've got a very busy day ahead of me,' said Babs, rising from the breakfast-table. 'By the way, I don't know what time I'll be home this evening, so don't keep supper waiting for me.'

Ray glanced up from his bacon and egg. 'Why, what are you up to?'

'I told you, I've got to go and set up our stand at the Exhibition,' said Babs.

'You mean you're going to be working there, inside the Palace?'

'Of course I am. Hawkins and Co have got a very good site in the middle of the Main Hall. I did tell you, but I suppose you weren't listening.'

Every year, one of the most popular events at the Crystal Palace was the South London Exhibition. Posters had gone up everywhere, advertising it as *The Great Annual Show Of Everything For House And Garden*; it was a local version of the Ideal Homes Exhibition at Olympia.

All the leading firms in South London were represented. Big stores like Kennards of Croydon, Grants and Allders put on special displays, and manufacturers of domestic goods – everything from basketware to kitchen gadgets, linoleum to china and glass – rented space in the Main Hall to show off their wares. This year for the first time Hawkins & Co had decided to take part as well.

'But what are you going to have on your stall?' Agnes wanted to know. 'You sell houses – you can't very well build a whole house, can you?'

'You'd be surprised!' said Babs. 'We're going to have a lot of model houses on show, and there'll be some beautiful photos of our different properties – and Crabbe and Carter have actually put up one of their new bungalows, completely furnished, so people can walk in and have a look round. You must come and see it when the Exhibition opens.'

Aggie exclaimed brightly, 'That would be lovely – can we all go?' Then her face fell. 'What about your dear mother? Do you think she'll be feeling strong enough to come with us?'

'Don't be silly, dear,' Ethel reproached her. 'You know perfectly well, Muriel hasn't left her room ever since – well, since poor Gerald's troubles began.'

'That reminds me.' Ray threw Babs a sardonic smile. 'If you should happen to run into Valerie while you're at the Palace, don't bother to give her my kind regards.'

Aggie recoiled in dismay. 'Oh dear, do you suppose she will be there? How very awkward.'

'Don't worry,' said Babs. 'I'll do my best to keep well out of her way.'

'And I expect she'll try and avoid you as well,' said Ethel. 'After all, it would be even more embarrassing for her.'

'Anyway, I can't stop here talking.' Babs picked up her handbag. 'I promised I'd get into work early.'

Ray swallowed a last mouthful of bacon, then stood up. 'Hang on a tick while I get my sandwiches. I can walk with you, part of the way.'

As they set off together, Babs said, 'You will come and see our display, won't you? I can't wait to show you the Crabbe and Carter bungalow. It's got all the latest labour-saving devices, just like the ones they're building on their new estate at Elmers End.'

'Sounds good,' he said. 'Maybe we'll have a place like that ourselves one of these days, eh?'

'If only we could.' She sighed, then linked her arm through his. 'So when are you going to come to the Exhibition?'

'I can't, can I? I'm out at work all day.'

'Yes, but we'll be open most evenings, and all day Saturday – you'll be free on Saturday.'

'Ah . . . No, 'fraid not. Not this Saturday.'

'Why, what's happening on Saturday?'

'I had an idea. I thought I'd go over to visit my dear old school – for auld lang syne.'

'The orphanage? You said once you'd never go back there.'

'I've changed my mind. Well, it struck me that I might be able to find out something about my family. I decided you were probably right. They must have all the papers tucked away somewhere, in the office.'

'But you said they never tell anyone who their parents were.'

He smiled. 'Maybe if I ask nicely, I can talk them into it.'

At lunchtime, the rest of the clerical staff at Colpoys & Co went off to lunch, but Ray stayed in the office, eating the sandwiches he had brought with him.

Today he got through them quickly, then washed his hands; it wouldn't look good if he got a smear of bloater-paste on the firm's notepaper.

Selecting a sheet of letterheaded stationery, he began to type, very slowly and very carefully since he was not an experienced typist:

To Whom It May Concern

This letter is by way of introduction; the bearer, Mr Duke, is a member of my staff. He is engaged upon an investigation into the family of a certain Raymond Potts who was, I am given to understand, in your care for several years. My firm is acting on behalf of a certain private individual who wishes to trace Mr R. Potts' parents; I am not at liberty to give you any further details at present, except to say that a satisfactory outcome will be to everyone's advantage.

I must add that this is all very confidential, and give you my personal assurance that my assistant, Mr Duke, may be relied upon to act with complete discretion.

Yours faithfully,

Pulling the letter from the machine, Ray read it through, feeling rather pleased with himself. He had borrowed a lot of the wording from phrases he had come across in various items of office correspondence; he wasn't quite certain what they all meant, but the general effect was impressive.

With a flourish, he forged his employer's signature – which he had been practising privately for some time: *William Colpoys*, then he folded the letter neatly, put it into an envelope, and slipped it into his breast pocket. That ought to do the trick.

Like Ray, Sir Henry Buckland rarely took time out for lunch, but stayed at his desk, going through the daily correspondence over a cheese-roll or a Cornish pasty.

Val often wished he would go to one of the Palace restaurants and enjoy a square meal instead. She felt sure it would benefit his digestion, and might even improve his temper.

Today, to make matters worse, there was a continual barrage of noise going on. An army of workmen, out in the Main Hall, were putting the finishing touches to the new Exhibition – sawing, hammering, shouting and whistling. And as if that were not sufficiently distracting, during the lunch-hour Sir Henry had asked someone to come and see him on an urgent business matter. Judging by the raised voices Val could hear through Sir Henry's door, the meeting was not going well.

He had given instructions that she should bring in a tray of coffee at one-thirty, and although she wasn't sure whether he would welcome the interruption, she did not like to disobey his orders. Tentatively, she rapped on the door, but the background noises were so loud, she couldn't make herself heard.

Taking her courage in both hands, she opened the door and went in. For a moment, neither of the men noticed her; they continued to glare at one another.

'What the deuce do you mean by it, eh?' bellowed Sir Henry, his moustache bristling.

His visitor, seated at the opposite side of the desk, retorted, 'There's no need to shout, I'm not deaf. You're the one who started all this – we didn't!'

'It's disloyalty, that's what it is!' Sir Henry thumped the desk. 'Treachery and disloyalty. Leaving us, after all these years!'

'Now just hang on a minute. If you hadn't put up your prices, we wouldn't be moving out.' The stranger was a good-looking young man; Val knew him by sight – he was the star motorcyclist on the Palace Speedway team.

'Economic necessity, Kirkwood. Prices are going up everywhere.'

The young man grinned. 'Not at New Cross, they're not. The manager over there is offering us a better deal than you are, old man, so we didn't have any choice, did we?'

'Blast your impertinence. Don't take that tone with me—' Sir Henry noticed Valerie in the doorway. 'Well? What do you want?' he snapped.

'Nothing, sir. Just the coffee,' she stammered.

'How dare you interrupt me in the middle of a private meeting?' Sir Henry roared, his face suffused with rage. 'Get out – do you hear?'

She fled; in all the years she had worked at the Palace, Sir Henry had never spoken to her like that. She retreated to her own office and poured herself a cup of coffee with shaking hands. It might be comforting – and it seemed a pity to waste it.

The acrimonious meeting did not continue for long. Very soon, the door opened again, and the young speedway rider emerged.

'Does he often get like that?' he asked Val.

'No. I've never known him quite so angry. He's usually very nice – very polite.'

'Well, I'm sorry if I set him off, but I couldn't help it.' Perching on the corner of her desk, he went on: 'We thought we had a good deal going for us here, with the speedway. Then out of a clear blue sky, we all got a stiff letter, saying His Lordship's putting up the rental – the money we have to pay for the lease of the track. He didn't even discuss it with us. There was just an ultimatum, take it or leave it – so we decided to leave it.'

'You're going to New Cross?'

'They've got a new stadium there, and they made us a very good offer, so we signed another agreement. And now your boss is calling us all the names under the sun – accusing us of treachery and going behind his back. Well, you heard the way he was carrying on.'

'I certainly did.'

He looked at her, and his face softened. 'Yes. Sorry about that. He shouldn't have taken it out on you.'

She tried to smile. 'I expect I'll get over it.'

He smiled back. 'All the same, I feel partly responsible.' Looking at the coffee cups, he added: 'Is this your lunch break?'

'It's supposed to be. I should really have an hour off, but I don't often take it.'

'Take it now. Come along to the refreshment room, and let me buy you a drink.'

'Oh no, really – there's no need for that.'

'But I want to. It's the least I can do.'

He really was very good-looking – and very charming. Suddenly, Val longed to get away from the four walls of this little office.

'All right,' she said. 'Just one drink – I mustn't be long.'

They went out through the Main Hall, through the chaos and confusion that preceded every new exhibition, picking their way through builders' ladders, piles of bricks and stacks of timber. Some of the stalls were already finished, and one or two hopeful exhibitors were trying out their sales-patter on anyone within earshot.

'Can I interest you in our new improved Kitchen Wizard?' asked a young lady in a white overall, wielding a stainless steel object with handles sticking out all over it. 'It's ideal for every kind of fruit and vegetable. It can peel, it can chop, it can core, it can slice—'

'Not tonight, Josephine,' said the young man cheerfully, and led the way into the bar. 'Now then, sit down,' he said to Val. 'What can I get you? A beer – a gin – or would you prefer a cocktail? Go on, name your poison.'

Val asked for a Green Goddess, which was the only cocktail she could remember. When it came, it was a dark, vivid green, and tasted a little sickly, but she enjoyed it anyway. The young man was very pleasant, and she found him easy to talk to.

At last she put down her empty glass. 'Thank you, that was very nice,' she said. 'Now I really must go. Sir Henry might want me.'

'Let him go on wanting. You're entitled to some time off, aren't you? Have another drink.'

'No, really—' She broke off, the words fading on her lips. Babs Glynn had just entered the refreshment room. It was a long time since they had last met; two old friends, who were friends no longer.

'Hello, Babs,' said Val.

Babs looked at her – and at her companion, and her eyes widened. Then she looked at the two empty cocktail glasses, and laughed. It was a brief, unattractive laugh.

'Well, I must say you're full of surprises,' she said. 'Does Steve know you go around picking up other men in your spare time?'

Val took a deep breath, then stood up and said to the young man, 'As I was saying, I really must go now. Thank you very much, Mr— oh, I'm sorry, I've forgotten your name.'

'I can tell you his name,' said Babs. 'He's Roger Kirkwood – and for your information, he's a married man – but I don't suppose you'd bother about a little thing like that.'

'Goodbye, Mr Kirkwood,' said Valerie. 'And goodbye, Babs.'

Then she walked out.

Roger watched her go, then turned to Babs, eyeing her appreciatively. 'Have we met somewhere?' he asked. 'I know I ought to remember, but – won't you sit down and keep me company? Have a drink.'

'No, thanks,' said Babs coolly. 'I'm particular about the company I keep.'

'Wait a minute! It's all coming back to me now . . . I'd just taken a spill and come off the bike – and you were there.' He grinned again. 'Of course I remember. You were just as bloody rude then as you are now.'

Babs drew back her hand and gave him a stinging slap across the face. He blinked, rocking back on his heels – then began to roar with laughter. She walked straight out of the refreshment room with the sound of his laughter ringing in her ears, and collided with a young lady in a white overall, who thrust a metal object at her and gushed: 'It's our new improved Kitchen Wizard – ideal for every kind of fruit and vegetable. It can peel, it can chop, it can—'

'It can go to hell,' said Babs, and walked on.

When Val returned to her office, the inner door was slightly ajar, and she heard Sir Henry calling to her. 'Would you come in for a moment, please?'

Bracing herself, she went into the other room. He looked up from his desk and said, 'Shut the door, please, I have something to say to you. Would you sit down?'

She obeyed, wondering what was to come, and he continued quietly, 'Twenty minutes ago, I was extremely discourteous, and I owe you an apology.'

'Oh no, you don't have to apologise.'

'Yes, I do. You were doing your duty, carrying out my instructions, and I lost my temper and shouted at you. That was unforgivable.'

'Really, it doesn't matter . . .'

'It matters very much; you don't deserve such boorish treatment. I'm also aware that I haven't been particularly civil to you for some time. I don't know how much interest you take in the financial side of our enterprise, but you probably realise that since the slump, it has been an uphill struggle, trying to keep the Palace on a secure footing. I've spent many a sleepless night wrestling with the situation, believe me.'

'Well, I knew things hadn't been going as well as you'd have liked,' she began.

'That is something of an understatement. And now we have this latest thunderbolt – the loss of our Speedway Motorcycle team, who are deserting us in order to move elsewhere. I can only claim that this seemed to be the last straw, and I'm sorry I lost control of my temper. It was wrong of me to treat you so abominably, and I hope you will forgive me.'

'Of course I do.' Val hesitated for a moment, then went on: 'I'm glad you told me because – well, just lately, I noticed that you seemed to be – not very pleased with me . . . I thought perhaps you disapproved of – of something you'd heard. Something I'd done.'

He raised his head, and their eyes met.

'Whatever you choose to do – whatever you choose *not* to do – outside these offices, and in your own time, is of no interest to me whatever,' he said. 'You do your work well, and I have no complaints to make. Apart from that, your private life is your own, and no concern of mine. And that is all I have to say.'

His moustache curved in the ghost of a smile as he added, 'Except – perhaps – if it is not inconveniencing you too much, I believe I would like that cup of coffee now, after all.'

On Saturday afternoon Ray made a cross-country expedition which entailed changing twice – taking a tram, then a bus, and then another bus, with long waits on draughty street-corners each time.

He finished up at Aldington Grove, a quiet residential road just off Woolwich Common, not far from the Barracks. At every step he took along the pavements, scuffing up drifts of fallen leaves, he felt his stomach churning with dread, and had an overpowering desire to turn and run away – away from the unhappy memories, away from his past.

But he forced himself to go on, and at last he reached the twin stone pillars, topped with two grim-faced stone lions, and the big wooden notice inside the railings bearing the legend: *The Lupton-Briggs Charitable Institute for Homeless Boys*.

Ray pushed one half of the rusting iron gates; it still squealed, just as he remembered it, and at once he was a small, frightened child again. He told himself not to be stupid – he had nothing to be afraid of any longer; he was not Raymond Potts now, he was Mr Duke, an up-and-coming solicitor, here on important business.

All the same, it was hard to ignore the pounding of his heart and the sweating of his palms when he looked up at the grey Victorian mansion with its rows of windows veiled by lace curtains. The building looked imposing enough – once upon a time it had been the home of a London banker and his family – but Ray knew only too well that behind those lace curtains, it was just another kind of barracks.

He walked up the path and climbed the three steps to the front door, where he tugged at the old-fashioned bell-pull. The sound of the cracked bell jangling at the far end of the passage made him feel sick, but he could not turn back now; he stood under the porch, and waited.

Footsteps clattered on the linoleum – he even knew the colour of the linoleum – and as the door began to open he had a sudden fear that he was about to see a face from his past – an ageing warden, who would recognise him instantly and bark: '*Potts . . . what are you doing here?*'

But it was all right. A young woman stood in the doorway; a plain girl, a little younger than Ray, who peered at him in a puzzled way.

'Yes?' she said. 'What do you want?

Courteously, he swept off his trilby hat and gave her a nice smile. 'My name's Duke,' he said. 'I'm here on business – I have a letter of introduction.'

'Oh.' She seemed to be at a loss, but stood aside, saying, 'You'd better come in, then.'

She led the way along the narrow hall. As he followed her, the smell of stale cabbage-water and unwashed small boys made his gorge rise, and he heard the old, familiar din of shouts and war-whoops coming from the back yard.

The young woman, feeling that this might require some explanation, said over her shoulder, 'It's the boys' afternoon break, you see. They're all outside in the playground.'

Ray nodded politely, but did not say that he had known this already, without being told.

She took him into the room he hated more than any other – the Principal's office, where boys who had misbehaved were sent to be punished. It had not changed much. The big desk was still in the middle of the room, the sepia photograph of the founder, the Rev. Horace Lupton-Briggs, still hung above the fireplace – but a second, smaller desk now stood in the bay window, with a typewriter upon it; that was new since Ray's time.

The young woman seated herself at the smaller desk, then said, 'I'm sorry – nobody told me you were coming, so I don't know what this is all about.'

'Perhaps you'd better read the letter,' he said, pulling the envelope from his pocket and handing it to her. 'This will tell you why I'm here.'

She read it through, then looked up blankly. 'I'm afraid I still don't understand. Mr Archer is out at the moment, and so is Mrs Archer – they always go shopping on Saturdays. And it being the weekend, most of the staff are away too. There's only two of them here, and they're both on playground duty. Who was it you wanted to see?'

Ray gave her another winning smile and said, 'I think it's you I want, really. There's no need to bother anyone else.'

She seemed slightly reassured by this, but demurred: 'I don't know if I'll be much help to you. This boy you're asking about – when was he here?'

'I believe he left some time before the end of the war,' Ray told her. 'It would probably have been nineteen-eighteen.'

'Yes, I see. The trouble is, I haven't been here very long myself.'

'Of course, I realise that,' Ray said gallantly. 'You're much too young. But I expect they keep records of all the boys who've lived here, don't they?'

'Well, yes, but they don't usually give out that kind of information, I'm afraid.'

'Not as a general rule, I'm sure – but this is a very special case, being a legal investigation,' Ray said glibly. 'I'm not supposed to tell you this really, but just between ourselves, there's some question of a legacy, and the executors have to make sure that they've found the right Raymond Potts . . .' He chuckled, as if struck by the humour of it for the first time. 'Poor chap – it's a terrible name, isn't it?'

She gave a little laugh. 'Yes, I suppose it is, rather. Well, I'll see what I can find, but it may take a little while. That cupboard's full of files, going back donkey's years.'

'That's all right. I'm not in any particular hurry. We could go through the files together, if you like?' he suggested. 'They do say that many hands make light work.'

'Well – yes, all right then.' She was beginning to enjoy herself. 'I'm afraid they'll be rather dusty.'

Opening the cupboard, she climbed up on a chair to fetch down the cumbersome old box-files; he stood close beside her, holding the chair steady and taking each file as she handed it to him, until they found the date they were looking for. Then he pulled the chair across to her desk and they sat side by side, going through the records – school reports, together with private notes on each of the inmates, and all the relevant details.

When they reached a file marked *Potts, R.* he felt a sudden wave of nausea, and was afraid he might vomit. There, on the desk, his childhood was laid out, year by year, with brief and hostile references to every broken rule, every failed test, every instance of bad behaviour, every punishment . . .

The girl glanced at him anxiously. 'Are you feeling all right?'

Choking back his bile, Raymond managed to say, 'Oh yes, I'm fine. This is what I've been looking for – we shan't be long now.'

Turning over the yellowing pages, he came to the earliest entry in his folder. There was no birth certificate, just a bald statement, recording the date of his arrival at Allington Grove when he was four years old, together with the name and address of his parents:

Gordon and Millicent Potts – 16, Low Water Lane, Thornton Heath.

Ray copied this carefully on to the back of the letter he'd brought with him, then slipped it into his pocket.

'Thanks a lot,' he said. 'You've been very helpful, Miss—'

'Norris,' she said. 'Janet Norris.'

'Janet?' He stared at her, as if he were thunderstruck. 'What an amazing coincidence!'

'What do you mean?'

'You, being called Janet. The moment I saw you, I thought how much you look like Janet Gaynor.'

'Janet Gaynor?' She laughed again. 'Me? Oh, you're just saying that.'

'I mean it. Just fancy, you being Janet as well – and she's one of my favourite film stars.'

'Mine too. Did you see her in *Adorable*?'

'Didn't I just? I thought she was wonderful.' He stood up. 'Now you must let me help you put those files away again, Janet – you don't mind if I call you Janet?'

'Not a bit. Can I ask you – what's your first name?'

He was about to say Raymond, but stopped himself just in time. Raymond Duke was a little too close to Raymond Potts for comfort.

'Richard,' he said, 'Richard Duke. And I'm really grateful to you for being so helpful.'

'Oh, it was nothing.' She looked at him shyly. 'Will you be coming here again, about your investigation?'

'I'm not sure. I might . . . But on the other hand, this might turn out to be the wrong Raymond Potts – you never know.' As he passed the box-files up to her, he added: 'As a matter of fact, it might be a good idea if you didn't tell anyone I'd been here today.'

'Oh? Why not?'

'Well, if this *is* the wrong chap, then you've been showing me a lot of confidential files I shouldn't really have seen at all – and that could get us both into serious trouble.'

'Oh, dear.' She stared at him nervously. 'Do you really think so?'

'But don't worry.' He patted her hand. 'I tell you what – don't tell anyone I've been here, and I won't mention you either. Then there'll be no harm done, will there?'

'All right.' Relieved, she put the last file away – and he heard a shrill whistle blowing outside.

He knew what that meant; in a few minutes, the house would be full of schoolkids, herded in like sheep by two barking members of the staff.

'Good Lord!' he exclaimed. 'I've taken up much too much of your valuable time – I really mustn't keep you any longer.'

As they shook hands on the doorstep, she said, 'Richard, can I ask you something? If it does turn out to be the right boy, do you think you'll be coming here again?'

'I don't really know.' He smiled at her. 'But I certainly hope so.'

'Yes,' she said softly. 'So do I.'

She watched him walk down the path and out through the gates, then closed the front door after him. When the boys came tumbling in, pushing and shoving as they raced up the stairs, she hardly even noticed them.

Janet Gaynor . . . she couldn't stop thinking about that, all day. It was the happiest day of her life.

★

461

That autumn, Ted Watt was in between jobs. He'd done a summer season at the Floral Hall, Bridlington, followed by a short tour, but now he was 'resting' until it was time to start rehearsals for pantomime.

Daphne was very glad to have him at home for a change, but the trouble was, he had nothing to do apart from the odd cabaret at a Ladies' Night, or an occasional radio variety show at the BBC's splendid new Broadcasting House, and when Ted wasn't working, he got restless.

One morning during the half-term holidays, after he'd enjoyed a long lie-in – because what was the point of getting up early, when you had nothing to get up for? – he came downstairs and found Daphne making pastry.

'Any chance of some breakfast?' he asked hopefully.

'Breakfast? It's nearly eleven,' she said. 'Would you settle for a cup of coffee instead?'

'I could do with something to eat,' he said.

'Can it wait? I'm in the middle of making a steak-and-kidney pie,' she told him. 'And if you have too much to eat now, you'll spoil your dinner. There's a few biscuits in the tin, and a bottle of Camp coffee in the larder. You can see to it yourself, can't you?'

'I suppose so.' While he was waiting for the kettle to boil, he noticed a letter propped up on the dresser, with some foreign stamps on it. 'Hello – what's this? Luxembourg?'

'Yes, it just came – but I was all over flour, so I didn't open it. You can read it if you like.'

Ted tore open the envelope, grumbling, 'I still wish your brother hadn't gone abroad. I'm sure I'd get more work at the BBC if he were still on the staff.'

'You never know, perhaps he's going to offer you a show of your own, on Radio Luxembourg!'

'Chance'd be a fine thing.' But as he glanced through it, Ted brightened up. 'D'you know, I believe you're right? He says he's helping to organise a new series—' But then, as he read on, he scowled. 'No, it's not a variety show, it's something for children. Listen to this. "*Quiz Kids – a series of general knowledge games, with youngsters from all over the British Isles taking part, to be recorded in London once a week during the coming winter*". He's not offering me a job – it's Annie he's after!'

'What? Show me.' Wiping her floury hands on her apron, Daphne took the letter from him and read on.

'"She's always been a bright girl, and I'm sure she could make a name for herself. The programme will be recorded at a sound studio in Marylebone Road every Saturday afternoon, and a fee of one guinea will be paid to each child taking part. The winning team will go forward to the following week, so with any luck Annie could become a regular radio celebrity and make herself some pocket-money as well . . ."'

Daphne put down the letter. 'Oh really, that's absurd.'

'What's absurd about it?' Ted took back the letter and re-read it. 'Sounds to me like a nice idea. I bet Annie would be very good.'

'That's not the point. She's got some important exams coming up, and she can't afford to play parlour-games when she should be studying. She has better things to do.'

'But he says they're recording the show on Saturdays – that wouldn't interfere with her schoolwork.'

'Of course it would. She needs to concentrate, to be single-minded. She's got her career to think about.'

'Oh, come off it. She doesn't even know what she wants to do with her life yet . . . and this could be the start of a career, for all you know. Like Gerry says, if she catches on, she might finish up as a broadcaster, and follow in her father's footsteps!'

Daphne continued to make pastry, pummelling the dough with unnecessary vigour. 'I certainly hope not,' she said. 'She's got a first-class brain – she could do anything if she sets her mind to it.'

Ted sighed. 'Well, OK, maybe you're right – maybe she could do better than her old man, but it's up to her, isn't it? Ask the girl what she thinks about it.'

Daphne looked doubtful. 'Do you think that's wise? She's still very young for her age in some ways – she might not realise what this entails. It's our duty to guide her along the right lines.'

'You can tell her what you think, of course, but in the end it's up to Annie to decide. This could be her big chance. You can't turn it down without even asking her.'

That morning, Annie had gone to the public library. When she came home with an armful of books, Daphne showed her the letter, with some misgivings, and Annie read it through carefully, before handing it back.

'Well, what do you think?' Ted urged her. 'How does the idea strike you?'

'I don't really want to do it,' said Annie. 'Would you mind if I say no?'

Ted said, 'Look, sweetheart, it might seem a bit alarming at first,

463

but I promise you, once you get started you'll enjoy it. You probably won't be nervous at all—'

'I'm not worried about that,' Annie told him. 'I just don't want to do it, that's all.'

Daphne hugged her daughter. 'I'm so glad,' she said. 'I told Dad, you're cut out for something better than that. Everyone at school says you'll do very well in the exams – you could even win a university scholarship! You don't want to waste time, playing silly games on the wireless.'

'I don't want to go to university either,' said Annie. 'That doesn't interest me.'

Daphne stared at her. 'But that's the way to get on in the world, to make something of yourself! I only got as far as Teacher Training College, but there are so many more opportunities for girls now.'

'You don't understand, Mum. When I said I didn't want to do the quiz show, it was because it would be on a Saturday. I go with Tony to see Crystal Palace play on Saturday afternoons.'

For a few seconds, her parents stared at her, then at one another. At last, Daphne said, 'Yes, I know – and that's very nice, but we're talking about your future – your whole life. You've got to look ahead and plan what you're going to do!'

'I know what I'm going to do,' said Annie. 'I've been meaning to tell you. Mrs Gunn hasn't been very well lately, and the doctor says she's got to rest a lot. Tony and his Dad are trying to run the shop on their own, but they can't manage it without some extra help. So I told them – when I leave school, I'm going to go and work there.'

There was another silence, and then Ted said gently, 'Helping out in a greengrocer's shop – is that what you really want?'

'Yes, Dad – and it's what Tony wants, too. We've got it all worked out.'

The days were getting shorter, and the weeks seemed to be racing towards the end of the year. As Christmas approached, there was always so much to be done – and at Carmichael Road School there was the usual end-of-term concert. Daphne had been given the task of directing the Sixth Form in some scenes from Shakespeare, and was busy with rehearsals. It was ironic, she thought, that now Ted wasn't working, she should be the one who went out rehearsing every night. Annie was involved in rehearsals too, because she had recently taken up the oboe, and the music mistress, who said she showed great promise, had persuaded her to play in the school orchestra.

Outside in the wider world, there was general rejoicing when, after a whirlwind romance, Prince George, the Duke of Kent, announced his engagement to Princess Marina of Greece; they were married with due pomp and ceremony at the end of November.

Early in December, Steve and Val went to the new Gaiety in South Norwood to see a comedy-thriller called *The Thin Man*, which everyone said was highly entertaining. After the big feature, they stayed on to watch the *Movietone News* – most of which was taken up with shots of the Royal Wedding. They saw the cheering crowds lining the processional route, and the open carriages arriving at the Abbey – and when the newly-weds emerged after the ceremony there was applause in the cinema as well, because the Prince was so obviously happy, and his bride looked like a Princess in a fairy-tale.

But all eyes were on the chief bridesmaid – Princess Elizabeth, aged eight and a half, who carried out her duties with immense and touching dignity. On the return journey to Buckingham Palace, she kept her younger sister in order when four-year-old Margaret Rose threatened to become over-excited.

When they left the cinema, walking home together, Steve noticed that Val was unusually quiet.

'I liked the big picture, didn't you?' he said.

'Yes.'

'I thought Myrna Loy was very good.'

'Yes.'

'So was William Powell. I even liked the dog.'

'Yes.'

'You enjoyed it too, did you?'

'Yes, it was very good.'

'Only . . . I noticed you were a bit quiet.'

'Was I?'

They walked on without speaking for some time, and then he said: 'It was that wedding, wasn't it?'

After a moment, she replied, 'I don't know what you mean.'

'Watching them getting married – and wishing it was us.'

Val sniffed, trying not to cry. 'Yes. I'm sorry – don't take any notice of me, I'll be all right in a minute.'

He put his arm round her. 'So that's why you've been down in the dumps lately. I wish you'd told me.'

'What's the good of talking? There's nothing we can do about it.'

She was still fighting back the tears when they found themselves face to face with Daphne and Annie, on their way home after a long evening at Carmichael Road.

'Well, hello!' exclaimed Daphne. 'Fancy seeing you! Where are you both off to?'

'Home. We've just been to the pictures,' Steve explained.

'And we've been rehearsing for our school concert,' said Daphne. 'So how are you keeping? You haven't been round lately, Val – you're quite a stranger.'

Steve took this as an ideal opening, and said abruptly, 'You haven't been to see us, either. Come to think of it, I don't believe you've ever seen our flat. Why don't you pop in, now you're here? We're only just round the corner.'

'Oh, yes!' said Annie eagerly. 'Can we, Mum? Please?'

'Well, I don't know.' Daphne thought fast; perhaps this would be a good way to bridge the gap that seemed to be widening between them. 'All right, then. If you're sure it's not inconvenient?'

Valerie, with her face averted, said in a stifled voice, 'Actually, I think it might be better if you came round some other time. It's getting awfully late, and I'm feeling rather tired. Come on, Steve.'

Taking his arm, she steered him away. As soon as they were out of earshot, Steve asked her, 'What did you do that for? They wouldn't have stayed long—'

'I'm sorry, I just couldn't. I didn't want Daff to see I'd been crying.'

When they got back to Sackville Road, Annie went up to get undressed, while Daphne told Ted about their unexpected meeting with Steve and Val. He had switched on the radio for a programme of dance-music and wasn't really listening to her, as he remarked, 'Pity you didn't drop in to see the new flat. It would have been a good opportunity.'

'That's what I'm trying to tell you! We would have gone – I wanted to, only Val said no. She said she was tired, but I could see she didn't really want us there. I don't know why.'

'Nor do I,' said Ted. 'What's the matter with the girl?'

'I suppose she still feels embarrassed – with the two of them living together like that. It's been awkward all round, ever since she moved in with him.'

'She's only got herself to blame.' Ted still wasn't giving Daphne his full attention. 'It was asking for trouble, setting up house with him. Why the hell did she do it?'

'What else could she have done? It was either that, or stop seeing Steve altogether.'

'She didn't have to break up her marriage, did she? She could have gone on seeing him on the quiet. Nobody need ever have known—'

In the background, a crooner was singing soulfully *I Only Have Eyes For You* – and suddenly Daphne couldn't stand it any longer. Walking over to the set, she switched it off, then rounded on Ted fiercely.

'I suppose that's what you'd have done, is it? Try to keep the affair secret – and hope you wouldn't get found out?'

He could not meet her gaze, but turned away. Without another word, he stood up and walked out of the room – and then she knew at last.

The next Saturday, since Babs was still on duty at the Exhibition, Ray found himself at a loose end.

All the week he had been trying to decide what he should do. Now he had the name and address of his parents, he should be feeling happy – he'd got what he wanted – but he still felt cheated.

It was a disappointment; he couldn't deny that. His hopes of a father who had been a famous man – even a celebrated criminal – were completely dashed. Nobody called Gordon Potts, living in Thornton Heath, could ever have been a hero.

All the same, when Saturday came around, and he had nothing to do, he decided to go and take a look at Number 16, Low Water Lane. Thornton Heath wasn't far away – this time, a single bus-ride would be enough – and he was curious to see what his parents' home looked like. He must have lived there himself, when he was a little nipper; he wondered if he would remember it when he saw it.

Jumping off the bus at Thornton Heath Station, he went into a newsagent's shop, asking for directions to Low Water Lane. it was easy enough to find, just ten minutes' walk along Brigstock Road, near Thornton Heath Pond.

When he reached the pond, he looked about him. A huddle of old cottages were reflected in the water; once upon a time, it must have been a picturesque scene – a wayside halt, where waggoners stopped to refresh their horses – but now the pond was a grubby puddle inside a concrete basin, with a dried-up ornamental fountain in the middle; the cottages were being converted into modern shops, overshadowed by a new super-cinema, and the waggons had been swept away by noisy trams, rattling along the London Road.

He soon found Low Water Lane, and that was being swept away too. Some houses had already been knocked down, and a small block of flats was going up in their place. But Number 16 was still there, squeezed in between Numbers 14 and 18 – a terrace of workmen's cottages, with a withered Virginia creeper trailing over the walls.

Staring at the little house in the middle of the row, he trawled for some childhood memory, but nothing rose to the surface. For a few moments he hung about, undecided, wondering whether he should walk up and bang on the front door . . . but what good would it do? After all these years, his parents could have moved on – there might be strangers living there. And even if he struck lucky, even if Gordon Potts opened the door to him, what would they have to say to one another?

Ray had seen at a glance what kind of place this was, and what kind of people lived here. With a sudden rush of anger, he turned on his heel and walked away. If his father had spent a lifetime in these drab surroundings, Ray wanted nothing to do with him.

'If this is the best you got out of life – I'm glad I never knew you.' He spat the words out, under his breath. 'Damn you, Dad!'

The daylight was beginning to fade, and he walked quickly past the pond, heading for the station once more. The outing had been a waste of time.

At the bottom of Brigstock Road, he saw a young man riding towards him on a light motorbike – and he stepped aside quickly, taking a sudden interest in a display of ladies' vests in the window of a draper's shop. Reflected in the plate-glass, he saw Steve Gunn ride by; he had heard that Steve was working at Croydon Airport again, and guessed he was on his way to work the night-shift.

Ever since their last meeting in the pub at Cawnpore Road, Ray had taken care to keep well out of Steve's way; running into him here would have been the last straw. One way and another, this had turned out to be a bloody awful day, and the sooner it was over, the better.

And yet, sitting on the top deck of the bus, jolting up the hill to Upper Norwood, one question still nagged away at the back of his mind . . . If his father was nothing but a failure – a loser – a nobody – why had Muriel Glynn reacted so strongly at the mention of his name? What was it she knew about Gordon Potts?

Daphne too wished the day would come to an end, and that Christmas was over and done with: she did not look forward to it.

For years now, Christmas had been an unhappy time for her –

from that first pantomime at Hastings, when she had watched Ted with Marta Linden, and felt the first sharp stab of jealousy, the first suspicion . . .

Now her suspicions had been confirmed; the look in Ted's eyes had told her more clearly than any words that he and Marta were lovers.

Of course they would be appearing together again this year – Daphne couldn't remember the name of the panto, and she didn't want to; she would not be going to see it. By mutual agreement, they did not spend Christmas holidays together any more.

But Christmas had to be faced, all the same. She had made the pudding and the cake, but there was still such a lot to be done – the mince-pies, the sausage-rolls, the cards to be written and posted, the tree to be bought and brought home and decorated – above all, there were the Christmas presents.

On Saturday afternoon, all the shops were packed with customers, and Daphne was fighting her way through the crowds in Catchpolls department store with two heavy shopping-bags, and too many names still to be crossed off the list.

Jostled and buffeted, she retreated into a side alcove, somewhere between Haberdashery and Soft Furnishings, and tried to check her crumpled shopping-list: *Valerie – Steve (?)*

The question mark meant that she hadn't decided whether to give them a joint present, or whether that would look mean. She wasn't certain how things stood now, between her and Valerie. For a long time, Val had been her best friend – but not now. Perhaps when you grew older, you didn't have 'best friends' any more. Perhaps friendships that sprang up when you were young gradually faded when you reached middle age, and no longer needed them.

Or perhaps she still needed Val, but Val didn't need her.

Looking down her list, she read: *Mother – Babs . . .*

She hardly ever saw them either, these days. Since her mother's pompous letter about the Watkins family, she did not often go round to Belmont. She didn't like to visit a house where her husband was not welcome.

Ted . . .

She had no idea what to give Ted for Christmas. She did not know what he wanted – except, presumably, Marta Linden. She only knew that, whatever Ted's needs might be now, his wife was not amoᵢg them.

Annie . . .

She could hardly read her own writing – the letters danced and blurred before her eyes, at the thought of Annie. In spite of all the plans and dreams they had shared, ever since she was a tiny child, Annie had turned her back on higher education, on a university degree, on a brilliant career in law, or medicine, or politics. She had set her sights on a perfectly ordinary suburban life – the kind of life that had imprisoned Daphne all these years. She wanted nothing but a job in a greengrocer's shop and a young man . . . and she didn't seem to want anyone else.

Screwing up the shopping-list, Daphne thrust it into her bag. If Annie didn't need her, then no one needed her. And if no one needed her – what was the point of it all? Standing alone in the middle of the shopping crowds, the loudspeakers blaring out recorded Christmas carols, the paper-chains and the tinsel, Daphne no longer knew who she was, or what her life was all about.

'Mrs Watkins? It is Mrs Watkins, isn't it?'

Startled, she looked up, unable at first to recognise the thin, grey-haired man who smiled shyly at her.

'Yes? I'm sorry,' she stammered. 'I'm afraid I can't quite—'

'Walter Faber . . . I used to have a furniture shop in Church Road. I knew your husband slightly – and your sister.'

'Oh yes, of course – how stupid of me. How are you, Mr Faber?'

'Pretty well, thank you. And you?'

'Yes, I'm very well. Rather exhausted at present. Well, you know how it is, Christmas shopping . . . It's never easy, is it?'

'Would you like to step into my office for a moment? I'm in charge of Furniture and Soft Furnishings. It's a little quieter there.'

'You're very kind, but I've still got so much to do—'

'Please, just for a minute or two. You can sit down – we can talk.'

So she allowed him to usher her into the tiny office. There was only room for a filing cabinet, a narrow desk and one chair; he insisted she had the chair, while he stood awkwardly with one elbow resting on the filing cabinet.

'Let me see – I seem to remember you had a little girl. She must be quite a big girl by now, I suppose?'

'Yes, Annie's in her last year at school. She – she's doing very well there.'

'I'm so glad.' He cleared his throat, then asked: 'And – your sister? How is Babs?'

'She's fine. She's working at Hawkins and Co – did you know that?'

'Yes, I did. In fact—' he pulled a folded handkerchief from his breast pocket and dabbed his upper lip '—it was Babs who helped me to sell my house and buy the flat where I'm living now.'

'Oh, really?'

'I actually chose it because it was the one she liked best. You see, there was a possibility at the time that she and I might – one day . . .' He left the sentence unfinished and began again. 'I moved in – by myself, of course, six years ago. It's very convenient in many ways, though it's rather too big for one person, really.'

Daphne did not know what to say, and after a moment Walter continued, stumbling over his words: 'That young man – Raymond Duke. I heard he'd moved back to Belmont, lodging with Babs' family. Is he still – I mean – are they—?'

'I believe they're more or less engaged, unofficially,' Daphne told him.

She glanced down at the shopping-bags on her lap, unable to look at the misery in his face, as he said quietly, 'Yes. Of course . . . I see.'

Outside the little office, the shop seemed to be noisier and busier than ever; there was a continual hubbub as the crowds swirled past, chattering and laughing, mingled with the tinny strains of *God Rest Ye Merry, Gentlemen*, and she hardly heard Walter's voice as he added: 'Loneliness can be a terrible thing, Mrs Watkins.'

'Yes,' she said. 'I know.'

Chapter Twenty-four

IT WAS A long while before Ray returned to Low Water Lane.

His first visit had been very unsettling, and for some time he tried to put it out of his mind. If that was all his family background had to offer, he wanted no part of it; he would reject Gordon and Millicent Potts, just as he had tried to wipe the orphanage from his memory.

But it wasn't that easy. Every time he saw Muriel Glynn, the same questions came back and tormented him. What did she know about Gordon Potts? What was she covering up?

He had given up asking questions. No matter how cunningly he introduced the subject, he came up against the same brick wall every time: she did not know what he was talking about – she refused to discuss it. If he persisted, she would be very angry.

One Sunday morning, an idea occurred to him.

He was putting on his best suit and a clean shirt, getting ready to go to church – he still went to Matins occasionally, not because he had any real interest in religion, but because it impressed other people, and there was always the possibility of making useful contacts there – when he had a sudden inspiration.

What a fool he had been, not to think of it before! If Muriel knew something about the Potts family, it was possible that they would know about her – and although she resolutely denied any connection with them, Mr and Mrs Potts might be more willing to talk.

There and then, Ray decided to make one more trip to Thornton Heath, and try to find out.

Going to the chest of drawers, he rummaged under his clean vests and found the forged letter he had written on *Colpoys & Son* notepaper. He shoved it into his pocket; if he needed any credentials,

472

it might come in handy. Running downstairs, he met Babs in the hall.

'Just off to church, are you?' she said. 'Don't be late for dinner, mind.'

'I might be,' he said. 'I'm thinking of going for a long walk after the service; it's a nice day, and I could do with a bit of exercise. I won't bother about dinner – expect me when you see me.'

'Where are you going? Somewhere nice?' Babs hated to be left out of anything. 'Can I come too?'

'No, I want to be on my own,' he said. 'I'm not going anywhere special – I just want a chance to think things over quietly.'

'What do you mean? What sort of things?'

'Oh, plans for the future,' he said vaguely. 'Plans for you and me. I'll tell you later, when I've got things sorted out.' And he left the house quickly, before she could start an argument.

In spite of what he had told her, he wouldn't bother with church this morning; now he had something more interesting to do.

When he reached Low Water Lane, it looked more depressing than ever. The new block of flats was finished, with To Let boards outside, and its smart modern lines and bright paintwork made Number 16 seem very shabby indeed.

Ray walked up the path and hammered on the door-knocker; he heard a dog barking inside, and then a man's voice shouting hoarsely, telling the animal to be quiet.

He waited, and eventually the door was opened a few inches. A grimy, unshaven face appeared, eyeing him suspiciously, and asking: 'Wotcher want?'

It was not a promising beginning, but Ray smiled politely. 'Good morning,' he said. 'I'm looking for Mr Potts.'

'That's me,' said the man. 'What about it?'

Ray's smile faltered. The man was in his seventies at least – surely this old codger couldn't be his father? He tried again.

'Mr *Gordon* Potts?'

'S'right.' Mr Potts turned the tables. 'Who wants to know? Who are you?'

'You won't know me – my name's Duke. But I'm a friend of Mrs Muriel Glynn, and I was wondering if—'

The effect of Muriel's name was instant. Potts' jaw dropped, revealing gappy, discoloured teeth, and his red-rimmed eyes looked suddenly haunted.

'No!' he snapped, pulling back his head like an ancient tortoise, and

Ray saw that he was very frightened. 'No – I don't know nobody of that name. You've made a mistake—'

He tried to shut the door, but Ray was too quick for him, and planted one foot across the threshold.

'I don't think so,' he said firmly. 'I believe you and Mrs Glynn were acquainted in the past. Perhaps I can refresh your memory?'

'No – you've come to the wrong house!' said the old man, struggling unsuccessfully to close the door.

'If you'd just let me in for a few minutes. This won't take up much of your time.'

Gordon Potts called over his shoulder: 'Kim! come here, Kim. See him off, boy!'

Growling, the dog pushed through into the narrow gap – a fierce black mongrel, with white hairs around its muzzle. Like its master, it was old and doddering, but it still had a lot of sinister yellow teeth and a threatening disposition.

'There's no need for that.' Ray tried to hold his ground. 'Down, boy – good dog . . . There's nothing to be alarmed about, Mr Potts. I've got a letter of introduction here – if you'll just let me show you – from my employer.'

He thrust the letter at the old man. Potts squinted at it briefly, but got no further than the letterhead before saying in a hopeless voice, 'I should've known. Him again – after all these years.' Pushing the dog out of the way with his foot, he moved back and let go of the door. 'If you're from Colpoys, you'd better come inside.'

Frustrated, the dog went off in a huff and flopped heavily on to the hearthrug.

Like most workmen's cottages of the time, Number 16 had no front hall or passage; the door opened straight into the living room, which had stairs leading up from it and a small scullery tacked on at the back. The place looked as if it had not been cleaned for years, and was extremely squalid; dirty cups and plates jostled for space with greasy saucepans and items of grubby underwear which Ray did not wish to examine too closely.

Gordon Potts pushed a pile of old newspapers off a chair on to the floor, and said wearily, 'Sit down if you want.' He sank back into an armchair which still retained the shape of his bony frame, moulded into the cushions. 'What's all this about then?'

By way of reply, Ray handed him the letter. It took Mr Potts some time to decipher it, frowning over the typewritten words. Finally he gave it back and glared sideways at Ray.

'What's all this got to do with me, eh?' he asked.

'You sent Raymond to school at Aldington Grove, I believe?'

'What if I did? It weren't no crime. They said it was a good school – he'd be well looked after . . . I ain't done nothing wrong.'

'He was four years old. You and your wife decided to send him away—'

'Not her – not Millie,' Gordon Potts broke in quickly. 'It wouldn't never have happened if she'd been alive.'

So his mother was dead. He realised that in a strange way he had been expecting this; he had been following a quest for his father – it was as if he had known all along that he had no mother.

'That's when everything went wrong, when Millie passed away,' muttered the old man. 'Well, what was I supposed to do? I wasn't a youngster, even then. I weren't going to find another woman to take Millie's place. How was I supposed to look after a kid, when I was out at work on the roads all day?'

'On the roads?'

'Working for the Council, I was, digging up roads, laying drains and that – hard work and long hours it was, till my back started giving me gyp and they laid me off. I've been on the Club ever since . . . I ask you – how could I bring up a kid on me own? I told Colpoys I couldn't manage it, and he helped make arrangements. I done everything what he told me, and I thought that was an end to it . . . What's he after now, sending you here and stirring things up? If he wants his bleeding money back, he's got another think coming, 'cos I ain't got none. You can see for yourself how things are. If it's money he's after, he can whistle for it!'

'Money?' Ray was sitting up now. 'What money would that be?'

'Why the money he—' Gordon Potts broke off, drawing in a long, rattling breath, then he leaned forward, screwing up his eyes. 'Didn't he tell you about the money? What've you come for, if it ain't the money?

Ray tried to bluff his way through this. 'Well, I know something about it, of course, but Mr Colpoys didn't go into details. How much money are we talking about? What was it for exactly?'

'He didn't tell you nothing about it, did he?' With rising indignation, the old man struggled to his feet. 'Look here, I dunno why he sent you, but I ain't telling you nothing. I don't trust you, whoever you are.'

Slowly, Ray stood up and faced him, saying, 'I'll tell you who I am. My name isn't Duke. I'm the boy you sent to the orphanage – Raymond Potts. I'm your son.'

Time seemed to stand still. Frozen, the old man stood and stared at him; then he began to utter a high-pitched rasping sound – and Ray realised that he was laughing.

'You bloody fool!' Between asthmatic crackles, Gordon Potts crowed, 'You got it all wrong, aincher? You don't know nothing about it! Get out of here. Go back to Colpoys and tell him not to try any more of his tricks on me. Get out, d'you hear?'

Ray attempted to interrupt him. 'No, wait. Let me explain!'

But the old man ignored him, calling to the dog: 'Kim – see him off, Kim! Go for him, boy!'

Like an old war-horse hearing a bugle-call, the dog lurched up, baring its fangs and barking menacingly at the intruder.

Ray backed away and beat a hasty retreat, while the old man called after him from the cottage door: 'Get out of my house! You don't know nothing, d'you hear? *Nothing!*'

'How is she today?'

'Much the same. Only don't tell her I rang you, Julie. She'll only start worrying.'

Steve led the way upstairs, to the flat above the greengrocery shop, and his sister followed. On the first landing, Alf Gunn stood in the sitting-room doorway, waiting for them. He kissed his daughter.

'Thanks for coming, girl,' he said. 'Good to see you.'

'You too, Dad.' She hugged him. 'How are you keeping?'

'Me? I'm right as rain – how's yourself? You're looking a bit washed-out, if you don't mind me saying so.'

'Oh, I'm not so dusty. I had rather a late night last night.'

'Did you? There now, I told Steve not to bother you with a phone-call this morning. I said to him: "She'll be wanting her beauty-sleep," I said, "working at that Corner House till all hours" – but he wouldn't listen.'

'No, I'm glad he called me. I didn't even know Mum had been poorly. Let me talk to her.' She was about to walk past her father, into the sitting room, but he put a hand on her arm.

'She's upstairs in bed. The Doc says she's got to take things easy.'

Julie looked at him. 'Mum – in bed? I don't believe it!'

'Come on,' said Steve. 'I'll take you up.'

'And I'll have a cuppa ready for you when you come down,' Alf told her.

Going up to the next floor, Julie asked Steve, 'When did Mum ever spend a day in bed? She must be really bad. When did all this start?'

'She's been under the weather for a while, only she wouldn't see the doctor. Until yesterday – then she didn't have any choice.' He opened the door of their parents' bedroom, saying: 'Look who's here!'

Freda was lying on the big brass bedstead, leaning back against the pillows. She was not in the middle of the bed, but kept to the side nearest the window because that was where she'd always slept, ever since her wedding-night, thirty-eight years ago.

Julie felt as if she were in a bad dream; Mum's face was so grey, and seemed more deeply lined than she remembered.

'Julie! You bad girl!' Freda scolded her daughter, just as she had always done, but now her voice was only a whisper. 'Fancy you coming down like this, without letting us know. I'd have smartened the place up a bit if you'd told us. I haven't made you a cake or anything.'

Julie sat on the bed and kissed her gently. 'I'm glad you didn't. You generally push so much food into me, I'm two stone heavier by the time I go back to town. How are you feeling, Mum?'

'Oh, there's nothing wrong with me. I'm an old fraud really, lying here in bed all day like Lady Muck. I told the doctor, I'm perfectly all right now, but he says I've got to stay here for a day or two, just to be on the safe side.'

'What happened exactly?'

'I don't really remember. I think I was lifting a sack of potatoes, to fill up one of the bins, and next thing I knew, I was up here on the bed.'

Steve explained: 'Dad and Tony were both in the shop, and things were a bit busy, so she went downstairs and started serving—'

'Well, you know what Saturday mornings are like. The two of them were run off their feet.'

'They told her they could manage, but she took no notice. Next thing they knew, she was lying in a heap across the runner beans . . . Well, Dad and Tony managed to get her up here, between them, while Annie rang for the doctor.'

'Annie?' Julie looked puzzled.

Steve grinned. 'Tony's girlfriend – Annie Watkins. She'd just arrived, to help out in the shop as well.'

'Girlfriend? That slip of a thing? She was just a schoolgirl last time I saw her!' exclaimed Julie.

'She still is, but not for much longer,' smiled Freda. 'Doesn't time fly?'

Julie bit her lip, but managed to smile back. The last time she came to Church Road, Mum had been the same as ever – busy, bustling, full of life – and now, while Julie wasn't looking, she had turned into a frail old lady.

'Annie's been coming in at weekends – this is her last term,' Freda went on. 'As soon as she leaves school, she's going to work for us full-time.'

'That'll make things easier for you and Dad,' said Julie. 'Specially now you're laid up.'

'Oh, I'll be up and about again in no time,' said Freda, 'when I get my energy back. That's the worst of it, I feel so useless. I asked your Dad to bring my knitting-bag up, 'cos I didn't want to lie here doing nothing, and I'm supposed to be making Grandad a new cardigan – only I don't seem to be able to put my mind to it somehow. I dare say I'll feel better tomorrow.'

Then Alf came in with a cup of tea for Freda, and told them theirs was on the table downstairs, and they shouldn't let it get cold. He rearranged Freda's pillows and helped her to sit up, staying with her while she sipped her tea.

On the way downstairs, Julie asked quietly, 'What does the doctor say about her?'

Steve stopped on the half-landing. 'It's her heart,' he said. 'She's overstrained it, trying to do too much. She doesn't know it yet, but she's going to have to rest for a long while.' He hesitated for a second, then added, 'I think it's probably my fault. She's not been her old self, ever since I went to live with Val.'

'Oh, don't be so daft. That's got nothing to do with it.'

'I'm not so sure. She never said much, but I know it upset her.'

Julie sighed. 'In that case, we can think ourselves lucky she never found out about me! Can you imagine what that would have done to—'

'Shut up about that,' he interrupted her. 'Come and say hello to the others, and we'll have some tea.'

Valerie and Grandad were playing bezique at the centre table; Julie kissed them both, and told her grandfather he was looking younger than ever. Then she went over to the young couple on the couch by the window.

'What happened?' Julie said to Annie. 'All of a sudden you're grown-up – and very pretty too!' As she kissed Tony, she whispered in his ear: 'You've got the right idea this time.' Aloud, she continued, 'So who's looking after you all, while Mum's poorly? Who made the Sunday dinner?'

478

'Val came round first thing – and Annie dropped in to lend a hand,' Tony explained.

From the table, old Jack added: 'Ah, our Annie's a good little cook, I can tell you. Not only that, did you know she can play the oboe? We're going to work up a duet, her and me – oboe and cornet. It'll be grand, having another musician in the family.'

Tony protested, 'Hey, give us a chance, will you? She's not even out of school yet!'

Valerie chimed in: 'Don't you worry, we won't let the family starve. We'll manage between us, until your Mum's feeling stronger. By the way, will you be here for supper? I can easily rustle up some bacon and eggs.'

'No, thanks all the same. I wish I could, but I've got to get back to town this evening. You know how it is, Joe Lyons keeps us very busy . . .' She had spoken lightly, without thinking, then she saw Steve turn away, and Tony looking embarrassed – and she went on quickly: 'But I'll come again very soon, I promise, and next time I'll stay longer.'

When Ray got back to Belmont, Babs remarked that he must have had a very long walk. She hoped he'd been able to solve all his problems?

'Not quite,' he said. 'I'm still working on them.'

'Oh. But what about your plans? You said you were making plans for us – you promised you'd tell me later.'

'So I will – when it's all sorted out.'

He did not tell her he had met his father at last; he was not proud of the way he had handled their meeting, or of his own ignominious retreat. But he wasn't going to be defeated by a stupid old man and a mangy dog. At least something had come out of it – he'd taken one step forward.

Inexplicable as it seemed, he knew now that Colpoys had been involved with his father at one stage. Colpoys had been instrumental in having him packed off to the orphanage.

The following day, while the rest of the office staff were at lunch, Ray swallowed his sandwiches rapidly and set out to do a little research of his own. He went up to the top floor, to the attics, where the old files were stored – hundreds and thousands of them, tied up in bundles with pink ribbon, gathering dust but still stored in alphabetical order on wooden racks, each rack with its date clearly marked on it.

He had worked it out; he had been four years old, so it would have been 1906. When he found the 1906 rack, he wandered along it, looking under P for Potts . . . At the end of the row, he cursed and began to work his way back again . . . but with no more success. There was no file for Gordon Potts.

He stood for a moment, chewing his fingernail. Perhaps he'd got it wrong. On second thoughts, it seemed highly unlikely that Mr Colpoys would have taken on a penniless old navvy as a client. But why else would he have gone out of his way to assist Gordon Potts?

Light dawned at last. If there had been some connection between Potts and the Glynn family, that could explain it. After all, hadn't Muriel admitted that at one time Colpoys had acted as her solicitor?

He began to make his way along the rack again – not under P this time, but under G – and there it was, a bulging file marked *Glynn – Belmont, Crystal Palace Park Road* . . . Treasure trove.

He brushed off the dust, and began to ferret through the faded pages. There was a lot of legal jargon he couldn't follow, but the subject was clear enough. It was something to do with a 'financial settlement' and 'division of property' – a 'judicial separation between the parties aforementioned' . . . Of course, Colpoys must have handled the break-up of the Glynns' marriage, when Muriel kicked Harry out.

But he wasn't interested in that; he was impatient to find some mention of Gordon Potts. He was still searching through the file when a voice made him jump. It was not loud, but very sharp and clear.

'What do you think you're doing, Mr Duke?'

The cardboard file slipped between Ray's fingers, disintegrating in a shower of paper at his feet. Nervously, he faced Mr Colpoys.

'Nothing, sir. I – I was just looking through some old documents, sir, out of interest. You told me always to keep my eyes and ears open; you said that was the way to learn.'

'I did not invite you to rummage about and spill important memoranda all over the floor. Pick them up at once and put them back where you found them.'

Hastily, he obeyed. From the doorway, Mr Colpoys asked: 'Were you looking for anything in particular?'

'Oh no, sir – nothing,' Ray lied, and stuffed the bulging file back, in between Ginsberg and Green.

'That's better,' said Mr Colpoys, slightly mollified. 'Now run along and go back to your desk. If you haven't enough to keep you busy, let me know. Satan finds work for idle hands, Mr Duke.'

Ray thanked his lucky stars that Colpoys had not bothered to investigate more closely, or discover which file he had been looking through.

Back at his desk, he did his best to buckle down to work – it was a laborious copying job, transferring details of a complicated lease into a proforma for a property conveyance – without making a single error, without omitting a single word or a single comma, and without making a single blot. It was a task of jaw-breaking boredom, and he was glad when Colpoys left the building. These days, he never arrived at the office until noon, and usually departed at tea-time.

Once the boss had gone, the atmosphere relaxed; the clerks chattered and laughed, swapping jokes between one desk and another. Under cover of this, Ray slipped away upstairs, climbing to the attics once again, eager to resume his examination of the 1906 Glynn file.

He worked along the row – then stopped and stared . . . it wasn't there. There was nothing between Ginsberg and Green. At first he thought he must have made a mistake, and put it back in the wrong place – but he hadn't; there was a smudge on the dusty shelf, showing where the missing file had been.

So old Colpoys had investigated closely after all. He had found out what Ray was reading – and removed it.

Suddenly shaking with rage, Ray brought down his clenched fist on the rack, sending up a cloud of dust that made him choke and splutter.

'You interfering bastard!' he gasped, between paroxysms. 'You think you've stopped me now, don't you? But one of these days I'll find out what you're hiding – and then there'll be trouble!'

Every year, at the height of the summer, the Royal Horticultural Society held a Flower Show at the Crystal Palace; it was always a popular event – especially the final day, when the stallholders sold off their exhibits to the general public at knock-down prices.

Daphne had arranged to go with Kate, and at the last minute Annie surprised them by saying that she would like to go too.

'Won't you be working at the shop?' Daphne asked, for it was a Saturday afternoon, and Annie always went to the Gunns' on Saturdays.

'They don't really need me today. Tony's sister is coming to stay for the weekend, so they'll have plenty of help,' Annie explained. 'I thought I'd buy a nice bunch of flowers to take back to Mrs Gunn.'

'Poor soul – she's no better then?' Kate asked.

'Not really. The doctor lets her get up for a few hours – she likes to sit by the window so she can see what's going on – but she still gets very tired. She's started knitting again – I suppose that's a good sign – but she gets cross with herself because she can't do the housework, or the cooking. That's why I wanted to take her some flowers; they might cheer her up.'

It was a very hot day, and inside the Palace it was hotter still. Visitors thronged the narrow aisles between the stalls, admiring the wonderful display of roses, delphiniums, and gladioli, bursting out in glorious explosions of colour.

'They're so bright, they almost hurt your eyes,' said Annie. 'I wonder if I could get some roses for her – I know they're her favourite.'

'I'm sure you could,' said Daphne. 'Only be careful not to take them if they're full-blown, or they'll start shedding petals on the way home. It's so warm in here – a lot of the flowers are starting to wilt.'

'I think I'm beginning to wilt a bit myself,' sighed Kate. 'Do you mind if we go on to the terraces for a bit, and get a breath of air?'

'Yes, let's. It will be cooler outside,' said Daphne. 'Are you coming, Annie?'

'I'll catch you up presently, when I've got the flowers,' said Annie, and disappeared into the crowds.

Kate and Daphne looked about for somewhere to sit and rest, and spotted an empty bench in a shady corner under the trees. As they reached it, a young lady with the same idea tried to overtake them.

'Excuse me – I think I saw it first!' she began, then stopped short. 'Oh, it's you.'

'Hello, Babs,' said Daphne. 'There's plenty of room for three. Why don't we all sit down?'

'Good afternoon, dear,' said Kate, smiling politely.

'Good afternoon, Mrs Watkins.' Babs did not smile, but sat at the other end of the bench, keeping her distance. 'I hope you're quite well?'

'Mustn't grumble,' said Kate.

'Oh, good.' Babs addressed herself to Daphne. 'And how are the rest of the family? How is Ted? And dear Annie?'

'They're both very well,' Daphne told her. 'Ted's away, of course – he's got a summer season on the pier at Clacton. We'll be going down there in a week or two . . . You'll see Annie in a minute – she's just gone to buy some flowers, then she'll be coming out to find us.'

'How nice.' Babs sounded preoccupied. 'As a matter of fact, I've been meaning to get in touch. There's something I feel I ought to tell you – but it's rather confidential.'

She threw a meaning glance in Kate's direction, and Daphne said coolly, 'I don't think you need make a mystery of it, whatever it is.'

'No – well – it's rather private, private and personal.' Babs was looking very embarrassed. 'Perhaps we could go for a little stroll, just the two of us?'

'Certainly not—' began Daphne, but Kate interrupted her, rising to her feet.

'No, no. You stay where you are. I'll just go and see if I can find Annie. She might not think to look for us here, under the trees. See you later.'

When she had gone, Daphne said angrily, 'How could you be so rude? That was unforgivable.'

'I couldn't help it. I've got something important to tell you, but I couldn't say it in front of her. You see, it's about her house.'

'Her *house*? What about it?'

'Well, I felt I ought to tip you the wink. You really should start looking for somewhere else to live.'

'Oh, for goodness sake, let's not start that again. Mother wrote to me ages ago, saying I ought to move out because of Valerie! I never heard anything so ridiculous in all my—'

'No, listen. This is nothing to do with Valerie. You know our firm are the agents for Crabbe and Carter, the builders? We handle all their paperwork, so I get to know what's going on. I knew about the new bungalows in Elmers End long before they happened . . . And now they're moving into another area.'

'What do you mean?'

'Maisonettes this time – a row of semi-detached maisonettes; one flat on the ground floor, one up above, with separate entrances. And they're going to be all along Sackville Road. That's why I couldn't tell you, in front of her. They're going to pull down those old houses.'

'No! Don't be silly. Kate Watkins has lived there all her married life – the landlord wouldn't turn her out after all this time.'

'The landlord hasn't got any say in it. He's sold all the houses on the north side, including Number 26, to Crabbe and Carter. They're putting up these new maisonettes in their place. I've seen the rough draft of their adverts already – the same old slogan – "Halfway to Heaven" . . . So you and Ted ought to look for somewhere else.'

'But that's disgraceful! Surely the Council wouldn't let people be turned out like that!'

'It's nothing to do with the Council either; those houses are private property – it's all perfectly legal. I shouldn't really be telling you this, but since you're my sister—'

'All right. Tell me where to find Messrs Crabbe and Carter, and I'll go and see what they've got to say for themselves.'

'No, don't do that. I might get into trouble, and you'd only be wasting your time,' said Babs. 'Honestly, there's nothing you can do about it.'

'Oh, yes, there is,' said Annie.

Babs and Daphne swung round; absorbed in their argument, they had not noticed her approaching. She stood there with her arms full of roses – all shades, from white, creamy-yellow and pink to darker reds and deep velvety crimson – but she was not thinking of the flowers as she spoke fiercely.

'I couldn't help hearing – it's our home you're talking about! I don't care what the landlord says, or the Council or anyone else – we're not going to sit back and let them turn us out, are we, Mum? Not without a fight!'

If only Ethel hadn't gone out shopping that afternoon, it might all have turned out differently. But Aggie had been to the shops in the morning, and it was so hot and oppressive, she got rather flustered and forgot some of the things she was supposed to buy. After lunch, Ethel told her to stay at home; she took the list and the shopping-basket, and went out to collect the marmalade and the large loaf and the battenberg cake that Aggie had overlooked – Muriel was very partial to battenbergs.

Left on her own, Aggie decided to make some biscuits. They wouldn't take long, and she'd got everything she needed – flour, sugar, butter, currants, and a little grated lemon-peel.

As she mixed them together, she kept one ear open for the little bell on Muriel's bedside table. If Mu wanted something, she would have to leave her baking and run up to her at once – but luckily the bell did not ring, and she was able to roll out the biscuit-mixture and make it into nice round shapes with the pastry-cutter, then transfer them to the baking-sheet and pop them into the oven. They would be ready in a quarter of an hour.

She was washing up the mixing-bowl when she heard the bell ringing, and trotted off at once. Halfway up the stairs, she realised it was not Mu's bell but the front-door bell, and had to retrace her steps.

Crossing the front hall, she opened the door.

A shabby old man – unshaven, with red-rimmed eyes and bad teeth – squinted at her short-sightedly. 'Who are you?' he asked, 'You're not Mrs Glynn – where is she?'

Aggie felt suddenly afraid, without knowing why. 'No – Mrs Glynn is my sister,' she said, stepping back slightly. 'I'm sorry, she's not well – she's in bed.'

'Tell her I gotta see her. The name's Potts.'

Something clicked at the back of Aggie's brain. It was the name Raymond had been asking about; she thought at the time it seemed familiar, but she couldn't place it . . . Now the memories came flooding back. This horrible man had called at the house once before, a long while ago. She couldn't remember much about him, except for one terrifying thing – he had made Muriel cry. Nobody else had ever done that.

'I'm sorry. It's no good – she won't see you,' she said, trying to summon up her courage.

'Oh yes, she will – she's got to.' To her horror, he pushed rudely past her into the hall. 'Just you tell her I'm here. Tell her it's life and death – she'll see me then, all right.'

'Oh, dear.' Her heart was in her mouth; she didn't know what to do. She would have to go and ask – Mu would tell her. 'Sit down, please,' she said. 'I'll just see what she says.'

She hurried upstairs, but Mr Potts did not take the chair she had offered him. Impatiently, he began to follow her.

Upstairs, Aggie knocked fearfully at Muriel's door and went in.

'Well! What is it?' Sitting up in bed, Muriel put down her copy of *The Lady*. 'Was that somebody at the door?'

'Yes. It – it's someone for you. A man . . . that dreadful man who came before – the one who made you cry. His name's Potts.'

Muriel's face hardened into a mask of rage. 'How dare he?' she exclaimed. 'Send him away at once – he's no right to come here!'

'I tried to tell him you weren't well, but he wouldn't listen.'

'You must be firm with him. Say that if he goes on making a nuisance of himself, I shall send for the police. Tell him I won't see him!'

'Oh yes, you will,' said Mr Potts, heaving to get his breath back as he staggered into the bedroom. 'Matter of life and death, this is – didn't she tell you that? I'm doing you a big favour, Mrs Glynn. Come here out of the goodness of my heart, I did, to warn you.'

'Warn me? What are you talking about?'

'It's him – he's come back,' puffed the old man, hanging on to the rail at the foot of the bed. 'The boy – Raymond – out to stir up trouble, he is. He's found out something—'

'Hold your tongue!' Muriel tried to silence him. 'Unless you leave my house this minute, I'll have you sent to prison!'

'Don't you understand? I'm telling you for your own good. He don't know the whole story, but he's cottoned on to something, believe you me. He'll be coming here and bothering you next, I shouldn't wonder.'

'I won't hear another word!' Muriel pointed a quivering finger at him. 'I know what you're after, but you're not getting another penny out of me—' Then she broke off, sniffing the air. '*Burning* . . . I can smell burning!'

Aggie, who had been listening dumbfounded, not understanding a word, suddenly moaned, 'Oh, the biscuits. The biscuits are burning!'

'You stupid woman!' Muriel screamed at her. 'If you've set my house on fire, I'll have you certified!'

In the confusion that followed, Potts made himself scarce; if the fire brigade were about to arrive, the police might follow, and he had no desire to be taken in for questioning.

Some time later, Aggie trailed miserably upstairs again and confessed to Muriel, 'It's all right, Mu. I was making biscuits when that man interrupted me, and now I've had to throw them away. It was all his fault . . . But he's gone now, dear, so you needn't worry any more. What was he talking about?'

Still suffering from the after-effects of shock, Muriel gave vent to her feelings and turned her wrath upon her sister. 'You idiot – I'll never forgive you for this! Letting that man into my house. Didn't you know any better?'

Aggie began to whimper. 'Don't be cross with me. I couldn't help it, he pushed his way in. What did he want?'

'Mind your own business! Ethel should never have left you in charge of the house – doesn't she realise you're a half-wit? I've a good mind to call the doctor and get him to put you away!'

Shaking with fear, Aggie clung to the memory of something Daphne had once said to her: '*Don't let her bully you. Stand up to her . . . If she shouts at you, shout back . . .*'

To her own amazement, she heard herself say, loudly and suddenly: 'Don't speak to me like that! Shut up, do you hear? *Shut up!*'

Incensed, Muriel raised her hand, about to strike her – but Aggie caught her wrist, and for a moment the two elderly women wrestled together, groaning and panting, just as they had done when they were children long ago.

It didn't last. Overcome by her own temerity, Aggie let go of Muriel and ran from the room, the tears streaming down her face.

When Ethel returned from the shops, she found a tray of black biscuits in the kitchen, and Aggie curled up on her bed, having sobbed herself to sleep – so she went to Muriel's room, and asked what on earth had happened. Muriel, who had combed her hair and put on more powder and lipstick, gave Ethel a brave, long-suffering smile.

'The usual thing, I'm afraid. Aggie began to make some biscuits, and of course they were all burned – so then she came up here, weeping and wailing – as if I were somehow to blame! When I told her not to be silly, she had a kind of brainstorm. She flew at me like a wildcat, and tried to scratch my eyes out. I had to speak to her quite severely. I'm sorry to have to say this, but she really is getting worse, don't you think so?'

'Oh Annie, it's ever so good of you, but you shouldn't have, really you shouldn't. I don't want you to go spending money on me,' said Freda, but she couldn't help admiring the huge bunch of roses Annie was arranging in a jug.

'It's nothing. They were practically giving them away,' said Annie. 'Mind you, I don't know how long they'll last, but I thought they'd brighten the room up a bit.'

'And they smell so beautiful. Come over here, Julie,' Freda called to her daughter. 'Have a sniff!'

Julie inhaled obediently, and agreed that the roses were lovely. 'I meant to bring you some flowers myself,' she added, 'only I didn't have a spare hand, with two suitcases to lug about.'

'Two cases?' Annie looked so surprised, Freda couldn't help smiling.

'Yes. Julie's not just staying the one night,' she said proudly. 'She's going to be here for a week or two – isn't that nice? I asked her what's going to happen to her job at the Corner House, but she says that'll be all right.'

'I'm taking a holiday,' Julie explained. 'I was due for some time off.'

'The only thing is, I do wish we'd got a proper bedroom for her.' Freda wrinkled her brow. 'It seems so silly, now Steve's moved out, 'cos there's a spare bed going begging in Tony's room, but she can't very well sleep there. I wondered if we could put Grandad in with Tony, only he does snore something chronic—'

'I told you, it's all right, Mum. When you go up to bed, I shall make myself comfortable on that sofa,' said Julie.

Freda came downstairs every afternoon, and always had the sofa in the window, with a good view of the street; she enjoyed being in the living room with her family around her and her knitting-bag on her lap – she had even resumed her long struggle with Grandad's cardigan. Now she began to argue.

'That's all very well for a night or two, but if you're going to be here any longer—'

'Don't fuss, Mum – I've got it all organised. Tomorrow I'm going to turn out the little box-room, and the boys can help me shift the spare bed in there; then I can have a room all to myself.'

'But that box-room's so tiny, and it's full of junk!'

'I know – I'm going to give it a proper clear-out. It'll be very cosy by the time I've finished with it.'

'I'd offer to come round and help, but I'm going to be busy at home tomorrow,' said Annie. 'My Auntie Babs gave us some bad news this afternoon.'

She told them about Crabbe & Carter and the maisonettes, and they were all suitably indignant.

'But they can't kick you out into the street!' Tony exclaimed. 'Where are you going to live?'

'We're not going anywhere – we're staying put! Mum and me are working out a plan of campaign. Tomorrow we're going to start writing letters to the Council, and to our MP – and anybody else we can think of. And my Nan's got a friend who's a lawyer – he'll tell us how to go about it.'

Annie did not stay to supper, though Tony wanted her to. This evening, she and Daphne were going to knock on every door in Sackville Road and pass on the news. If they could enlist enough support, and everyone banded together, Crabbe & Carter would have to think again.

When she had gone, and Alfred had put up the shutters in the shop, Julie laid the table and the family sat down to eat.

'What a pity Annie couldn't stop,' Freda said, as Alf settled her in her chair at the table. 'Still, in a way it's rather nice to be on our own for once. Just the family – together again.'

Valerie wasn't there either; she was working late this Saturday, helping to wind up the last day of the flower show and dividing the takings with the organisers.

Steve began to protest, 'Val's part of the family too, isn't she?' – but Julie kicked him under the table and changed the subject.

'Sorry it's a cold supper, but I hoped you wouldn't mind, this weather.' She had brought plenty of food down with her – smoked fish and roll-mops, spiced ham and some exotic varieties of salad.

'I suppose you got all this from the Corner House, did you?' asked Alf, with his mouth full.

'No, I did some shopping in Soho, on my way. You can always get a good selection there.'

Helping herself to ham, Freda paused, saying anxiously: 'Are you sure they don't mind about you taking time off at such short notice? How long are they giving you? When are you going back?'

Julie knew that Steve and Tony were looking at her, and kept her eyes fixed on her plate as she answered her mother. 'I don't know yet. I'm going to stay here as long as I can make myself useful. Until you're on your feet again, anyhow.'

Now they were all staring at her.

'But that could be weeks . . .' Alf said. 'Surely Lyons won't keep your job open for you all that time?'

'I don't know, and I don't really care.' Julie lifted her head, looking directly at Steve as she continued. 'I've got rather fed up with my job, as a matter of fact. I've been doing it too long – and I'm not getting any younger, either. I told the other girls to look around for someone else to share the flat. I've got a bit of money put by and I'm going to give myself a break.'

Freda was torn between joy and dismay.

'Oh Julie, that's lovely – but when I get better, you'll be wanting to go back to work, won't you? And then you'll be out of a job, with nowhere to live.'

'You're fussing again, Mum! You leave me to worry about that, eh? When the time comes, I'll decide what I'm going to do, but until then, I'm staying here. For as long as you'll have me.'

'What did you think?' asked Ray.

'I didn't like it much,' said Babs.

They had just come out of the Rialto and were walking home; the cinema had been packed with a Saturday-night audience, watching H. G. Wells' fantastic vision of the future: *The Shape Of Things To Come.*

'Why not?' Ray frowned. 'I thought it was good – what was wrong with it?'

'Do you really think the world's going to be like that one day?'

'You mean – rockets flying off into space? Yeah – anyhow I hope so.'

'What about the other part? The war – aeroplanes dropping bombs, killing people . . . That frightened me.'

'Don't be so soft! It's only a story, nothing to be frightened about.'

'I can't help it. Sometimes I get scared about things that might happen.' She shivered a little, and repeated unhappily, 'Things to come . . .'

He put his arm round her waist; though the sun had gone down, the air was still warm and Babs had no coat on. He pulled her closer, his hand sliding up to her breasts.

'That's what I like,' he said softly. 'Thinking about things to come . . . Making plans for the future.'

'You keep saying that, only you never tell me what the plans are!' she objected, but little thrills of pleasure were running through her, and she did not pull away from his inquisitive fingers.

'Things are going to start happening for us one of these days,' he whispered in her ear. 'Just you wait and see.'

When they got back to Belmont, they found Ethel and Aggie sitting in the kitchen. Ethel was looking very concerned, and Aggie's face was still blubbered and tear-stained.

'What's the matter?' asked Babs. 'What happened?'

'I'm afraid Aggie has had one of her nasty turns,' said Ethel, rather tight-lipped. 'She had a disagreement with your mother about – well, about something she imagined she'd seen.'

'I didn't imagine it!' Clearly, it would not take much to set Aggie off again. 'At least, I don't think I did.'

'But Aggie dear, you heard what Muriel said. There wasn't anybody here. There wasn't a man trying to force his way into the house. You must have been daydreaming . . .'

'I don't know why she said that. I *saw* him . . . Well, I thought I saw him – and it was the same man.' Aggie gulped, trying to cling to the few details she remembered, or thought she remembered. 'He came in through the front door. He said he'd got to see Mu. He came once before, a long time ago and . . . and he made her cry.'

'Well, I certainly don't remember him.' Ethel shook her head. 'I'm quite sure that if this Mr Potts had come here and upset Muriel, I wouldn't have forgotten it.'

'You weren't here the last time, either. You must have been at your office then.'

'Did you say Potts?' Ray cut in sharply. 'Would that be Gordon Potts?'

'Yes!' Aggie grabbed Ray's hand hopefully. 'You know him too don't you? You must do – you asked me about him!'

'That's right, so you did,' said Ethel, looking at him doubtfully. 'Do you understand what this is all about, Raymond?'

'Not quite, but I'm going to.' Ray made for the door. 'Where's Mrs Glynn? Up in her room, I suppose?'

'Yes, but it's late. She won't want to be disturbed—'

'Too bad,' said Ray pleasantly, and walked out.

Babs hurried after him. 'Ray, you mustn't. She might be asleep—'

He took no notice, but said over his shoulder, 'Didn't I tell you things were going to start happening?'

Nothing would stop him now. It was as if he had been working on a huge, complicated jigsaw puzzle, and now the last pieces were beginning to slot into place.

Babs tugged at his elbow, but he walked straight into Muriel's room without bothering to knock. She had been dozing, and the bedside light was still on, but when she opened her eyes and saw Ray at the foot of the bed, she sat up, gathering the bedclothes defensively around her.

'Have you taken leave of your senses?' she demanded. 'How dare you march into my bedroom like this. Babs, take him away at once!'

'Sorry to disturb you, but we're going to have a little talk,' said Ray, and pulled up a chair. 'Sit yourself down, Babs. I want you to hear this too. It's about my father.'

Muriel had wiped off her make-up before settling down for the night, and without the rouge and powder, her face looked much older; under a tracery of fine lines, her skin had an unnatural pallor.

'I don't know what you're talking about,' she said sulkily.

'Oh yes, you do. I'm talking about my old Dad – Gordon Potts. You said you'd never heard of him, but he came to see you today – and according to Aunt Aggie, he was here once before, years and years ago. You and Mr Colpoys helped him put me into the orphanage, didn't you, when I was just a little kid? I believe you gave him some money, as well. What I want to know is, why did you do it?'

For several moments the room was very quiet, except for the sound of Muriel's laboured breathing. Then she loosened her grasp upon the bedclothes and flopped back upon her pillows, defeated.

'Very well,' she said at last. 'I suppose I shall have to tell you.'

Closing her eyes, she cast her mind back to the beginning of the story.

'It all started a long time ago – before any of us knew what was happening. And it began with my so-called husband. I need hardly tell you he was the cause of all the trouble . . . Harry Glynn.'

Ray frowned. 'What's he got to do with it?'

'He had everything to do with it. Although I did not suspect it at the time, that man was conducting one of his sordid affairs with a woman of the lower classes – the wife of Gordon Potts – and she became pregnant.'

Ray drew in his breath – but she would not allow him to interrupt her. Opening her eyes, she went on.

'When she told her husband, he forgave her. He even agreed to give the child a name, and the baby was brought up as if it were his own son. Even then, we might never have known anything about it, but a few years later the woman was taken ill and died suddenly. You can imagine his situation. The wretched man could not raise a small child on his own – he had no one else to turn to, but he knew the name of the child's natural father. That was when he came here the first time, begging for help. I saw him, and the whole shocking story came out. It's true that I was reduced to tears – Aggie was right about that.'

'Oh my God.' Ray was struggling to understand. 'But – what did you do?'

'My own marriage had not been a happy one, and this revelation put an end to everything. I sent for Colpoys, who was our solicitor in those days, and we agreed that the child must be provided for. We gave Mr Potts some money, and Colpoys arranged for the boy to be taken into the care of an orphanage. He also drew up the legal documents for our judicial separation.'

She looked solemnly at Ray, as she concluded: 'I am sorry to have to break this terrible news to you, Raymond, but you insisted on ferreting out the truth. And after all, perhaps it's as well that you did. You see now why I said I could not allow you to marry my daughter. You are the son of Harry Glynn – and Barbara is your half-sister.'

Chapter Twenty-five

THEY LOOKED AT one another, unable to speak.

At last Ray said, 'No . . . It's not true. I don't believe it.'

Babs tried to say something, but could only shake her head helplessly.

Muriel sighed, and told Ray, 'You don't believe it because you don't want to believe it. I'm very sorry, my dear boy – more sorry than I can say – but you had to know the truth. You both have the same blood in your veins – tainted blood. That man's blood.'

Babs buried her face in her hands as her mother continued, 'I know you have become very close – very fond of one another. When I realised, I tried to keep you apart, but you would go your own way. We can only be thankful that your little romance never—' she chose her words cautiously '—never took a more serious turn.'

Babs uttered a wordless sound – a shuddering groan, as if she wanted to retch but could not, and scrambled to her feet, running from the room. Compassionately, Muriel watched her go, then turned and addressed Ray.

'Perhaps she thought it was serious. I blame myself – I should have taken a firmer line from the beginning, but by the time I found out, it was too late.'

'When was that?' Ray asked her. 'When did you know – about me?'

'Not until Babs told me your real name. By then she had already made up her mind that you were to be married. Of course I was appalled – I did my best to put a stop to it, but she seemed to be completely infatuated.'

'We love each other,' said Ray stubbornly. 'Nothing can change that.'

'Now you're talking nonsense, Raymond. You must see that this changes everything. In every possible way – legally and morally – the idea of marriage is completely unthinkable. You must accept that. You must say goodbye to one another, and never meet again.'

'No, we can't. You don't mean that—' he began. But when he looked into her eyes, they were hard and determined, and he saw that she meant every word.

'I'm sorry,' she said again. 'I shall be sad to see you go, but under these circumstances—'

'Go?' he cut in. 'Go where?'

'Anywhere you like – that's entirely up to you. Anywhere, as long as it's at a suitable distance from this household. You must find other lodgings immediately.'

'But that's not fair! I've done nothing wrong—'

'I sincerely hope you have not, but you must see I can't run any more risks. I can't allow you to stay under this roof, knowing how you and my daughter feel about each other. It wouldn't be right.'

At first he had been numb with shock, but as his feelings were aroused, he grew indignant. 'You can't turn me out like this! I've got nowhere to go!'

'I understand how you feel, dear boy. I realise this must have come as a bolt from the blue – naturally it will take time for you to find suitable accommodation elsewhere, and I don't wish to be unreasonable. You must have sufficient time to find another address – shall we say three weeks? Yes, I think that should be ample. And if you happen to find somewhere before then, well, the sooner the better, obviously. Now I must ask you to leave me in peace. It's been a long, trying day, and I'm feeling very tired. Good night, Raymond. I do hope you sleep well.'

On Sunday afternoon, another family conference took place, this time at Sackville Road.

Kate was expecting Mr Colpoys to arrive for one of his regular Sunday visits. In the morning, at church, she prayed hard that Harry Glynn would not gatecrash this tea-party, as he so often did; today, she needed the undivided attention of Mr Colpoys.

She went to a lot of trouble, putting out the best tea-service and the best lace tablecloth, and making egg-and-cress sandwiches. Fortunately, she had already made one of her special chocolate layer cakes a few days earlier – that was one of his favourites.

When he arrived, and saw everything laid out on the table, he exclaimed, 'It all looks most attractive, Mrs Watkins. You spoil me, you really do.'

'Well, I wanted to make a bit of an effort today, because I'm afraid I've got a favour to ask. I hope you don't mind, but I've invited Daphne to join us – and Annie.'

Perhaps he was a little put out – he really preferred to have Mrs Watkins all to himself – but he tried not to show it. Instead, he smiled politely. 'That will be a great pleasure. I should like to see Daphne again, and your little granddaughter.'

'She's not so little now – you'll be surprised. In the ordinary way, I wouldn't have asked them, only – well, like I said, we've got a favour to ask.'

'All three of you?' He eyed her quizzically over his gold-framed pince-nez. 'Dear me – a favour to three generations at once sounds a tall order! What seems to be the problem?'

'I'd rather not start on that till they join us. Daff's the one who knows all about it, she'll explain better than I can. They won't be long – would you like a cup of tea while we're waiting?'

So they drank their tea and talked of other things, and after a few minutes Daphne and Annie came in and sat down. Mr Colpoys went through the usual procedures, telling Annie that he'd never have recognised her, she'd grown so much.

They attacked the egg-and-cress sandwiches, though Kate said she didn't really fancy anything. Since Daff had told her the news last night, she seemed to have lost her appetite.

They all exchanged glances. Mr Colpoys put aside his plate, saying, 'Well, now. Won't someone tell me what it is that's worrying you so much?'

So Daphne repeated what Babs had told her about Messrs Crabbe & Carter, and their plans to tear down half the street.

Mr Colpoys took off his pince-nez and polished them judicially. 'Let us take this step by step. The first thing I must point out is that so far the story is only hearsay. I am relying on evidence that is no more than a tale told to you by a third party. Until we have somehow verified it, we have no means of knowing whether it is true or otherwise.'

'I think we can take it that it's true,' said Daphne. 'Babs is my sister, and though she does exaggerate sometimes, she wouldn't have invented it. She's seen all the preliminary paperwork; our landlord has sold the property to Crabbe and Carter, so he isn't our landlord any more, and they're already drawing up a prospectus to start advertising their new flats.'

'I see. But there's many a slip 'twixt cup and lip, as the saying goes. It's an ambitious project. They may not be able to raise the necessary capital – they may not be able to carry it through.'

'I don't think there will be any problem about that,' said Daphne. 'They've done this before, very successfully. They bought those old houses at the top of Sydenham Hill and pulled them down, then turned them into Westwood Court – and they did the same thing at Elmers End, with that big estate of bungalows, so they're not exactly beginners.'

'And they're not fools either,' Annie chipped in. 'I mean, I bet they wouldn't spend good money buying up these houses if they didn't have enough to go ahead and finish the job, would they?'

Mr Colpoys gave her a wintry smile. 'You have a point, young lady, but nevertheless . . .' He addressed Kate. 'Mrs Watkins, would you mind telling me how much you pay in rent, per annum?'

When she told him, he nodded gravely, but made no comment, and she asked, 'What do you think? Is it going to be all right? I can't bear to think of being turned out, not after all these years.'

'Don't worry, Nan, we won't let it happen,' said Annie. 'Will we, Mr Colpoys?'

Replacing his pince-nez on the end of his nose, he put the tips of his fingers together and said regretfully, 'I fear we may not be able to prevent it.'

The three Watkins ladies looked at him in dismay, and Daphne exclaimed: 'But surely there must be something we can do!'

'From a strictly legal viewpoint, if the situation is as you have described it to me, I'm sorry to say that Messrs Crabbe and Carter may have a watertight case. If they have become the owners of the property, they can do what they please with the bricks and mortar – demolish the houses – rebuild them – make a bonfire of the whole street, if they feel like it!'

Kate clutched Daphne's hand. 'I knew it! What did I tell you?'

Daphne tried to calm her mother-in-law. 'It's all right, dear, just a minute. Mr Colpoys, surely they passed an Act of Parliament a few years ago, giving protection to tenants? I thought, as long as Mrs Watkins always paid her rent and behaved herself, she couldn't be thrown out – isn't that the law now?'

'You're quite right, but unfortunately the Act you are referring to only applies to certain properties at the bottom end of the scale. This house is reasonably spacious, and the rental Mrs Watkins pays puts it just outside the protected category. I'm sorry to disappoint you, but I'm afraid nothing can be done. The new landlords will have to serve notice on all tenants, giving due warning of their intentions and allowing you a certain time to quit the premises, but after that, I fear you will be obliged to move out.'

'Suppose we sit tight and refuse to budge?' said Annie.

'Then they could have you evicted. Mind you, there is always a silver lining to every cloud. As sitting tenants, you certainly have *some* rights – you cannot be treated unfairly, and if there is any question of undue force being brought to bear, or resulting hardship, the courts would probably take a sympathetic view of your plight. It strikes me that you might even be entitled to claim some form of compensation.'

'What do you mean, compensation?' asked Annie.

'A sum of money to help tide you over, to enable you perhaps to put down a deposit on rented accommodation elsewhere. If you want me to act on your behalf in this matter, I would be more than happy to take a strong line with the new landlords and ensure that—'

But Daphne interrupted him. 'I'm sorry, you don't understand. It's very good of you, and we're very grateful, but we don't want compensation. We want our house. We want to stop them throwing us out.'

'That's right, Mum!' Annie backed her up. 'We're not going to give in – we're going to fight!'

'But you haven't any legitimate grounds to contest it,' Colpoys tried to explain. 'Legally, there's nothing you can do.'

'We can stir up a fuss, can't we? We can get together with all the other tenants in the street, not just the ones on this side, but the ones across the road as well,' said Daphne. 'I've talked to some of them already, trying to make them realise – they may be sitting pretty today, but the same thing could happen to them tomorrow! We want to band together, and demand a fair deal.'

'Daff's already started sending off letters to all the local bigwigs,' said Kate proudly. 'I told her she ought to write to the King and Queen as well. They may not know Sackville Road personally, but I'm sure they'd be very concerned if they heard – and my husband died for King and Country, don't forget that!'

'I'm certainly going to write to all the newspapers,' added Daphne. 'Not just the local ones, but the national dailies too. And to the BBC

– I'd go on the wireless and tell the whole nation what's going on here, if they let me.'

'And if that doesn't do the trick, it's going to be full-scale war!' exclaimed Annie. 'Barricade the streets – stop the demolition men getting in. Fight them off with sticks and stones and milk-bottles . . . we're not giving in without a struggle!'

'I admire your spirit, young lady,' said Mr Colpoys, 'but I must warn you that if you follow that course of action, you will be placing yourselves on the wrong side of the law.' He turned solemnly to Daphne. 'And once you step outside the law, I shall be unable to help you. You will be fighting a lone battle.'

'She won't be alone,' said Annie, putting her arm round her mother's shoulders. 'We'll fight them together.'

Since Muriel's shattering revelation, Ray had hardly seen Babs at all. Last night, he had gone to his room and waited for her to join him there, as she did almost every night – but eventually he had fallen asleep, still waiting. This morning she had not come down to breakfast, sending a message by Aunt Ethel to say she had a sore throat and would stay in bed until lunchtime.

She put in an appearance at one o'clock, but Ray only saw her across the dining-table; when he addressed her, she answered in monosyllables, without looking at him, and when the meal was over she said she was going out for a walk.

Ray caught her up at the front gate and offered to go with her, but she told him she would prefer to be alone. Quoting his own phrases back at him, she said: 'I'm not going anywhere special. I just want a chance to think things over quietly. I'm sure you understand.'

In a bad temper, he went to the cinema on his own. That was one good thing that had happened in the last few years, anyway. At least now they'd changed the laws, you could go to the pictures on a Sunday. When he came home that evening, Ethel informed him that Babs had already gone to bed.

His black mood returned; he went to his room and got undressed, then lay on his bed for some time. When he heard that the old ladies had retired for the night, he got up again. Slipping on his dressing gown, he crept along the passage and turned the handle of Babs' door . . . It was locked.

He said quietly, 'Babs, it's me. Let me in.'

She replied in a muffled tone, 'No – go away.'

'I must talk to you. Unlock the door.'

'No! Don't be silly – go back to bed.'

'If you don't let me in, I shall kick up such a row, it'll wake the whole house. I'll break the door down if I have to.'

He heard her getting out of bed; a moment later, the key turned and the door opened.

'That's more like it,' he said, entering the room.

She was in her nightdress, but when he tried to lead her back to the bed, she resisted him. 'No. Please, Ray, you shouldn't be here.'

He perched on the side of the bed and patted the eiderdown, inviting her to sit beside him. 'I told you, we've got to talk. Come and sit down.'

Unwillingly, she did so, keeping a little gap between them and saying, 'I don't know what there is to talk about, after what Mummy told us.'

'There's millions of things to talk about. We're not going to let her stop us seeing one another, are we? I still love you, you know I do.'

'You mustn't say that, not any more. It's all over.'

'No, it isn't over.' He took her hand, pulling her a little closer. 'I can't help the way I feel – and neither can you. We still want each other, don't we?' He was running his hand along her arm now, stroking her gently; his other hand rested lightly on her knee.

She was trembling as she whispered, 'No, Ray, we mustn't. You know we can't—'

But she did nothing to stop him, so he moved closer still and kissed her – a long kiss, full on the mouth.

When their lips parted, he asked: 'After all the times we've been together – what does once more matter?'

'Of course it matters! You're my brother,' she protested faintly, as he began to pull up her nightdress.

'Half-brother,' he corrected her. 'And you want it as much as I do, you know you do.' He lowered his head, beginning to kiss her thighs, and she started to cry, unable to resist him, betrayed by her own weakness. He stood up, throwing off his dressing gown; naked, he pulled her down on to the bed, and took possession of her once again.

Afterwards they lay together, breathless and exhausted. She was still weeping softly, and he asked impatiently, 'What's the matter now? You enjoyed it, didn't you?'

'Yes – that's what's so awful. But we shall never do it again,' she told him.

'Why not? If it's what we both want, what difference does it make?'

'You don't seem to realise . . . you won't be here any more.

Mummy says we mustn't see each other . . . We can never be married.'

'We can if we want to. You don't think I'm going to let you go, do you? We can get married in secret, like I always wanted to – and as soon as your mother's safely out of the way, there'll be nothing more to worry about, will there? We'll be husband and wife, living happy ever after!'

'No!' She was horrified. 'That's a terrible thing to say. It would be wicked and sinful—'

'Who cares? Once the old folks have all popped off, we'll be on Easy Street. You'll come into a lot of money by then – the family fortune—'

'There isn't any family fortune! I told you, there's nothing left, apart from the interest on a few shares, and this house.'

'And will that be divided between you and your brother and sister?'

'Ethel and Aggie get the shares; the house is left to me, because Gerry and Daphne don't need it—'

'And because you're her favourite, right? Well, there you are – the house must be worth a packet. We can sell it and move into a little modern flat, just the two of us – the way we always wanted.'

'Stop it, do you hear? *Stop it!*' Her voice was rising hysterically and she pushed him away. 'You don't love me at all. It's the money you want, isn't it? I knew it all along! Get out of my room – go on. Get out!'

He hit her then, a hard blow with the back of his hand, across the face, and when she gasped and flinched away from him, he hissed: 'Don't you tell me what to do. Shut your row, for God's sake. Do you want to wake the whole bloody family?'

Crouching at the foot of the bed, sobbing in a mixture of rage and grief, she turned on him like an animal at bay. 'I don't care any more! If you don't leave me alone, I'll scream for help. I'll tell them you burst in here and raped me, then they'll send for the police and you'll be arrested. I don't ever want to see you again – *you make me sick!*'

He stood up and pulled on his dressing gown, looking down at her. 'You stupid bitch,' he said. 'You don't know what you're saying . . . But you'll be sorry when I've gone. Oh yes, you'll be sorry.'

The hot weather continued, week after week: the sun shone mercilessly from a copper sky, until the heat became a burden. By the end of the summer, the humid weather brought widespread storms, and the electricity in the air played on people's nerves and frayed their tempers.

When Ted's summer season finished, he came home from Clacton on a close, muggy evening. Daphne heard a taxi pull up and went out to meet him; when he had paid off the driver, she helped to carry his luggage into the house. On the doorstep, he glanced up at the home-made banner stretched across the road – *Save Our Street – Make Your Voice Heard!* – and grinned.

'Very nice, but you needn't have gone to all this trouble, just to welcome me home. A plain red carpet would have done.'

'We're doing our best to whip up a bit of neighbourhood support,' said Daphne.

'I know, I'm only kidding,' he said. 'So that's still going on, is it?'

'I'm afraid so.'

As soon as they were inside the house she took him in her arms, and they kissed; it was their first kiss for a long time.

'I've missed you,' she said.

'I missed you too,' he told her. 'But I always do – you know that.'

She led the way downstairs, and when he walked into the kitchen, he asked, 'Where is everyone? I was expecting the full turn-out, with a brass band.'

'We thought you'd be home by tea-time – that's what you said on your last postcard.' She smiled. 'So when it got to seven o'clock, we had to send the brass band away . . . Then your Mum went off to the Harvest Festival supper at the Church Hall, and Annie's gone to an orchestra rehearsal at the Palace.'

'Orchestra?' Ted raised an eyebrow. 'I knew she was going on with the oboe – I didn't realise she was that good.'

'Old Jack Gunn got her into the Crystal Palace orchestra – apparently they had some vacancies in the woodwind section. Do you fancy a cup of tea? It won't take me a minute to put the kettle on.'

'Don't bother, love. I'd sooner have a scotch.'

'Oh – I'm afraid I haven't got any whisky.'

'That's OK, I have.' He pulled a half-bottle from his pocket. 'For my next trick, all I need is a tumbler and a drop of water – how about you? Do you want to join me in a wee dram?'

'No, thanks.' She watched him pour it out, adding, 'And I bet that's not your first, either. Is that what made you so late? Having a farewell party with your pals?'

'Just a bit of a celebration, that's all.' He raised his glass. 'Here's to us – and to our future!'

A flash of lightning at the kitchen window took them by surprise; to the south, over the Surrey hills, the sky was an angry purple, and they heard a rumble of thunder.

'Sorry I'm late,' he said. 'The time just slipped by before I realised, and then I missed the train at Charing Cross – that's why I took a taxi instead.'

'A taxi? All the way from Charing Cross?'

'Why not? It's not that far – I've done it before.'

'Once – when you came home, the night you left the Army. But that was a special occasion.'

'This is a special occasion too.' Taking his jacket off, he flung himself into the armchair. 'I told you – I had something to celebrate. A bit of good news.'

'That'll make a change. We don't seem to have had any good news round here since Crabbe and Carter decided to pull the house down.'

'Ah, you don't have to worry about the house any more.' He winked at her over the rim of his glass. 'That's not going to be a problem.'

'What do you mean?'

'You won't be living here much longer anyway. We'll be moving out soon.'

'Ted, what are you talking about?'

'You haven't heard the news yet. I've been offered a new contract – the best I've ever had.'

'If you mean you're off on another tour—'

'Only three weeks in Manchester, for the try-out – then one week in Birmingham – and then we go straight into the West End,' he said happily. 'Yours truly – starring in a new musical comedy, with my name up in lights on Shaftesbury Avenue – *Duet in Springtime* – with *Ted Watt* . . . How about that?'

'Congratulations – you deserve it! But what's that got to do with moving out of the house?'

'If the show's a hit, I could be in town for six months or more – years, even. And they're paying me pots of money – old Percy's done me proud this time. We can afford to get ourselves a luxury flat Up West somewhere. Well, I shall have to live near the theatre. Can't traipse all this way every night after the show, can I?'

'But we can't live in the West End! School starts again next week—'

'No, it doesn't. Annie left at the end of last term, didn't she? You told me she doesn't have to go to school any more—'

'But I do! I'm still teaching at Carmichael Road – remember?'

'You don't seem to realise . . .' Ted began to laugh. 'That's something else you needn't worry about now. You don't have to go out teaching any longer. You're going to be a lady of leisure.'

'Ted – I like teaching. It's my job! Besides, I'm sure Annie wouldn't want to leave Norwood either, and neither would your Mum.'

'Oh, we can sort them out later.' He pulled a face. 'I dunno – anyone would think this was bad news, the way you're carrying on.'

Daphne looked at him for a moment, then asked, 'This show, what's it called? You said something about a duet.'

'*Duet in Springtime* – what about it?'

'Is Marta Linden in it too?'

He hesitated for a split second, then said casually, 'Of course she is. I'm playing a cockney barrow-boy at Covent Garden, and she's a famous opera star . . . The public seem to like seeing us together – you know how it is.'

'Yes, I know how it is.' The electric storm was making Daphne's head ache, but she forced herself to go on. 'I know this is a very big thing to ask you, but it's important – to both of us. I want you to turn it down.'

He stared at her as if she had gone mad.

'A chance like this? Shaftesbury Avenue – top billing – and you're asking me to turn it down? What for?'

'Because I want you to.' She moved across the room and knelt beside his chair, taking his hands in hers and looking up into his face. 'Please, Ted. We can manage without it – we don't need pots of money. You haven't signed the contract yet, have you? You can still get out of it?'

'No, I can't,' he said. 'You don't know what you're asking. The show's been written specially for us – for me and Marta. This means a lot to me.'

'I know,' she said. 'It means a lot to me as well.'

There was another rumble of thunder, and the kitchen was momentarily lit by another burst of unearthly white light. Caught in it – two startled faces in a flashlight photo – they stared at one another like strangers. Slowly, Ted withdrew his hands, then stood up.

'I'm sorry,' he said. 'I can't let them down now.' He moved away, turning his back on her.

'I see,' she said at last. 'All right, then – go ahead. Sign the contract and do the show. Go and live in the West End if you want to. But I'm not coming with you, Ted . . . You're on your own now.'

The past few weeks at Belmont had been very difficult for Ray.

Babs stayed out of his way as much as she could. Her bedroom door was kept locked at all times, and he knew it would be a waste of time to try and see her on her own.

Ethel and Agnes had been informed that he would be leaving them soon, though they had no idea why. They asked no questions, but watched him speculatively, their curiosity touched with a kind of pity which he found infuriating.

Two or three times he tried to see Muriel, but was always told that it 'wasn't a convenient moment', or that 'Mrs Glynn is feeling very tired – she's taking a little nap' . . . Everyone was avoiding him.

It was all the more surprising when Ethel met him in the hall one evening when he came home from work, and addressed him affably. 'Ah, there you are, Raymond. What a nasty evening . . . Do you think there's going to be a storm?'

'Looks like it. It's been close all day.'

'Yes, hasn't it? At least the rain's held off – you were lucky to get home in the dry.' She seemed to be making conversation, and he wondered what she was working up to. She cleared her throat, then began again. 'If you can spare a minute, my sister would like a word with you.'

He brightened up. 'Yes, of course – right away!' Perhaps Muriel had relented after all.

Ethel escorted him as far as the bedroom, and was about to leave him there when Muriel called to her: 'Ethel! Don't go, dear – I'd like you to stay. This won't take long.'

She had put on her best bed-jacket – a confection of pink ribbons and organdie frills – and she had spent time and trouble over her hair and her make-up. She was all smiles, looking younger and happier, and for the first time Ray could see a hint of Babs in her fair, doll-like prettiness as she held out her hand to him.

'Come and sit by me, dear boy. We don't seem to have had a chance to talk lately, do we?'

'I tried to see you once or twice, but . . .' He shrugged. 'Seemingly I always picked the wrong moment.'

'What a shame. I've been thinking about you such a lot lately. Anyway, here you are, and looking very well, too. I expect you can guess why I've sent for you?'

His heart leapt; he was sure that she had changed her mind. 'No. I don't know,' he said hopefully.

'Really? I'd have thought it was obvious. The last time we met, you were about to start looking for somewhere to live; we agreed that you should have three weeks to find suitable accommodation – isn't that right?'

'Well, yes, but—'

'And it's over a month already. So I want to know what's happening. You have been looking around, haven't you?'

His hopes dashed, Ray said, 'Oh yes, of course.' It was a lie. He had glanced at some of the adverts in the columns of the local paper, and cast an eye over the cards in the newsagent's window when he passed it on his way to work, but that was as far as it went. 'I've been looking, but I haven't found anything I fancied,' he went on.

The truth was, he had felt certain that if he bided his time and picked the right moment to tackle her, he would eventually manage to soften the old woman's heart and wheedle her into letting him stay. But it seemed that she was immovable.

'That's a pity,' she said. 'Because it looks rather as though you will have to settle for somewhere you don't fancy. I'll give you one more week, Raymond, and if you haven't moved out of this house by then—'

She paused, and he prompted her: 'If I haven't – what then?'

Muriel smiled sweetly. 'We could always put your luggage out on the front steps and get a man in to change the locks – but I do hope it won't come to that.'

'Now just a minute.' He was getting worried now, and when he was worried, he became angry. 'I'm doing my best. You can't hurry these things! I'll go on looking, but—'

'Of course you will. And I think you should start looking right away, my dear. You've only got one more week, remember. Run along now – and let's hope you have better luck this time.'

He stood his ground for a moment, refusing to be browbeaten – and in that moment he had a bright idea. 'All right,' he said. 'I'm going. I know somewhere I can try, somewhere I hadn't thought of before.'

When he had gone, Ethel said, 'Don't you think you're being a little hard on him, Muriel? He's not a bad boy at heart. I'm sure he means well—'

'Thank you, Ethel dear, I think you can leave me to deal with him.

That young man is being very difficult. I shan't rest until he has moved out.'

Ethel sighed, and was about to leave the room when Muriel called her back again. 'Just one more thing. Could you possibly make a telephone-call on my behalf?'

'Yes, certainly. Who do you want me to telephone?'

'Do you know the office where Raymond works – Colpoys and Son? You may remember, William Colpoys was our solicitor for a short time, many years ago. I don't have the number, but you can easily find it in the directory. I want you to speak to Mr Colpoys and ask if he will be good enough to come and see me as soon as possible. Say that it's very important – and very urgent.'

The thunderclap made Valerie jump, and she shut her eyes, turning away from the window.

Steve had not been home long; he was still having his daily wash-down when the storm broke, and at the first crash of thunder he came tearing out of the bathroom, dripping wet, wearing nothing but a towel round his waist.

'Oh Steve, you shouldn't!' she said nervously. 'Whatever would Mrs Pilling think if she saw you on the stairs like that?'

'She'd think your husband's a fine figure of a man!' he chuckled. Then he saw Val's face and added quickly: 'Well, you know what I mean. As far as the Pillings are concerned, I'm your husband, aren't I?'

She lowered her head unhappily, and he went to put his arm round her, but she shook him off, saying, 'No, don't. Go and dry yourself – and get some clothes on.'

'Sorry. I was only trying to cheer you up. I know you've been a bit miserable.'

'I'm not exactly miserable – it's just the weather. I don't like thunderstorms.'

'Don't you? I do – that's why I came out of the bathroom. I didn't want to miss all the fun!'

Another dazzling flash cracked the sky, and he moved to the window, exclaiming, 'Hey! Look at this – talk about a Brock's Benefit!'

She called to him sharply. 'Oh, do come away from the window!'

'It's all right, I've got my towel on – I'm quite decent!'

'No, come away. It's not safe! You might be struck by lightning.'

Steve laughed. 'I'm not scared of lightning – I enjoy a good storm.'

'I hate it!' she said violently, and as the thunder broke overhead, she shrank back, putting her hands over her ears. When he saw the terror in her face, he was immediately contrite, and pulled the curtains shut.

'There – is that better?' he asked.

'A bit,' she muttered, keeping her head well down.

'Poor old Val . . . You're really scared, aren't you? I didn't realise.' Quickly, he towelled himself dry and began to pull some clothes on.

'I've always hated lightning,' she said. 'Fires and lightning – my two nightmares. I suppose they go together, in a way. Houses catch fire if they're struck by lightning.'

'It'll be all right, don't you worry. I don't expect it'll last long.'

'It's been coming on all day; I could feel it in the air. I'm sorry to be such a fool, but storms always upset me.'

Buttoning his shirt, he said quietly, 'It isn't just the storm though, is it?'

'Of course it is – what do you mean?'

'You've been a bit down for a while now. It started long before the weather changed.'

She would not look at him. 'Oh, have I?'

'You know you have. I could see there was something wrong, but you wouldn't tell me.'

'It's just a mood I'm going through. It doesn't mean anything.'

'It must mean something. There's got to be a reason . . . If you're unhappy, that makes me unhappy.' He came over and put his arm round her. 'Just when everything seems to be turning out so well, too.'

'Does it?'

'Well, doesn't it? I should think you'd be feeling cheerful. Mum's getting stronger every day – she's been much better since Julie came home . . . And Tony's bucked up no end. He and Annie seem to be really hitting it off, don't they?'

She nodded, but said nothing. After a moment, he went on: 'I'm sorry, I'm being selfish again. Telling you everything in the garden's lovely for the Gunn family – I was forgetting about Sackville Road. You're worried about those builders moving in, aren't you?'

'No, it's not that.'

'What is it then?' Cupping her chin in his hand, he turned her face gently towards him. 'It's not about me, is it? You're not having second thoughts or anything?'

'You know I'm not.'

'Well, I couldn't help wondering. Just lately, you've been sort of looking through me, as if I wasn't here.'

'Oh, Steve.' She sighed. 'All right, I'll tell you – but you're not going to like it. It's still the same old thing – I can't help feeling badly about not being married.'

'Is that all?' He held her tightly, trying to comfort her. 'But that's not half as bad as it was. Mum and Dad think of you as one of the family now, and you said yourself, Daphne and your mother are beginning to come round to the idea.'

'Not any more,' said Val flatly. 'They're going to hate it more than ever when they find out.'

'What do you mean? Find out what?'

'That I'm going to have a baby,' said Val, and buried her face in his shoulder.

Aggie, too, was terrified of storms, and Ethel was having a very trying time, doing her best to take her sister's mind off the crashes and bangs that rolled round the darkening sky. They sat together in the kitchen with the blinds drawn, but every thunderclap made Aggie squeak with terror, and when the front doorbell jangled suddenly, it startled both of them.

'Oh! My nerves must be as bad as yours,' said Ethel.

'Whoever can that be?' asked Aggie. 'On a night like this, too.'

'We shan't know until we go and find out, shall we?' Ethel stood up. 'Are you coming with me?'

Aggie half-rose, uncertainly. 'Yes – no – oh dear . . .' Another loud bang decided her. 'You go – I'll stay here.'

Alone, Ethel went to answer the door. When she opened it, she could see nothing but a large black figure, looming up against the stormclouds.

'Miss DeWitt? We spoke on the telephone – my name is Colpoys.'

'Oh yes, of course. I'm sorry, it's so dark I could hardly see you.'

He came in, and she switched on the hall light; even then, she did not really recognise him. He had not been to the house for thirty years, and he had never been a frequent visitor.

'I know I said I'd call sometime tomorrow, but after I rang off, I thought – I had nothing particularly pressing to do this evening, and by the tone of Mrs Glynn's message, it sounded as if it might be some sort of emergency. Did she give you any idea what it was about?'

'No – you'll have to speak to her yourself. May I take your coat?'

'Ah, thank you. It's not too late to disturb her, I hope? You said she was more or less a permanent invalid. She may be asleep, perhaps?'

'I don't think so. She doesn't usually settle down this early, and with the storm going on, I'm pretty sure she'll be awake.'

'The weather certainly is atrocious, but I was lucky in one respect: it hasn't begun to rain yet.'

'I wish it would – the air would be so much fresher.' Ethel ushered him to the staircase. 'I'd better go first, to tell her you're here.'

'Tell her – if it's inconvenient, I can call back tomorrow.'

He waited outside the bedroom door, and after a few moments Ethel reappeared, saying, 'I'm sorry to have kept you waiting. She wanted to make herself presentable. You can go in now.' She held the door open. 'Here's Mr Colpoys, Muriel. Don't hesitate to ring your little bell if there's anything you want.'

And she left them alone together.

They stood and looked at one another, each thinking how the other had aged.

'Come closer,' said Muriel. 'Come here, where I can get a good look at you.'

He obeyed, and entered the circle of lamplight by the bedside. 'Do we shake hands?' he asked.

'Of course.'

Their hands touched briefly; two dry palms, faintly warm, with only a little life left in them.

'Well . . .' he said at last. 'It's been a long time.'

'Yes – thirty years is a very long time,' she said. 'Have I changed so much?'

He took up his gold pince-nez and placed them carefully on his nose, then said, 'No. You seem – astonishingly the same.' It was not altogether a lie; behind the painted face and the carefully arranged fringe of curls, he could see something of the woman he remembered.

'The years have been kinder to you than to me,' she said. 'It's good of you to bother to visit a poor, helpless creature.'

'Don't fish for compliments!' he said. 'May I sit down?'

'Before you do that . . .' she lowered her voice. 'I want you to go and open the door – suddenly.'

'But I—'

'Please – do as I say. Quickly and quietly.'

He pursed his lips, but did not argue with her. When he opened the door, there was no one in the passage.

'Thank you – one can't be too careful,' she said. 'That's a lesson I am beginning to learn. Now pull up a chair, and sit by me.'

'Very well.' It was a spindly bedroom chair, unsuited to a man of his build, but he settled himself as comfortably as he could, then resumed. 'I'm glad to know that we are still on speaking terms. I'm only sorry that our last meeting was rather – what shall we say? Acrimonious?'

'Perhaps . . . But I hope sufficient time has elapsed to allow us to bury the hatchet.'

'I hadn't even remembered a hatchet.' He allowed himself the ghost of a smile. 'That's all forgotten now – the past is over and done with.'

'If only it were,' she said. 'But it isn't – and that's why I sent for you. You have a clerk working in your office, who calls himself Raymond Duke.'

'Ah . . .' The faint smile disappeared. 'I was afraid that young man might be the cause of the trouble. He's your lodger, I gather?'

'He has been our paying guest – but not for much longer. I've told him he must go; I can't allow him to stay here.'

'He's been making a nuisance of himself?'

'He has. That's why I sent him packing – and you must do the same.'

Colpoys frowned. 'You mean – dismiss him from his post?'

'Of course – and as soon as possible.'

'I can hardly do that without giving him some reason. His conduct is satisfactory enough, he's not a fool, and as long as we keep an eye on him, he's a reasonably good worker. Apart from—' He paused, then finished: 'Apart from a tendency towards inquisitiveness.'

'What do you mean by that?'

So he explained how he had caught Raymond looking into the *Glynn* file – the one dated 1906 – and Muriel gasped, 'You don't mean to say you leave private documents lying about for any Tom, Dick and Harry to read?'

'Certainly not. There was nothing especially confidential in the file; just details of the deed of separation drawn up between you and your husband. In any case, I took the precaution of removing it to a place of safety before he could satisfy his curiosity. I suppose you're going to tell me now that he has started asking awkward questions about it?'

'Yes. That's why you must get rid of him!'

Colpoys sighed. It all came back to him now. This was how every conversation had turned out, in the old days – they always finished

510

up by having an argument. Automatically, he put his hand in his pocket and took out his pipe, remarking, 'If I may say so, I think you're making rather too much of this, dear lady. I feel sure there's nothing to be alarmed about . . . By the by, would you mind if I smoke?'

'In my bedroom?' She was outraged. 'I should object very strongly!'

'Forgive me – force of habit, you know. Then I won't light it.'

He stuck it in his mouth, sucking at the empty bowl, as Muriel went on: 'I don't think you appreciate how serious the situation is. Raymond Duke has already uncovered far too much, with his poking and prying. I believe he's been to the Lupton-Briggs Home – he certainly dug up the name and address of that man Potts from somewhere.'

Colpoys bit on the pipe-stem. 'No, that's impossible.'

'Potts came here in person, to tell me so. Yes, and he's another one out to make trouble. I told you from the start, I never trusted him.'

'But – how could Duke have found out?'

Muriel leaned forward impatiently. 'Don't you understand yet? Haven't you realised? His name's not Duke. He's Raymond Potts – the boy we sent to the orphanage!'

There was a clatter as the pipe fell to the floor; Colpoys sat motionless. 'That boy?' he gasped, paralysed with shock. 'Oh, my God . . .'

Then his words were drowned by a spattering noise which became steadily louder and more insistent, like a drumroll upon the window-panes. The clouds had broken, and the rain had begun at last.

Harry Glynn was trying to finish a painting, though he only had one naked electric bulb in his room, and he detested working by artificial light at the best of times. Still, he had promised to deliver the picture tomorrow – a pretty little watercolour of a summer garden, which he had been copying from a black-and-white snapshot.

A woman in Dulwich had commissioned it, telling him what the various flowers were; she was very proud of the pink climbing roses on the pergola, and the herbaceous border. Harry, whose knowledge of gardening was rudimentary, had only a hazy notion what colours they were supposed to be. He seemed to remember that those tall things at the back were delphiniums – they were blue, weren't they? – but as for the others . . . He had decided to lay on some washes of various pastel shades, and hope for the best. If necessary, he would tell the woman this was not meant to be Nature, but Art.

He put his head on one side; it was looking a bit chocolate-boxy by now, but he suspected that was the way she wanted it. And he had to finish it tonight, because she'd agreed to pay cash on delivery, and he was practically stony-broke again. If he didn't pay his rent soon, Miss Preece would throw one of her tantrums.

Concentrating hard, with his tongue between his teeth as he added the finishing touches, he barely noticed the sound of the rain lashing the windowpanes. Slowly, through the noise of the storm, he became aware of something else – a kind of knocking. Someone at the front door.

At first he tried to ignore it. It wasn't his house, after all – it wasn't his job to answer the door – but then it occurred to him that Miss Preece, up in her room, might not be able to hear it. And by the sound of that rain, whoever was standing out on the step would be getting soaked to the skin. With a sigh, he laid aside his paintbrush and went out into the hall.

When he opened the door, a sudden squall of wind and rain buffeted him and he said to the stranger, 'Come in, whoever you are. You must be half-drowned . . . Come inside, so I can shut the door.'

The stranger obeyed, but was he a stranger? By the dim light in the hall, Harry peered at him doubtfully, trying to place him. 'Do I know you?' he asked. 'Your face seems familiar, somehow, but . . .'

'We have met,' said Ray.

He was wet through. The rain had begun just as he turned the corner, with not much more than twenty or thirty yards to go, but in that short distance the heavens had opened and now he was completely drenched. Rain streamed down his face and dripped from the brim of his hat; his cheap mackintosh had done nothing to protect him, and all his clothes were sticking to him. From his sodden boots, a puddle spread slowly across the lino.

'If it's the landlady you're wanting, I'll give her a call,' Harry began, but Ray stopped him.

'It's you I came to see, Mr Glynn, though I'd like to talk to her as well, presently. Do you know if she's got a room to let?'

'I'm not sure – she might have.'

'You see, I've been staying at Belmont, till your wife turned me out. She's given me a week's notice, and I've nowhere else to go.'

Harry struggled to make sense of this. 'You were lodging at Muriel's house? I don't understand.'

'I was a friend of Babs, you see; she took me there in the first place. Then I became a friend of the family, as you might say.'

'Ah yes, I seem to remember. I've seen you about with Babs once or twice.' Harry frowned, as another memory surfaced. 'Wait a bit – wasn't there some sort of trouble? Weren't you the chap who—'

Delicately, he left the sentence unfinished, and Ray said simply, 'I made one mistake – but I've paid my debt to society. Since then, I've gone straight. I'm on the side of the law now – I've got a good job in a solicitor's office . . . Colpoys and Son.'

'Gad, yes – it's all coming back to me now.' Harry scratched his head, then added, 'Anyhow, you'd better not stand here, catching cold. Come in out of the draught.'

He took Ray into his own room. There was an oil-stove in the corner which gave out a small amount of heat, and he encouraged Ray to take off his hat and coat and try to get warm.

Ray glanced at the picture on the easel, and commented, 'Nice . . . Babs told me you did pictures. I've often thought I'd like to take it up myself, if I had the time. I've got the artistic whatsit – the temperament.'

'Oh, yes?' Still at a loss, Harry pressed on. 'But I don't understand – what made you come here?'

'I told you, I've nobody else to turn to. Mrs Glynn kicked me out.'

'Yes, but that's nothing to do with me, is it?'

'In a way, it is. You see – she found out who I am.'

This baffled Harry completely, and he repeated blankly, 'Who you are? What do you mean?'

'Well, I generally call myself Ray Duke, but that isn't my real name.' He paused to give the words their full dramatic effect. 'My name is Potts . . . Raymond Potts.'

He had expected an immediate reaction, but he was disappointed. Harry merely said, 'Well? What about it?'

He tried again. 'My mother was Millicent Potts.'

Harry shook his head. 'I'm sorry, I don't know what you're talking about.'

Ray said angrily, 'All right, it was a long time ago – but you can't have forgotten!'

So then he threw the facts baldly at the old man – the names, the dates, the whole story – but Harry continued to shake his head.

'There must be some mistake. Mind you, I won't pretend I was a saint in my younger days – there have been other women in my life from time to time, but no, I never knew a Millicent. I'd have remembered.'

He broke off as the door opened and Miss Preece entered the room, saying, 'I thought I heard someone—' Then she stopped short, and her face changed as she recognised Ray. 'What's he doing here?' she asked, in a low voice.

'I can't make head or tail of it. Muriel's been filling his head with all manner of rubbish, telling him he's the son of a woman I never even heard of, and claiming I was his father!'

Miss Preece looked very bizarre. She was in a nightgown, with a black and crimson shawl draped around her, and she had taken the combs from her hennaed hair, letting it fall to her shoulders. Her kohl-rimmed eyes were wild, and as she gazed at Ray he thought of an illustration he'd seen once in a children's book – a picture of an old witch.

'I – I've got nowhere else to go,' he faltered. 'I was hoping you might have a room to let—'

She moved slowly towards him, gazing at him with a kind of horrified fascination. 'Give me your hand,' she said.

Half-hypnotised, he obeyed, and as their hands touched, a shudder ran through her; for an instant she closed her eyes, forcing herself to hold on to him by an effort of will. Then she let his hand drop, and turned to Harry.

'There is a link that binds you together – I've always known that – but it is not a blood tie . . .' The formal words might have sounded ludicrous in her hoarse cockney voice, but they did not. 'The connection is mysterious and deeply buried. I can't understand it – but I can tell you one thing . . . he is not your son.'

She addressed Ray. 'There is no place for you here. I'm sorry, there are no vacancies. You must leave this house at once.'

Under other circumstances, he might have tried to argue, but there was something about this room – the harsh light and the dark shadows, the eerie atmosphere, and above all, the look in the old woman's eyes – they all combined to terrify him, and an icy sweat ran down his spine, along with the raindrops.

'Don't worry, I'm not stopping,' he said thickly, and made for the door. Outside the house, even the downpour was a welcome relief.

Miss Preece breathed a long sigh. She felt suddenly weak; shaking, she sat down to rest on Harry's unmade bed.

'Are you all right, old girl?' he asked.

'Better, now he's gone,' she said. 'Once before, I touched him – that was bad enough – but this time it was worse, much worse.'

'Why? What was it like?'

'It was like touching a corpse,' she said slowly. 'He carries death with him, everywhere he goes. Death and destruction, all around.'

Harry sank on to the bed beside her. 'What's going to happen? Do you know?'

The two old people huddled together for comfort, as she replied, 'No, I can't tell you. But whatever it is, it's getting nearer . . . It will come soon now. Very soon.'

Chapter Twenty-six

'HOW MANY HAVE you got on your list?' asked Daphne.

Kate sighed, looking at the paper in her hand. 'Not very many,' she admitted. 'Some of them said they'll try to come on the day if they can spare the time, but I got the feeling they were just saying that.'

'So – how many are definite?'

'Only three, really. Mr and Mrs Harrington, and old Miss Casey. She's very keen – she says if the landlord turns her out, she'll have to go into a home, and she doesn't want that.'

'But she's so lame! How will we ever get her to the Town Hall?'

'I was thinking – perhaps Val's Steve might help, if we asked him nicely?'

'I can't quite see Miss Casey on the pillion of a motorbike, somehow.'

'I didn't mean his bike. I wondered if Steve could borrow his Dad's greengrocery van? We could take a lot of people in that, sitting in the back – on cushions.'

'Well, perhaps.' Daphne looked at her own list with a sinking heart. 'Not that there's likely to be that many going anyway. I've only got five names on my list – definite promises, that is. Which means, including you and me and Annie, it looks like being eleven altogether. Not what you'd call a vast multitude.'

After a moment, Kate ventured hopefully, 'Mrs Langdon from number ten said she'd think about it. She promised to let us know if she decides to come – that would make twelve.'

'*If* she decides to come. Why are they all being so half-hearted about it? You'd think they'd be up in arms. I was sure I'd be able to drum up a lot of support this week.'

It was a Tuesday morning at the end of October, and the schools were all on half-term holiday, so for once Daphne had some spare time.

'Most of them say protesting's no use. And p'raps they're right. You remember what Mr Colpoys said – legally, there's nothing we can do to stop them.' Kate turned away, gazing blindly at the kitchen range. Her voice quavered a little as she added, 'Looks like we're just going to have to make up our minds to it. But it's going to seem very funny, moving out of this house after all these years.'

Daphne put her arm round her mother-in-law, saying fiercely, 'Don't talk like that! There must be something we can do. Annie says she's getting a lot of names on the petition now. She keeps it in the shop, and she asks every customer who comes in if they'd like to sign it.'

'Oh, bless her. She's trying so hard, I know. I only wish all the neighbours felt the same way—' Kate broke off at the sound of someone climbing the front steps, and brightened up a little. 'There, now! That might be Mrs Langdon come round after all.'

Without waiting for the door-knocker, Daphne made for the stairs, but then they heard the front door being unlocked.

'That's never Annie, home already?' exclaimed Kate.

Daphne hesitated. 'I suppose it might be Ted,' she said doubtfully.

'Oh, you never said. Are you expecting him?'

'No, not really . . .' But she held her breath as the newcomer descended the basement stairs, and then said flatly: 'Oh, it's you.'

'Well, that's what I call a real warm welcome.' Valerie walked into the kitchen. 'Thanks very much!'

She kissed her mother, who hastened to explain, 'We thought it might be Ted, didn't we, Daff?'

Val turned to Daphne. 'Oh – is he on his way?'

'Not as far as I know.' She changed the subject. 'We couldn't think who it was. What are you doing here, this time of day? Why aren't you at work?'

'I wasn't feeling too grand first thing. When I rang in and told them, they said I'd better take the day off.'

'Oh, you poor soul!' Kate began to fuss over her. 'Come and sit down. What do you think it is? Something you ate? Can I get you anything for it? Have you tried bismuth?'

A little embarrassed, Valerie smiled. 'It's OK, Mum. To be honest,

I'm a lot better than I was first thing, but Steve's at the airport, and I got bored with my own company so I thought I'd pop round to say hello.'

'That's right – you take it easy, my girl.' Kate began to fill the kettle. 'You're quite a stranger.'

'I suppose I should have gone into the office, really. They'll be up to their eyes with all the last-minute arrangements for Guy Fawkes – this is always a busy time for us.'

'Good gracious me, that's next week, isn't it?' Kate clucked. 'I don't know where the time goes, really I don't.'

Val's eye fell on the lists they had been compiling, and she asked Daphne, 'What's this? Still rounding people up for the protest rally? How's it going?'

'Not very well. It's probably my fault; I don't think I'm much good at persuading people.'

'You ought to get Ted on to it,' Val suggested. 'He's got a good line of patter – he could always charm the birds off the trees.'

'Yes, I expect he could – but he's not here.'

'Well, when he comes home—'

'He doesn't come home very often,' said Daphne shortly. 'Since he's been renting that flat in Chelsea, he stays there most of the time.'

Setting out cups and saucers, Kate chimed in, 'He's so busy, you see, working on his new show.'

'Oh. Have they started rehearsals already?'

'Not exactly.' Daphne made herself useful, getting out the biscuit tin and arranging chocolate digestives on a plate. 'There's been some sort of a hold-up, he said – but he has to be there, all the same. I don't know why.'

For the past month, Ted had been living in a second-floor flat in Cale Street, near the Kings Road; it called itself a 'flatlet', but in reality it was not much more than a bed-sitting room. Still, it was reasonably cheap, and he wouldn't start getting paid until the rehearsals began.

He knew Marta and Franz had been trying out some of her numbers already, but every time he asked when they were going to make a start on his music, Franz told him that the composer hadn't quite finished working on the score.

This morning, he decided he was fed up with waiting around and doing nothing, so he telephoned Percy Thring to ask what the hell they were playing at? The try-out date in Manchester was getting dangerously close, and he hadn't even seen the final script yet.

Over the phone, he heard Percy clearing his throat, wheezing a little, before saying cheerily, 'Ah, now there's a coincidence! It's funny you should call, I was just going to ring you. It's about the show. I'm afraid I've had to re-negotiate your contract, old man. There's been some changes made.'

At the end of their conversation, Ted replaced the telephone slowly. He felt quite dazed, and could not believe what he had just been told. He sat there for some time, staring at the wall and wondering what to do next. Then he made up his mind; he would go round to Marta and Franz, and ask them what it all meant.

The Neumanns' flat was only a few minutes from Cale Street, but he walked so quickly, he was out of breath by the time he arrived there. When Marta opened the door, she saw at a glance that something was wrong.

'I'm sorry – I had to see you—' he began.

'Yes, of course.' She kissed him on the lips, then took him into the living-room. Franz was sitting at the piano, pencilling some corrections into the score on the music-stand. He looked up, smiling, but Marta threw him a meaning look, and his smile faded.

'So – they have told you, I suppose?' he asked.

Ted was beginning to get angry. 'You both knew about this, didn't you?' he said.

'*Liebchen* – we wanted to tell you, but they had forbidden us to say a word. They made us swear to keep it a secret until everything was fixed,' began Marta.

'What do you mean by "everything"?' Ted demanded. 'I've just been talking to Percy, and I'm not sure if I'm on my head or my heels. For God's sake, tell me what's going on!'

'Sit down, my darling. Franz, get him a whisky.' Marta perched on the arm of Ted's chair while Franz went to the drinks cabinet. 'My poor love, I know this must be a big shock for you, but I'm sure it will be for the good of the show in the end – and we all want it to be a big success, don't we?'

'But Percy says my part's been cut down – why is that good for the show? They promised me equal billing—'

'That was before they started rewriting the script. They've got some new ideas now, to bring it up to date. Everyone thought the opera star and the cockney boy at Covent Garden was a little old-fashioned, so now the hero is going to be a tap-dancer instead.'

Franz handed Ted a large scotch, adding, 'And I think they are right – it will be better so. It's a good contrast, you see. She sings romantic operettas and he prefers swing.'

'They're changing the title, too,' Marta threw in. 'It's *Duet In Swingtime* now.'

Totally confused, Ted shook his head. 'But I've never done tap-dancing. I suppose I could learn, but there isn't much time—'

'No, darling, you're still playing the same character – the lovable costermonger. They've signed Chuck Vernon for the leading role.'

'You mean – the film star?'

'He's already on his way from Hollywood. He can sing and he can tap – and he has so many fans over here, everyone says we're bound to be a smash hit.'

Still struggling to understand, Ted asked: 'But if he's playing the lead – if he's the one who gets the girl – where do I come in?'

'You're the comedy relief, darling – the one who brings us together. A sort of cockney Cupid, really.'

Franz put his hand on Ted's shoulder and squeezed it. 'It's still an excellent part – the show will run and run . . . And in the end that's what matters, isn't it?'

Marta smiled at him. 'Once you get used to the idea, I'm sure you're going to love it. After all, we shall still be working together, my darling. We're going to have a lot of fun.'

Soon after his unsatisfactory encounter with Mr Glynn and Miss Preece, Ray had found himself a room in a cheap lodging house in Penge. It was cramped and dingy, but he scarcely noticed that; he could think of nothing but his obsession. Time and again his attempts to trace his parents had seemed to be on the point of success, only to be frustrated by further contradictions and confusion.

Once or twice he had tried to speak to Mr Colpoys, but each time he was told that the head of the firm was a very busy man, and could not be disturbed – and nowadays he did not come to the office as often as he used to.

But this morning Ray knew he was in the building, and when the heard the Head Clerk say to the office-boy: 'Take these ledgers in to Mr Colpoys, please, he's waiting for them' – Ray stepped in quickly.

'That's all right,' he said. 'I'll do that for you, I've got to see him about something else anyway.'

He took the leather-bound books from the boy and made his way to Mr Colpoys' office on the first floor. Tucking them under one arm, he knocked deferentially at the door, and waited.

'Come in,' said Mr Colpoys.

Ray entered the room; Colpoys, sitting at his desk by the window, looked up – and his face changed. 'What do you want?' he asked.

'I've brought the ledgers you asked for, sir,' said Ray, shutting the door behind him.

Colpoys frowned slightly. 'Thank you. Put them on the side table, will you? I'll attend to them later. That will be all.'

'Before I go, sir, I wonder if you could spare me a few moments?'

'I'm afraid I'm very busy today. Some other time, perhaps.' Colpoys was obviously disconcerted, and would not meet Ray's eye; taking off his pince-nez, he began to polish the lenses with great care.

'This won't take very long, sir. It's about Mrs Glynn.'

'I've no idea what you're talking about. As I say—' Colpoys waved his handkerchief dismissively. 'I'm far too busy to discuss it now.'

But Ray held his ground. 'It's very important to me, sir. And you're the only person I can turn to.'

Colpoys was becoming agitated. 'I've already had to speak to you once about prying into matters that do not concern you. I must warn you that if you persist—'

'But these matters do concern me, sir – very much so. I'm trying to find out the truth about my parents. Mrs Glynn fobbed me off with one story, but it turned out to be a pack of lies – and you must know the truth, better than anyone.'

Startled, Colpoys glanced up, and for the first time they looked at one another directly.

'What do you mean by that?'

Then, all at once, something very strange happened. Looking straight into the old man's eyes, Ray saw his own eyes looking back at him . . . And then, at last, he understood.

'You ought to have told me,' he said softly.

With that, he turned on his heel and walked out. Colpoys called after him: 'What are you saying? Come here! Come back, will you?'

Ray ignored him. He did not return to his own desk, but walked on down the main staircase, through the front office, and out into the street.

He went on walking – along Thicket Road, past the entrance to the Palace grounds, then turned left into Crystal Palace Park Road.

As he climbed the hill, he saw someone coming out of the front gate at Belmont; it was Ethel DeWitt, carrying a shopping-basket. He dodged behind a milk-cart and stayed out of sight until she had passed by. This was a stroke of luck – he wanted to have Muriel all to himself today.

When he reached the house, he was about to ring the front doorbell – Aggie would answer it, but he knew she would not be able to prevent him from walking in – and then he heard someone singing, in a shrill, cracked soprano, and he changed his mind. Treading softly, trying to make no sound on the gravel path, he went round to the side of the house. Aggie was some way off, in the back garden, sweeping up fallen leaves and singing tunelessly to herself:

> '*Early one morning, just as the sun was rising,*
> *I heard a maid singing in the valley below . . .*'

She was clearing the leaves from the path, pushing them down towards a big pile at the bottom of the lawn – and the side door had been left wide open.

Ray almost laughed aloud; his luck was really in today, and no mistake! While she had her back to him, he slipped in at the open door and shut it behind him – the key was on the inside, and he locked it. Now he could be certain that he would not be interrupted.

Unhurried, he went through the house and up the stairs; he did not bother to knock on Muriel's door, but walked straight in.

Muriel was sitting up in bed. When she was reading the serial in her weekly magazine, she did not like being disturbed, and she snapped, 'Well, Aggie? What is it now?'

'It's not Aggie,' he said. 'It's me.'

She looked up instantly, then sat quite still, as if she had been turned to stone. At last she managed to say, 'What are you doing in my house? You have no business here – who let you in?'

'I let myself in,' he said. 'We've got to have a talk, you and me.'

'No! Go away – leave me alone!'

The magazine slid through her fingers on to the carpet as she fumbled for the little bell upon the bedside table. He was there before her, and snatched it away, out of reach.

'You needn't bother with that,' he said, sitting on the side of the bed. 'We don't want anyone else in here, do we? The things we've got to say to each other are private things. It's better like this – just you and me. That's the way it should always have been, right from the start.'

'I – I don't know what you're talking about,' she stammered, and then started calling out, 'Ethel, come here! *Ethel!*'

'Ethel's gone to the shops, didn't you know? She won't be back yet a while – and Aggie's down the garden.'

'How dare you break into my house?' Taking a deep breath, she shouted as loudly as she could: '*Aggie! Come here at once!*'

He smiled. 'She's right down the other end – she can't hear you.'

But Aggie did hear, or thought she did – and then she wondered if she had imagined it. Putting down the broom, she listened again, but the wind was making so much noise, tearing at the trees, it was hard to be sure. So she trotted up the path to the house and tried to open the side door – and found that she could not.

She rattled the handle helplessly for some time. It couldn't possibly be locked; there was no one else in the house apart from Mu, and she was upstairs. Of course, there had been a lot of rain lately. They said that the wood sometimes swelled up when it got damp. The door must have jammed . . . such a nuisance!

Oh well, Ethel would be home presently, and she'd have the key to the front door in her purse, so that would be all right. Aggie listened at the door, but could hear nothing inside the house. Perhaps she had been dreaming, after all.

Reassured, she went back to the bottom of the garden, and resumed her sweeping-up:

> '*Oh, don't deceive me. Oh, never leave me.*
> *How could you treat a poor maiden so?*'

Upstairs, Ray put his hand on Muriel's arm.

'Why did you have to tell me lies?' he said quietly. 'Why couldn't you tell me the truth?'

She was trembling violently; he could feel the fear within her – and that pleased him.

'I didn't—' She forced the words out in spasms. 'I never – told you – lies.'

'Course you did! Not all the time, p'raps. It was true about you and Mr Colpoys sending me to the orphanage, I know that. But you said Mr Glynn was my dad and Mrs Potts was my mum – and that wasn't true, was it? Mr Glynn didn't know anything about it – he told me so.'

'That man's a liar – he always was. He's the one telling you lies,' she broke in desperately, and the sweat running down her face left rivulets in the paint and powder. 'You are Barbara's half-brother – I swear it.'

523

'Yes, I know I am. But not the way you said. When I got to thinking about it – why should you and Colpoys go to all that trouble to cover up for Mr Glynn? And today the penny dropped. William Colpoys is my father – and you're my mother.'

As she shrank back, his hand tightened on her arm.

'As soon as I was born, you had me sent away,' he said. 'You shouldn't have done that.'

Kate glanced at the kitchen clock.

'Look at the time,' she said, 'and us sitting here talking! Well, this won't buy the baby a new bonnet. I'll never get round the shops at this rate.' She stood up and began to put on her hat and coat, asking, 'Do you want to come with us, Val?'

'I think I'd sooner sit here a bit longer, d'you mind?'

'Course not – if you don't mind us leaving you all on your ownsome,' said Kate. 'Daff, are you ready?'

Under the table, Val trod gently on Daphne's foot, and she understood the message.

'I think perhaps I'll stay as well,' she said. 'To keep Val company, is that all right?'

'Just as you like. Anyway, I shan't be long.'

As soon as Kate left the house, Val said, 'Thanks. I've been dying to talk to you, but I never seemed to get the chance.'

'What is it?' Daphne studied her more closely. 'You're not still feeling badly?'

'No, I'm OK now – honest.'

'That's good. Only I noticed you didn't have your chocolate biscuit – that's not like you.'

'I've been a bit off sweet things, lately. This morning, I was too sick to manage any breakfast.'

Daphne was immediately concerned. 'I knew there was something wrong. Have you been to the doctor?'

'Not yet. You see, I know what it is. I'm going to have a baby.'

'Oh, Val!' Impulsively, Daphne threw her arms around her. 'I'm so glad. You must be so pleased – aren't you?'

'Sort of. Steve's really happy about it, but he doesn't realise what it's going to be like. We haven't told anyone yet, I daren't tell Mum – it'll break her heart. You know what she's like about babies, the ones she calls "out of wedlock".'

'Does it have to be? Out of wedlock?'

'Don't be silly – we can't be married!'

'Have you talked to Gerry about it?'

'No!' Val looked horrified. 'I couldn't . . . Besides, it wouldn't do any good.'

'He might change his mind. I believe he was hanging on to the idea that you and Steve would split up, and then you'd go back to him, but now . . . You've really got to tell him.'

'What – go to Luxembourg and beg him for a divorce? I can't do that.'

'You could write to him. He's not really a monster, you know, and he's got to be told.'

Val sighed. 'I suppose so. Sometimes it's hard to remember he's your brother. All right – I'll try and write him a letter.' She fidgeted with her empty cup and saucer for a moment, then said abruptly: 'Talking about brothers, can I ask you something?'

Daphne tensed slightly. 'Yes – what?'

'It's about Ted. I know he's got to be in London because of this new show, but every time you talk about him, you seem a bit – I don't know – you get a funny look in your eye. Have you had a row, or what?'

'How can we have a row when we never see each other?' countered Daphne.

She began to clear the table, taking the cups and saucers to the sink, but Val persisted: 'No, tell me honestly. Is everything all right?'

'Oh, I don't know . . .'

Daphne didn't mean to talk about her problems – she was determined not to say anything – but before she knew it, she found herself pouring out the whole miserable story, and it was such a relief, she couldn't stop.

When she had finished, Val said, 'Marta Linden – she's the one we saw at the Croydon Empire, isn't she? I never liked her much, even then. What a cow.'

In spite of herself, Daphne couldn't help smiling. 'She's not that bad – and she's been a big help to Ted. You must admit, they do work well together.'

'All that girlish charm and broken English? I suppose it's all right if you like that kind of thing.'

'Well, it seems Ted does – so that's that.' Daphne began to wash up the cups and saucers, saying over her shoulder, 'The peculiar thing is, she's a married woman, but I suppose her husband doesn't care. Perhaps theatrical people always carry on like that . . . Anyhow, that's the way things are, and there's nothing I can do about it.'

'But there is! You're not going to let her walk off with your husband, are you? Haven't you even talked to him about it?'

'I did try once, but we didn't really get very far. If it comes to choosing between her and me, he'll stick with her, for the sake of his career.'

'Then he's a damn fool – and you're as bad as he is. What's wrong with you both? You've got to go and see him – have a stand-up row if it comes to that – but don't just sit here, doing nothing!' She pointed an accusing finger at her sister-in-law. 'You told me I've got to talk to Gerry – well, it's about time you and Ted did some straight talking yourselves.'

For a long moment, Daphne stood still, up to her wrists in soapy water. Then she wiped her hands on a teacloth and said, 'All right. Come and finish off the washing-up – and when your Mum gets back, you can give her a message for me. Say I've gone up to London and I don't know what time I'll be home. Tell her I'm going to talk to my husband.'

When Aggie had swept all the leaves into a tidy heap, she went and tried the side door again, but it still wouldn't budge. Mournfully, she retreated to the ramshackle arbour at the bottom of the garden; the trellis was broken in several places, and climbing roses straggled over it, unpruned and uncared for, but it sheltered a small rustic bench, so Aggie sat down and made herself as comfortable as possible, hoping that Ethel would soon be home.

Then she remembered with dismay that Ethel would be away for a long time. She hadn't gone to the shops down the road – today was the day she was catching a bus into Croydon, to buy some winter underclothes. Too late, Aggie remembered Ethel telling her that she was going to have a midday snack at Wilsons' coffee shop, because she wouldn't be home until some time this afternoon. She had left strict instructions that Aggie should make sardines on toast for lunch, and take Muriel's up to her on a tray. Ethel would be so cross with her for making a muddle of it – and Muriel would shout at her if she missed her lunch.

Huddled up on the rustic bench, Aggie began to cry quietly; the whole thing was too difficult for her to deal with. In her despair, she closed her eyes – and she went on crying until she had cried herself to sleep.

Up in her bedroom, Muriel too had been crying. Sweat and tear-stains had ruined her make-up, and for the first time Ray saw her as she really was – an old, defenceless woman – talking on and on, trying to justify herself.

'. . . Babs was only a few months old. I should have been very happy, but when I discovered what a rotter my husband really was, I felt as if I were alone – alone in the world. You know, he used to have one of these rooms as his studio, and when he was painting he wouldn't let anyone go in because he didn't like to be disturbed – that's what he said – but I found out he was making improper advances to one of the girls he hired to model for him, right under my own roof, too! That was when I turned him out. I sent for my solicitor, to draw up a deed of separation, and he forced that dreadful man to sign it. I made sure he would never get a penny of Papa's money . . . The house – the furniture – all our treasures – they belonged to the DeWitts. They belonged to *me*!'

She dabbed at her eyes, smearing her mascara as she continued. 'After that, I felt lonelier than ever. William Colpoys had come here several times, to discuss various legal details. He was such a charming man in those days, and he flattered me disgracefully – well, he was a widower, you see, so of course he was lonely too. Anyway, that's how it – it happened . . . Afterwards, when I discovered I was – with child – I was absolutely horrified. William wanted me to have an operation and get rid of it, but of course I told him that was unthinkable. It was an impossible situation altogether.'

'But if you'd divorced Mr Glynn, you could have married him, couldn't you?' asked Ray.

'Certainly not. There has never been a divorce in our family. Well, you know yourself – even after the way that Watkins girl behaved, Gerald refused to divorce her – and quite rightly. We do have some standing in society – we have a reputation to maintain. So I told everyone I was unwell, and I went away to a private nursing home in Bournemouth; that was where the birth took place.'

'And after that – you had me adopted?'

'It seemed to be the best plan. Somehow William got to hear of this working-class couple who were unable to have a child of their own, and he arranged everything – he's very clever, in his own way. It all happened so quickly. They pretended she'd had the baby at home, prematurely, without the assistance of any midwife or doctor, and the birth was officially registered as such . . . It all cost money, of course. William and I shared the expenses.'

'But – the orphanage—'

'Four years later, Mrs Potts died. She had some incurable disease, poor creature, I don't remember the details. I realise that it left Mr Potts in a difficult position, but we had a strict understanding that there was to be no further contact of any kind between us, and he broke the agreement by coming to this house. It upset me very much at the time. He begged and pleaded with me to take the child back—'

'Me – that's who you're talking about. That child was *me*!'

'Yes, well – anyway, I had to refuse. How could I have agreed to such a preposterous idea? What would people have said? I consulted William Colpoys again, and we agreed that the best solution was for the child – for you – to be sent to a – well, it was a kind of boarding school.'

'I know what it was. It was an orphanage.'

'Yes – something of that sort. But we did our duty by you. We arranged things so you were well brought up, and given a good education. I consider we did everything that was necessary.'

'Do you? Is that really what you think?'

'Certainly,' she said firmly. 'And if you hadn't met Barbara, there need never have been any unpleasantness . . . It was all extremely unfortunate.'

Stretching out a hand, she picked up a small vanity mirror, and recoiled from her own reflection.

'Oh heavens, just look at the state I'm in – and it's all your fault, coming in and upsetting me like this. Quick, give me my bag. Hold the glass for me, will you?'

He obeyed, and she began to repair the ravaged make-up as best she could, still trying to convince herself that in spite of everything that had taken place, she had never been to blame in any way whatever.

Ray watched with fascination as she put back the mascara, covering the wrinkles with powder and rouge, and outlining her lips with carmine.

'So here we are – the two of us,' he said dreamily. 'Together again after all this time. You – and your son.'

'Oh no, you must never say that, Raymond.' A tiny wrinkle puckered her brow. 'That's one thing I was never really happy about. I do wish the Potts family hadn't called you Raymond. It's not a very nice name, is it?'

'It's better than Potts,' he said. 'What would you have called me, if you'd ever given me a name?'

'I don't know – I never really thought about it . . . Henry, perhaps,

528

she said, still concentrating on her lipstick. 'That was my father's name – Henry DeWitt.'

'Henry DeWitt.' He tried out the sound of it. 'Yes – that's not bad.'

'Well, now – that's done!' She put away her cosmetics, and for the first time she smiled at him. 'How do I look, Raymond?'

'You look beautiful,' he said – and at that moment, he really meant it. She looked years younger, and there was something about her smile and the sparkle in her eyes that reminded him of Babs. He took both her hands in his as he repeated: 'You look really beautiful. Only – don't call me Raymond. I'd like you to call me Henry.'

'Ah, if only . . .' She sighed. 'If only things had been different.'

'They could be different, couldn't they? I'm still the grandson of Henry DeWitt, still your son and heir.'

'No! Gerald is my son. I'm sorry, but you have to understand – you can have no place in this family.'

'But I've got a right to it! You know that, in your heart of hearts. You ought to do something for me.'

'What do you mean?'

'You could alter your will – you could still slip me in somehow—'

She turned her head away. 'No, that's impossible. Whatever would people think? I couldn't possibly explain it!'

'What does that matter? Babs told me you'd left her the house. I deserve to get *something*, don't I? Come on, fair's fair.'

'You're being very silly – it's out of the question.'

'All right, then, I've got a better idea. You told Babs she was my half-sister – you can tell her now you made a mistake. Say you'd got it all wrong, then we can get married after all. That way I'll still be part of the family.'

She stared at him with growing horror. 'Do you know what you're saying? That would be incest!'

'Nobody would ever know except you and me – and Mr Colpoys, I suppose, but he's not going to spill the beans, is he? Come on, let me marry Babs—'

'I've never heard anything so disgusting in my life!' she told him angrily. 'I really think you must be raving mad!'

'Don't say that.' Suddenly he was a child again; in the bleak, grey playground, surrounded by a ring of jeering boys who chanted at him: '*Potty Potts – Potty – that's what you are* . . .' He felt the same fear, the same helpless fury welling up inside him as he turned on her furiously. 'Don't you ever call me that . . .'

There was something in his eyes that frightened her. 'That's enough – I want you to go. Leave my house at once, or I shall call the police.'

'Oh no, I'm staying here. This is where I belong. It's my house, by rights.'

She tried to get out of the bed. 'I warn you, I'm going to telephone the police station—'

But he grabbed her arm. 'Oh, yes? And what if I was to tell them the truth, eh? How would you like that, Mummy dear?'

'Nobody would believe you!' she threw the words into his face. 'They'd take you for a lunatic—'

'*Don't call me that!*'

He pushed her back on to the bed and threw himself across her; she struggled wildly – trapped under blankets and eiderdown, she could not free herself. Pressing down upon her, he thought again of Babs, and felt an urgent desire growing in his loins, as he realised that he had her at his mercy.

'Kiss me, Mummy,' he said, thrusting his mouth down upon hers.

She tried to hold him off, and began to scream for help. During their struggle, the pillows tumbled aside; to silence her, he snatched one up and pressed it over her mouth.

'Shut up, you bitch,' he panted. 'Shut up! Do you hear?'

The thickness of the bedclothes and the weight of his body pinned her down, but she clawed at him desperately, wriggling and jerking beneath him. His excitement mounted, overwhelming him, until the tension became unbearable, and relief flooded him. At the same moment, she stopped struggling and lay still.

He lay on top of the bed for some time, and his passion slowly ebbed away, leaving him drained and empty. Then he rolled off; sitting up, he waited for her to say something.

But when he lifted the pillow from her face, she did not speak. Her sightless eyes stared at the ceiling, and he realised that she would never speak again.

'*Jesus Christ . . .*' he whispered.

He stood up, and went along the passage to the bathroom, where he cleaned himself up and adjusted his clothing. He looked at himself in the mirror, automatically straightening his tie and smoothing down his hair, then he went on, along the passage and down the stairs, without once looking back. He unlocked the side door and peered out cautiously; at the bottom of the garden he saw Aggie, curled up on the bench in the arbour, fast asleep.

So then he knew that there was a God after all, and that God was on his side, and he walked out of the house, leaving the door unlocked. He walked on and on, regaining strength and confidence at every step, until he reached the offices of Colpoys & Son, and went in, taking his place at his desk.

The Head clerk looked up crossly, asking, 'Where the devil have you been?'

'Mr Colpoys sent me out on an errand,' said Ray calmly, and picking up his pen he went on with his work.

If anyone asked, Colpoys would back up his story. He wouldn't want the facts coming out, would he? He was his father, after all.

Ray smiled to himself. From now on, he felt sure everything was going to turn out right for him. And nobody would ever call him 'Potty' again.

Southern Railway's new electric trains were fast and frequent, and Daphne reached Chelsea early in the afternoon.

She had to ask a policeman for directions to Cale Street, but when she found it, she looked about her in surprise. She did not know Central London very well, and her trips to the West End were usually confined to the big department stores of Oxford Street and Kensington.

Cale Street was quite different. These shops were small and homely – a butcher's, a bakery, a grocery on the corner. There was a triangular open space, with a public bench, a drinking-fountain, and a few trees; some pigeons crooned and squabbled over fresh horse-dung on the road. And there was a strange light over everything. The autumn air was very crisp and clear; in the sunshine every detail stood out sharply.

She felt that she was on the threshold of a new world and her spirits rose, as if something important and unexpected might happen at any moment. Perhaps this would be a new beginning for both of them.

Walking along Cale Street and looking at the numbers on the doors, she suddenly found herself thinking of her mother. Daphne hadn't been round to Belmont lately; she must make an effort and visit Mother at the weekend – perhaps Annie would come too.

What had put that thought into her head at this particular moment, she wondered? And then she realised that there was a kind of parallel between her parents' lives and her own. Harry Glynn had never been a model husband; absorbed in his work as an artist, he had often neglected Muriel. From time to time he had been involved with other women, too – and when that happened, Muriel did not make any effort to understand, or try to put things right between them. She had turned him out of the house and out of her heart, closing both against him.

Daphne stopped walking. This blue door with the paint peeling off it was the one she had been looking for. There was a row of electric bells, with names beside them; she selected the one marked *Watt* – not Watkins, she noticed – and pressed it firmly. Whatever happened now, she was determined she would not follow the pattern laid down by her mother.

She waited for some time, slowly realising how silly she had been. Why had she expected to find Ted at home in the middle of the day? He would probably be with his agent, or with the producer – or with Marta. But then she heard the sound of light, running footsteps, and she knew that they were Ted's; nobody else ran downstairs like that.

He opened the door, and looked at her in blank astonishment.

'Hello,' she said.

'Hello, Daff,' he said – then asked immediately: 'What's happened? Is something wrong?'

'There's nothing wrong,' she said. 'I wanted to see you, that's all. Can I come in?'

He hesitated for a split second, and it occurred to her that Marta might be there, upstairs – but then he said, 'Yes, of course you can. Shall I go first?'

She followed him up the narrow staircase, and into the flatlet on the second floor.

'It's a bit of a pigsty,' he said, as she looked around. 'I don't get many visitors, so I don't often bother with tidying up.'

It was small, and very cluttered, and he had left things lying about on every available surface. There was an unmade divan bed, a table, two chairs, and some wall-shelves – all covered with books and papers and open suitcases and glossy photographs, along with a telephone, and a black japanned make-up box, some grubby towels and neckties and a pullover, a dinner-jacket on a wire coat-hanger, a half-empty bottle of scotch and a dirty glass, and a full cup of tea – stone cold, with a skin on top of it.

'I could soon make a fresh pot, if you like?' he offered politely, as if she were a stranger. 'There's some clean cups in the kichen.'

Through a half-open door, she could see into the little kitchenette, where washing was hanging up to dry – a vest, a pair of pants, a shirt – on a clothes-line above the sink and the gas-stove.

'No, don't bother,' she said. 'It's all very—' She searched for the right word. 'It's very compact, isn't it?'

'You'd be surprised. They even managed to fit a bath in there as well,' he said.

'In the kitchen? Where?'

'You lift up the draining-board, and it's underneath . . . I have to sit in it with my knees up to my chin,' he added, with the faintest hint of a smile. Then he cleared a pile of newspapers from a chair by sweeping them on to the floor, and said, 'Here, sit down. Why didn't you ring up and tell me you were coming?'

'I don't know – I didn't stop to think. I decided I had to talk to you, so I got on the next train, and . . . I hope you don't mind?'

'I don't *mind*, but you haven't picked a very good day, that's all.'

'Oh. Are you going out?'

'No, it's not that. I've only just come in, as a matter of fact. I had to go and see – some people – about the show.'

'Have you started rehearsals?'

'Not yet – they're having the first read-through on Friday. I'm supposed to be getting a script tomorrow. Oh God, it's all such a mess.'

Then he told her what Percy Thring had said, and how he had gone round to see Marta – and Franz, of course. He told her about the salary-cut he would have to take, and the fact that he would only be playing a supporting role, and finished by saying: 'The fact is, I still don't know what to do. It hasn't turned out the way I hoped. For two pins, I'd tell them what they can do with their bloody contract.'

He was slumped on the divan, and Daphne got up and went over to him, putting her arms round him. 'I'm sorry, Ted – I'm really sorry. You'd been looking forward to this so much.'

He kissed her – then kissed her again, and began to caress her, as if by embracing her he could blot out his unhappiness.

'You don't have to do the show if you don't want to,' she told him. 'Why don't you say no?'

'It's not as simple as that. They're relying on me – I'd be letting them down.'

'Ted, they've let *you* down. You don't owe them anything!' She held him close to her. 'They can always find someone else. Come home with me, and let's begin again. This is the moment for us to make a fresh start, I know it is.'

'You don't understand – I can't do that. This will be my first West End show. They've got a theatre booked already, on Shaftesbury

Avenue – I might never get another chance like this. All right, it's not top billing, but I'll be seen by everybody who matters. This could still be my big break.'

She drew her head back, and looked at him. 'You've let Marta talk you into it, haven't you?'

'It wasn't just Marta. Franz said the same – and Percy. They're sure this is right for me. They're all pro's – they know what they're talking about.'

'And I don't. Ted – I love you. I want you with me. That's all I know.'

'I love you too.' He went on kissing her, with a kind of hunger. 'There's nobody like you – there never will be. And I want you – now.'

He drew her down beside him, and there was nothing more to be said. It was a couple of months since they had last made love, but they slipped easily into the old, familiar rites of passion – old, but always new – familiar, yet continually surprising. At last they lay still in each other's arms, together and at peace.

After a long while, Ted murmured: 'How about that cup of tea now?'

'Yes – all right.'

She went on lying there, while he threw on his old dressing gown and pottered about in the kitchen; she listened to the kettle being filled, and the pop and roar of the gas-stove, and felt blissfully contented.

While they waited for the kettle to boil, he came back and sat beside her, lazily stroking her hair.

'You do know I love you, don't you?' he said.

'Yes, I know. But what's going to happen to us?' she asked. 'Is it always going to be like this? You and me, in two different worlds?'

'It'll be better than this. One of these days I'll be a big star with my name up in lights – you'll see. I'll buy a luxury flat in Mayfair—'

'And where shall I be? Living at Crystal Palace, coming up to see you every now and then – for afternoon visits?' She smiled wryly. 'But not on matinée days, of course.'

'Oh, Daff.' He kissed her again, tenderly. 'We'll work things out, somehow. I promise.'

The kettle began to whistle, and he went back to the kitchen. Naked, she got up and followed him, standing beside him as he filled the teapot.

'This is what we want,' he said. 'A nice hot cuppa.'

She lifted her arms, stretching luxuriously, and saying, 'What I really want is a nice hot bath.'

'Well, why not? I've only got to put a tanner in the meter and lift up the draining-board,' he said, adding with a grin: 'Pity it isn't big enough for two.'

'That's the worst of living in your world,' she told him, as he cradled her in his arms. 'It isn't big enough for two.'

By the time Aggie woke up, the sun was going down behind the trees, and the afternoon had turned quite chilly. For a moment she couldn't remember where she was; slowly it came back to her – but vaguely, in bits and pieces. She knew that she had shut herself out of the house, and that Ethel had gone off to do some shopping. It must be getting quite late.

Her joints creaked painfully when she stood up, and she realised that she had been asleep on the bench for some time. She began to walk towards the house, and dicovered she was hungry – she had had nothing to eat since breakfast. With a sudden shock of dismay, she remembered that Mu hadn't had any lunch, either.

She tried the side door again – and to her surprise she found that it was open.

Perhaps Ethel had come home, after all. She went into the house, calling out, 'Ethel! Are you there, dear?'

But there was no answer, and when she went through the little lobby that led into the hall, she saw that Ethel's hat and coat were not in their usual place on the pegs, so that meant she must still be out. How very strange that the door should have opened so easily this time, when it had been so tightly shut before.

Well, the first thing to do was to go up and see Mu, and say she was sorry about the sardines on toast. Perhaps she might like to have them now instead, as a sort of 'high tea'?

As she went up the stairs, she started to feel horribly nervous. She felt sure Mu would be very cross indeed, and shout at her – and then she would be so frightened, she wouldn't be able to explain properly. She wouldn't be able to do anything except cry, and that always made Mu angrier still.

She must try to be brave; she must try and stand up for herself. If Mu shouted, she would shout back at her – but sometimes, when she was really angry, Mu took hold of her and shook her so hard she couldn't think straight – she could hardly breathe! Well, if that happened, she would just have to make the first move. She would get hold of Muriel and shake her really hard, and see how she liked it!

Buoyed up by this resolution, she walked into Muriel's bedroom – and saw her lying there like an untidy parcel, sprawled half on and half off the bed.

'Oh dear, whatever's happened?' Aggie gasped, hurrying to her side. 'Mu, dear, try and sit up. Can you hear me? *Muriel!*'

She tried to drag her back on to the bed, tugging at her with all her might, and whimpering: 'Mu, dear, speak to me. Do say something – please . . .'

One of the pillows had fallen on to the floor, and Aggie picked it up, trying to lift Muriel's shoulders and slip it under her head, but when she touched her skin, it felt so cold – and her face was such a strange colour . . .

Pulling and pushing at Muriel, making little moaning noises, Aggie did not hear the sound of footsteps coming along the landing, until Ethel appeared in the doorway. She stood there, dropping the heavily laden shopping-basket and letting her purchases roll out over the carpet, as she exclaimed in terror: '*Oh, Aggie – whatever have you done?*'

Chapter Twenty-seven

WHEN DAPHNE CAME home that evening, she found Kate waiting for her, looking frightened and anxious.

'Oh Daff, thank goodness you're back! I've been so worried.'

'Why? I went up to see Ted – didn't Val tell you?'

'Yes, she said, but you've been gone so long – I didn't know what time you'd be coming home.'

'It's only half-past seven. It's not late . . . There were things we had to talk about. He sent you his love, by the way.'

'That's nice.' Kate continued to plait her fingers nervously as she went on: 'It's just so dreadful you had to go off today, of all days.'

'What do you mean?'

'They've been phoning you from Belmont – Babs was trying to get hold of you. She's ever so upset, poor girl. I promised you'd go round there right away.'

'Oh, lor' – what is it this time?' Daphne began to take her coat off, saying, 'She might at least give me time to sit down and get my breath back!'

'No – I'm ever so sorry, but – I think you ought to go now.' Moistening her lips, she forced herself to say: 'I don't know how to tell you this. It's your mother.'

With her coat half on and half off, Daphne asked sharply: 'What's the matter with her? Is she ill?'

'I'm afraid it's worse than that, dear – much worse.' Kate took a step towards her. 'She – she's dead.'

Daphne put a hand on the table to steady herself. 'When? What was it – a heart attack?'

'No. It seems like – there's been a terrible accident. Babs was almost hysterical when she rang up – I couldn't follow what she was saying. She seemed to think your mother had been—' Kate broke off, shaking her head. 'But it couldn't be that – she must have got it wrong . . . I'm sure it must have been an accident.'

Daphne broke in: 'What did Babs say, exactly?'

Kate's voice was almost a whisper. 'She said – she said it was – murder . . .'

From that moment, Daphne found herself in a waking nightmare – a jumble of meaningless horrors.

She went straight to Belmont. As she arrived, an ambulance was turning out of the drive; there was a police car parked by the front door, which stood wide open. A uniformed constable tried to stop her as she entered the house, but when she told him who she was, he let her go in.

There were strangers everywhere; some in uniform, some in plain-clothes – a man with a camera – and the Glynns' family doctor, who took her aside, saying in a hushed voice, 'I've had to give your Aunt Agnes a sedative, and your sister, too. They're a little calmer now.'

'And where is – my mother? Can I see her?'

'I'm sorry; she's not here. As soon as they'd taken the photograph, and the police surgeon had made his examination, the body was—' He corrected himself quickly: 'She was taken away. There will have to be an inquest, I'm afraid.'

'I see. So it wasn't an accident?'

He looked at her in amazement. 'Oh, no. I beg your pardon, I thought you knew . . . Mrs Glynn had been smothered – with a pillow.' He put his hand on her arm: 'I think you'd better sit down. I could give you something to calm you?'

'No, thank you. I'll be all right . . . Where's Babs? Where are the others?'

He escorted her to the drawing room. Sitting on the sofa, with her face distorted after hours of crying, Aggie was almost unrecognisable. Ethel sat beside her, with one arm round her shoulders. 'It's all right, dear,' she was saying in a soothing voice. 'You're all right. Nobody's blaming you. Everything's going to be all right.'

Babs was staring at herself in the looking-glass above the fireplace; when she saw Daphne entering the room she turned and ran towards her with arms outstretched, like a child seeking comfort. The two sisters embraced without a word, holding one another in a desperate silence.

At last Babs let her go, saying plaintively, 'I needed you – where were you?' Daphne tried to explain, and Babs interrupted: 'But I *needed* you! You should have been here. It wasn't fair, leaving me to do it all on my own. I feel terrible. My head's aching—'

'Why don't we go into your room? Then you can lie down and rest, and try to tell me about it.'

Before they left the sitting room, Daphne went over to speak to her aunts. Aggie looked vaguely up at her, saying in a strange, faraway voice, 'I'm very sorry, Daphne dear – I'm afraid I've been very naughty. But I didn't mean to hurt her. I don't know what came over me . . .'

Appalled, Daphne exclaimed: 'Oh no, you didn't! You couldn't—'

Ethel said immediately, 'Of course she didn't. That's what I keep trying to tell her, but she won't listen.'

'I must have done it; there wasn't anyone else,' Aggie persisted, in the same high, plangent tone. 'I can't quite remember how it happened – but that's because I make mistakes, and forget things. I didn't mean to do it.'

'Of course you didn't, Auntie Ag,' said Babs impatiently. 'You're just being silly.' Taking Daphne's arm, she dragged her off to her own room, where she threw herself on to the bed, sighing, 'At least the doctor's quietened her down at last. She's been driving us all mad, saying she'd had a quarrel with Mummy, and got so cross with her, she killed her! It's been so awful, you can't imagine.'

'But Aggie would never do such a thing—'

'Well, of course she wouldn't. You've only got to look at her. She's over seventy, she hasn't got the strength . . . The police doctor says he's absolutely certain she couldn't have done it.'

'Then why does she keep saying—'

'According to Auntie Eth, it was Ag who found Mummy – and the shock seems to have driven everything else out of her head. She kept trying to confess; it's a good job the police didn't take her seriously. By the time I got home from work, the place was swarming with policemen – asking questions, taking pictures, looking for clues . . .' Babs rested her head on her pillow and closed her eyes. 'I'm so tired. I feel as if I could go to sleep for a hundred years.'

'I still don't understand.' Daphne probed gently. 'If it wasn't Aggie – what really happened?'

So Babs tried to put the sequence of events together, from what she had been told. Ethel's shopping trip to Croydon, and Aggie's attempt to do a little gardening: 'And while she was down the garden, the side door was left open. At least, she said the door must have blown shut and jammed at one stage, but then she changed the story and told us it opened itself again. I expect she'd been turning the handle the wrong way, you know what she's like . . . So it was probably standing wide open for hours – anyone could have walked in.'

'You mean it could have been a burglar?'

'Must have been, though there doesn't seem to be anything missing. But the Inspector said Mummy might have disturbed him. He could have tried to stop her calling for help, and – that's how it happened. Afterwards, when he saw she was dead, he was so scared he ran out of the house without taking anything.'

One of the policemen knocked at the bedroom door, and asked Daphne if she could spare a few minutes to speak to the Inspector. He had chosen to use the kitchen as his temporary office, and as they faced one another across the kitchen table, against the familiar background of the china on the dresser, the gas-stove, the sink and the draining-board, the situation seemed more than ever like a crazy bad dream.

Having expressed his regrets and condolences, the Inspector asked a few routine questions about Daphne's movements during the day, and in particular her whereabouts at the time of the murder. She explained that she had been with her husband in London during the afternoon, and he went on to ask when she had seen her mother last. For the first time she felt tears pricking at her eyes as she replied unhappily, 'Not very recently. Several weeks ago, in fact. I'm sorry, I can't remember the exact date. Does it matter?'

'No, madam – don't upset yourself. I only wanted to know whether she had seemed at all apprehensive or preoccupied recently. I suppose you don't happen to know if there was anyone who might have fallen out with her – someone with a grudge against her, perhaps?'

She began, 'No, I'm sure there wasn't. She'd have mentioned it, if—' Then she hesitated, as the thought of Ray Duke crossed her mind.

As if he were telepathic, the Inspector continued, 'I believe there was a young man who had been lodging here for some time – a Mr Duke. She had asked him to find other accommodation, I understand?'

'Well yes, but surely you're not suggesting—'

'No, no. I gather he moved to new lodgings about a month ago. Your sister told me he was sorry to leave. Well, that's understandable enough, but she said that in the end he and Mrs Glynn parted quite amicably. So that hardly explains this kind of motiveless assault, does it?'

'No, but whoever did it – there must have been some motive?'

'Not necessarily. We do sometimes come across the odd, inexplicable crime, without any motive whatever. They're the most difficult to understand, or to solve. But don't worry; I assure you we shall leave no stone unturned.'

Later that evening, the Inspector called on Mr Duke at his new address.

Ray was very shocked when he heard the news, saying he would do anything he could to help the police in the their enquiries, but he was unable to add anything to the information they already had.

When he was asked to describe his feelings about the deceased, he said quietly, 'Of course, we had our differences of opinion now and again, me and Mrs Glynn – she was a very strong-minded lady! – but I shall always have fond memories of her. Being an orphan, like I am, I can only say she was almost like a mother to me.'

He was so frank and open, and so obviously grieved by the tragedy, the Inspector was quite touched.

To the Glynn family, it seemed at first that the nightmare would never end, but as time went on, the pain and shock began to fade, little by little. Even the unthinkable, inexplicable horror of Muriel's death slowly receded into the past, and with each day that dawned the family discovered that life could still go on, after all.

The police enquiries continued, but turned up no fresh evidence. When the inquest was held, in the light of the inconclusive facts brought forward, the coroner was forced to bring in a verdict of 'Unlawful killing by person or persons unknown'.

He gave instructions for the body to be released from the mortuary and sent to the undertakers, and the funeral took place a few days later.

It was a miserable morning in late November; the last leaves had been whipped from the trees by the autumn gales, and the churchyard was exposed to the raw, bleak weather.

A north-easter brought fitful bursts of rain, and at the graveside, the mourners wrestled with their umbrellas. As soon as the ceremony was over, they retreated to take shelter under the lych-gate; Harry Glynn met Daphne and Ted and mumbled a few conventional words of regret. Then he turned to Babs, saying, 'Sorry not to have seen more of you over these last few years, Babs, but let's hope we meet more often in future, eh?'

'I shouldn't think so,' she said coldly, ignoring his outstretched hand, and went off to talk to Val and Mrs Watkins.

Daphne kissed her father. 'Never mind, Dad. She'll come round, don't you worry. Give her time.'

Ted put a hand on the old man's shoulder and said, 'That's right – things'll be better from now on. Look here, why don't you come round to Sackville Road with us? Babs decided not to ask people back to the house – well, it doesn't seem right, does it – but you'll be very welcome to have a cup of tea and a sausage-roll – or perhaps a glass of something stronger, to keep the cold out. How about that?'

Daphne added, 'Yes, do – then you can see Annie as well. She was only saying just now, she hasn't seen you for ages.'

'Oh, is Annie here?' Harry looked disapproving. 'I can't say I agree with youngsters attending funerals—'

'She's hardly a youngster now, Dad. In fact, she's here with her young man – didn't you see her in church?'

'Good Gad – that tall, pretty girl? I didn't recognise her. She must come round to my studio one of these days – I'd like to do some sketches of her.'

'Come back home with us and tell her so,' grinned Ted. 'I know my Mum will be glad to see you.'

'Thanks, lad – some other time, perhaps.' Harry shook his son-in-law's hand in a firm grip. 'Good of you to ask, but I've got to be on my way. Miss Preece will be getting dinner ready, and she doesn't like to be kept waiting.'

As he hobbled away, he almost collided with Mr Colpoys, who raised his hat stiffly to the old rogue as they passed. He stopped and spoke to Daphne and Ted for a few minutes, then moved on to Aggie and Ethel, who were sheltering from the rain under the yew trees.

Both ladies were in deep mourning, but they had begun to recover from the first shock of Muriel's death, and when Mr Colpoys expressed his sympathy for their sad loss, Aggie said brightly, 'We try not to think about it now, do we, Ethel?'

Ethel agreed. 'You see, she'd been an invalid for such a long time – and we know that she's gone to a better place.'

Aggie nodded eagerly. 'And we're going to a better place as well, aren't we? Next week!'

Seeing Mr Colpoys was looking rather taken aback, Ethel explained: 'Babs has decided to sell the house – well, it's much too big for us, and now Muriel's gone there's nothing to keep us here. We've been invited to go and live with some cousins of ours – so kind of them to offer us a home – the Wittekinds. They have a farm in Dorset.'

Puzzled, Mr Colpoys repeated the name. 'Wittekind? I don't seem to recollect—'

'They're on Papa's side of the family. Grandpapa was a Wittekind originally, from Hamburg. He changed his name to DeWitt for business reasons, you know.'

'No, I didn't know.' Mr Colpoys was quite stunned. 'I had no idea . . .'

'No, well, we never talked about it very much – especially during the war when feelings were running so high.'

'But the Wittekinds are so kind – and it will be lovely to live in the country, on a farm,' said Aggie cheerfully. 'We're really looking forward to it, aren't we, dear?'

Under the church porch, Mrs Watkins was asking Babs, 'So when are you going to move out of Belmont?'

'Oh, goodness knows. I've got to find a buyer for it first. And it's going to take ages to get the furniture packed up and put into store – and of course I've still got to find myself somewhere else to live.'

Val began to say, 'That shouldn't be too difficult for you, working in an estate agent's—' Then she broke off and caught her breath, looking over Babs' shoulder at someone coming up the path towards them. Babs saw the look in her eyes, and swung round at once, then hurried to meet her brother.

'*Gerry!* You did come, after all.'

'Sorry I'm so late, old girl. The damn ferry was delayed – gale-force winds in the Channel. We were kept hanging around outside Dover for a couple of hours, waiting to get into harbour,' said Gerald. 'I suppose it's all over, by now?'

'I'm afraid it is. Still, you're here – that's what matters.' Then Babs remembered Val and said awkwardly, 'By the way, Daphne asked Valerie and Mrs Watkins.'

Politely, he shook hands with Kate, then turned to face Valerie. 'Hello, old dear. It's good to see you.'

'You too,' she said, with an effort. 'I hope you're keeping well?'

'Yes – nothing to complain of. Living abroad seems to suit me. How's the world treating you?'

Mrs Watkins put a hand on Babs' arm and murmured, 'Do you think we could go and look at the wreaths for a minute or two?'

'Oh yes, all right.'

They walked away, leaving Gerry and Val alone together. She took a deep breath and nerved herself to ask, 'Did you get my letter?'

'Yes.' He stroked his moustache. 'Yes, I did, actually.'

'You never answered it. I suppose you're still very angry.'

'No – it wasn't that. Fact is, I wasn't too sure what to write. I didn't know whether congratulations were in order? You're looking damn good, I must say.'

'Thanks. But you – you won't change your mind – about a divorce?'

'I was just coming to that. Matter of fact, I've been meaning to get my lawyer chappie to drop you a line, and let you know it's all going ahead.'

'What? You really mean it?'

'Of course. There shouldn't be too much difficulty, seeing I've left the country. You could probably sue me for desertion! – with adultery thrown in, if you like – I don't give a damn. Between you and me and the gatepost, I've decided to take the plunge again myself, as soon as I'm a free man.'

'You're going to get married?'

'Yes, I've fallen on my feet, really. When I first moved to Luxembourg, I rented a room in a very decent house – and the lady of the house turned out to be a widow . . . A real charmer. We seemed to hit it off straight away. I think we'll make a go of it . . . So – do we wish each other better luck next time, and shake hands – or what?'

'Of course we don't shake hands!' Val threw her arms round him and hugged him. 'Oh Gerry, I'm really glad. And I wish you all the luck in the world.'

Some time later, when the last mourners were about to leave, Babs asked Daphne and Ted if they wanted a lift in the hired car, with Gerry and the aunts, but Daphne said, 'No thanks, it'll be rather a squash. Besides, the rain seems to have let up at last. We don't mind walking, do we, Ted?'

As they left the churchyard, she looked round for Annie, but there was no sign of her, and Ted said, 'I think I saw her go off with young Tony. She'll turn up presently.'

'I expect so.' Daphne breathed a long sigh of relief. 'Well – thank goodness it's all over.'

He glanced at her sympathetically. 'Poor old Daff. It must have been a bit of an ordeal.'

'Not really – not as bad as I expected. In fact—' She paused for a moment, then the words came tumbling out in a rush. 'To be honest, I'm beginning to get used to the idea that Mother's gone. Oh, the first few days were terrible – but that was mostly the shock, the way it happened. But now I can't really say I'm grieving any more. Isn't that dreadful?'

'Well, let's face it – you and your mother never really got along that well, did you?'

'No, we didn't. I loved her, and I often felt sorry for her, but – I never really liked her much. I suppose I've had more arguments with her than anyone, including you! The sad part is, I don't think she was ever a happy woman. She always wanted things she didn't have, and she never enjoyed the things she'd got. Most of the time she lived in a kind of dream world, because real life never came up to her expectations.'

Ted smiled. 'She's probably giving St Peter a proper earful right now, telling him it's high time he polished those pearly gates.'

'More than likely . . . Anyway, I shall try not to make the same mistake she did. It's no good crying for the moon.' Remembering Crabbe & Carter's slogan, she added ruefully: 'Better live halfway to heaven than have no heaven at all.'

Ted considered this for a moment, then asked: 'Is that meant to be a dig at me, by any chance?'

'No, of course not. Why?'

'I wondered if you thought – me, wanting to be a West End star – is that crying for the moon?'

'Certainly not! That's ambition – it's a different thing altogether.' Then she continued, as an afterthought, 'You haven't said how that's been going. I know you signed the new contract – did they let you off rehearsal today, to come to the funeral?'

'No. I haven't been called to rehearsal yet. They've started working on the principals, and the chorus numbers – I'm not needed till Monday.'

'But didn't you say the show's opening in Manchester very soon?'

'Manchester's been cancelled, because of all the changes. They've postponed the opening till the week before Christmas.'

'So you're just sitting around, kicking your heels? Why didn't you come home, if you're not working?'

'Oh . . .' He wouldn't meet her eye, but gazed straight ahead as they walked towards Sackville Road. 'I've been making contacts – seeing people, that sort of thing. Percy's hoping to get me a couple of BBC dates – you know they've just started these new television broadcasts? Well, they do the odd variety show now and then, and he seems to think I stand a good chance. And there's a possibility of a film, as well. Marta's going to introduce me to some American director she knows – he's got this idea for a musical comedy movie for the two of us . . . That's why I have to stay up in town. You've got to keep in touch with what's going on.'

Daphne said, 'Yes – I suppose you have.'

Suddenly she felt very tired. Nothing had changed, after all. It seemed that Ted would never change – she would just have to remember her mother and try to be content with life the way it was, instead of the way she would like it to be.

They walked the rest of the way home in silence.

Ray had asked the Head Clerk at Colpoys & Son if he could take the afternoon off to attend the funeral of his ex-landlady. Muriel Glynn's mysterious death had been widely reported, not only in the local papers, but as a column-filler in some of the nationals, and the story had become a nine days' wonder.

'Of course, you knew Mrs Glynn, didn't you?' the Head Clerk had asked him, unable to conceal his fascination. 'What was she like? Have you got any idea why a total stranger should want to do her in like that?'

'I can't imagine,' said Ray truthfully. 'As far as I know, she hadn't got an enemy in the world. At least, she was always very good to me. That's why I feel I ought to go to the funeral . . . with your permission, sir, of course.'

Grudgingly, the Head Clerk gave his permission, and Ray left the office at lunchtime.

In actual fact, he never had any intention of going to the church. He felt reluctant to meet the family and exchange pointless platitudes – an inner voice warned him that for the time being, the less he saw of them, the better. But he certainly wasn't going to miss the chance of a half-day's holiday with pay.

For convention's sake, he had sent round a cheap bunch of chrysanthemums with a note attached – *In loving memory – Ray* – but after that he felt he had done his duty, and decided to while away a couple of hours at the Rialto instead.

He was halfway up Anerley Hill when he saw Mr Colpoys walking towards him, dressed in black from head to foot. Obviously he had been to the funeral . . . *shit*! Of all the rotten luck . . . The old man hadn't been near the office for weeks; since the day of Muriel's death, he had stayed at home, and it was understood that he had been unwell. And here he was now. If he'd just left the church, he'd realise Ray couldn't have been among the congregation.

Averting his face, Ray changed course and turned sharp right, through the gates into the Crystal Palace grounds, hoping that the old man hadn't spotted him.

As it happened, William Colpoys had seen him. He had noticed the sudden start, and the change of direction – he knew that Ray Duke was avoiding him, and he wondered about that.

He had not set eyes on the young man since their last meeting in the office – that disastrous meeting, when Ray had appeared to read his thoughts, and uncover his secret – the day that ended more disastrously still, with the death of Muriel Glynn . . . A moment ago, he had seen the lightning-flash of fear and guilt in Ray's eyes, before he turned and fled – and now he began to ask himself: what was Ray Duke afraid of?

A hundred yards away, safely through the gates and out of sight among the trees, Ray was still walking very fast – as fast as he could, without breaking into a run and drawing attention to himself.

He was almost certain Colpoys had recognised him, and he cursed himself for his moment of stupid panic.

'If he did see me,' he thought, 'he'll wonder why I'm running away. I was a bloody fool to sheer off like that. I should have brazened it out and said hello, instead of letting him see I was rattled . . . Well, I won't make that mistake again. Next time I see him, I'll go straight up and have a chat with the old sod, cool as a cucumber. Show him I've got nothing to hide.'

Relaxing a little, he began to breathe deeply, slowing down to his normal pace. He could always go to the pictures later on. For the time being, it might be a good idea to lie low and keep out of sight. With this in mind, he stepped off the path, threading his way through the shrubbery, going towards the lake.

The daylight was fading fast, and shadows closed in upon the young couple who were walking through the park.

'It gets dark early now, doesn't it?' said Tony Gunn. 'Soon be the shortest day.'

'And then it'll be Christmas,' said Annie. 'It won't seem the same, this year.'

'You mean – because of your Grandma?' asked Tony cautiously.

'That, too – and my Dad being away so much. Everything's different, somehow.'

547

They were walking along the winding path that led through the oak-tree plantation. When the funeral was over, Tony had offered to take Annie home, but she said she'd rather go for a walk, so they had made a detour through the grounds.

Ahead of them, Annie noticed one or two other couples strolling in the dusk, with their arms entwined; she and Tony walked side by side and hand in hand, as they had always done.

'It's going to be a problem,' he said suddenly.

'What is?'

'Christmas – buying you the right present.' With a chuckle, he reminded her: 'I haven't forgotten last year! I thought for a minute you were going to throw it at me.'

'I nearly did! Honestly, fancy buying me a teddy-bear,' she said indignantly. 'As if I was a little kid!'

'I didn't mean it like that. The woman in the toyshop said lots of grown-ups bought them. I thought it would make you laugh.'

'Well, it didn't. Whatever made you go to a toyshop in the first place? It just shows how you think of me – as if I was about ten years old!'

'All right – I promise. No more teddy-bears.' He squeezed her hand. 'After all, I did take it back, didn't I? I got you that jumper instead.'

'Only because I went with you and told you which one. This time, why not try choosing something yourself?'

'Oh blimey, I couldn't do that! I wouldn't know what to get.'

'Something you'd like to see me wearing – something that suits me.'

He thought hard for a moment. 'How about another jumper?'

'I don't *need* another jumper. I tell you what I would like—' She plunged in. 'How about a nightie – a really pretty one?'

He laughed. 'Catch me going in and asking for a lady's nightie!'

'Why not? Men do buy them, you know – for their girlfriends.' Then, as he was still laughing, she stopped walking and tugged at his arm, pulling him round to face her. 'Why won't you ever take me seriously? You never even look at me properly!'

He saw that she was angry, and stopped laughing. 'What's the matter?'

'Look at me now! How old do you think I am? Twelve? Fourteen? Aren't you interested in me at all?'

He was completely lost. 'I don't know what you're on about. I thought we were talking about what you want for Christmas.'

'All right, I'll tell you what I want for Christmas! If you really want to know, I'd like you to buy me a ring – or is that too much to ask?'

'A ring?'

Her eyes were blazing. 'Do you have to be told everything? An engagement ring! And it's not very nice of you to leave me to do the asking!'

He stared at her – and for one terrible moment he nearly laughed again, but he managed to choke it back, and said, 'Annie, listen. That's very flattering – I really appreciate it – but don't you think you're a bit young to start talking about engagement rings?'

'Don't talk such rubbish!' she said furiously. 'I love you – I thought you loved me!'

'Oh, for goodness sake!' Now he was beginning to get angry too. 'Of course I love you – you know I'm very fond of you – but you're practically a schoolgirl! I'm years older than you are.'

'There's only about four years' difference. What does that make you – Methuselah? Don't you understand? I love you, you idiot, and I want to marry you – but it seems as if I might as well talk to a brick wall. You don't really give a tuppenny damn about me, do you?' She pulled away from him and began to walk off, with her head held high.

'Don't go! Annie, don't be silly. Come back here!'

He started to follow, and she quickened her steps, calling back over her shoulder, 'Leave me alone, can't you? I've finished with you, Tony Gunn!'

He began to walk a little faster, but his lameness was a handicap; she broke into a run, and he had to let her go.

As soon as she turned the corner of the path, Annie slowed down, then carried on walking under the trees until she saw the gleaming surface of the lake, reflecting the last glimmer of daylight. Suddenly, out of the undergrowth, a hideous face loomed up, and she stifled a scream, then she recognised the glaring eyes of a gigantic iguanodon – one of the huge prehistoric monsters guarding the lake.

Ever since she was a child, she had always been scared of the monsters; when she was little, the labyrinthodont's toothy grin and the cruel mask of the megalosaurus used to haunt her dreams. At this time of the evening, they took on still more menacing proportions, seeming to tower above her, out of the darkness.

With a shiver of fear, she was about to move on when, just behind her, a voice said: 'Hello, stranger. What are you doing here, this time of night?'

It was Ray Duke.

Annie had never liked him much, but after her encounter with the lakeside monsters she was relieved to see somebody she knew, and greeted him with relief.

'Oh, hello. I was just – I've been for a walk.'

'All on your own?' he asked.

'Yes. Well, not exactly, but—' Having no wish to explain, she concluded: 'I was with a friend, but I'm just going home now.'

'I'm going that way myself. Why don't I keep you company?' Ray suggested, falling into step beside her, and offering his arm.

'All right – thank you.' Shyly, she took his arm.

As they walked on, he remarked: 'Turning quite chilly, isn't it? "Winter drawers on", as the saying goes.' He broke into a loud laugh, and she joined in politely, though it was a very old joke. Then he said, 'Matter of fact, it's a bit too parky for comfort. I'd been thinking I might pay a visit to the pictures – how about coming with me? It's nice and warm in the Rialto.'

'Oh no, thanks all the same. I'd better go home – Mum will be expecting me back for supper.'

'Get away! They think you're out with your boyfriend!' He sniggered a little, pulling her closer. 'You've been having a bit of a barney with him, haven't you?'

'How did you know?' She was horrified. 'Did you hear me?'

'I should think they heard you all the way to Peckham Rye,' he said cheerfully. 'Mind you, I was on your side. He shouldn't go treating you like a kid at your age. I don't think of you like that, even though I've known you since you were so high. You used to sit on my lap sometimes, when you were a little nipper – but you're a grown woman now, and no mistake. I wouldn't mind having you on my lap again.' Still holding her, he began to steer her purposefully away from the path, into the bushes.

'What are you doing? I've got to go home—'

'You don't want to do that. We're going to have some fun, you and me,' he said. There was just enough light for her to see the expression on his face: his eyes and teeth were gleaming – cold and cruel as the face of the iguanodon.

She began to struggle. 'Please, let go!'

'Don't be silly,' he whispered, and his hands began to roam over her body, pulling open her coat, fumbling with the buttons of her blouse. 'That stupid berk doesn't know what he's missing. He doesn't appreciate you the way I do . . .'

Then he tried to kiss her, and his breath was hot and sour and so disgusting, she lashed out instinctively. Her right hand caught him squarely across the jaw and she heard his teeth click as his head jerked up.

'You bloody little bitch!' He staggered back, then made a grab for her throat. 'Two can play that game!'

But she was already running – running for dear life – away from the bushes, along the side of the lake, the way she had come, imagining she could hear him pounding after her. Turning a bend in the path, she ran headlong into Tony's arms.

'Hold me!' she gasped. 'Hold me tight!'

'What's the matter?' he began, and she blurted out: 'He grabbed me! He tried to – he wanted to—'

'Who did?' Tony's voice hardened. 'Who was it? Where did he go?'

'I – I don't know.' She pulled herself together. If she told him it was Ray Duke, it would mean endless trouble, and she didn't want that. 'I don't know who it was,' she lied. 'I've never seen him before . . . but he's gone now. He ran off the other way. I'm all right.'

'Yes – you're all right now. Come on, I'll take you home.'

'No, not yet. I want to stay here for a while – and talk.' Annie struggled to get her breath back: 'I'm sorry for what I said, but I do love you, Tony. I can't help it.'

Holding her in his arms, he kissed her gently. It was a long time before they spoke again, and then it was Tony who broke the silence.

'I love you too,' he said. 'And tomorrow morning, you and me are going out to buy that engagement ring.'

'Come on, Roger. I'm sure you can manage to finish up the last of the trifle,' said Valerie. 'It won't keep – it'll only get thrown away otherwise.'

'Well, if you put it like that—' Roger Kirkwood handed over his plate. 'It does seem a pity to waste it.'

'You want to watch out, mate,' Steve teased him. 'If you're not careful, you'll be too heavy to get on the bike!'

Since the old days at the speedway track, Roger and Steve had always kept in touch, thanks to their shared enthusiasm for motor-cycles; from time to time he would come round for a bite of supper and a game of cards.

'You cheeky devil,' retorted Roger, with his mouth full. 'Can I help it if Val's such a good cook?'

'Doesn't your wife like cooking?' asked Val, without thinking.

'No,' he said shortly.

She bit her tongue. Roger never talked about his wife. Privately, she suspected that his marriage might have broken up – he seemed to be something of a lone wolf. She couldn't help feeling sorry for him, especially this evening, when she and Steve were so happy.

Firmly, Roger changed the subject, asking Val how things were going at the Crystal Palace.

'I haven't been near the place since the speedway moved to New Cross,' he said. 'I had the feeling Sir Henry wouldn't exactly put out any red carpet for me.'

'Don't be silly, you know you're always very welcome,' Val told him. 'You ought to drop in and see us one of these days. We've got a very good exhibition of photographs at the moment.'

'Sunset across the duckpond?' He shook his head. 'I'm not much of a one for pretty pictures.'

'You'd like these. They were sent over from Germany – photos of this year's Olympics in Berlin. All the athletics, and the races—'

He raised an eyebrow. 'But no speedway, of course?'

'Well, no – but there are some wonderful pictures of the runners – that American, Jesse Owens, winning the hundred metres *and* the two hundred metres. And do you know, when he went up to get his gold medal, Herr Hitler wouldn't shake hands with him, because he's a black man?'

At the end of the meal, Steve opened a bottle of sparkling white wine, explaining to Roger that they had something to celebrate. As soon as Val was a free woman again, they would be married.

Roger raised his glass. 'Here's to a happy divorce, and many of 'em,' he said, adding ironically: 'Some people have all the luck. When did you get the good news?'

'Today,' said Valerie. 'I saw my husband for the first time since he went abroad. He came back for his mother's funeral . . . you know – Mrs Glynn.'

'Muriel Glynn? Of course . . . I'd forgotten that.' Like everyone else, Roger had read the story in the papers.

They went on talking about the Glynn family for some time. Roger had never met Daphne, but when Valerie mentioned Babs, he exclaimed: 'I know her! She's a real beauty. Any rate, I've met her once or twice. Remember when you and me were having a drink together at the Palace, just after I had my dust-up with Sir Henry? She slapped my face.'

Valerie laughed. 'I don't remember that!'

'It happened after you left. I must have said something to upset her, and suddenly – wham! I got a real fourpenny one.'

'I'm sorry. Babs can be a bit difficult sometimes.'

'I tried not to take it to heart,' Roger grinned. 'I think she was probably going through a bad patch at the time.'

'She's going through a worse one now,' said Steve.

'You mean because of her mother? Yes, I suppose so – poor kid.'

'It's not only that,' added Valerie. 'Her aunts have left London and gone to live in the country.'

Roger looked thoughtful. 'So she's all alone in that big house?'

'Val tried to persuade her to move out, but she won't hear of it,' Steve told him. 'She says there's too much to do, packing the furniture and shutting the place up.'

'I offered to stay with her for a while, to keep her company,' said Val, 'but she says she's perfectly all right. All the same, I don't like to think of her at Belmont, on her own – not after what happened.'

On the last Saturday in November, Ray Duke went to Gipsy Hill.

It was not an area he often visited. Since the night he'd met Steve and Valerie in the Railway Bell at Cawnpore Street, he had given the district a wide berth – but today he had no choice.

Coming from Westow Hill, at the highest point in Upper Norwood, he turned northward, and began to walk down the steep descent of Gipsy Hill, looking for the address he had been given. Before him, the whole of central London lay at his feet – St Paul's to his right, Westminster away on the left, and in the far distance, the misty heights of Hampstead – but Ray did not give the great panorama a single glance. He had more important things on his mind.

Why had Colpoys sent for him? What was it about?

He found the house without any difficulty – a trim, four-square Victorian villa with a neat little garden. A gravel path led straight from the front gate to the door, between two narrow beds of rosebushes. Although it was nearly December, one or two late roses were still trying to bloom.

William Colpoys opened the front door, wearing a large apron. 'Come in,' he said. 'You are very prompt.'

'Well, I got your note. I thought I'd better come as soon as I could.'

'I'm much obliged to you. Follow me, please.' He led the way along the hall, through a second door and into the kitchen. 'You find me still clearing away after my lunch,' he said. 'I hope you don't mind if I carry on while we talk?'

'No – you go ahead.' Ray looked round the spotless kitchen, with its quarry-tiled floor and white-tiled walls. Everything was bright and shining, with no trace of dust – not a crumb anywhere. 'Nice place you've got here. I must say you keep it spick and span.'

'Thank you.' William continued to wash up the plates and utensils, putting each item carefully on the draining-board to dry. 'I do my best.'

'And your front garden looks really good. I didn't see any weeds,' smiled Ray. 'Keen on gardening, are you?'

'A single man has to have a hobby,' said William. 'Perhaps you would care to see the back garden later? That keeps me pretty busy. I've been mowing the lawn this morning – the last time before winter sets in.'

'Very nice too.' Ray was getting a little restless. 'What was it you wanted to see me about?'

'Oh, I think it's time we had a talk, don't you?' said William vaguely. Then, indicating the joint of cold ham on the table, he broke off to ask: 'By the way, have you had lunch? Can I give you something?'

'Not for me, ta. I had my sandwiches, same as usual.'

'Well, if you're quite sure . . . Yes, I think we should talk. I know you were eager to ask me some questions – perhaps this is a suitable occasion?'

'I don't think there's anything I need to know, really. In the end I worked it out for myself, didn't I? And when I talked to my mother, she had to admit I'd come up with the right answers.'

'Ah, so you did speak to her again. I'd been wondering about that,' said William.

'Yeah – so now we can put our cards on the table, can't we?' asked Ray. 'You and me – father and son . . .'

A kind of shudder passed over William's face. 'I think I would prefer you not to use those particular words, if you don't mind,' he said. 'I don't think of you as a son . . . I had a son once; he died on the battlefield, and no one will ever take his place.'

'Well, I'm very sorry about that, but it doesn't alter the facts, does it? A long time ago, you managed to pull Muriel Glynn into bed with you – and here I am. And whether you like it or not, that makes you my Dad.'

William frowned slightly. 'She told you that, did she?'

'Yes, she did. So I reckon you owe me something for the way you treated me – sending me away like you did, without even giving me a name. I've got your blood in my veins, haven't I?'

William turned to look at him. His expression was so odd and enigmatic, Ray felt a touch of unease.

'You have tainted blood in your veins,' said William. 'Bad blood – enemy blood . . . I only discovered that the other day.'

'What are you talking about?' Ray shifted uncomfortably. 'I don't understand.'

'Never mind.' William took a teacloth and began to dry the cutlery. 'So that's what your mother told you – but *when* did she tell you?'

'After I left your office, I went to Belmont and—' Ray broke off, realising what he had said.

'Yes, I'd guessed that much. The other day, I asked my Head Clerk where you were that afternoon—'

'No, that was a different day. I was in the office!' Ray began to talk a little too quickly. 'I was at my desk that afternoon – working hard.'

'Oh, no. He told me you went out to run an errand; he said that I had sent you – and we both know that I did not. But now I know where you went . . . straight to Belmont.'

'Well, I had to see her, didn't I?'

'Of course you did. You had to see her that day – just as I had to see you this afternoon.'

William's voice was still quiet and slow, his sentences measured, as he continued to move around the room, putting the cutlery away in a drawer, picking up the carving-knife from the table, moving behind Ray's chair.

'As you say, there are certain things we have to do. Things that have to be done—'

The blade caught the light as it flashed down upon Ray's throat. William Colpoys stood and watched the young man as he pitched sideways – watching with faint disgust, but no regret whatever. He was only surprised by the amount of blood – he had not expected it to spurt so violently from the severed artery – but afterwards it would be quite simple to wash his apron and the tiled floor and the tiled walls, and then everything would be spotless once again.

Chapter Twenty-eight

ON MONDAY, BABS did not go in to work at Hawkins & Co.

Since her mother's death, she had spent a lot of time at home; her employers were very considerate, and agreed to manage without her until she felt able to resume her normal duties. Babs explained to them that there was so much to be done at Belmont, closing up the house and putting it on the market. As soon as that was disposed of she would return to the office.

She tried to deal with each room methodically, going through every cupboard, turning out the drawers, clearing the shelves. She sorted the jumble into three different piles: things of value, which would have to go into store for the time being – personal possessions which she would take with her when she moved out – and the third and largest pile, which was simply rubbish, put on one side to join the growing heaps of junk that would be taken away by the dustmen.

The job seemed never-ending, and she found it a terrible strain; it was harder to bear because of the absolute stilless and silence within the house. Every sound she made echoed and re-echoed along the passages, where doors opened on to lifeless, empty rooms.

And all the time, she had a strange feeling that her mother was still there – listening to her, watching her.

Late on Monday afternoon, when the light was beginning to go, Babs went round the whole house, switching on every lamp. At all costs, she felt she had to keep the darkness at bay. When the doorbell pealed suddenly, it sounded so loud that she flinched, digging her nails into the palms of her hands to prevent herself from trembling.

She had no idea who it could be – she wasn't expecting anyone; she held her breath, hoping whoever it was would go away.

After a few moments, the bell rang again. Afraid to answer the door, and afraid not to, she went slowly downstairs.

At first she did not recognise the broad-shouldered man under the porch, but when he smiled she knew him at once.

'Hello,' he said, in a friendly way. 'Remember me?'

'No,' she said – but it wasn't true, and he knew it.

'My name's Kirkwood – Roger Kirkwood. We have met.'

'Oh yes? What do you want?'

'I'm a friend of Valerie and Steve. I was round at their place for supper the other night, and they were talking about you. I just wanted you to know – I'm very sorry.'

'Sorry? What for?'

'Sorry for you. You've been having a rough time, haven't you?'

'I'm quite all right. It's a pity Valerie hasn't anything better to do than gossip about me to strangers,' she began, trying to close the door.

He did not seem at all disconcerted, but leaned against the doorpost, still smiling. 'I'm not a stranger,' he said. 'I told you, I'm a friend of theirs. And I'd like to be a friend of yours as well. Seems to me you could do with a friend, right now.'

'You . . .' She was at a loss for words: 'You came here – just to say that?'

'Not exactly. I happened to be going past, and I saw all the lights were on. Is it all right if I come in?'

She was about to say no, but something stopped her. Speechlessly, she stood back, letting him into the house.

'They told me you were busy packing things up. Do you want me to give you a hand?'

'No! How could you? You wouldn't know where anything goes. You don't know anything about – anything . . .'

'I'm a quick learner. Between the two of us, we'll get the job done in half the time. Just tell me what needs doing.'

She wanted to tell him to go away and leave her alone, but she didn't seem to have any will of her own. And perhaps she didn't really want him to go.

'Very well,' she said. 'This way.'

She took him upstairs. Her mother's sitting room was the first room she had tackled; she had moved all the furniture into one corner and rolled up the carpet, and when the doorbell rang she had been filling an empty tea-chest with ornaments and bric-à-brac, every single item carefully wrapped in old newspaper.

Propped against the wall was an assortment of looking-glasses of all shapes and sizes, from heavy overmantel pieces to small mirrors in silver frames, and the tiny vanity-mirror from her mother's dressing table.

'You've got a lot of looking glasses in here,' remarked Roger.

'I collected them from all over the house; it was the first thing I did.'

'Why was that?'

She turned away. 'I didn't want to look at myself.'

He glanced at her, but made no comment except to say: 'When was the last time you had anything to eat?'

'Oh – this morning, I think, some time. Why?'

'Got any bread and cheese in the house? Right – point me in the direction of the kitchen. I'm going to make us both some Welsh rabbit. Can't expect to get much work done on an empty stomach, can you?'

When William Colpoys arrived at Sackville Road, about an hour later, it was already dark.

Kate had not long said goodbye to Annie – her music-case in one hand and her oboe in the other, she was off to a rehearsal with the Crystal Palace Orchestral Society – and she was just settling down to a cup of tea in the kitchen when the front-door knocker banged.

'There now!' Kate clucked to herself as she went up to answer the door. 'What's she forgotten this time?'

By the light of the hall lamp, Mr Colpoys looked rather pale, and when he walked in he seemed very agitated.

'Good evening!' exclaimed Kate. 'Well, this is a nice surprise. When you didn't turn up yesterday, I was afraid you might be ill.'

'No, I – I'm perfectly well.' He frowned. 'Did you say – yesterday?'

'That's right. I was expecting you round for tea, seeing it was Sunday afternoon.'

'Oh.' Taking his hat off, he ran his hand through his thinning hair. He was always so neat and tidy, she was startled to see that his hair needed combing – and it looked as if he hadn't shaved recently. 'What day is it today?' he asked.

'Monday,' she told him, more and more puzzled. 'Monday, November the thirtieth.'

'I'm so sorry. I do beg your pardon, how stupid of me. I felt sure it was Sunday today.' He tried to smile. 'The fact is, I haven't been out very much lately, and staying at home I seem to have lost all count of time. I hope I haven't called in at an inconvenient moment? Perhaps I'd better come back another day—'

'No, of course not. I'm very glad to see you. As a matter of fact, I'm all on my own. Annie's gone to a practice with the orchestra, and Daphne's stayed on at school, rehearsing for their end-of-term pantomime. Let me take your coat.'

'You're sure I'm not imposing on you?'

'Not a bit. I was having a cup of tea anyway; I'll make a fresh pot.'

From force of habit, he began to go towards the sitting room, and she said apologetically, 'Oh dear, I'm afraid I haven't lit the fire in there, 'cos I wasn't expecting company. Would you mind very much sitting in the kitchen, just this once?'

'Of course not. It will be a pleasure.'

Seeing him more clearly under the kitchen light, she was shocked by his appearance. As she made the tea, she asked, 'Are you sure you're not feeling poorly?'

'No – why do you ask?'

'I wondered if that's why you'd been staying at home, not going out.'

'No – I'm in very good health, I assure you. But I've decided I shan't be going to the office in future. I believe it's time I retired altogether. There are plenty of men there, ready to take my place – abler and better men, I've no doubt.'

'I expect you're a bit tired; it's probably the weather. You'll feel different when the spring comes round again, I dare say.'

All the same, she felt quite concerned about him. He didn't seem to be his usual self at all – there were dark circles under his eyes, and a nerve kept twitching at the corner of his jaw. He sipped his tea, but soon lost interest in it and put it aside, asking, 'Would you have any objection if I smoke a pipe? Perhaps you don't care for the smell of tobacco in your kitchen?'

'Oh, that won't bother me at all. Eddie used to smoke a pipe sometimes – Mr Watkins, I mean. I'm quite used to it.'

With trembling fingers, he managed to fill the bowl of his pipe, spilling some threads of tobacco on to the tablecloth, but when he tried to light it, although he kept flicking the little wheel of his lighter, he could not produce a flame.

'Dashed nuisance. The thing must have run out of juice,' he muttered.

'I've got a box of matches somewhere.'

'No, no. Don't bother. I never use matches – the smell of sulphur spoils a good smoke,' he told her. 'As it happens, I've got a bottle of fluid in my coat pocket, so with your permission—?'

'That's all right – you carry on.'

She watched him carefully; his hands were so shaky, she was afraid he would spill it over the table. However, he managed it at last, and when he began to puff away at his pipe, he seemed a little calmer.

'That's one of the old wartime lighters, isn't it?' she asked. 'I remember Eddie having one like that.'

'I'm sure he did.' William nodded. 'He would have done – they made them for the troops. This one belonged to my son; it was sent home to me with the rest of Jack's personal effects, after – well, you know about that . . . My son – your husband – both gone to glory.'

'You still miss him very much,' Kate said gently.

'Just as you miss your husband, I'm sure.'

'But it's been different for me, with the children growing up – and now little Annie as well. Of course I still think of her as a tiny mite, but would you believe it? She's talking about getting married! A nice young man too; his family have the greengrocery, up Church Road. Gunn – you probably know them.'

'Do I? Yes, perhaps I do . . .' Leaning back in his chair, William gazed at the little wreath of blue smoke floating above his head; his thoughts were far away. For some minutes there was silence in the kitchen. He seemed to be in a kind of reverie, and Kate did not like to disturb him.

At last he said, 'When Jack was taken from me, I had no one but myself to blame. It was a punishment, you see – a terrible punishment – and all the worse because I brought it down upon myself.'

'Oh, I'm sure that's not true—' Kate began.

He did not seem to hear her, but went on: 'I'm ashamed to say that I had committed a great sin. I was unfaithful to my dear wife – to her memory.'

Again, Kate tried to interrupt him. 'Please, you don't have to tell me anything. You mustn't upset yourself—'

'But I want to tell you. I loved her so much – she died when Jack was born, and I was left alone, with our baby son. He should have been a consolation, I know, but I missed her so much, I – I have to confess there were times when I almost hated him, because in a sense he had killed her. And I was so lonely – so very lonely . . . Can you understand that?'

'Yes, I understand.'

'A few years later I met a certain lady, in connection with my business. We became – very close. She was a married woman, but her husband neglected her; she was lonely too. By all the laws of professional etiquette, I should have stopped seeing her, but – she offered herself to me. She offered a sort of comfort . . . I was still a comparatively young man in those days – selfish and stupid – and I couldn't resist. We sinned – and now we have both been punished for our wickedness – the most horrible punishment. My son was taken from me in that hideous war and later – years later – one horror seemed to pile up on another, each one worse than the last, until I thought I should go mad . . .'

He turned to Kate, his face so harrowed with misery, her heart went out to him as he said, 'You're a God-fearing woman. Tell me truthfully, do you think He will ever forgive me?'

Kate went to him, taking his ice-cold hands in hers. 'Of course He will. God is merciful – God is love.'

'I don't know what love means any more,' he said, in a voice drained of everything but weariness. 'It was so long ago – I've forgotten.'

'You mustn't let yourself give way like that, my dear – it's not like you.' Kate tried to rally him. 'I think it's on account of you shutting yourself up in that house and not going out – not seeing anyone. You must make the effort to get out more, meet people—'

'Where would I go? Who would I see?'

'There's lots of places to go – you must try and cheer yourself up. You could go to the pictures, or how about a whist drive? It'll be Christmas soon; there's always plenty going on, this time of year.' Racking her brains, she thought back to the first time they had met, and suggested: 'Why don't you go to the Crystal Palace?'

He uttered an unhappy sound, something between a sob and a laugh. 'To the Circus, perhaps? To watch the performing elephants?'

'No! They have all sorts of interesting things there.' She remembered something Valerie had mentioned recently. 'There's ever such a good exhibition of photographs on at the moment – Val says it's really worth seeing. Perhaps we could both go? Pictures of this year's Olympic Games – they got them over specially from Berlin—' She broke off, as an extraordinary change came over him. His unhappiness seemed to vanish in a moment, like a blackboard wiped clean – but it was replaced by a kind of frenzy.

Scrambling to his feet, he began to cry out, shaking his head as if he were in physical pain. 'Germany – always Germany! When will it ever end? When will we learn our lesson? Didn't you see the papers, just a few months ago? The Germans have marched into the Rhine-land again, in spite of all the regulations. They've torn up the peace treaties – they're preparing for another war. More bombs, more deaths – more young men to the slaughter—'

She tried to stop him, but he brushed her aside, struggling into his overcoat and stumbling blindly for the door.

'They must be stopped! They must be removed, the murderers, the enemy . . . They come to this country – and we're such fools, we do nothing. We let them in, to cheat us all over again. That man at the furniture shop – the woman singing in the theatre – each and every one. We must put an end to them, before they destroy the whole world!'

He blundered up the staircase, out of the house and into the darkness. Helplessly, Kate heard him going away down the street, still calling out defiantly, '*Stop them . . . Remove them . . . Destroy . . .!*'

'Drink, *liebchen*?'

'Hey, steady on! I've already got enough there to float a battleship!'

Ted tried to put his hand over his scotch-and-soda, but Marta insisted on topping up his glass, saying, 'Such nonsense! This is a very special occasion – your first day at rehearsal. It's so wonderful to be working with you again, my darling.'

She smiled at him, and her smile was so intimate and full of meaning, he felt a thrill of desire stir within him; it was a long time since he and Marta had made love.

'But it's not like it used to be, is it?' he said, keeping his voice down so that no one else would hear him. 'In this show, we don't play any love-scenes.'

They were in the Neumanns' flat; at the far end of the living room, Franz was sitting at the piano, running through one of the new numbers with their American star, Chuck Vernon.

Marta laughed. 'Don't tell me you're jealous of Chuck?'

'Ssh – he'll hear you.'

'He's a very sweet man, and I enjoy working with him – but you will always be very special to me, my dearest . . .' Then she kissed him – lightly, teasingly – adding, 'And you will enjoy working with Chuck too, I promise, when you get to know him. That is why I wanted so much that you should both come to supper with us this evening – to break the ice.'

Ted had not found his first day of rehearsal for the new show very easy. They had been setting his scenes in Act One – early morning at Covent Garden, where he met Marta in the flower-market – another when he found her later, alone and unhappy in St James's Park, after a lovers' tiff with her American boyfriend – and then the scene where Chuck's racy little sports car, driving on the wrong side of the road, ran smack into Ted's costermonger barrow, and the two men were supposed to have a blazing row.

'We didn't exactly hit it off this morning, if that's what you mean,' Ted admitted.

'I know, darling, and that is why it was so difficult for you. When you and I had to rehearse a quarrel sometimes, it was always great fun, wasn't it? – because we were really fond of each other. But you and Chuck were so cold and polite with one another—'

'What's this? Talking about me behind my back, eh?'

Moving with a dancer's catlike grace, Chuck took them by surprise. Not in the least embarrassed, Marta smiled at him.

'Of course – I was just telling Ted how wonderful you are, my sweet. Oh, but your glass is half-empty – that will never do. Franz – give Chuck another drink at once!'

Chuck made an unconvincing protest. 'What are you trying to do to me? I'll finish up under the table at this rate. Oh hell, maybe my drink could do with freshening up a little, at that.'

As Franz led him away to the drinks cabinet, Marta whispered to Ted, 'Trust me . . . Once we all get to know each other, you won't have a thing to worry about.'

Ted pulled her a little closer, murmuring in her ear, 'Except he still gets to play the love-scenes – and I don't.'

'You think not?' She laughed softly, with a throaty catch in her laughter that excited him even more. 'Just you wait and see.'

Half an hour later, Kate had another unexpected visitor. When Steve turned up at Sackville Road, she was still very worried, but she made an effort to greet him cheerfully. 'Is Val with you, by any chance?' he asked her.

'No, I'm all on my own.' She explained that Annie and Daphne were both out, adding, 'But I haven't seen anything of Val. Why – were you expecting to find her here?'

'I wasn't sure. When I got home from work, she wasn't at the flat – and she hadn't left me a note or anything. I couldn't help worrying. I mean, in her condition, anything could have happened.'

'Perhaps she's gone round to Church Road, to your mother?'

'No, I don't think she'd do that. We – er – we haven't seen much of my family, lately.'

Kate looked at him shrewdly. 'You mean you still haven't told your mother about the baby?'

'Well, no. We're waiting till the divorce is all settled, then we can tell her we're going to get married as well. That'll make it easier for her.'

'But . . .' Kate frowned. 'You told me.'

'Val said we ought to. She said you'd understand.'

'I see.' Her expression softened. 'Anyway, I'm sure Val's all right – she'd have phoned. I expect she's probably working late.'

'I suppose so, though she usually tells me at breakfast if she's got to stay on and do some overtime.'

'Perhaps it was a last-minute thing – some sort of emergency.'

'Perhaps. Oh well, sorry to have bothered you. I think I'll just nip round to the Palace. I'll probably meet her coming down the hill.'

He was about to leave, but Kate put a hand on his arm. 'Steve, before you go – could I ask you a favour?'

'You know you can. What is it?'

'Well, I know this sounds daft, but I'm a bit concerned about my friend, Mr Colpoys.' She tried to explain what had happened, but Mr Colpoys had been so confused himself, she found it hard to remember exactly what he had said. 'Something about the Germans – the enemy, that's what he called them. Something about stopping them – destroying the world.'

Steve snorted with laughter, but then he saw she was really upset, and put his arm round her shoulder. 'I wouldn't take it too seriously, if I were you. Maybe the old boy dropped in at the pub on the corner, on his way, and had one too many before he arrived.'

'Oh no, he'd never do a thing like that! Besides, it wasn't even opening-time then. I know it seems silly, but I think he was having some sort of brainstorm. The way he sounded – the way he looked – I'm afraid he might do himself a mischief.'

'Yes, well, I'm very sorry, but I don't really see what I can do about it—' Steve began.

'He doesn't live very far away – somewhere in Gipsy Hill. You wouldn't be very kind and call in there, before you go and meet Val, would you? If you could just knock at his door and make sure he's all right, it'd put my mind at rest.'

Steve sighed; he'd only met Colpoys briefly once or twice, and he felt reluctant to go and confront the chap in his own house, but Kate was so obviously worried he hadn't the heart to refuse her.

'OK then, I'll see what I can do. Whereabouts does he live, exactly?'

'I've never been there myself, but I think it's fairly near the top of the hill. I've got the address written down somewhere – we always send each other cards at Christmas . . . Hang on a tick, while I find it.'

With a sigh of relief, Valerie put the cover on her typewriter and went to fetch her coat from the peg behind the door. Thank goodness, she had finished work at last – now she could go home.

Before she left the office, she took a last look round, calling out, 'Minnie? Where are you, Min?' There was no answering *miaow*, and she called again: 'Minnie! Stop playing hide-and-seek. I've put down a saucer of milk for you.'

Getting no response, she pulled on her beret and prepared to leave. She had been on the point of leaving some time ago; in fact she had actually been putting her coat on, when Sir Henry had called her into his office to explain that there were several changes which had to be made immediately in the calendar of next year's events.

'Oh, but I've posted the copy to the printers, sir. You initialled it yourself,' began Valerie.

'I know. Some of the participating groups have been extremely difficult, changing their dates at the last minute. I've jotted down a revised schedule; this will have to go round to the printers by hand, first thing tomorrow,' he told her. 'I'm very sorry to trouble you like this, but I shall be extremely grateful if you could re-type it this evening – then it will be ready to go in the morning.'

'The whole calendar for 1937?' Val's face fell.

'I do apologise – is it a great inconvenience? Had you made other plans for the evening?'

'Well, no, not really.' She accepted the inevitable. 'It's all right. It shouldn't take me very long.'

In the end, it had taken her more than an hour and a half – but at last the job was done.

As she left her office, she thought she heard a sort of rustling sound in the corridor, and glanced round hopefully – could it have been Minnie? She called the cat again, but the sound was not repeated. Valerie shrugged, and turned away.

Not far off, a door closed with a quiet click, and she stopped again. 'Hello?' she said. 'Who's that?'

Silence. She tried once more. 'Is there anybody there?'

Nobody answered; it sounded as if it came from the direction of the ladies' room, but Val knew that all the office staff had long since gone home. Oh well, it was probably a door blowing shut in a draught; anyway, she really couldn't hang about any longer. Making up her mind, she walked briskly out of the office section and into the Main Hall.

One or two lights had been left on, because the orchestra were still rehearsing in the Garden Room, but most of the Palace was in darkness. Behind closed doors, she could hear the distant strains of some eerie, oriental music, with lots of pizzicato strings and stabbing percussion.

As she made her way along the main aisle, among the palm trees and giant ferns, she was surprised to see Steve's brother sitting on one of the benches. 'Hello!' she exclaimed. 'What are you doing here?'

Tony stood up sheepishly. 'Hello, Val. I'm just waiting for Annie – do you mind? She said it would be all right.'

'Well, I don't mind – but they don't usually allow visitors after closing-time. How did you get in?'

'I told them I had to see somebody in the orchestra, and they let me through the staff entrance.'

'Oh, I see.' Val made a mental note to have a quiet word with the Chief Commissionaire tomorrow. Of course Tony wouldn't cause any trouble, but the men on the gate weren't to know that. 'Have you got any idea how much longer Annie's likely to be?'

'She said they generally finish about eight o'clock. It shouldn't be much longer now.'

'Well . . . the only thing is, if one of the night-staff comes along and find you, he might ask you to leave. I tell you what – why don't you come and sit in my office till the rehearsal's over? You'll be able to hear the orchestra from there; when it stops, you can slip out and find Annie.'

'OK – thanks.' As they strolled back towards the office, Tony added, 'I don't think much of their choice of music, do you? Annie said they were going to do a piece called *A Tale Of Old Japan* – all that plinking and plonking – it's about as tuneful as a bunch of cats out on the tiles!'

'There's no accounting for tastes,' laughed Val. 'And that reminds me, you haven't seen Minnie anywhere about, have you?'

'Minnie?'

'She's a big, beautiful tabby. She lives in the office and helps to keep the mice down, but she's been very jumpy all day today – wouldn't settle down for two minutes. Finally she disappeared altogether. You didn't happen to notice her when you came in?'

'No, sorry.'

'Oh, dear. She didn't come for her milk at tea-time either – I do hope she hasn't got shut in anywhere.' Switching on the office light, she told him: 'That's my desk, over there. Make yourself comfortable . . . I hope the rehearsal doesn't drag on too long. If you want something to read, I think there's a *Daily Sketch* lying about somewhere.'

'That's OK – I won't bother, thanks.' Tony seemed a little embarrassed as he went on: 'I wouldn't be here at all, in the usual way, only . . . well, Annie had a bit of a scare the other night. Some filthy beggar jumped out when she was walking through the park, and tried to grab her. That's why I don't like her being out on her own, after dark.'

'I'm not surprised! Did she report it?'

'No, she didn't – and she wouldn't let me say anything about it, either, so don't let on I told you, will you?'

'Well, if you think that's best. Anyhow, I mustn't stop. I should have been home hours ago – Steve will be wondering whatever's happened to me. You're sure you'll be OK here, all on your own?'

'Course I will. Besides, I'm not exactly on my own, am I?'

At the doorway, she turned, slightly puzzled. 'What do you mean?'

'Well, there's that other chap – the old feller your Mum knows. What's his name? Colpoys. He was here a little while ago – I saw him.'

'Mr Colpoys?' Valerie stared at him, then smiled. 'Whatever gave you that idea? He never comes to the Palace at all, and certainly not when we're closed! What would he be doing here at this time of night?'

'I don't know, but it was him all right; he came in just after me. I heard the chap on the gate stop him and ask where he was going. Old Colpoys muttered something – I couldn't catch what it was – and the doorman said: "Oh, you'll be one of the Orchestral Society, I expect?" – then he let him in.'

'But Mr Colpoys hasn't got anything to do with the orchestra. I can't imagine what he's doing here!'

'Then a bit later on, while I was sitting in the Hall waiting, he walked right past me. I thought he was talking to me at first, but when I said, "Beg your pardon?" he just went straight on like I wasn't there. I think he was talking to himself.'

'He must be ill . . . I'd better go and find him. I can see I'll never get home at all at this rate – Steve's going to kill me! Did you happen to notice which way he went?'

'Well, the last I saw of him, he seemed to be heading in this direction, towards the offices.'

They went out into the corridor – and Val suddenly remembered the rustling noise she had heard, and the door that had shut quietly, all by itself. She called out tentatively: 'Mr Colpoys? Are you there?'

There was no answer, but then she became aware of a faint but persistent crackling – and at the same moment, Tony sniffed and said, 'Can you smell burning?'

Less than a quarter of a mile away, in his study at Rockhills, Sir Henry Buckland had been writing a letter to an old family friend in Harrogate. While admitting that the Crystal Palace had been going through some difficult times since the slump, he said he had every confidence that they had turned the corner now; the coming year would be a new beginning, and he saw bright prospects ahead.

Satisfied, he slipped the letter into an envelope, addressed and sealed it, then went into the hall to put on his hat and coat.

His twenty-year-old daughter Chrystal was coming down the stairs. 'Hello. Are you going out?' she asked.

'Only as far as the pillar-box, my dear.' He pulled his gold watch from his waistcoat pocket. 'Twenty to eight – I should just catch the last collection.'

'Can I come with you? I've been indoors all day and I'd like a breath of air.'

So they set out together, turning left at the gate and walking along the Crystal Palace Parade. To one side of them, the huge building seemed to float in the night sky, as the street lamps were caught and reflected in countless glittering panes of glass. Suddenly Chrystal said: 'That's funny – what's going on inside?'

'There's nothing on tonight, except a rehearsal for the next orchestral concert. Why do you ask?'

'Well, there's a sort of glowing light. Look, through the ground-floor windows.' She pointed, and Sir Henry saw the red glow, which seemed to brighten and spread as he watched it – and he knew what it was.

'*Fire!*' he exclaimed. 'Fire in the offices . . . Dear God – Valerie Watkins was working late this evening. She could still be there!'

He broke into a run, and Chrystal followed him.

As soon as Valerie had opened the door leading to the ladies' room, she saw the whole place was ablaze; the draught from the doorway fanned the flames and tongues of fire licked greedily at the walls. Slamming the door shut, she clutched Tony's arm; she felt sick with fear – her private nightmare had become a reality – but she knew she mustn't let herself think about that.

'We must get help!' she gasped. 'There are always firemen on duty – they'll know what to do.'

She led the way. Following her through the Main Hall, Tony stumbled and nearly fell – his foot struck against a small object which clanked and rolled away into the darkness.

Remembering his game leg, Val said, 'What was that? Are you all right?'

'Yes. I nearly tripped over something – I'm OK.'

He had caught a brief glimpse of shining glass as it skidded aside, under the ferns. As a non-smoker, he did not recognise the coloured label; it was an empty bottle that had once contained lighter-fuel.

In the Garden Room, the members of the orchestra were wrestling with the oriental complexities of the score; the conductor tapped his baton crossly on his music-stand every time someone played a false note.

'Oboes! That's a B-flat, not an A. Please try to pay attention!'

'I'm sorry, that was my fault,' Annie confessed. 'Only it's not very easy to concentrate with all that noise going on.'

'Noise? What noise?'

They all stopped and listened. Somewhere outside the rehearsal-room, they could hear running feet, and people shouting, and in the distance, a strange, roaring sound.

'Oh really, this is too bad!' snapped the conductor. 'Will we never be allowed to work in peace?'

Then the door opened, and Annie saw Valerie standing in the doorway, white-faced. She was saying: 'I'm sorry to interrupt, but I thought you should know – a small fire has broken out at the other side of the building. There's nothing to worry about. The firemen are dealing with it now – it will soon be under control.'

She spotted Annie across the room, and tried to smile reassuringly. Annie waved back, and the conductor said coldly, 'Thank you, but since there is no danger, perhaps we may be allowed to continue with our rehearsal?'

Valerie apologised again and went away, as he tapped with his baton once more. 'We'll take it from the top of the page, if you please. The fourth bar after Letter G . . . One, two, three—'

As the Crystal Palace burned, the orchestra went on playing.

When Valerie returned to the scene of the fire, she found Sir Henry and his daughter talking to Tony, who had been trying to explain what he was doing there, and how they had discovered the fire. As Val approached, Sir Henry greeted her with relief.

'Thank heaven you're safe,' he said. 'They tell me that now the men have got the hose connected, they should be able to extinguish the blaze in next to no time.'

But as he was still speaking, one of the fire crew came running out of the offices, saying breathlessly, 'It's no good, sir! We've only got the one branch, y'see, and the blaze is getting out of hand now. We'll never keep it under on our own. We'll have to call in the Fire Brigade.'

'I'll go and ring them,' said Valerie, automatically moving towards the offices, but the man gripped her arm.

'Not that way, miss. All them wooden partitions could go up at any minute – it'd be a death trap.'

'Use the telephone at the refreshment-rooms.' Sir Henry took charge of the situation. 'Call the exchange and say this is an emergency . . . Hurry!'

Remembering the child within her, Valerie did not dare to run, but walked away as quckly as she could. Luckily, Sir Henry had already turned away, and was addressing the fireman. 'You and your colleagues must do the best you can. Keep playing water on to the flames – try to contain the fire as far as possible.'

Annie was still struggling to get through the score without making any more mistakes, when the door burst open again, and a young woman she did not recognise rushed into the room, saying: 'Stop! You must stop! My father says you've all got to get out of the building at once!'

Confused and uncertain, they stared at her, then at one another, and the conductor threw down his baton. 'This is beyond a joke,' he complained. 'I will not have these constant interruptions while I am trying to—'

'Oh please, do listen – it's terribly important!' exclaimed Chrystal, almost in tears. 'Don't you understand? The Palace is blazing! You must go at once. Run – run for your lives!'

Chapter Twenty-nine

WHEN STEVE ARRIVED at Gipsy Hill, he rang the doorbell, but nothing happened.

The house was in darkness. He rang again, without really expecting to find Mr Colpoys at home. After all, there was no reason to suppose he had returned there after he left Sackville Road – he could be anywhere by now.

Turning away, Steve was about to give it up as a bad joke, but then he paused. He could smell a familiar, homely smell – someone was cooking a meal. The aroma floated by him, wafting away on the westerly breeze; when the wind dropped for a few seconds, he caught it again. It was a smell he knew very well, because Freda Gunn had never been the best-organised of cooks, and would sometimes forget she had put a joint in the oven, leaving it there until it began to char at the edges. If Mr Colpoys had put his supper on before he went out, he had left it to burn.

It occurred to Steve that if Colpoys had gone wandering off in a distressed state, leaving the oven on, it might have serious consequences; burning fat could blaze up – the oven could catch fire – the whole house might go up in flames. He decided he'd better investigate a little further.

At the side of the house there was a narrow alley, which he presumed must lead to the back garden, so he walked slowly along it – cautiously, since he did not know the way, and he was moving through darkness.

As he turned the corner, the darkness lifted a little, and he saw that a light had been left on in one of the downstairs rooms at the back. The curtains were drawn, but there was a small chink between them, and Steve peered in, feeling very foolish, hoping he would not come face to face with a furious Mr Colpoys, accusing him of spying at his windows and trespassing on private property.

The kitchen was brightly lit, but there was nobody there – and no signs of any preparation for a meal. Everything had been left meticulously tidy and spotlessly clean; as far as he could tell, the stove was not lit.

Yet the smell of burning was much stronger now – and then, looking around him, Steve noticed a faint gleam of light at the end of the garden, and recognised the tang of woodsmoke. Of course! That was it – it wasn't a cooking smell at all, but the incense of an autumn bonfire.

Colpoys must have been doing some late gardening, collecting and burning the fallen leaves; a little smoke was drifting towards the house, and he realised that there was still some life in the bonfire – at the bottom of the dark heap, he could see a few red embers glowing.

That could be dangerous too; it might flare up and spread. For safety's sake, he decided he should try to put it out before he left.

Walking down the garden in the dark was like an obstacle-course; he trod on some flowerpots, breaking one underfoot, and he was slapped in the face by the overhanging branch of an unseen tree. Eventually he reached the bonfire. The smell was very strong here, and it was not a pleasant one, either; mingled with the woodsmoke, there was still that underlying stink of burning meat and bone, as if Colpoys had thrown the remains of his Sunday joint on to the fire as well.

Steve turned the ashes over with the toe of his boot, and some dead leaves caught fire. As they flared up for a moment, he saw the shape of the bonfire more clearly – a sprawling heap of leaves and twigs, nearly six feet long – but some of the leaves must have been too damp to burn, because the fire was hissing, on the point of going out.

Then another twig caught, and a bright flame blazed. He noticed that it was reflected in a circle of glass; the glass of a wristwatch. Then he saw a man's hand, sticking out of the funeral pyre – charred, but still quite recognisable.

The flame fizzled and went out, leaving Steve in darkness once more, as he realised at last what the stench was – the cremation of human flesh.

He dropped to his knees on the wet grass, and started to vomit . . . When he could move, he pulled himself up on to his feet and set off to find the nearest telephone-box, and to call the police.

*

Inside the Palace, the heat was almost overpowering, and the general office section was now one mass of flame. The staff firemen were forced to retreat, step by step, though they kept a steady jet of water directed on to the blaze.

At the other side of the building, Val and Tony were standing near an open doorway that led out on to the terrace; even at that distance, they could feel the scorching heat, and they had to put their hands up to shield their faces.

'Where's Annie?' Tony kept asking. 'What's happened to her?'

The members of the orchestra were running out of the Garden Room by now, in twos and threes, pausing for an instant to stare open-mouthed at the dazzling conflagration, then plunging on, out of the building – grateful for the night air – thankful to be alive.

Sir Henry, standing in the main transept by the ornamental fountain, ordered his daughter to go after the musicians and make her escape, telling her he would follow her directly. Seeng Val and Tony lingering in the open doorway, he gesticulated angrily, shouting at them above the roar of the flames, 'Get out at once! Get out while you can!'

As he spoke, the upper galleries on the west wall, unsupported, fell in upon the offices below – and at once a gigantic explosion of white-hot flame soared up to the roof.

Chrystal Buckland rushed past Val, gasping, 'You must do as he says – only keep away from the glass, whatever you do!'

Val looked up at the colossal wall behind her. Normally transparent, it was no longer clear, but seemed to be on the move, continually bubbling like simmering water – and then she realised that the panes had started to melt; molten glass was slipping and sliding down from the frames, like a waterfall in hell.

And all the time, the smoke was getting thicker, rolling towards them. Tony began to choke, wiping away the tears that streamed from his eyes, desperately trying to see through the murky orange clouds – and then—

'Annie!' he yelled. 'Over here! This way . . .!'

As the last refugees fled from the Rehearsal Room, stumbling towards him, he left Val's side and raced to meet Annie, catching her in his arms and dragging her to safety.

'It's all right,' he kept saying. 'I've got you. You'll be all right now . . .'

The firemen had to retreat still further from the inferno, and Sir Henry was forced to move back with them. Shepherding the last of the musicians out, he turned angrily to Val. 'What the devil are you waiting for? Do you want to be killed?'

'No. I'm coming, in a minute,' she said. But even when she was outside on the terrace, taking in gulps of blessedly cool air, she could not quite bring herself to leave the Palace.

'You go on,' she told Tony. 'I'll catch you up. I thought I saw someone, still inside . . .'

Roger looked at the Chinese vase with dragons chasing each other round it, and took it from Babs' hands.

'Leave that,' he said. 'You've done enough for one day; you must be dead on your feet.'

'No, really, I've only got to wrap it and—'

'Shut up,' he ordered, kindly but firmly. 'It can wait till tomorrow. I don't know why you want to keep it anyhow. It's a bloody monstrosity.' She smiled, despite herself, and he said, 'That's more like it. Do you know, that's the first time I've seen you looking halfway cheerful since I got here? Come and sit down; you need a rest.'

He steered her towards one of the few pieces of furniture that wasn't piled high with books and boxes and bundles, and sat her down beside him, on the sofa.

'Right – now you can tell me,' he said.

'Tell you what?'

'Why you don't like looking at yourself in the glass,' he said.

'I should have thought that was obvious. I don't like my face.'

'Well, I do,' he said. 'What's wrong with it?'

'Oh, for heaven's sake! I'm old and ugly and horrible – and getting worse every day.'

'Hello, what's all this? Fishing for compliments?'

'Don't be stupid. I'm too tired to argue – anyway, it's true, and you know it.' She tucked her feet under her and curled up at the end of the sofa, hugging her knees and gazing into space; she felt so exhausted, she didn't really care what she said. 'I'm thirty-five years old. After Mummy died, I looked at myself in a mirror for the last time, and I thought what a damn fool I'd been. Half my life gone by, and what have I got to show for it? Nothing at all. I used to be Mummy's darling – her little treasure – and now she's gone, and I'm nothing.'

'That's a daft thing to say. You're a lovely girl, you've got a nice home, a nice family – you've got friends—'

'No, I haven't. Nobody likes me – I'm always having rows with people. The last time you saw me, you said I was bloody rude.'

'So you did remember.' Roger threw back his head and laughed. 'Well, you were bloody rude, and that's a fact. And the first time I met you, you practically bit Steve's head off. I've never forgotten you, that day I took a spill on the bike. When I came round, I thought you were a blooming angel.'

'Some angel . . .' She ran a hand through her untidy blonde hair. 'I bet I look a real mess.'

'You look about sixteen years old, sitting all curled up like that. How about boyfriends? You must have plenty of blokes after you.'

'Only one – well, there was only one that really counted. I was in love with him for a while – but he turned out to be no good. I haven't seen him lately. There's never been anyone else.'

'There's me,' Roger said.

'You?' Dumbfounded, she turned and looked at him. 'But you—'

'Why else do you think I came round here this evening?' he asked, and then, with a complete change of tone, he said suddenly: 'My God – what the hell's that?' He was looking past her, staring out of the window; she followed his gaze, and caught her breath.

Behind the bare winter branches of the trees at the end of the garden, the entire sky was blood-red. Together, they jumped up and ran to the window, and saw the most extraordinary spectacle. On the brow of the hill, the whole of the Crystal Palace was outlined in fire.

'Blimey,' said Roger, under his breath. 'Talk about a Brock's Benefit . . .'

'You seem to be rather down in the dumps this evening,' said Daphne, from underneath a towel.

'Me? Oh no, not really.' Kate hesitated, then admitted; 'But I can't help feeling worried about Mr Colpoys – I told you.'

'Oh, I shouldn't worry about him.' Rubbing her hair briskly, Daphne dismissed Kate's anxiety. 'Lots of people get upset about Germany nowadays. You read such awful stories in the papers, about the way Hitler's treating the Jews. And didn't Mr Colpoys lose his son in the war? Well then, it's not really surprising if he lets off steam sometimes.'

'He wasn't letting off steam,' said Kate unhappily. 'I'm afraid he might have been taken ill . . .' But she made an effort to change the subject. 'Anyhow, you're not exactly a ray of sunshine yourself tonight. What's up?'

'I'm just a bit tired. I felt cross and scratchy – that's why I decided to wash my hair, to buck myself up. Well, you can imagine. Teaching all day, and then trying to rehearse the little darlings in *Puss in Boots*.' She was sitting on the floor, close to the kitchen range, turning her head from side to side as she dried her hair. 'The Head came in and watched us for a while, and when I asked her afterwards what she thought of it, she said: "Such a pity you can't persuade your husband to come and supervise the rehearsals. Being a professional, he'd be able to give it that little extra polish". I could have killed her.'

'Have you heard from Ted lately?'

'I've spoken to him on the phone once or twice since the funeral, that's all – why?'

'I was wondering if he'd be able to get down to see the play, at the end of term,' Kate mused. 'I mean – if he can spare the time.'

'I sincerely hope he can't. I'd never hear the last of it!' Daphne tossed back her hair, and began to comb it. 'Luckily, he'll be up to his eyes with his own show by then. They're opening the week before Christmas.' Then she paused, and turned towards the window. 'Whatever's all that noise outside? I keep hearing people running past – and there's somebody shouting.'

Kate got up and went to the window, but as the kitchen was in the semi-basement, looking out on to the area and the coal-cellar under the pavement, she couldn't see much. But when they listened, they heard a boy's voice shouting something about a fire – and words that sounded like 'the Palace' . . .

'Did he say Buckingham Palace was on fire?' asked Kate, very shocked.

'No – it sounded more like the Crystal Palace.' Wrapping the towel round her head, Daphne ran upstairs and opened the front door.

The boy was freewheeling past on his bike, yelling excitedly: 'The Crystal Palace is on fire! The whole blooming place is going up in flames!'

Horrified, Kate followed Daphne up the stairs. 'Oh no, it can't be true!'

'I think it's true enough.' Daphne was looking upwards; in every direction the sky appeared to be one enormous sunset, all round the horizon.

'But it can't be!' said Kate. 'Glass wouldn't burn!'

With a sickening jolt at the pit of her stomach, Daphne suddenly remembered: 'Oh, my God – *Annie*.' She went straight to the hall-stand and grabbed her hat and coat.

As she scrambled into them, Kate protested, 'You can't go out like that! Your hair's still wet – you'll catch pneumonia!'

'Annie's there,' said Daphne shortly. 'I've got to find her' – and just as she was, she ran out of the house and away up the road.

Kate called after her: 'And Val, too! Steve said she might be there!' – but Daphne had already disappeared.

As soon as Daphne turned the corner into Anerley Hill, she saw it – the South Tower of the Palace, silhouetted against a wall of flame – and she joined the throng of people hurrying in the same direction, all making their way to the top of the hill, to watch the fire.

By the time she reached Crystal Palace Parade, the street was so packed, it was almost impossible to push through the crowds, but she dared not pause for a moment. She had to find Annie – she had to make sure her daughter was safe.

Her heart was pounding, and the heat from the fire was making it hard to breathe, but she ploughed on, squeezing in between people, gasping: 'Excuse me . . . I'm sorry – I must get past. I'm looking for my daughter. I'm very sorry – please let me through . . .'

Outside the main entrance to the Palace there was a small forecourt, normally used as a car park; now there were fire engines trying to get in, and a group of policemen, helped by volunteers from the crowd, labouring to shift the parked cars.

Daphne recognised the orchestra conductor, expostulating furiously as one of the police constables went from car to car, deliberately smashing the windscreens with his truncheon.

'How dare you?' she heard him exclaim. 'I saw you do that! That's my car!'

'These vehicles were locked, sir,' the constable told him. 'The fire's spreading fast – we're trying to move them out of harm's way. Which would you sooner have – a broken windscreen, or a burnt-out Morris?'

Daphne knew the conductor slightly – she had been introduced to him after a previous concert – and she tugged at his arm, saying urgently: 'I'm looking for Annie Watkins – have you seen her?'

'What? Who?' He stared at her, so numb with shock, he could barely understand what she was saying.

'Annie Watkins – my daughter. She was at the rehearsal tonight. Where is she now?'

'I don't know. She got out – everyone got out. She'll be all right, I expect.' He turned back to mourn over his shattered windscreen. 'Look what they've done to my car . . .'

'Get it moved, please, sir,' snapped the constable. 'Quick as you can. There's fire-appliances coming from all over – we've got to make way for them.'

The Penge Fire Brigade had been the first to arrive, at eight o'clock. This was soon followed by the Beckenham engine, tearing through Penge High Street at top speed with the bell clanging, then careering up Crystal Palace Park Road at sixty miles an hour. The West Norwood alarm had brought the entire London Fire Brigade into action, and within the next half-hour more and more engines arrived, each crew hunting for fire hydrants and running out branches, until the roadway was ankle-deep in tangled fire-hoses, twisting and turning like a giant snake-pit – and the more hoses they used, the more the water-pressure dropped.

The Fire Officer in charge was shouting orders through a megaphone, telling his men that there was another source of water at the other end of the Palace – the boating-lake in North Tower Gardens was a standing reservoir.

Close to Daphne, a joker in the crowd called out: 'How about the Crystal Fountain indoors? Only mind you don't frighten the goldfish!'

Daphne felt like hitting him; how could he make stupid jokes at a time like this? Turning away, she continued to search for Annie.

On the far side of the building, Valerie lingered on the terrace, straining her eyes, looking for any sign of life within the Palace . . . but she was beginning to think it was hopeless.

By this time the smoke was a pall of yellow fog. Behind the fog there was nothing but fire, and still more fire; with no dividing walls to break its progress, the central transept had become a wind-tunnel filled with flame – a roaring monster that devoured everything in its path.

One by one, the mighty steel girders buckled in the heat, cracking under the strain; the roar of burning and the thunder of crashing glass and metal sounded terrifying. In the midst of the noise and the chaos, Val could hear something else, more eerie and still more terrible; a series of ghastly groans, as if a giant were crying out in agony. A passing fireman told her what these sounds were. As the great organ in the concert hall caught fire, the heat made the bellows expand and contract, producing that unearthly wailing noise.

Then, as she stood watching and waiting, she forgot the noise and the heat and the danger – she forgot her own terrors – because she saw someone walking through the fire . . . and she knew it was Mr Colpoys.

If she could attract his attention, he might realise there was still one way of escape – he might get out in time. Very conscious of the child she carried within her, Valerie knew she must not take any risks, but she could not leave Mr Colpoys to certain death. Moving towards the open doorway, she called his name as loudly as she could.

He must have heard her, because he turned and saw her. Now, she thought – now he would come and join her. But he did not. Instead, he raised one hand in a last gesture – whether it was hail or farewell, she never knew – and then he turned and walked away, into the heart of the fire.

High overhead, the great arched roof began to give way, and as it fell in a shower of dazzling, incandescent sparks, a fireman appeared from nowhere, seizing Val and dragging her to safety. Above them, a volcanic eruption of flames shot upwards, nearly a hundred and fifty feet high.

The fireman panted, 'Good thing I caught you, miss. Is this the little lady you were looking for? I just managed to grab hold of her tail, and I pulled her out.'

Purring loudly, Minnie leaped into Val's arms, and she burst into tears.

That night, they saw the red sky all over London and the Home Counties; it could be seen for miles – from Hampstead, from Enfield, from Iver and from Sevenoaks. The crimson glow was watched by people in Brighton, and from ships in mid-Channel. At Hillside Road in Streatham, an enterprising trader was hiring out field-glasses at 'tuppence a look'. It was the biggest blaze London had seen since the Great Fire of 1666.

To most of those watching from a distance, the location of the fire remained a mystery until nine o'cock, when the BBC made an announcement in its evening news bulletin. At Langham Place, four members of the Outside Broadcasting Department leaped into action and left immediately, hellbent for the Crystal Palace, but all over south-east England, thousands of others were doing the same – they ran for their cars, or jumped on bicycles, or simply set off on foot. Soon a massive traffic jam built up, stretching for miles in all directions. Inevitably, the blocked roads and the vast number of spectators hampered the efforts of the Fire Service, who were still doing their best to get through.

At the height of the fire, over eighty pumps and other appliances were in action, manned by more than four hundred men, while all around them crowds of up to a hundred thousand people stood and watched, as the Crystal Palace collapsed in a last blaze of glory – a bigger audience than any of their celebrated firework displays ever had.

Ted had no idea what the time was; his brain was fuddled, and his eyelids kept drooping. He seemed to remember sitting down to supper at the Neumanns' candlelit dining-table, but he hadn't the faintest idea what he had eaten – if anything. He could only recall Franz filling his wineglass again and again. On top of the scotch he had been drinking earlier, it had been an unwise mixture.

All he wanted now was to lie down and go to sleep, but he forced himself to sit upright and stay awake, trying to listen to what Franz was saying.

'. . . And Marta is very, very fond of you – you must know that, surely? She has told me many times, there is nothing in the world she would not do for you.'

'That's nice.' Screwing up his eyes, Ted looked around the living room; he appeared to be alone with Franz. 'Where is she?' he asked. 'Where did she go?'

'She is not far away,' Franz smiled. 'She thinks you are a very attractive man, with so much sex-appeal . . . and I rather agree with her.'

As Franz leaned closer, his face seemed to blur. Ted squinted, trying to keep him in focus. 'And where's the other bloke?' he asked. 'The film-star chap – what's his name? Has he gone home already? Is it that late?'

'Oh no, it's not late at all. Chuck is around somewhere.' Franz put a hand on Ted's knee. 'But Marta gave me a message for you. She wants you to go and find her . . . she is waiting for you.'

'What are you talking about?' None of this made any sense to Ted. 'You mean she's hiding somewhere? Is it some kind of game?'

'Yes, it's a game.' Franz nodded eagerly, and moved closer still, until his smile seemed to fill the whole room. 'The best game in the world. Come, my friend – I will show you where to find my beautiful wife.'

He pulled Ted on to his feet, leading him out of the room and along the passage. Ted knew where they were going. This was the way to Marta's bedroom – he had been there often enough. But tonight he felt oddly reluctant – he had promised himself he wouldn't get lured into Marta's bed again. It wasn't right – it wasn't fair to Daff. Remembering Daphne at this moment, thinking of her all by herself at home, he would have given anything to be with her.

'Look, I think I'd better be going,' he began, trying to pull away from Franz's guiding hands. 'Time for me to be on my way.'

'Don't be foolish. Marta expects you – you mustn't keep her waiting.' With that, Franz opened the bedroom door and gave him a gentle push.

Ted was too tired to resist. The room was heady with Marta's perfume, and he found himself thinking of the way she had smiled at him – when was that? – sometime before dinner? It seemed a lifetime ago. But she was certainly a gorgeous creature – he was beginning to feel excited again – and besides, Daff would never know . . . Just once more wasn't going to hurt anybody, was it?

The room was dimly lit; one pink-shaded lamp shone beside the bed, and as he moved towards it, Franz whispered in his ear, 'Why don't you get undressed, my friend? Do you want me to help you?'

Shaking him off, Ted began to unbutton his shirt, tugging at his necktie, unbuckling his belt – and there was Marta, as lovely as ever, smiling up at him from the pillows and saying, 'My darling, what took you so long? We couldn't wait – we just had to start without you . . . But you'll soon catch up, won't he, *liebchen*?'

'Sure thing,' said Chuck lazily. 'Jump in, feller – it's party time.'

Then Ted realised Marta was not alone; she and Chuck Vernon were lying naked on the unmade bed, their arms and legs entwined – and they were reaching out for Ted, inviting him to join them . . .

There were two mirrors, angled at either side of the bed, and as Ted shook his head in disbelief, he saw an infinite series of reflected images – pink, naked limbs – greedy, eager faces . . . He stepped back, but Franz was close behind him, barring his way, and laughing.

'You knew?' asked Ted, and Franz replied gleefully, 'But of course! I enjoy it. I like to watch you play your little game.'

Suddenly Ted recognised another face in the mirrors – his own, open-mouthed and stupid, reflected again and again in ludicrous expressions of disillusion and disgust. With a shock of terrifying clarity, he realised that most of all, he was disgusted with himself.

Pushing Franz aside, he made for the door. Marta called after him, telling him not to be silly and pleading with him to come back, but he was already grabbing his hat and coat, fumbling with the front-door handle.

Out in the street, the night air hit him like an ice-cold shower, and he began to sober up. When a cruising taxi came along, he hailed it; the driver opened the door, 'Where to, Guv?'

'Cale Street,' he said thickly, and fell into the back seat as the cab accelerated.

But he didn't want to go back to Cale Street. He wanted what he had lost. He remembered with longing the life he had thrown away – he thought of Daphne and the love he had wasted. He would have given everything he had to be with her now . . .

'Didja hear the news?' Over his shoulder, the driver was making conversation. 'Terrible, innit?'

'What's that?'

'About the Crystal Palace.'

'What about it?'

'Oh, doncha know? Bloody place is on fire – all gone up in flames, so they say. People are gonna miss it, ent they? I meanter say, where's everybody gonna go now, Bank Holidays and Bonfire Nights?'

'The Palace – on fire?' Ted repeated slowly. 'Are you sure?'

'Look at that sky! Anyhow, it was on the wireless. Not much of it left, by the sound of things. Soon be burnt to the ground.'

Ted thought fast. 'Never mind about Cale Street, can you take me to Upper Norwood? I've changed my mind. I'm going home.'

More and more police had to be called in from all the surrounding districts; as the night wore on, nearly seven hundred and fifty men were needed in order to control the enormous crowds, and they had other duties to perform.

A new and terrible danger had arisen, for the fire continued to blaze, and the flames went on spreading. Fanned by the wind, they moved inexorably towards the South Tower. Standing at the top of Anerley Hill, it dominated the landscape, poised above the maze of narrow streets that ran down the hillside; row upon row of small terraced houses that were home to hundreds of families. If the fire engulfed the Tower, it would almost certainly collapse. No one could tell exactly where it would fall, but in such a closely packed area, it would create immense damage and innumerable casualties.

There was only one thing to be done.

Kate was listening to the report on the wireless, trying to keep calm, and trying to pray for all her loved ones who might be in danger, when there was a loud knock at the front door. Anxious for news, she hurried up to answer it, and a policeman told her as quickly as possible that all the streets within a few hundred yards of the Tower were being evacuated. She was told to take any small objects of value she could easily lay hands on, and leave the house as fast as possible.

'Whatever happens, you've got to get out of here right away,' he told her. 'Don't stop to think about it – there's no time. Pick up everything you can carry, and get out fast. That Tower could come down any minute.'

'But what shall I do?' she asked, trembling. 'Where can I go?'

'That's up to you, ma'am. All I can tell you is, you've got to get away from here. They say they're taking in women and children at St John's Parish Hall. You'll be out of danger there.'

Up at Crystal Palace Parade, Valerie was still cradling Minnie in her arms as she tried to make her way through the crowds. She had lost sight of Annie and Tony, and was hoping to find them again. Passing a couple of policemen, who were exhorting the public to keep back and let official vehicles through, she heard one of them say: 'All the side streets off Anerley Hill are being evacuated. They're sending the occupants out of harm's way.'

Val realised that this must include Sackville Road, and thought of her mother. Thank goodness she had Daphne with her – Daff would know what to do. But then she had an uneasy feeling – didn't Mum say something about Daff having to stay on at school some evenings this week? Suppose Mum had been left all on her own – whatever would she do?

Valerie was torn with indecision. Should she go and make sure her mother was all right, or stay here and try to find Annie and Tony first?

'Keep back there!' a policeman warned her. 'Stand well back – you might get hurt!'

A police car swerved past her, and Minnie miaowed indignantly as it missed her tail by inches. Val stepped back, on to the toes of the people behind her. The car screeched to a halt, the doors swung open, and two uniformed sergeants scrambled out – followed by a solemn, grey-faced Steve Gunn.

She shouted, '*Steve!*' – so loudly, everyone turned and stared at her, but she didn't care. She fell into his arms, laughing and crying with relief.

'Are you OK?' he asked. 'You shouldn't be here – you ought to be at home.' Then, as he embraced her, Minnie protested vigorously, and he exclaimed: 'Hello – where did the cat come from?'

'Minnie's our office mascot. She's OK – and so am I.'

He held her carefully, as if she were fragile and in danger of breaking, and said, 'I'm taking you home – thank God I found you.

When I left the police station, I told them I was coming to look for you, and they gave me a lift.'

'What were you doing at the police station?' she asked at once. 'You're not – I mean, there hasn't been any trouble?'

He nodded. 'There's been some trouble, all right – bad trouble, but not for me. The police were looking for Mr Colpoys, only they got a call to drop everything and come here instead. But when they do find him—'

Val interrupted quietly: 'They won't find him,' she said.

'What d'you mean? Where is he?'

'He was in there . . .' She gestured hopelessly at the twisted, derelict shell of the Palace, still ablaze from end to end. 'I saw him – he walked straight into the fire.'

For nearly two hours, Roger and Babs had been standing at the upstairs window at Belmont, while the Palace was slowly engulfed in flames. They did not say much; there was nothing to be said and nothing to be done, except stand there, side by side, watching. At one moment, when there was a particularly dazzling burst of fire, Babs felt for Roger's hand. He said nothing, but held her hand tightly, reassuring her.

Finally she turned away from the window. 'I can't bear it any more,' she said, and she pulled the curtains together, shutting out the spectacle.

'Don't be afraid,' he told her. 'You're safe here.'

'I know. If I'd been on my own, I should have been frightened, but as long as you're here, it's all right. Except – it seems all wrong, somehow, us standing here like this. In a way, it's so beautiful, you can't stop looking – and yet it's so terrible . . .'

There were tears in her eyes, and she brushed them away with the back of her hand, trying to pull herself together, and asking politely, 'Would you like a drink? I believe there are still a few bottles of wine downstairs.'

'No, thanks. I don't want anything.'

She was aware of his steady gaze, and went on in a matter-of-fact tone: 'It must be getting very late. I expect you'll have to go soon?'

Without taking his eyes from her, he said, 'I'm in no hurry. Unless you want me to go?'

There was a pause that seemed to last for a long time – and then Babs managed to say, 'But your wife – she'll be worried about you, won't she?'

He took a long breath, and said: 'I haven't got a wife.'

She stared at him. 'Oh, but I thought Steve said . . .'

'Come and sit down.' Roger moved to the sofa, patting the cushions. 'You're going to think I'm a lousy bastard, but you might as well know the truth. I've never been married. I used to pretend I was, because it made life easier.'

She sat beside him, totally lost. 'I don't understand.'

'I enjoyed picking up girls, having a good time, and I thought, if I was single, they'd start to get their hooks into me. Before I knew it, they'd be dropping hints about going steady, and settling down. I didn't want any of that – I was having too much fun, being a bachelor. So I let everybody know I was a married man.'

'But didn't that put the girls off?'

'Some, it did – the ones who were serious. But I didn't care. I was having too much fun with the other kind.'

'I see.' She looked away, and seemed to shrink a little.

'That's shocked you, hasn't it? I knew it would . . . The fact is, I've never told anyone this until now – but you had to find out, sooner or later.'

'Why?' Her words sounded flat, drained of any emotion. 'Why did you tell me? You could have gone on pretending – I'd have believed you.'

'I wanted you to know. I want you to know all about me, like I want to know all about you.'

Looking into his eyes, Babs said, 'I told you before – you don't know anything about me. I'm not a very nice person – I've done some horrible things.'

'I'm not very nice, either. There's a lot of girls who'd tell you I'm a regular villain. But perhaps we'll be good for each other?'

He gave her a questioning smile, and she said in a small voice, 'So, you don't really have to go after all?'

'I'll stay as long as you want me to,' he said.

On the west side of Crystal Palace Parade there was a row of single-storey shops, and on the flat roof of one of those shops the BBC's Outside Broadcasting Department had managed to rig up a microphone.

The Chief Commentator, 'Lobby' Lotbinière, stood with his back to the wind, trying to shield the mike as he delivered his running commentary.

'. . . All the while you see coming down molten bits of metal and glass, like a firework display. I should think the whole steel framework to the north nave may collapse at any moment. It doesn't look to me as though there's any hope of any rain coming from anywhere. It's a pretty clear sky, and a moment ago there was almost a full moon looking straight at me, across this blaze of smoke and ruins . . .'

He glanced upward; he could just pick out the navigation lights of some small aircraft, circling high overhead. As the news spread, some enterprising pilots had begun offering charter-flights at £1 a trip, to fly over the scene.

'The Croydon aerodrome people have evidently been doing a roaring trade, giving people a view from the air,' Lobby continued. 'Now the building just between me and the South Tower is beginning to blaze up, and I can see smoke coming through the tiles on the roof, and flames shooting out of the four chimneys, but I should think – even if that does go—'

A second commentator took up the story; he had been making a tour of the Palace grounds, and reported that the long South Wing, leading down to the Low Level railway station, was now ablaze.

'As those of you who have been here may remember, there are all sorts of these shrouded females and vast statues there, waiting in the dark to be burned. The flames are moving at the rate of about a yard every five minutes, and the roof is coming crashing down in sections . . . A good dozen hoses inside and outside are squirting away for all they're worth, but even now there's quite a considerable blaze on the roof of the building, right under the Tower . . .'

In his little studio in Penge, old Harry Glynn switched off his newly-acquired wireless set.

'I've heard enough of that – I can't stand any more. Gad, all those beautiful statues, gone for ever. It's like the end of the world.'

Miss Preece went on gazing out of the window; too far away to see the Palace itself, she watched the blood-red sky, and the occasional eruptions of yellow flame exploding above the rooftops.

'The end of one world – the start of another,' she said.

'What d'you mean by that? It's not the start of anything. Fire's a devil – sheer wickedness – burning everything, destroying everything!'

'Yes, the flames destroy, but they're cleansing too. They burn away the past, to make way for the future.'

Harry waved this aside impatiently; he could only think that this was the end of an era. With a sudden surge of inspiration, he pulled out a blank canvas and stuck it on the easel, dragging it across the floor to the window, muttering to himself: 'Oils, I think. Yes, oils – this isn't a subject for watercolour. Stand back, old girl, I've got work to do. Chrome yellow – cadmium – crimson – burnt umber . . .'

Miss Preece watched him as he made his preparations, setting out his tubes of paint, his palette and brushes, and she smiled faintly.

'That's right,' she said. 'Catch the moment, and keep it for ever.'

Under the threatening shadow of the South Tower, Steve had managed to guide Val safely through the crowds, down Anerley Hill. When they reached the pub at the corner of Sackville Road, they saw Annie and Tony standing there, along with Kate, who had a shawl thrown round her shoulders and a thick book under her arm.

Thankfully, Val hugged her mother. Kate explained that she had been warned to leave the house at a moment's notice, in case the Tower should collapse. She had just had time to put on her coat and shawl, and grab her valuables.

'What valuables?' asked Valerie. 'I didn't know we'd got any!'

'Well, my handbag – and my old photograph album. I wasn't going to leave the family snapshots behind, was I?'

Annie took Minnie in her arms, petting and stroking her, and the cat purred with satisfaction; then they all began to talk at once, telling one another where they had been and what they had seen – although Steve and Valerie said nothing about Mr Colpoys.

Suddenly Val looked round, and asked, 'Where's Daff? Isn't she here?' – and they all fell silent.

At the top of the hill, the streets were still jammed with people. Ted's cab-driver did his best to reach the Palace, using all the side streets and back-doubles he could find, but when he reached Upper Norwood the traffic was solid and immovable, and he had to admit defeat.

Ted said, 'Thanks, anyhow. You did a good job, mate' – and paid him off, then jumped out and continued on foot.

Even then, the press of people was so great, he could only get through with difficulty. Near the end of Church Road, he passed a motorcar that had been parked overnight; now it was being used by sightseers as a viewing-platform, but with so many standing on top of it, the vehicle had collapsed under their weight, like a broken-backed camel – its front wheels were spreadeagled, and all four tyres completely flat.

At the top of Anerley Hill he was brought up short, seeing the extent of the fire for the first time. Only the two towers remained; the whole of the enormous Palace between them had gone. Nothing remained of it but a tangle of broken steel girders and a sea of yellow flame, beginning to die down at last.

The crowd had started to thin out a little; people who had been standing there for a couple of hours or more were leaving regretfully, like a theatre audience at the end of a performance. The best of the show was over; it was time to go home.

As the sightseers turned away from the ruins, Ted saw an army of strangers coming towards him – men and women, old and young, some with sleepy children riding on their shoulders – and over a hundred yards away, in the middle of that multitude, he saw one face he knew.

Daphne saw him at the same moment, and at once the crowds ceased to exist; they might have been the only two people in the world. Ted shouldered his way forward, against the human tide, and they walked toward one another; even then, it was several minutes before he reached her and took her hands in his.

They did not speak; they had no need for words.

She lifted her face to him, and they held one another for a long time, oblivious to the shoving and jostling of the passers-by, clinging together in an embrace that seemed as if it would never end.

Then, through the din around them, they gradually became aware of another sound – confused shouts, which swelled and spread, and finally turned into a full-throated cheer.

The efforts of the firefighters had been rewarded; they had succeeded in halting the progress of the fire, just fifteen feet from the base of the South Tower.

Arm in arm, Ted and Daphne joined the throng streaming down Anerley Hill, and at last she asked: 'How did you know where to find me?'

'I didn't know. I was in a taxi, on my way to Cale Street, when I heard the news – and I told the driver to bring me home.'

'But you've got a rehearsal tomorrow, haven't you? How will you get back?'

'I'm not going back. I won't be going to rehearsal any more.'

'But you must! The show's opening soon.'

'I'll ring Percy in the morning; he can explain to them. It's a lousy part, in a lousy show, and I don't want to do it.'

'You can't break your contract – they could sue you!'

'It wouldn't do them a lot of good – I haven't got much money. I'll probably be signing on at the Labour Exchange next week, but who cares?'

She stopped walking, staring at him, trying to understand. 'What about the flat? What about Marta?'

'I told you – I'm not going back. I'm giving up Cale Street; I'm giving up – all that. I'm coming home.'

When they reached Sackville Road, they found the rest of the family standing on the corner, and there was another joyful reunion.

Val explained: 'The police came round to tell us the Tower's safe. Mum can go home, only I can't persuade her to budge. You try telling her.'

Ted hugged Kate. 'There's nothing to worry about, Mum. It's OK now.'

'Yes, I know.' But Kate remained where she was, gazing up at the tall tower outlined against the dying flames, and the tears ran down her face as she said, 'I just want to take a last look at it. The Palace has always been there, as long as I can remember. It was like watching my whole life burning up, in front of my eyes.'

Chapter Thirty

FIRST THING NEXT morning, Steve took Tony and Val to the police station, to see the Inspector who was investigating Ray Duke's death. They were able to tell him that Tony had recognised Mr Colpoys entering the Palace before the fire broke out, and Val said she was certain she had seen him walking into the flames.

But there was no real evidence, and his body was never recovered from the Palace ruins. Amazingly, in spite of the enormous damage done by the fire, there had been no fatal accidents; only four firemen were injured, treated in hospital for burns to their faces from particles of molten glass.

Officially, the cause of the fire was never discovered. Rumours began to circulate: had a burning cigarette-end fallen through a crack in the floorboards? Was it deliberate sabotage, or even an attempt at an insurance swindle? Possibly it had started with a fault in the electrical wiring system, somewhere in the building, but nothing was ever proved.

When Valerie left the police station, she went straight to the Palace, reporting for duty with the rest of the staff.

There was nowhere for them to go. They wandered around like ghosts, staring at the terrible scene of desolation; exhausted firemen were still on duty, hosing the smouldering ashes, damping down the wreckage.

Someone asked: 'What happened to the goldfish in the ornamental fountain? Boiled alive, I suppose, poor things.'

One of the groundsmen said, 'No, they weren't. They didn't look much like goldfish when I found them – the heat had turned them black – but they were still alive, so I took them down to the pond.

Give 'em a day or two, they'll soon perk up. Probably go back to their original colour, I shouldn't wonder.'

In the middle of the wreckage, Valerie found Sir Henry Buckland, as trim and smart as ever, in his homburg hat and grey plus-fours, picking through the ashes with the point of his cane – but when he turned to greet her, his face was haggard.

'Well, my dear, it's all over. My Crystal Palace is finished – there will never be another.'

She said helplessly, 'I'm so sorry – so very sorry. I just came to see if there was anything I could do.'

'There's only one thing to be done now, though I hate to do it. I have to give notice to the staff – nearly two hundred people to be thrown out of work. Some of them can pick up temporary jobs, helping to clear away the debris, but after that – there will be nothing more for them here. It breaks my heart.'

That night, when Val got home, she said to Steve, 'I'll never forget the look in his eyes. I know it's terrible for everybody, but for Sir Henry it's a tragedy.'

Steve tried to cheer her up. 'Still, look on the bright side. You'd have had to give in your notice before long, anyhow.'

'That's true.' She attempted to smile. 'It had been worrying me. I didn't know how I was going to explain it to Sir Henry! It'll be hard enough, breaking the news to your mother.'

As the weeks went by, everyone began to accept the disaster. Gradually, the wreckage was cleared, but there was still a gaping hole between the two towers – a gap in the landscape, and a sad loss in the lives of so many people.

But there was one unexpected scrap of good news.

After those few hours of panic, when the local residents had been evacuated, the Anerley Hill district didn't seem quite as safe; and the splendid vista of the Palace and its park had become a wasteland. Upper Norwood was no longer the desirable residential area it used to be.

A few days before Christmas, Daphne ran downstairs to the kichen, brandishing the local newspaper, and showed it to Ted and Kate at the breakfast-table. It was only a small item, tucked away at the foot of a column, but she pointed it out in triumph.

'It says here that under the circumstances, Messrs Crabbe and Carter have decided not to proceed with their plans for this area. "*There will be no redevelopment in Upper Norwood!*" How's that for a Christmas present?'

On Christmas Day, the whole family came to Sackville Road for dinner at midday. Somehow Kate had managed to squeeze the turkey into the oven, and Ted did the honours, carving the bird, while Daphne passed the plates around, to Steve and Val, Annie and Tony, Roger and Babs.

Afterwards, they went up to the sitting room and opened their presents, and when the ritual was over and the floor was deep in coloured ribbon and wrapping paper, Daphne asked Ted, 'Do you feel like a breath of air? Come on, let's go for a walk before it gets dark.'

'Slave-driver. All right, anything for a quiet life.'

They walked up the hill; there was a frosty nip in the air, but the sky was clear, and the two glass towers threw a glitter of gold back at the setting sun.

Surveying the scene, Ted said wryly, 'It'll never be the same again.'

Daphne tucked her arm through his. 'I'm beginning to get used to it.' Glancing up into his face, she added: 'Do you still mind – very much?'

'About the Palace?'

'No, I meant about the show. About not being in the West End.'

'No, I don't. It just means we'll have to tighten our belts a bit, that's all.'

Once Percy Thring had recovered from the shock of the broken contract, he had done his best. Of course, it was far too late to try and fix up a pantomime for Ted this year, but he'd managed to get him some local dates at smoking concerts, and Masonic Ladies' Nights, and working-men's clubs.

'When I talked to him yesterday, he said he's pencilling in a tour for me, starting in February – and after that a summer season, on the pier at Southend, with any luck.'

'Back where you started, almost.'

'Well, what's wrong with that?'

Since the Palace had gone, the view from the top of the hill had opened up; in the sunset, they could see across the North Downs, across Kent and Surrey, into the far blue distance.

Pulling Daphne closer, he murmured, 'Whatever Crabbe and Carter may say, we're still "halfway to heaven" . . . and that's not such a bad place to be.'